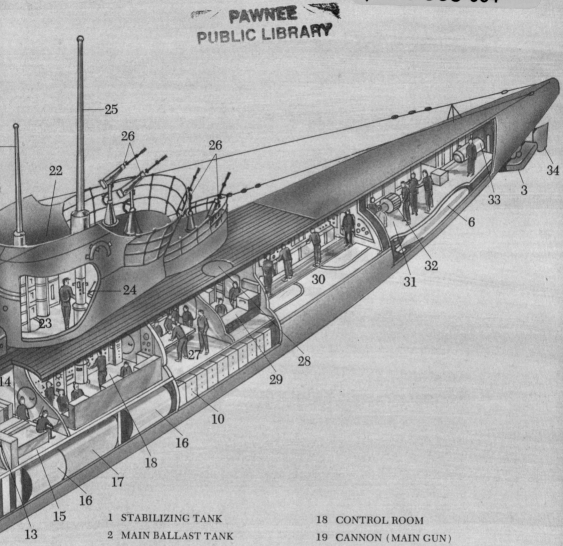

1 STABILIZING TANK	18 CONTROL ROOM
2 MAIN BALLAST TANK	19 CANNON (MAIN GUN)
3 HYDROPLANE	20 RADIO DIRECTION FINDER AERIAL
4 BOW TORPEDO TUBES	21 SKY PERISCOPE
5 FORWARD TRIMMING TANK	22 BRIDGE
6 TORPEDO STOWAGE	23 CONNING TOWER
7 BOW COMPARTMENT	24 COMMANDER'S SEAT AT PERISCOPE
8 TORPEDO SUPPLY HATCH	25 ATTACK PERISCOPE
9 HEAD	26 ANTI-AIRCRAFT GUN
10 BATTERIES	27 U-ROOM, PETTY OFFICERS' QUARTERS
11 QUARTERS	28 GALLEY HATCH
12 WARDROOM, OFFICERS' MESS	29 GALLEY
13 SOUND ROOM	30 ENGINE ROOM (DIESEL)
14 RADIO SHACK	31 MAIN MOTOR ROOM (ELECTRIC)
15 COMMANDER'S QUARTERS	32 E-MOTORS
16 FUEL TANK	33 STERN TORPEDO TUBE
17 MAIN BALLAST TANKS	34 RUDDER

The Boat

Lothar-Günther Buchheim

A Novel
The international bestseller about a
German submarine in World War II

THE BOAT

THE BOAT

Lothar-Günther Buchheim

Translated from the German by Denver and Helen Lindley

 Alfred A. Knopf · New York · 1975

THIS IS A BORZOI BOOK
PUBLISHED BY ALFRED A. KNOPF, INC.

Copyright © 1975 by Alfred A. Knopf, Inc.

All rights reserved under International and Pan-American
Copyright Conventions. Published in the United States by
Alfred A. Knopf, Inc., New York. Distributed by
Random House, Inc., New York. Originally published
in West Germany as Das Boot by R. Piper & Co.
Verlag, Munich. Copyright © 1973 by R. Piper & Co. Verlag.

Grateful acknowledgment is given to E. P. Dutton & Co., Inc.,
for permission to reprint an excerpt from The Mirror
of the Sea by Joseph Conrad. Everyman's Library Edition.

Library of Congress Cataloging in Publication Data
Buchheim, Lothar-Günther.
The boat.
Translation of Das Boot.
I. Title.
PZ4.B9198Bo3 [PT2662.U3134] 833'.9'14 74-21314
ISBN 0-394-49105-X

Manufactured in the United States of America

First American Edition

CONTENTS

i	BAR ROYAL	3
ii	DEPARTURE	27
iii	FRIGGING AROUND: 1	81
iv	FRIGGING AROUND: 2	113
v	FIRST ATTACK	147
vi	STORM	179
vii	CONTACT	234
viii	SECOND ATTACK	255
ix	PROVISIONING	316
x	GIBRALTAR	356
xi	RETURN VOYAGE	415

THE CREW
OF THE BOAT

OFFICERS:

Commander (the Old Man—also addressed as Herr Kaleun, the standard naval abbreviation of his full title, Herr Kapitänleutnant)

First Watch Officer

Second Watch Officer
Chief Engineer (the Chief)
Second Engineer
Narrator—a naval war correspondent

PETTY OFFICERS AND SEAMEN ("LORDS"):

Ario–diesel stoker
Bachmann ("Gigolo")–diesel stoker
Behrmann ("Number One")–bosun
the Bible scholar–control-room assistant
Bockstiegel–seaman
Dorian ("the Berliner")–bosun's mate
Dufte–seaman
Dunlop–torpedo man
Fackler–diesel stoker
Franz–chief mechanic
Frenssen–diesel mechanic mate
Hacker–torpedo mechanic
Hagen–E-stoker
Herrmann–sound man
Hinrich–radioman

Isenberg ("Tin-ear Willie")–control-room mate
Johann–chief mechanic
Katter ("Cookie")–cook
Kleinschmidt–diesel mechanic mate
Kriechbaum–navigator
Little Benjamin–helmsman
Markus–helmsman
Pilgrim–E-mate
Rademacher–E-mate
Sablonski–diesel stoker
Schwalle–seaman
Turbo–control-room assistant
Ullmann–ensign
Wichmann–bosun's mate
Zeitler–bosun's mate
Zörner–E-stoker

and fourteen others unnamed. The normal crew for a boat of this class was 50; on this voyage, however, the Second Engineer was a supernumerary, on board for duty training.

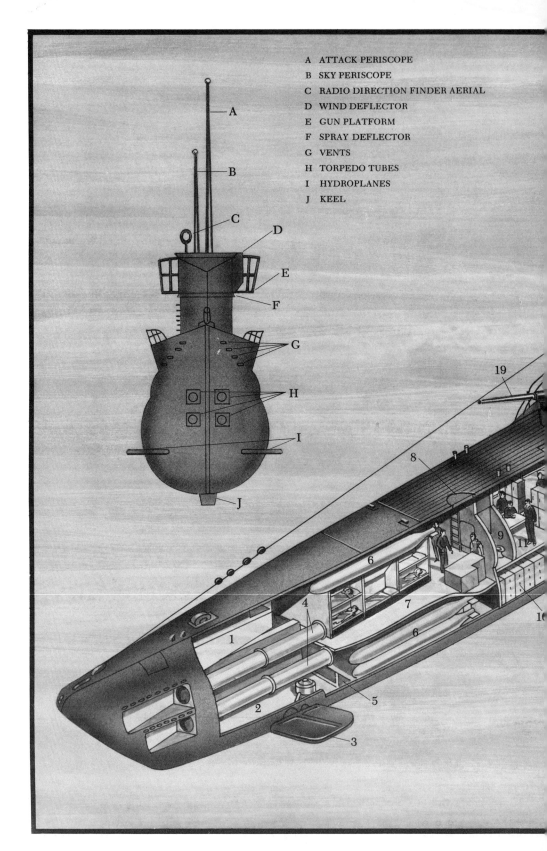

A ATTACK PERISCOPE
B SKY PERISCOPE
C RADIO DIRECTION FINDER AERIAL
D WIND DEFLECTOR
E GUN PLATFORM
F SPRAY DEFLECTOR
G VENTS
H TORPEDO TUBES
I HYDROPLANES
J KEEL

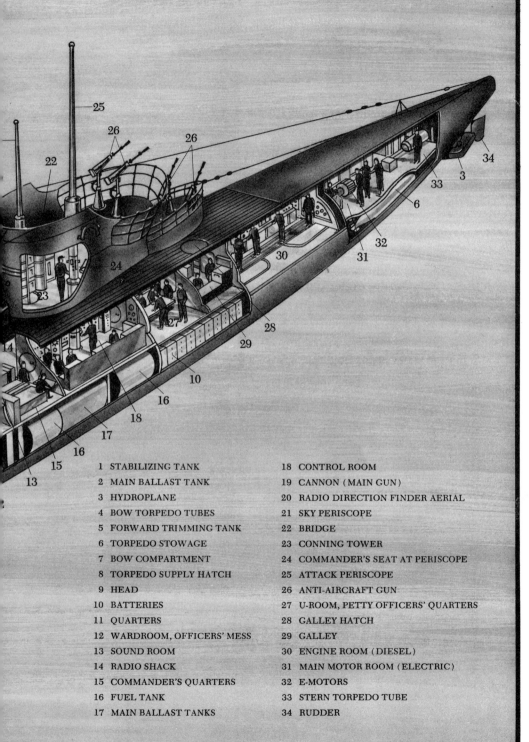

1 STABILIZING TANK	18 CONTROL ROOM
2 MAIN BALLAST TANK	19 CANNON (MAIN GUN)
3 HYDROPLANE	20 RADIO DIRECTION FINDER AERIAL
4 BOW TORPEDO TUBES	21 SKY PERISCOPE
5 FORWARD TRIMMING TANK	22 BRIDGE
6 TORPEDO STOWAGE	23 CONNING TOWER
7 BOW COMPARTMENT	24 COMMANDER'S SEAT AT PERISCOPE
8 TORPEDO SUPPLY HATCH	25 ATTACK PERISCOPE
9 HEAD	26 ANTI-AIRCRAFT GUN
10 BATTERIES	27 U-ROOM, PETTY OFFICERS' QUARTERS
11 QUARTERS	28 GALLEY HATCH
12 WARDROOM, OFFICERS' MESS	29 GALLEY
13 SOUND ROOM	30 ENGINE ROOM (DIESEL)
14 RADIO SHACK	31 MAIN MOTOR ROOM (ELECTRIC)
15 COMMANDER'S QUARTERS	32 E-MOTORS
16 FUEL TANK	33 STERN TORPEDO TUBE
17 MAIN BALLAST TANKS	34 RUDDER

This book is a novel but not a work of fiction. The author witnessed all the events reported in it; they are the sum of his experiences aboard U-boats. Nevertheless, the description of the characters who take part are not portraits of real persons living or dead.

The operations that form the subject of the book took place primarily in the fall and winter of 1941. At that time the turning point was becoming apparent in all the theaters of the war. Before Moscow, the troops of the Wehrmacht—only a few weeks after the battle of encirclement at Kiev—were brought to a standstill for the first time. In North Africa the British troops went on the offensive. The United States was providing supplies for the Soviet Union and itself became—immediately after the Japanese attack on Pearl Harbor—a nation at war.

Of the 40,000 German U-boat men in World War II, 30,000 did not return.

THE BOAT

I BAR ROYAL

FROM THE OFFICERS' BILLET in the Hotel Majestic to the Bar Royal the coast road describes a single extended curve three miles long. The moon is not yet up, but you can make out a pale ribbon of a road.

The Commander has the accelerator all the way down, as if this were a race. Suddenly he has to brake. The tires scream. Brake, release, brake again fast. The Old Man handles it well, and without skidding, the heavy car comes to a stop in front of a wildly gesticulating figure. Blue uniform. Petty officer's cap. What insignia on his sleeve?—U-boat man!

He's standing just outside the beam of our headlight, waving his arms. His face in darkness. The Commander is about to start forward slowly when the man begins to beat with the palms of his hands on the radiator hood, bellowing:

> *You bright-eyed little fawn, I'll get you,*
> *I'll break your little heart in two . . .*

A pause, more fierce drumming on the hood and more bellowing.

The Commander's face is grim. He's about to explode. But no, he shifts into reverse. The car leaps, and I nearly crack my head on the windshield.

Low gear. Slalom curve. Screeching tires. Second gear.

"That was our Number One!" the Commander informs me. "Tight as a tick."

The Chief Engineer, sitting behind us, swears unintelligibly.

The Commander has barely gotten up speed when he has to brake again. But he has a little more warning this time, because the swaying line caught in our headlights is still some way ahead. At least ten men straight across the road, all sailors in shore uniform.

Flies open, cocks out, a single cascade of urine.

The Old Man sounds the horn. The line parts and we drive between two rows of men pissing at attention.

"We call that the watering cart—they're all from our boat."

Behind us the Chief growls.

"The rest are in the whorehouse," the Commander says. "They'll be doing rush business there tonight. You know Merkel is moving out in the morning too."

For almost a mile not a soul to be seen. Then in our headlights a double file of military police.

"Let's hope none of our boys are missing in the morning," says the voice from behind us. "When they're drunk they like to go after the shore patrols—"

"Don't even recognize their own Commander," the Old Man mutters to himself. "That's going too far."

He's driving slower now.

"I'm not feeling so fresh myself," he says half over his shoulder. "Too much ceremony for one day. First the funeral this morning—for that bosun who caught it in the air attack at Châteauneuf. And in the middle of the funeral another attack—terrific fireworks. It isn't decent—particularly during a funeral! Our flak brought down three bombers."

"And what else?" I ask the Old Man.

"Nothing today. But that execution yesterday turned my stomach. Desertion. Clear case. A diesel engineer. Nineteen years old. Let's not talk about it. And then in the afternoon that hog slaughter at the Majestic. Probably meant to be a banquet. Pudding broth, or whatever the stuff's called—nobody liked it."

The Old Man stops in front of the *établissement*; on the garden wall a sign in letters three feet high proclaims BAR ROYAL. It's a creation in concrete, shaped like a ship, between the shore road and a secondary road coming in at a sharp angle from the pine forest. Straight across the front—on the ship's bridge—a picture window like a great superstructure.

Monique's the entertainer in the Bar Royal. A girl from Alsace who knows only scraps of German. Black hair, dark eyes, all temperament and tits.

Besides Monique, the attractions are three waitresses with peekaboo blouses and a three-man band, nervous and insipid except for the drummer, a mulatto, who seems to enjoy what he's doing.

The Todt Organization had requisitioned the place and had it repainted. Now it's a mixture of Fin de Siècle and German House of Art. The mural above the orchestra platform represents the five

senses or the Graces. Five Graces—three Graces? The U-boat Commander-in-Chief took the place away from the Todt Organization
on the grounds that "U-boat soldiers need relaxation"; "U-boat
officers can't spend all their time in whorehouses"; "We need a more
refined atmosphere for our men."

The more refined atmosphere consists of tattered carpets, split-
leather chairs, white latticework adorned with artificial grapevines
on the walls, red shades on the wall lights, and faded red silk curtains
over the windows.

The Commander looks around the room with a grin, stares magis-
terially at the groups at various tables, his chin pulled back and his
forehead furrowed. He then methodically straightens a chair, lets
himself drop heavily into it, and stretches his legs out in front. The
waitress Clementine immediately comes tripping up to him, breasts
bobbing; the Old Man orders beer all round.

Before it arrives, the door bursts open and a group of five men
crowds in, all lieutenant-commanders by the stripes on their sleeves
—and behind them three lieutenants and a second lieutenant. Three
of the lieutenant-commanders are wearing white caps: U-boat officers.

Against the light I recognize Flossmann. An unpleasant, irascible
individual, square-built and blond, who recently boasted that during
his last patrol, in the course of an artillery attack on an unescorted
vessel, the first thing he had done was to open fire on the lifeboats
with a machine gun, "to make our position clear . . ."

The other two are Kupsch and Stackmann, the inseparables, who
were heading home on leave when they got stuck in Paris and since
then have been overflowing with whorehouse talk.

The Old Man growls, "Another hour and the whole U-Force will
be here. I've been wondering for a long time why the Tommies
haven't smashed this shop in one of their dashing commando raids,
along with the Commander-in-Chief in his little castle at Kernével.
Can't understand why *that* shop hasn't been taken—so close to the
water and right next to all that mess around Fort Louis. As for us
sitting here, they could take us with a lasso if they wanted to. This'd
be a good night for it."

The Old Man has neither the thin, thoroughbred face nor the
wiry figure of the picture-book U-boat heroes. He looks rather
ordinary, like the captain of a Hamburg–America liner, and he
moves heavily.

The bridge of his nose is narrow in the middle, bends to the
left, and broadens out. His bright blue eyes are hidden under brows
that are permanently frowning from so much concentrated staring at
the sea. Usually he keeps his eyes so nearly closed that you only see

two slits and, at their outer corners, a burst of wrinkles. His lower lip is full, his chin strongly modeled; by early afternoon it is covered with reddish stubble. The rough, strong features give his face a look of gravity. Anyone not knowing his age would put him in his forties; he's really ten years younger. But given the average age of commanders, he is already an old man at thirty.

The Commander is not given to grandiloquence. In his official reports, his accomplishments sound like child's play. It's hard to get anything out of him. Usually we understand each other by an exchange of fragmentary phrases, tangential speech. A mere hint of irony, a slight pursing of the lips, and I know what he really means. When he praises U-boat Headquarters, looking crosswise past me, it's clear what he means to convey.

Our last night ashore. Beneath the babble of talk always the nagging anxiety: Will it be all right? Will we make it?

To calm myself I reason it out: the Old Man—a first-class commander. Unflappable. No slavedriver. No crazy, bloodthirsty daredevil. Reliable. Has served on sailing ships. Has always come through. Two hundred thousand tons—destroyed a whole harborful of ships. Always got away, even out of the worst jams . . .

My heavy sweater will be useful if we head north. I've told Simone not to come with me to the harbor. It would only cause trouble. The Gestapo idiots watch us like lynxes. Envious pigs. The Dönitz Volunteer Corps—they can't touch us.

No notion where we are really headed. Mid-Atlantic probably. Not many U-boats out there. A very bad month. Strengthened defenses. The Tommies have learned a lot of new tricks. The tide has turned. The convoys are excellently guarded these days. Prien, Schepke, Kretschmer, Endrass all attacked convoys. And they all got it at almost the same time—in March. For Schepke it was especially nasty. Jammed between the periscope housing and the tower's armor plate when the destroyer rammed his bombed-out tub. The aces! There aren't many left. Endrass's nerves were shot. But the Old Man is still intact, a model of perfect calm. Introverted. Doesn't destroy himself with booze. Seems completely relaxed as he sits there lost in thought.

I have to leave for a minute. In the toilet I hear two officers of the watch standing beside me at the yellow-stained tile wall. "Have to go unload it."

"Don't stick it in the wrong place. You're really pissed."

When the first one is already halfway through the door, the other roars after him, "While you're at it, stuff in greetings and salutations from me too!"

Men from Merkel's boat. Drunk, otherwise they wouldn't be spouting filth like that.

I return to the table. Our Chief Engineer is angling for his glass. An entirely different man from the skipper. Looks like a Spaniard, with his black eyes and pointed black beard, a portrait by El Greco. Nervous type. But knows the ropes from A to Z. Twenty-seven years old. The Commander's right hand. Has always sailed with the Old Man. They understand each other without much talk.

"Where's our Second Watch Officer?" the Old Man wants to know.

"On board. Still on duty, but he'll probably turn up."

"Somebody has to do the work. And the First Watch Officer?"

"In the cathouse!" says the Chief, grinning.

"Him in the cathouse? Don't make me laugh! Probably writing his will—that's one man who always has everything in order."

About the apprentice engineer, who is going to be joining the crew on this voyage and is supposed to take over the Chief's job afterward, the Old Man doesn't ask at all.

So there will be six of us in the Officers' Mess, a lot of men at one small table.

"What's become of Thomsen?" asks the Chief. "He wouldn't just stand us up."

Philipp Thomsen, a commander of the UF and very recent recipient of the Ritterkreuz, had reported in during the afternoon. Seated deep in a leather chair, elbows propped up, hands folded as though in prayer, his eyes staring grimly over them at the opposite wall. ". . . we were then harried for three quarters of an hour by depth bombs. Right after the explosion, at a depth of about two hundred feet, we took six to eight canisters fairly close to the boat. Flat pattern. One especially well placed, about the height of our gun and over two hundred feet to one side, hard to be more precise. The others all fell eight hundred to a thousand yards away. Then an hour later, another series. That was in the evening, about 23.00. At first we stay down and then make a silent run, rising slowly. After that we surface behind the convoy. Next morning a cruiser makes a dash in our direction. Wave force three, and moderate wind. Rain squalls. Rather cloudy. Very favorable for surface attacks. We submerge and position ourselves for the attack. Fire. Wide of the mark. Then again. Destroyer proceeding at slow speed. Make a try with the stern tube. That works. We then run behind the convoy until we receive orders to turn about. The second convoy announced by Zetschke. We maintain contact and supply running reports. Toward 18.00 we catch up with it. Weather good, sea two to three. Fairly cloudy."

Thomsen paused. "Very odd; all our successes were on days when one of the crew was having a birthday. Really extraordinary. The first time it was the diesel stoker's. The second, a radioman's. The unescorted ship went down on the cook's birthday, and the destroyer on the torpedo technician's. Crazy, isn't it?"

Thomsen's boat had four pennants on its half-raised periscope when it ran in early this morning with the flood tide. Three white ones for merchant vessels and a red one for the destroyer.

Thomsen's hoarse voice rang out like the bark of a dog over the oil-covered, brackish water. "Both engines twice stop!"

The boat still had headway enough to glide noiselessly up to the pier. Its outlines were sharp; out of the sticky, oily scum of the stinking harbor water it rose like a tall vase with a much too tightly bunched bouquet in it. Not much color—a bunch of dried flowers. Blossoms like pale patches amid the dark moss of beards. As they approached, the patches became emaciated white faces. Chalky skin. Deeply shadowed hollow eyes. Some glittered as though with fever. Dirty, gray, salt-crusted leather clothes. Mops of hair under caps that were almost sliding off. Thomsen actually looked ill: thin as a scarecrow, his cheeks cavernous. The grin on his face—certainly meant to be friendly—looked frozen.

"Respectfully report UF back from action against the enemy!" Whereupon we: "Heil UF!" at full pitch.

From Supply Depot One an echoing squawk, and then another, weaker, from the Penhoët wharf.

The Old Man is wearing his oldest jacket to show his contempt for all the fancy dressers. The front of this ancient peajacket has long since ceased to be blue and is more of a faded gray filmed with dust and spots. The once-golden buttons are green with verdigris. His dress shirt is also an indefinable color—lilac shading into blue-gray. The black, white, and red ribbon of his Ritterkreuz is no more than a twisted string.

"This is not the old gang," the Old Man complains, casting an appraising glance over a circle of young watch officers at the center table. "These are the tadpoles—all booze and big talk."

Lately two groups have formed in the bar: the "old warriors," as the Old Man's crewmates call themselves, and the "young strutters," the philosophically oriented youngsters with faith in the Führer in their eyes, the "chin-thrusters," as the Old Man calls them, who practice intimidating looks in front of the mirror and clench their asses extra-tight, just because it's in style to move springily on the balls of the feet with buttocks held in and body inclined slightly forward.

I stare at this assemblage of young heroes as though I were seeing them for the first time. Hairline mouths with sharp grooves on either side. Rasping voices. Swollen with their own superiority and crazy for medals. Not a thought in their heads but "The Führer's eyes are upon you—our flag is dearer than life."

Two weeks ago in the Majestic one of them shot himself because he'd caught syphilis. "He gave his life for Volk and Vaterland," was what they told his fiancée.

In addition to the crew of old warriors and young recruits there is also the outsider Kügler, who sits with his first lieutenant close to the washroom door. Kügler of the oak leaves, who keeps aloof from everyone. Kügler, noble knight of the depths, Parsifal and torch-bearer, unshakable believer in Final Victory. Steel-blue eyes, proud bearing, not an ounce too much fat—an immaculate example of the Master Race. With tapered index fingers he shuts his ears when he prefers not to hear cowardly misgivings or the sneers of doubting cynics.

The flotilla surgeon occupies a neighboring table. He too has a special position. His brain is stuffed with a collection of the most astounding obscenities. Hence he is known concisely as "the filthy pig." Nine hundred and ninety-five years of the thousand-year Reich are already gone, in the opinion of the flotilla surgeon, an opinion broadcast whenever he sees fit or is drunk.

At thirty, the surgeon enjoys universal respect. On his third sortie against the enemy he took over command and brought his boat back to base after the commander had been killed during a concentrated attack by two aircraft and both lieutenants lay badly wounded in their bunks.

"Somebody die around here? What is this, a wake? What kind of place is this anyway?"

"There's enough noise as it is," growls the Old Man, taking a quick swallow.

Monique must have grasped what the surgeon was saying. She brings the microphone close to her scarlet lips as though she means to lick it, flourishes a bundle of violet-colored ostrich feathers with her left hand, and bawls in a smoky voice, "*J'attendrai—le jour et la nuit!*"

The drummer uses his brushes to evoke a sexy whisper from his silver-mounted drum.

Shrieking, sobbing, moaning, Monique acts out the song with contortions, undulating her opulent blue-white, shimmering breasts, valiantly exercising her derrière and performing a lot of hocus-pocus with the feather fan. She holds it behind her head like an Indian war bonnet and taps her pouting lips rapidly with the flat of her hand. Then she draws the fan up from behind and between her legs— ". . . *le jour et la nuit*"—and rolls her eyes. Tender stroking of the feathers, bumps and grinds toward the feather bush—drawn up again from below—hips swaying. She pouts again and blows on her fluttering prop.

All at once she winks in the direction of the doorway, over the heads of the men around the tables. Aha, U-boat Commander with his adjutant! This beanpole topped by a diminutive schoolboy's face is hardly worth more than a brief wink. He doesn't even give a smile of recognition, but glares around as if looking for another door to escape through unobserved.

"A highly distinguished visitor come to consort with the mob!" roars Trumann, an especially recalcitrant member of the old guard, in the midst of Monique's sobbing— ". . . *car l'oiseau qui s'enfuit.*" He actually staggers over to the Commander-in-Chief's chair. "Come on, you old Aztec, how about charging the front line? Come on, here's a good spot—orchestra seat—the whole landscape from underneath . . . not interested? Well, one man's meat is another man's . . ."

As usual, Trumann is dead drunk. His spiky mop of black hair is covered with a drift of cigarette ash. Three or four butts have become entangled in it. One still smoldering. He may burst into flames at any moment. He wears his Ritterkreuz back to front.

Trumann's boat is known as "the barrage boat." Since his fifth patrol his bad luck has become legendary. He's seldom at sea for more than a week. "Crawling back on knees and nipples," as he calls it, has become a regular routine for him. Each time he has been caught during his approach to the theater of operations: bombed by flyers, harried by depth bombs. And there were always malfunctions —broken exhaust pipes, ruptured compressors—but no targets. Everyone in the flotilla is privately amazed that he and his men can bear up under their totally disastrous lack of success.

The accordion player stares over his folded bellows as if he'd seen a vision. The mulatto is cut off somewhere around the level of his third shirt button by the moon of his big drum: either he's a dwarf or his stool is too low. Monique makes her roundest and most carplike mouth and moans into the microphone. "In my solitude . . ." And Trumann leans closer and closer to her until he suddenly shouts, "Help—poison!" and throws himself over backward. Monique falters. He thrashes about, then starts to get up again and bellows, "A real flame-thrower—she must have eaten a whole string of garlic—god-oh-god-oh-god!"

Trumann's Chief, August Mayerhofer, appears. Since he wears the German Cross on his jacket, he's known as "August of the Fried Egg."

"Well, how did it go in the whorehouse?" Trumann yells at him. "Are you all fucked out? It's good for the complexion. Old Papa Trumann certainly ought to know by now."

At the next table they're bawling in chorus: "O thou We-es-ster-wald . . ." The flotilla surgeon is leading the halting choir with a wine bottle. There is a big round table close to the podium, which by tacit consent is reserved for the old guard; in the leather chairs around it only the Old Man's friends and contemporaries sit or sag, more or less drunkenly: Kupsch and Stackmann, "the Siamese Twins"; Merkel, "the Ancient"; Kortmann, "the Indian." They are all pre-maturely gray, naval gladiators from the word go, who act non-chalant although they know better than anyone what their chances are. They can loll for hours at a time—almost motionless. On the other hand, they can't lift a glass without shaking.

They all have more than half a dozen difficult missions behind them, they all have been through the worst kind of nervous tension, refined torture, hopeless situations that swung around to their ad-vantage by some sheer miracle. Not one of them who hasn't come back with a wrecked boat, against all expectation—upper deck demolished by aircraft bombs, conning tower rammed in, stoved-in bow, cracked pressure hull. But each time they did come back, they were standing bolt upright on the bridge, acting as though the whole mission had been mere routine.

To act as though everything were a matter of course is part of the code. Howling and chattering of teeth are not allowed. U-boat Headquarters keeps the game going. For Headquarters, anyone who still has a neck and a head and all four extremities attached to his torso is all right. For Headquarters, you're certifiable only when you start to rave. They should long ago have sent out fresh, unscathed men to replace the old commanders in the front-line boats. But, alas, the unscathed novices with their unshaken nerves happen to be far less competent than the old commanders. And the latter make use of every conceivable trick to keep from parting with an experienced watch officer who is really ready to become a commander.

Endrass should never have been allowed to put to sea again in his condition. He was completely done in. But that's the way it goes: U-boat Headquarters has been struck by blindness. They don't see when someone is on his last legs, or they don't want to see. After all, it's the old aces who brought in the successes—the con-tents of the little basket for special communiqués.

The combo takes a break. I can again hear fragments of conversation.

"Where is Kallmann?"

"He certainly won't be coming!"

"You can see why!"

Kallmann came in the day before yesterday with three victory pennants on his half-raised periscope—three steamers. He sank the last one, in shallow coastal waters, with his cannon. "It took more than a hundred rounds! We had a heavy sea. With our boat hove to, we had to shoot at an angle of forty-five degrees. We got the one before that at about 19.00 in the twilight—an underwater shot. Two hits on a twelve thousand gross registered tons—one miss. Then they were after us. Tin cans for eight long hours. They probably used up everything they had on board!"

With his hollow cheeks and his wispy blond beard, Kallmann looked like Jesus on the cross. He kept twisting his hands as if each word were being dragged out of him.

We listened intently, disguising our uneasiness with an exaggerated show of interest. When would he finally ask the question we were dreading?

When he had finished, he stopped twisting his hands and sat motionless, palms pressed together. And then gazing past us over his fingertips he asked with forced indifference, "What news of Bartel?"

No answer. The Commander-in-Chief let his head nod fractionally.

"So—well, I guessed it when there was no further radio contact." A minute of silence, then he asked urgently, "Doesn't anyone know anything at all?"

"No."

"Is there still a chance?"

"No."

Cigarette smoke hung motionless in front of their mouths.

"We were together the whole time at dock. I ran out with him too," he said finally. Helpless, embarrassed. It made you want to vomit. We all knew what close friends Kallmann and Bartel were. They always managed to put to sea together. They attacked the same convoys. Once Kallmann had said, "It stiffens your spine if you know you're not alone."

Bechtel comes through the swinging door. With his pale, pale hair, eyelashes, and eyebrows, he looks half scalded. When he is as pale as this, his freckles stand out.

A big hello. He's surrounded by a group of the younger men. He has to stand them drinks, because he's been "reborn." Bechtel has gone through an experience that the Old Man described as "really remarkable." After a fierce pursuit with depth bombs and all sorts of damage to his ship, he surfaced in the gray of dawn to find a hissing canister lying in front of his cannon on the upper deck. The corvette still in the neighborhood and the live bomb in front of the conning tower. It had been set to go off at a greater depth and so hadn't exploded when it fell on Bechtel's upper deck at two hundred feet. He immediately ordered both diesels full speed ahead and the bosun had to roll the depth charge overboard like a barrel of tar. "It blew twenty-five seconds later. So it was set for three hundred feet." And then he had to dive again and took twenty more depth charges.

"I would certainly have brought that firecracker back with me," Merkel shouted.

"We'd have liked to. Only we couldn't stop that damn hissing. Simply couldn't find the button. Absolutely hilarious!"

The room is getting more and more crowded. But Thomsen is still missing.

"Where d'you suppose he can be?"

"Perhaps he's getting in one last quick one."

"In the shape he's in?"

"With the Ritterkreuz around your neck, it must give you a whole new sensation."

During the awarding of the Ritterkreuz by the Commander-in-Chief of the U-boats this afternoon, Thomsen had stood as rigid as an iron statue. He had such a grip on himself that there was practically no color in his face. In his condition he could hardly have heard a word of the C-in-C's rousing speech.

"He'd better look out or I'll eat that lousy cur of his," Trumann had muttered at the time. "The bitch is there every time he reports in. We're not running a zoo here."

"Toy soldier!" he now adds as the Commander-in-Chief withdraws after a manly handshake and a piercing glance. And, cynically to those in the circle, "Great wallpaper," pointing at the photographs of the dead on the three walls, one little black-framed picture after another. "There beside the door, there's still space for a few more!"

Already I can see whose photo is going to appear next: Bechmann's.

Bechmann should have been back long ago. The three-star announcement is sure to be issued very soon. They took him off the Paris train stinking drunk. It required four men to get him out—the express had to wait while they did it. You could have hung him over a clothesline. Completely fucked out. Albino eyes. And that's the shape he was in twenty-four hours before putting to sea. How in god's name did the flotilla surgeon get him on his feet again?

Probably an airplane caught him. Shortly after he cleared port, reports from him ceased. Hard to believe. The Tommies are coming in now as close as channel buoy Nanni I.

I'm reminded of Bode, the naval staff officer in Kernével, a solitary old man who used to get drunk all alone late at night in the wardroom. Thirty boats had been lost in a single month. "You could turn into a drunk, if you drank to each of them."

Flechsig, heavy and uncouth, one of the Old Man's last crew, throws himself into the last empty chair at our table. He got back from Berlin a week ago. Since then, he's hardly said a word. But now he breaks out. "D'you know what this idiot monkey said to me, this dolled-up staff heinie? 'The right of commanders to wear white caps is not expressed in any of the regulations regarding uniforms!' I said, 'Would respectfully suggest that the omission be rectified.'"

Flechsig takes a couple of powerful swigs of Martell from a tumbler and methodically wipes his mouth with the back of his hand.

Erler, a young lieutenant who has completed his first patrol as commander, keeps opening the door so hard that it bangs against the doorstop. From his breast pocket dangles the end of a rose-colored slip. Back from leave just this morning, by afternoon he was in the Majestic waxing eloquent about his experiences. As he told it, they had held a torchlight parade for him back in his home town. He could prove it all with clippings from the newspapers. There he stood on the Rathaus balcony, his right hand raised in the German salute: a German sea hero hailed in his home town.

"Well, he'll quiet down later on," mutters the Old Man.

In Erler's wake come the radio commentator Kress, an oily, intrusive reporter with exaggerated ideas of his own importance, and the former provincial orator, Marks, who now writes inflated inspirational articles on Endurance. They look like Laurel and Hardy in Navy uniforms, the radio creature tall and lanky, the enduring Marks fat and nobbly.

At their appearance the Old Man gives an audible snort.

The favorite word of the radio people is "continuously," the "continuously increased effort" in munitions, victory statistics, will to attack. Everything must press on con–tin–u–ous–ly.

Erler plants himself in front of the Old Man and snappily invites him to a round of drinks. For quite a while the Old Man does not react at all, then he lays his head to one side as if for a shave and announces distinctly, "We always have time for a quick swig!"

I already know what comes next. In the middle of the room Erler demonstrates his method of uncorking champagne bottles with a single sharp blow of the back of a knife against the bulge in the neck. He's great at it. The cork and the glass lip fly off without leaving a splinter and the champagne shoots up as though from a foaming fire extinguisher. I am instantly reminded of an exercise of the Dresden fire department. In front of the Opera House they had erected a steel mast with a swastika made of pipes in celebration of Reich Fire Prevention Day. Around the mast a herd of red firewagons had been drawn up. The immense square was jammed with an expectant crowd. The command was barked from the loudspeaker: "Foam, forward march!" and out of the four ends of the swastika shot the foam; it began to rotate, faster and faster, becoming a spouting windmill. The crowd went "Aaah!" And the foam gradually turned rosy, then red, then violet, then blue, then green, then yellow. The crowd applauded while an ankle-deep slime of analine spread out in front of the Opera House . . .

Again the door crashes open. It's Thomsen—at last. Half supported, half pushed by his officers, he staggers in, glassy-eyed. I quickly drag up a chair so that we can take him into our circle.

Monique is singing: "Perhaps I am Napoleon, perhaps I am the King . . ."

I gather the wilted flowers from the table and strew them over Thomsen's head. Grinning, he allows himself to be adorned.

"Where's the Commander-in-Chief hiding?" asks the Old Man.

It's the first time we realize that the C-in-C has disappeared again. Before the real celebration has begun. Kügler is no longer here either.

"Cowardly bastards!" Trumann growls, then rises laboriously and staggers off between the tables. He returns with a toilet brush in his hand.

"What the hell's that thing for?" the Old Man bursts out.

But Trumann only staggers closer. He places himself in front of Thomsen with his left hand propped on our table, breathes deeply a couple of times, and at the top of his voice roars, "Silence in the cathouse!"

Instantly the music stops. Trumann moves the dripping toilet brush up and down right in front of Thomsen's face and babbles tearfully, "Our magnificent, esteemed, abstinent, and unwed Führer, who in his glorious ascension from painter's apprentice to the greatest battle-leader of all time . . . is something wrong?"

Trumann wallows for a few seconds in boozy emotion before going on to declaim, "The great naval expert, the unexcelled ocean strategist, to whom it has occurred in his infinite wisdom . . . how does it go from there?"

Trumann throws a questioning glance around the circle, belches deeply, and starts up again. "The great naval leader who showed that English bedwetter, that cigar-smoking syphilitic . . . ha, what else has he dreamed up? Let's see . . . has shown that asshole of a Churchill just who knows which end is up!"

Trumann lets himself sink back into his chair exhausted, and blows his Cognac breath straight into my face. In the bad light he looks green. ". . . we dub him knight—we consecrate the new knight! The shitty clown and the shitty Churchill!"

Laurel and Hardy force their chairs into our circle. They're brown-nosing Thomsen, using his drunkenness to learn something about his last patrol. No one knows exactly why they spend their time trying to get interviews for their clichéd articles. But Thomsen is long past the point of communication. He stares at the two almost idiotically and simply growls as they busily put words in his mouth: "Yes, exactly right—blew up promptly—as expected! A hit just beyond the bridge—Blue-Funnel Steamer. D'you understand? No, not *funny*—funnel!"

Kress feels that Thomsen is stringing him along and swallows dryly. Looks like a fool with his Adam's apple bobbing up and down.

The Old Man is enjoying his embarrassment and wouldn't dream of helping him out.

Thomsen is finally incapable of taking in anything at all.

"All shit! Shitty fish!" he shouts.

I know what he means. In the last few weeks there's been one torpedo failure after another. So many defects are no accident. There's been talk of sabotage.

Suddenly Thomsen springs to his feet, terror in his eyes. Glasses fall and break. The telephone has rung. He must have mistaken it for the alarm bell.

"A can of pickled herring!" he now demands, swaying heavily. "Pickled herring all around!"

I half hear fragments of what Merkel is reporting to his group, behind me.

"The chief petty officer was good. First-class man. The diesel mechanic I've got to get rid of, he's a dead loss . . . The corvette was at position zero. The chief was slow in getting the lifeboat down . . . There was one man swimming around in the drink. Looked like a seal. We ran up to him because we wanted to know the name of the ship. Black with oil. Hanging onto a buoy."

Erler has discovered that it makes a murderous noise if you run an empty wine bottle along the ribs of a radiator. Two, three bottles burst, but he doesn't give up. Scattered glass crunches under foot. Monique throws him a furious look because she can hardly make her groans heard over the uproar.

Merkel staggers to his feet and gives himself a thorough scratching between the legs through his trouser pocket. Now his Chief Engineer appears. This man is universally envied for his ability to produce a tune on two fingers. He can do anything: the fanciest whistling, commando signals, wild musical arabesques, tremulous fantasies.

He's feeling expansive and immediately agrees to teach me. First, however, he has to go to the can. When he comes back he says, "Get going, wash your paws!"

"Why?"

"If you're going to be difficult—okay—one hand will do."

After I've washed, Merkel's Chief thoroughly examines my right hand. Then decisively pops my index finger and middle finger into his mouth and begins to whistle a couple of trial notes. Soon a whole melody emerges, getting gradually shriller and sharper.

He rolls his eyes as he plays. I'm stunned. Two more cascades of sound, and finish. I examine my wet fingers with respect. I must pay attention to the finger placement, says the Chief.

"Good." Now I try it, but only extract a couple of honking noises and the sputter of a leaky pressure hose.

Merkel's Chief rewards my attempt with a despairing glance. Then with an air of assumed innocence he puts my fingers in his mouth again and out comes the sound of a bassoon.

We agree that it must have something to do with the tongue.

"Unfortunately, they're something you can't trade!" says the Old Man.

"Youth without joy!" Kortmann roars unexpectedly during a pause in the hubbub. Kortmann with his eagle's face: "the Indian." At U-boat Headquarters in Kernével he's been in disgrace since the incident with the tanker *Bismarck*. Kortmann, the disobeyer of orders. Rescuing German seamen! Taking his boat out of action to do so. Failing to follow orders out of sentimentality! Could only happen to Kortmann, one of the old guard with the antiquated credo branded on his brain: "Concern for the fate of the shipwrecked is the first duty of every seaman!"

Much good it'll do him to roar, old-fashioned Herr Kortmann, whom U-boat Headquarters finds a little slow on the uptake and who has not yet noticed that requirements have become more rigorous.

Of course bad luck came into it as well. Did the English cruiser have to turn up just when Kortmann was securely connected by fuel hose to the tanker? The tanker had really been intended for the *Bismarck*. But the *Bismarck* didn't need any more fuel oil. The

Bismarck was at the bottom of the ocean, along with twenty-five hundred men, and the tanker was wallowing along, full to the brim and with no takers. Then Command decided the U-boats should suck it dry. And just as Kortmann was partaking, it happened. The Englishmen shot the tanker away from under his nose, the fifty-man crew was floundering in the drink—and warm-hearted Kortmann couldn't bring himself to let them go on floundering.

Kortmann was still proud of his catch. Fifty seamen on one VII-C boat, where there's hardly room for the crew. How he stowed them away is his secret. Probably by the canned sardine method: head to toe, and no unnecessary breathing. Good old Kortmann certainly thought he'd performed a miracle.

Drunkenness begins to wipe out the boundary between the old warriors and the young strutters. They all try to talk at once. I hear Böhler reasoning, "After all, there are guidelines—explicit guidelines, gentlemen! Orders! Perfectly clear orders!"

"Guidelines, gentlemen, clear orders." Thomsen imitates him. "Don't make me laugh. Nothing could be less clear!"

Thomsen glances up sideways at Böhler. Suddenly he has a devilish gleam in his eye and is entirely aware of what's going on. "Actually, it's part of their plan, all this uncertainty."

Saemisch sticks his carrot-colored head into the circle. He's already half smashed. In the murky light, the skin on his face looks like a plucked chicken's.

Böhler begins to lecture the carrothead. "Here's the way it is. In total war the effect of our weapons can . . ."

"Pure propaganda rubbish," Thomsen jeers.

"Let me finish, will you? Now take this as an example. A support cruiser fished a Tommy out of the drink who'd already been overboard three times. What does that imply for us? Are we carrying on a war or just a demolition campaign? What good is it if we sink their steamers and then let them fish out the survivors so they can just sign on again? Of course, there's a lot of money in it for them!"

Things are really hot, now that Böhler has opened up the burning topic that is usually taboo: destroy the enemy himself or merely his ships?

"That's neither here nor there," Saemisch insists. But here Trumann breaks in. Trumann the agitator feels himself challenged. A thorny problem that everyone ducks—except Trumann.

"Be a little systematic for once. U-boat Headquarters gives orders: Destroy the enemy, with unswerving warlike spirit, with unfaltering severity, implacable effort, and so on—all that crap. But

U-boat Headquarters hasn't said a word about attacking men who are struggling in the water. Am I right?"

So leather-faced Trumann is wide enough awake to play provocateur. Thomsen immediately jumps in. "Well, of course not. It has simply been made un-mis-tak-ably clear that it is precisely the loss of crews that hits the enemy hardest."

Trumann looks sly and stokes the fire a little. "So what?"

Thomsen, inflamed by the brandy, promptly protests. "Then everyone has to decide for himself—very smart!"

Now Trumann really fans the flames. "There's one person who's solved the problem in his own way and makes no bones about it. Don't touch a hair of their heads, but shoot up the lifeboats. If the weather happens to help them sink fast, so much the better—that's that! The conventions have been respected. That's right, isn't it? U-boat Headquarters can consider itself understood!"

Everyone knows who is meant, but no one looks at Flossmann.

I have to think about the stuff I want to take with me. Only what's absolutely necessary. Certainly the heavy sweater. Cologne. Razor blades—I can do without them . . .

"The whole thing is a farce." Thomsen again. "As long as a man has a deck under his feet you can shoot him down, but if the poor bugger is struggling in the water, your heart bleeds for him. Pretty ridiculous, isn't it?"

Trumann starts up again. "I want to explain what it really feels like . . ."

"Yes?"

"If it's only one man, you imagine it could be you. It's only natural. But no one can identify with a whole steamer. That doesn't strike home. But a single man! Instantly it all looks different. That's getting uncomfortable. So they patch an ethic together—and presto, everything's beautiful again."

The heavy sweater that Simone knitted for me is terrific. Collar reaching to the middle of the ears, all done in cable stitch; and it's not an ass-freezer either, but nice and long. Maybe we'll really go north. Denmark Road. Or all the way up. The Russian convoys. Lousy that no one has any idea.

"But the men in the water really *are* defenseless," Saemisch insists in a plaintive, righteous voice.

It starts all over again.

Thomsen gestures in resignation, murmurs, "Oh shit!" and lets his head slump.

I feel an urgent desire to get up and get out, to go pack my things properly. One or two books. But which ones? No more brandy

fumes! The atmosphere in here would flatten a prize fighter. Try to keep my head clear. Last night ashore. Extra films. My wide-angle lens. The fur-lined cap. Black cap and white sweater. I'll certainly look silly.

The flotilla surgeon is supporting himself on outspread arms, one hand on my left shoulder, the other on the Old Man's right, as though about to perform on the parallel bars. The music has started up again; over it he roars at the top of his voice, "Are we here for a Ritterkreuz celebration or a philosophy session? Cut the bullshit!"

The surgeon's bellow startles a couple of officers to their feet and they immediately proceed as if on cue. They get up on chairs and pour beer into the piano, while a lieutenant-commander pounds the keys like mad. One bottle after another. The piano swallows the beer unprotestingly.

The combo and the piano don't make enough noise, so the phonograph is turned on. At maximum volume: "Where's that tiger? Where's that tiger?"

A tall blond lieutenant rips off his jacket, leaps smoothly into a squat on the table and starts flexing his stomach muscles.

"Ought to be on the stage!"—"Fantastic!"—"Cut it out, you're making me horny!" During the frenetic applause one man wraps himself up comfortably in the red runner on the floor, puts the life preserver, which has been hanging as a decoration on the wall, around his neck, and goes right to sleep.

Bechtel, hardly one of nature's exhibitionists, stares into space while clapping in time to a rumba that is demanding the utmost from the belly dancer.

Our Chief, who until now has been sitting silently, thinking, also gets out of hand. He climbs up the latticework attached to the wall above the platform and, imitating a monkey, plucks away at the artificial grapevine in time to the music. The lattice sways, remains standing for a moment two feet from the wall, as in an old Buster Keaton film, then crashes down with the Chief onto the platform. The piano player has his head bent way back—as if he were trying to decipher some notes on the ceiling—and bangs out a march. A group forms around the piano and bawls:

> We'll march, march, march,
> Though heaven rains down crap.
> We're heading home to Slimeville,
> From this asshole off the map.

"Classy, virile, Teutonic," growls the Old Man.

Trumann stares at his glass, and is galvanized; he springs to his

feet and roars, "*Skoal!*" From a good six inches above his mouth he pours a stream of beer into himself, sending a broad flow of slobber down his jacket.

"A real orgy!" I hear from Meinig, the dirtiest mouth in the flotilla. "All that's missing is women."

As though that were a signal, Merkel's Numbers One and Two get up and leave. Before reaching the door they exchange meaningful glances. I thought they had already gone.

"Whenever you're scared, go get laid," mutters the Old Man.

From a neighboring table I make out:

> *Whenever passion seized him,*
> *He'd leap up on the kitchen table*
> *And screw the hamburger . . .*

That's the way it always is. The Führer's noble knights, the people's radiant future—a few rounds of Cognac washed down with some Beck's beer and there goes our dream of spotless, shining armor.

"Remarkable," says the Old Man, reaching for his glass.

"This shit of a chair—can't get up!"

"Ha!" comes from someone in the neighborhood circle. "That's what my girl says too. Can't get up again—can't get up again!"

The table is a wild mess of champagne bottles with broken necks, ashtrays swimming with butts, pickled herring cans, and shattered glasses. Trumann glances thoughtfully at this rubbish heap. When the piano finally stops for a moment, he raises his right hand and roars, "Attention!"

"The tablecloth trick!" says our Chief.

Trumann carefully twists one corner of the cloth like a rope; he takes a good five minutes because it gets away from him twice when it's half ready. Then with his free left hand he gives a signal to the piano player, who almost seems to have rehearsed the act, for he strikes a flourish on the keys. Trumann settles his feet with the concentration of a weightlifter, stands perfectly still for a moment staring at his two hands as they grip the twisted corner of the cloth, and suddenly with a primitive war whoop and a mighty swing of the arms, he pulls the cloth halfway off the table. A jarring cascade of smashing glass, splintering crash of bottles and plates falling to the floor.

"Shit—fucking shit!" he curses, and staggers crunching through the shattered glass. He steers uncertainly for the kitchen and bellows for a broom and shovel. Then amid the mad laughter of the whole crowd he crawls around between the tables and grimly clears up the

litter, leaving a trail of blood behind him. The handles of the brush and the garbage shovel are immediately smeared with it. Two lieutenants try to take the implements away from Trumann but he obstinately insists on gathering up every last splinter. "Clear up—everything—must first be ord—ly, cleared up—always just right, shipshape . . ."

Finally he lets himself down in his chair, and the flotilla surgeon draws three or four splinters out of the balls of his thumbs. Blood continues to drip on the table. Then Trumann rubs his bloody hands across his face.

"Hell's teeth!" says the Old Man.

"Doesn't matter a shit!" Trumann roars, but allows the waitress to apply small adhesive bandages, which she brings with a reproachful look in her eyes.

He has hardly been in his chair five minutes when he pulls himself to his feet again, yanks a crumpled newspaper out of his pocket and yells, "If you've nothing else to say, you boneheads, here—here are some golden words."

I see what he's holding: the will of Lieutenant-Commander Mönkeberg, who died ostensibly in combat but actually lost his life in a completely unmilitary fashion, to wit, by breaking his neck. And his neck broke somewhere in the Atlantic in a smooth sea, simply because the weather was so fine and he wanted to go swimming. Just as he dived from the conning tower, the boat rolled in the opposite direction and Mönkeberg cracked his head against the ballast tank. His manly swan song was printed in all the papers.

Trumann holds the clipping out at arm's length. "All alike—one for all—all for one—and so I say to you, comrades, only a unique determination to fight—the background of this dramatic battle of world-historic significance—anonymous heroic courage—historic grandeur—wholly incomparable—standing alone—imperishable chapter of noble endurance and martial sacrifice—the highest ideal—those living now and those yet to come—to be fruitful—to prove oneself worthy of the eternal heritage!"

Still holding the sodden and illegible piece of paper, he sways back and forth, but he doesn't fall. His shoes seem stuck fast to the floor.

"Crazy bugger," says the Old Man. "No one can stop him now."

A lieutenant sits down at the piano and starts playing jazz, but this makes no difference to Trumann. His voice cracks. "We comrades—standard-bearers of the future—life and spirit of a human élite with the concept of 'service' as the highest ideal—a shining example for those left behind—courage that outlives death—lonely resolve—calm acceptance of fate—endless daring—love and loyalty of such boundlessness as you rabble couldn't begin to conceive of— more precious than diamonds—endurance—*jawohl*—proud and manly—hurrah!—finds his grave in the depths of the Atlantic. Hah! Deepest comradeship—battle front and homeland—willingness to sacrifice to the utmost. Our beloved German people. Our splendid God-sent Führer and supreme Commander. Heil! Heil! Heil!"

Some of them join in. Böhler looks severely at Trumann, like a governess, pushes himself up out of his chair to his full height, and disappears without a word of farewell.

"You—you there, get away from my tit!" Monique screams. She means the surgeon. Apparently he has made himself too companionable.

"Then I'll just crawl back inside my foreskin," he yawns and the circle bursts into uproarious laughter.

Trumann collapses onto his chair and his eyelids droop. Maybe the Old Man was mistaken after all. He's going to pass out right in front of us. Then he leaps up as though bitten by a tarantula, and with his right hand fishes a revolver out of his pocket.

An officer near him has enough reflexes left to strike down Trumann's arm. A shot hits the floor, just missing the Old Man's foot. He simply shakes his head and says, "Not even much of a bang with all this music going on."

The pistol disappears, and Trumann sinks back in his chair, looking sullen.

Monique, who has been slow to recognize the shot, springs out from behind the bar, sashays her way past Trumann, stroking him under the chin as though she were soaping him for a shave, then leaps quickly onto the platform and moans into the microphone. "In my solitude . . ."

Out of the corner of my eye I see Trumann rise in slow motion. He seems to divide each movement into its individual components. He stands, grinning craftily and swaying for at least five minutes until Monique has finished her wailing, then during the frantic applause he feels his way between the tables to the back wall, leans there a while still grinning, and finally whips out a second pistol from his belt and shouts, "Everyone under the table!" so loud that the veins in his neck stand out.

This time no one is close enough to stop him.

"Well?"

The Old Man simply stretches his feet out in front of him and slides out of his chair. Three or four others take cover behind the piano. The piano player has fallen to his knees. I too crouch on the floor in an attitude of prayer. Suddenly there is dead silence in the room—and then one bang after another.

The Old Man counts them aloud. Monique is under a table screaming in a high voice that cuts to the bone. The Old Man shouts, "That's it!"

Trumann has emptied his magazine.

I peer over the edge of the table. The five ladies on the wall above the platform have lost their faces. Plaster is still trickling down. The Old Man is the first to get up and observe the damage, his head cocked to one side. "Fantastic performance—rodeo standard—and all done with wounded fists!"

Trumann has already kicked the pistol away and is grinning with delight from ear to ear. "About time, don't you think? About time those loyal German cows got it, eh?"

He's almost delirious with self-satisfaction.

Hands in the air, shrieking in a high falsetto as if afraid for her life, ready to surrender—enter the "madam."

When the Old Man sees her, he slides down out of his chair again. "Take cover!" someone roars.

A miracle that this over-rigged old frigate, who functions as the hostess here, has taken till now to put in an appearance. She has dolled herself up Spanish-fashion, spitcurls plastered down in front of her ears and a gleaming tortoiseshell comb in her hair—a wobbling monument with rolls of fat bulging out all over. She's wearing black silk slippers. There are rings with huge imitation stones on her sausage-like fingers. This monster enjoys the special favors of the Garrison Commander.

Ordinarily her voice sounds like bacon sizzling in the pan. But now she's yowling away in a string of curses. "Kaput, kaput," I manage to distinguish in the general yammer.

"Kaput—she's right about that," says the Old Man.

Thomsen lifts a bottle to his mouth and sucks at the Cognac as if from a nipple.

Merkel saves the situation. He clambers onto a chair and vigorously begins to conduct a choir:

"Oh thou blessed Christmastide . . ." We all join in enthusiastically.

The "madam" wrings her hands like a tragedienne. Her squeaks only occasionally cut through our performance. She looks ready to tear her spangled dress from her body, but then simply tears at her hair with her dark-red lacquered nails instead, screeches, and rushes off.

Merkel falls from his chair, and the chorus ebbs away.

"What a madhouse! Christ, what a racket!" says the Old Man.

In any case, I think, I must take the warm bodyband along. Angora wool. First-rate stuff.

The flotilla surgeon draws Monique onto his lap; he has hold of her rear end with his right hand and with his left is raising her right breast as if weighing a melon. The voluptuous Monique, straining in her scrap of a dress, shrieks, tears herself loose, and collides with the phonograph so that the needle shoots across the grooves with a dull, groaning fart. She's giggling hysterically.

The surgeon pounds the table with his fists until the bottles jump, and turns red as a turkey cock with repressed laughter. Someone puts both arms around his neck from behind to embrace him, but when the hands disappear, the surgeon's tie is cut short directly under the knot, and he doesn't even notice. The lieutenant with the shears has already chopped off Saemisch's tie, and then Thomsen's, and Monique, watching all this, falls over backward on the stage having hysterics, and her wildly kicking legs reveal that she's wearing only tiny black panties under her dress, just a kind of G-string. "Wooden eye" Belser already has a siphon in his hand and is directing a sharp stream up between her thighs, and she's squealing like a dozen little pigs whose tails are being pinched. Merkel notices that the ends of his tie are missing, the Old Man murmurs, "Clean-cut raid," and Merkel seizes a half-filled Cognac bottle and hurls it into the tie-cutter's stomach, doubling him up.

"Neat—perfect throw," the Old Man says approvingly.

And now a piece of the lattice flies through the air. We all duck except for the Old Man, who sits there unmoved and grinning.

The piano gets another swallow of beer.

"Schnapps makes you im-po-tent!" Thomsen stammers.

"Back to the cathouse again?" the Old Man asks me.

"No. Just sleep. At least a couple of hours still."

Thomsen laboriously pulls himself to his feet. "With you—I'm coming—fucking den of thieves—let's go—just one more stop at the waterhole, one last good leak!"

The white moonlight beyond the swinging door hits me like a blow. I wasn't prepared for light: a glitter of flowing silver. The beach a blue-white strip in a cold fire of pure radiance; streets, houses, everything bathed in icy, glowing neon light.

My god! There's never been a moon like this. Round and white like a Camembert. Gleaming Camembert. You could read the paper by it with no trouble at all. The whole bay a single sheet of glittering silver foil. The enormous stretch from coast to horizon a myriad of metallic facets. Silver horizon against velvet-black sky.

I narrow my eyes. The island beyond is a dark carp's back in the dazzle. The funnel of a sunken transport, the fragment of a mast—all sharp as a knife edge. I prop myself against the low concrete wall; the feel of pumice on the palms of my hands. Disagreeable. The geraniums in the flowerboxes, each blossom separate and distinct. Mustard gas bombs are supposed to smell like geraniums.

The shadows! The roar of the surf along the beach! I have the groundswell in my head. The gleaming, spangled surface of the moonsea bears me up and down, up and down. A dog barks; the moon is barking . . .

Where is Thomsen, the new knight? Where the hell is Thomsen? Back into the Royal again. You could cut the air with a knife.

"What's become of Thomsen?"

I kick open the door to the can, careful not to touch the brass knob.

There lies Thomsen, stretched out on his right side in a great puddle of urine, a heap of vomit beside his head, blocking the urine in the gutter. On top of the grating over the drain is a second great mess of it. The right side of Thomsen's face is resting in this concoction. His Ritterkreuz dangles in it too. His mouth keeps forming bubbles because he's forcing sounds out. Through the gurgling I can make out, "Fight on—victory or death. Fight on—victory or death. Fight on—victory or death."

In a minute I'll be vomiting too. Rising nausea against the roof of my mouth.

"Come on, on your feet!" I say between clenched teeth and seize him by the collar. I don't want that mess on my hands.

"I wanted to—wanted to—tonight I wanted to—really fuck myself out," Thomsen mutters. "Now I'm in no shape to fuck anything."

The Old Man appears. We take Thomsen by the ankles and wrists; half dragging, half carrying, we get him through the door. The right side of his uniform is completely drenched.

"Give me a hand with him!"

I have to let go. I rush back into the can. In one great torrent the entire contents of my stomach gush out onto the tile floor. Convulsive retching. Tears in my eyes. I prop myself against the tile wall. My left sleeve is pushed up and I can see the dial of my wristwatch: two o'clock. Shit. At six thirty the Old Man is coming to drive us to the harbor.

II DEPARTURE

THERE ARE two roads to the harbor. The Commander takes the somewhat longer one, which runs along the coast.

With burning eyes, I observe the things we go past, the antiaircraft batteries with their mottled camouflage in the gray morning light. The signs for HEADQUARTERS—capital letters and mysterious geometric figures. A wall of shrubbery. A couple of grazing cows. The shattered village of Réception Immaculée. Billboards. A half-collapsed kiln. Two cart horses being led by the halter. Late roses in untended gardens. The splotched gray of house walls.

I have to keep blinking because my eyes still smart from all the cigarette smoke. The first bomb craters; ruined houses that announce the harbor. Heaps of old iron. Grass withered by the sun. Rusted canisters. An automobile graveyard. Parched sunflowers bent over by the wind. Tattered gray laundry. The half-riddled base of a monument. Parties of Frenchmen in Basque berets. Columns of our trucks. The road descends into the shallow river valley. Thick fog still hangs over this low ground.

A weary horse in the heavy mist hauling a cart, its two wheels as tall as a man. A house with glazed roof tiles. A once-enclosed verandah, now a mass of splintered glass and twisted ironwork. Garages. A fellow in a blue apron, standing in a doorway, the wet butt of a cigarette stuck onto his fleshy lower lip.

The clanking of a freight train. A siding. The riddled railway station. Everything gray. Innumerable nuances of gray, from dirty plaster-white to yellowish rusty-black. Sharp whistling of the shunting engine. I feel sand between my teeth.

French dockworkers with black hand-sewn shoulder bags. Astonishing that they go on working here despite the air raids.

A half-sunken ship with patches of red lead showing. Probably an old herring boat that was to have been rebuilt as some kind of patrol vessel. A tug pulls out into the shipping lane with a high forecastle and the lines of its hull bulging underwater. Women with huge asses in torn overalls, holding their riveting machines like machine guns. The fire in a portable smithy glows red through the gray murk.

The cranes on their high stilts are all still standing—despite the constant air attacks. The pressure waves from the detonations meet with no resistance in their iron filigree.

Our car can't go any farther in the confusion of the railroad yard. Rails bent into arches. The last few hundred yards to the bunker we have to cover on foot. Four heavily bundled figures in single file in the mist: the Commander, the Chief, the Second Watch Officer, and I. The Commander walks bent over, his eyes fixed on the path. Over the stiff collar of his leather jacket his red scarf has worked its way up almost to his spotted white cap. He keeps his right hand deep in the pocket of his jacket; the left is hooked into the jacket by the thumb. Under his left elbow he carries a bulging sailcloth bag. His bandy-legged gait is made even heavier by his clumsy seaboots with their thick cork soles.

I follow two paces behind. Then comes the Chief. He walks in a kind of unsteady bob. Rails that don't even check the Commander's stride force the Chief to proceed in short, springing hops. He's not wearing leather gear like us but gray-green overalls—like a mechanic wearing an officer's cap. He carries his bag properly by the handle.

Last in line is the Second Watch Officer, the shortest of us all. From his mutterings to the Chief, I make out that he's afraid the boat will not be able to put out on time because of the fog. There is not so much as a breath of air stirring in the dripping mist.

We go through a landscape of craters. In the depths of each shellhole the fog has settled like thick soup.

The Second Watch Officer has the same kind of sailcloth bag under his arm the Commander and I do. Everything we're taking on this patrol must fit into it: a big bottle of cologne, woolen underwear, a bodyband, knitted gloves, and a couple of shirts. I'm wearing the heavy sweater. Oilskins, seaboots, and escape apparatus are waiting for me on the boat. "Black shirts are best," the navigator had advised me and added knowledgeably, "black doesn't show dirt."

The First Watch Officer and the apprentice engineer are already on board with the crew, readying the boat for sea.

Over the harbor to the west the sky is still full of shadows, but eastward above the roadstead, behind the black silhouette of the freighter lying at anchor, the pale dawn light has already reached the zenith. The uncertain half-light makes everything strange and new. The skeletal cranes that tower above the bare façade of the refrigeration depot and the low roofs of the storage sheds are like charred black stakes for giant fruit. On the tarpaper roofs, ships' masts have been erected; along them coil white exhaust steam and oily black smoke. The plaster on the windowless side of the half-bombed house has been attacked by leprosy; it's falling away in big pieces. In huge white letters across the dirty red background of the ruins swaggers the word BYRRH.

Overnight, hoar frost has spread like mildew over the rubble still left from the last air raid.

Our path leads between ruins. Instead of the stores and inns that once lined the streets there are now only splintered signs above empty windows. Of the Café du Commerce only the "Comme" remains. The Café de la Paix has disappeared into a bomb crater. The iron framework of a burned-out factory has folded inward into a gigantic thistle.

Trucks are coming toward us—a column of them, carrying sand for the construction of the bunker channel. The wind from their passage picks up empty cement bags and blows them against the legs of the Commander and the Second Watch Officer. White plaster dust takes our breath away for a moment and clings like meal to our boots. Two or three shattered cars with Wehrmacht numbers lie overturned, their wheels in the air. Then more charred timbers and blown-off roofs, lying like tents amid the twisted railroad tracks.

"They've certainly messed the place up again," growls the Commander. The Chief takes this for an important communication and hurries up to him.

Then the Commander stops, clamps his sailcloth bag between his legs, and systematically digs out of the pocket of his leather jacket a shabby pipe and an old battered lighter. While we stand about, shivering and hunched over, the Old Man carefully lights the already full pipe. Now, like a steamer, he trails white clouds of smoke as he hurries along, frequently turning back toward us. His face is twisted in a mournful grimace. Of his eyes in the shadow of the visor of his cap nothing at all is visible.

Without taking his pipe from his mouth he asks the Chief in a rasping voice, "Is the periscope in order? Has the blur been fixed?"

"*Jawohl*, Herr Kaleun. A couple of lenses came loose in their cement bedding, probably during an air attack."

"And the trouble with the rudder?"

"All fixed. There was a break in the cable connection with the E-machine. That's why contact was intermittent. We put in a whole new cable."

Beyond a line of billboards there is a long row of freight cars. Behind them, the way leads straight across the tracks, then along a mud-choked road deeply rutted by the transport trucks.

Slanting iron bars armed with a thicket of barbed wire flank the road. In front of the guardhouse, sentries stand with raised collars, their faces hidden, like phantoms.

Suddenly the air is filled with a metallic clatter. This rattling ceases abruptly and an increasingly shrill whistle from a siren, as visible as a cloud of steam, hangs in the cold damp wind that smells of tar, oil, and rotten fish.

More bursts of metallic sound. The air is heavy and pregnant with them: we are in the wharf area.

To our left yawns a gigantic excavation, long strings of tip-cars disappear into its murky depths. They puff and rattle about below.

"There are going to be new bunkers all over this area," says the Old Man.

Now we're headed for the pier. Dead water under wads of fog. Ships moored so close beside and behind one another that the eye can't even distinguish their shapes. Battered, salt-encrusted fishing steamers, now serving as patrol boats, strange floating vehicles such as lighters, oil barges, harbor defense boats lying next to one another in packets of three—the bedbug flotilla—that wholly un-aristocratic confusion of shabby, wornout work and supply boats that is now a part of every commercial harbor.

The Chief points into the fog. "Over there—a bit to the right on that six-story house—there's a car up there!"

"Where do you mean?"

"Over the gable of the supply shed—the house with the wrecked roof!"

"How the hell did it get there?"

"Day before yesterday in the attack on the bunker. Bombs coming down as big as phone booths. I saw that buggy fly up and land on the roof—right on its wheels!"

"A circus act!"

"And the way the Frenchmen suddenly vanished. Couldn't believe it."

"What Frenchmen?"

"There's always a whole dockful of fishermen. You'll always find some right beside the entrance to Pen Number One. You just can't get rid of them."

"Of course they must have been keeping watch for the Tommies —which boats go out and which of them make it back—with exact times!"

"They're not spying any more. When the alarm sounded they just sat where they were, twenty or thirty of them—and then one of those huge bombs smashed into the pier."

"It caught the bunker too."

"Yes, a direct hit—but it didn't penetrate. Twenty feet of reinforced concrete."

Metal plates bend under our feet and spring back into their old positions. A locomotive whistles a piercing cry of woe.

Beyond the heavy, bouncing figure of the Commander there slowly emerges a concrete shape looming over everything. Its side walls are lost in the fog. We hurry toward a bare front without cornice, doors, or window openings. It looks like the side of a mighty foundation for a tower planned to climb far above the clouds. Only the twenty-foot-thick covering seems slightly out of proportion—a heavy load; it looks as though it had jammed the whole structure some distance back into the earth.

We have to make our way around blocks of concrete, railroad tracks, piles of boards, and pipes as thick as a man's thigh. Finally we come to the narrow side of the structure, an entrance protected by heavily armored steel doors.

Furious riveting greets us from the dark interior. The rattling stops occasionally, only to resume and grow to a thunderous uproar.

There is half darkness in the bunker. Only through the entranceways from the harbor basin can a pale light penetrate into the concrete caves. Two by two, the U-boats lie moored in their pens. The bunker has twelve pens. Some of them are constructed as dry docks. The boxes are divided from one another by huge concrete walls. The entrance to the pens can be protected by lowering steel bulkheads.

Dust, fumes, the stink of oil. Acetylene torches hiss, welding torches sputter, crackle, and howl. Here and there fireworks shoot up from the blow torches.

We go in single file along the concrete ramp that leads straight through the bunker at right angles to the docks. We have to be scrupulously careful. Loose material is lying around everywhere. Snakelike cables are trying to snare our feet. Railway cars block the path. They're bringing in new machine parts. Vans are drawn up close to the freight cars. On them, cradled in special supports, are the dully shimmering torpedoes, dismounted cannon and anti-aircraft guns, and everywhere pipes, hawsers, more cables, heaps of camouflage netting.

From the left, warm yellow light streams out of the windows of the workshops, carpenter shops, smithies, machine shops, torpedo, artillery, and periscope shops. Under this concrete roof a whole shipyard has been installed.

The Commander turns back. The sudden flaming of a welding torch illuminates his face with bluish light. Blinded, he squints. When the noise lessens for an instant he shouts at the Chief, "Did anything special turn up in dry dock?"

"Yes. The starboard propeller—bent blade."

"Aha, that was the singing noise we had at silent run!"

"New propellers—we've got brand-new propellers, Herr Kaleun!"

"Noiseless? Does the hydroplane work?"

"Yes, sir—the gear—took it apart—replaced the wheel—rusted places—cogwheel—everything in order!"

In the pens to the right lie wrecks, disabled boats with patches of rust and red lead showing. Smell of rust, paint, oil, putrid acids and burned rubber, benzine, seawater, and rotten fish.

Beyond the flooded pens are the dry docks. Far below, inside one of them, a boat lies with open belly, like an eviscerated whale. A whole crowd of dockyard men are at work on it—small as dwarfs, insects around a dead fish. At the moment large pieces of the outer skin are being cut away with blow torches. The damaged hull shows its jagged edges in the light of the flames. Compressed-air hoses in thick bundles and electric cables hang out of the boat's interior. Vitals and entrails. The round steel cylinder of the pressure hull is laid bare for the whole length of the foreship. Over the diesel room there is an opening. Yellow light streams from the inside of the boat. I can look deep into its guts. The huge blocks of the diesel engines, the tangled mass of pipes and conduits. Now the hook of the crane descends over the boat. A new load is attached. It looks as if the boat were to be completely emptied out.

"They went through a heavy depth charge attack," says the Chief.

"Sheer miracle they got back with that bombed-out tub!"

The Commander leads the way to a concrete stairway descending into the dry dock. The steps are smeared with oil; running down them are insulated cables in thick bundles.

Again the hissing flame of a welding torch leaps up, plucking part of the flooded bunker out of the half darkness. Farther back in the pen more welding flames, and the whole boat is caught in their flickering light. These are not the familiar stylish lines of surface vessels; from the flat sides the forward hydroplanes extend like fins, amidships the hull is distended. Thick rolls curve out to the right and left from the belly—the buoyancy tanks. They are welded onto the boat like a saddle. Everything is in a circular curve: a completely sealed and rounded-off creature of the deep, with its own special anatomy. The ribs here are closed rings.

Along one side of the bow a steel plate moves, opening up a dark slot. Slowly the plate moves farther back, enlarging the hole. It widens into a gaping mouth: an uncovered torpedo tube.

Two dockworkers try waving their arms in order to communicate above the racket of the pneumatic hammers.

The torpedo tube cover closes again.

"Looks worse than it is. Pressure hull—still perfectly good—all in order!" roars the Old Man.

I feel someone grasp my arm. The Chief is standing beside me, his head cocked to one side. He is looking up over the rounded belly of the boat.

"Fantastic, isn't it?"

From above, the guard looks down, his machine gun over his shoulder.

We clamber over piles of scaffolding toward the stern. The ground plan of the boat can be seen quite clearly. The extended steel cylinder encloses the power plants, the batteries, and the living quarters. This cylinder together with its contents is almost as heavy as the water it displaces. It is a VII-C boat, like ours. I remember: length 220 feet; width 20 feet; displacement 1,005 cubic yards on the surface and 1,138 cubic yards submerged—a very small difference. The boat simply has very few parts that rise above the surface. Draft on the surface 16 feet—an average figure, for actually the draft is variable. One can alter it inch by inch. The draft corresponds to the displacement of 660 tons of water when the boat is on the surface.

In addition to our type, there is also Type II with 275 tons and Type IX-C with 1,100 tons on the surface and 1,355 tons submerged. The VII-C boat is the fighting craft best adapted to the Atlantic. It can dive quickly and has great mobility. Its range of operations is 7,900 nautical miles on the surface at 10 knots, 6,500 nautical miles at 12 knots. Submerged, 80 nautical miles at 4 knots. The maximum speed is 17.3 knots on the surface and 7.6 knots submerged.

"He got it in the stern too. Rammed by a sinking steamer!" the Chief yells in my ear.

Here and there Jupiter lamps stand on tripods. Plates that have been dented are being hammered into shape again by a crowd of dockyard workers. Not serious: this is only a part of the outer skin, which is not pressure-resistant.

Of the true cylindrical core of the ship, the pressure hull, only a portion is visible amidships. Toward stern and bow this hull is covered by a thin outer skin, which camouflages the inflated deep-sea fish as a low-lying surface vessel when it comes up for air. Along the entire length of the boat the outer skin is pierced by holes and slits for flooding so that water can penetrate into the spaces between it and the real pressure hull. Otherwise the light disguise would be crushed like a cardboard box by the weight of the water pressing on it.

The weight of the boat can be precisely controlled with the trim tanks and the ballast tanks. Through a system of cells placed partly outside and partly inside the pressure hull, the boat can be raised high enough in the water for surface operation. The fuel tanks also lie outside the pressure hull.

On the underside of one of the ballast tanks I catch sight of the flooding hatches, which stay open when the boat is on the surface. The ballast tanks, like air cushions, keep the boat floating. If the air escapes through the valves in the top of the tanks, the water can rush in through the flooding hatches. The lift disappears, the boat dives.

I let my eyes roam along the boat: the thick bulge is the fuel oil tank. The hole over there is the cold-water intake for the diesels. Somewhere here must be the submersion cells. They are pressure-resistant, as are the trim cells and the ballast tanks.

A worker begins to hammer furiously at some rivet heads.

The Commander has gone farther toward the stern. He points upward: the boat's propellers are completely concealed by wooden scaffolding.

"He really got it," says the Old Man.

"Propeller shafts—getting—new lignum vitae bearings," roars the Chief. "Probably making noise—depth bomb pursuit."

Directly above the propellers, the cover for the stern torpedo tube. Halfway up, the flat surfaces of the stern hydroplanes grow out of the curve of the side like stunted airplane wings.

A workman spattered with paint from head to foot almost knocks me over. He has an enormous brush on an extra-long broom handle. While I'm waiting for the Old Man, he begins to paint the belly of the boat dark gray from underneath.

When we reach flooded Pen Six, the Commander once more turns aside toward the boat moored at the right of the pier. "Here's the boat that took a direct hit from a plane—Kramer's!"

Kramer's story is still in my ears. "Just as we're getting to the surface I see a plane. The bomb doors open, down comes the bomb straight at the bridge. I jerk my shoulder back for fear the bomb will hit it. The thing actually crashes into the bulwark of the bridge— but a little bit askew, not head on. And instead of blowing up, it just flies to bits. A dud."

The Commander inspects the conning tower from forward and aft, the bizarre strip of rolled-up metal that the bomb has torn from the covering of the tower, the broken cutwater. A sentry from the boat, bundled up against the cold, advances and salutes.

"By rights, he should have been flying around in a white night-gown for a good week already," says the Chief.

The basin of Pen Eight is also flooded. Reflections shiver and intertwine on the surface.

"Our boat," says the Chief.

In the semi-darkness of the bunker the hull is hardly distinguishable from the water. But against the pale wall the outlines rising above the low pier are more clearly defined. The upper deck lies only a bare yard over the oily brackish water. All the hatches are still open. I explore the entire length of the boat with my eyes as though to imprint it on my mind for all time: the flat wooden deck that reaches forward in one uninterrupted sweep to the bow; the conning tower with its squat, bristling, anti-aircraft guns; the gently sloping stern; the steel cables of the net guards with their interlaced green porcelain insulators slanting forward and aft from the conning tower. Everything of the utmost simplicity. A VII-C boat, the most seaworthy of ships.

I catch a crooked grin on the Commander's face, like an owner before a horse race.

The boat is ready for sea. Its tanks are filled with fuel oil and water—cleared for departure. And yet it isn't throbbing with the quivering, high-pitched hum of a ship ready to sail; the diesels aren't yet running, although the wharf crew with their heavy gloves stand ready with the hawsers.

"The official farewell takes place in the channel," says the Commander. "With all the idiocy that goes with it."

The crew is drawn up on the upper deck behind the tower. Exactly fifty men. (And me.) Eighteen-, nineteen-, and twenty-year-olds. Only the officers and petty officers are a few years older.

In the semi-darkness I can't really make out their faces. Roll is being called, but their clearly enunciated names escape me.

The upper deck is slippery from the fog that pours in through the bunker gates. The grayish misty white is so dazzling that the outlines of the exits are indistinct. The water in the basin is almost black and looks as turgid as oil.

The First Watch Officer reports, "All hands present and accounted for except control-room assistant Bäcker. Engine room ready, upper and lower decks cleared for departure!"

"Thanks. Heil UA!"

"Heil, Herr Kaleun!" resounds throughout the pen above the wailing of machinery.

"Eyes front! At ease!"

The Commander waits until the shuffling has subsided.

"You know that Bäcker's had it. Bombing raid on Magdeburg. A good man—what a mess. And not even a single score on his last cruise."

Long pause. The Old Man looks disgusted.

"All right then—not our fault. But let's make sure we do things better this time. Buck up."

Grins.

"Dismissed!"

"A fine speech," the Chief murmurs. "My respects!"

On the long, narrow upper-deck, fenders, cables, and new hawsers are still lying about. Warm steam pours out of the open galley hatch. Cookie's face appears. I hand my things down to him.

Noiselessly the periscope rises. Polyphemus eye turning in all directions, it rises to full height on its gleaming silvery mast, then sinks down again and disappears. I climb onto the conning tower. The paint is not yet entirely dry and comes off on the palms of my hands. The torpedo supply hatch on the upper deck is already closed. Aft, the galley hatch is now sealed. The single remaining entrance to the boat is the conning tower hatch.

Below, disorder reigns. One can move nowhere without pushing and shoving. Hammocks bulging with loaves of bread swing to and fro. Everywhere in the passages boxes of provisions, piles of canned food, sacks. Where is all this stuff to be stowed? The last inch of space is already full.

The designers of our boat have dispensed with the storage rooms that on surface vessels are normally many and capacious—just as they have dispensed with washrooms. They have simply built their machines into this war tube and have persuaded themselves that, given the most sophisticated deployment of the jungle of pipes and huge propulsion engines, there would necessarily be enough nooks and crannies left over for the crew.

The boat has taken on fourteen torpedoes. Five are in the tubes, two in the upper-deck torpedo holders, and the remainder under the floor plates—both aft and in the bow compartment. In addition,

120 shells for the 8.8 millimeter cannon and a quantity of anti-aircraft ammunition.

The navigation officer and the bosun—Number One, in nautical language—have their hands full. Number One is a powerful fellow called Behrmann, who towers by a head over most of the crew. I already know him: "*You bright-eyed little fawn, I'll get you . . .*"

Still a half hour to sailing. I have enough time to take a look around the engine rooms—an old love of mine, the engine rooms of ships cleared for sea. In the control room I sit down for a moment on the water distributor. All around me pipes, ventilators, hand wheels, manometers, auxiliary engines, the confused tangle of intertwined green and red electrical connections. In the half-darkness I recognize the hydroplane-position indicators, one electrical and one mechanical—almost all the systems are duplicated, for safety. Above the hydroplane station with its push-button controls for electrical underwater steering, I can just make out the trimming scales, one approximate and one exact. The Papenberg—a depth indicator between the round dials of the depth manometers with their clock-like hands—looks like a huge thermometer. During precise maneuvering it shows the depth for periscopic observation to within three inches.

The control room has pressure-resistant hatches fore and aft that can withstand greater pressure because of their half-spherical shape. The boat can be divided into three compartments by these two hatches.

There is not much advantage for us in this, for if one of the three compartments is flooded, the boat is no longer able to float. The designers probably had shallow waters in mind, like those of the Baltic.

The forward compartment has the torpedo supply hatch as the emergency exit, the after compartment has the galley hatch.

The engine room—my goal—lies aft of the galley.

All doors have been opened.

I painfully work my way aft over chests and sacks through the petty officers' quarters, where I am to sleep, and on through the galley, which has not yet been cleared up either.

Our engine room cannot compare with the engine rooms of big ships, those lofty halls usually extending from the top to the bottom of the whole craft, with their many stages of gratings and stairways glistening with oil, leading from story to story in a luster of polished copper and shimmering steel beams. Ours, on the contrary, is a narrow cave in which the two mighty diesels with all their auxiliary machines have to crouch like cowering animals. Around them, no small corner amid the welter of pipes is unused; there are cold-water pumps, lubrication pumps, oil separators, compressed-air starting cylinders, fuel pumps. In between are the manometers, thermometers, oscillation gauges, and every possible kind of indicator.

Each of the two diesels has six cylinders. Together they develop 2,800 horsepower.

When the hatches are sealed, the public address system is the only link with the control room. During battle, the floor here in the narrow gangway between the mighty diesels is especially tricky, for the diesel room holds most of the outboard plugs, the most vulnerable points in the pressure hull.

The two master mechanics are still hard at work. Johann is a tall, quiet, very pale, high-cheeked fellow who always looks calm and resigned; he has wretched posture, is blond and almost beardless. The other, Franz, is square, dark, and has a beard. He too is a chalk color, and stoops. He looks bad-tempered.

At first I assumed that they were both called by their first names. Now I know that Johann and Franz are family names. Johann's first name is August, and Franz's is Karl.

Farther aft is the motor room. The E-motors are run by batteries, which in turn are charged by the diesels. The E-motors develop 750 horsepower. Here everything is as clean, cold, and hidden as in a power station.

The housing of the motors rises only a little above the gleaming silvery floor plates. On both sides of the switching boxes are black signs and a mass of ampere meters, output gauges, and voltage controls. The motors work without drawing any air from outside. They are direct-current machines which during underwater navigation are attached directly, without gears, to the driving shafts behind the diesels. During surface operations, when the diesels are running, they also serve as dynamos to charge the batteries. At the after end of the room is the floor breach-lock of the rear torpedo tube. Left and right of it stand the two compressors, which supply the compressed air for emptying the diving tanks.

I wrestle my way back into the control room and clamber up through the hatch.

In line with the stern post our boat is being drawn out of the bunker by its E-motors and emerges into a mother-of-pearl brightness that makes the damp deck shimmer like glass. The Typhon, our signal horn, emits a hollow groan. Once, twice. A tug replies on an even deeper note.

In the diffused foggy light I see it glide by as if it were a black cardboard cutout. A second tug, heavy and powerful, pushes by so close I can make out the line of automobile tires it wears as fenders, the way Viking longboats carried their shields. A stoker sticks his ruddy face out of a porthole and shouts something to us, but in the sudden howl of our Typhon, I can't understand him.

The Commander himself is giving engine and rudder orders. He has propped himself up well above the bulwark of the bridge so that he can survey the boat from bow to stern for the difficult maneuvering through the harbor narrows.

"Port engine stop! Starboard engine slow ahead! Rudder hard to port!"

Cautiously the boat swings yard by yard into the mist. It's still cold.

Our pointed bow sweeps past a row of vessels lying close together. Small fry—harbor defense craft, a patrol boat among them.

The harbor water stinks more and more of tar and refuse and seaweed.

Over the fog banks now, individual steamer masts begin to appear, followed by a mass of derricks. The black filigree of the cranes reminds me of rigs in an oil field

Workmen making their way to the wharf along a suspension bridge are concealed up to the neck by its rusty brown side: a procession of severed heads.

In the east above the pale gray of the cold-storage plants, a reddish gleam gradually blends with the milky mist. A great block of buildings slips very slowly aside. Suddenly through the framework of a crane the sharply incised ball of the sun blazes out—only for an instant, then over it sweeps a puff of greasy smoke from a tug towing barges filled with black sand and coal.

I shudder in the damp wind and hold my breath, so as not to get too much of the suffocating vapor into my lungs.

On the channel wall a crowd has assembled: harbor workmen in oil-smeared overalls, sailors, a few officers of the flotilla. I recognize Gregor, who wasn't there last night, Kortmann, the Siamese twins Kupsch and Stackmann. Trumann is there too, of course, looking completely normal; no traces of last night's drunk. Behind him I notice Bechtel, he of the depth charge on the upper deck, and Kramer, of the aircraft bomb. Even the swaggerer Erler has turned up, surrounded by a crowd of girls carrying flowers. But no Thomsen.

"Just let me catch sight of that goddam dumb carbolic whore,"

I hear from a seaman beside me who is coiling up a stream cable.

"Boy, those bitches are crazy!" I hear from another one.

"The third from the left, the little one, I laid her!"

"Bullshit!"

"Word of honor. It's true."

To port, near the stern, a sudden surge of water. Waves of foam dance around the boat. Buoyancy Cell One is being blown out until it is completely filled with air. A moment later, water spurts up foaming along the sides: one cell after the other is being blown—our upper deck rises higher above the water.

An artillery man from above shouts, "A ship this size!" and stretches out his arms like a fisherman bragging about his catch; one of our men on the upper deck sticks out his tongue. A variety of insults, grins, funny faces. All in good humor—but that won't last.

Now it's really time to cast off. Commander, officers, and all the crew are aboard. For Bäcker, the one who got it in Magdeburg, there's a substitute: a pale, spindly eighteen-year-old.

High tide an hour ago. We should get through smoothly.

Our crew on the upper deck act out the standard farce—how wonderful to be on our way at last! And the ones left on the pier pretend they're dying of envy. You're off on this splendid cruise! You get to see enemy action and grab all the medals, while we poor bastards are stuck here in shitty France frigging around with shitty whores!

I straighten up in my still stiff leather clothes. There I stand, hands belligerently thrust into the pockets of my felt-lined jacket—it reaches to my knees. I stamp up and down on the grating in my heavy boots which are cork-soled against the icy chill of the iron.

The Old Man is grinning. "Impatient?"

The men in the military band with their steel helmets look at us blankly.

A slovenly bassoonist in the second row is licking the mouthpiece of his instrument for the fifth time, as though it were a lollipop.

When he has completely licked away his bassoon, one second of eternity will have . . .

The jackbooted bandmaster raises his baton and the brasses blare out; another second and all talk is drowned in the screeching impact of the music.

The two gangplanks have been hauled in.

The first watch has taken up maneuver stations. The off-duty watch remains on the upper deck. The First Watch Officer whistles to cast off. The Commander acts as though none of this concerns him in the slightest, and puffs away on a thick cigar. Up on the pier Trumann has also lit one. They salute each other, cigars between index and middle fingers. The First Watch Officer looks away in irritation.

"Where's Merkel?" the Old Man asks when the band stops playing, gesturing toward the pier.

"Not yet cleared for sea."

"Ach, shameful!"

The Old Man squints at the sky, then wraps himself in an especially heavy cloud of smoke, like a steam tug.

"Cast off all lines except mooring cables!"

Hawsers fore and aft are cast off by soldiers on the pier. The men on the upper deck haul them in, working smoothly together. The result of seven earlier patrols.

"Port engine dead slow ahead, starboard engine slow astern! Both engines stop—midships!"

Now the mooring cable splashes into the water.

Our fenders glide along the rounded belly of the outer bunker. The bubbling gurgle of water from the propellers makes me look toward the stern.

The boat has freed itself from the pier, a dismal ferry on an oily black Styx, with a cargo of leather-armored men on the antiaircraft platform behind the circular enclosure of our bridge. No exhaust visible, no engine noise. As though by a magnet, the boat is drawn away from the pier.

Small bouquets of flowers fall onto the bridge. Members of the watch stick them into the ventilation ducts.

The dark strip of water between the gray steel of the boat and the oil-smeared wall of the pier keeps widening. Now there is a commotion in the crowd on the pier. Someone is forcing his way through from behind, parting the mob: Thomsen! He stretches both hands in the air, his new decoration glittering on its neckband, and roars across the brackish water, "Heil UA!" And again, "Heil UA!"

With an indifference uniquely his, the Old Man waves his cigar.

The boat is making its way slowly into the misty outer basin and the horizon expands. The bow points toward the open sea.

Gradually the smoky mist lifts from the water. On the black iron girders of a crane the sun climbs higher. Its brilliant red fills the whole eastern sky. The edges of the clouds are dappled with red foam. Even the seagulls catch the splendor. With folded wings they fall through the glowing light almost to the water and at the last instant swing upward, screeching wildly.

The clouds of mist dissipate completely and the oily water burns in the glare. A floating crane quite close to us emits a gigantic cloud of steam that the sun instantly stains red and orange. Beside it, even the red BYRRH sign looks pale.

Quickly the sky becomes green-yellow and the clouds take on a dull dove-gray.

A green wreck-buoy slides past. Looking to starboard, I see the red roofs of the bathing huts crowded together and slowly sinking behind the gleaming yellow derricks.

All of a sudden a high choking sound. Then comes a harsh singing and rumbling. The deck begins to shake. The rumbling grows louder and takes on a regular rhythm: our diesels have started.

I put my hands on the cold iron of the bridge bulwark and feel the pulsing of the machinery.

The sea is running against us. Short, choppy waves break against the buoyancy tanks. The head of the breakwater moves past and recedes.

A freighter slips by, camouflaged green, gray, black.

"About six thousand tons!" says the Commander. No wave at the bow; the freighter is lying at anchor.

Our route now runs so close to the coast that we can see all the landmarks. Soldiers wave at us.

We move at the speed of a slow cyclist.

"Clear upper deck to dive!" the Commander orders.

The bollards to which the lines had been made fast retract, the boat hooks are lashed down, the lines and fenders stowed in spaces under the gratings. The seamen push home and lock all the openings on the upper deck, bring in the flagpole, clear the machine guns, lay out the ammunition.

Number One watches with a sharp eye to see that everything is done properly; during silent run there must be no noise. The First Watch Officer rechecks, then reports to the Commander, "Upper deck cleared for diving!"

The Commander orders increased speed. Between the gratings, foam boils up and spray strikes the tower.

The rocky coast recedes behind us. Dark shadows still lie in its clefts. The anti-aircraft installations have been so well camouflaged that I can hardly find them, even with binoculars.

Two patrol boats—rebuilt trawlers—join our boat to provide anti-aircraft protection.

After a while a mine sweeper turns up to accompany us, a big camouflaged ship stuffed full of barrels and other highly buoyant cargo. Its upper deck bristles with anti-aircraft guns.

"What a job," says the navigator. "They go around on trampolines so their bones won't be broken if a mine just happens to go off. Every day the same thing—out—in . . . Thanks, but no thanks!"

Our boat stays precisely in the middle of the broad bubbling wake of the mine sweeper.

I get the long bay of La Baule in my glasses: a thick row of dollhouses. Then I turn toward the stern. Saint Nazaire is now a thin streak, with the tall cranes no more than pins outlined against the sky.

"Complicated channel here. All sorts of wrecks lying around— look!—tips of masts! That was an Allied transport sunk by Stukas, a bomb straight down the funnel. It's exposed at low tide. There's another one. The thing in front of it is a light-buoy."

When hardly anything more than the north shore of the estuary can be seen, the navigator orders the optical bearing-finder brought up. He places the apparatus on its stand and bends over it.

"Hey, move over!"

The guard on the starboard deck aft moves over.

"What's your landmark?" the Commander inquires.

"Tip of the church steeple there—you can hardly see it—and the top of the rocks to starboard."

The navigator sights carefully, reads off the numbers, and calls them down. "Last landmark," he says.

We have no harbor as destination. The goal that draws us from our base out into the expanse of the ocean is a square designated by two numbers on the map of the mid-Atlantic.

The Operations Division of U-boat Headquarters has divided up the ocean into a mosaic of these small squares. This simplifies exchange of information, but it makes it hard for me, accustomed to the usual coordinates, to recognize our position at a glance on the map.

At eleven o'clock the escort is dismissed. The patrol boats fall rapidly astern. The mine sweeper swings away in a wide curve and unfurls a dark, broad-flowing smoke banner against the sky. A last wave of farewell.

Now the navigator determinedly turns forward with his whole body, holds the binoculars to his eyes, and props his elbows on the bulwark.

"Well, Kriechbaum, here we go again!" says the Commander and disappears down into the conning tower.

The boat is now alone on its course.

One of the bridge guards pulls the flowers out of the ventilation ducts and throws them overboard. They quickly drift astern in the swirling wake.

I prop myself up high, in order to see the boat from bow to stern over the bridge bulwark.

A long groundswell is coming toward us. Again and again the bow dips and splits the waves like a plow. Each time, water shoots up foaming, and sharp showers hiss across the bridge. If I run my tongue over my lips I taste the Atlantic—salty.

In the blue vault of the sky hang a few stratocumulus clouds like the foam of beaten egg whites. The bow descends, rises high again, crashes down, and the whole forward deck is covered for minutes at a time with foam. The sun brings out the colors of the spectrum in the watery mist; little rainbows arch over the bow.

The sea is no longer bottle-green but a deep dark-blue. Thin white streaks of foam run irregularly along the blue surface like veins of marble. When a wad of cloud moves in front of the sun the water turns to blue-black ink.

Astern, a broad path of milky waters; our wide, roiling wake dashes against the groundswell and shoots up in white manes. These gleaming tresses extend as far as the eye can see.

Propping my feet against the periscope housing I climb a little higher out of the bridge and lean back, supporting my arms on the net guard. Seagulls with bent swordlike wings shoot around the boat and watch us with stony eyes.

The noise of the diesels alters constantly; it ebbs away when the exhaust vents on either side of the boat are submerged in the sea, then rises when they come free and the gas can escape unhindered.

The Commander returns to the deck, narrows his eyes, and raises his binoculars.

Ahead, a cloud like a gray fleece hangs over the water. The Commander eyes it sharply. He compensates so precisely with his knees for the motion of the boat that he has no need of a hand-hold.

"High time we put to sea again!"

The Commander increases speed and orders a zigzag course. At each change of direction the boat heels to one side. The wake twists to right, then left.

"Look out for bubble tracks—this area—very risky!" and then turning to me: "The gentlemen of the other firm are accustomed to lie in wait for us here. After all, they know exactly when we cast off. Not much of a trick—they can easily find out. From the harbor workers, from the cleaning women—from the whores. What's more, they can peek in themselves while we're docked."

Again and again the Commander glances distrustfully toward the sky. Washboard wrinkles in his forehead, his nose twisted to one side, he shifts impatiently from one foot to the other. "Any minute now the flyers could surprise us. They're getting bolder all the time!"

The clouds gradually draw closer together. Only now and then does a piece of blue sky shine through.

"Very risky indeed," the Old Man repeats, and murmurs under his binoculars, "Better get below just now. When there's an alarm— as few people on deck as possible."

That means me. I disappear promptly from the bridge.

My bunk is in the petty officers' quarters, the U-room, the most uncomfortable on board: it has the most through traffic. Anyone who wants to get to the galley, or to the diesels or the E-motors, has to come through here. At every change of watch the men from the engine room squeeze through from astern, and the new watch comes through from the control room. That means six men each time. And the stewards have to work their way past with their full dishes and pots. In fact, the whole place is nothing more than a narrow corridor with four bunks on the right and four on the left. In the middle of the passage, screwed to the floor, there's a table with folding leaves. The space on both sides is so narrow that at mealtimes the men have to sit on the lower bunks with their heads bent. There is far too little space for stools. And there is muss and confusion whenever someone has to get from the engines to the control room or vice versa during a meal.

Meals are so arranged that the officers and the crew are already finished in the forward compartments when the petty officers crowd around their own table—so the stewards don't then have to go back and forth between the bow compartment and the galley. Nevertheless there is constant disturbance. It's my good luck that I don't have to eat in the U-room; a place is laid for me in the Officers' Mess.

Some of the bunks are used by two petty officers in rotation. I am the happy possessor of a bunk all to myself.

The petty officers from the off-duty watch are still busy arranging their lockers. Two men going to the engine room have to get through to the stern, and there's a mix-up right away. My bunker rail, a kind of narrow aluminum ladder, has come down, which adds to the confusion.

My bunk is still covered with canned food, a bundle of fur-lined jerkins, and some loaves of bread. A seaman brings oilskins, leather clothing, seaboots, and rescue gear. The lined leather jacket is still uncreased. The boots are lined with felt, but are big enough to wear over heavy socks.

The rescue gear is in a dark-brown sailcloth bag with a zipper. Brand new. "Pure decoration," says the control-room mate, "really meant for the Baltic!"

"But very useful when the diesel stinks," says a big dark-haired fellow with bushy eyebrows: Frenssen, the diesel mechanic mate. Nevertheless, the rescue gear has its use; if I turn the nozzle slightly, the little steel flask immediately emits oxygen.

I stow the brown bag at the foot of my bunk. For my possessions I have a tiny locker, not even big enough to hold the absolute necessities. So I put my writing materials and camera in the bunk between the light mattress and the wall. Just enough space remains for my body—it's like being in a suitcase. I want to look around a little before the noon meal and I go forward through the control room.

Aside from the petty officers, the rest of the crew, including the Commander and officers, sleep in the foreship. The Commander lives directly beyond the control-room hatch. Behind a green curtain there's a bunk, a couple of lockers on the wall and ceiling, and a very small writing table, really only a writing board—and that's it. He too has to make out as best he can. Closed rooms on either side of the passageway, such as you find in surface vessels, don't exist. Opposite the Commander's "room" are the radio shack and the sound room.

Farther forward is the Officers' Mess—the wardroom, which also serves as living quarters for the Chief, the apprentice engineer (our Second Engineer), and the First and Second Watch Officers.

The mattress on which our Commander and the Chief sit at mealtimes is really the Chief's bunk. The railroad berth above it is folded up during the day; it's the Second Watch Officer's berth. The berths of the First Watch Officer and the Second Engineer are more favorably placed on the opposite wall. Since these don't have to be put away during the day, the First Watch Officer and the Second Engineer can stretch out during their free time.

The table, screwed fast to the floor, is on the side away from the passage. It's designed for four: the Commander, the Chief, and the two Watch Officers. However, six of us will be eating there.

In the adjoining compartment, the Quarters, which is separated from the O-Mess simply by lockers, live the navigator Kriechbaum, the two chief mechanics Johann and Franz, and the bosun Behrmann. Under the floor plates lies Battery One, which together with Battery Two under the U-room supplies the energy for running underwater.

The bow compartment is separated from the Quarters by a nonpressure-resistant hatch. Despite its cavelike appearance, the bow compartment is the closest thing we have to a room. Strictly speaking, it is a combination work-storage space for torpedoes and a battle station. "Torpedo room" is therefore an accurate designation. Here live most of the crew. On each side are six berths, two by two, one above the other. In them the sailors, or "lords," sleep, plus the torpedo men, the radioman, and the stokers.

Because they stand six-hour watches, two stokers share each bunk. For the others who go on watch in trios, there are two bunks for every three men. No one has a bunk to himself. When a sailor gets up to begin his watch, the man he relieves lies down in the stale air he's left behind. Nevertheless, there still aren't enough bunks; four hammocks dangle from the ceiling.

The men off-duty rarely stay undisturbed. During mealtimes they all have to get up. The upper berths have to be snapped shut and the lower ones cleared so that the "lords" can sit down on them. When the torpedoes in the four bow tubes are being "adjusted," the room is transformed into a machine shop. Then the bunks are taken down and the hammocks stowed away.

The reserve torpedoes for the forward tubes are stowed under the raised floor plates. Until they are loaded, the lack of space will be painful. So for the men in the bow compartment, every torpedo fired means added freedom of motion. But they do have at least one advantage: no through traffic.

Right now the place looks like a devastated arsenal: leather clothing, rescue gear, sweaters, sacks of potatoes, teapots, uncoiled rope, loaves of bread . . . Unimaginable that all this will disappear to make room for twenty-six seamen and the torpedo mechanic, who is the only petty officer not living in the U-room.

It looks as if everything they couldn't find space for right away has been shoved in here. Just as I appear, the bosun is urging two seamen on. "Hurry up—the lettuce crate between the torpedo tubes! Lettuce! You'd think this was a fucking grocery store!"

The bosun points out the narrowness of the ship as if it is a special attraction. He acts as though it were all his own idea. "It's a matter of give and take," he says. "The heads, for example: there are two of them, but we have to use one for provisions, so there's more space for food and less for shitting! You try to make sense out of it!"

In all the compartments, thick bundles of cables and pipes run

under the floors. If you open a locker door, more of them are revealed—as if the woodwork were only a pretty veneer over the
technological maze.

At lunch I have to sit on a folding chair in the gangway next
to the Second Watch Officer. The Commander and the Chief are
on the "leather sofa," the Chief's bunk. The apprentice engineer and
the First Watch Officer sit at the ends of the table.

If someone wants to get through, the Second Watch Officer and
I either have to get up or jam our stomachs against the table and
bend over so that the man can wriggle past. Standing up is the lesser
evil, as we quickly discover.

The Commander wears a disreputable sweater of indefinable
color. He has changed his blue-gray shirt for a red-checked one, its
collar showing over his sweater. While the steward is serving, he sits
with folded arms, leaning back in his corner and occasionally inspecting the ceiling as though fascinated by the veins in the wood.

The apprentice engineer is a full lieutenant, new on board. He's
to replace the Chief after this patrol. A blond North German with a
broad, rather square-cut face. While we eat, I see little of him
except his profile. He looks to neither right nor left and doesn't
utter a sound.

The Chief sits opposite me. When you see him next to the Commander he looks even thinner and more haggard than he really is: a
sharp, curved nose that shows the bone, black hair combed back
flat. His receding hairline gives him a real thinker's forehead. Very
dark eyes. Prominent cheekbones and temples. Full lips but a firm
chin. The men call him "Rasputin," mainly because he goes on
tending his pointed black beard with devotion and patience long
after every patrol, until finally making up his mind to shave it off
and rinse it away with the lather.

He's been on board since the boat's first patrol and is the second
most important man here, the undisputed ruler of all technical
matters. His domain is completely separate from that of the sea
officers; his fighting station is the control room.

"The Chief's first-rate," says the Old Man. "He keeps a steady
course and that's what counts. Does it by feel. The new man will
never be able to. He simply doesn't have it in his fingertips. You
can't do it just by knowing things. You have to sense the reaction
of the boat and act before a particular tendency can take effect.
A matter of experience and feeling! Not everyone can do it. Not
something that can be learned . . ."

As he sits there beside the Old Man, with his small lively hands, his dreamy eyes, his long, dark hair, I can imagine him in all kinds of roles: a croupier or a crap-shooter, a violinist or a movie actor. His build is almost that of a dancer. Instead of boots he wears light sport shoes, instead of the cumbersome U-boat clothing a kind of overalls, like a gym outfit. Getting through the circular hatches is easier for him than for anyone else. "He slips through the boat like oil," I heard the control-room mate remark this morning.

From the Old Man I know that the Chief is unflappable, for all his racehorse nervousness. While we were in harbor he was seldom at the flotilla mess. He was on board from morning till night busying himself with the smallest details.

"On this boat not so much as a wooden screw goes in without the Chief's supervision. He has no confidence in shipyard work-men."

On account of his small stature, the Second Watch Officer is known to the crew as "the Garden Gnome" or "the Baby Officer." I have known him and the Old Man and the Chief for quite a while. The Second Watch Officer is just as conscientious as the Chief. He always looks alert—almost sly. If you speak to him, his face soon crinkles into laughter. "He stands firm on his hind legs on deck," says the Old Man. The skipper sleeps soundly when the Second Watch Officer is on duty.

The First Watch Officer has been out on patrol only once before. I hardly ever saw him in the mess during our time in port. Toward both him and the Second Engineer, the Commander's manner is strained—either noticeably reserved or exaggeratedly friendly.

In contrast to the Second Watch Officer, the First Watch Officer is a gangling, pale, colorless type with a frozen sheepface. No real self-possession or assurance, so he's always trying to appear quick and decisive. I soon discover that he obeys orders but has no initiative or common sense. The upper portions of his ears are strangely undeveloped and the lobes lie close to his head. His nostrils are flat. His whole face looks unfinished. Also he has an unattractive way of glancing disapprovingly out of the corner of his eye, without moving his head. When the Old Man produces one of his little jokes, he smiles sourly.

"If we have to put to sea with nothing but schoolboys and super-annuated Hitler Youths, things must be getting pretty bad," the Old Man had murmured to himself in the Bar Royal, no doubt with the First Watch Officer in mind.

"Cups over here!" the Commander now directs, and pours tea for all of us. There's no longer room for the hot teapot on the table. I have to hold it between my knees and bend over it to get at my food. Damn hot! I can barely stand it.

The Commander sips with visible enjoyment. He forces himself farther and farther into the corner and draws up one knee so that he can brace it against the table. Then with a slight nod he looks around at us, exactly like a contented father with his brood.

His eyes sparkle with mischief. His mouth widens: the Second Watch Officer has to get up again. I of course have to get up too, along with the teapot, because Cookie wants to go forward through the passage.

The cook is a vigorous, shortish fellow with a neck as wide as his head. He grins at me trustingly, from ear to ear. I suspect that he's come through the mess right now to be congratulated on his food.

"I'll tell you a story about him sometime!" the Old Man says, chewing, as the cook departs.

Crackling in the loudspeaker. A voice comes on. "First watch prepare for duty!"

The First Watch Officer gets up and begins systematically to dress himself up. The Old Man watches with interest as he finally manages to get into the huge boots with their thick cork soles, wrap a scarf meticulously around his neck, and muffle himself up in the thick-lined leather jacket; he gives a military salute and departs.

Shortly afterward, the navigator, who has been in charge of the previous watch, comes through, his face reddened by the wind, and reports: "Wind northwest, tending to veer to the right, visibility good, barometer one thousand and three."

Then he makes us get up because he wants to go through to his quarters to change. The navigator has also been on board since the boat was commissioned. He has never served on surface vessels, only on U-boats. Way back in the old Reich Navy in those tiny, single-hulled crafts.

The navigator would probably be a failure as an actor. His facial muscles are stiff, so that he seems to be wearing a rigid mask. Only his deep-hollowed, heavy-browed eyes are full of life. "He has eyes in the back of his head," I heard someone in the bow compartment say of him approvingly.

In so low a voice that the navigator can't pick it up next door, the Old Man whispers to me: "He's an ace at dead reckoning. Sometimes in bad weather we can't see stars or sun for days or weeks at a time, but our position checks with astonishing precision. I often wonder how he does it. Has a lot to do on board. In charge of the third watch in addition to all that navigational stuff."

After the navigator, it's the bosun who wants to go forward. Behrmann is a chunky fellow, red-cheeked and bursting with health. And then, as though to illustrate the contrast between seamen and engineers, comes the white-faced chief mechanic Johann. "The Sorrows of Christ," the Commander calls him. "A real expert. Married to his machines. Hardly ever comes on deck, a real mole."

Five minutes later three men of the new watch struggle through the mess toward the stern.

It no longer matters to me—when the First Watch Officer got up I had quickly planted myself in his seat.

"The next to last was Ario," the Chief says. "And the last one, the little fellow, was the new—what's his name?—the replacement for Bäcker. Control-room assistant. He's already got a nickname, 'the Bible Scholar'—apparently he reads tracts."

Soon the watch that has been relieved comes through. The Chief leans back and drawls, "That's Bachmann, 'the Gigolo': diesel stoker. Absolute balls! There's nothing to stoke any more, but in the Navy traditions survive longer than ships. Hagen: E-motor stoker. Even less to stoke. Turbo: the other control-room assistant. First-rate boy."

Then from the opposite direction appears a tall blond fellow, Hacker, the torpedo mechanic and senior man in the bow compartment. The only petty officer who sleeps there. "Maniac," says the Old Man. "Once he got a completely screwed-up torpedo out of the upper-deck compartment with a huge sea running, took it apart and repaired it, below decks of course. That was our last fish, and we knocked out one more ship with it, a ten-thousand-ton steamer. *His* steamer, strictly speaking. He'll get the fried egg soon—he's earned it."

Next through the compartment is a small man with very black hair carefully plastered back and slit eyes that twinkle confidingly at the Chief. His forearms are tattooed; I catch a fleeting glimpse of a sailor hugging a girl against a red sun.

"That was Dunlop. Torpedo man. He looks after the workshop. The big harmonica in the sound room belongs to him."

Finally we get Franz, also a master mechanic. The Chief casts a disgruntled look after him. "Tires too easily. Johann, the other one, is the better man."

The meal is over and I'm making my way from the O-Mess to the petty officers' quarters.

The bosun must be a terrific housekeeper. He's divided up the provisions and stowed them away so perfectly everywhere that the trim of the ship hasn't suffered—and, as he proudly assures me, in such a way that perishables will come to hand before things that last. No one else knows where the mountains of food have disappeared to. Only the hard sausages, the sides of bacon, and the loaves are visible. The supply of sausage hangs from the ceiling of the control room as though in a smokehouse. The fresh bread fills the hammocks in front of the sound room and radio shack. Every time someone wants to get past, he has to stoop and work his way through the loaves.

I climb through the second circular hatch. My bunk is free now. The equipment is laid out properly on the blanket, the bag with my belongings at the bottom end. I can pull the green curtain shut and close out the world. Wood paneling on one side, green curtain on the other, white lacquer above. The life of the boat is now reduced to voices and sounds.

In the afternoon I go up onto the bridge. The Second Watch Officer has just begun watch. The sea is bottle-green. Close beside the boat, almost black. The air is damp, the sky completely clouded over.

After I have stood for a good while beside the Second Watch Officer he begins to talk from beneath his binoculars. "It was about here that they fired a spread of four at us. Patrol before last. We saw one fish shoot by the stern and another one cut past the bow. Made quite an impression!"

Choppy little waves have risen on the low groundswell. However benign the water may appear, the shadow of each of these short waves may hide the enemy's periscope eye.

"Have to be damn careful around here!" says the Second Watch Officer from between his leather gloves.

The Commander comes up. He growls a curse at the weather and says, "Look out, youngster, keep your eyes open! Damn bad spot here!"

Suddenly he snarls at the starboard lookout aft. "Keep it down or we'll have to hang you over a laundry line!" And after a while, "If you can't take it, you shouldn't be here. But since you are, you'll have to find your sea legs any way you can."

He orders a practice dive for 16.30 hours. After her long period in dock, the boat is to submerge for the first time and be balanced out, so that when an alarm comes there won't have to be a lot of trimming and flooding first. It's also important to make sure all the vents and plugs are working.

The order "Clear bridge for dive!" initiates the maneuver. The anti-aircraft ammunition disappears into the tower. The three lookouts and the Officer of the Watch are still on the bridge.

Orders, reports, ringing of bells. Aft, the diesels are stopped and disengaged. The E-motors are geared to the drive shafts and set at high speed. Simultaneous with the stopping of the diesels, the big conduits leading to the outside—for the exhaust and for air intake —are closed. From the diesel room the signal *Ready to Dive* is flashed to the control room. The bow compartment also gives its *All Ready* signal. The lookouts on the bridge have come below. Looking up the shaft of the tower, I see the Watch Officer hastily turning the hand wheel that presses the tower hatch home in its bed.

"Clear the air-release vents!" the Chief orders. Reports come in quick succession to the Chief. "One!" "Three, both sides!" "Five!" "Five clear!"

It sounds like a magic incantation.

"All vents clear!" the Chief reports.

"Flood!" comes from below.

"Flood!" the Chief repeats for his crew.

The sailors in the control room swiftly open the emergency evacuation vents. The air that gave the boat buoyancy escapes with a thundering roar from its tanks. The hydroplane operators set the forward plane hard down and the after-plane ten down. The boat dips and becomes noticeably bow heavy; the pointer on the depth manometer moves slowly over the numbers on the dial. One more wave crashes against the tower and then suddenly all noise ceases: the bridge has slid underwater.

Oppressive silence—no breaking of waves, no more vibration of the diesels. The radio is silent. Radio waves cannot penetrate the depths. Even the humming of the ventilators has stopped.

I pay close attention. Someday it may be up to me.

The Chief orders, "Forward up ten, aft up fifteen!" The bow heaviness is corrected. The current from the propellers strikes the upward-tilted hydroplane and slowly the boat grows stern heavy. The final bubbles of air that have clung to the corners of the buoyancy cells and might give unwelcome lift now escape.

The Chief reports to the Commander, "Boat balanced!"

The Commander orders, "Close vents!"

The exhaust vents on top of the buoyancy cells are closed by hand wheels and connecting rods in the control room.

"Proceed to ninety feet!" The Commander is leaning motionless at the chart table, his elbows braced behind him.

The Chief stands behind the two hydroplane operators, so that the hydroplane indicators, depth indicators, trim indicators, water-depth gauges, scales, and manometer needle are in full view.

The hand of the manometer turns. Forty feet, sixty, seventy-five.

Now there is only the soft humming of the E-motors. Somewhere water drips into the bilge with a thin, lost sound. The Chief looks up. With his pocket flashlight he goes searching among the pipes on the port side. Then the dripping stops by itself. "That's that," the Chief murmurs.

A shudder like a chill runs through the boat.

The Old Man seems completely unconcerned. He appears to be just staring blankly ahead, but now and again he glances around quickly.

The indicator on the manometer approaches ninety. Its movement becomes steadily slower. Finally it stops. The boat is no longer descending; it hovers in the water like a zeppelin, but you can feel that it is still stern heavy. There is no upward or downward motion, but it's not yet on an even keel.

The Chief begins the trimming operation. "Pump water forward!" The control-room assistant Turbo turns a valve behind the periscope shaft.

The Chief orders a readjustment of the hydroplanes. Now the boat rises, without any water having been expelled. Very slowly the hand of the manometer moves backward over the dial. Simply by use of the hydroplanes and the forward thrust of the propellers the required depth is reached—dynamically.

Now and again the Chief gives an order to the hydroplane operators. Finally the Commander speaks. "Proceed to periscope depth!" He gets up with a jerk and clambers heavily into the tower.

"Forward up twenty, aft down five!" The Chief.

The column of water in the Papenberg is already slowly sinking. The Chief bends to one side, tilts his head back, and reports to the tower, "Periscope cleared!"

Every up or down movement of the column of water in the Papenberg means a rise or fall of the boat. The hydroplane operators have to try through expertly timed setting of the planes to counteract a rise or fall before these motions show in the Papenberg, for then it is too late: either the periscope has risen too high out of the water, betraying the boat to the enemy in case of attack, or it has plunged beneath the surface so that the Commander sees nothing at all at the decisive moment.

The Chief has not once taken his eyes off the Papenberg. Neither have the two hydroplane operators. It barely rises or falls. Total silence in the boat, only an occasional low humming from the periscope motor.

"Bridge watch stand by! Oilskins on!" The voice of the Commander from the tower.

The bridge lookouts tie their sou'-westers under their chins and put on their oilskin jackets, then form in a group under the tower hatch.

"Prepare to surface!"

Aft, the stokers now pump oil so that the diesels can start immediately.

"Surface!"

The Chief has the forward hydroplane turned up full and the aft up five degrees. He orders the tanks blown.

With a sharp hissing sound the compressed air streams in.

"Equalize pressure!"

Suddenly there is a pain in my ears; the excess pressure has been reduced. A stream of fresh air bursts into the boat from above: the tower hatch is open. The ventilators are turned on and draw a mighty draft into the boat.

There follows a series of orders for the engines.

"Port diesel ready!"

"Port E-motor stop! Change gears!"

"Port engine slow forward!"

The trim cells are flooded again. After that the Commander orders, "Blow tanks with the diesels!"

The diesel exhaust gases now force the water out of the buoyancy cells. This saves compressed air. And the procedure has another advantage: the oily exhaust gases help prevent corrosion.

One buoyancy cell after the other is blown out. From the bridge the Commander can tell by the air bubbles that rise along the sides of the boat whether the buoyancy cells have been properly cleared. After a while he calls down, "All blown. Dismiss from diving stations!"

The boat is a surface vessel again.

The Commander orders, "Starboard diesel stand by! Starboard E-motor stop! Shift over! Starboard engine forward slow!"

The Chief stands up, wriggles his shoulders, stretches, and looks quizzically at me. "Well?"

I nod submissively and, like a defeated boxer, sink down on the sack of potatoes leaning against the chart table. The Chief seizes a handful of prunes from the chest that stands open for everyone beside the table, and holds them out to me. "Spiritual refreshment! Yes, we're not exactly your simple, straightforward kind of boat."

When the Old Man has disappeared, the Chief says quietly, "Things are going to stay lively today. 'Working the weariness out of dissipated bones!' is what the Old Man calls it. Nothing gets past him. He has his eye on everyone. All we need is a single mistake and we'll be in for one exercise after the other."

On its table under a thick celluloid cover lies the sea chart. At present it's still a blank, showing only the edges of the coasts. The land masses behind the coasts are empty, as though uninhabited; no roads, no towns. A sea chart. What's behind the coasts has no meaning for the seafarer. At most a few landmarks and the designated lighthouses. On the other hand, all shoals and sandbars near the entrance to rivers are here. A zigzag pencil line extends from Saint Nazaire. There is a cross on it—our last bearing.

Our general course is three hundred degrees, but I keep hearing orders to the helmsman. Danger from enemy submarines still keeps us from steering a straight course.

In the control room an off-duty member of the watch is talking with Turbo, the assistant, who preserved his reddish beard while the boat was in harbor and now looks like an imitation Viking. "Wonder where we're off to this time."

"Looks like Iceland!"

"Naw, I bet on the south! A long southern patrol. Look at all the stuff we took on board."

"That doesn't mean a damn thing. And why should we care anyway? There's no getting ashore for a quick lay whichever way we go."

Turbo has been aboard a long time. With the blasé manner of a man of experience, he draws down the corners of his mouth, half hidden under his tangle of beard, taps the other man indulgently on the shoulder, and explains to him, "Cape Hatteras in the moonlight—Iceland in the fog—you certainly see the world when you're in the Navy."

Before the evening meal the Commander orders a trial deep dive.

He wants to find out whether the outboard plugs will hold at greater depths.

The VII-C boats have been approved for a depth of three hundred feet. But because the effect of depth charges decreases the deeper they are when they explode (the denser water reduces the impact of the pressure wave), the boats must often go below three hundred to escape pursuit. To what depth the pressure hull can really hold out—i.e., what the maximum diving depth is—who knows? Men who have gone very deep can never be sure they've actually reached the extreme limit. And a crew only finds out once at what depth its boat cracks.

The afternoon's series of diving commands is repeated. But we don't reach equilibrium at ninety; instead we go deeper and deeper. The boat is as quiet as a mouse.

Suddenly a sharp screeching, a frightening, ear-splitting sound. I catch alarmed looks, but the Old Man makes no move to stop the oblique downward motion.

The manometer needle stands at five hundred. Again the shrieking, combined with dull, scraping sounds.

"Not exactly an ideal spot here," murmurs the Chief. He has sucked in his cheeks and glances expressively at the Commander.

"The boat has to be able to take it," says the Old Man laconically. Then I realize the boat is scraping over rocks on the bottom.

"Purely a matter of nerves," whispers the Chief.

The ghastly sound continues.

"The pressure hull will hold up all right . . . But the screws and rudder . . ." the Chief complains in a mutter. The Old Man seems to be deaf.

Thank god—the screeching and scraping stop. The Chief's face is gray.

"Sounded exactly like a streetcar on a curve," says the Second Watch Officer. The Old Man's manner is that of a benevolent pastor as he explains to me, "In the water noises are magnified five times. Makes a great racket, but doesn't mean much."

The Chief gulps in air as if he'd just been saved from drowning. The Old Man looks at him like an interested psychiatrist, then announces, "That's enough for today. Surface!"

The litany of orders for the surfacing maneuver is run through. The hand of the depth manometer moves backward over the dial.

The Commander and the watch go above. I follow them and take up a position behind the bridge enclosure in the "greenhouse." There is plenty of space around the four anti-aircraft guns. I can look straight through and down between the crossbars of the greenhouse railing. Although we're traveling at cruising speed, the water foams and swirls violently. Myriads of white bubbles stream up, strips of foam interweave only to disperse again. I feel entirely alone. Isolated on an iron raft. The wind presses against me, the iron vibrates with minute oscillations. New patterns drift by constantly. I have to tear my eyes away to keep from dozing off.

Suddenly behind my back I hear the deep drawling voice of the Old Man. "Beautiful, isn't it?"

Then follows his usual bear dance. "Stretching his legs," he calls it.

I squint at the sinking sun, which has broken through a hole in the clouds.

"A pleasure cruise in the middle of the war! What more could a man ask!"

He stares at the foreship and says, "The most seaworthy ship there is—with the greatest radius of action."

Then we both look astern over the waves.

"Tsch—our wake! A pretty illustration of mortality: you're still watching—and it's gone!"

I don't dare look at him. "Philosophical hot air," is what he would call this kind of profundity if he heard it from anyone else. But he goes on to spin the thread further. "Even Mother Earth is a little more considerate; at least she allows us the illusion."

I press my tongue against my front teeth and hiss softly.

But the Old Man won't be put off. "Perfectly clear. She allows us the illusion that we've immortalized ourselves on her—engraved records, erected monuments. All she's doing is giving herself a little more time than the sea does to level things out again. A couple of thousand years if necessary.

"The Navy's famous clarity strikes again!" is all I can find to say, embarrassed.

"That's the way it is," says the Old Man, grinning straight into my face.

My first night aboard: I try to go limp, to extinguish all thought. Waves of sleep finally reach me, draw me away for a while, but before I can settle down properly they reject me again. Am I asleep or awake? The heat. The stench of oil. The whole boat quivers with a thin vibration: the engines communicate their rhythm to the smallest rivet.

The diesels run all night. Every change of watch startles me wide awake. Each time the hatch opens or is slammed shut in its frame, I'm dragged back from the verge of unconsciousness.

It's very different from awakening on a conventional ship. Instead of the ocean foaming beyond a porthole, there is only harsh electric light.

Heavy-headed, lead in my skull from the engine fumes. For half an hour now deafening radio music has been rasping at my nerves.

Beneath me I see two bent backs, but no place to put my dangling foot. If I were to get out of my bunk now, I would have to step between the half-finished food and the scraps of white bread turning to mush in puddles of coffee. The whole table is a slimy mess. The sight of pale-yellow scrambled eggs makes my gorge rise.

From the engine room comes the stench of lubricating oil.

"Dammit, man, get that hatch shut!"

Hinrich, the radioman, looks despairingly at the ceiling. When he discovers me, he stares, his eyes still gummed half shut, as though I were an apparition.

"Give us another shot of that coffee from the clap hypo," says the E-mate Pilgrim.

Clearly I should have got out of my bunk earlier. I can't trample through their breakfast now, so I let myself sink back and listen. "Come on, get your fat ass out of there!"

"Like baby shit, these scrambled eggs! I can't stand the smell of this powdered stuff!"

"Want to keep hens in the control room?"

The thought of chickens—white leghorns—in the control room nesting on the trim-valve controls cheers me up. I conjure up a vivid picture of their greenish-white muck smeared on the floor plates amid clotted chicken feathers, and I can hear their silly cackling in my ears. As a child I hated to touch chickens. I can't stand them now either. The smell of boiled chicken feathers—the pale yellow skin—the fatty pope's nose . . .

The loudspeaker thunders through the boat, "I am Lilli, your Lilli from Najanka. That's in the Cameroon, right on the Tanka . . ."

The loudspeaker can be turned down a little, but it can't be turned off since it's also used to transmit commands. So we have to acquiesce to the whims of the radioman or his assistant, who selects the records in his shack. "Lilli" seems to have caught the assistant's fancy. He's playing it for the second time this morning.

I shudder at the realization that it's *really* only between four and five a.m. But to avoid the process of conversion in radio communications, we operate on German summer time. Besides, we are now so far west of the prime meridian that between the sun time of our position and the time shown by our clocks there must be more than another hour's difference. Essentially it doesn't matter when we set the beginning of the day. The electric light is on twenty-four hours, and the changing of the watches occurs at intervals that have nothing to do with the time of day.

It's time to drag myself out of the covers. I say "Excuse me," and force one foot between the two men who are squatting on the bunk below.

"All good things come from above!" I hear Pilgrim say.

While I search for my shoes, which I thought I had safely jammed behind two pipes, I carry on a morning chat with the control-room mate, who is sitting close beside me on a folding chair.

"Well, how does it look?"

"*Comme ci, comme ça,* Herr Leutnant!"

"Barometer?"

"Rising."

I thoughtfully scratch the fluff from the wool blankets out of the stubble on my face. The comb I run over my head turns black immediately—my hair catches the particles in the oil fumes like a filter.

From my locker I dig out a washcloth and soap. I would like to wash in the forward head, but a quick glance through the circular hatch tells me that's impossible at the moment: the red light is on. So I simply wipe my eyes and stow the washcloth and soap in my trouser pocket for the time being.

The light signal was rigged up by the Chief. It goes on as soon as the latch on the inside is turned to "Occupied." One of the nice inventions that reduce wear and tear, for now no one needs to work his way in uncertainty along the narrow gangway from one end of the boat to the other, only to be brought up short in front of a locked door.

As I leave the wardroom I hear Pilgrim croon, "The morning shit comes soon or late, although till evening you may wait," and immediately there is a rumbling in my belly. I apply the Coué method: "There is no rumbling in my belly. In my belly there is peace. In my belly there is quiet and serenity!"

The Chief comes in from his morning visit to the engine room, his hands oily. The First Watch Officer is nowhere to be seen, nor is the Second Engineer. The Commander is probably washing. The Second Watch Officer is still on duty.

The cook had been wakened at 06.00. Along with the pale scrambled eggs that come to the table cold, there is bread, butter, and black coffee called "nigger sweat." Against this brew my stomach protests violently; the cramping and rumbling in my gut get worse. I take a quick look to see whether Cabin H is finally free.

"Don't you like it?" the Chief inquires.

"I don't know—it isn't exactly a taste thrill."

"You ought to try brushing your teeth first, then perhaps it'll taste better," the Chief advises, chewing with both cheeks stuffed. The Commander comes out of his cubbyhole with toothpaste spattered on his cheek and his beard darkened with moisture. He says, "Good morning to you, unwashed heroes of the sea," edges himself into his corner, and stares into space.

No one dares say a word.

Finally he asks for the code word of the day.

"*Procul negotiis*," the Chief proposes and translates immediately, so as not to show anyone up, "Far from business cares."

The Commander nods. "Education, education—excellent!"

The loudspeaker blares a torch song.

Now the heavy morning traffic has started up. Every few minutes someone forces his way through the Officers' Mess. Since I sit on my folding chair in the middle of the gangway I have to get up each time. My guts are now in upheaval. Dammit! When will the idiot in there finally come out?

The whole thing would be no problem if demand for the head were evenly spaced. If there were no rush hour like this morning. Midnight is just as bad, because the watch from the bridge and the watch from the engine room go off duty simultaneously. Eight people then want to use it at the same time. Last night, two of the men still waiting in the control room were doubled up as though they'd been kicked in the belly.

At last the door to Cabin H opens. The First Watch Officer! I snatch my things and almost tear the door out of his hand. Over the tiny wash basin in Cabin H there is even a faucet for fresh water. It isn't running, but in any case it's only to be used for brushing teeth and a cat's lick with a washcloth. I can use the salt-water tap and manage to achieve a sort of half lather with the salt-water soap provided, but I can't make myself gargle with the briny water. When I turn up again in the Officer's Mess everyone is still sitting around the table in silence, following the Commander's example.

From the loudspeaker a melting voice inquires, "Do you love me? It was only yesterday that you said no . . ."

The Chief sighs audibly and rolls his eyes.

I take a large swallow of coffee and swirl it back and forth until it's foaming, force the brown liquid through the narrow openings between my teeth, let it gurgle through a gap, and shoot it from my right cheek into the left until all the encrusted spittle and deposits are washed away—then I swallow. Ah! Now I can breathe better through my mouth. Next a deep breath through my nose. My throat and respiratory tract are clear. The coffee tastes better too. The Chief was right.

After breakfast the Commander goes to work on the ship's log with undisguised reluctance. He announces special instruction for the petty officers an hour later. The Chief disappears aft again, the First Watch Officer busies himself with some kind of paper work.

The steward comes to clear away: ship's routine.

On my way aft I pass through the control room, and the round opening of the tower hatch is still filled with black night. The air coming in from above is cold and damp. Let's go, I say to myself, and put my left foot on the aluminum ladder, although I don't feel the slightest desire to go on deck. Now the right leg!

I'm at the level of the helmsman, who is sitting bent over his dimly lit dials in the tower.

"Permission to come onto the bridge?"

"Granted!" The voice of the Second Watch Officer.

I push my head over the rim and politely say good morning.

It takes a while for my eyes to adjust themselves to the darkness so that I can make out the horizon. High in the sky a few pale stars still shimmer faintly. Above the eastern horizon a red band of light is slowly emerging. Gradually the water brightens too.

I shiver.

Kriechbaum the navigator comes up. Silently he looks around, sniffs hard, and has the sextant handed up to him.

"Stopwatch ready?" he shouts down in a hoarse voice.

"Aye aye, sir!" comes the report from far below.

The navigator points his instruments at Saturn and puts his right eye to the eyepiece. For a while he remains motionless, then he lowers the sextant and turns the screw: he brings Saturn from the heavens and places it precisely on the horizon.

"Attention—Saturn—zero!" he shouts below.

In the control room the time is recorded. The navigator has difficulty reading the figures in the half-light. "Twenty-two degrees, thirty-five minutes," he announces to the man below.

From the time of day and the height of the planet a base line can now be calculated. *One* base line, however, does not give a ship's position—we need a second.

The navigator raises the sextant once more.

"Attention—Jupiter—zero!"

A pause, and then: "Twenty-two degrees, twenty-seven minutes!"

Cautiously he hands the sextant down, then follows it. I climb after him. Once below, he takes off his peajacket and pulls up to the chart table. He has no spacious map room such as navigation officers have on the big steamers. He has to make do with the tiny table in the control room, placed to port amid a confusion of switches, speaking tubes, and valves. Above this table is a locker for the sextant and the starfinder and a shelf with nautical almanacs and tables of times and azimuths, navigational handbooks, catalogues of lighthouses, charts of the weather and tides.

The navigator picks up a pencil and calculates. He is on intimate terms with sines, cosines, tangents, and their logarithms.

"It's sort of nice that we're still making use of the stars," I say casually, just to put an end to the silence.

"What's that?"

"I simply meant—that with all the technical perfection here in the boat, it's really astounding that you still use the sextant to find the ship's position . . ."

"How else could I do it?"

I can see my observations are out of place. Perhaps it's too early in the day, I say to myself, and perch on the chart chest.

The navigator picks up the celluloid sheet that covers the chart. The map of our area of the sea is now uniformly blue-gray. No coastal edges, no shallows—only a thick network of squares with numbers and letters on the perpendicular and horizontal lines.

The navigator holds the dividers between his teeth and mutters, "There it is—a pretty little error, fifteen miles—well, so it goes!"

With a stroke of the pencil he connects our last position with the new one. He points to a square on the chart. "Things were really wild here once, almost 'Lash the helm and take to prayer!'"

Apparently the navigator is ready for a little more give and take. He points his dividers at the spot where things were so wild.

The control-room mate now comes up and looks at the network of squares.

"That was on the fourth patrol. Typical hallelujah voyage. One attack on top of another. They were after us from the word go. Depth charges all day. You lost count . . ."

The navigator keeps his eyes on the dividers as though they still hold signs and portents for him. Then he takes a deep breath, snaps them together, and abruptly thrusts them away.

"Wasn't at all funny."

I know that he won't say anything more. The control-room

mate also gets back to work. The navigator carefully fits the sextant back into its case. A tiny hole from the point of his dividers remains in the chart.

Since there is still considerable confusion in the boat I clamber back onto the bridge so as not to be in the way.

The clouds are now sharply defined mosaics inlaid in the gray-blue sky. One of them drifts in front of the sun. Its shadow wipes away the greenish-white radiance from the sea. The cloud is so large that its lower edge dips beneath the horizon, but there are holes in it through which the sun's rays dart at an angle. The beams seem to come from a projector, traversing the sea; one of them sweeps directly over our boat, and for a while it illuminates us like a huge theatrical spotlight.

"AIRCRAFT ON THE LEFT!"

Bosun's mate Dorian's shout hits me like an electric shock. For a fraction of a second I catch sight of a dark point against the gray background of cloud and then I'm at the conning tower hatch. Its locking lever bangs into my coccyx. I almost scream with pain. As I slide down the ladder I have a clear vision of the leather guard that should be covering this protruding iron handle.

Below, my leap to the side is too short. The next man is already on his way down. One of his boots hits me in the neck. I hear the bosun's mate land with a crash on the floor plates.

"Too damned close!" he exclaims, gasping for air.

The Commander is already standing open-mouthed under the tower, looking upward.

"*Flood!*" the Second Watch Officer shouts down. The exhaust doors are drawn aside. From above crashes a wall of water, out of which the Second Watch Officer emerges dripping.

The needle of the depth manometer moves very slowly, as though overcoming strong resistance. The boat seems to be glued to the surface.

The Chief roars, "All hands forward!"

The men rush stumbling and crouching through the control room. The boat finally becomes bow heavy and tilts forward. I have to hold on to keep my footing.

Breathlessly, the Second Watch Officer reports to the Commander. "Plane from the left. Out of a hole in the clouds. Type not identified!"

Once again, through closed lids, I can see the black point in front of the cloud banks. The same sentence goes on repeating itself inside my head—"Now he's going to drop them—now he's going to drop them!" And then the word "bombs!"—"bombs!"—"bombs!"

Gasping breath. The Commander doesn't take his eyes off the depth gauge. His face is expressionless, almost indifferent. Water drops in the bilge—*tip—tap—tip*. The electric motors hum very softly.

The electric motors? Or is that the gyrocompass?

Nothing?

"Diving stations!" the Chief commands. The men work their way back up the incline, seeking handholds on either side, like mountain climbers.

"Both hydroplanes up!"

I stand straight, take a deep breath. A piercing pain like a hot iron shoots through me down to my feet. For the first time I realize how heavily I hit the hatch lever.

"It's gone!" says the Commander. "Proceed to a hundred feet!"

"Shit!" mutters the navigator.

The Commander stands in the middle of the control room, hands in his trouser pockets, cap pushed to the back of his head.

"They've spotted us. Here's hoping all hell doesn't break loose." Then he turns to the Chief. "We'd better stay down a while." And to me, "I told you yesterday—they know exactly when we put to sea. We're in for trouble."

I have my second aircraft scare a few hours later during the navigator's watch. He roars "ALARM!" and I catch a glimpse at forty-five degrees—a thumb's breadth above the horizon—of a point in the gray. And I'm already letting myself slide down the metal ladder, guiding my fall with both hands and feet.

The navigator shouts, "Flood!"

I see him hanging onto the closing wheel of the hatch cover and searching with his feet for a toehold. Finally he turns the spindle tight.

"Five!"—"Three, both tanks!"—"One!" A loud gurgling of water rushing into the buoyancy tanks. "Aircraft at forty-five degrees, distance ten thousand feet. Not coming directly at us!" reports the navigator.

The ventilating shafts and exhaust vents of the diesels have been made fast and both E-motors are coupled to the driving shafts. They are running at full speed. Instead of the roar of the diesels there is now only their vibratory hum.

We hold our breath again.

"Boat plunging fast," the Chief reports, then quickly commands, "Blow submersion cells!" These cells are flooded when the boat is on the surface, to give it additional weight and to help overcome surface tension during a quick dive. They have a five-ton capacity; the boat is now too heavy by this amount. With an explosive roar, compressed air is released into them, driving the water out with a deafening hiss.

Still no bombs!

It couldn't have taken us more than thirty seconds to submerge completely. But the water at the point where you dive remains turbulent for about five minutes. It is into this surge that the Tommies like to drop their depth charges.

Nothing!

The Old Man expels his breath. The navigator follows suit but less violently. The control-room mate gives me a faint nod.

At 250 feet the Chief, with complete confidence, has the bow first pointed upward by the hydroplanes, then downward.

"Boat's in balance!" he now reports. "Close the exhaust vents!"

We stand around in silence for a good five minutes. Finally the Old Man has us brought up to periscope depth. Both hydroplanes are set hard up, the E-motors switched to half speed ahead.

The next command startles me. The Chief orders flooding in the tanks, although the boat is meant to rise. Admittedly not much is involved; nevertheless the order to flood seems nonsensical. I have to think hard before I remember: if we rise, the boat expands because the pressure on it decreases, hence we lose specific gravity; and that must be equalized so we don't shoot up too fast. To be able to stop the boat at precisely the desired depth, you have to maintain an exact balance.

"Perhaps he didn't see us at all!" says the Old Man.

The third aircraft alarm comes four hours later. This time it is the First Watch Officer who roars the order to flood. "Came straight out of the sun!" he gasps.

"All hands forward!"

More slipping and sliding, wild confusion in the control room. Anything to get down!

The Chief uses a different trick to get the bow down faster. Only when the boat has been tipped forward by setting both hydroplanes hard down does he order the escape vents of the rear buoyancy cells opened. For a moment he is able to utilize their lifting power to force the bow down more quickly.

"Third and last strike," mutters the First Watch Officer when it's clear no bombs are falling.

"I wouldn't tempt Providence quite that far," the Old Man says dryly.

"They're getting ruder all the time!" The Chief. "No manners these days!"

"We'll stay down a while. You can't always count on Kramer's kind of luck."

We move into the O-Mess. "Good job by the First Watch Officer," says the Old Man, loud enough to be heard in the control room. The First Watch Officer has earned this by spotting the aircraft in time. Not easy, when a clever bastard sits in his cockpit and flies at you straight out of the sun. Nine times out of ten it's seagulls. They glide at you with their rigidly extended wings from just above the horizon and the alarm cry is out before you realize what they are. In the glittering, blinding, glassy radiance that dissolves all contours, the illusion is perfect. But the tenth time, the approaching gull turns into a plane.

"When attacked from the air, always turn to windward," says the Old Man. "The First Watch Officer did it just right. The plane gets too much wind on its wing as it banks and it's forced outward. Doesn't make that much difference, but we need every foot we can get."

"I'll remember."

"As for the flyers they're sending out now, all you can say is— hats off!" The Old Man bites his lower lip, nods a couple of times, narrows his eyes, and says, "There they sit in their windmills, absolutely alone, and yet they attack like Blücher at Waterloo. They could simply drop their bombs into the drink and shoot their machine guns into the blue—who'd know the difference?"

He continues to sing the praises of the Royal Air Force. "The bomber pilots that attack our bases aren't exactly lily-livered either. How many was it we brought down last time?"

"Eight," I reply. One crashed almost on our roof in La Baule— right between the pine trees. I'm never going to eat calves' brains on toast again."

"What do you mean?"

"There were still three men inside. The cockpit was completely ripped open. They had brought a lot of sandwiches with them. Snow-white bread top and bottom, roast meat and lettuce in between, and all over one of them, the pilot's brains. I wanted to get hold of the papers—anything at all—but the plane was already on fire and suddenly the machine-gun ammo started going off, so I had to scram."

I try to read a nautical handbook. After a while I just catch the Old Man's voice. "The pilot that got the *Gneisenau* must have been quite a boy. No emergency rations in his pocket, just condoms . . ."

I put the book away.

"Obviously he was planning to finish off his mission with a visit to the whorehouses on the Rue de la Paix. The Canadians are practical about these things," says the Chief.

"Alas, that's where he made his mistake," says the Old Man. "But what a mad performance! Down in a spiral glide. Nobody noticed anything at first. No flak! No shooting! And then to position himself perfectly and release the bomb. Pure circus stuff! It was a shame he didn't come out of it! They say he hit the water like a stone. Well, we might as well try again . . ."

I climb into the control room behind the Old Man and the Chief.

The Chief reports, "Boat ready to surface!"

"Surface!" orders the Commander and climbs up the ladder.

"Blow the tanks!"

The Chief stares at the sinking of the water column in the Papenberg, then reports, "Conning tower hatch clear."

The Commander's voice comes from above. "Tower hatch being opened!"

"Equalize pressure!" calls the Chief.

"Let's hope those damn mosquitoes leave us alone now," I hear the navigator say.

The control room a half hour before midnight. The soft humming of the ventilators. Through the open tower hatch the diesels suck in a stream of fresh air. The few lights are shielded so that no rays can find their way upward and betray us to a night flyer. The darkness extends the room to infinity. Out of the uncertain depths of the shadows gleam the green phosphorescent arrows that direct us to the tower hatch in moments when all lights fail. These indicators are fairly recent. They were installed only after the disaster on Kallmann's boat. In the fall of 1940 in the Brunsbüttel channel, Kallmann collided with a Norwegian freighter. His little boat, without watertight bulkheads, was hit directly behind the control room and split open so completely that it sank in seconds. Only those on deck escaped. When the boat was raised—Kallmann had to be present—some of the crew were found in the control room crowded together not under the tower but on the other side of the periscope shaft. In exactly the wrong place.

But are our green arrows really any use? If the boat sinks here, it will sink thousands of feet and the pointers can go on gleaming till Doomsday.

In the semi-darkness the control room is huge. The only gleam of light is forward, where it sharply defines the circle of the hatch opening and the other end of the compartment. The light comes from the radio shack and from the lamp burning in the passage to the Officers' Mess. I can make out two men in the glow. They're sitting on the chart chest, peeling potatoes. Dimly visible, the officer of the watch in the control room is leaning against a stand-up table and noting down in the daily log the contents of the trim tanks. Gurgling and hissing, the bilge water sloshes back and forth under the floor plates. The two closed hatches beyond the petty officers' quarters lessen the noise of the diesels; it sounds filtered. The waves running alongside the boat fill the control room with a fluctuating roar.

I climb through the forward hatch. The radioman, Hinrich, his headset on his ears, is deep in a book. He's supporting himself with his elbows on the tabletops, right and left, that hold his apparatus. He looks as if he's on crutches. The green curtain has been drawn in front of the Commander's bunk opposite the radio shack. But a narrow slit is emitting light; so the Commander is not asleep either. Very likely he's writing in bed as usual, letters he won't be able to send until we return to base.

With no one sitting at the table, the O-Mess now seems unnaturally large. The Chief is asleep in his bunk behind the table. Close above his face, his watch dangles on its short chain, a random pendulum swinging in all directions.

In the lower berth to port, behind the curtain, the First Watch Officer is sleeping before going on duty. The door to the bow compartment opens with a crash. The Chief turns over with a grunt and goes on snoring, his face toward the lockers. A man with a rumpled topknot of hair comes in, mutters a sleepy greeting, blinks uncertainly for several seconds, and then resolutely draws back the First Watch Officer's curtain. "Twenty minutes to, Herr Leutnant."

The sleep-fuddled face of the First Watch Officer emerges into the light from the deep shadows of the bunk. He works one leg out from under the covers, pushes it stiffly over the bunk railing, and rolls his body after it. The whole performance looks like a slow-motion film of a high jump. I don't want to irritate him by watching, so I go on forward.

In the bow compartment the master mechanic Johann is sitting at the table with a woeful expression on his face. He yawns and says, "Morning, Herr Leutnant!"

"Bit early for that!"

Johann ignores this and slowly raises himself to his feet.

Two weak bulbs provide the bow compartment with no more than half-light. A heavy, sour fug meets me: sweat, oil, bilge, the smell of wet clothing.

Here, toward the bow, is where you feel the rolling of the boat most. Two shadowy figures are staggering back and forth in front of the torpedo tube supports. I hear them cursing. "Anti-social bastards! Enough to drive you to revolution. Middle of the night!"

From the hammocks emerge two men, then a third from a port-side bunk.

"Fuck it all!" That must be Ario.

Since the boat is rolling heavily, the two of them make a number of fruitless attempts before they succeed in getting their seaboots on.

"Filthy weather, eh?" one says. "Going to get our feet wet again!" They work their way into heavy sweaters and wrap towels around their necks so that no water can get in under their collars once they put their rubber jackets on in the control room.

The men of the preceding watch come down the ladder stiffly. They are soaking wet. The navigator has turned up his collar and drawn his sou'wester down over his face. The faces of the others are whipped red by the spray. All of them hang their binoculars over hooks and undress as silently as the new watch dressed, peeling themselves awkwardly and heavily out of their rubber jackets. Then they help one another off with their rubber pants. The youngest member of the watch loads himself with the whole mass of wet oil-skin trousers, jackets, and sou'westers, and carries it aft. The spaces between the two electric motors and on both sides of the stern torpedo tube are the best for drying.

The men who have come off duty gulp down a mouthful of hot coffee, polish their binoculars, and stow them away.

"Bearing up?" the navigator asks me.

Bosun's mate Wichmann moves aft, the navigator with the two lookouts forward.

For a while there's only the roar of the sea and the drone of the engines, until the control-room mate turns on the bilge pump.

All at once there's heavy traffic in the control room. The new engine-room watch is going on duty. I recognize the diesel stoker Ario and the E-stoker Zörner.

In the U-room Wichmann has planted himself at the table. Chewing hungrily.

I climb into my bunk. Now I can hear the waves close to my ear rushing past the boat. There is a long scraping and gurgling that rises and falls and sometimes mounts to a whistling hiss.

The hatch from the galley is kicked open. Bosun's mate Kleinschmidt and E-mate Rademacher appear.

"Leave something for us, you glutton! Whenever I see you, you're stuffing yourself."

"Crap!"

Through a crack in my curtain I see Wichmann unembarrassedly scratching his crotch. He even lifts himself slightly to get at it better.

"Get your joystick out of the way, man! This is no place for a hand job."

"I'll fuck *you* in a minute!" Wichmann retorts.

This dialogue has apparently aroused a memory in Kleinschmidt. He giggles so audibly that everyone stops to listen.

"Something happened to me in a Paris bistro. I'm just sitting there at a table and opposite me on a kind of sofa there's a Negro with a whore and she keeps on feeling him up under the table. In Paris there's no holds barred."

Rademacher nods in agreement.

"All at once the Negro begins panting loudly and rolling his eyes. I think, 'This has got to be seen,' and push my chair back, and I see him just as he comes—all over my shoe!"

"You're joking!"

"What did you do then?" Rademacher wants to know.

"I just sat there thunderstruck. But you ought to have seen them —they took off like greased lightning!"

"Holy shit—the things that happen." Rademacher is still astounded.

Wichmann has apparently taken till now to digest the story properly. He leans back and announces, "Those French are real swine!"

It takes another good quarter of an hour for the U-room to settle down.

In the battle log, the first two days have been recorded as follows:

SATURDAY
08.00 *Departure.*
16.30 *Trial dive.*
18.00 *Deep-dive test.*

SUNDAY
07.46 Aircraft alarm with emergency measures and deep dive.
10.55 Aircraft alarm.
15.44 Aircraft alarm.
16.05 Cruising in attack area.

"You've still got eyes like an albino rabbit," the Chief needles me. It's the third day at sea.

"No wonder—those last days on shore were pretty rough."

"That's what I heard. They say you were right there for the famous brawl in the Majestic. That was the night before Thomsen—right?"

"Exactly. You really missed something. You should have seen the Commissioner of Works flying through the plate-glass window!"

"How did it happen?"

"You know all about Scholle yourself—how he considers himself essential to the war effort? Well, this clod starts out by paying for a round of drinks. The men are being halfway polite. Herr Scholle seems to have had a few already and is obviously feeling on top of the world. Nothing can stop him. He's actually acting as if he belongs—as if everyone has been waiting for him!"

I see the dueling scars—red whipmarks—on his two hamster cheeks. I see Herr Scholle gesticulating wildly, then wavering slowly back and forth, beginning to orate, beer foam smeared around his mouth. "Fantastic, simply fantastic. This magnificent success! Splendid fellows—sterling characters! *Jawohl!*" I see the contemptuous glances of the crowd and hear the loud question, "What in hell is this asshole doing here?" But Herr Commissioner Scholle is deaf to everything but himself. "Stiffen your spines—bring Albion to her knees. *Jawohl!* The fighters at the front can rely on us. Sacrifice everything for the Homeland! Dedicated knights!"

"He was talking absolute garbage," I tell the Chief. "The whole propaganda bullshit about unflinching spirit at the front and so on. And obviously including himself right up there. Markus has been boiling for quite a while, but he's behaving himself. It's only when Scholle claps him on the shoulder and shouts 'Up and at 'em,' then belches, and to top it all off hollers, 'Ach, just a few shitty depth charges!' that Markus blows a fuse. You should have seen it. He went bright red and gagged on his words, as though he'd lost his breath. But the others—they were up on their feet in a single motion. Table and chairs, everything knocked over. They grabbed the Commis-

sioner by the wrists and ankles and off they went through the bar—
half dragging him, half carrying him—right down the corridor. The
idea was to heave him through the door with a kick in his brass-hat
ass. But the bosun suddenly had a better one. Probably because
they were holding the Commissioner at both ends like a hammock,
the bosun had them line him up, roaring and struggling, parallel
to the big plate-glass window, then ordered, 'One good hard swing
and at the count of three, let go!' They got the idea. 'One—and two—
and three'—you should have seen it. The Commissioner sailed
through the air, there was the crash of breaking glass, and he was
lying on the street."

I can still hear the impact and the splintering of the glass on the
pavement and the bosun saying, "That's that!" But it isn't. Silently
the four about-face, march back through the long room to their
places, dust off their hands as though they had been touching
something dirty, and reach for their glasses. "Stupid pig!" says one
of the crew.

Suddenly someone else yells, "There he is again!" and points toward the entrance. Through the haze in the doorway looms a
bloody face.

"He's looking for his Himmler spectacles!"

They're on their feet again. Drunk as they are, they're at the door
in a flash and dragging the Commissioner of Works across the thresh-
old. One of them kicks loose the Commissioner's leg, which is
caught in the door jamb. Then the door is slammed. "Perhaps he's
had enough now, the stupid cunt!"

"And then all that business with the military police?"

"Apparently they turned up an hour later when only the petty
officers and the men were left, and there was a real brawl. One of the
police got a flesh wound in the upper thigh."

"Throughout the flotilla there was general regret," said the Chief,
"that it was not something else that got hit."

I know why the Chief has such a grudge against the watchdogs
and all so-called security agencies. He was on his way back from
leave in Paris on the Admiral's train and had made himself comfortable for a doze in the midday heat—bottom button of his
jacket undone, slumped down in his seat, alone in the compartment
with a lieutenant—when the door was pushed open and the comedy
began. He described the whole thing to me in the Royal. "Suddenly
some sweaty bastard was standing there all in field gray, helmeted,
booted and spurred, leg-o'-mutton breeches of course, full war paint
—a cannon at his waist. And through the two side windows his two

watchdogs staring in like oxen. 'Your travel orders, Herr Ober-leutnant, and will you kindly look to your uniform. You are *not* on board ship here!' "

The Chief, according to him, got to his feet but did not do up the button. Instead, he undid all the others, fumbled for his papers, handed them to the steel-helmeted heinie, and shoved his hands down into his trouser pockets.

"You should have seen him. He almost exploded! He was bel-lowing like a steer. 'I shall report you! I shall report you!' "

At which point I said to the Chief, "That so? Maybe that's why they decided to replace you and send us that Hitler Youth as your understudy. U-boat Headquarters probably decided they could no longer regard you as the kind of model our Führer wants for the crew!"

I can still see the Chief gaping in astonishment. But then he began to glow like a lighted Christmas tree. Apparently I'd said the right thing.

Monday evening in the Officers' Mess. 20.00. I can't grasp the fact that this is only our third day at sea. The land lies so far astern that we could already be hundreds of miles away. I have to make an effort to convince myself that it was only last Friday evening at this time that the brawl was beginning in the Bar Royal.

"Deep thoughts?" inquires the Old Man.

"No, not exactly. I was just thinking about Thomsen."

"That uniform! He'd better get rid of it," says the Old Man.

Tuesday. Fourth Day at Sea. The Chief is strolling about, ap-parently at leisure. A good opportunity for me to coax some technical information out of him. All I need to say is, "It's all so damned complicated," and he's off. "You can say that again. A damned sight more complicated than ordinary steamers, which simply float out to sea on the same principle as a washtub on a pond. They've all got their own characteristic trim and their own constant buoyancy. So-and-so-many gross registered tons and so-and-so-many tons of cargo. And if they load more on, the scow just sinks a little lower and the water comes up over the Plimsoll line. That's all there is to it, nothing to worry about. At worst it's a matter for the Maritime Authorities. But with us any excess weight demands special counter-measures . . ." The Chief stops, nervously hoods his eyes. I'm afraid he may not go on, and keep staring at him. He lets me wait.

Floating, being borne up by water, is a phenomenon I've always found hard to grasp. Not wooden rowboats—but iron ships seemed like a miracle to me as a child. Iron floating on water! I even saw concrete ships with sides as thick as bunkers on the Elbe one day, and I couldn't believe those vast masses would float, let alone carry cargoes.

Although I understand the functioning of the ship's equipment and the sequence of maneuvers, diving and resurfacing continue to baffle me. The fact that a U-boat can eliminate its own buoyancy and get it back again at will never ceases to fascinate me.

When the Chief starts up again he sounds like a lecturer. "The so-to-speak fundamental difference is this: we achieve our buoyancy not like ordinary scows, through the water we displace, but through the air in the cells. So what keeps us on the surface is a kind of life preserver. When we blow the air out, we sink."

The Chief stops until I nod.

"We have to watch our weight like hawks. It must always remain the same. At an alarm, there's no time for fumbling around. Everything goes insanely fast. So we have to trim the boat for diving in advance—that is, while we're still traveling on the surface. This means we must keep the weight steady by means of the trim cells. Then when there's an alarm, all we still have to do is eliminate the lift in the buoyancy cells. Once the boat is underwater, its own weight doesn't tilt it up or down."

The Chief pauses to inquire, "Got it?"

"Yes, Chief."

"At the desired depth, the weight of the boat must exactly equal that of the water it's displacing, so that the boat hovers perfectly, ready to react precisely to the smallest push from the propellers and be easily maneuvered up or down, right or left, by the hydroplanes or the rudder. It mustn't have any tendency to sink or to rise. Unfortunately the boat's weight changes every day, through the consumption of provisions—water and fuel, for example. The crazy thing, however, is that not even the weight of the water displaced by the boat remains constant. So everything is always changing. You can never stop calculating. You hardly dare to cough."

He pauses for breath. Gets a bottle of apple juice from the locker. Pulls the tin cap off on the hinge of the locker door and raises the bottle to his mouth.

He has hardly wiped his lips when he starts up again. "The thing that gives us the most trouble is the changing specific gravity of water. If we were diving in fresh water everything would be simpler. Then all we'd have to do every day would be to add the same weight of water to the trim cells as we used up in food, oil, and water, and that would be that. But in salt water it's very tricky. There's no getting away from it. In this pond, water is not just water. Our buoyancy changes from day to day—even from hour to hour."

He pauses again and glances at me to observe the effect he's having.

"The specific gravity of salt water is influenced by every imaginable factor. Depth, temperature, the time of year, the various currents. Even the sea life—plankton, for example—affects it appreciably. A little more plankton in the water and we have to pump. And it depends on the sun as well."

"On the sun?"

"Yes, the sun causes evaporation, which increases salt content. Greater salt content in the water and the specific gravity goes up."

"But aren't the differences minimal?"

He ponders for a while, frowning deeply. "A difference in the specific gravity of the water—well, let's take a really minimal one, of one one-thousandth—that means that the weight of the boat, to maintain its balance, must also be changed by one one-thousandth. Now assume that the boat weighs eight hundred and eighty tons. So: a change of one one-thousandth gives us a bit over sixteen hundred pounds. That much of a difference would make for a serious mistake in calculating the content of the trim cells. To keep the boat adequately poised, we have to weight it out with the help of the trim tanks to within eleven pounds. I say adequately because in practice it's impossible to weigh out the boat so accurately that it remains poised without the help of propellers and hydroplanes. Even a pint—as a matter of fact, even a thimbleful—too much of water in the tanks would make it rise. So every day that God the Cloudmaker allows to dawn, we have to use the densimeter to determine the specific gravity of the seawater around us."

The Chief is enjoying the sound of his own eloquence. He's blossoming, as though the whole science of submarining had originated with him.

The Commander, who has been listening for some time, goes by and asks, "Well, professor, is all that stuff really true?" as he climbs through the forward hatch.

Immediately the Chief is disconcerted. When he begins again, it's in a plaintive tone. "All the Old Man's interested in is balancing the boat precisely—not a quart too much, not a quart too little . . ."

The Chief seems to have finished. However, I can see he's searching for a suitable closing sentence.

"Hell," he says finally, "the fact is, we put to sea with a lot of physics . . ."

"And chemistry."

"Yes, and chemistry too—that we don't really use. Keep your fingers crossed," says the Chief. "If it ever really does come down to chemistry, we'll be needing psychology too. And at that point we'll be right up the ass of the Prophet!"

He suddenly has to leave. I have no chance to ask him what he means.

At the noon meal the Old Man looks merry. No one knows what's cheered him up so. He's even joking in a way I haven't noticed before. The Chief appears at last.

"Well, Chief?" he asks in a self-satisfied undertone.

"All in order, Herr Kaleun!"

The Commander cordially invites him to sit down on the corner of the bunk. This deliberate friendliness alarms the Chief. Furtively he peers at each of us. I can imagine what's about to happen: as I was coming through the control room I saw the Commander secretly slip a small note into the hand of the control-room officer.

Within a few minutes the alarm bell peals. The Chief has difficulty scrambling to his feet. On the ceiling the flooding valve rods begin to turn. The plates on the table start slipping.

"Hold tight!"

The Chief shoots an embittered glance at the Old Man, but it does no good—he has to struggle into the control room.

"Very good. Quick as a weasel!" the Old Man jeers after him.

The uproar coming from the control room confirms my belief that this is not a simple test alarm; it sounds very much like a disaster exercise.

Everything on the table skids forward, crashing and clattering—I'm already stepping on splintered plates.

The bow is getting steadily heavier.

A questioning glance from the Second Watch Officer. But the Commander continues to behave as if all this had nothing to do with him.

From the control room comes the alarm cry: "Breach above the water gauge!"

Instead of leaping to his feet, the Commander favors the Second Watch Officer with a broad grin, until the latter finally grasps that this is a carefully prepared accident.

The Old Man takes fiendish pleasure in the curses and uproar coming from the control room. He gets heavily to his feet and lumbers his way there like a cautious mountain climber. Rattling and tinkling everywhere, then a loud crash. Some massive object must have tipped over. The boat is now attempting a headstand.

The First Watch Officer is looking surly. We gather the knives and forks together in a corner of the leather sofa. Goddam mess! The whole table is smeared with remains of food. Unfair of the Old Man to choose a mealtime!

"The crew has to get used to this sort of thing. The Tommies have no consideration either—practice is half the battle!" The Old Man's mockery only adds to the confusion.

Thank god. The boat is gradually coming back to an even keel. Now he turns considerate. He fixes the depth at two hundred feet. The steward comes and silently cleans up the mess.

After a quarter of an hour the Chief appears, completely drenched and out of breath. The Commander loans him his own fur-lined vest and pours out his tea with exaggerated courtesy.

"It all went off very well!"

The Chief acknowledges the praise with a sour look.

"Now, now, now!" says the Commander.

The Chief leans back against the wall and lays his hands in his lap, palms up. They are smeared with oil. The Old Man looks at him disapprovingly. "But Chief—what will our First Watch Officer think if you appear at the table like this?"

The First Watch Officer instantly turns red. The Chief pushes his hands into his trouser pockets and asks, "Better this way? As a matter of fact, I've already eaten."

"But Chief! You're starting to lose weight. Eat, drink, and be merry my children." The Old Man is munching away with bulging cheeks. Then in the same derisive tone he asks, "Wasn't there something you wanted to fix on the port diesel? Now's the time. And perhaps you'll have the starboard diesel overhauled while you're at it? We can stay down as long as it takes. Anything you like!"

What can the Chief do but disappear aft looking resigned?

The Old Man grins around the table and says, "Let's get some life into this damn tub! That endless loafing around back at base still sticks in my throat."

Ever since we've been at sea, the Commander has appeared to be in high spirits, or at least quietly content. He even came back early from leave. The boat could perfectly well have been readied without him, but no, he had to be there.

From his sacrifice of a whole week's leave, the crew has naturally enough concluded that he's not exactly rolling in domestic bliss.

Apparently no one knows anything definite about his private life. Even I can construct a picture of it only from reluctant reminiscences, cynical marginalia, and my own observations. From time to time he looks through letters, all of them written in green ink with enormous handwriting. The lady who wrote them is said to be a flyer's widow. Her father is a magistrate. The Old Man once let something fall about a piano with candelabra—red candles—and "very beautiful evening dresses." Looking disgruntled, he made occasional remarks about this last leave as well. He "constantly" had to keep his decoration around his neck; he had to go shopping with her. "And that wasn't all I had to put up with. Ridiculous. Every evening something going on. Endless company. Makes you dizzy. I was even supposed to give lectures in schools—I just said 'count me out.'

"What people like us want on leave is simply a change of clothes, and hours in the bathtub. Not to be bothered, no newspapers, no radio, turn everything off, stretch out. But then they lay out a beautifully pressed Sunday afternoon dress uniform, complete with dagger and scabbard. Snowy-white shirt, silk tie, black lisle socks, and crown it all with the hand-polished decoration on an absolutely spotless black, white, and red rep ribbon. God almighty!"

Work in the engine room is over in an hour. The Commander orders us up.

The bridge watch gets ready under the tower hatch.

"Surface!"

"Forward hydroplane up ten, aft hydroplane up five!" The Chief initiates the maneuver.

"Blow the tanks!"

Compressed air hisses out of the steel cylinders into the buoyancy tanks. The water is being driven out through the open flooding doors on the bottom.

"Boat rising. Conning tower free. Boat surfaced!" reports the Chief. The tower hatch is opened and the excess pressure equalized. "Ventilate with diesels!"

The watch climbs up. The rocking of the boat has already

changed to a forward motion. The lapping of the waves becomes a sharp hissing. When the ventilation has been completed the Commander orders, "Dismiss from diving stations!"

A stoker climbs up into the tower. He lights a cigarette, crouches down on his haunches to the left of the helmsman and gives himself up with closed eyes to the pleasures of tobacco. Before he has finished, there are cries from below of men waiting in line for his place.

Afternoon. The boat has been running on the surface for two hours—at "twice half speed" for a change, but without the dynamos turning, since the batteries are already fully charged. At this speed, the boats make from fourteen to fifteen miles an hour, no faster than a good cyclist.

ALARM! The bell strikes straight to my heart. I catch my breath.

A man tumbles out of the head with his trousers half down. "Go ahead, shit your fill," I hear someone behind him call.

The diesels have stopped—the boat is already tilting.

Now what's going on? Isn't the Chief ever going to stop the dive?

All at once it dawns on me that this alarm is for real.

We stay submerged for no more than a quarter of an hour. Then the waves are hissing along our steel hull again.

"That strikes me—as being enough—for one day," the Chief remarks.

"Balls," says the Old Man.

"The Old Man and the Tommies are a perfect team," I hear from bosun's mate Zeitler in the bow compartment. "They keep you moving."

⦀ FRIGGING AROUND: 1

Wednesday. Fifth Day at Sea. Strumming from the radio half wakes me, then the door to the galley slams into its frame. The room resounds with a confusion of voices. The E-mate Pilgrim. "Steward, what's this cunt mess doing here on the table? Get cracking! Out it goes!"

I glance below through the crack in the curtains. The bosun's mate Wichmann is staring at a blob of mixed-fruit jam on the table and growling, "Looks as though the lady of the house was flying Pennant Z." Pilgrim and Wichmann seem to have one-track minds, but sometimes I don't understand either their vocabulary or their references.

"Little Snow White and Rose Red," Wichmann says. His eyes are set wide apart and protrude slightly, so his face, despite its narrow chin, is rather like a frog's. To keep his black hair combed straight back and lying flat, he carefully squeezes a tube of pomade between the teeth of his comb and then distributes it conscientiously over his head. He likes to describe the kind of life he wants— theater, nightclubs, lots of good company—this is what he calls his "dream." A bragger, who keeps harping on his interrupted college education. But despite his loud talk, Wichmann is considered a good sailor; he is said to have been the first to spot more than one convoy.

The E-mate Pilgrim is from Thuringia, like his colleague Rademacher; he's small and pale, with a pointed beard. Only he talks more than Rademacher.

Pilgrim and Wichmann are swapping stories about a certain lady in the sailor's cathouse.

"I can't take her constant whining. 'Don't go off in my hair.' That's her problem. Too much ladylike crap!"

"But she knows her stuff all right otherwise."

"She's got a good ass, you have to admit that."

Pause. Then Pilgrim's voice again. "I screwed that little girl from the flower stall on a bench in the park. But I didn't get a scumbagful till I got home and went to work on myself."

I struggle out of my bunk.

My tongue is sticking to the back of my mouth like a piece of leather. Nausea fills my throat.

Finally I make it to the control room and manage a clear enough voice to ask, "Permission to come on the bridge?"

"*Jawohl!*" The Second Watch Officer cries from above.

Bending over the boat's railing, I stare at the water shooting along below me, roaring and hissing, churned up with air into a milky froth. Bubbles and streamers of foam combine in an endless tapestry of constantly changing patterns. My eyes are drawn aft by the white streamers. A long path a few yards wide marks our course. On it, the high choppy waves are smoothed out as though the train of a long dress had swept over them and flattened all the flashing crests.

I ask the Second Watch Officer, "What is Pennant Z?"

He responds promptly. "The signal for attack. It's red."

"Filthy swine," I exclaim involuntarily.

The Second Watch Officer stares at me in surprise.

"Thanks," I say, and disappear again down the hatch.

The helmsman in the tower hardly needs to touch the rudder. The same number on the compass card swings back and forth under the central mark. Two hundred sixty-five degrees. We are running on a constant course. According to the navigator, it will take us ten days at cruising speed to reach our area of operations. We could be there sooner if we ran the diesels at high speed. But we've chosen cruising speed in order to save fuel. We need all our reserves for the hunt.

At breakfast I wait in vain for the Commander.

The alarm bell makes me jump. *Airplanes*, I think. Fucking vermin—you can always count on them!

Then I catch sight of the Old Man through the circular hatch in the control room. He's looking at his stopwatch. Thank god. Practice alarm. He's seeing how long it takes the boat to get under water.

I squeeze to one side out of the way of the sudden scramble.

The boat is already pitching downward. I try to keep the plates on the table, but two or three slide off.

I can't help thinking of all the things that have happened during practice alarms. On Kerschbaumer's boat, they closed the intake valve to the depth manometer by mistake. Kerschbaumer wanted to take his boat down 250 feet fast. The boat went down all right, but the manometer needle didn't move, so Kretschbaumer thought the boat was stuck on the surface and ordered more flooding, then more, until suddenly they noticed the mistake. But by then the boat was already 600 feet down—with a shipyard guarantee of 300!

We're at our midday meal when the next practice alarm takes place. The Chief jumps up, knocking a full soup tureen from the table straight into the Second Watch Officer's lap.

The Old Man still appears dissatisfied after this second alarm. Not a word of appreciation.

At 16.00 on the dot comes the third.

The teacups on the table are smashed to bits.

"If this goes on, we'll be eating with our paws and drinking out of buckets," I hear the bosun complaining.

At last the Commander says, "Okay that time!"

Seated at the chart table in the control room, I'm trying to learn more about technical matters. An incipient row between Frenssen and Wichmann—the eternal conflict between engineers and sailors— is headed off by the arrival of the navigator. There's only enough time for Wichmann to call Frenssen's diesels "farters" and Frenssen to shove his oil-smeared fists in Wichmann's face.

With peace restored, I return to concentrating on the layout of the cells. In the diving arrangements of a U-boat the buoyancy cells take first place. There are three of them, located inside and outside the pressure hull. The inside cell is so large that if the two outer ones are damaged the boat can go on floating.

On the underside of the buoyancy cells are the flood doors, above them the air vents. Both must be opened before we can dive. As the air escapes through the vents, the water pours in through the flood doors to replace it. The boat has buoyancy tanks as well as buoyancy cells. These lie in the outer ship, and when the boat leaves base they are full of fuel oil. Only when this oil has been used up do they start to function as air reservoirs, giving the boat additional lift.

In addition to the buoyancy cells and tanks the boat has both regulator and trim cells. Weight lost by consumption of food, water, and fuel is made up for by taking seawater aboard in the regulator cells, located on the ceiling of the control room.

The trim cells serve to control the position of the boat underwater. If the boat is either bow heavy or stern heavy, it can be brought back to even keel by exchange of water between the two cells—that is, by achieving trim state zero. The trim cells are of the utmost importance; they are our balancing pole, for underwater the boat has a tendency to rock lengthwise as well as from side to side. With surface vessels it's different; in a rough sea, naturally, they roll heavily from side to side, but they don't tend to stand on their head.

With U-boats underwater, however, pitching of as much as forty degrees is common. In contrast to surface ships the U-boat in its submerged state is extremely sensitive to changes in weight and is hard to keep on an even keel. For this reason the designers gave the trim cells the greatest possible effectiveness by placing them at the extreme ends of the boat.

If a hundredweight of potatoes is moved from the control room to the bow compartment when the boat is submerged, bow heaviness results. To compensate for this, water has to be pumped from the control room to the stern cell—only half the weight of the potatoes, though, because the water for the trim cell is taken from the opposite end of the boat. The foreship is thereby made lighter by one half the weight of the potatoes. If a hundredweight of potatoes were taken from the E-motor room into the bow compartment, the trim calculation would, of course, be different. In that case water would have to be pumped from the bow to the stern.

I memorize the rule of thumb: control cells regulate rise and fall of boat; trim cells regulate position in water.

After the evening meal I climb as quickly as possible into my bunk, dog-tired.

God knows the sailors I share the compartment with are at no pains to restrain themselves out of any consideration for me. When I'm lying in my bunk, they return with complete abandon to topic number one. Apparently all I need to do is close my curtain and I cease to exist for them. I remind myself of a zoologist: the animals I'm studying have become accustomed to me.

The day began with Pilgrim and Wichmann; now Frenssen and Zeitler see me to bed. Their obscene imaginations appear to be inexhaustible. I would give a lot to find out whether they really have had all the adventures they're always boasting about. Are they actually the seasoned whorehouse veterans they pretend to be? It's not hard to credit them with almost anything.

The bosun's mate Zeitler is a North German. His pale, innocent face with its sparse growth of beard suits neither his cynical talk nor his weightlifter's build. He's said to be a first-rate sailor; nothing upsets him. He belongs to the first watch. If I'm not wrong, the Old Man thinks more of him than of the First Watch Officer.

The diesel mechanic mate Frenssen is a thick-set fellow who exudes arrogant self-assurance wherever he goes. Not the slightest hint of self-doubt ever creases his forehead.

Frenssen comes from Kottbus. He likes to appear hard-nosed; the perfect cynical desperado from a third-rate cowboy film. His grim, slit-eyed stare is something he must have practiced in front of a mirror. The diesel stokers Ario and Sablonski, who are in his watch, can't have a very easy time of it. He's not more than twenty-two. His bunk is directly under mine.

Through my half-drawn curtain I hear, "It stinks like a pigpen in here."

"What do you expect it to smell like—a cathouse?"

Groans and yawns.

"So something really happened?"

"I'll say!"

For a while there is only munching to be heard.

"You're just jealous because you only got your finger up."

"Fuck off! Anything you can do with your cock I can do better with my big toe."

"Yeah, if you come from Kottbus, you do it with your toe!"

Sounds of the exhaust pumps, organ-like yawns and gasps.

"In any case, no more fucking now. Somebody else is humping them all, yours included."

"What a brain! You ought to get yourself promoted to the General Staff with a bright little head like yours. They need people like you to stick the little flags in."

"Ought to have corked her up to keep out any cunt-mates!"

Rattle of dishes, scraping of boots.

My curtain bulges inward as someone makes his way between the table and the starboard bunks. Then I hear their voices again.

"A little recreation wouldn't hurt at all after a leave like that. One air raid after another. It's downright peaceful here by comparison."

"Just keep your fingers crossed!"

"Can't get laid properly any more. Not even at noon in the arbor."

Then comes the explanation: "You know, they have a garden with a kind of summerhouse in it. Sofa, icebox—everything ready to go. But you barely get started when the fucking sirens go off, and the dumb twat gets nervous—and there's the end of your fun!"

Thursday. Sixth Day at Sea. In the morning, before breakfast, I'm on the bridge with the Commander.

The sky is covered with turquoise batik clouds bound together by fine veins. Everywhere a reddish background shows through. Slowly the background begins to brighten and outshine the blue of the clouds. A red glitter takes over the eastern sky, breaking through at every opening. The expanses of cloud are penetrated by brilliant points of light. Then slowly the flashing and glittering grow paler, as though the light were going out. The colors soften; the sun has risen behind the cloud cover.

"Pleasant sea today!" says the Commander.

At the changing of the watch I think I've discovered new faces.

"Never seen that man," I mutter as another unknown comes out of the tower hatch.

"Fifty men are a lot," says the Old Man. "There have been times when I myself didn't recognize members of my own crew. Some of them are real masters of disguise, of course, absolutely unrecognizable when their Passion-play beards are gone. After getting back to port, when they've shaved and then come on watch, I ask myself how on earth I could have put to sea with this kindergarten. They're just kids, nurslings who belong at their mothers' breasts . . . I've often thought: please, god, only photos of returning boats for the newsreels and the papers; with bearded crews. No departure pictures, if only out of consideration for the enemy's feelings."

As usual the Old Man leaves me a while to puzzle out what he means by that. "The Tommies really would have something to be ashamed of if they saw just who was making life such hell for them: a kindergarten with a few Hitler Youths for officers. You feel old as the hills among all these kids—it's a real children's crusade."

The Old Man has changed; I've never seen him the way he is now. He used to be discontented, yet introverted, meditative, phlegmatic. Now he's talking openly—with pauses, as is his custom, but consecutively.

Things have now found their permanent place in the boat. No chart chest to block the passage, and you don't have to run around ducking your head. The crew no longer has swollen eyes. A rhythm has been found, the ship's routine established—a blessing after the confusion of the first days. Nevertheless I feel as if there were a thin membrane stretched between me and reality. I seem to be living in a kind of trance. The consternation that I felt at first when presented with the many pipes, manometers, machines, and valves has at last subsided. Now I know about the various pipes—which cells they lead to and even by which valves they can be shut off; hand wheels, levers, and the tangle of cables have sorted themselves out into a comprehensible system, and I feel a respect for this world of machinery dedicated to practical purposes. Nevertheless, there is still a great deal I can only accept with astonishment, as purely miraculous.

I still don't comprehend the Second Engineer. I can't tell whether his failure to react to the Commander's provocations is due to obstinacy or lack of wit. Even when the Commander meets him more than halfway with jovial good humor, he fails to respond. He's probably completely devoid of imagination, the typical product of a one-sided education designed to turn out mass-produced, brainless, dutiful performers, utterly committed to the Führer.

His private life I know only in broadest outline, hardly more than what is recorded in the personnel file. But I'm just as ignorant about the other officers too.

I do learn something about the Chief's home life. His wife is expecting a child. His mother is dead. During this last leave he visited his father. "Not a success," he informed me. "My father goes in for trays inlaid with iridescent blue butterflies. And cut-glass liqueur glasses. And liqueurs he makes himself. He used to be director of a waterworks. I brought him all sorts of supplies, but he refused to eat any of them—'food taken out of the mouths of men at the front,' and that kind of nonsense. In the mornings he would march up and down beside my bed, up and down, never a word, only silent reproaches. The room I had to sleep in was a nightmare; the Sistine angels over the bed, a piece of birchbark with picture postcards glued to it. Pathetic, really, a widower like that. The way he lives: soup three times a day and one hot drink in the evenings. It's funny, everything about him is blue: face, hands, clothes—all blue. In the evening he lays his clothes over four chairs, picks them up again, lays them down again. Once he designed a sink. He's still living on the strength of it today. Inventor's fame. Now he twists wires into vegetable baskets and barters them for food. He grows the yeast for his bread himself. Horrible stuff. 'Extremely palatable,' he says. 'I'm going to give some to the ladies. It's important to give pleasure to others.' That's also a kind of slogan of his. He's always trying to prove he's not what he seems to be. For example, he thinks of himself as a great lady's man. He carries a worn picture around in his wallet. 'My passion, 1926' written on it—a publicity still? Who knows . . ."

In the bow compartment. The new control-room assistant inquires cautiously what the Commander is like. Someone fills him in. "The Old Man? He's an odd one. I'm always amazed how happy he is when we put to sea. It seems he's got himself engaged to one of those Nazi bitches. You can't find out much about her. Flyer's widow. Looks like she's trying out the services one by one: first the Air Force, now the Navy. In any case, the Old Man isn't getting much out of it. Must be one of those stuck-up types. That's about all you can make out from the photo—long legs, decent enough front—sure! But he deserves something better."

"They say those Nazi bitches aren't so bad." Schwalle.

"What makes you think so?"

"They get all kinds of special instruction at the Reich School for Brides. For example, they have to hold a piece of chalk in their assholes and write 'otto-otto-otto' on a blackboard. Makes them supple."

General uproar.

Several times in the course of a day through the open door of the radio shack I catch a passing glimpse of Herrmann, the sound man, who relieves Hinrich at the radio. He has a complicated way of squeezing himself between the table tops where his instruments stand. There's almost always a book in his hands. He's twisted his headset so that only one earpiece is in place. This way he can hear incoming Morse signals and still have an ear free for orders.

Herrmann has been on board since the commissioning of the boat. His bunk is in the petty officers' quarters opposite mine. His father, as I learned from the Commander, was a deck officer on a cruiser, and went down in 1917.

"The boy has had an absolutely typical career. First business school, then the Navy. In 1935 he was sound man on the cruiser *Köln*, then on a torpedo boat, then submarine school, and after that the Norwegian expedition with me. He's earned his Iron Cross First Class a couple of times. He's due for the fried egg soon."

Herrmann is a quiet, strikingly pale man. Like the Chief, he moves easily through the boat, as though there were no obstacles in his path. I've never seen his face relaxed—it's always tense, giving him a somewhat animal look. His behavior is timid and withdrawn. He keeps himself apart, even among the petty officers. He and Ensign Ullmann are the only ones who never play cards; they prefer to read.

I bend over Herrmann's table and from the earpiece of his headset hear thin sounds like the soft chirping of crickets. Not one of us—not even Herrmann—knows whether the message being transmitted at this exact instant, hundreds or thousands of miles away, has anything to do with us.

Herrmann looks up, his eyes alert. He hands out a sheet of paper with a meaningless sequence of letters on it. The Second Watch Officer takes it and quickly gets to work deciphering it.

After a few minutes he has the clear text: "To Commander-in-Chief U-boats: Out of a convoy, two steamers five thousand and six thousand registered tons—seven hours depth charge pursuit—driven off—am pursuing—UW."

The Second Watch Officer enters this message in the radio log-book and gives the book to the Commander. The Commander signs the message and hands the book on. The First Watch Officer reads it and initials it as well. Finally the Second Watch Officer hands it back to Herrmann, whose arm is already stretched out of the shack ready to receive it.

A typical message, relating in the meagerest detail the story of an attack: success, narrow escape after seven hours of underwater bombardment, and pursuit despite enemy defense.

"Eleven thousand gross registered tons—not so bad. UW—that's Bischof," says the Old Man. "Pretty soon he'll have a sore neck from all those decorations."

Not a word about the seven hours of depth charges. The Old Man acts as though the radiogram had never mentioned them.

Some minutes later Herrmann hands out the book again. This time it's a signal from the Commander-in-Chief to a boat stationed in the far north: to proceed at full speed to another attack area. Apparently a convoy is thought to be in the region in question. Invisible threads of radio are now drawing the other boat to a specific point in the Atlantic, the boat under remote control, thousands of miles from the Commander-in-Chief and his broadcasting station.

The hunt is being taken up out of sight of the enemy. On the huge map in the C-in-C's Headquarters someone is moving a small red flag to indicate the boat's new position.

There are intervals of calm during the daily trial dives, and these are used for inspecting the torpedoes.

The bow compartment is transformed into a machine shop. The hammocks are stowed away and the berths snapped shut. The seamen discard their shirts. Block and tackle are secured to the loading carriage. The floor breach of torpedo tube number one is opened. The first fish—fat, heavily greased, and dully gleaming—is drawn partway out of its tube, its weight borne by the hoist rings. At the command of the torpedo mechanic, everyone hauls on the horizontal hawser as if in a tug-of-war. Slowly the half-exposed torpedo emerges from its tube to hang free on the loading carriage, where, despite its full weight of 1½ tons, it can easily be moved forward, backward, or to either side.

Each man has his own special assignment. One tests the motor, another the bearings and axles. Special pipes are attached and the compressed-air tanks filled, rudder and hydroplane controls tested, the lubrication points filled with oil. Then, after much shouting and shoving, the fish is finally pushed back into the tube.

The same procedure goes for the second torpedo. The crew seems to have hit its stride. "Come on, out of the lady," roars Dunlop. "This is no damn good at all. There're people standing in line outside and the man simply won't budge. Damn pimps—not one of you is willing to work."

Finally the floor breaches are sealed again, the tackle knocked off the loading carriages, the carriages removed, and the tackle stowed away. The bunks can be pulled down again. Gradually the room is transformed back into a cave dwelling. The bow-compartment crew is exhausted; the men crouch on the floor plates that hide the second load of torpedoes.

"It's about time these beasts did a little hunting," Ario complains.

No one has to give a thought to the 8.8 shells. The highly sensitive torpedoes, however, require constant attention. They're quite different from shells—more like little ships with an extremely complex technology. In addition to the usual rudders they also have hydroplanes. Essentially they're self-sufficient miniature U-boats loaded with a cargo of 800 pounds of TNT.

In the old days people used to talk about "launching" torpedoes, —not about firing them—which is much more to the point. We simply give them a push out of their tubes and direct them on their way. After that they run on their own power—compressed air or electricity—and follow a predetermined course.

Four of the fourteen torpedoes are in the bow tubes, one in the stern: G7A's, motor-driven, with compressed-air tanks. Two are for concussion explosion, three for remote-control explosion. On contact with a steamer the percussion caps detonate the load of explosives and tear holes in the sides of the vessel. The more complicated and therefore more sensitive remote-control detonators, which are activated magnetically, explode at the appropriate depth just as the torpedo is passing under the ship. This detonation causes a pressure wave that strikes the vessel at its structurally weakest point.

The days pass in constant alternation of watch and off-watch, the same routine that governs every ship afloat.

The first watch is obviously the one that worries the Old Man. The First Watch Officer seems conscientious enough, but he can't fool the Commander, who thinks he's too lazy.

I am to take the place of one of the guards on the second bridge watch who is apparently down with flu. That means night watch from four to eight ship's time.

It's three o'clock when I wake up, half an hour too early. Silence in the control room. The bulbs have been shaded. Again I have the impression that the room stretches away into infinity.

The control-room mate reports on the weather. "Not much water coming over, but cold!" That means my woolen scarf and thick sweater, and perhaps even my woolen executioner's hood over the sou'wester. I get my things together.

The other bridge guards turn up: the Berliner and the ensign.

"Pretty damn cold," the bosun's mate mutters finally. "The second watch is always the shittiest!" Then louder, "Five minutes till time!"

At this moment the Second Watch Officer comes through the circular hatch, so bundled up that almost nothing of his face is visible between his sou'wester and the edge of his collar.

"Morning, men!"

"Morning, Lieutenant!"

The Second Watch Officer pretends he can't wait to go. He's the first to climb up and out. It's a tradition to spare the retiring watch the last five minutes.

The First Watch Officer, whom we're relieving, announces the course and speed.

I have the starboard sector aft. My eyes quickly adjust to the darkness. The sky is a little brighter than the black sea, so the horizon is clearly defined. The air is very damp. The binoculars quickly cloud over.

"Leather cloths to the bridge!" the Second Watch Officer shouts below. But it isn't long before the wipers are saturated too, and they begin to smear. Soon my eyes are burning and I have to shut them for seconds at a time. No one says a word. The pounding of the engines and the hissing and roaring of the waves quickly merge into the general silence. Now and again someone bumps his knee against the tower wall, producing a dull boom.

The port lookout astern gives a sigh and the Second Watch Officer whirls around. "Pay attention. Keep your eyes skinned!"

I feel an itching on my neck, but I'm wrapped up like a mummy. Can't scratch properly. Even monkeys can do that much! But I don't dare fumble around with my clothing. The Second Watch Officer gets uneasy if you undo so much as a single button.

He comes from a suburb of Hamburg. Was supposed to go to college but gave it up. Studied banking instead. After that he enlisted in the Navy. That's all I know about him. He's always cheerful, well thought of by commanders, petty officers, and seamen alike; no stickler for rules, does his job with relaxed matter-of-factness and no fuss. Although this shows that his ideas of duty are very different from those of the First Watch Officer, he's still the only person who manages to stay on halfway decent terms with the latter.

The wake is phosphorescent. The night sky black. Black with diamond embroidery. The stars stand out brilliantly in the heavens. The moon is dull, its light pale and bleached and tinged with green. It looks spoiled—like a rotting melon. Visibility over the water is very bad.

Clouds move in front of the moon. The horizon has almost disappeared. What's that—Shadows?—Announce them?—Or wait?— Goddam strange clouds! I stare until my eyes water, until I feel certain that it's nothing, no shadows.

I sniff hard to clear my nose so that I can smell things more easily. Many a convoy has been caught in pitch darkness by the far-reaching scent of smoke or escaping fuel oil from a damaged steamer.

"Black as a bear's bottom," complains the Second Watch Officer. "We could run straight into a Tommy!" We don't need to be on the lookout for lights. The Tommies are extremely careful not to show any. Even the glimmer of a cigarette could spell destruction.

The Zeiss binoculars are heavy. My arms begin to fail. The triceps ache. Always the same routine: let the glasses hang for a moment on their strap, stretch and wave your arms around. Then up with the heavy glasses again, press the eyepieces against your browbones, support the binoculars on your fingertips to cushion them against the vibration of the boat. And constantly scan the ninety degrees of horizon and sea for signs of the enemy. Move the glasses very, very slowly from one side of the sector to the other, feel out the horizon inch by inch, then put the glasses down and scan the whole sector in a single glance, then back to the horizon from left to right, inch by inch.

Now and again the wind whips spray over us. The forward lookouts bend down stiffly to shield the lenses with their hands and the upper part of their bodies. When thick clouds move across the moon, the water is stained black.

I know that the Atlantic here is at least ten thousand feet deep—ten thousand feet of water under our keel—but we might as well be gliding with idling engines across a solid surface.

Time drags. Growing temptation to let one's eyelids close and surrender to the motion of the boat, to enjoy being cradled up and down, lulled to sleep.

I'm tempted to ask the Second Watch Officer for the time but decide against it. In the east a trace of pale, reddish light shows above the horizon. The soft, bleached glow only colors a thin band of sky because a drift of blue-black clouds lies low over the horizon. A long time passes before the light makes its way up behind them, setting their edges aflame. The foreship is now recognizable as a dark mass.

It takes a while before there is enough light for me to be able to make out the individual gratings on the upper deck. Gradually the men's faces become clear: weary, gray.

One of the crew comes up to have a pee. He directs his face into the wind and pisses leeward through the railing of the "greenhouse." I hear the stream spatter on the deck below. Smell of urine.

Again the question: "Permission to come on deck?" One after another they emerge for a breath of air and a quick pee. The scent of cigarette smoke, fragments of conversation.

"All we need is for them to sell rubbers, and the ship's store would be perfect."

A little later the Second Watch Officer reports. The Commander has appeared on the bridge—he must have come up very silently. A quick side glance and I see his face, red in the glimmer of his cigarette, but then I call myself to order. Don't listen, don't let yourself be distracted, don't move. Don't remove your eyes from your sector. You have only one duty: to peer until your eyes come right out of their sockets.

"Tubes one to four—torpedo doors open!"

So the Old Man is going to have another firing-control exercise. Without turning my head I hear the First Watch Officer give the angle of aim. Then the report from below: "Torpedo doors one to four open!" Again and again the First Watch Officer repeats his monotonous incantation. But from the Old Man not a sound.

The horizon grows sharper. In the east the light has spread out along it; soon it will have encircled the skyline completely. Red fire now glows in the slit between the horizon and the blue-black clouds. The wind freshens, and suddenly in the east the gleaming upper portion of the sun appears. Soon snakes of fiery red are darting and twisting across the water. I have only a brief glimpse of the sun and the color of the sky, for the lighting is made to order for enemy flyers. Bright enough to reveal the boat and its foaming wake, but still too dark for us to spot airplanes quickly against the background of the sky.

Goddam gulls! They're harder than anything else on the nerves. It would be nice to know how many alarms have been sounded on their account.

I'm profoundly grateful that I don't have the sunlit sector.

The First Watch Officer goes on issuing commands. "Tubes one to three—ready—one and three tubes fire—distance twelve hundred —width of spread two hundred fifty—angle?"

"Angle ninety," comes from below.

The ocean is now fully awake. The short waves flash with the first light. Our bow begins to glitter. In rapid succession the sky now becomes red-yellow, yellow, then blue-green. The exhaust gas from the diesels extends its bluish veil to a few clouds of pink tulle. Our wake throws up myriad sparks of sunlight. The next man turns his face toward me, flooded with the red light of dawn.

Far off amid the waves I suddenly discover a few dark points . . . and then they're gone. What were they? The port lookout has seen them too.

"Porpoises!"

They approach like badly trimmed torpedoes, shooting first through the water, then through the air. One of the school has noticed the boat and they come flying toward us as though on signal. Soon we have them abeam on both sides. There must be dozens of them. Their bellies shimmer bright green; their dorsal fins cut the water like the prows of ships. Effortlessly they keep pace. This isn't swimming, but a constant flowing succession of leaps and bounds. The water seems to offer them no resistance. I have to remind myself not to watch them, but to pay attention to my sector.

Short gusts of wind ruffle the waves. Gradually the sky clouds over. Light trickles down and seems to be reaching us through a gigantic horizontal pane of milk glass. Soon our faces are dripping with flying spray. The motions of the boat increase.

The porpoises abruptly abandon us.

As I go off-watch my eyes seem to be swollen out of their sockets, at the end of tentacles. I press them with the palms of my hands and have the feeling that they actually are allowing themselves to be pushed back into place.

I'm so stiff that I can scarcely move as I peel off my wet oilskins and clamber exhausted into my bunk.

Still half an hour until change of watch. For the thousandth time I concentrate on the pattern of veins in the woodwork beside the bunk: nature's indecipherable hieroglyphics. The lines around a knot look like the airstream around the lifting surface of a plane.

Sudden jarring of the alarm bell.

I'm out of my bunk and reeling on the floor before I'm really conscious. The navigator has the third watch. What in the world can have happened?

As I try to get into my boots I'm caught in a crowd. The whole room is suddenly full of frantic commotion. Blue smoke billowing out of the kitchen. Looming through it the face of one of the stokers. With forced indifference he asks what's up.

"Whatever's not tied down, you dumb pig!"

The boat is still on an even keel. What does it mean? An alarm—and we're still horizontal?

"Belay alarm! Belay alarm!" rings out from the loudspeakers, and finally the report comes from the control room: "False alarm!"

"What?"

"Helmsman hit the alarm bell by mistake!"

"What a shit!"

"Which goddam asshole was it?"

"Markus!"

Speechlessness for a while, then general rage.

"I could kick that swine overboard."

"Fucking shit!"

"What a beat-up asshole!"

"That's what my girl says too . . ."

"Shut your trap!"

"They ought to use your ass for a fender."

"Between cruisers if possible!"

I smell a real fight.

The navigator is beside himself. He doesn't say a word, but his eyes are blazing.

Lucky for the helmsman that he's sitting in the tower. Even the Chief looks ready to tear him limb from limb if he ever gets his hands on him.

Politics is taboo in the Officers' Mess. Even if I touch on political matters when talking privately with him, the Old Man instantly puts an end to any serious conversation with a mocking twist of the lips. Questions about the meaning of the war and our chances are absolutely out. At the same time there's no doubt that when the Old Man takes to brooding all day long, staring at nothing, it's the political questions that bother him, not his personal problems.

He's good at camouflage. Only occasionally does he open a small crack in his visor, venture a cryptic remark, and for a few instants betray his real opinion.

Especially when enraged—the radio news almost always puts him in a fury—he reveals his hatred of Nazi propaganda. "Bleeding the enemy of shipping capacity, they call it! Destruction of tonnage. Heinies! Tonnage! It's good ships they're talking about. Fucking propaganda—turns us into official executioners, wreckers, slaughterers . . ."

The cargoes of the sunken ships, which are usually much more valuable to the enemy than the actual ships, hardly interest him at all. His heart is with the ships themselves. For him they're living things with pulsing hearts of machinery. It is abominable to have to destroy them.

I often wonder how he can possibly come to terms with this inescapable inner conflict. Apparently he has reduced all problems to a single common denominator: Attack so as not to be destroyed. "Submit to the inevitable" seems to be his motto. But he will have nothing to do with the rhetoric.

Sometimes I feel compelled to coax him out of his reserve, to ask him whether perhaps he isn't playing a game like all the others, though in a more complicated fashion than most; whether it doesn't require an infinite capacity for self-delusion to be able to live with the conviction that all doubts are silenced by the concept of duty. But he neatly evades me every time. Most of what I learn comes from his dislikes and antipathies.

Again and again it is the First Watch Officer or the new engineer who annoys the Old Man.

Even the way the First Watch Officer sits down so precisely irritates him. And there's his demonstrative cleanliness. And his table manners. He handles a knife and fork like dissecting instruments. Every canned sardine is subjected to a formal post-mortem. First he excises the ribs and backbone with the utmost care, then goes to work to remove the skin. Not the slightest scrap is allowed to escape him. By this time the Old Man is beginning to glower.

In addition to the canned sardines there is a kind of dried sausage with an especially thin skin that simply cannot be peeled off. This is a favorite object for the First Watch Officer's dissections. He captures the skin in tiny slivers; in the deep folds it can't be loosened at all. Everyone else devours the sausages skin and all. Although he fiddles about, naturally he can't get it off. He finally cuts so much of the sausage away from around the skin that there's almost nothing left. The Old Man can contain himself no longer. "Perfect ornament for the garbage pail!" But even this is too subtle—the First Watch Officer doesn't get it. He simply looks up expressionlessly and goes on scraping and cutting.

The new engineer obviously doesn't go down any better. What disturbs the Old Man most about him seems to be his vulgar way of grinning and his arrogance. "Second Engineer isn't up to much, is he?" he recently inquired of the Chief. The Chief merely rolled his eyes and wobbled his head back and forth like a mechanical dummy in a store window—a gesture he'd picked up from the Old Man.

"Come on, spit it out!"

"Hard to tell! A Nordic type, as they say."

"But a very damn slow Nordic type. Just the man we need for Chief Engineer! Down to a 'T'!" And after a while, "All I want to know is how we're going to get rid of him."

At that moment the Second Engineer turns up. I study him carefully: chunky, blue-eyed, the perfect model for textbooks. All hair cream and indolence, he's the exact opposite of the Chief.

Because he doesn't feel welcome in our mess, the Second Engineer tends to seek out the petty officers. The Commander disapproves of such crossing of lines and glowers at him out of the corner of his eye whenever he disappears into the petty officers' mess. Not being very perceptive, the Second Engineer is quite unaware of this, but perches on the sofa when there's room and babbles away to the petty officers about this and that. No wonder the atmosphere is less than congenial when the First Watch Officer and Second Engineer eat with us.

Conversations remain entirely neutral. Thorny subjects are avoided, but occasionally the Old Man gets out of control. One day at breakfast he said, "The gentlemen in Berlin seem to be working full steam ahead to invent new epithets for Herr Churchill. What's he called in today's official notices?" The Old Man glowers. No answer from the circle, so he answers his own question. "Sot, drunkard, paralytic . . . I must say that for a drunken paralytic, he's giving us one helluva time."

The First Watch Officer sits bolt upright and looks mulish. The world is suddenly incomprehensible to him. The Chief, in his usual position with his hands clasped around his knees, stares at a spot between the plates as though it contained some remarkable revelation.

Silence.

The Old Man won't let himself be put off.

"What we need is some music—perhaps our Hitler Youth leader would be kind enough to put a record on."

Though no one looks at the First Watch Officer, he feels the remark is meant for him and leaps to his feet, bright-red in the face. The Old Man thunders after him, " 'Tipperary,' if you please."

As the First Watch Officer returns and the opening bars start blaring through the boat, the Old Man needles him. "The record won't undermine the foundations of your philosophy, First Watch Officer, will it?" Then he solemnly raises his forefinger and announces to the table: "*His* Master's voice—not ours!"

In the bow compartment, close to the door, I sit on the floor plates, with my knees drawn up. It's the only possible way to sit in there, torpedoes underneath, and my back against the wall of the Quarters.

Conversation flows freely. Nothing like the constrained atmosphere in the Officers' Mess. The leaders in the bow compartment are always the same—Ario and Turbo along with Dunlop and Hacker. Some of the less articulate men withdraw from the argu-ments—leaving the others to talk and show off to one another—and creep into their bunks and hammocks like nocturnal animals into their burrows.

"Once a whore pissed all over my back," a voice comes from a hammock high up. "Man, that was a sensation!"

"You slob!"

"Sensations! I'll give you sensations!" Ario asserts. "On our steamer we had a character who always said, 'Get a cork with a nail in it and a violin string attached, push the cork up your ass and then have someone fiddle a tune on the string!"

"You can't get much more complicated than that, can you?"

"They say it gives you an amazing buzzing in the ass," Ario insists.

Now I hear fragments from way ahead in the bow. "Emma still doesn't know who knocked her up."

"How so?"

"How so? Christ, are you that dumb? Just try holding your bare ass against a circular saw and then say which tooth cut you first!"

Uproar.

For the first time I see the chief mechanic Johann on the bridge. Here in the bright light he looks twice as bleached and emaciated as he did down there in the electric light of the engine room. Although he's only just got here, he's already shivering as if he belongs in bed.

"Not used to fresh air, Johann?" I ask. Instead of answering, he stares grimly over the bulwark with something like disgust. The sight of the sea obviously makes him uneasy. I've never seen him so sour before. He usually seems cheerful, but that's because he's looking at pipes and manometers. The silvery gleaming floor plates of the E-room are the true foundation of life for him, the fine smell of oil a balm for his lungs. But up here—nature in the raw—the hell with it! A disgusted sweeping glance makes clear that no doubt the sight of the sea may be all very well for primitive creatures like sailors, but not for specialists who are on intimate terms with highly complicated machinery. His face set, Johann disappears below in silence.

"Now he's pouring out his woes to his machines—all about the wicked, wicked sea," the Second Watch Officer says. "Funny heinies, these machinists. Fresh air seems to damage their delicate lungs, daylight screws up their retinas, and seawater is pure hydrochloric acid."

"It's not like that with the Chief," I remark.

The Second Watch Officer is never at a loss for a quick answer. "He's simply perverse!"

For me, visits to the bridge are pure salvation.

Luckily two men are allowed topside in addition to the guards. I take advantage of this as often as possible. The moment I stick my head through the tower hatch, I feel liberated. I climb out of the mechanical cage, out of confining walls, out of the stench and dampness into the light and the pure air.

First I search the sky for weather signs, then give a quick sweeping glance around the horizon. Then I turn my head to and fro and finally tilt it all the way back. Through a few holes in the clouds I look out into space. Nothing to distort my view of the heavens—a huge kaleidoscope that offers a constant succession of images with every hour that goes by. I watch the panorama of the sky as it changes: now, for example, it's deep-blue high overhead. All the holes in the rapidly moving cloud cover are filled with deeper blues. Only toward the horizon is the cover torn. Here the blue is thinner, washed out by the drifting water vapors. To the east a touch of red still hangs above the horizon; in it floats a single dark violet-blue cloud.

Presently, something marvelous occurs behind the boat. Half-way up the vault of sky a moist patch of steel-blue light spreads until it blends with a flood of pale ochre, rising from behind the horizon. At first the fringes take on a soiled, greenish tone, but then they are slowly shot through from behind by a dull, luminous blue with the merest shimmer of green remaining: Verona blue.

At noon the sky becomes filled with cool silvery-gray. The piles of cloud have disappeared and only a few silky cirrus clouds veil the sun, scattering its light in silvery glints and flashes. A quiet pastoral scene unfolds, drawn in nacreous, subtle tints—like the inside of an oyster shell.

In the afternoon, to starboard, yellow and orange bands shimmer behind dark blue clouds. Their color is rich, heavy, almost oily. The clouds surge upward as though from a prairie fire: an African sky. I picture table mountains, giraffe acacias, gnus, and antelopes.

Far off to port beside a pile of dirty woolen clouds a rainbow rises in the sky. A second, paler one arches over it. In the middle of this semi-circle floats a dark ball like an explosion of shrapnel.

In late afternoon the stage sets above me change completely. The alterations are not achieved by drawing a few curtains or changing the shades of color; instead, a magnificent procession of clouds arrives, quickly filling the heavens.

As though the pattern of forms were not striking enough, the sun breaks through a rift, shooting oblique spears of light into the tumult of clouds.

After the evening meal I climb up to the bridge again. The day is dying, dissolving. The only color left is dabbed here and there on the clouds that float in the western sky, lined up like beads on an abacus. Soon only a small fleecy cloud retaining the last of the light is there to hold the eye. The glow of the setting sun lingers a while above the horizon, but then that too grows cold. Now the day is finished. In the east, night has already come. The water is transformed under the violet shadows. Its murmuring grows louder. Like the breathing of a sleeping man, the waves sweep by beneath the boat.

I am always awakened at midnight by the change of watch in the engine room. Both watches have to pass through the petty officers' mess. For a while both doors to the diesel room stand open. The roaring fills the room and the engines suck in great drafts of air, making the curtain of my bunk billow up. One of the men coming off-duty forces his way past the unfolded table, pulling the curtain all the way back. It will be some time now before peace is restored.

I keep my eyes shut and force myself not to hear the voices. But another light is turned on. The glare of the bulb in the ceiling strikes me straight in the face, and I'm fully awake. There's a strong smell of diesel exhaust. The petty officers who have been relieved are pulling off their oil-smeared jackets and trousers, taking a few drags of apple juice from their bottles, and climbing into their bunks, chatting in subdued voices.

"Big fancy to-do." I hear Kleinschmidt. "Coffee at my future in-laws, with vases of flowers and gold-trimmed dishes. Very nice people. The old man's sixty-five and she's already seventy. Pound cakes and plum cakes. Before that, black currant liqueur, homemade —all first class. My fiancée was in the kitchen making the coffee. I was sitting there on the sofa—with my arms sort of spread out, and I happened to push my right hand down into the crack between the seat and the upholstery at the back—you know?"

"Of course, then what?"

"Guess what I fish out?"

"How the hell would I know?" That must be the control-room mate Isenberg. "Don't overdo the suspense."

"Well, a five-pack of condoms. Three still in it. Two missing. What d'you say to that?"

"You're great at arithmetic!"

"So I slammed the package down on the table. The old folks were gaping at me. Then I walked out—end of dream!"

"You're crazy!"

"What d'you mean? Maybe you think I should have invited my Herr Cunt of a brother-in-law to join us for coffee, eh?"

"Take it easy."

"Either—or! There's no third way as far as I'm concerned!"

"You're a nut case! What makes you so sure she really . . ."

"Oh come on, don't talk crap. Do you want me to believe the old man needed them?"

I turn over again toward the plywood wall but the door is thrown open with a bang and the last man appears, bosun's mate Wichmann. He slams the door shut behind him and turns on a second bright light. I already know from other nights what will happen next. But some damn curiosity makes me watch again.

Wichmann strikes a pose in front of the mirror on the door and makes faces at himself. Before bringing his hair forward over his face he runs his thumbnail a couple of times in both directions over the teeth of the comb. After a series of attempts he succeeds in getting the part exactly right. When he takes a few steps back, I can see that his face is shining in an ecstasy of concentration. Now comes the moment when he inspects himself from left to right, his head cocked on one side. Then he goes to his locker and rummages about. When he reappears in front of the mirror he has the tube in his hand. He carefully applies the pomade between the teeth of the comb, then draws it through his hair again and again until he achieves a completely flat surface that's like a mirror.

Finally he packs away his utensils, takes off his jacket, removes his shoes without unlacing them, and rolls into bed, leaving the light on.

Five minutes later I climb down to turn it off. In passing I glance at the bosun's mate's bunk: the splendor is destroyed.

Friday. Fourteenth Day at Sea. I meet the Old Man in the control room. Affable. Apparently happy to have a conversation. This time I make a start by asking his explanation of why so many men volunteer for U-boat service despite the heavy losses.

The usual minutes for reflection. Then, with pauses: "You won't get much out of the children themselves. Obviously they're tempted by the aura. We're what you might call the *crème de la crème*, the Dönitz Volunteer Corps. And then, of course, there's the propaganda . . ."

Long pause. The Old Man keeps staring at the floor plates. Finally he's ready to talk again. "Perhaps they simply can't imagine what's ahead of them. After all, they're nothing but blank pages— three years' schooling, then drafted immediately, and the usual training. They haven't seen anything yet—nor experienced anything —and, besides, they have no imagination."

A ghost of a grin spreads across his face as he turns halfway toward me. "Footslogging around with a gun over your shoulder—can't say I'd find it exactly inspiring either. How would *you* like to go plowing through the countryside in jackboots? God knows, we're better off in that respect. They give us a ride. We don't have to drag ourselves along getting blisters on our feet. Regular meals—mostly hot food. Where else can you find that? Besides, we have real bunks. And excellent heating. And lots of good invigorating sea air . . . And then shore leaves, with stylish marine uniforms and all the pretty decorations. If you ask me, we're better off than the ordinary troops: certainly a U-boat crew is way ahead of the Navy shit-shovelers. Everything's relative, after all."

At the word "shit-shovelers" I see myself practicing "individual review with salutation." The division commander roars the order at the top of his voice. Each roar jerks him up on tiptoe. "Kindly get your goddam rifle up faster or I'll have the piss streaming out of your nose and ears before I've finished with you!"

And before that, labor service . . . August Ritter von Karavec was the name of the bastard they assigned to us as chief instructor after he had been transferred several times for disciplinary reasons. "When properly commanded, a division should be distinguishable from the terrain by nothing but the whites of their eyes" was his basic principle. By putting us through wheeling maneuvers and parade march in a bog, he could get us plastered from head to foot with ice-cold mud in five minutes flat; there wasn't a boot left on anyone's foot—they were stuck in the slime, and we were soaked to the skin. Two hours later this madman had uniform inspection and found something in everyone to bellyache about. Which meant: Dump all belongings in a single heap in the middle of the room, and then let twenty men sort out their possessions again. As "punishment" there was also the great wheeling maneuver performed on a slope. This was even worse than the bog, because the men on the wings almost burst their lungs racing uphill. And that bastard made sure that everyone had to take his turn on the outside . . .

The cynical grin was gone from the Old Man's face before he picked up from where he'd left off.

"Perhaps you can only do this kind of thing with kids, because they're still what you might call underexposed. No ties. The one person to make it out of a tight spot is almost always an officer. With a wife and children at home! Funny thing. Once we were picking up seamen from a sunken destroyer—one of ours—pulled them out of the drink. We must have got there something like two hours after she sank, which is pretty soon as these things go. It was summer, so the water wasn't too cold. But most of the young ones were hanging in their life preservers—already drowned. They'd simply given up—let their necks go limp, although there was only a medium to heavy sea. Only the older ones struggled. There was one of them—over forty and seriously wounded—and *he* survived even though he'd lost a lot of blood. But the eighteen-year-olds who were completely un-injured—they didn't." The Old Man is silent for a few moments, apparently searching for the best words to sum it all up. Then: "The older ones generally get through—the kids would rather give up."

The Chief has arrived, and glances at me for a moment in astonishment. The Commander goes on.

"Actually we ought to be able to get along with a lot fewer men. I keep imagining a boat that would only need a crew of two or three. Exactly like an airplane. Basically we have all these men on board because the designers have failed to do a proper job. Most of the men are nothing but links in a chain. They fill the gaps the designers have left in the machinery. People who open and close valves or throw switches are not what you'd call fighting men. I can't listen these days when the C-in-C U-boats tries to get everyone all excited with his advertising slogans: 'Attack—Defeat—Destroy'—it's all pure bullshit. Who does the attacking? The Commander and no one else. The seamen don't see so much as a trace of the enemy."

The Old Man pauses. No need to say anything now. No prompting necessary today.

"Damn shame old Dönitz has joined the bigmouths. We swore by him at first," he says in a low voice.

I've known for some time what's been eating the Old Man. His re-lations with the Commander-in-Chief have not been good since his last report.

"We used to see him as a kind of sea Moltke. But now it's 'One for all, all for one'—'One Reich, one Volk, one Führer'—'The Führer has his eye on you'—'The Führer, the Führer, the Führer' . . . You can hardly bear to listen. Always stuck in the same groove. And then he keeps going on about the 'German woman, our noblest possession.' 'When I leave the Führer I always feel a mere nothing.' That sort of thing's enough to floor anyone."

The Old Man has talked himself into real bitterness.

The Chief stares straight ahead and pretends he's heard nothing.

"Tsch, the volunteer crews!" The Old Man is back where he started. "Comradeship—the togetherness of all men aboard—'sworn fellowship'—*that's* not just hot air, as a matter of fact. It really attracts people. And more than anything else so does the feeling of belonging to an élite. You only have to look at the fellows on leave.

They swell up like pouter pigeons with their U-boat insignia on their uniforms. Seems to have some effect on the ladies too . . ."

The loudspeaker crackles. Then: "Second watch stand by!" This time the order applies to me too. I'm going to stand one watch as stoker, attending the exhaust doors and the diesels.

The Chief has given me cotton for my ears. "Six hours of diesel noise is quite enough, I can tell you."

The suction of the machines holds the diesel room door so tight that I need all my strength to open it. Immediately the noise of the engines breaks over me like a hail of blows. The staccato chatter of the push rods and rocker arms forms the percussion accompaniment to the contained torrent of explosions within the cylinders and the deep thundering roar issuing, I assume, from the blower. However, only the starboard diesel is running, at half speed, while charging batteries; the port engine is silent. So the deep roar can't be the blower after all, since it's only used to increase the air supply when the machines are running at full speed.

The diesels reach almost to the rounded ceiling. Along the flank of the starboard engine the links between the rocker arms and push rods move in perfect unison, sending out wave after wave of vibrations over the huge machine.

The chief mechanic Johann is on duty. For the time being he pays no attention to me. He's concentrating on the behavior of the tachometer; its needle is moving sharply. All of a sudden it will jump several marks on the scale and shiver nervously as our screws meet varying resistance in the rough sea. Even without the tachometer, I would be more aware here in the after part of the ship than in the control room of how the waves cling to the boat, then release it and hurl it forward again. The screws labor at first, then the boat fights its way free, and they race all the faster.

Johann checks the oil pressure and the cold-water pressure, one after the other, then with the abstracted look of a lab worker he reaches for the fuel oil line, which branches off under the lubricating pumps, and tests its temperature. Finally he mounts the silvery, gleaming step that runs along the side of the diesel and touches the rising and falling rocker-arm hinges: all with very slow, precisely calculated movements.

He shouts my instructions at me: see to it that nothing gets too hot, keep feeling the cold-water pipes and inspecting the rocker arms on the push rods, the way he's just done it. And if he gives the sign, shut the exhaust gas doors. I've watched this procedure often enough.

Johann returns to the control station, cleans his hands with brightly colored cotton waste, reaches into a chest beside his small standing table for a bottle of juice, and tilts his head back to take a couple of deep gulps.

The vibrating joints drip with oil. I feel them one after the other, absorbing the heavy impact through my hand. All of them are uniformly warm. The explosions in the cylinders follow one another in uninterrupted sequences. I repeat to myself: intake stroke, compression stroke, power stroke, exhaust stroke.

After a quarter of an hour Johann opens the door to the galley and turns a hand wheel on the ceiling. At the same time he roars an explanation. "I'm closing—the—bottom valve of the diesel—now it's—drawing air—from inside the boat—gives a fine—through draft!"

An hour later the chief mechanic leaves the control station and comes along the gangway between the two engine blocks. One after another, he opens the inspection petcocks on the side of the diesel that's in use. Each belches a stream of fire. Johann nods, reassured: ignition in all cylinders, everything in perfect running order. Funny, I think to myself, smoking is forbidden, but this flame-throwing is all right.

Swaying like a tightrope walker, Johann makes his way back again to the control station—rubbing a few oil flecks from a polished surface in passing—and cleans his hands again with a handful of cotton waste. The waste is tucked between the pipes near the door. After a while he reaches over his head and turns on a high-pressure valve to increase the flow of fuel oil. Then he glances at the electrical telethermometer, which registers the temperature in all the cylinders and the combined exhaust pipes. Using a pencil stub so short that he has to hold it with the tips of his fingers, he makes his entries in the engine-room log: consumption of oil, temperatures, variations in pressure.

The helmsman, just off duty and both arms full of wet oilskins, comes crashing through the door more by suction than his own momentum, squeezes past me, and works his way aft along the support bars of the diesel toward the E-motors, where he hangs the dripping clothes around the stern torpedo tube to dry.

The diesel mate is sitting on a low tool chest opposite me in front of the port diesel control station, poring over a battered book. His machine is idle so he has nothing to do. He has to stay on duty, however, because the machine may be called upon at any moment.

Again and again I sway along the polished iron runway on the side of the starboard diesel. The gauges show normal pressure.

The chief mechanic signals to me: I am to sit in the doorway to the E-room. The brown bags with the escape gear hang close to the door on switchboxes. They are an oppressive reminder that the control room and the bridge are a long way off. A long escape route to the tower hatch. Not a pleasant post for someone with a lively imagination. You can tell yourself a dozen times that it makes no difference whether the escape route is long or short once the boat has been sent to the bottom. The feeling of being shut up all the way in the stern eats away at your nerves just the same.

Besides, the boat can just as easily be wrecked on the surface— by being rammed, for instance—and in that case everyone knows that the guards on deck and the men in the control room may be rescued, but the engine-room crew, never.

A bell shrills above the noise of the diesel. A red lamp goes on. A stab of fear. The diesel mate is on his feet. What's up? Johann makes a reassuring gesture. I understand: the port diesel has been ordered into action. Now I have something to do: open the exhaust gas vents for the port diesel. The diesel mate couples the engine to the driving shaft. Compressed air hisses into the cylinders. The chief mechanic has already opened the fuel-oil throttle. Rockers click, and there is the crack of the first explosion. The push rods begin to move: the port diesel is roused from inactivity. Ignition of all cylinders, and already their noise is blending in with the sound of the starboard engine. Another stretch with nothing to do. The gauges show that the engines are getting all they need: fuel, air, and water for the cooling system.

Three hours of the watch are over: halftime.

The air has become rapidly hotter and heavier since the port diesel has been running.

At ten o'clock Cookie brings around a pail of lemonade. I drink thirstily out of the ladle.

Johann jerks his thumbs up toward the ceiling: time to shut the exhaust gas doors. We don't dare neglect them. They cover the exhaust lines from the diesels while we are submerged, and they must be absolutely watertight to prevent any flooding of the engines. When we're traveling on the surface, however, there's incomplete combustion in the engines. This leads to a buildup of carbon deposits and could prevent the doors from shutting tight during a dive. At the beginning of the war, as a matter of fact, boats were lost simply because the doors were jammed open by the residue, and water rushed into the boat. To prevent this we "grind in" the doors every four hours.

The red light flashes on again. The engine-room telegraph jumps to half speed ahead. The chief mechanic pulls the throttle up. Less fuel is reaching the cylinder pumps and the starboard diesel begins to turn more slowly as the rhythm of the combustion falters. Johann puts the throttle at zero and the diesel stops. He raises his fist, signaling me to close the outer gas exhaust door by turning the big hand wheel on the ceiling. I seize the spokes and turn with all my might, driving the exhaust-door plate back and forth against its housing to scrape off all the carbon deposits. Back and forth, back and forth, until Johann lets me stop.

Bathed in sweat and panting hard, I stand there as the starboard diesel springs to life again. Shortly thereafter the port diesel is stopped and the same procedure begins again. I now have no real strength left and have to use every muscle to turn the spokes. Sweat is streaming down my face.

The two diesels haven't been running long when the chief mechanic's face goes tense. He listens to the pulse of the engines as if turned to stone. Reaches for pocket flashlight and screwdriver and pushes his way past me. Close to the after door he lifts a floor plate, shines his light down, and beckons me closer. Underneath is an even wilder confusion of pipes, filters, valves, and faucets. This is part of the water-cooling and oil-lubrication system and the fuel supply.

Now I see it too: one of the pipes is releasing a fine spray of water. Johann glances at me eloquently, then works his way between the pipes, twisting like an acrobat, and is at the trouble spot with his tools. After a while he hands me some nuts and bolts. He's removed a packing from the pipe. I can't understand what he's roaring at me; he has to raise his head from the tangle of pipes before I get it. The diesel mate is to cut a new packing. Suddenly everyone has something to do. The repair is not a simple one. A large black patch of sweat appears on Johann's back. Finally he hauls himself out of the jungle, smeared with oil, and winks—so whatever he did has worked. But how did he detect the fault in the first place? He must have a sixth sense for his engines.

At five minutes to twelve the new watch comes in. One last mouthful of apple juice, rub the hands with cotton waste, and then no thought but to get out of this cave of an engine room and into the control room for the first gulp of fresh air.

Fifteenth Day at Sea. Two weeks. The waves today are low. They collide helter-skelter without any clear sense of over-all movement. The boat rides them uneasily, unable to settle into any rhythm. An old groundswell, which can be felt at long intervals under the choppy surface, adds yet another variation to the motion.

For days we've seen nothing except one barrel, a few boxes, and, once, hundreds of bottle corks—a sight that baffled even the Commander. "Can't be left over from a binge—just corks and no bottles—it's crazy!"

I'm on watch with the navigator. My biceps at least are being kept in training. I can feel every muscle in my upper arm all the way down into my shoulder blades from holding up the heavy binoculars. I'm lowering the glasses more often than I did in the first hour of the watch. The navigator can hold his for hours at a time: you'd think he'd been born with his arms fixed at right angles to his body.

"We lead what you might call a double life," he begins, out of nowhere.

I don't know what he's getting at. The navigator is anything but articulate, so his words emerge hesitantly from between his leather gloves. "Half on board and half ashore, so to speak." He wants to say something more but obviously can't find the right words.

We both busy ourselves with scanning our sectors.

"The way it is," the navigator finally resumes, "here we are, dependent on ourselves—no mail, no communications, nothing. But we still have a kind of link with home."

"Yes?"

"For example, there are things that bother you. You keep wondering how things are going at home. And even more, how your folks are. They don't even know where we really are, swanning around the way we do."

Another pause. Then, "When we put to sea"—he lets the sentence dangle for a while—"we're already half gone. If something really happens to the boat, it's months before they announce the loss."

Silence. Then he abruptly begins again. "If a man's married, it makes him as good as useless." This uttered as a maxim beyond dispute.

Finally light dawns. He's talking about himself. But I pretend we're still talking generalities.

"I don't know, Kriechbaum, whether wedding rings matter all that much . . . How long is it the Chief has actually been married?"

"Only a couple of years. Stuck-up kind of lady—blond hair, with a permanent."

Now he's talking easily, without hesitation, relieved that it's no longer about his own problems. "She delivered a sort of ultimatum.

'Not going to let my life be all messed up,' that sort of thing. Not that she looks as if she'll lack for entertainment while we're promenading around out here. Nice mess for the Chief. Now she's pregnant, too."

Another silence, then when Kriechbaum starts up once more he's as hesitant as he was at first. He's obviously talking about himself again. "You find yourself carrying so much ballast around—better not to think about it too much!"

We devote ourselves to the horizon again. I scour it with my glasses, inch by inch. Then I rest the binoculars and look out across the sea and sky to relax my eye muscles. Then I squint and raise the glasses again. Always the same routine: search horizon, lower binoculars, take a look all around, raise binoculars again.

Ahead of the boat, two points to port, there's a fog bank—a clump of dirty, gray-green wool—clinging to the horizon. The navigator concentrates on that area. Fog banks are always suspect.

A good ten minutes pass before he takes up the thread again. "Perhaps it's the only thing to do—away with the whole *menkenke!*"

This goes around in my brain for a while: "*Menkenke*"—isn't that Jewish for "bag of tricks" or something? Where can he have come across "*menkenke*"? "*Fisimatenten*"—that's another one—for "fuss." "*Menkenke*" . . . "*fisimatenten*"—you could go nuts speculating over things like that.

I remember Ensign Ullmann. He has his troubles too. Ullmann is from Breslau. With his snub nose and those sparse freckles scattered all over his face, he looks like a fourteen-year-old. At the base I saw him once in his blue dress uniform. With his big peaked cap on his head, he looked like a clown done up in a costume that had been bought too large so he could grow into it.

The ensign is popular. He seems to be a tough fellow. Actually, he's not so much small as compact, and, viewed close up, he's older than he looks at first: He didn't get all those creases in his face just from laughter.

One day when I was alone with him in the petty officers' mess he started behaving oddly: fiddling aimlessly with the utensils on the table, pushing them here and there, laying a knife parallel to a fork and glancing up from time to time to catch my attention.

I realized that he wanted to tell me something.

"D'you know the flower store next to the café, À l'Ami Pierrot?"

"Of course, and the two salesgirls. Pretty thing, Jeannette, and what's the other one's name?"

"Françoise," the ensign said. "As a matter of fact, I'm engaged to her—secretly, of course."

"Tst!" I sputtered in sheer astonishment: our little ensign with his porcupine haircut and his outsized dress uniform engaged to a French girl!

"She's nice," I said.

The ensign was sitting on his bunk, hands palms up on his thighs, looking helpless—his confession seemed to have worn him out.

Gradually it all came out. The girl is pregnant. The ensign is not so naïve as to be unaware of what it would mean for her to have a child. We are the enemy. Collaborators usually get short shrift. The ensign knows how active the Maquis are. The girl obviously knows it even better.

"Besides, she doesn't want the child!" he said, but so hesitantly that I asked, "Well?"

"Not if we get back!"

"Hmm," I said. Embarrassed, I could think of nothing better than, "Ullmann, that's no reason to be so depressed. Everything will straighten out. You're imagining things!"

"Yes," was all he said.

Up with the glasses again. They ought to make them lighter. The navigator beside me says bitingly, "The gentlemen at Headquarters ought to see all this just once—nothing but ocean and not a trace of the enemy. I can just imagine how they picture it: we put to sea, run around for a few days, and hey presto—here come the freighters, sailing along, crowds of them and all loaded to the gunwales. A daring attack—fire everything we've got. A few depth charges in return just to teach us not to get too uppity. The victory pennants on the periscope for a lot of fat tankers, and tie up at the pier grinning from ear to ear. Brass bands and decorations, of course. But there really ought to be a film of all this: closeups of pure shit. Horizon bald as a baby's bottom, a couple of clouds—and that's it. Then they could film the inside of the boat: moldy bread, filthy necks, rotten lemons, torn shirts, sweaty blankets, and, as a grand finale, all of us looking utterly pissed-off."

Sixteenth Day at Sea. The Chief seems to be in a good mood today. Probably because he succeeded in making an especially complicated repair on one of the engines. He's even persuaded to whistle for us.

"Ought to be in vaudeville!" says the Old Man.

I only have to close my eyes for a second to see every detail of the scene in the Bar Royal, with Merkel's Chief trying to teach me to whistle on two fingers. The art of whistling—in this flotilla, at least—is apparently a specialty of the engineers.

How long ago it seems. The musicians with their empty, staring eyes, and crazy Trumann. Thomsen, lying in his own piss, bellowing slogans through a cloud of bubbles.

"Haven't heard from Trumann in a long time," the Old Man says suddenly, as though he'd read my thoughts. "He must have put out long ago!"

Nothing from Kortmann either, nor from Merkel.

We have only heard Kallmann and Saemisch by accident, when they were ordered to report their positions. Plus the reports that our radioman also picked up of Flechsig's and Bechtel's boats.

"This is going to be a shitty month," growls the Old Man. "The others don't seem to be having any luck either."

Another hour and ten minutes until dinnertime—seventy minutes, four thousand two hundred seconds!

The radioman Hinrich comes in and delivers a message addressed specifically to us. The Chief takes the slip of paper, gets the deciphering machine out of the locker, puts it down among the plates, carefully tests the setting, and begins to strike the keys.

The navigator turns up as if by accident, and watches out of the corner of his eye. The Chief pretends to be completely absorbed. Not a muscle moves in his face. Finally he winks at the navigator and gives the deciphered radiogram to the Commander.

It's only an order to report our position.

The Commander and the navigator disappear into the control room. Won't be long before the radioman spits out a brief signal with our coordinates.

iv FRIGGING AROUND: 2

THE BOAT continues to wander around with its cargo of fourteen torpedoes and one hundred twenty shells for the 8.8 millimeter cannon. Only the amount of 3.7 ammunition has been slightly reduced by practice firing. And a good deal of our 114 tons of oil has gone. We are also the lighter by a fair amount of our provisions.

So far we have contributed nothing to the war effort of Greater Germany. We haven't inflicted the slightest damage on the enemy. We have added no luster to our name. We haven't loosened Albion's death grip, or added a single new leaf to the laurels of the German U-boat Command, blah blah blah . . .

We have merely stood watch, gobbled food, digested it, inhaled bad smells, and produced a few ourselves.

And we haven't even got off any misses. They would at least have made space in the bow compartment. But all the torpedoes are still here, expertly tended, greased to perfection and regularly tested.

The sky grows darker, and the tattered sheets of water that hang from the net guards after every plunge of the boat are as gray as laundry washed in wartime soap. All around us there is nothing but gray on gray; no line of division between the gray of the sea and the gray of the sky. Higher up, where the sun ought to be, the gray is only a shade lighter. The sky looks like watered-down gruel.

Even the foam on the occasional breaking wave is no longer white. It is soiled, second hand.

The howl of the wind sounds like the yowling of a kicked dog, spiritless and depressing.

We are heading against the sea. The boat stamps along like a rocking horse: up and down, up and down. The strain of peering ahead becomes a torment. I have to keep cheering myself up lest I fall prey to the sick hopelessness that engulfs us all and sink into apathy.

The gray light seems filtered through gauze and weighs on the eyelids. The watery mist makes it dimmer still. There is nothing solid in this soup to catch one's attention.

If only something would happen! If only the diesels would run at full speed for a while, if the boat would throw up a bow wave again instead of jouncing around at this soul-destroying jogtrot. Head stuffed with cotton, heavy limbs, aching eyes.

Shitty sea, shitty wind, frigging around!

As the oldest man in the bow compartment, the E-stoker Hagen commands universal respect. And he obviously knows it. In the dim light all I can see of his face is eyes and nose. The high, curled ends of his mustache reach almost to his eyelids. Forehead hidden under a thick thatch of hair. His black beard is thick and long, since he didn't sacrifice it even during our time in port. From a favorite phrase of his, he's known on board as "the Plain, Straightforward Fellow." He already has seven patrols behind him, six of them on another boat.

"Tsch!" says Hagen, and at once everyone is silent.

I stretch my legs, brace my back against the frame of a lower bunk, and wonder what's to come.

Hagen savors this expectancy to the full, wipes the palms of his hands thoroughly on the hair of his chest, and drains the teapot into his cup. Relaxed, he then savors his tea, swallowing it in great gulps.

"Well, out with it, O Gracious One! Speak, Lord for Thy servant heareth!"

"I was once so angry at the Tommies!—"

". . . in my plain, straightforward way!" This last from a bunk; Hagen answers it with a glance of truly theatrical contempt.

"It was hellish weather—just like—today, and they got us by the nuts off the Orkneys, a great batch of escort vessels standing over us. No decent depth under our keel. No chance of escaping underwater. Surprise packages of depth charges all day long—"

He takes a mouthful of tea, but doesn't swallow it immediately. Instead he swishes it noisily around a few times between his teeth.

"Nice bombing job. Then the Tommies went quiet. Simply waited up there for us to surface. The second night, our Commander went mad, used every trick he knew, including the thin silhouette, and suddenly we're up and away. The Tommies must have been sleeping on the job. I can't understand it even now. The very next day we sank a destroyer. Nearly ran into it in the fog. Had to fire at almost point-blank range."

Hagen falls into a trance, and someone plays midwife again. "Come on, out with the rest!"

"We got the destroyer at angle zero!" Hagen demonstrates with two matches. "Here's the enemy destroyer, and here's our boat." He arranges the matches with their heads facing each other. "I was the first to spot her—in my plain, straightforward way!"

"Now we're getting it—didn't I tell you?" The voice from the bunk again.

Hagen cuts the story short. Pushing the matches around, he demonstrates the attack. "Sank in a matter of seconds."

He reaches for the match representing the destroyer and breaks it in two. Then gets up and tramples it under his boot.

The helmsman Little Benjamin pretends to be fascinated. He gazes straight into Hagen's face, simultaneously trying to make off with a piece of bread that Hagen's just buttered for himself. But Hagen is on the alert and slaps his fingers smartly. "Not so fast with my bread and butter."

"My mistake," Little Benjamin says apologetically, "as the hedgehog remarked when he got up off the toilet brush."

Control-room assistant Turbo also has something to contribute. He's cut out a cigar and a plum from the advertisements in a magazine and pasted them together to make an obscene montage that he now proudly hands around.

"Swine!" says Hagen.

For three days and three nights the radioman has picked up nothing but position reports from other boats. No victory announcements. "Never known such a total washout!" says the Old Man. "Absolute bottom."

The sea seethes and boils. The wind keeps whipping up the surface into a gray-white plain. Not a single patch of the usual beer-bottle green, only dull white and gray. When our bow works its way free of the waves it seems to be festooned on both sides with dripping decorations of stucco.

Brooding bleakly at breakfast time, the Old Man simply forgets to chew. It isn't until the steward enters to clear the meal away that he suddenly comes to with a start, moves his lower jaw busily for a few minutes, then drifts off again with his thoughts. Finally he pushes his plate away indifferently and pulls himself together. He gives us a friendly glance and opens his mouth to speak but seems unable to find a single word. He saves himself with a few official announcements: "09.00, practice dive; 10.00, instruction for petty officers! Maintain course until 12.00." Same old thing.

The First Watch Officer is not the least of the causes of the Old Man's depression. The expression on the man's face—at best faintly critical, often openly contemptuous—grates on the Old Man's nerves. His pedantic mannerisms unsettle all of us, both on watch and off, in much the same way as a driver who sticks exactly to the rules produces chaos in traffic. Most of all, however, it is his thinly concealed political convictions that irritate the Old Man.

"He really seems to hate the Tommies," the Old Man says just after the First Watch Officer has gone on duty. "Thoroughly indoctrinated. At least he's got it all worked out to his own satisfaction."

I'd give a lot for a half hour's walk—or a cross-country run through the woods. My calf muscles have gone slack. My existence consists of nothing but lying down, standing up, and sitting still. Some hard physical exercise would be a big help. Felling trees, for instance. The very thought makes me smell the pines. I can almost picture orange-red chips of felled timber, the cabins we used to build ourselves, hear the rustling of reeds, see myself hunting water rats. Dear god . . .

The radio has picked up a message. We behave with elaborate indifference, yet each of us is longing for a radio order that will put an end to all this frigging around. After a contemptuous glance at the decoding machine, the Commander reads the slip, noiselessly moving his lips, and disappears without a word through the circular door.

We look at one another.

Plagued by curiosity, I move into the control room. The Commander is bent over the sea chart. For the moment I must wait in vain. In his left hand he holds the slip and with his right he's manipulating the dividers.

"It's possible—not altogether out of the question," I hear him murmur. The First Watch Officer can no longer endure the uncertainty and begs for the slip of paper. "Convoy in Square XY. Zigzag course around sixty degrees, speed eight knots—UM." One glance at the chart and I feel sure we can reach Square XY.

The navigator clears his throat, looking totally indifferent, and asks the Commander for the new course. You'd think the radiogram had brought us nothing more than the new retail price of potatoes.

The Commander isn't giving away anything either. "Wait and see," he says.

Everyone falls silent. The Chief bores into a tooth with his tongue. The navigator becomes absorbed in his fingernails while the Commander measures angles and lays off distances with the dividers —the problem of interception.

The navigator peeps over the Old Man's shoulder as he works. I get myself a few prunes from the box and move the pits back and forth in my mouth, trying to pick them clean. The control-room mate has nailed a milk can to the wooden wall for the pits. It's already half full. Mine are by far the cleanest.

UM—that's Marten's boat. Marten, who used to be the Old Man's First Watch Officer and is now serving with the Sixth Flotilla in Brest.

New radio messages tell us that three boats have been ordered to join in pursuit of the convoy, then four, then finally five.

We're not one of them.

"They ought to be sending in everything that can move," is the Old Man's comment. What he probably wants to say is, "Hell and damnation, when are we finally going to get our orders?"

Hour after hour goes by, and still no radio message for us. The Commander squats in the corner of his bunk and busies himself with a collection of colored folders full of all sorts of memoranda: secret orders, tactical regulations, flotilla orders, and all the other paperwork that's always going the rounds. Everyone knows that he detests this sort of official waste paper, that he's only taken the folders out to hide how tense he really is.

Toward 17.00, another radio message finally arrives. The Commander lifts his eyebrows: his whole face lights up. A personal message for us! He reads it and his face shuts tight again. Almost absentmindedly he pushes the note over to me: it's an order to report weather conditions.

The navigator makes out the report and hands the sheet to the Commander for his signature: "Barometer rising, air temperature five degrees, wind northwest six, cloud, cirro-stratus, visibility seven miles—UA."

Not wanting to be infected by the Old Man's depression, I head for the control room and climb up the ladder. The thin veil of cirrus has grown thicker. The tattered blue gradually disappears behind it. The sky will soon be clothed in gray-on-gray. The light becomes duller. All around, dark clouds have piled up heavily against the horizon. Their lower edges merge shapelessly into the gray of the surrounding sky. It's only higher up that they're clearly silhouetted against the whiter gray. I push my hands deep into the pockets of my leather jacket and stand there balancing with bent knees against the motion of the boat while the clouds swell slowly higher as if inflated from within. Dead ahead, the wind tears a hole in them, but more clouds pile in at once from either side to seal the hole again. They form a mighty phalanx that will soon threaten to conquer the whole sky. And then, as if the many collisions and occlusions weren't already causing enough confusion, the sun comes bursting through a rift: its beams slant down like spears to make a dramatic play of light and shadow on the tumultuous mass. Next, a bright flash touches the sea, broad on the starboard beam; then the spotlight wanders on over a trailing, padded rim of cloud, making it flare into brilliance. It darts back and forth, never lingering anywhere for more than a moment, crowning one cloud after another with a halo of light.

The Second Watch Officer is not impressed by the transformations of the sky. "Damned flyer's clouds!" For him the magnificent scenery is riddled with trickery. Again and again he trains his glasses on it.

I climb down and busy myself with my cameras. Evening comes. Up onto the bridge again. Now the clouds are sprinkled with iridescent colors. Suddenly the light of the sun abandons them, and they immediately revert to their own dreary gray. High in the sky there's a pale phantom, the last quarter of the waning moon. 18.00.

After the evening meal we sit tongue-tied, still expecting another radio message. The Commander is uneasy. Every fifteen minutes he disappears into the control room and busies himself at the chart table. Five pairs of eyes are fixed on him each time he returns. Futile. He says nothing.

The Chief finally makes an attempt to coax the Commander out of his sullen silence. "About time that contact man reported again."

The Commander pays no attention.

The Chief reaches for a book. All right, if there's not going to be any talk, I can pretend to read too. The Second Watch Officer and the Second Engineer thumb through newspapers, the First Watch Officer immerses himself in official-looking folders.

I'm on my way to my locker and just passing the radio shack

when I see the radioman, eyes half closed in the light of his small lamp, scribbling down a message.

I stop dead in my tracks. Back into the Officers' Mess. The Second Watch Officer quickly starts deciphering it. Suddenly a look of consternation comes over his face. Something's wrong.

The Commander holds the message in his hand and his face slowly assumes the same bewildered expression you see on boxers after a hard blow to the chin.

He reads out the message. "Surprised by destroyer coming out of rain squall. Four hours' depth charges. Contact lost, am pursuing in Square Bruno Karl—UM."

At the last words his voice dies away. He stares for a good minute at the radiogram, audibly takes a deep breath, stares again, then finally blows the air out of both cheeks. He also lets himself sink back in the corner of his sofa. Not a word, not a curse, nothing.

Later we're sitting on the railing in the "greenhouse" behind the bridge.

"This is madness," says the Old Man. "It feels as if we're bouncing across the Atlantic all on our own. And at the very same time—right now, sure as fate—there are hundreds of ships at sea and some of them are probably not far away. Except they're beyond the horizon." With bitterness in his voice, he adds, "Curvature of the earth is something the dear Lord must have invented just for the English. What can we possibly see from way down here? We might as well be sitting in a canoe. Pathetic that nobody's come up with a solution yet."

"But they have," I say. "Airplanes!"

"Oh yes, airplanes. The *enemy* has those. Where are our own sea scouts keeping themselves, that's what I'd like to know. A big mouth is all Fatbelly Goering supplies. That Reichsmaster of Hounds!"

Luckily the Chief bobs up. "Just grabbing a mouthful of fresh air."

"It's getting a bit crowded here," I say and disappear below.

A glance at the sea chart. As usual—the pencil line that records our course tacks back and forth like a folding yardstick out of control.

The Old Man also comes below. He sits down carefully on the chart chest, and there's a pause before he takes up where he left off. "Perhaps we'll still be lucky. If they send in enough boats, there's a chance someone will make contact again."

Next morning I read a radiogram picked up during the night. "Square Bruno Karl search a failure—UM."

. . .

The next day is the worst since our departure. We avoid speaking and keep out of one another's way as though we had scurvy. I spend most of the time on the sofa in the Officers' Mess. The Chief doesn't even emerge from the engine room for meals. The Second Engineer also stays with his machines. We three, the First Watch Officer, the Second Watch Officer, and I, don't dare say a word to the Old Man, who stares holes in the air and only consumes a few spoonfuls of thick soup.

Silence also reigns in the next door Quarters. The radioman carefully avoids putting a record on the turntable. Even the steward works with downcast eyes as though he were serving at a wake.

Finally the Commander opens his mouth. "The other lot just aren't making mistakes any more!"

Later, Zeitler starts up again with another of his knowing remarks: "Y'know . . . first thing in the morning's really the best." It doesn't take a genius to know what subject we're back on. Wichmann and Frenssen are all ears.

"I was in Hamburg one time . . . had to deliver a letter for my Chief. It was when I was still serving with the minesweepers. Anyhow, there I am, I ring the bell, and who comes to answer it but this little blond bombshell. Mother's out, just gone to the post office, back in a minute, do come in . . . so I do. Inside there's a kind of hall with a couch in it. I get a scumbag on and her skirt off in no time flat, and just as we finish banging, the door starts . . . her mother's opened it and got stuck by the safety chain! Luckily the couch is too far to one side, so she can't see us through the crack. Missy shoves her panties out of sight under a cushion, but I almost forget to zip up before shaking stinkfingers with the old lady. Zeitler, how d'you do, pleased to meet you, 'fraid I have to run, due back, you know how it is . . . and I'm out of there. It's not till I'm taking a piss hours later that I realize I've still got my rubber on. Or rather, it's not till *after* I take the piss and I find myself looking down at this huge yellow cucumber. What a mess! And the guy standing next to me is laughing himself sick . . ."

The First Watch Officer's daily shave is the talk of the bow compartment. "Upsetting the whole place—whoever heard of such a thing—spending all your time in the can, shaving."

"The Old Man ought to issue an ultimatum."

"One shithouse for the whole crew and we have to have a bathing beauty like that on board!"

Pilgrim pulls some photographs out of his wallet. One of them shows a man on a pier. "My father!" he explains to me. He sounds as if he's introducing us. "Died in the prime of life—that's the way I want to go too."

What on earth is there to say? I don't dare look Pilgrim in the face but simply mutter, "Fine photo."

He seems satisfied.

"The emotional life of most of the crew is a complete mystery to me," the Old Man said to me once. "How can you know what the men are thinking? Once in a while you find out something, and it knocks you right off your feet, like the story of Frenssen's donna—Frenssen the diesel mechanic mate. He met this lady on leave. Then he left on patrol and she got no mail from him so she went to a fortune teller. Apparently there are still some around. He'd neglected to tell his lady that we don't often get to the post office. Apparently the fortune teller put on a big act, then gasped, 'I see water—nothing but water.'"

The Old Man was doing both voices: the fortune teller's and the lady's. "'And no U-boat?' 'No, water—only water—nothing but water!' The donna, who considered herself our diesel mechanic mate's fiancée, started screaming, 'He must be dead!' The fortune teller remained as silent as the Oracle itself. D'you know what happened next? The donna put her hands to her head and wailed, 'Oh god—and I'm still wearing red!' Wrote one letter after another to the flotilla. To me too. I had the rest of the story from Frenssen. He didn't go to Paris on his last leave. He'd had enough!"

I'm sitting alone with the Old Man in the Officers' Mess. We pick up a radiogram addressed to Bachmann. It's the third time in four days that Bachmann's boat is being ordered to report.

"All quiet on the Western Front," murmurs the Commander. "Very likely he's caught it too. The shape he was in, he should never have been allowed to put to sea." The old story: When does a commander become "ripe" for retirement and have to be relieved? Why are there no medical men to make sure that the boats don't put to sea with commanders on the verge of total breakdown?

Ziemer sailed with Bachmann as First Watch Officer. Ziemar drowned? I see him with the waitress from the flotilla mess, lying in the sun. Always eager to learn, he was having her anatomy explained to him in French. Practicing on a live model. First he took hold of her breasts and said, *"Les duduns."* *"Les seins!"* the waitress corrected him. Then he pushed his hand between her legs and said, *"Lapin!"* Whereupon she put him right: *"Le vagine"*; and so it went.

From next door we can hear the First Watch Officer giving a class in security precautions. "They'll gabble just the same!" the Old Man comments. He broods for a while, then: "This whole secrecy business is a farce. The Tommies have had an undamaged boat of ours for ages now."

"Really?"

"Yes, one that surrendered. Ramlow's boat. South of Iceland in the open sea; all our secret material, all the codes, everything—the Tommies got all of it in one fell swoop!"

"That must have made the C-in-C happy!"

"When you think that Ramlow may even have been a secret agent—you can't even trust your own right hand. He managed to talk his officers into it—hard to believe!"

Only one more day at cruising speed till we reach the new field of operations. A radio message is picked up. Tension while we wait for it to be decoded.

It's addressed to Flechsig. Ordered to shift his position seventy miles westward. Apparently a convoy is expected to pass through at that point. The navigator shows me the spot on a small-scale chart. It's close to the American coast, i.e., many days sailing away from us. A little later we pick up a radio signal directed to a boat stationed near Iceland, Böhler's boat; and to a third operating near Gibraltar —UJ—that's Kortmann. Kortmann, who was involved in the foul-up with the *Bismarck* tanker.

A boat reports that it's unable to dive. Meinig's. Foul-mouthed Meinig. If it's unable to dive, a boat is practically lost.

"Shit!" says the Old Man. "Not even pursuit escort—too far away. All we can do is keep our fingers crossed."

He bends forward and raps three times underneath the table. "Let's hope he makes it. Meinig, it would be Meinig!"

We all sit there silent. The Old Man's lips move noiselessly. Perhaps he's figuring out how long it will take Meinig's boat to reach Saint Nazaire at cruising speed.

A cold shudder runs down my back: Just what will they do if the Sunderlands appear? Or destroyers? As a surface vessel the U-boat is hopelessly inferior to its opponents. Too little engine power to get away, no armor, guns too small. More vulnerable than almost any other ship: a single hit on the pressure hull and that's it.

"Boy, oh boy!" is all the Chief can say. It's obvious how completely he's identifying with his colleague on the other boat. He's actually gone white.

"Meier Two or Three is with Meinig, isn't he, Chief?" asks the Old Man.

"Meier Two, Herr Kaleun—in my class at the academy!"

No one opens his mouth. We stare at the table as though there's something—anything—to be seen there. I can hardly breathe. I also know one of the men in that boat—Habermann—the Balt Habermann who was with me on that wretched inspection cruise to Götenhafen: midwinter, twenty-five degrees below zero and an east wind.

I can remember him sitting on the cold linoleum—stark naked —legs stretched out stiff in front of him, back braced against the silk-covered wall of the *Cap Arcona*, head on his chest, dribbling. No respect for the impressive interior appointments of the former luxury liner now a floating barracks.

I am overtaken by a nervous fit of the giggles: old barefoot Habermann—that was when he'd just got over his third dose of the clap.

Later he told me that he'd been looking for the washroom and had lost his way. Naked and desperate, he had just sat down and waited for a rescuer.

Pneumonia? Not a chance! Never one for domestic comforts, he couldn't be knocked out by spending hours sitting on his naked ass. Not even ten doses of clap could do that. But now it looks as though the Tommies have managed it. A three-star announcement will be coming up. Flemming, Habermann—there aren't many left!

The Old Man is the first to speak. He means to change the subject but actually stays with it. "A *proper* submarine, now that would be something. We're not really a submarine. All we have here is a diving boat."

Silence. Only after a surprised look from me does he explain, between pauses, "after all, the capacity of our storage batteries is only enough for short attacks at periscope level or a quick run underwater to escape pursuit. Actually, we're completely dependent on the surface. It's impossible to do more than eighty miles underwater even when we're conserving power as much as we can. If we run underwater at our top speed of nine knots, the batteries are flat in one to two hours. Not exactly luxurious. And yet the batteries are an enormous dead weight. Those lead plates weigh more than all the rest of the boat's machinery put together. Now a real submarine would be able to travel underwater, with no diesels requiring air and producing exhaust gas. It wouldn't be as vulnerable without all the equipment we need now—all those openings in the pressure hull. What we need is some form of engine that's independent of the atmosphere."

We have barely reached the new area of operations when a radio message comes in. We are to be marshaled into a group with other boats, i.e., form a reconnaissance patrol. The area to be covered lies a good distance farther to the west. It'll take us two days to get there at cruising speed.

"They've christened the group 'Wolf Pack'—marvelous!" says the Old Man. "Apparently they have a kind of court poet at Staff Headquarters who thinks up this bullshit—'Wolf Pack'! 'Daisies' would have done just as well, but no: keep banging the drum . . ."

To the Old Man, even "area of operations" sounds too high-flown. If he had his way, the usual naval rhetoric would be thoroughly deflated. He himself can spend hours thinking up the worst possible banalities for his entries in the war log.

I read over what I've written in my blue notebook:

Sunday. Sixteenth day at sea. Report of convoy headed east. We are on course at ninety degrees to direction of convoy.

Monday. Seventeenth day at sea. Given new base line. Farther south. Dragnet being drawn that way. Probably only five boats in our new patrol—some dragnet!: either the mesh is too big or the net is too small. Speed eight knots. Let's hope the ship's positions tally. Also that the General Staff has taken due account of the unfavorable weather conditions in our area.

No machine-gun practice because of bad visibility. "Might just as well throw it away." We dive to listen.

Wednesday. Nineteenth day at sea. Another new tack. Only slight groundswell, no artillery practice possible. The weather must have joined the Allies.

Thursday. Twentieth day at sea. Radio silence except for enemy reports. More than five boats now assembled in our area. The enemy mustn't learn that we're gathering. Results of search: nil. Moderate sea. Light wind from northwest. Strato-cumulus clouds. But heavy layer of mist down close to the water. No trace of convoy.

Friday. Twenty-first day at sea. We've been assigned yet another new outpost patrol.

"God knows where the bastards are bucketing around!" growls the Commander.

Twenty-second Day at Sea. The watches seem to go on forever. Sky like beef suet. All day long, this huge heavy dome of fat weighing down on the dark sea—and no sun to melt it.

Today we have a superb, unbroken horizon. Nothing on it. Not a single bristle of a mist. Nothing. If only we could get up higher! That, of course, has often been tried. Take the kite experiment. They sent a man up on a kite back during World War I, but apparently it wasn't much of a success.

Twenty-third Day at Sea. The wind has picked up, and the sea has become a gigantic field of breakers. The waves don't rise all that much, yet all of them break. This makes the sea look gray-white and ancient.

The sky is dismal, a uniform gray cloth stretched over our heads. A sagging curtain of rain begins to fall from the gray, over to starboard. A single patch of light on the horizon glows faintly through the streaks. The wall of rain is slate-gray, with a trace of violet in it. Haze spreads out like fog on all sides. The wall is advancing slowly but directly at us, so the Commander has his oilskins and sou'-wester brought up. He's swearing.

We're in the midst of a cloudburst. No longer any air. The flail of the rain raises welts on the waves, which hunch their backs under it. No more rising crests, not the slightest glitter of reflection. Only our heavily dripping bow that tears them apart and tosses spray into the air. Streams of rain and spray mix on our faces.

The glassy green of the water has faded, the white veins have disappeared; the sea has grown older by a thousand years. It is gray, miserable, pock-marked.

No shimmer, no color. Nothing but uniform, soul-destroying gray.

The bridge guards stand like blocks of stone beneath a sky that is turning itself inside out. Six of us try to penetrate the wall of water; no point in using glasses now—they'd mist over immediately. It's as though the rain were trying to drown us.

Only toward evening does the wild fury of the downpour abate. It's night before it stops entirely.

Twenty-fourth Day at Sea. In the control room. The Old Man is talking half to me and half to himself. "Strange how little time one side or the other can hold the upper hand thanks to a new weapon. Never lasts more than a few months. We invented the tactic of hunting in packs, and the enemy built up their defense system. Which also worked. Prien's boat, Schepke's, Kretschmer's, all of them were lost against a single convoy. Now we have the new acoustic torpedo with its homing head, and the Tommies are already towing those damned rattling buoys along on a long steel cable— they divert the torpedoes because they make more racket than the screws. Action and counteraction—always the same. Nothing stimulates the brain cells like a desire to wipe out the other side."

For more than three weeks now we have been voyaging into emptiness. The uniform days flow one into another.

The boat drew a blank on its last patrol. Returned to base after a long, exhausting voyage without having fired a single torpedo. "The bastards seem to be avoiding us," says the Second Watch Officer, the only one who still keeps up an attempt at the odd joke. It takes us a half day to traverse the attack area assigned to us and reach its northern border. "Time to change course!" the helmsman shouts up through the open hatch.

"Hard a-port! New course one hundred eighty degrees!" The Watch Officer.

Slowly the bow swings through a semicircle of the horizon. The wake curls like a snake, and the sun, distorted into a white patch by multiple layers of cloud, pushes itself to the other side of the boat.

"Heading one hundred eighty degrees!" The voice of the helmsman again.

The course indicator now stands at 180 degrees. It was at 360 degrees. Otherwise nothing has changed.

Not much to see from the bridge. The sea has dozed off. Only a few ruffles on a tired, elderly groundswell. The air is motionless. The clouds stand still like captive balloons.

Bone-weary, I still find myself keeping a watchful eye on the stolid progress of the minute hand around the dial above the galley door. Finally I fall into a semi-trance.

The thin shell of sleep is suddenly ruptured: the alarm bell shrills. The floor is already tilting.

Sleep-tousled, the Chief crouches behind the hydroplane operators. The Commander stands motionless beside them. The navigator, who gave the alarm, is holding fast to the ladder. He's still breathing hard from the effort of sealing the hatch.

"Raise the stern—forward ten—aft fifteen—up slowly!" the Chief orders.

"A shadow—at ninety degrees—quite distinct!" the navigator finally explains to me.

The sound gear is in action; the operator's head is thrust forward into the gangway. His eyes are blank as he slowly searches the water for noises. "Sound of screws at seventy degrees—receding!" And after a while, "Sounds growing weaker—fading out!"

"That's how it goes," the Commander says, unmoved, and shrugs slightly. "Course one thirty degrees!" and he disappears through the circular hatch. So—we'll remain submerged for a while.

"Thank god, it's quiet!"

"Some fast vessel sailing unescorted—not a chance when it's *this* dark."

I'm hardly back in my bunk when I pass out.

"Enemy convoy in sight—UX."

"Convoy in sight Square XW, one sixty degrees, speed ten knots —UX."

"Enemy following zigzag course around fifty degrees. Speed ten knots—UW."

"Convoy traveling in several columns. Surrounded by escort vessels. Course twenty degrees. Speed nine knots—UK."

The radio spares us nothing. We know everything that's going on in the Atlantic theater of war. But we can't reach a single one of the reported convoys; they're all in the North Atlantic. We're positioned much too far to the south of them.

"If it goes on this way, we'll still be at sea come Christmas," Zeitler says.

"Well, what of it?" Rademacher answers. "That won't cause any embarrassment. We've got a Christmas tree on board."

"Come on!"

"I'm telling you! It's an artificial, collapsible thing—like an umbrella—in a cardboard carton. If you don't believe me, go ask Number One."

"Typical of the Navy!" says Ensign Ullmann. Then to my surprise he starts telling us about his Christmas experiences. "Someone always died at Christmas in our flotilla. New Year's Eve, too. In 1940 it was a bosun. It was around twelve o'clock on Christmas Eve when he played his little joke. Wanted to be a daredevil; put his automatic to his forehead and actually crooked his finger around the trigger while we stood and gaped at him. Of course, he had taken the magazine out beforehand. Only he wasn't smart enough to remember there was already a shell in the barrel—and bang—off flew the back of his skull. Made one hell of a mess!"

The shattered skull reminds Hinrich of something. "Once we had a fellow who blew his whole face off—New Year's Eve. That was when I was still serving on a patrol boat. We were all dead drunk. At twelve o'clock on the dot one of the petty officers came on the bridge carrying a kind of hand grenade. Those miserable things were still around at that time and you lit them exactly like a firecracker, with a fuse. He stood beside the railing and put a cigarette to the fuse and blew on it just right. Only then he got his paws mixed up: he hurled the cigarette into the drink and went on holding the grenade right in front of his snout. Of course, it exploded—that was some mess too!"

I don't want to listen to any more.

In the U-room, instruction for petty officers is in progress again. First Watch Officer lecturing. ". . . fell in action against a convoy . . ."

The Old Man rolls his eyes and looks furious.

" 'Fell'? That's another of those damn fool expressions. I suppose he tripped? I've seen thousands of photos of soldiers who 'fell.' Well, they didn't look so good after they 'landed.' Why doesn't anyone have the guts to say that the man they're talking about was drowned? I get ill when I come across all the nonsense they churn out about us."

He pushes himself to his feet and heads for his cubbyhole; comes back holding a news clipping. "Got something here—kept it especially for you."

" 'Well, First Watch Officer, that's it! Another five thousand gross registered tons. But tomorrow is my wife's birthday. We should do something to mark it. Honor our womenfolk! We must never forget that!' The First Watch Officer grins understandingly and the Commander lies down *on his hard couch to make up for lost sleep. But hardly an hour has passed when the First Watch Officer shakes him awake. 'Birthday steamer, Herr Kaleun!' The Commander shoots to the bridge: everything happens very fast. 'Tubes one and two stand by for underwater shot!' Both torpedoes are hits. 'At least six thousand gross registered tons!' says the Commander. 'Is Herr Kaleun satisfied with his birthday present?' 'Very!' replies the Commander. And the face of his First Watch Officer is transfigured with joy."*

The Old Man starts cursing again. "And that's the kind of stuff people are given to read. Incredible."

Wherever I look—nothing but clenched teeth, faces dull with disgust, irritation, discontent.

Almost impossible to imagine there's still dry land somewhere. Houses. Pleasant rooms. Lamps. The warmth from the stove.

The warmth from the stove. Suddenly I catch the smell of baked apples, wafting through the iron grating of the green stove that reached to the ceiling in our living room at 28 Bahnhofstrasse. There were always baked apples at this time of year. I inhale their sweet, spicy smell; I juggle one—hot, hot, hot—rejoicing in the play of color of the burst skin: smooth, gleaming, polished. Apples from our own trees, the kind with red streaks on a yellow background; at the center of the red rays is the blossom. It looks as if transparent red lacquer had been dripped over each one.

"Nice here. No mail, no telephone," the Old Man remarks suddenly, sitting down on the leather sofa beside me. "Well-ventilated boat, handsome wood veneer, open house. On the whole we've made out pretty well."

". . . horse shit," says the Chief, appearing like a jack-in-the-box. "He's certainly made out all right, hasn't he? And he doesn't have to worry about promotion any more—he's even allowed to smoke."

The Old Man is thoroughly disconcerted.

Meanwhile the others have assembled around the table for the daily squeezing of lemons, a self-imposed task that little by little has assumed the character of ritual. We are haunted by images of the devastation that can result from a lack of vitamin C. I see the circle around the table as hideous, toothless ghosts painfully gumming hard crusts of bread: that's scurvy.

Everyone has his own method of downing lemon juice. The Chief first cuts the fruit in two, systematically pierces the juice cells in each half as though expecting to spend the whole evening at it, then sticks a small piece of lump sugar into each of the halves and sucks the juice noisily through the sugar. No regard for etiquette.

The Second Watch Officer has hit upon a particularly striking procedure. He squeezes the lemon juice into a glass, mixes it with sugar and then adds a dash of condensed milk. The milk curdles immediately and the whole thing looks loathsome. It makes the Old Man shudder every time, but the Second Watch Officer pays no attention. He proudly names his drink "The U-boat Special," inquires if the rest of us are jealous, and then slowly swallows the concoction, rolling his eyes in ecstasy.

The Second Engineer is the only one who takes no trouble at all. He follows the vulgar practice of sinking his healthy teeth into the two halves and eats the pulp along with the juice.

The Old Man watches him with obvious disapproval.

I can't get over the Second Engineer. At first I decided he was simply obstinate. But now I know that he's just a man devoid of natural sensibility and equipped instead with a hide like an elephant's. He plays up his imperturbability and calm, emphasizes his strength of character, when he's nothing but dull and thick-skinned. Also he's very slow to think and just as slow to act—mentally and physically the exact opposite of the Chief. God knows how he happened to hit on becoming an engineer, and how—given his ponderous ineptitude—he wangled his way through the courses and examinations.

That's the difference between him and the Old Man: the Old Man pretends to be ponderous and indolent—while the Second Engineer really is.

For a while we all concentrate on our lemons. As the squeezed or sucked-out halves in the middle of the table turn into a mountain, the steward appears and with a sweeping gesture of his arm collects them all in his garbage pail. Then he mops up the vitamin-rich juice with an evil-smelling rag.

The ship's day still has about six hours to run. Our little gray cells are on vacation. We simply sit and vegetate—like old-age pensioners on a park bench. Actually all we lack are walking sticks to lean on.

The Second Watch Officer has immersed himself in French newspapers. He makes a practice of reading them all the way through, including the advertisements. This time he's come across an item he can't understand. Over a photograph of five girls is a large headline stating: "*On a couronné les rosières.*" It has to do with the bestowal of a prize founded by a now-deceased lady of Nancy for virtuous daughters of that city. I have to translate the whole article, including the songs of praise to the virtue of the five chosen virgins. There is a touching description of how the young ladies made a pilgrimage to the cemetery where the founder was buried and adorned her grave on the Sunday when the prizes were given out.

"How much per capita!"

"Two hundred francs apiece."

The Second Watch Officer is dumbfounded. "That's only about ten marks, isn't it?" It takes him some time to draw the obvious conclusion. "It's crazy. If the ladies had forgotten about their virtue, they'd have shown a much tidier profit . . ."

"Nicely put."

There is a real library on board. In a locker on the side wall of the Commander's cubbyhole. But it's far less popular than the detective stories strewn around in the bow compartment. They have covers with bloodthirsty scenes and titles such as *The Black Cotton Noose, Shot in the Back, Three Shadows at the Window, Expiated Sins, The Innocent Bullet.* Most of them have been passed from hand to hand so often that the covers are in rags and the greasy pages are coming apart at the seams. As of now, seaman Schwalle holds the record. On the last cruise he's said to have got through twenty of them; this trip he's already up to eighteen.

Twenty-seventh Day at Sea. A radio signal comes in. "To Wolf Pack: Assume new advance patrol position. Course three hundred ten degrees. Speed seven knots. Advance position will be reached on twenty-third at 07.00—BdU (Dönitz)." This means a new course, otherwise no change.

A voice from the radio, ". . . unyielding martial spirit . . ."

"Shut it off!" The Chief shouts so loud that I jump.

"It seems as if they've got the hang of it now," says the Old Man and looks at me grimly. "Just read through the last radiograms. 'Dive to escape flyers—forced away—contact lost—dive to escape destroyers—depth charges.' Always the same story. It's beginning to look as if the balance has swung their way. I'd hate to be in the BdU's skin right now. The Greatest Field Marshal of All Time, old Adolf, will make mincemeat out of him if nothing comes through soon for the special announcement basket."

"Well, after all, the balance can swing both ways."

The Old Man looks up. "Do you really believe . . . ?"

"Believe—sounds too much like church."

But the Old Man won't allow himself to be provoked.

"Where exactly are we?" Frenssen the diesel mechanic mate asks as he comes off duty into the control room.

"Almost off the coast of Iceland."

"Well, what do you know? And I thought we were close to America."

I can only shake my head in amazement: typical of an engine-room man. They don't give a damn *where* the boat is operating. It's the same on all ships: engine-room people mend and tend their diesels and motors and don't care whether it's day or night. They shy away from fresh air and are baffled by the real sailors.

Our little seafaring band is riddled with caste divisions. The two main ones are the sailors and the engineers. Upper deck and lower deck. Below decks is subdivided into electricians and diesel men. In addition, there's a control-room caste, a torpedo mechanics' caste, and the small select caste of radio and sonar men.

It comes out that the bosun has some cans of pigs' feet hidden among his supplies. Plus some cans of sauerkraut. The Commander immediately orders a feast for the next day. "About time, too!" is all he adds.

At noon the steward comes in with the steaming dishes, and the Commander's face lights up as if this is Christmas dinner. He leaps to his feet in anticipation, sniffing the fragrant steam that rises from the rose-gray mound of pork on a great aluminum platter with the jagged bones and white cartilage showing. The huge pieces are garnished with slices of onion and pickle and arranged in the proper way—on a bed of sauerkraut.

"Beer wouldn't be bad with this," hints the Chief, knowing perfectly well that only a single bottle per man is on board, to be opened after a victory. But the Commander seems ready for anything today. "Must celebrate holidays as they come. A half bottle of beer per man—that's one full bottle between every two men!"

The news is flashed to the bow compartment and a roar goes up. With a sharp jerk on the hinge of a locker the Chief opens the three bottles that come to the Officers' Mess, and even before we can seize our glasses, thick white froth streams out of the bottlenecks, like foam out of a fire extinguisher.

"*Prost!*" the Commander lifts his glass. "Here's to the end of this damn frigging around!"

The Chief drains his glass at a single gulp and tilts his head right back to catch the last drops. Then he licks the foam from the inside of the rim and smacks his lips. He concludes with groans of sheer pleasure.

When the bare bones of the feast have been carried away, the steward appears once more. I can't believe my eyes. He's bearing a large cake covered with black chocolate icing.

The Commander has the cook summoned immediately. The cook looks confused but is ready with his excuse: the eggs had to be used; otherwise they would have gone bad.

"How many cakes have you baked?"

"Eight, three slices per man!"

"And when?"

"Last night, Herr Kaleun."

Permission to grin can be read in the Old Man's face.

The debauch is followed by contented calm. The Old Man folds his arms across his chest, hunches his head down against his shoulders, and smiles amiably at us all.

The Chief settles himself properly in his corner of the sofa: an intricate procedure. He takes as long as a dog to find the best position. He has just managed it when word comes from above. "Chief to the bridge!"

Cursing, he struggles to his feet. He's got only himself to blame. The minute anything of interest occurs topside he wants to be informed. Only the day before he was angry because he hadn't been called when three whales surfaced quite close to the boat.

I climb up after him and get my head above the edge of the hatch just in time to hear him ask angrily, "What the devil is it then?" And the Second Watch Officer replies obsequiously, "Thirteen white gulls flew around the ship!" Even from behind them, I can tell that the bridge guards are grinning. "They've just disappeared over the horizon," he adds.

The Chief yells, "Just you wait!" Then he goes below to the control room, obviously to plan revenge.

This time the Old Man saves him the trouble. While the Second Watch Officer is still on duty he sounds the practice alarm. The boat cuts under the surface before the Second Watch Officer has sealed the hatch and he gets a tremendous dousing. As he climbs down into the control room the Chief favors him with a happy smile. The Second Watch Officer suddenly runs his hand in panic through his hair.

"Anything wrong?" the Commander asks solicitously.

The Second Watch Officer takes a deep breath. His mouth sags open and he looks crushed. "My cap—on the bridge," he stutters. "I took it off and hung it over the torpedo sight."

The Commander adopts the ingratiating tones of a headwaiter.

"Would the gentleman like us to surface immediately, reverse our course, and undertake a search?"

The Second Watch Officer lets himself drop into a chair.

A fly darts aimlessly back and forth under the lamp above the chart table. It's a puzzle. After all, flies are not albatrosses: They can't just sail straight across the Atlantic. When we left Saint Nazaire it wasn't the right time of year for flies—already too late in the season, too cold, even for France. It's possible the fly was brought aboard as an egg, pre-embryonic maybe, along with a thousand other ones that had less luck in hatching. Perhaps our fly got into the torpedo tubes as a maggot. Perhaps it grew up in the bilges, constantly pursued by the inveterate fanatical cleanliness of Number One. A true miracle, this fly's life, as everything here is soldered shut. No pieces of cheese lying about. No idea how it has survived.

One knows altogether too little about one's neighbor. Here we sit, in the same boat—in the most literal sense of the word—and yet I have no inkling of this fly's view of the world. I know nothing whatever about the emotional life of the common housefly. As to the fruit fly, however, I can at least give it its Latin name: *Drosophila melanogaster*. Short-winged and long-winged *Drosophila* were popular during my time in school. We had a fair number of each in test tubes with mashed bananas. The biology lecturer combined carefully counted specimens in a third tube, but the results of the cross-breeding never checked out because we secretly put a few additional short-winged flies in among the long-winged ones. There stood the lecturer trying to juggle the numbers till we all shouted, "Cheat!"

A fly's eye under the microscope—a true marvel. Flies have to be caught from in front because they can't take off backward. Clear as daylight. But this one isn't going to be caught. It's under my personal protection. Perhaps it will even have babies, which in turn will have more babies—one generation of shipborn flies after another, and I their patron. And I'm not even that fond of the creatures.

We had barely fished my classmate Swoboda out of Binsen Lake when those fat bluebottles began to settle in the corners of his eyes. Rigor mortis had made him stiffen in a strange bent position with his knees drawn up. The scent of acacias was almost overpowering in the Mecklenburg summer heat. The rigor mortis finally wore off by evening, so we could straighten him out. It was then that

I discovered clots of yellow fly eggs as big as peas in the corners of both his eyes.

I wonder if our ship's fly is getting ideas . . .

The First Watch Officer is instructing the petty officers again. Through the clatter of dishes, which the steward considers an indispensable part of his work, comes the fragment of a sentence. ". . . to break the stranglehold . . ."

The Old Man gives a pained glance at the ceiling and raises his voice to reach the bow compartment. "Are you settling accounts with Albion again, First Watch Officer?"

The navigator has spotted and reported an object at thirty degrees. The Commander climbs to the bridge the way he is, in sweater and drill trousers. I at least get down my rubber jacket from its hook. Luckily I'm wearing leather trousers and cork-soled shoes.

The flotsam is easily visible to the naked eye. The Commander scrutinizes it for a good two minutes through his binoculars, then orders the helmsman to steer straight for it. It rapidly grows until it becomes a boat with its bow at an angle of two hundred degrees to us.

The Old Man sends the two lookouts below and mutters an explanation: "No reason for them to have to look at it too."

It quickly becomes clear, however, that this move was unnecessary: the lifeboat is empty.

The Old Man has both engines stopped. ". . . a bit closer, navigator, and read the name."

"Stel—la Mar—is," he says slowly. The Old Man has the bridge lookouts come on deck again. "Make a note for the log," he tells the navigator, and gives course and engine orders.

After a couple of minutes we are back on our old course. I climb down behind the Old Man. The lifeboat wallowing in the gray-green sea must have stirred a memory in him. "A boatload of people once rowed directly at us. Odd story . . ."

Well, out with it.

But he says nothing more for the time being. One of these days he's going to drive me mad with all his foibles and five-minute delays. I have to summon up all my self-control not to nag at him.

But I soon realize that the Old Man isn't putting on the usual act. His face is troubled. He doesn't really know how to tackle his story. Very well, we'll wait. I push my hands deep into my trouser pockets, straighten my back, and shift my weight from one buttock to the other to find the most comfortable position. We're certainly not pressed for time.

While I listen to the patter of the spray and the crash of the waves, the Old Man finally begins to talk. "I once sank a steamer—that is, it was really her own speed that sank her—on my third patrol. The torpedo tore away the bow and the steamer went down forward immediately; it was still making so much headway that she dived like a U-boat. You'd hardly believe it. Gone in a flash. Practically no survivors."

After a while, he adds: "Funny, it was actually a bad hit—but that's the way it goes!"

I find myself thinking that it's not the story he'd really wanted to tell, interesting and typical though it is: a factual account of his professional experiences—curiosities and oddities—memorable departures from the norm. But the real story? A lifeboat must have come into it somewhere. I'll have to give him a lead. "So they never got to the lifeboats at all . . . ?"

"*They* didn't!"

I deprive him of the satisfaction of being prodded again and wait. He snorts twice, quickly, then wipes his nose with the back of his hand. "People shouldn't get so cynical, you know . . ."

Now it's up to me to indicate my interest by a turn of the head. Nothing more. But he stares stolidly in front of him. That's all right too. Don't rush. I wait for the pause to be completely played out before I ask, as casually as I can, "What d'you mean? Why shouldn't they?"

The Commander chews a while longer on his pipe stem before he starts to talk rather haltingly again. "I was just thinking about it—had an experience once—men in a lifeboat, English, overwhelmed me with thanks, and I'd just sunk their ship!"

I can no longer pretend indifference. "So?"

The Old Man takes a few more gurgling drags on his cold pipe, then finally launches out. "The steamer was called *Western Star*. Beautiful big ship. Ten thousand tons. Unescorted. Pure luck. By sheer chance we were in the necessary forward position. I fired a spread of four, but only one hit and it did astoundingly little damage. The scow simply settled a little deeper in the water and slowed down. Then we scored another with our stern tube. But she was still far from sunk. I could see the people getting into the boats; then I surfaced.

"They'd launched two lifeboats. Steered directly toward us. Came right within earshot and one of the men just couldn't stop thanking us for being such splendid people. Took me quite a while to realize they thought we weren't taking any further action so that they'd have a chance to pull away from the steamer. Thanked us for our fair play. Truth was we simply hadn't a torpedo in the tubes. They of course had no idea we'd already let fly with three other fish. Our crew was slaving like crazy, but reloading takes quite a bit of time. They thought we were postponing the coup de grace—"

Half a glance sidewise and I see the Old Man's grinning. "That's how you achieve nobility before you know what you're doing!"

The radio assigns us a new area. We're not to proceed to any definite destination; by way of a change we're to chug along at a fixed course and speed again. At a predetermined hour the boat is then to reach the spot where the C-in-C's Operations Division wants us to close a gap in the line. We will then proceed up and down as usual: half a day at minimum speed northward, half a day south.

To my amazement the Old Man is optimistic again. "Something'll happen yet . . . The dear Lord isn't going to desert his frigging little Wolf Pack! Or don't you believe in the dear Lord God?"

"I do, of course I do," says the Chief, busily nodding his head. "Of course I believe in the great Gas in the sky."

"You really are an evil bastard," mutters the Old Man. Which doesn't bother the Chief a bit. Simply to get a rise, he announces that he once had a vision of the Virgin Mary—"right on the net guard—soft rose-pink with a shimmer of violet—but completely transparent—gorgeous! The Lady pointed upward and blew out her cheeks!"

"She probably wanted you to volunteer immediately for the Air Force. Balloon division."

"That wasn't it," the Chief replies dryly. "I'd forgotten to ventilate with the diesels after we'd surfaced!"

The Old Man's trying not to laugh, which would mean losing the game. "You should report that to the Pope. He'll canonize you on the spot—only takes twenty-five years, as is usual with the Holy See!"

We're unanimous in our opinion that the Chief would make a handsome saint. "Pious and noble," says the Old Man. "And even more ethereal than he is now—an ornament to the Church."

. . .

As I go through the Quarters, the navigator is busy arranging his locker. I sit down at the table and leaf through a seaman's handbook. The navigator digs some photographs out of a worn wallet and hands them to me: badly underexposed pictures of some children. Three little boys, bundled up against the cold and sitting on a sled one behind the other in descending order of size. In another picture they're in bathing suits. There's an embarrassed smile on the navigator's face. His eyes are fixed on my lips.

"Sturdy little fellows!"

"Yes, all boys."

But immediately he seems to feel that it's not the place for tender emotions, here between these steel walls damp with condensation. He snatches the photographs back as if he'd been caught doing something improper.

Twenty-eighth Day at Sea. The sun is the color of boiled chicken, and the sky grayish-yellow, like chicken broth. Little by little the horizon sinks into the mist; an hour later streamers of fog unfurl from the water around the boat.

"Visibility zero!" the navigator reports from above. The Commander gives the order to dive.

When the boat reaches 150 feet we make ourselves comfortable in the control room. Legs up, boots propped against the chart chest. The Commander is sucking and gurgling on his well-chewed pipe-stem. He seems lost in thought. From time to time he nods to himself, far away in his memories.

Thirtieth Day at Sea. The horizon is still empty. An east wind has sprung up, bringing the cold. The guards on the bridge wrap themselves up like mummies. Inside the boat the electric radiators are on.

A radio message arrives. The Commander signs for it and hands it to me.

"To Wolf Pack: Advance patrol area from point G to D to be occupied on the twenty-eighth at 08.00. Distance ten miles. Course two thirty degrees. Speed eight knots—BdU."

The Commander unfolds the big transatlantic map and points with a pencil to the position of our ship. "This is where we are— and this is where we have to go." His pencil moves far south. "Any

way you look at it, this means a good three days' sailing. The whole
operation seems to have been broken off. Something completely
new. No idea what's behind it. This way we'll be on a latitude with
Lisbon."

"And out of the cold, thank god," the Chief breaks in, shivering.

Cookie bobs up. He's furious. "Shit—what a fuck-up! Five big
cans of sardines have leaked in the hold. Straight into the sugar!"
He's beside himself. "Goddam mess—now we can throw all the
sugar away!"

"I think we'd better keep it," says Ario. "You never can tell—
sometime you may want sugar on your fish."

Three days pass at cruising speed, south-southwest, without the
guards on the bridge seeing a trace of the enemy; only empty casks
and drifting wooden cases.

The dull shuttling to and fro of a scouting patrol begins again.
The eternal sameness has made all sense of time long since disappear. I don't know how long this frigging around has lasted already. Weeks? Months? Or has the boat been driving around in
the Atlantic for half a year? Even the distinction between day and
night seems to be getting blurred.

Our supply of stories has long since run out. We try to cheer
one another up with stale jokes.

A new catchword of approval has spread through the boat like
the plague: "Bomfortunal." No one knows who invented this nonsense, but all at once everything is "bomfortunal." There's also a
new unit of measurement everywhere, the word "jet." At first it
cropped up only at breakfast time: "Just one more jet of coffee if
you please." Then it bobbed up as a unit of time. "Sure I'll do it, but
just wait a jet." And now the Chief asks me if I would please move
a jet to one side.

I stay in the control room, sitting on the chart chest and trying
to read. After an hour, the Commander clambers heavily down from
the tower.

"Very pretty!" he says, lines of anxiety creasing his forehead.
He paces the room three or four times, nervous as a cat, then lowers
himself onto the chart chest beside me; instead of saying anything, he drags at his pipe, long since extinguished. I put aside my
book because I feel he wants to talk. Wordlessly, we stare straight
ahead.

I wait for him to speak first. He draws a tattered letter written
in green ink out of his pocket and strikes the paper a couple of times

with the back of his hand. "Here, I just came across this a little while ago. What a crazy notion they must have of the way we live!" Green ink, as I know, is the mark of the Commander's fiancée, the flyer's widow.

He thrusts out his lower lip and shakes his head. "End of subject," he says brusquely and gestures as if to wipe his own remarks off a blackboard.

So, I think: no go.

Although we're sailing with open hatch, thanks to the improvement in the weather, the petty officers' quarters stink to high heaven. Of moldy bread, rotting lemons, rotting sausage, of oily exhaust from the diesels, of wet foul-weather gear and leather boots, of sweat and semen.

The door is yanked open and a cloud of diesel stench comes in along with the engine-room watch just relieved. Curses and imprecations. Locker doors slammed shut. The diesel mechanic mate Frenssen suddenly bursts out singing like a drunk. "Love and love alone drives our ship and steers it home . . ."

Of course. Frenssen—as usual.

"We could use a nice beer right now!"

"Just cool enough, with a head as white as a lily—and then another—and another—let them hiss down your throat. Christ!"

"Shut up! You're driving me insane!"

Today the sky is as slimy as sour milk. No motion. The water seems to have become more viscid. The waves simply stoop over, round-shouldered and weary; no more crests. Only occasional white veins showing in their black-green. The Atlantic has turned one single color: this blackish-green—not a sight anywhere to cheer us up.

Big ships at least offer the eye some color here and there. Funnel insignia, white-painted ventilator hoods, red markings. But with us everything is gray. Not a dab of color in the whole ship—only gray, and even the same shade throughout. We ourselves blend into our background superbly well: our skin is gradually turning the same pale, sickly gray. No more bright pink cheeks like the ones children paint on the faces they draw. Even the bosun, who was positively apple-cheeked when we sailed, now looks as if he's just got up from a sickbed. Still, he certainly hasn't lost his voice. Right now I can hear him bellowing at someone: "Look with your goddam eyes, not your goddam asshole!"

All of us need a psychiatrist. He could thrash out the First Watch Officer's elaborate affectations—some job! Also that trick of wrinkling his nose, and his sensitive, oh-so-considerate smile.

The Second Watch Officer's laugh lines are another matter: they would have to be retained; the baby face is still really in pretty good shape. But the Chief would need intensive treatment, nervous and overstrained as he is—the tic at the outer corner of his left eye, the way his mouth twists, his habit of sucking in his cheeks, the meaningless pursing of his lips, and above all his jumpiness—that sudden shudder at the slightest noise. At least a small piece of the Second Engineer's thick hide needs to be transplanted onto the Chief. And it might help the Second Engineer as well. He needs a thinner skin.

Then there are the Old Man's compulsive noisy mannerisms: scratching his beard, sucking on his pipe, making the bowl gurgle so that it sounds like fat frying on a low fire, snorting through his nose. Sometimes he forces spittle through a hole in his teeth till it hisses.

Johann is getting to look more and more like Christ. When he pushes his mass of pale-yellow hair back off his high forehead, he only needs to lower his eyes to produce a perfect likeness of the Holy Handkerchief.

Ensign Ullmann really worries me. At first I thought he looked full of energy. Now it's vanished. I've seen him a few times crouched on his bunk, sunk in gloom.

By radio we learn that Meinig's boat has sunk a refrigerator ship of nine thousand gross registered tons, an unescorted vessel.

I stare at the radiogram: almost incredible! How the hell could he have done it with his disabled boat? Meinig has reported—so Habermann is alive too. Might have guessed it: Nothing's going to put *him* out of commission so quickly.

"He must have had plenty of luck," says the Old Man. "You can't accomplish that sort of thing these days without it. If you're not lucky enough to be in a forward position and be able to station yourself until one of their scows runs right in front of your tubes . . . everything that's going unescorted these days is going fast. Pursuit from astern is pointless. A fast refrigerator ship simply outruns you. I've tried to overtake one often enough—but it's been nothing but a waste of fuel every time. Even if we run at maximum r.p.m. we barely make one to two knots more than a fast, unescorted single vessel—and if she tacks in a favorable direction and we're too slow in following, it's all over and done with."

Thirty-third Day at Sea. The calendar says Wednesday. At eight in the morning we receive a report: "Convoy headed west to be intercepted Square Gustav Fritz."

Bent over the chart table, the Old Man emits a skeptical, "Well now!" Five minutes of reckoning and he says, "Not exactly favorable, but nevertheless—with a little luck—we might get there—just about." New course, higher speed. Otherwise no change.

"It's about time we shoved a few tons toward the bottom," says the Second Watch Officer, and immediately looks embarrassed, because he realizes that in our present state of irritation his remark sounded much too confident.

Midday. I climb up behind the First Watch Officer, who's just going on duty. The air is heavy and stagnant. The sea has subsided under the diffused light and covered itself with a gray skin that only occasionally shows a small buckling or swelling: visual boredom that dampens our spirits.

That evening, however, during the Second Watch Officer's watch, color appears. Single flat banks of cloud stretched above the horizon begin to glow like the fire in a forge. The whole sky quickly turns red and the sea is overrun with the magnificent glow. The boat moves with throbbing engines through this blazing hallucination. The whole bodywork gleams. The foreship looks like a huge anvil. The faces of the bridge guards are flooded with red. Two colors—red and black—would be enough to paint all this: sea, sky, ship's hull, and the faces under the sou'westers.

For a quarter of an hour sky and sea are in conflagration, then the crimson glow fades from the clouds and they instantly return to a dim, sulphurous gray. Now they look like mountains of ashes covering the glowing heart of a small fire.

Suddenly a spot flames out in the gray wall directly ahead: bellows seem to fan the glimmer into life. But again, a few minutes later, the red glory shrinks; it gleams for a time like the mouth of a blast furnace and finally is extinguished completely: the sun has sunk beneath the horizon.

High above the parade of clouds, the heavens still hold a lingering glow. Only very slowly does it grow thin and striated, and in its place comes saffron-yellow, which gradually turns greenish and slowly sinks to the horizon. The sea mirrors this poisonous color. It lies rigid, paralyzed under its sickly-colored skin.

The Commander comes up and observes the sky. "Gaudy but not beautiful!" he announces sourly.

When the Old Man isn't on the bridge, he spends hours like a hermit behind his green curtain or on the periscope saddle in the tower. Sometimes I hear the machinery start up. The Old Man is bored, and is riding his carousel.

The crew doesn't hear a sound out of him from one day to the next. They could well believe that the boat is voyaging the seas without a commander. The Chief is another one who's badly affected by all this frigging around. He's lost a lot of his liveliness, and looks as though he'd put green eyeshadow under his eyes to turn himself into a demon. But the greenish rings are genuine. For a long time now he's given up puttering around—when he's not checking his engines, you seldom see more of him than his bowed head with the bright line of the part in his hair: he has succumbed to furious reading. He only lifts his head at mealtimes, and the Commander says, "Good day!" to his pallid face. Sometimes he just sits around and bitches.

Yet the unspoken understanding between the Chief and the Commander persists despite all the irritability. Between the two of them all tensions have apparently long since been worked out. Seven patrols together already.

We're almost three thousand miles away from base. The boat has an action radius of about seven thousand miles. But since we've burned up so much fuel wallowing back and forth on patrol, there's only a small "margin." With such a reduced supply we could hardly be brought from any great distance to attack a convoy. Our reserves would be barely sufficient for the lengthy positional maneuvering at high speed that's inevitable when attacking.

The First Watch Officer makes the Chief nervous, opening and shutting his locker, clattering his keys, and scribbling in his colored looseleaf notebooks. No one knows what he's putting down in them.

"He's memorizing the order of the cathouses for our return to harbor," is the Chief's theory, as the First Watch Officer disappears in the direction of the control room. One of his notebooks is lying on the table. I can't resist the temptation to leaf through it. *Personnel Management on a U-boat* is the red title on the first page. I begin to turn the pages and can't tear myself away.

Point I: Peculiarities of U-boat Life.

Life on board for long periods is monotonous. One must be able to endure long weeks of lack of success. When depth bombs are added to this, it becomes a "war of nerves" which weighs principally upon the higher-ranking officers.

More red pencil: *The morale of the crew is dependent on:* and underneath, point by point, in blue ink:

1. *The discipline of the crew.*

2. *The success of the Commander. If the Commander is successful, then he may be a fool, but the crew will always love him more than an unsuccessful one. But it is precisely the unsuccessful Commander who most needs a high level of morale among his crew.*

Red pencil: *Discipline*; then more blue:

The Commander's duty is to ensure that the spirit of the good soldier predominates on his boat and that the opinions of the bad soldier count for little. He must be like a gardener who pulls up the weeds and tends the good plants.

Another red title: *Quotation from a Speech by Lieutenant-Commander L.*

I am well aware that women can destroy the fighting morale of the soldier, but I also know that they can strengthen their husbands in their attitudes, and I have found that married men in particular return from leave well rested to begin the new patrol against the enemy. One must tell married petty officers what they should expect from a soldier's wife. I was happy to have the opportunity to entertain the wives of most of my men at a coffee party in my home, to come to know them and to be able to tell them that a brave attitude on their part was expected. I believe that many of them gained new backbone from this, and I have requested my wife to write to them and to keep in touch with them.

Appeal must be made to the iron will to sustain health and overcome small difficulties. If two soldiers are eligible for the Iron Cross and only one Cross can be awarded, I prefer to give it to the man who stays on board and continues to sail rather than to the one whose good luck has made it possible for him to become a petty officer or a sergeant and who must therefore return to land duty. Finally the Iron Cross is no pilgrim's medal but a reward for bravery in the face of the enemy which, once won, must immediately be earned again.

I can hardly believe my eyes: so this is our First Watch Officer's primer! I don't have to read far to come across another gem.

On long patrols against the enemy a great deal of crockery is broken by young soldiers. It is well known that admonishment does little good, especially as the sea often makes serving difficult. I now have an inventory of crockery made every week. If too much is missing, the stewards must eat out of tin cans for three days. Another severe penalty is the prohibition of smoking. For card lovers, being forbidden to play for three days works wonders.

Now comes a mimeographed page.

It is a matter of honor, and I regard it as such, that etiquette should be maintained on board. In harbor—more than at sea, naturally, where it must suffice that someone shout "Attention" the first time the Commander enters a room—the senior soldier present should report what is being done, just as the Watch Officer reports on the bridge. In harbor, during refitting, there must be an assembly for inspection at least once a day. I lay especial emphasis on the raising of the flag. At sea the condition of the lockers must also be checked from time to time and neatness throughout the boat constantly maintained . . .

At sea I have had one dead man and a couple of wounded. As substitute I secured a volunteer ordinary seaman from a German steamer. He was nineteen years old, had been abroad on German ships since he was under fourteen. He came aboard with a straw hat on his head and said, " 'Day, Cap'n, I'm to come aboard here." He had no inkling of the outer forms of soldiery. I turned him over for guidance to my best petty officer, who taught him to walk and stand, and indoctrinated him with basic principles. After fourteen days we swore him in. For this event we dived, the bow compartment was adorned with flags, and we made the oath-taking a properly solemn occasion. The man had learned the oath by heart in advance. In my address I told him about the duties of a German soldier. The crew sat there in their brown tropical uniform shirts. In honor of the day they had all given one another proper haircuts and had decided in advance on the songs to accompany the celebration, so that the singing really went off very well. In addition we presented the young seaman with "The Duties of a Soldier." One of the men had written it out in an elegant script.

The heading Feasts and Celebrations makes me particularly curious.

At Advent time every compartment glowed with electric Advent candles on Christmas wreaths that had been made by twisting together napkins and toilet paper painted green. The Christmas baking took fourteen days and everyone had a taste of it, just as at home. On Christmas Eve the festively bedecked bow compartment features a Christmas tree made by ourselves. Saint Nicholas appears, wrapped in a simple sheet, since we are in the tropics, and gives every soldier *sweets and an inscribed book, all appropriately accompanied by beautiful songs and suitable speeches . . . on board, we say a great deal with music. If we dive, then the off-duty watch learns about it by hearing the stirring diving march that is played to our Chief when he's supervising the hydroplanes. And when the watch is to prepare for surfacing, they are alerted by the march "Today We Plow Through the Open Sea."*

v FIRST ATTACK

THE RADIOMAN hands a message out of the shack. Nothing on his face but that perpetual, harmless grin.

The First Watch Officer, all importance, puts the decoding machine on the table, lays the radioman's strip of paper beside him, cocks his head first to one side and then to the other like a rooster looking for a kernel of corn, checks the alignment, and finally taps the keys.

During this procedure the Chief manages to look as bored as a British racing-stable owner. The Second Watch Officer, who's off duty, doesn't even look up from his book. I join in the general pretense of indifference.

The First Watch Officer has barely decoded the last word when the Commander snatches the strip of paper out of the machine—with an eagerness that contradicts his look of contempt—reads it with a grim expression, gets up and heads for the control room without saying a word. Through the circular door I see him carefully adjusting the lamp over the chart table.

The Chief and I exchange pregnant glances.

"Aha!"

I control my curiosity for a suitable interval before I go into the control room after the Commander. The navigator is there already—as if conjured up by magic.

The Old Man's torso is bent over the sea chart; in his left hand he has the radiogram, in his right the dividers. He doesn't look at us.

"Not too bad," he murmurs finally. Then he silently pushes the radio message over to me. "0810 hours convoy sighted Square Bruno Max. Steering northerly course. Driven off by flyers. Enemy out of sight—UR."

The Commander points the dividers at Square Bruno Max. Not far from our present position.

"At a rough guess, we should be able to get there in twenty-four hours at top speed."

Now we have to wait and see whether UR establishes contact again: only then would we be ordered in pursuit of the convoy.

"Maintain course and speed for the time being."

The next couple of hours are rife with speculation: "Looks like the convoy's heading for America. But then it could always be Gibraltar. Can't be sure," I hear the navigator say.

"UR—that's Bertold," says the Old Man. "Good man. No beginner. He won't let himself be shaken off so easily . . . they must have put to sea a week after us; they were having trouble with their periscope."

An inviting gesture to me to come and sit beside him on the chart chest. Expectancy and excitement have made him cheerful. "Always these shitty airplanes," he says. "Lately they've been working in hunting units along with destroyers, and once a pack like that gets its teeth into you . . . There used to be hardly any flyers around here—those were the days, all right. All you had to do was keep watch on the surface and you knew pretty well what you had to reckon with."

The control-room mate, who is standing at a little desk making entries on the diving log, pauses in his writing.

"They're trying everything to shake us off. For a long time now they've stopped stationing their destroyers close to the herd of shipping. They've got the hang of it. The destroyers patrol at top speed at a considerable distance from their precious steamers. That way, even if we make contact at the farthest limit of visibility, they can force us to withdraw, or go underwater. As for their sweepers, they have them cavorting around way ahead of the convoy . . . there's just no more brotherly love these days. They've even managed to rebuild big freighters as auxiliary aircraft carriers. And they form protective groups of small carrier-based planes and destroyers that really make things hot for us. All they need is proper training in precise coordination and it's guaranteed that any boat spotted by one of their busy bees will be worked over by the destroyers till their precious freighters have run so far the enemy hasn't a ghost of a chance of finding them again. Which means you do nothing but beat yourself to death and burn up a hellish load of fuel."

The Old Man seems completely relaxed. Even talkative. "We really should have taken the offensive much earlier—before the Tommies woke up and got themselves organized. Still, when war broke out we had only fifty-seven boats, and no more than thirty-five of them were suitable for the Atlantic. Obviously nowhere near enough to blockade England. Just a tentative sort of stranglehold. And the arguments! To risk everything on U-boats or to build battleships as well. We were never really trusted by the old fogeys in the Imperial Navy. They wanted their proud fleet, regardless of whether battleships were still any use or not. We're what you might call a con-serv-a-tive club!"

Later, as I am stretching my legs in the control room, a new radiogram comes in. "09.20 hours dived to avoid aircraft. One hour underwater. Enemy convoy in sight again. Square Bruno Karl. Position of enemy uncertain—UR."

"I tell you, he's not going to let 'em slip through his fingers. Navigator, does the convoy seem to be running on a parallel course?"

This time the Commander takes only a few minutes at the chart table, then turns abruptly and orders, "Course two hundred seventy degrees. Engines full speed ahead!"

Orders are acknowledged. The engine telegraph rings. A heavy shudder runs through the boat, and the pounding of the engines rises to a fierce roar.

Oho, so the Old Man's going to get into it! He isn't even waiting for an order from Kernével.

The roar of the diesels swells, sings in a higher key, then once again sounds dull and rumbling, almost smothered: the diesel music of the sea. The muffled tone means a big wave meeting the bow, the clear singing that the boat is shooting through a trough.

Everywhere men are at work reinspecting the connections, as they have so often before. They do it of their own accord, inconspicuously, almost surreptitiously.

"Permission to come on the bridge?"

"*Jawohl!*"

First I look at the wake. It's boiling-white, the huge, thick, gleaming train of a dress stretching as far as the eye can see, thinning to bottle-green at the horizon in individual tattered strands, as if it had parted at the seams. Both sides are banded in light green, the shade of translucent beer-bottle glass. Over the gratings drift blue-white fumes from the diesels. I turn toward the bow and get struck in the face by a whiplash of spray. Sea head-on and the diesels at full speed—should have expected what it would be like.

Water drips from my nose.

"Congratulations," says the Second Watch Officer.

I squint to look at our foreship from the protection of the bulwark. We're tearing along so hard that the bow is throwing out sheets of water, and broad streaks of foam boil up around the sides.

The Commander's hands are thrust deep into the pockets of his leather trousers. His once-white, battered cap with its green-tarnished insignia is pulled far down over his face. He's searching sky and water with narrowed eyes. Again and again he urges the bridge guards to keep a sharp lookout.

He doesn't go below, even to eat.

A full hour passes before he climbs down to have a look at developments on the chart. I go too.

The navigator is still busy calculating.

A new small pencil cross on the hydrographic chart shows the last position of the enemy. Now our own chart allows us to read off his course and speed. Another pencil cross: the intersection of his assumed course with ours. Our thoughts are drawn compulsively to this point, like a compass needle to the north.

Hour after hour goes by. Fuel racing through the pipes.

"This is burning up a pretty load!" I hear Dorian say. The Chief is supposed to be out of earshot.

The Second Watch Officer comes in with a new radiogram.

"Aha!" says the Commander with obvious anticipation. He even condescends to read it aloud. "To UA: Proceed immediately at top speed against convoy reported by UR—BdU."

"Watch Officer: Steer three hundred forty degrees. Further orders to follow." The repetition of the command echoes back from the helmsman in the tower.

On the chart the Commander points out first the position of the convoy, then ours. "We ought to be there tomorrow morning around six o'clock."

Bertold dare not attack now. It's more important to maintain contact—not to let the enemy escape, to send short signals until other boats can assemble from the far reaches of the Atlantic.

"Surely it's going to work," I comment cautiously.

"No wedding reception before the church service," the Commander warns me.

Questioning faces appear in the round opening of the doorway. To their great amazement the men see their Commander hopping around and around the control room, from one foot to the other, like a bear with a sore head.

"You see!" says Dorian. "Just what I always suspected—"

The Commander takes the microphone of the public address

system to announce to all compartments: "The boat is operating against a convoy located by UR. Starting at six tomorrow morning we can anticipate contact." A crackling in the loudspeaker. Nothing more.

The Commander tilts his head way back. His elbows are propped between the spokes of the hydroplane handwheel. He frees his right arm, takes the pipe out of his mouth, makes an all-embracing gesture with the stem, and begins abruptly, "Marvelous thing, boat like this. Some people are against technology. Supposed to stultify you, impair your drive, nonsense like that!"

He pauses, and a good ten minutes pass before he takes up the thread again. "But there's nothing more beautiful than a U-boat like this. Don't mean to sound fanatical—god forbid!"

He takes a deep breath and produces a few snorting sounds in self-mockery, then goes on talking. "Sailing ships are marvelous too. Nothing in the world has more beautiful lines than a sailing ship! Served on a three-master years ago. Her bottom yard was forty feet above the deck. A good hundred and seventy all the way up. In bad weather no one wanted to climb up to the skysail. And if anyone fell you could hear the impact all over the ship. Happened three times on a single voyage. Special kind of thud—dull but penetrating—and everyone immediately knew what had happened."

The Old Man pauses and lets us listen to the gurgling of his cold pipe.

"Wonderful ship, that. Each hold as big as a church—the nave of a church—probably why they call them naves. Usually had sand as ballast. A good deal of it was different from this." The Old Man grins. "For one thing, we could stretch our legs properly!"

For a while the fist with the pipe remains poised in mid-air. Then, without putting the pipe away, he pushes his cap far back on his head. His tangled blond hair protrudes from under the peak, giving him a daredevil look. "Nothing I love more than the sound of these diesels running flat out. And some people cover their ears if they so much as hear them!" The Old Man shakes his head. "There're some who can't even stand the smell of gasoline. My fiancée can't abide the smell of leather. Funny!"

He suddenly clams up, like a boy who's let something slip.

No appropriate question occurs to me, so we both sit in silence staring at the floor plates. Then the Chief appears to ask whether the port diesel can be stopped for fifteen minutes. Reason: suspected damage to the crank shaft.

The Commander suddenly makes a face as if he'd bitten into a lemon. "Tsch, Chief—if we have no choice."

The Chief disappears, and a few moments later the tone of the diesels slackens. The Commander bites his lower lip.

Only when a new radio message is handed to him does his face light up again. "Last observed position of enemy Square Bruno Anton—UR."

The second watch assembles in the control room and makes ready. Safety belts are no longer in use. As the big hand of the clock approaches twelve, the four men climb up. "Course three hundred forty degrees, starboard diesel running full speed—port diesel stopped," the helmsman reports as the watch changes.

The lookouts who have been relieved come down. Their faces are the color of boiled lobster. The navigator, who is the last to descend into the control room, comes to attention. "Reporting from watch. Light cloud cover from northwest. Wind northwest to west. Veering counterclockwise. Shipping a lot of water due to high speed."

As though in confirmation, a surge of water lands on the floor plates.

"Thanks." The four salute, then shake themselves like dogs. Water from their rubber coats flies all over the control room. One of them ventures a question. "How far now from the scows?"

"Still a whole jet!" replies the control-room mate.

The steward comes through. Seems to be feeling his oats, tripping along like a headwaiter. Surprising he hasn't got a napkin clasped under his arm.

After the steward it's the cook on his way to the bow compartment. He has the ingratiating smile of a tavern-keeper.

"Pure play-acting today," says the Old Man, not noticing that he himself is performing the leading role as he sits in his corner benevolently surveying his children like a contented father.

It's as though we had broken out of a clinch and could breathe freely again. No more aimless searching, no more patroling up and down in the same area, a clear course at last, full speed ahead toward the enemy. The only one who takes no joy in the diesel roar and the hissing of the waves is the Chief. "There's a lot of my oil gone to hell," he growls with a look of disgust. But even he sounds satisfied when he announces that the port diesel is ready again.

"Fine, Chief, good to hear it!" says the Old Man. "Now let's see what you can do with your second wind."

I move off in the direction of the bow compartment. As soon as I open the door I notice that the excitement has taken hold here too. The cook appears behind me with a big pitcher of lemonade. The off-duty watch gathers around him like a horde dying of thirst.

"Here's hoping something comes of it all this time," Little Benjamin proclaims stoutly, almost before he's finished drinking.

"I can wait!" says Schwalle, hard-nosed.

"Well, I'm fed up with this frigging around!"

"Hero!" jeers someone out of the half darkness farther forward.

"Don't let your courage run away with you, little one. You're okay the way you are!"

"You've probably been swilling funny water again," says the same voice from the darkness.

"Something not suit you? These negative types give me a pain in the ass."

For a while there's nothing but the sleepy thrumming of radio music to be heard over the fluctuating roar of the waves. All at once the conversation turns to the reported convoy. "If the Old Man wants to get anything done, he's got to get there tonight," the torpedo mechanic asserts.

"Why's that?" the bridge johnny asks.

"Because tomorrow is Sunday, you imbecile!" Little Benjamin sputters. "It's in the Bible. Thou must honor the Sabbath and not violate thy sister."

I feel as if I'm in a road company. Our seagoing amateur theatricals are a play about imperturbability, coolness, and heroism; the actors are also talking away their fear.

The sea grows rougher during the night. I can feel it clearly as I doze.

Shortly after five o'clock I climb up to the bridge. The Second Watch Officer is in charge. The Commander's there too. Morning half light. The boat buffets the dark waves. Streamers rise like smoke from their crests, and more watery smoke fills the valleys between. An agony of watchfulness: if the convoy has tacked in this direction, we may intercept its course at any instant.

The sun rises astern, a milky disk. Ahead of us the sky is blocked by black walls of cloud. Very slowly they free themselves from the horizon as though drawn out of a sail loft: patches that are no further use. It remains misty.

"Damned poor visibility," growls the Second Watch Officer.

Soon more dark cloud cover comes creeping toward us just above the water, draped like a dingy curtain. Immediately in front of us it begins to fray out. The strands are black-gray like the clouds themselves, and stretch down to the water. The horizon disappears.

Another cloud a few points to port can no longer hold its burden of rain. Before long the trailing fringes of the two come together.

Already a few drops are falling. They make little pecking sounds on our sou'westers and jackets. The rain front swells out on both sides. Larger and larger sections of the horizon vanish into the blinding mist. A dark net is being thrown around the boat; it's already closing behind us; now there's no range of vision at all.

Intently, inch by inch, we search the gray curtain for some sign of the enemy. Every gray wall may hide a destroyer, every racing cloud a diving plane.

Spray comes flying over the bulwark; my tongue tastes of salt. My sou'wester is a roof. The rain pounds down on it, and I can feel the sharp blows of each drop on my scalp. Our blue-green oilskins glitter in the wet, and rain shoots down the folds in torrents. We stand like blocks of stone while the sky empties itself over us.

Must be seven o'clock now. We should have made contact with the convoy around six.

I hear Dorian cursing. "This weather is for the birds. I'm fed to the teeth with it!" The Second Watch Officer immediately turns on him to shout, "Look out, man, you're meant to be on watch."

Despite the Turkish hand towel wrapped around my neck, the water has soaked down as far as my belly.

I climb inside, and the control-room mate greets me expectantly. To his disappointment I produce nothing but a sigh of resignation. I go off to change my clothes and put the wet things in the E-room.

"Wind northwest five, sea running four, sky overcast, visibility poor," runs the text prepared for the war log. The rolling of the boat is getting steadily worse.

The last reported contact is now three hours old. "Enemy changing course to one hundred ten degrees. Proceeding in wide formation. Four columns. About thirty steamers." Since then no further news. Our diesels are still running full speed.

I hear the sea firing salvo after salvo against the tower. We seem to be caught in the aftermath of a high groundswell and the wind is whipping it up again.

At eight o'clock the watch is changed.

"What's it look like?" Isenberg asks the Berliner.

"Well, the light rain's gone. Now it's just pouring buckets!"

"Cut the crap—what's really happening?"

"Blown itself out—nothing doing—fog."

Suddenly the Old Man begins swearing. "Damn and fuck this filthy weather! Always just when we don't need it. Could easily go racing past and miss them by a couple of miles. Goddam pea soup!" And then, "If only Bertold would make a move!"

No new signal arrives.

Without another contact report we're up the creek: our calculations were never that accurate to begin with. The boat that made contact can't have had the chance to take an astronomical fix in the last forty-eight hours. The sky must certainly have been as constantly overcast for them as for us. So they've reported a position arrived at by dead reckoning. Even if the navigator on Bertold's boat has calculated exactly, he can only guess at the displacement of the boat by the sea and the wind.

Silence from headquarters. Has Bertold been forced to dive? Surprised by a destroyer?

No chance of getting a sighting from the other boats sent after the convoy. After all, they were farther away than we were; it's natural enough that they have nothing to contribute. But Bertold, the contact boat—surely he ought to know something.

"Must be stuck in the same pea soup," says the Old Man.

The engines throb steadily. There isn't much for the Chief to do now. "This weather must be giving our colleagues a bad time."

It takes me a while to realize he's sympathizing with the crews of the enemy ships. Then he adds, "Those destroyer crews really take a beating—tin cans."

He sees my startled expression and continues: "It's true. Our own destroyers no longer put out to sea if there's the slightest storm cloud outside the harbor wall."

The control room is filling up. Everyone with any kind of legitimate excuse to be there seems to have appeared. In addition to the Commander, the navigator, and the control-room mate with his two assistants, I see the First Watch Officer, the Second Engineer, and Dorian.

"We've had it! Take it from me!" says Dorian, but so softly that only I can hear. The others are silent—they seem to be suddenly struck dumb.

The Old Man jerks up his head and orders, "Prepare to dive!"

I know what he has in mind: a sonar search. The sounds of enemy engines and propellers carry farther in deep water than we can possibly see on the surface.

The usual series of orders and maneuvers follows. I glance at the depth manometer. The pointer begins to turn and suddenly the roaring of the waves ceases.

The Commander has the boat level off at a hundred feet and crouches in the passageway beside the sound room. The face of the hydrophone operator, lit from below, looks absolutely expressionless. His eyes are empty. With the headpiece clamped over his ears, he's conducting a search in every direction to pick out some trace of the enemy from the general underwater sounds.

"No target?" The Commander asks again and again. And after a while, impatient and tense, "Nothing at all?"

For a moment he presses one of the earpieces to his own head, then passes the instrument to me. I hear nothing but a surging hum like the noise from a conch shell when you press it against your ear.

The boat has been running underwater for an hour. No hydrophone directional bearing. "That's the way it goes," murmurs the Chief, who keeps running his fingers nervously through his hair.

"Fucked!" says someone half under his breath.

The Commander is about to pull himself to his feet and give the order to the Chief to surface when he catches sight of the hydrophone operator: eyes closed, mouth tight shut, and face contracted as if in pain. He swings his equipment slowly right, then left. Finally he moves the wheel a fraction of an inch: a noise! Struggling to control his excitement, he announces, "Sound bearing sixty degrees—very weak!"

The Commander straightens up with a jerk and grabs one of the earpieces. His face takes on an intense expectancy.

Suddenly the operator gives an almost imperceptible shudder and the Commander sucks his lips between his teeth.

"Depth charges! They're raking somebody. What's the bearing now?"

"Seventy degrees—moving astern—long way off!" The Commander climbs through the circular door into the control room. His voice is harsh: "Course fifty degrees! Prepare to surface!" And then to the navigator, "Note for the war log: 'Despite condition of weather decided to proceed on surface against convoy.'"

The weather has grown even worse. Low-hanging squalls of rain darken the sky around us. All the daylight is gone: It might as well be evening. Wind-driven spray covers the watery landscape with a pale mist.

The boat's rolling heavily. Waves coming from the port beam. Water spurts through the open hatch, but we have to keep this open because the enemy may surprise the boat at any moment.

The propellers race, the diesels are running flat out. The Commander is rooted to the bridge. Under the rain-slicked, downturned brim of his sou'wester he searches the sea. He stands motionless; only his head pivots slowly from side to side.

After a quarter of an hour I climb down to inspect developments on the chart table. The navigator is hard at work calculating. Without lifting his eyes he says, "Here we are—and here's where we can expect the convoy. Unless it's tacked again."

Standing around aimlessly embarrasses me. I already have my left hand on the aluminum ladder when I tell myself that all this climbing up and down makes me look nervous. Just take it easy: relax. Whatever's happening, I'll find out in good time. How late is it really? Past twelve? Well, I just have to act as though none of this is out of the ordinary, so I peel off my wet things.

I sit in the mess, trying to read a book, until the steward finally brings in plates and cups for lunch. The Commander doesn't appear.

We've scarcely sat down at the table—the Chief, the Second Engineer, and I—when there's a roar from the control room. The Chief looks up quickly. A report comes down from the bridge. "Masthead off the port bow!"

Almost without thinking, I'm halfway to the control room: the convoy.

I'm ahead of the Chief to the bridge. The rain is worse. My sweater is immediately soaked from spray and the downpour. I was in such a hurry, I forgot to grab my oilskin from its hook.

I hear the Commander. "Hard to starboard. Steer one hundred eighty degrees!"

A bridge guard hands me his binoculars unasked. I start searching the same area as the Commander. Gray streamers of rain. Nothing else. Holding my breath, I force myself to stay calm, search the right-hand edge of this banner of water and then swing my glasses very slowly across it to the left. There—in the streaks of gray—a hairbreadth line that immediately disappears again. An illusion? Imagination? I take a deep breath, relax my knees, give myself a gentle shake, balance the glasses on my fingertips. The boat heaves under me. I lose my bearings, then reorient myself by the Commander. There it is again.

It trembles and dances in the glasses. A mast! No doubt of it. But—a mast and no accompanying plume of smoke? Only this single hairline? Hard as I look, I can find nothing else; it seems to be pushing its way slowly over the horizon.

Every steamer is supposed to have a plume of smoke that betrays it long before its radio masts appear. So this can't be a steamer.

Hell and damnation—where is it? Now I have it again. I should be able to see it with the naked eye. I put down my glasses and search—there it is all right!

The Commander is chewing his lower lip. He takes up the binoculars again, muttering half to himself—"Shit! Destroyer!"

A minute goes by. My eyes are glued to the thin line above the horizon. I'm choking with excitement.

No more doubt about it: It's a radio mast, so the destroyer is coming directly at us. Without slow engines there's no chance we can get away on the surface.

"They must have seen us. Goddammit!" The Commander's voice hardly changes at all as he gives the alarm.

One bound and I'm down the tower hatch. Boots ringing on the floor plates. The Commander is the last in. He pulls the hatch shut. Even before it's completely sealed he orders, "Flood!"

He stays in the tower. In a steady voice he calls instructions down to the control room. "Proceed at periscope depth!" The Chief balances the boat. The needle of the depth manometer stops, then slowly moves backward over the scale. Dufte is beside me, breathing heavily in his wet oilskins. Zeitler and Bockstiegel are sitting in front of the buttons of the hydroplane controls, their eyes glued to the water column in the Papenberg. The First Watch Officer bends forward to let the rainwater run off the brim of his sou'wester.

No one says a word. Only the electric hum of the motors can be heard, as if through padded doors, coming from the stern.

From above us, the voice of the Commander finally breaks the silence. "Report depth."

"Seventy feet!" from the Chief.

The water column in the Papenberg sinks slowly: the boat is rising. The lens of the periscope soon comes clear.

The boat is not yet on an even keel, so the Chief orders water pumped from the forward trim tank toward the stern. Slowly the boat attains the horizontal. But it doesn't stay there. The waves roll us in all directions. Sucking, dragging, pushing. Periscope observation is going to be damned difficult.

I listen intently, waiting to hear from the Commander, when the hydrophone operator reports, "Destroyer hard on the starboard beam!"

I pass the report up.

"Acknowledged." Then, just as dryly, "Man battle stations!"

The operator is bent out of the sound room into the passageway, his eyes wide and blank. The direct lighting makes his face a flat mask, the nose simply two holes.

Along with the Commander, the operator is now the only one in contact with the world outside our steel tube. The Commander can see the enemy, the operator hears him. The rest of us are blind and deaf. "Auditory contact stronger—moving slowly astern!"

The Commander's voice sounds choked. "Flood tubes one to four!"

Just as I thought: The Old Man is going to take on the destroyer. He wants a red pennant. The only thing still missing from his collection. When he ordered periscope after the alarm, I knew for sure.

His voice comes down again. "To control room—Chief—hold our exact depth!"

How can he possibly do it, I ask myself, in this rough sea? The muscles in the Chief's gaunt face tense and relax rhythmically. He looks as if he's chewing gum. If the boat rises too far, and the upper part of the hull breaks the surface—disaster: it will betray us to the enemy.

The Commander is astride the periscope saddle in the narrow space between the periscope shaft and the tower wall, his face pressed against the rubber shell, his thighs spread wide to grip the huge shaft. His feet are on the pedals that enable him to spin the great column and his saddle through 360 degrees without making a sound; his right hand rests on the lever that raises and lowers it. The periscope motor hums. He's lowering it a little, keeping its head as close to the surface of the water as he possibly can.

The Chief is standing immobile behind the two men of the bridge watch who are now operating the hydroplanes. His eyes are glued to the Papenberg and its slowly rising and falling column of water. Each change in it means the boat is doing the same.

Not a word from anyone. The humming of the periscope motor sounds as if it's coming through a fine filter; the motor starts, stops, starts again, and the humming resumes. The Commander ups periscope for fractions of a second and immediately lets it sink below the surface again. The destroyer must be very close.

"Flood tube five." The order is a whisper.

It's passed on softly to the main motor room. We're in the midst of battle.

I sink down onto the frame of the circular door. The whispered report comes back from astern, "Tube five ready to fire when torpedo door opened."

So—all tubes are flooded. All that's needed is to open the doors and release a blast of compressed air to send them on their way. The Commander wants to know the position of the helm.

Suddenly I notice that I still have a half-chewed bit of bread in my mouth. Mushy bread and sausage fat. It's beginning to taste sour.

I have the feeling that I've lived all this somewhere before. Images shift about in my mind, jostling, overlaying one another, merging into new combinations. My immediate impressions seem to be being transmitted by a complicated circuit to my brain center from which they re-emerge into my consciousness as memories.

The Old Man's mad—attacking a destroyer in this sea.

But it has its advantages too. Our periscope can't be all that visible. The streamer of foam that would betray it must be hard to distinguish among the cresting waves.

The drip in the bilge is deafening. Sounds as if it's coming over a loudspeaker. Lucky that everything's worked so far: no problem maintaining depth. The Chief was well prepared, had it all figured out.

If the Old Man decides to fire, the Chief must flood at once to make up for the weight of the torpedo. Otherwise the boat will rise. A torpedo weighs three thousand pounds—so an equivalent weight of water has to be taken on for each one launched. Multiplied by the number of torpedoes fired—it's a lot.

Not a word from the Commander.

It's very difficult to hit a destroyer. Shallow draft. Easily maneuverable. But score a hit, and it's gone in a flash, blown away. The explosion of the torpedo, a geyser of water and torn steel, then nothing.

The Commander's steady voice comes down. "Open torpedo doors. Switch on tubes one and two! Enemy course fifteen. Bow left. Direction sixty. Range one thousand!"

The Second Watch Officer puts the figures in the calculator. The bow compartment reports torpedo doors opened. The First Watch Officer relays the message softly but distinctly. "Tubes one and two ready to fire!"

The Commander has his hand on the firing lever and is waiting for the enemy to move into the crosshairs.

If only we were able to see!

Imagination runs riot in this silence. Visions of catastrophe: a destroyer swinging until it's at angle zero. The foaming bow, the white bone in its teeth, towering over us, ready to ram. Staring eyes, the sharp rending of metal, jagged edges of steel, green surge of water through fissures like opened stopcocks.

The voice of the Commander, as sharp as a descending whiplash. "Close torpedo doors. Dive to two hundred feet. Fast!"

The Chief is only a fraction of a second behind him. "Hard down both—both engines full ahead! All hands forward!"

Loud confusion of voices. I flinch, press myself to one side, have trouble staying on my feet. The first man is already forcing his way through the circular door aft, staggers, recovers his balance and rushes, half crouched, past the sound room toward the bow.

Wide-open questioning eyes fixed on me. Chaos: slipping, stumbling, hurrying, staggering. Two bottles of lemonade come tumbling in from the petty officers' mess and smash noisily against the wall of the control room.

Both hydroplanes are hard down. The boat is already distinctly bow heavy, but the men keep coming from astern. They slide through the tilted control room as if it's a chute; one falls full length, cursing.

Only the engine room personnel are left in the after part of the ship. The floor slips away beneath me. Fortunately I manage to grab the periscope stanchion. The sausages swing out at an angle from the wall. I hear the Old Man's voice from above us, cutting through the scuffling and stamping of boots. "Depth charges next!" He sounds perfectly calm, as though passing on a piece of casual information.

He climbs down with exaggerated deliberation, as if it's an exercise. Traverses the slope, hanging on to both sides, and props one buttock on the chart chest. His right hand grasps a water pipe for support.

The Chief slowly levels the boat out and orders, "Man diving stations!" The seamen who rushed forward now work their way back hand over hand up the slope. The sausages act like a scale: we're still a good thirty degrees bow heavy.

Rrabaum!—Rrum!—Rrum!

Three crashing sledgehammer blows spin me around. Half stunned, I hear a dull roar. What is it? Fear claws at my heart: that roaring! Finally I identify it: it's water pouring back into the vacuum created in the sea by the explosion.

Two more monstrous explosions.

The control-room mate has hunched his head into his shoulders. The new control-room assistant, the Bible Scholar, staggers and seizes hold of the chart table.

Another explosion, louder than the rest.

The lights go out. Darkness!

"Auxiliary lighting gone," someone calls.

The orders from the Chief seem to come from a distance. Pocket flashlights cut whitish cones in the darkness. Someone calls for a damage report. The section leaders' replies come through the speaking tubes. "Bow compartment in order!"—"Main motor room in order!"—"Engine room in order!"

"No leakage," says the navigator. His voice is as matter-of-fact as the Commander's.

Before long, two double explosions make the floor plates dance.

"Pump out torpedo cell one!" With a sharp hum the bilge pump springs into action. As soon as the roar of the detonations has subsided, the pump will be stopped again. Otherwise it could supply a bearing to the enemy's hydrophones.

"Raise bow!" The Chief to the hydroplane operators. "Boat's in balance," he reports to the Commander.

"There'll be more," says the Old Man. "They actually saw our periscope. Amazing—with the sea running this high."

He looks around. No trace of fear on his face. There's even an undertone of scorn in his voice. "Now it's psychological warfare, gentlemen."

Ten minutes pass; nothing happens. Suddenly a violent explosion shakes the whole boat. Then another and another. It quivers and groans.

"Fifteen!" counts the navigator. "Sixteen, seventeen, eighteen!"

The Chief stares at the needle of the depth manometer, which jumps a couple of points at each detonation. His eyes are huge and dark. The Commander's are closed to obliterate his surroundings and concentrate on his calculations: our own course, enemy course, ways of escape. He must react with lightning speed. He's the only one among the lot of us who's actually fighting. Our lives hang on the correctness of his orders.

"Hard a-port!"

"Helm hard a-port!"

"Hold zero bearing!"

The Commander never stops calculating. The basic factors in his reckoning change with each report; he must determine an escape route according to the strength of the sound of propellers and the approach angle of the destroyer. His senses no longer supply him with any immediate information; he must guide the boat like a pilot flying blind, his decisions based on indications given him by the instruments.

Against closed eyelids I see the gray-black cans twisting heavily as they shoot downward from the launchers, plunge into the water, spin lazily into the depths leaving bubbling trails, and then explode in the darkness—blazing fireballs of magnesium, incandescent suns.

Water transmits pressure much more strongly than air. If an intense pressure wave hits a boat it rips it apart at the seams. To destroy a submerged U-boat, depth charges don't have to hit it; they need only explode within the so-called lethal radius. The small depth charges dropped by airplanes weigh about 150 pounds, the destroyer bombs about 500 pounds. At a depth of 350 feet, the lethal radius extends about 275 to 350 feet. Once you've learned something, it sticks. I feel a kind of satisfaction that I now know this kind of thing by heart.

For a while all is quiet. I strain my ears. No propeller noise, no splashing of bombs. Only the thin humming of our electric motors. Not even the sound of breathing. The Commander suddenly seems to remember that we're here. He doesn't move, but he glances around and whispers, "I could see them clearly. They were standing on the bridge, gaping straight at us. There were three men in the crow's nest. A corvette!"

He bends forward and whispers through the circular door to the sound man, "See if they're going away." Still bending forward a minute later, his question becomes more urgent: "Louder or weaker?"

The operator answers immediately. "No change." It's Herrmann: face like a Noh-mask—colorless, eyes and mouth thin lines. The Old Man orders us down farther.

Our pressure hull can withstand a good deal. But the flanges, all those damned pierced sections, are our Achilles' heel. And there are too many of them.

The most dangerous bombs for the boat are those that explode diagonally under the keel, because the underside has the largest number of flanges and outboard plugs. The deeper you go, the smaller the lethal radius: the water pressure, which is itself a threat at such depths because of the overloading on the seams, also limits the effective radius of the bombs—at 130, it's perhaps 160 feet.

Suddenly a handful of pebbles rattles against the boat.

"Asdic!" I hear a voice from the stern end of the control room. The jagged word suddenly stands out in my head in glaring capitals.

A shudder runs down my spine: *Anti-Submarine Development Investigation Committee*; the supersonic detection system!

It's the impact of the directional beam against our side that produces this low tinkling, chirping sound. In the absolute silence it has all the force of a siren. Time between impulses: about thirty seconds.

"Turn it off!" I want to shout. The chirping grates on my nerves. No one dares so much as lift his head or speak, even though it will find us even if we remain as silent as the grave. Against it, silence is useless. So is stopping the E-motors. Normal hydrophones are outclassed by the E-motors, but the Asdic isn't dependent on sound, it reacts to our mass. Depth no longer affords any protection.

The nervous tension is infectious. My hands are shaking. I'm glad

I don't have to stand up; instead I'm able to sit in the frame of the circular doorway. I try out actions that require no major bodily movement: swallowing, blinking, grinding my teeth, making faces— a crease to the right, a crease to the left, forcing saliva between my teeth.

The operator whispers, "Getting louder!"

The Commander frees himself from the periscope shaft, makes his way past me almost on tiptoe. "Any change in direction?"

"Bearing still two hundred ninety-five degrees."

Four detonations in quick succession. The roaring, gurgling surge of the explosions has barely subsided when the Commander says in a low voice, "She was well camouflaged, a fairly old ship, rather squat."

A hard blow against my feet jolts me badly. The floor plates rattle.

"Twenty-seven—twenty-eight!" the navigator counts, trying to imitate the Old Man's elaborate casualness.

A pail goes rattling partway across the floor plates.

"Hell and damnation—quiet!"

Now it sounds as if the pebbles are in a tin can, being shaken this way and that; in between is a louder, singing sound, with an underlying quick, sharp chirping, like crickets—the whirling propeller blades of the corvette. I stand rigid, frozen. I don't dare make the slightest movement; it's as if any motion, even the smallest slithering sound, would bring the beating propellers closer. Not a flicker of an eyelash, a twitch of the eye, not a breath, not a quiver of a nerve, not a ripple of the muscles, not even a goose pimple.

Another five bombs! The navigator adds them to the total. My expression doesn't change. The Commander raises his head. Clearly emphasizing each word, he speaks into the echo of the crashing water. "Keep calm—calm, gentlemen. This is nothing at all."

His quiet voice does us good, eases our jangled nerves.

Now we are struck by a single ringing blow, like a giant cudgel on a sheet of steel. Two or three men begin to stagger.

The air is hazy, hanging in blue layers. And again the heavy explosions.

"Thirty-four—thirty-five—thirty-six!" This time the counting comes in a whisper.

The Commander remains firm. "What in the world—is bothering you?" He withdraws into himself once more, calculating courses. It's deathly still in the boat. After a while the whispering voice comes again. "What's his bearing now?"

"Two hundred sixty degrees—getting louder!"

The Commander raises his head. He's reached a decision.

"Hard a-starboard!" And immediately afterward, "Sound room—we're turning to starboard!"

A wrench has to be passed through to the stern. I reach for it eagerly and hand it on. Dear god, to be able to *do* something—turn handwheels, adjust levers, man the pumps . . .

The operator leans out into the passageway again. His eyes are open but he's staring into infinity. He sounds like a medium speaking. "Sounds growing louder—two hundred thirty—two hundred twenty."

"Nonessential lights out," the Old Man orders. "Who the hell knows how long we may need the current!"

The operator reports again, "Attacking again—sounds bearing two hundred ten degrees—getting louder fast! Quite close!" The excitement has upset his delivery.

The Commander orders: "Both engines full ahead!"

The seconds stretch out. Nothing. No one moves.

"Let's hope they don't get their friends in on it!" The Old Man voices a fear that's been in my bones for a long time: the sweepers, the killers . . . a pack of dogs is death to the hare.

Whoever has us on the hook now is no beginner, and we're defenseless in spite of the five torpedoes in our tubes. We can't surface, we can't come speeding from behind cover and throw ourselves on the enemy. We haven't even the grim assurance to be had from simply holding a weapon in your hand. We can't so much as shout at them. Just creep away. Keep going deeper. How deep are we now? I can't believe my eyes: the pointer of the manometer stands at 465. "Shipyard guarantee three hundred" flashes through my mind.

Ten minutes pass and nothing happens.

Another handful of pebbles hits the boat high up on the port buoyancy tank. I can see from the operator's face that more depth charges are coming. He's moving his lips, counting the seconds before detonation.

The first is so well aimed that I feel the shock all the way up my spine. We're in a huge drum with a steel plate for a drum head. I see the navigator's lips moving but I hear nothing. Have I gone deaf?

But now I can hear the Commander. He's ordering higher speed again. He raises his voice to be heard over the pandemonium. "All right! Carry on just as you are, gentlemen, pay no attention to this nonsense! At home there are . . ."

He breaks off in mid-sentence. Suddenly there's a humming stillness. Only the occasional swish and slap from the bilge.

"Bow up! Steady!" the Chief orders the hydroplane men. His

whisper sounds too loud in the silence. Once again the E-motors have been reduced to crawling speed. Bilge water gurgles toward the stern. Just where does it all come from? Wasn't it properly bailed in advance?

"Thirty-eight . . . forty-one!" the navigator counts.

With the roaring and bursting of the bombs still in my ears the silence that follows seems like a bizarre acoustical black hole, bottomless. Probably just to keep the silence from becoming too painful, the Commander whispers, "I'm not sure whether those characters up there are in contact!" At the same moment new detonations shake the depths: the answer is plain.

Once more my ears can't distinguish one explosion from the next. Nor have I any impression of whether the bombs are exploding right or left, above or below the boat. But the Old Man can obviously locate them. He's probably the only one who knows our position relative to our tormentor. Or is the navigator calculating too? In any case I no longer have the slightest clue. I see only the needle of the depth manometer moving slowly forward over the dial. We're going deeper again.

The Chief is bending forward toward the hydroplane operators. His face is thrown into unnatural relief against the dark background, like that of an actor lit only by the footlights, every bone emphasized by dark lines or shadow. His hand looks waxen. There's a black streak across his right cheek. He's narrowed his eyes as if dazzled by the light.

The two hydroplane operators crouch motionless in front of their control buttons. Even when they change the hydroplane settings one sees no movement. The slight pressure of a finger requires no shift of their limbs. Our hydroplanes are power-operated. What more could we possibly want? Except for some piece of equipment that would allow us to observe the enemy from way down here.

A breathing space? I try to settle myself more firmly. The corvette certainly won't keep us waiting long. It's simply circling again; even when it's moving away from us, the goddam Asdic keeps us cornered. The people up there have got every man they can spare on the bridge, peering at the choppy sea, searching the marbled foam for some sign of us. Nothing—zebra patterns drawn in green; green and white oxgall paper streaked with black . . . but it's the iridescent sheen of oil they're really after.

Still no move from the hydrophone operator: no sounds to report.

A strange clicking noise. A new device to locate us? Minutes pass. No one moves a muscle. The clicking stops; in its place another handful of pebbles strikes the boat, small gravel stones this time.

Abruptly the Commander raises his head. "D'you think we'll get them—again?"

Get them again? Does he mean the convoy, or the corvette?

He leans forward and speaks softly to the hydrophone man. "Find out if she's going away." Seconds later he asks impatiently, "Louder or weaker?"

"Staying the same," replies the operator, and after a while, "Getting louder."

"Any deviation?"

"Bearing still two hundred twenty degrees."

The Commander immediately has the rudder put hard to starboard. So we're going to double back again.

And now he orders both motors slow ahead.

Drops of condensation punctuate the tense silence at regular intervals: *Pit-pat—tick-tack—pitch-patch.*

A hard blow makes the floor plates jump and rattle. "Forty-seven—forty-eight." And then, "Forty-nine—fifty—fifty-one."

A glance at my wristwatch: 14:30. When was the alarm? Must have been shortly after twelve. We've been under pursuit for two hours!

My watch has a red second hand on the same pin as the two main hands, so that it's constantly circling the dial in a series of jerky movements. I concentrate on this hand, measuring the interval between the individual detonations: two minutes, thirty seconds—another one; thirty seconds—the next; then twenty seconds.

I'm happy to have something to do. Nothing else exists. I take a tighter grip with my right hand as though to focus my concentration. It has to come to an end. *Has to.*

Another hard, sharp blow: forty-four seconds this time. Up to this point I've been mouthing syllables noiselessly, but now I can clearly feel my lips spread into a flattened oval, baring my teeth. Now I need my left hand to hang on with too.

The Commander orders us down another seventy feet.

Almost seven hundred now. A loud crackling and snapping runs through the boat. The new control-room assistant glances at me in fear.

"Only the woodwork," whispers the Commander.

It's the wooden paneling that creaks and snaps so loudly. The interior structure can't stand the compression. Seven hundred feet. Every square inch of steel skin now has to withstand a weight of 284 pounds, which means over twenty tons per square foot. All this on a hull less than an inch thick.

The crackling's getting sharper.

"Unpleasant," murmurs the Chief.

The excruciating tension exerted on the steel skin is torture to me: I feel as if my own skin were being stretched. Another crack resounds, as loud as a rifle shot, and my scalp twitches. Under this insane pressure our hull is as fragile as an eggshell.

The ship's fly appears less than two feet away. I wonder how she likes this infernal drum solo. Each of us chooses his own fate: it's as true for the fly as it is for me. We both embarked on this undertaking of our own free will.

A double blow, then a third, not much weaker than its predecessors. The people up there are fishing for us with an even tighter net.

Renewed clattering of floor plates and deafening after-roar.

Peace lasts only a couple of heartbeats. Then two shattering blows and the glass plates of the depth manometers fall tinkling to the floor. The light goes out.

The cone of a pocket flashlight wavers across the walls and comes to rest on the dial of the depth manometer. I make a terrifying discovery: the hands of both manometers are gone. The water gauge between the two hydroplane operators has cracked and is shooting a hissing stream of water straight across the room.

"Leak through the water gauge," I hear a shaky voice report.

The Commander snarls, "Nonsense, cut the dramatics!"

The empty dials stare like the eyes of a corpse. We can no longer tell whether the boat is sinking or rising.

My scalp crawls again. If the instruments have failed us, we have no way of telling our position.

I stare intently at the black ends of the shafts, but without a pointer they are meaningless.

The control-room mate fumbles about among the pipelines by flashlight. Apparently trying to reach some valve that will close off the spurting stream of water. He's soaked to the skin before he finds it. Although the flow is choked off, he continues to feel about on the floor. Suddenly he's holding a pointer. Cautiously he lifts his precious find and places it on the square shaft of the small manometer, the one that registers the lowest depths.

It feels as if all our lives depend on whether the thin strip of metal will move or not.

The man takes his hand away. The needle quivers and slowly begins to turn. Silently the Commander nods approbation.

The manometer shows six hundred feet.

The hydrophone man reports, "Sounds getting louder—two hundred thirty degrees—two hundred twenty degrees!"

The Commander takes his cap off and lays it on the chart chest.

His hair is matted with sweat. He takes a deep breath and says, "Keep it up!"

For once his voice isn't entirely under control. There is an unmistakable undertone of resignation in it.

"Noises bearing two hundred ten degrees! Growing louder—attack beginning again!"

The Commander immediately orders full speed ahead. A sharp jolt runs through the boat as it leaps forward. The Commander leans against the shining oily column of the sky periscope, resting the back of his head on it.

Long-forgotten images rise in my mind: two cardboard disks painted in spirals and spinning in opposite directions on the ice cream machines at country fairs. The tangle of red and white completely fills my head and becomes the trail of two depth charges, flaring comets that consume everything in a blaze of white.

The hydrophone operator startles me. Another report. I stare at his mouth, but his words don't penetrate.

More waiting, more holding my breath. Even the smallest sound is painful, a touch on a raw wound. As if my nerves had escaped the outer layer of skin and were now exposed. I have only one thought: they're up there. Right overhead. I forget to breathe. I'm stifling before I slowly, cautiously, fill my lungs with oxygen. Against closed eyelids I see bombs tumbling perpendicularly into the depths trailing sparkling air bubbles, exploding into fire. Around their incandescent cores all the colors of the spectrum flare up in mad combinations, leaping and dying again but growing steadily more intense until the whole interior of the sea glows like a blast furnace.

The control-room mate breaks the spell. Gesturing and whispering, he calls the Chief's attention to a corner of the control room where a can of lubricating oil is overflowing. This is about the most trivial problem imaginable right now, but it upsets him.

The Chief nods permission for him to do something about it. The pipe that is dripping oil reaches straight into the can. He can't simply take the can away from under it, but has to tilt it to get it out. As a result, more oil spills onto the floor plates and forms an ugly black puddle.

The navigator shakes his head in disgust. The control-room mate withdraws the overfilled can as cautiously as a thief trying to avoid setting off a burglar alarm.

"Corvette noises receding astern!" reports the operator. Almost simultaneously, two more bombs explode. But the roar of the detonations is weaker and duller than before.

"Way off," says the Commander.

Rwumm—tjummwumm!

Even fainter. The Commander seizes his cap. "Practice maneuvers! That's the sort of thing they ought to work on at home!"

The control-room mate is already busy fitting new glass tubes into the broken water gauges; he seems to know that the mere sight of the breakage effects us like poison.

When I stand up, I'm stiff all over. No feeling in my legs. I try to put one foot in front of the other—feels like stepping into the void. I hold fast to the table and look at the chart.

There is the pencil line showing the boat's course, and the pencil cross indicating its last position. And here the line suddenly stops— I'm going to make a note of the latitude and longitude of the place if we get out of this.

The operator sweeps the whole circumference of his dial.

"Well?" asks the Commander. He acts bored, pushing his tongue into his left cheek till it bulges.

"Going away!" the operator replies.

The Commander looks around. Satisfaction personified. He even grins. "As far as I can see, gentlemen, the incident is over."

He staggers a little. "Very instructive, of course. First, all that damn chasing around and then a real bomb scare!" He climbs through the circular door and into his cubbyhole.

"Bring me a piece of paper!" Is he going to compose something really profound for the war log or a report for the High Command? No, it's sure to be nothing more than, "Surprised by corvette in rain squall. Three hours of depth bomb pursuit." I wouldn't bet on anything more colorful than that.

Five minutes later he's back in the control room. He exchanges a glance with the Chief, then orders, "Take her to periscope depth!" And climbs deliberately to the tower.

The Chief has the hydroplanes adjusted.

"Report depth!" The Commander's voice comes down.

"One hundred twenty-five feet." Then in sequence: "Sixty feet. Forty-five feet—periscope above surface!"

I hear the periscope motor hum, stop, hum again. Minutes pass. Not a word. We wait. Not a sound from the Old Man.

We look at each other questioningly. "Something wrong?" the control-room mate murmurs.

Finally the Commander breaks the silence. "Crash dive! Deep! All hands forward!"

I repeat the order. The hydrophone operator passes it on. From astern I hear it in multiple echoes. Tense with anxiety the crew rushes through the control room toward the bow.

"Goddam filthy weather!" the Chief curses under his breath. The hand of the manometer moves forward again: sixty, one hundred, one hundred fifty feet . . .

The Commander's seaboots appear. He clambers slowly down into the control room. All eyes are fixed on his face. But he merely smiles sardonically and orders, "Both motors slow ahead. Course sixty degrees." Finally he enlightens us.

"The corvette's lying six hundred yards away. Stopped, as far as I could see. Wanted to surprise us, the bastards." The Old Man bends over the chart. After a while he turns to me. "Fucking maniacs. You can't be too careful. Well, let's crawl our way comfortably westward for the time being."

Then, to the navigator, "When does twilight begin?"

"At 18.30 hours, Herr Kaleun."

"Good. We'll stay down for the time being."

There no longer seems to be any immediate danger: at least the Commander was speaking loudly enough. He inhales with a deep snort, arches his chest, holds his breath, and nods from one of us to the other.

"After the battle," he says with a meaningful look at the confusion of broken glass, strewn oilskins, and upturned buckets.

I see drawings by Dix: horses lying on their backs, bellies torn open like exploded ships, all four legs stretched rigidly toward the sky, soldiers sunk in trench slime, teeth bared in final madness. Here on board, however, we may have just narrowly escaped destruction, but there are no sprawling tangles of entrails, no charred limbs, no lacerated flesh bleeding through canvas covers. A few fragments of broken glass, damaged manometers, spilled cans of condensed milk, two crushed pictures in the gangway—these are the only traces of battle. The steward appears, casts a disgusted look at the debris, and begins to clean up. The photo of the C-in-C U-boats, alas, has not been touched.

But there's been a lot of damage in the engine and motor rooms. The Chief recites a long list of technical details. The Old Man nods patiently.

"Just let her plow along steadily. I have a feeling we're still going to be needed around here." And then to me, "Time to eat. I'm starving!" He takes his cap off and hangs it on top of the oilskins on the wall.

"The fried eggs have probably gone cold," the Second Watch Officer remarks and grins.

"Hey, Cookie, fry up some more eggs," the Commander shouts toward the stern.

I'm in a daze. Are we really still here or is it an illusion? There's a ringing in my inner ear, as if someone's playing back a recording of the bombs going off. I can't really grasp the fact that we've come through the storm in safety. I sit there silent and shake my head to try to banish the sights and sounds that haunt me.

Still less than an hour since the last depth charges fell, and the radioman is putting a record on the phonograph. Marlene Dietrich's voice is soothing. "Put your money away—some other time you can pay . . ." It's a record from the Old Man's private collection.

At 19.00 the Commander gives the order over the loudspeaker to surface. The Chief swings himself through the circular door and gives the necessary instructions to the hydroplane operators. The bridge watch climbs into their rubber clothes, stands ready under the tower hatch, and fumbles with their binoculars.

"Two hundred feet—one fifty—boat rising rapidly!" reports the Chief. When the manometer hand reaches a hundred the Commander orders a hydrophone check in every direction. No one makes a sound. I hardly dare breathe. Nothing.

The Commander climbs the ladder. When the boat is at periscope depth I can tell from the sound of the gears that he's doing a complete sweep.

We wait intently: nothing!

"Surface!" Compressed air rushes hissing into the diving cell. The Commander retracts the periscope. It takes a while for it to settle into place with a click. Only then does he remove his face from the rubber eyepieces.

"Tower clear," the Chief reports upward and then, "Equalize pressure!"

The First Watch Officer turns the hatch spindle, and the hatch springs back with a snap like a champagne cork. Pressure equalization can't have been complete. Fresh air pours into the boat. Cold and damp. I gulp it in eagerly. It's a gift—and I savor it to the full, pumping it into my lungs, tasting it on my tongue. The boat pitches and tosses.

"Prepare to blow tanks! Clear for ventilation! Diesel room stand ready to dive!"

The Chief nods his approval. The Commander's on his guard, doesn't want to run any risks.

The circle of the hatch still frames the dark sky. A few scattered stars. Sparkling and twinkling, tiny lanterns wavering in the wind.

"Stand by port diesel!"

"Port diesel ready!"

The boat drifts, rocking. The hatch wanders back and forth beneath the shining stars.

"Port diesel slow ahead!"

A trembling shudder runs through the boat. The diesel fires.

The Commander orders the bridge watch and the navigator to the bridge.

"Radiogram to be sent!" I hear someone say.

The navigator is already on his way down. I peer over his shoulder and can't repress a grin: the text he's writing out is almost exactly what I had predicted.

He can't understand why I'm smiling, and looks offended.

"Lapidary," I say. But he doesn't understand that either. He makes his way to the radio shack and I see him shaking his head.

"Permission to come on the bridge?"

"*Jawohl!*" and I climb up.

The cloud curtain is parting to reveal the moon; where its beams strike the water, the sea glitters and glistens. The cloud curtain closes, and now the only brightness comes from a few scattered stars and from the water. Behind the boat the foam phosphoresces —luminous green magic. Waves hiss over the bow like water poured onto hot iron plates, but beneath the sharp hissing is a continuing dull roar. Occasionally a larger wave rises and strikes the boat's side with the heavy, hollow boom of a gong. *Bomm—bomm—tsch— jwumm!*

Rather than being buoyed up by water, the boat seems to be gliding along between the depths and the heights on a thin, scarred skin—abyss above, abyss below: a thousand stories of darkness in either direction. Wandering thoughts—confused, hardly focused: We are saved. Voyagers to Orcus who have found our way home.

"All the same, it's a good thing this pond is three dimensional!" the Commander says close beside me.

I'm at the table. Breakfast. Fragments of conversation from the Quarters. Going by the voice, it must be Johann. He seems to be in the middle of a story:

". . . turned out the only thing there was a stove. God oh god, was that a runaround! Nothing to be had. Not even with U-boat insignia on my jacket. The kitchen cabinet was no problem, thank god. My brother-in-law's a prison inspector. He's having it made in the prison . . . Of course there's no baby carriages to be had either! Right away I said to Gertrude, 'Do you really have to have a carriage like that these days? Black women carry their babies around in shawls!' We still need a standing lamp to make our little sitting room complete. But the old man can go ahead and pay for that . . . Gertrude's already as big as a house. Six months! I'd like to know whether we'll be moved in when the time comes . . . Nah—no rugs—who needs rugs? Besides, how'd you get one except by heisting it? My other brother-in-law can take care of that, he's a painter. Likes to call himself an interior decorator. As I always say, 'If only the house is still standing!' They've had eight raids in one week!"

"Well, one more patrol and then off to the training course," someone says in a comforting tone. The bosun.

"We can paint the table white and make a little box around the gas meter."

"The men at the dock could make that for you. You could take a little box like that away without any trouble. After all, it's not the biggest thing in the world." That must be the navigator.

"If I were you I'd have them make the baby carriage at the same time—after all, they're equipped for that sort of thing," the bosun teases him.

"Thanks for the tip. If I need a bulletproof one, I'll remember it."

He's managed to have the last word, but he doesn't stop there. "All that fuss about hoarding provisions. Why not give everyone a couple of cans? Gertrude could make good use of them."

Next morning around nine o'clock we come on an expanse of wreckage. One of our boats must have scored a hit on a convoy. Our bow wave parts planks smeared black with oil. A rubber dinghy bobs up. There's a man in it. He looks as if he's sitting in a rocking chair, his feet dangling over the bulge of the side, almost touching the water. His forearms are raised as if trying to read a newspaper. I'm surprised how short they are. Then we draw nearer and I realize that both his hands are gone. The blackened stumps are stretched toward us. His face is a burned-out mask with two gleaming rows of teeth. For a moment, the illusion of a black stocking pulled over his head.

"Dead!" says the navigator. He could have saved his breath.

The dinghy and its corpse slide rapidly past, rocking violently in our stern wave. The "reader" seems to enjoy being cradled in this comfortable position.

No one ventures a word. Finally the navigator says, "But he was a *civilian* sailor. I just can't work out where he got the dinghy. They usually have rafts on freighters. The dinghy—that's very funny. Looked exactly like the Navy."

A technical observation at this juncture does us good. The Old Man is glad to pursue the subject. The two of them spend quite a while discussing whether or not steamers have been carrying naval personnel for some time. "Otherwise who would man the guns?"

There's no end to the flotsam. The sunken steamer has laid a broad swatch of wreckage in the water: black fuel oil, crates, splintered lifeboats, charred remains of rafts, life preservers, complete superstructures. In between, three or four drowned men hanging from their life jackets with their heads under water. And there are more: a whole field of floating corpses, most of them without life jackets, faces submerged, many mutilated.

The navigator took too long to spot the dead men among the wreckage. There's no time for us to alter our course.

The Old Man's voice goes cold and he orders higher speed. We shear through the scattered, torn remnants, bow throwing everything aside like a snowplow. The Old Man stares straight ahead. The navigator surveys his sector.

I see the starboard lookout swallow as a corpse slips past, draped head down over a white-striped timber.

Wonder how he got it.

"There's a life preserver!" says the Old Man, and his voice grates, suddenly rusty.

In quick succession he gives two or three orders for engines and rudder, and our boat swings slowly toward the red and white life preserver, which is only momentarily visible among the waves.

The Commander turns to the navigator and says, much too loudly, "I'll take it on the port side. Move—Number One!"

I keep my eyes fixed on the dancing life preserver. It quickly looms larger.

The bosun reports breathlessly on the bridge, then climbs down the iron steps on the tower. He's carrying a small grappling hook.

Although we've known all along what the Old Man has in mind, he says, "Just want to see what the scow was called."

The navigator's up as high as he can go, hanging far out so as to be able to keep the entire boat in view for maneuvering. "Port engine slow ahead! Starboard engine full speed ahead! Rudder hard aport!"

The helmsman in the tower acknowledges the orders. The life preserver disappears from time to time in the troughs of the waves. We have to keep a sharp lookout so as not to lose track of it.

The navigator has the port engine stopped and the starboard

run slow speed ahead. Once again I'm aware that all the boat's otherwise famous maneuverability doesn't amount to much in a high sea. Given its length, it's so narrow that the propellers are far too close together.

Now where's the life preserver? What's become of the damned thing? It ought to be almost dead on our port beam . . . thank god, there it is.

"Port fifteen points, steer one hundred degrees—both engines slow ahead!"

Slowly the boat homes in on the life preserver. The navigator brings the helm around and sets a direct course. Seems to be working right.

The bosun holds the grappling iron in one hand and the line coiled like a lasso in the other. Advancing cautiously, hanging onto the net guard for support, he moves over the slippery gratings toward the bow. The life preserver is already level with us. Damn: the letters seem to be on the other side. Or have they been washed off?

Slowly it comes within ten feet of the boat. Could hardly be better. The bosun takes aim and throws his iron. To one side! I groan aloud, as if I'd been the one to be hit. Before he's reeled the iron in again, the life preserver has already drifted far astern.

"Both engines stop!"

Damnation, what now? The boat still has a lot of headway. We can't just put on the brakes!

The bosun has run to the stern and now he makes a cast from the afterdeck, but this time he jerks on the line too soon. The iron splashes into the water two feet this side of the life preserver, and he looks up despairingly.

"Another approach, if you please," the Commander says frostily. The boat describes a great circle, while I concentrate on keeping the life preserver in range of my glasses.

This time the navigator goes so close that the bosun could have caught the thing with his hand if he'd stretched himself out on the upper deck. But he still relies on the grappling iron and this time makes a hit.

"*Gulf Stream!*" he shouts to the bridge.

In the Officers' Mess the Old Man says, "I hope our activities don't make difficulties for anyone."

The Chief looks up questioningly. So does the First Watch Officer.

But the Old Man takes his time. Finally he reveals haltingly what's going through his head. "Assuming our colleagues didn't find out the name of the ship they sank and then greatly overestimated it in their success report—and assuming they've reported a fifteen thousand tonner—now we report that we've found the wreckage of the steamer *Gulf Stream*—and it turns out that she's in the register at only ten thousand tons—"

The Commander pauses to see whether we're all with him and says, "Could be embarrassing, really embarrassing, don't you think?"

I examine the linoleum tabletop and silently wonder what we're gabbing about. Whether a commander can make a fool of himself or not? First a grisly paper chase and now these guessing games.

The Commander has leaned back. I look up to see him stroking his beard with the back of his right hand. At the same time there's a nervous twitch in his face. Of course—it's an act: he's playing hard-nosed to inoculate us with his own firmness. He feels it all very keenly. He overacts, entertains his audience with observations and conjectures—just to keep us free from haunting scenes of nightmare and horror.

But the dead seaman won't leave me alone. He blots out my visions of the devastation around him. He was the first dead foreign seaman I had seen. From a distance he looked as though he'd made himself comfortable and would go on happily paddling away, his head tilted slightly backward, the better to see the sky. The burned-off hands—other people must have lifted him into the dinghy. He couldn't have managed it without hands. A total mystery.

No survivors to be seen. They must have been picked up by a sweeper. In a convoy people who lose their ship still have a chance. But the others? Those on lone vessels?

The Commander is at the chart table again, calculating. Before long he orders both engines full speed ahead.

He gets to his feet, straightens up and squares his shoulders, shakes himself thoroughly, clears his throat for a good minute, and tests his voice before uttering a single word. "If we're not square on the course of the convoy I'll eat my hat. Probably missed a whole batch of radio reports while we were submerged, dammit. Let's hope the contact boat calls in again—or anyone else who has the scent now."

And then suddenly, "A depth charge is the most inaccurate weapon there is!"

The Chief stares at him. The Old Man nods with a trace of self-satisfaction. Everyone in the control room has heard. He's just got around to drawing the moral of the corvette attack: You don't score hits with depth charges. After all, we're the proof—the living proof —of that.

Bertold is repeatedly requested to report his position. We wait just as intently as the people in Kernével for his answer.

"Hm," says the Old Man and gnaws at a few hairs in his beard. Then again, "Hm."

vi STORM

Friday. Forty-second Day at Sea. The nor'wester is blowing harder. The navigator has an explanation. "Apparently we're south of a family of cyclones that's being drawn toward Europe by way of Greenland."

"Funny customs these Cyclops and their families have," I say.

"What do you mean—Cyclops?"

"The Cyclops is a one-eyed wind."

The navigator favors me with an openly suspicious glance. It's probably high time for me to stick my head out into the fresh air again.

The sea is now a dark blue-green. I try to define its shade. Arborvitae? No, rather bluer than arborvitae. Onyx? Yes, onyx is closer.

In the distance the sea appears almost black under a mass of low-hanging cloud. Scattered about the horizon a few single clouds, dark gray-blue and bloated. Halfway to the zenith and directly ahead of us hangs another that looks more solid. On either side, arranged in orderly rows, dirty wisps of gray—like large weaver's shuttles. And—directly above—wind-torn cirrus hardly distinguishable from their background; really not clouds at all but just carelessly slapped-on whitewash.

The only violent movement in the sky is in the east, where new clouds well up over the rim of the sea, growing visibly plumper until they finally free themselves from the horizon like balloons with sufficient gas to float up. I watch them take over the sky. From the dark, massed army close to the horizon in the west the first scouts set out, little groups of clouds that gradually feel their way forward to the zenith. Only when they have established an outpost does the whole black horde move up. It rises, slowly pushed sideways by the wind, but already there are new clouds underneath, thrusting their ragged edges above the horizon—forced upward out of some apparently inexhaustible reservoir. Rank upon rank of them.

Seaman Bockstiegel, nineteen, comes to Herrmann, who doubles as the medical orderly, with an itching inflammation of the armpits.

"Crabs! Down with your pants!" says Herrmann.

Then suddenly he explodes. "Are you completely nuts? There's a whole lousy army running around here. They'll finish off a mouthful like you in no time!"

The orderly reports to the First Watch Officer, who orders an inspection at 19.00 for those off-duty, and for the current watch an hour and a half later.

The Commander, who was asleep, finds out about it an hour later in the Officers' Mess. He's like a bull stopped in his tracks by the cape as he glowers up at the First Watch Officer. Then he strikes his forehead with the flat of his left hand, fighting to control his anger.

Word gets around in the bow compartment. "Knocks you sideways, doesn't it?"—"Nasty business."—"This on top of everything else."—"What a nerve!"

Now we seem to have ship's crablice as well as a ship's fly. We'll soon be a kind of Noah's ark for the lower orders of animal.

Five men on the off-duty watch are found to have crabs. Soon the sweetish smell of petroleum spreads through the boat. Extermination is in progress.

The wind comes roaring at us like compressed air through a narrow nozzle. Sometimes it ceases for a moment while the bellows are replenished, then suddenly it lets loose again with increased fury.

With each moment that passes the water surges to fiercer heights in the grip of the gusts. Streaks of foam flicker out in every direction like cracks appearing in dark glass. The waves look more and more sinister—a seething, swirling cauldron. Again and again the spray sweeps hissing over our bows and spurts up through the gratings. The wind sweeps through the showers, to send whiplash after whiplash of water smacking against the faces of the forward lookouts.

Humidity in the control room gets worse. Bit by bit, everything is coated with a film of damp. The ladder is wet and cold to the touch.

Without oilskins and sou'wester I can no longer remain on the bridge. Once below, the first thing I look at is the barograph. Its needle has described a descending staircase. It looks like the cross-section of a cascade. The bad-weather line is falling so steadily that it'll soon reach the bottom of the paper.

The barograph is a fascinating instrument. The weather seems to take up a pen and write its autobiography on a drum that slowly revolves on its vertical axis. This line, however, is broken at regular intervals by sharply rising peaks.

Since I can make no sense out of these spikes I ask the navigator what they mean.

"They're the record of our daily practice dives—the barograph reacts not only to variations in the pressure outside but also—naturally enough—to variations inside the boat. The spikes mean excess pressure."

The weather is obviously worrying the Commander. "Lows of this sort sometimes move at one to two hundred miles an hour, which means severe disturbances and oscillations between subtropical and polar air," he explains. "They create violent turbulence—the wind can go completely crazy."

"You're in for a treat," the Chief says tauntingly, grinning at me. The Old Man bends over the chart, the navigator peering over his shoulder.

"These North Atlantic storm fronts are no joke. There'll be cold air behind the retreating low. It'll probably bring squalls and, with any luck, better visibility. Of course we could go farther north, but then we'd get deeper into the eye of the squall. And dodging south is unfortunately out on tactical grounds. Well, Kriechbaum; only one thing to do—praise the Lord and go slap through the middle. Too bad we've got the sea dead on our port beam."

"It's going to be a real rodeo," says the navigator hollowly.

A few of the off-duty seamen are busy using light lines to lash down the provision chests. Otherwise there isn't much to do: none of the storm preparations you get on a surface vessel. The Old Man can be comfortable, his big hands resting idly on his thighs.

At lunch we have to put up the plate rails; even so, we spend our time trying to keep the soup from slopping over.

All at once the Chief says casually to the Second Engineer,

"What's with your eyelashes and eyebrows? You ought to show that to the doc."

After the two Watch Officers and the Second Engineer have departed, he says—just as casually—"Crablice."

"What—how's that again?" snaps the Old Man.

"What the Second Engineer's got in his eyebrows and the roots of his eyelashes."

"You're joking."

"Seriously. When they start breeding *there*, things have gone pretty far."

The Old Man inhales violently through his nose and stares at the Chief—disconcerted, forehead a washboard of wrinkles, mouth half open.

"With all due respect to the range of your knowledge, is that supposed to mean your successor is . . . ?"

"Tsch—perhaps one oughtn't to assume the worst straight off!"

There is a cynical grin on the Chief's face. The Commander shakes his head as if to test his vertebrae. Finally he says, "The Second Engineer has just gone up in my estimation. I'm curious to see what he'll do next."

Now it's the Chief's turn to gape in astonishment.

The boat gradually goes quiet. You can hear the humming of the ventilators. Only when the door to the bow compartment opens for a few instants do we hear snatches of song and the gabble of voices. I get up and make my way forward.

"Great ruckus in the cable locker," says the navigator with an approving nod as I pass through the Quarters. The bow compartment is even murkier than usual.

"What's going on here?"

"Jubilation and riot!" a chorus of voices shouts back at me. The men off-watch are squatting close together tailor-fashion on the floor plates. It looks like an impromptu version of the robber scene from *Carmen*, with amazingly tattered costumes improvised out of oil-smeared drill jackets and streaked sweaters that they've dug out of some rummage heap.

The boat suddenly heels sharply. Leather jackets and oilskins swing out from the wall. We have to hold fast to the bunk ropes. Sharp curses from the depths of the compartment. I peer into the darkness between the heads and the hammocks. Someone is dancing about naked.

"The bridge johnny! He's keeping his precious body fit," is the explanation I get from Little Benjamin. "Does it all the time. He's mad about himself."

Mournful singing comes from the forward bunks and one of the hammocks. Little Benjamin gets his harmonica out, ceremoniously empties it by tapping it in his palm, slides it back and forth a couple of times across his tightened lips, holding it in the hollow of his hand, and finally strikes up a melody to which he adds a light tremolo, with soft, quick taps of his free hand. Hagen hums in tune. One after another the seamen join in. Bockstiegel leads the chorus.

> She took the train to Hamburg
> Her mood was black as black.
> At Flensburg Junction out she got
> And lay upon the track.
> The engineer, he spied the girl
> And took the brake in hand.
> Alas, the train sped blithely on.
> A head rolls in the sand.

"Hell and damnation, it's ten to, already!" Fackler announces suddenly. "What a life. You no sooner sit down than you have to get up again. Shit!" Cursing, he leaves the group.

Schwalle gets up too, methodically tightening his belt, and disappears through the door, saying, "Off to work!"

"Give it my love!" Bockstiegel shouts after him.

The Chief is still sitting in the Officers' Mess. He looks at me expectantly and asks, "What does the glazier do when he's got no glass?"

My look of bewilderment does me no good. No mercy to be had.

"He drinks out of the bottle."

Wearily I ignore the joke.

From the control room the sound of water gushing through the hatch is like a cloudburst. Occasionally a gigantic fist rises and strikes the hull. The rumble is so loud it makes me jump. The Commander grins. "Just the sea elephants trying to rub their spawn off on the boat!"

More dull rumbling. The Chief gets up, braces himself carefully, lifts one of the floor plates, and motions me toward him. "There goes one of them now!"

I stick my head through the hole and in the light of a flashlight see a small car suspended from two rails. There's a man lying on it all twisted up.

"He's testing the acid concentration in the batteries."

"Nice job in this kind of sea!"

"You can say that again."

I reach for a book but soon discover that I'm much too weary and bruised to concentrate. The only thing now would be to tie one on—go on a real bender—put myself an entire world away from this wretched sense of suffocation and living death. Beck's beer —Pilsner Urquell, good Münchner Löwenbräu—Martell—Hennessy, the fine three-star stuff!

Suddenly I notice that the Chief is looking intently at me. He jeers. "Abstracted—that's the word. Our abstracted ship's poet!"

At this I whirl around, bare my teeth, and snarl like a wild animal. This pleases the Chief. He keeps on grinning for quite a while.

Saturday. I'm on morning watch with the navigator. The wind has whipped the groundswell into foaming crests and swift green valleys. High mat ridges, their sides dull like slabs of slate. Luckily we no longer have the sea abeam but directly head on. Who knows what circumstance we have to thank for this overnight change of course.

We might as well be standing still, as the mountains of water beat down on us in closed ranks, one after the other.

About halfway through the watch a wall appears directly ahead of us, looking like gray-black plaster. It reaches from the horizon right into the sky. Gradually it stirs into life. Arms grow out of it and slowly extend over half the visible heavens, until they extinguish the last pale radiance of the sun. The air becomes heavier and heavier with brute pressure. The hiss and roar of the waves sounds all the louder because there is a sudden lull in the howling of the wind.

And now the storm is upon us. It advances in a sudden assault, racing toward us out of the wall ahead, ripping away the greenish-white skin from the waves as it comes.

The air is a slab of unbroken mouse-gray. Only the occasional dark fleck betrays the fact that the whole sky is in wild flight.

From time to time, individual waves rise above the rest, but the storm challenges them instantly with searing blasts, and whips the high-tossed water backward.

The piping of the net guard cable grows steadily shriller.

The storm tries out all its possible voices, and at every possible strength: shrieking, yowling, groaning. Whenever the bow plunges downward and the net guard goes underwater, the whining ceases momentarily. But as soon as the bow springs clear of the mottled green whirlpool, it resounds again. The banner of water hanging from the net guard is ripped and torn to rags by the wind—in seconds it's gone.

I brace my back against the periscope housing and inch my way upward to look over the bulwark of the bridge at the whole length of the foreship. Screaming blasts of wind instantly strike my head. This is no longer air—no volatile element—but a solid, tangible mass that forces itself between my jaws whenever I open my mouth.

The storm! I want to roar aloud with delight. I screw up my eyes in concentration, taking mental snapshots of the action of the waves, instant home movies of the origin of the world.

The flying spray forces me into the protection of the bulwark. My eyelids are swollen. My seaboots full of water. Poorly designed: The water forces its way into them from the top. The gloves are no good either. They were completely soaked through, so I handed them down some time ago. The knuckles of my hands are dead white—washerwoman's hands.

We are enveloped in sheets of foam, and I don't dare straighten up for minutes at a time.

These metal bathtubs, open at the back, into which we duck like defensive boxers, don't deserve the name bridges. They have nothing in common with the bridges of ordinary ships, which extend across the whole superstructure and are properly glassed in, dry and warm: a sure protection from which one can look down on a stormy sea from a height of thirty, forty, fifty feet—as one might from the upper story of a house. Those bridges have rapidly rotating glass disks that retain not a drop of water.

Our bridge, on the contrary, is nothing more than a big shield, a sort of breastplate. The wind deflectors that are built in around the upper edge of the bulwark are intended to protect us by turning the horizontal force of the wind into an upward current, thus forming a kind of wall of air, but a storm of this strength nullifies any effectiveness they may have. And toward the stern, the bridge offers no protection whatever; our position is entirely exposed and the water floods in continuously.

I spend most of the watch standing in swirling water that rises around me like a tearing, sucking, raging river. Barely has one whirlpool rushed out astern through the watergates when the Second Watch Officer shouts, "Hold fast!" and the next surge hurls itself onto the bridge. I dodge around this boxing ring, chin pressed down against my chest. But the water has feints of its own. It strikes blows to the face from below, real driving uppercuts.

So I won't be swept off my feet, I wedge myself between the TBT post and the wall of the bridge. Brace yourself tight, breathe deep, make yourself heavy! You can't just rely on the safety belts, however sturdy and solid they may look.

Still dazed, I have barely raised my head to take a quick glance round the sector when the Second Watch Officers shouts, "Look out!" and another wave roars in. Head down again. Another crack across the back followed by a second blow from underneath. My hands cramp in a desperate hold until the knuckles stand out in ridges. I snatch a quick glance astern: Through the bars of the railing and past the mounting of the anti-aircraft gun the aftership is invisible—buried under a thick blanket of seething foam. The gas exhaust flaps have disappeared, smothered by the whirlpool, as have the air intake valves; the diesels must now be drawing their air from the inside of the boat.

Within seconds another wave crashes dully against the tower and shoots high in the air like a breaker meeting a cliff. Two tearing, blinding walls of spray converge over the aftership, collide, and shoot roaring upward. Then the water rushes whirling and gurgling over the aftership and the boat's hull forces its way up again through its smothering burden of foam to shake off every remaining rivulet of water. For a few moments the whole upper deck is free. Then the boiling waves strike again, punching the aftership down. Fight free and dodge away, duck down and up again, in a never-ending sequence.

I can no longer feel a thing as I climb down, soaked. Groaning, I peel off my rubber jacket. Beside me the bridge johnny is cursing. "Whoever designed *these* togs must have been a real asshole."

He continues to gripe as he peels the wet clothes from his body.

"Complain to Headquarters," Isenberg needles him. "The C-in-C's delighted to have suggesions from the fighting forces; you can bet your life on that."

"Fairly rough," is the Old Man's comment on the sea. He's sitting at the table leafing through his blue and green notebooks. I want to tell him that the adjective "rough," for me at least, may serve to describe sandpaper but not this waterbound insanity—but what's the point? The Old Man seems to have no stronger word to describe it.

He reads aloud in a grumble. "Unobserved by the enemy, the U-boat can infiltrate any area of the sea in which it wishes to be of military service. Thus it is the most suitable mine-layer for use in direct action against enemy coasts, the mouths of enemy harbors, and estuaries. Here, at the focus point of enemy commerce, the U-boat's limited load factor is also less of a disadvantage. Likewise, this limited number of mines offers optimal chances of success."

He looks up, staring me straight in the face. "Wishes to be of service—mines offer optimal chances! Well, that's style for you, eh?"

Soon he finds another passage that provokes him to read aloud. "The U-boat man loves his fighting unit. It proved its daring spirit in the First World War, and to this day the U-boat Command preserves this same determination and daring to the best of its ability."

"Pretty, isn't it?"

"I'll say!" says the Old Man and snorts. "The C-in-C's very own work."

A bit later he shakes his head and reads something aloud from a newspaper. "Helios surprise tip to win the Cup." He closes his eyes for a moment, then mutters, "And people think they've got troubles."

How far away it all seems!

I realize that we hardly ever think of the mainland. Rarely does anyone talk about home. Sometimes I feel we've been on patrol for years. If it weren't for the radio news, we could imagine we were voyaging the globe as the last specimens of *Homo sapiens* in existence.

I play with the notion that High Command might forget us altogether. What would happen then? How far could we get, using all our reserves? Under our feet of course we have the ship that's known to have the maximum operating range. But what about provisions? Our twilight world could certainly function as a mush-room farm. The climate here on board is ideal—the mold on our bread is proof of that. Or watercress. You're supposed to be able to grow watercress under electric lights. The bosun could certainly find a place for it, just under the ceiling in the gangway, for example. Watercress gardens overhead, suspended on gimbals.

Finally, we could catch algae. Algae have a high vitamin C content. Perhaps there's even a species that would flourish in the bilge, using the grease as a kind of fertilizer.

Sunday. "There ought to be crisp fresh rolls on the table," the Chief says at breakfast time. "Smothered in salted butter, melting a little because the rolls are still warm inside—straight from the baker! And a cup of hot cocoa, not sweet—the bitter kind—but hot. That would hit the spot."

The Chief raises his eyes ecstatically and dramatically fans the imaginary fragrance toward his nose.

"You'd make it in burlesque," says the Old Man. "Now show us a breakfast of powdered scrambled eggs, compliments of the Navy."

On cue, the Chief gags and gulps, making his Adam's apple bob violently up and down; his eyes are bulging, fixed rigidly on a spot before him on the table.

The Old Man is satisfied. But the First Watch Officer, whose expressionless demonstrations of zeal extend even to mealtimes, where he methodically consumes every last scrap of the rations assigned to him, finds this more than he can bear. He casts a pained expression around the table.

"Clear away!" the Commander shouts into the control room, and the steward appears with his smelly rag. The First Watch Officer turns up his nose in disgust.

After breakfast I take myself off again to the petty officers' quarters. I want to catch up on a little sleep. "We're still going to get knocked around a bit" is the last thing I hear from the Old Man in the control room.

However hard I try, whatever new position I experiment with, I cannot wedge my body into the bunk so as not to be rolled and tossed around. I could get used to the rolling if only it had some rhythm to it. But the hard jolts when the bow falls or a heavy wave strikes the foreship drive me to desperation. And there are sinister new sounds. Roaring blows against the tower that carry an unfamiliar accompaniment, a ceaseless rasping, whirring, scraping, scratching, and—whole octaves higher—a threatening, rhythmless drumming, plus a nerve-destroying series of yowlings, screeches, and whistles. Not a minute passes without a violent shuddering running the length of the pressure hull or noises piercing you to the very bone. Against this unending misery, and the orgy of sound, the only defense is dull resignation.

The hell of it is that the din doesn't stop at night; as the boat falls quiet, the uproar of the waves seems to increase. At times it sounds as if waterfalls were plummeting into the molten contents of a blast furnace. I lie awake and try to differentiate the sounds that make up the clamor outside: in addition to the rasping and hissing there is lapping, smacking, and chiseling. Then the mighty crashing blows begin again, making the boat resound continuously like a giant drum. *Davy Jones!* I think—muffled drum and drunken gong.

The storm must be sweeping along now at a good sixty-five miles an hour.

As the bow makes its crashing curtsy, the compartment drops forward, slanting, steeper and steeper. Our clothes stand out from the wall at forty-five degrees. My curtain shoots open of itself, my legs rise helplessly into the air. My head is thrust down—and the room goes around in a circle as the boat tries to free itself sideways. It doesn't want to stand on its head. From astern our propellers sound as if they've spun themselves into a cocoon of cotton wool. The boat shivers feverishly, some iron part rattles violently against some other one: a rolling of drums.

Frenssen favors me with a bored look, then rolls his eyes. "Bumpy, isn't it?"

"Yes, you might say so."

Finally the propellers race free again. The compartment returns to horizontal. Our clothes resume the vertical against the walls. And then I shut my curtain. Why bother? the boat's on its way into the next wave already.

Monday. I haven't been on the bridge for some while. It's time for me to clamber up again and air myself out. But what's the point? Face lashed by the waves, blows from a cat-o'-nine-tails, body soaked to the skin, limbs frozen stiff, aching bones, smarting eyes.

These are, after all, valid objections. Why not stay put? It's still the best place, here in the Officers' Mess—dry.

A book has fallen from the table. I must have noticed it fall, but it's only after it lands on the floor that I *see* it for the first time. There must be a delay between actual vision and perception. Our nerves are overstretched like used elastic. I feel a definite urge to pick the thing up: it can't just lie there! But I ignore this inner voice. I shut my ears, let the last ounce of initiative seep away. After all, the book's not doing anyone any harm down there.

The Chief comes in from his engines, sees the book, bends down and picks it up. So that's that!

He braces himself in his bunk with his knees drawn up and gets a newspaper out from under his bolster, all without saying a word. He just sits there sullenly, smelling of oil.

After a quarter of an hour the ensign appears and asks for new cartridges for the recognition signal. The Chief's reactions are slipping too: he doesn't hear the ensign, who has to repeat his request in a louder voice. Finally the Chief looks up angrily. Observing him sideways I can see his mind slowly trying to tick over. He's struggling to make a decision. The recognition cartridges are, of course, a serious matter. And they're in the locker behind his back. Heaven knows whether we'll ever use them, but their daily change is part of the sacrosanct routine.

Finally he gets up and opens the locker with an expression of the most extreme repugnance. You'd think someone was holding shit under his nose. His newspaper slips down off the bunk and lands in a puddle no doubt left over from the last meal. He suppresses a curse and crouches back in his corner. This time he draws his knees up even higher. He seems to be trying to take cover.

Crouching burial, I think; the Chief is re-enacting a crouching burial. I want to communicate my idea, but I'm too lazy even to speak.

Barely five minutes pass and the ensign is back again. Perfectly clear: the old cartridges have to be locked away. There can be no careless handling of recognition cartridges: they can't be left lying around. I expect the Chief to explode like a bomb. But he doesn't utter a word. He even gets up with a certain alacrity, shoots a disgusted look at me, clamps his newspaper under his arm, and disappears aft. Two hours later I find him in the E-motor room. He's sitting in the general reek of fumes, on an up-ended chest of prunes, with his back against the stern torpedo tube, still perusing his newspaper.

After the evening meal my inner voice reminds me that I haven't been on the bridge all day. I silence it by arguing that it's almost dark up there by now.

I do need a change, however, so I go off to the bow compartment, where I'm hit by a solid stench of bilge, remnants of food, sweat-drenched clothes, and rotting lemons. Two weak lightbulbs give the place the dim glow of a whorehouse.

I can make out Schwalle holding a big aluminum pot between his knees. There's a dipper sticking out of it. Around him is a confusion of bread and sausage and pickles and open sardine cans, and overhead two low-sagging hammocks weighted down by the bodies of the sleeping off-watch men. The upper berths to left and right are also occupied.

The motion of the boat is worst here in the bow. Every few minutes the compartment begins to roll and sway violently and each time Schwalle has to seize the pot so it won't spill over.

Dunlop the torpedo man comes out of the depths of the compartment on all fours with two lamps, one red and one green, in his hand; he wants to substitute them for the white ones. It takes him a while to accomplish this, but he's in ecstasies over the result. Bengal festival lights! His very own handiwork!

"Sexy," says a complimentary voice from one of the hammocks.

I hear the Gigolo talking to Little Benjamin. "Perfectly clean, isn't it? How long would you guess I've been wearing this shirt?"

"Certainly since we left port."

"Wrong!" There's triumph in his voice. "Two weeks before that!"

Along with Schwalle, Ario, and the torpedo man Dunlop, Gigolo Bachmann, Dufte, Fackler, and Little Benjamin (he of the Menjou mustache) are all sitting on the floor.

The Commander has had the watches shortened. This means that people are now being thrown together who never used to see one another during their off-duty hours.

The boat gives an unexpectedly violent jolt. The aluminum kettle slips out from between Schwalle's legs and splashes soup all over the bread. The boat heels and begins to corkscrew madly. Next to the door a waste bucket tips over, spilling its contents of moldy breadcrusts and squeezed lemon rinds all over the floor. The bilge water gurgles. The bow falls with a crash and the whole room shivers. The bilge water shoots forward roaring.

"Dammit to hell!" Schwalle shouts.

"A pain in the ass—damn, shit, fuck!" Little Benjamin rolls cursing across the floor, pulls himself up to a sitting position, and hooks one arm around a bar of the bunk to keep himself upright, cross-legged like a Buddha.

"Don't take up so much room," Ario snaps at him.

"Just give me a minute and I'll breathe myself flat!"

Ario avoids being knocked about too by pushing his left arm around the taut lifeline that runs along a lower bunk, then he collects the heavy loaves of bread that are covered with green mold and uses a big knife to cut off massive pieces. The unspoiled parts are now no larger than plums. His biceps bulge from the effort.

The boat heels again. But Ario's hooked arm hangs on.

"Like a monkey on a stick!" Schwalle teases him.

"You think it's funny?"

"Take it easy now—I've got first-class references from people who've been punched in the face by me. All of them were completely satisfied."

New clattering and scraping. Forward between the bases of the torpedo tubes a bucket is banging back and forth. No one gets up to make it fast again. A towel hanging from one of the starboard bunks slowly unfurls and remains for some time extended diagonally into the room as if heavily starched.

Ario gives it his full attention. "Fifty degrees at a guess."

The towel slowly sinks back into a reasonable position, then is plastered against the railing: the boat has heeled to starboard.

"Shit, fucking shit," groans the torpedo man, who has wedged a pail between the rails and is trying to wash up. His cloth fills the whole room with a sour stench. The dirty water that was a quiet puddle a few minutes before is creeping over the floor plates to where the men are sitting. Ario is starting to get to his feet when the water stops as though hypnotized and slowly recedes.

Ario wipes the sweat from his forehead with the back of his hand, clumsily stands up, leans crosswise on a bunk, still careful to keep firm hold of the bunk support, and peels off his jacket. Black hair sticks out like stuffing from a torn mattress through the holes in his shirt. His whole body is dripping with sweat. Snorting, he sits down and tells everyone that to hell with the weather, he's going to fill his belly so tight we'll be able to squash fleas on it with our thumbnails. We see at once that he really means it. Using a not completely moldy remnant of bread as a base, he carefully heaps it with butter, sausage, cheese, and sardines.

"The perfect tower of Babel!" is the tribute from the Gigolo. Ario knows his reputation is at stake and placidly smears a thick layer of mustard on top. Sounds of noisy enjoyment. The hard dry bread gives his jaw muscles a thorough workout.

"It's still better than some junk out of a can," he growls.

He finally washes the thick mush down with reddish-yellow tea. Grease shines at the corners of every mouth: cannibals seated around their pot. Everyone's legs are interlaced like those in a full railway car. Now and again a belch from Ario indicates his satisfaction. A bottle of apple juice goes the rounds.

The door bangs open.

"Jesus! Look at this room!" the bridge johnny complains indignantly, shaking water from his face and hands.

He's answered with a roar of laughter.

"Say that again!" Fackler jeers.

"The room! Look at this room!" The Gigolo imitates the bridge johnny and goes on to ask him, "Perhaps something's not quite satisfactory?" The Gigolo can't contain himself. "Man oh man, what an expression! 'This room'—almost as good as 'Get the bullets up out of the cellar.' "

"What's all this about getting bullets out of the cellar?"

"That's the order some imbecile of a watch officer gave during the last artillery practice. Hadn't you heard? 'Get the bullets up out of the cellar,' he said, instead of, 'Pass the shells up from the hold'!"

A grin spreads across the bridge johnny's face. He's so plump that he looks more like the boat's cook than a seaman. His face is in constant motion. A small black beard is its only fixed feature. He must be good-natured, for he doesn't mind the kidding; he searches quietly for a place in the circle and wriggles his way forcibly into an opening.

"Don't take up so much room!" Fackler snaps at him.

But the bridge johnny only smiles at him in a friendly way and doesn't budge an inch. Fackler becomes incensed. "You're a real pile of blubber!"

At this the Gigolo takes the bridge johnny's part and addresses him in pastoral tones. "Now now, don't let the nasty boys upset you."

There's peace for a while. The rattling of the bucket forward between the torpedo tubes and the noise of eating echo all the louder.

Dunlop the torpedo man steps into the red light of the lamp and busies himself at his locker. A mass of bottles comes to light. Whatever he's searching for must be at the very back.

"What d'you want?" Fackler finally asks from his bunk.

"My face cream."

As though this were their long-awaited cue, the whole crowd lets go at once. "Look at that gorgeous little bathing beauty!"— "He'll soon be rubbing ointments into his lovely alabaster body!"— "Please, please, you're making me horny!"

The torpedo man turns on them in a rage. "You bastards, you don't even know there's such a thing as hygiene."

"Come on, don't get so excited!"—"You're a real advertisement for shipboard hygiene! No doubt you've had a good shit today!" "Just look at him! Screaming about hygiene while his cock stinks like Gorgonzola!"—"It would have to be you that talks about hygiene. That's what I like: filthy as a wild ass and you spread that mess on top. Some hygiene!"

Hacker, the senior man in the bow compartment roars, "Jesus Fucking Christ, is there going to be peace here or not?"

"Not," says Ario, but so low that the torpedo mechanic can't hear him in his bunk.

Tuesday. The sea's running even higher. The boat pancakes so suddenly that a violent shudder runs through every rivet—and lasts for half a minute. The foreship's been rammed so deep into a wave that it seems unable to free itself. The boat rolls from right to left; I can feel it struggling to break out sideways. Finally the bow lifts, the screws pick up speed, and we feel like a boxer breaking out of a clinch.

I try to keep my breakfast down and even to do some writing. But the compartment drops so fast that my stomach heaves. We hold on with all our strength because experience teaches that each downward swoop ends with a sudden jolt. But this time it goes off smoothly. The screws are driving powerfully again.

The midday meal consists of sausage and bread. Hot food has been struck from the menu. There's only cold chow out of cans because the cook can't keep his pots on the stove. It's a marvel that he even succeeds in supplying us with hot tea and coffee.

When the meal is over, the Commander wrestles his way to the bridge, after putting on a thick sweater under his oilskins. Instead of a sou'wester he's wearing a waterproof rubber hood that sits tight on his head, leaving only his eyes, nose, and mouth uncovered.

In less than five minutes he's back, dripping wet and sputtering barely articulate curses. Sullenly he works his way out of the gleaming wet rubber clothing and drags the sweater over his head; he shows me a big dark patch that has formed on his shirt during the short time he was up there. He plumps himself down on the chart chest, and a control-room mate pulls the boots from his legs. Water pours out of them and gurgles into the bilge.

While he's wringing out his sodden socks like a mop, there's a gush of water splatters down from above and hisses back and forth a few times on the floor before it too finds its exit in the bilge.

"Start the pumps!" he orders, hops barefoot over the wet floor plates, climbs through the circular door, and hangs up his wet clothes to dry over the gleaming red heater in the sound room.

He communicates his observations to the navigator, who's pushing his way past him. "Wind veering to port. So far, all according to program."

So our storm is behaving correctly, conforming entirely to expectations.

"Are we to hold course?" the navigator asks.

"Yes, we've got to! As long as we can—and so far we seem to have managed it."

As though to contradict him, a sharp heeling of the boat sends the accordion case shooting out of the sound room. The big box smashes against the opposite wall of the gangway.

"Here's hoping it was empty." The box hurls itself against the opposite wall, breaks open, and disgorges the instrument. The Chief thrusts his head into the gangway, examines the wreckage, half curious, half concerned, and announces, "That's not going to do it any good."

The control-room mate comes crawling rather than running and gathers up the fragments of the case together with the accordion.

The Commander totters his way through to the Officers' Mess and settles himself firmly in his corner at the narrow end of the table. He twists this way and that, shuts his eyes for seconds at a time as though having to remember how he used to arrange his body, and tries out various positions until he finds enough support not to be lifted out of his seat by the next roll of the boat.

All three of us keep our heads bent over our books. After a while he looks up. "Just read this! It's a perfect description!"

I find the paragraph he's pointing to.

"The caprice of the winds, like the willfulness of men, is fraught with the disastrous consequences of self-indulgence. Long anger, the sense of uncontrolled power, spoils the frank and generous nature of the West Wind. It is as if his heart were corrupted by a malevolent and brooding rancor. He devastates his own kingdom in the wantonness of his force. Southwest is the quarter of the heavens where he presents his darkened brow. He breathes his rage in terrific squalls and overwhelms his realm with an inexhaustible welter of clouds. He strews the seeds of anxiety upon the decks of scudding ships, makes the foam-striped ocean look old, and sprinkles with grey hairs the heads of ship-masters in the homeward-bound ships running for the Channel. The Westerly Wind asserting his sway from the south-west is often like a monarch gone mad, driving forth with wild imprecations the most faithful of his courtiers to shipwreck, disaster, and death."

I turn to the title page: Joseph Conrad. *The Mirror of the Sea.*

Wednesday. "One good thing about this filthy weather," says the Old Man. "At least we don't have enemy flyers on our necks."

Hardly any sleep during the night. My bunk tries to toss me out in spite of the railing—or roll me up the plywood wall. Twice I climb out because I can't stand it up there any longer. Now I feel as if I hadn't slept for a week.

The storm shows not the slightest sign of letting up. The day passes in exhausted dozing. The whole crew is letting itself sink further and further into apathy.

Thursday. The Commander himself reads the final words of the entry that he has written in the war log. "Wind south-southwest, 9 to 10. Sea 9. Hazy. Barometer 711.5. Heavy squalls."

"Hazy"—his usual understatement. Steam bath would be more

like it. Overhead it looks as if water and air have united, leaving the
world only three elements instead of four. The storm has grown still
wilder—exactly as the Old Man prophesied.

I get my oilskins down from the hook, wrap a hand towel around
my neck as usual, and fetch my rubber boots from the sound room,
where they've been standing near the heater to dry. I intend to
stand watch with the navigator. Just as I have one boot halfway
on, the floor goes out from under me. I roll in the middle of the gangway like a beetle on its back. As soon as I find my feet, another lurch
knocks me over again. I finally manage to hoist myself up on the
water distributors.

The boots are wet inside. My extended foot will not go into the
shank. It never works very well standing up, so I try it sitting down.
That's better. Should have done it the first time. The next roll
pushes the Commander's green curtain all the way open. He's
composing the war log again, chewing on his pencil. The sentence he's
written probably contains one word too many. The Old Man always
acts as if he's concocting an overseas telegram and each word costs
a fortune.

Now the oilskin breeches over the boots. They're wet inside too.
Oilskins—another one of those antiquated expressions; in fact they're
made of rubberized cloth. I suffer some minor dislocations getting
the trousers as far as my knees. Okay, up off your rear end and on to
your feet! The damn pants continue to fight me. I'm in a sweat before
I finally drag them up over my leather clothes.

And now the oilskin jacket. It's tight under the arms because
I have on two sweaters. They say it's very cold topside. After all, it's
November and we're pretty far north. I really ought to get my bearings again from the chart. We must be plowing around in the
sixties. Probably not far from Iceland. Actually, we were originally
supposed to be heading for the latitude of Lisbon.

Now the sou'wester. Inside, it's sopping wet. The cold on my
scalp makes me shudder. The straps have been left tied, and the
damp has swollen the knots so much that they can't be undone.

The Commander stops composing his telegraphese, gets up,
stretches, sees me struggling with the straps, and needles me. "Hard
life at sea, isn't it?"

Everything that was hanging is now standing straight out from
the walls. A pair of seaboots slides from one side of the compartment to the other. I climb elegantly through the hatch, only to be
caught in the control room by the reverse roll. I grab for the low
railing on the chart table and miss, lose my balance completely,
and sit down hard on the flooding and pumping distributor. The

Old Man's intoning his damnfool refrain: "Take care, my pretty pet, you'll lose your balance yet!" Must have been a hit before my time.

The room tips to port. I'm sent flying against the rounded housing of the gyrocompass but manage to grab onto the ladder. The Old Man swears he once saw a Cuban rumba that was absolutely amateurish compared to my performance. Derisively he acknowledges my balletic gifts . . . and my obvious predilection for national and native dances.

You have to admit that he's never caught off balance. He'll start to stagger, and quick as a flash he'll be looking for a suitable landing place. Taking advantage of the impetus he's given by the rolling of the boat, he steers himself so as to end up in a dignified sitting position. Then he usually looks around calmly, as though the one thing he'd had in mind was to rest his backside on the chart chest.

The Second Watch Officer comes down dripping. A great shower shoots in behind him. "A hogfish leaped straight over our cannon— right over it! We had one of those steep waves at an angle to port, and the hogfish jumped out of it as if it was a wall, straight over the cannon! Could hardly believe it!"

I sling the broad safety belt with its heavy snap hook around me and climb up after him. It's dark in the tower, except for the pale gleam of the helmsman's instrument dials. Above us there's a gurgling sound on the bridge. I wait a few seconds until it lets up, then force the heavy hatch cover up as fast as I can, climb out, and slam the cover down again. Success! But instantly I have to duck behind the bridge bulwark along with the rest of them to avoid the next hissing wave. The waterfall crashes on my back, and eddies tug at my legs. Before they can pull me off my feet, I attach the snap of my safety belt to the TBT post and jam myself between the periscope housing and the bridge partition.

Now I can venture my first glance over the bulwark. My god, that's no ocean out there! What meets my eyes is a quivering gray-white snow landscape; with the wind stripping a blizzard of foam from its hills. Dark fissures run through the white: black bands that heave this way and that, constantly creating new shapes and patterns. No vault of sky, just a flat gray plate that's almost resting on the gray-white wasteland.

The air is a fog of flying salt water—an overpowering fog that reddens the eyes, stiffens the hands, and quickly sucks all warmth out of the body.

The rounded form of our saddle tank rolls lazily out of a foaming eddy. The wave that bore us up begins to sink, the boat heels farther and farther to port and remains there for seconds at a time at an extreme angle, dropping deeper and deeper.

One white-fluted wave after another moves indolently toward the boat. Now and again there's one that towers over the rest with a mighty crest of foam. Immediately in front of the boat the wall of water begins to curve, slowly at first, then faster and faster, until it breaks on the foreship with a crash like a monstrous hammer.

"Stand by, danger ahead!" roars the navigator. A geyser foams up the side of the tower—and breaks over us. A blow on the shoulders, then water that whirls up from below to rise as high as your belly. The bridge quivers and quakes. The boat is racked by a violent shudder. Finally the foreship emerges. The navigator shouts, "Look out—one of those—tear you right out of the bridge!"

For a couple of seconds the boat is racing through a valley. Mountainous white waves cut off the view. Then we are lifted once more, gliding up a gigantic slope. Our circle of vision widens as the boat rises higher and higher, until it reaches the foaming crest of the wave, and we look out over the stormy sea as if from a watch-tower; it's no longer the old dark-green Atlantic out there but the ocean of some planet that's still being torn by the pangs of creation.

The duty period for those on bridge watch has been cut in half. More would be unendurable. Two hours of ducking down, staring, and ducking down again, and you're finished. I'm glad I can still move sufficiently, when my time is up, to get myself below.

I'm so exhausted that I'd be glad to let myself drop onto the floor plates, wet clothes and all. I'm only vaguely, foggily aware of what I'm doing.

My eyelids are inflamed. I feel it every time I close them. Best thing to do is shut your eyes, let yourself go, stretch out. Right here in the control room. But I'm still conscious enough to make my way aft. As I lift my right leg to climb through the hatch I almost scream with pain.

Undressing is only possible given long pauses to get my breath. Again and again I have to clench my teeth to keep from groaning aloud. And now the worst, the gymnastics of hoisting myself into my bunk. No ladder like those in sleeping cars. That final push with the toes of the left foot, like mounting a horse. My eyes are wet when I finally lie down.

A whole week of storm! How long is this going to last? Incredible that our bodies adjust to these torments. No rheumatism, no sciatica,

no lumbago, no scurvy, no diarrhea, no colic, no gastritis, no serious
inflammations. Apparently we are as sound as a bell, as resistant as
our racing diesels.

Friday. Another day of depressed dozing and laborious attempts
to read. I'm lying in my bunk. I can hear the sharp splash of water
landing in the control room. The tower hatch must be closed but
not made fast, so when the cockpit is flooded a gush of water always
pours through.

The navigator appears from forward and announces that a new
man in his watch has been hit hard. "He's sitting on the floor plates
vomiting nonstop. . . ."

To our amazement he accompanies this with vivid pantomime.
We also learn from him that one of the stokers has come up with an
invention that's catching on fast: he's hung a tin can around his
neck like a gas mask. Three men are already following his example
and running around with "vomit cans," he tells me without a trace
of malice.

I can't stay in the same position for more than five minutes at a
time. I use my left hand to hold on to one of the bars of the bunk
railing and twist my body so that I can brace myself against the wall.
But the cold of the iron soon penetrates the thin wood and even
the bunk railing sends icy chills into my hand.

The hatch to the galley opens. I feel the pressure on my ears and
every sound goes flat. The diesel intake doors have gone underwater
in the heavy sea, so the diesels can no longer draw their air through
the outboard pipes. Low pressure—high pressure. Eardrums in, eardrums out—and you're supposed to be able to sleep. I turn on my
stomach and push my left arm over the edge of the bunk for added
support. Before long a stoker coming off duty lurches in and bangs
my arm with the full weight of his body.

"Ouch!"

"What's that?—Oh! Sorry."

The bunk, which at first sight had seemed too narrow, is now
much too wide. However many different positions I try, I can't find
any firm hold. Finally I remain on my stomach, legs spread wide
like a wrestler trying not to be turned over on his back. Sleep
is out of the question.

Hours later I hit on the idea of jamming my bolster between my
body and the bunk railing. Broadside it won't fit but with the narrow end it works. I now lie firmly wedged between the wooden
wall and the bunk railing.

I see myself as an illustration in my anatomy textbook, printed in red, in an affected pose, with numbers showing the various muscle groups. The practical advantage of my anatomy course is that now at least I can name each muscle that's hurting me. Ordinarily I carry these fibrous bundles of flesh around on my bones, conscious at most of satisfaction at the way they contract and relax—a self-sufficient, practical system intelligently arranged and operating flawlessly. But now the system will no longer function; it rebels, makes trouble, sends warning signals: a stitch here, a tearing pain there. For the first time in my life I become aware of the component parts of this apparatus of mine: the platysma that I need to move my head; the psoas muscle for moving the bones in my hip. I have the least trouble with my biceps—they're in training. But my pectoral muscles are a real problem. I must have been lying all cramped up—otherwise why should they hurt like this?

Saturday. A note in my blue exercise book: "Senseless—joyriding around in mid-Atlantic. No sign of the enemy. Feels as if we're the only ship in existence. Stench of bilge and vomit. The Commander finds the weather perfectly normal. Talks like a veteran of Cape Horn."

Sunday. The daily test dives, usually a bore, have become a blessing. We long for every minute of relaxation they bring. To be able to stretch, go limp, breathe deeply and freely for a while instead of ducking and grasping for handholds; to stand safely, upright and relaxed.

With the command "Stand by to dive!" the ritual begins. "Stand by to blow tanks!" is next. The Chief has stationed himself behind the two hydroplane operators. The control-room mates at the compressed-air controls report, "One!"—"Three, both sides!"—"Five!"

The Chief shouts up to the tower, "Ready to blow!"

"Flood!" comes the voice of the Second Watch Officer from above.

"Flood!" the Chief repeats. The control-room mates open the valves.

"Forward hard down—aft neutral!" The Chief. At "neutral" he has to raise his voice to be heard over the roar of the water rushing into the diving cells. At fifty feet he has the trim cells emptied. Instead of the crashing of the waves we hear the hiss of compressed air and then at once the roar of water being forced out of the trim cells.

At a hundred feet the hand of the depth manometer stops. The boat is almost on an even keel but is still rocking so violently that a pencil on the chart table rolls back and forth.

The Chief has the blowing of the diving cells stopped and the Commander orders, "Take her down and level off at a hundred forty feet." But even at that depth the boat is still not at rest. The Old Man takes up his customary position with his back against the periscope housing. "Take her to a hundred seventy!" And after a while, "So, peace at last!"

Thank god! The torture has stopped, this time for at least an hour, as I learn from the Old Man's directions to the Chief.

My head is still full of roaring and crashing, as if I were holding big seashells to my ears. Quiet only gradually reasserts itself in my echoing skull.

Now, not a single minute to waste! Quick, up on the bunk. Jesus God, these pains! I go heavy all over—my stiffly outstretched arms laid parallel to my body with my hands palm down on the mattress. With my chin drawn in I can see my ribcage rising and falling. Although I haven't yet been on the bridge today, my eyes are burning. After all, they're not fish eyes, designed to peer through salt water. I suck my lips between my teeth and taste the salt. I lick around my mouth and taste more salt. Very likely my whole body is covered with it. Sea water has managed to creep in everywhere. I'm as salty as a well-cured ham or *Kasseler Rippchen*. *Kasseler Rippchen*—with sauerkraut, bay leaves, peppercorns, and lots of garlic. With goose fat, even better, and with a glass of champagne, a feast. Funny thing: the moment the stomach-churning and jouncing stops, my appetite comes back. How long has it been, in point of fact, since I last ate?

It's beautiful in my bunk. I've never known how magnificent it can be just to be here. I make myself as flat as a board and feel the mattress with every square inch of my back, the back of my head, the inside of my arms, the palms of my hands. I curl the toes of my right foot and then the left, stretch out first one leg, then the other. I'm growing, getting longer all the time. In the loudspeaker there's a sound like sizzling fat, then a gurgle, and, finally, a record the Old Man brought aboard:

> *Sous ma porte cochère*
> *chante un accordéon,*
> *musique familière*
> *des anciennes chansons.*

Et j'oublie la misère
quand vient l'accordéon
sous la porte cochère
de ma vieille maison . . .

I bet *this* record wasn't a present from his donna, the lady of the green ink. Where it came from I can only guess. The Old Man? —Still waters run deep.

Here comes Isenberg to report that lunch is served.

"So early?"

I learn that the Old Man has advanced the midday meal by an hour so that the men can eat in peace.

At once I begin to worry about the other end of this process. Eating in peace is all very well—but how are we going to get rid of what we've digested? I shudder at the thought of the head.

My hesitation is certainly not shared by the Old Man. He consumes gigantic slices of head cheese spread with thick layers of mustard, with pickles, sliced onions, and canned bread on the side. The First Watch Officer painstakingly excises a piece of rind that has a couple of white bristles in it from his head cheese and pushes it disgustedly to the edge of his plate.

"Whiskery bastard, isn't it!" says the Old Man, and then, chewing vigorously, "What we need is beer—and fried potatoes."

But instead of the longed-for beer the steward brings tea. The Second Watch Officer gets ready to clamp the pot between his thighs as usual, then realizes that this is no longer necessary and strikes his forehead theatrically with the palm of his left hand.

The Old Man extends the time underwater by another twenty minutes "because it's Sunday!"

The men in the petty officers' quarters make use of the underwater interlude in their usual fashion. Frenssen reports that there was a bombing attack on the train during his last leave, so he only got as far as Strasbourg, where he promptly found the cathouse.

"She said she had a specialty. Wouldn't tell me what. I went along. She gets undressed, lies down. I think, let's see what the surprise is, and I'm about to hump her, when she says, 'You want a fuck, sweetheart? My god, how primitive.' And suddenly she takes her eye out, a glass eye, naturally, and leaves a kind of red role. 'Go ahead, now you can really eye me!'"

"You goddam pig!"—"Tell that to your grandmother!"—"Of all the filthy buggers!"—"You make me puke!"—"They ought to cut your prick off!"

But when the cursing has subsided the diesel mechanic mate says equably, "Still it's a first-rate idea, isn't it?"

I feel nausea rising in my throat. I stare at the ceiling and see a pale blurred face and a dark red hole in the plywood background. Was that true? I wonder. Do these things happen? Can anyone actually invent such monstrosities? Isn't Frenssen simply putting on an act?

I'm still in my bunk when we surface. My whole body is aware of how the boat begins to move—gently at first. Then I feel like a driver going around a curve in winter when his rear wheels start to skid. Soon the whole compartment starts to reel. I hear the first waves batting at us like huge paws. We're on the surface, and the St. Vitus dance begins again.

Noises from the control room. The man in there is cursing out loud because water keeps pouring down on him. I duck through the hatch. When he sees me he begins again, "Goddam mess! Soon there won't be a safe place left."

Monday. The orderly has work to do. Several men have been injured. Bruises, a smashed finger, a nail turned violet, blood blisters—nothing serious. One man was flung out of his bunk, another in the control room was hurled against the ventilator. A seaman had his head banged against the sonar. It's a puncture wound and looks nasty.

"What a mess! I hope he can cope because otherwise *I'll* have to take a hand," says the Old Man.

I get ready for the Second Watch Officer's watch at 16.00. One of the lookouts is sick. I'm to take his place.

Before I can so much as lift the hatch cover I'm soaking wet. I wedge myself between the periscope housing and the bridge bulwark as quickly as I can, and snap on the hook of my safety belt. Only then do I attempt to force my body upright so that I can look out over the bulwark.

Another sight to take my breath away. Chaos! The waves override their own ranks, falling on one another's backs as though to tear them apart.

The boat is poised on the tip of a gigantic wave: a piggyback ride on a leviathan. For seconds I can look out over the age-old seascape as if I'm in the gondola of a ferris wheel. Then the boat begins to waver. The bow searches this way and that, trying to find its goal. Then the roaring downward slide begins.

Before the boat can right itself in the valley, a second gigantic wave—tons of crushing weight—smashes down on our upper deck in furious uproar, rams us behind the knees, covering us completely, whirls and seethes around our bodies. It seems an eternity before the boat finally shakes itself free. For just a second the whole length of the foreship is visible, then the next paw strikes.

The back of my neck is soon burning, rubbed raw by the stiff collar of the oilskins. The salt water only increases the pain; it burns like acid.

I have a cut on the ball of my left thumb. It won't heal as long as sea water can find its way into the wound. The brine is slowly eating us away. The hell with it all!

And then there's this fierce cold wind. It flays the white skin from the waves and carries it off in horizontal tatters. It turns the driven spray to buckshot. When it sweeps over the bridge we have to take shelter behind the bulwark.

The Second Watch Officer turns around. He grins at me, his face beaten red. He wants me to see that he's not a man easily impressed by this sort of knocking about. Above the roaring and the hissing he shouts, "Wouldn't it be something—weather like this and no ship under your feet! And a heavy suitcase in each hand!"

Another blow strikes the tower. A heavy wave smashes down on our bent backs. But the Second Watch Officer is already up, his eyes focused on the horizon. He continues to roar. "Water, water, everywhere, and not a drop to drink!"

I have no desire to compete with the weather, so I simply touch my forehead when he turns to look at me.

Every time I take the binoculars from my eyes, water runs down my arms. There's always trouble with the oilskins and more damn trouble with the glasses! Most of the time there isn't a single pair on the bridge because they've all been hopelessly fogged by salt water. The men are always working on them in the control room, but as soon as a pair is well polished and handed up, it's a matter of minutes for the salt water to ruin them again. We've long since given up trying to make any use of our sodden polishing leathers.

Suddenly I grin, remembering the storms they make in sea movies, in a tank with model ships, and for close-ups a piece of the bridge mounted on rockers and tilted left, then right, while buckets of water are being thrown from all sides in the actors' faces. And instead of ducking down, the heroes stare all around, looking threatening.

Here they could take lessons in the real thing: we're only visible for seconds at a time. We bend our heads, hunch over, presenting nothing but the tops of our skulls to the waves. An instant to observe your sector out of closely narrowed eyes, then down with the face. No matter how we dodge, the thin whiplashes of spray strike home.

There's no protection against them. A real wave that smashes you straight in the face is always easier to bear than these fierce, under-hand lashes. They burn like fire.

Immediately I have to take another gurgling cascade full in the back. Looking down, I see the water eddy around the sides of my boots, flood up, and ebb sucking away, leaving them like the piles of a wharf. Another flood, and then another.

The change-over ahead of time is a blessing. The Second Watch Officer may act as tough as he likes—not even he could endure a full stint.

Undressing is hard work. Just as I have one leg halfway out of my trousers, the floor goes from under my feet. I land full length on the floor plates. Lying on my back on the hand wheels, I finally get both legs free.

The control-room mate throws me a hand towel. I still have to get out of a dripping wet sweater and soaked underclothes before I can dry myself with one hand while I brace myself with the other.

I am terrified of the night. How will I be able to get through the hours on a mattress that is bucking, swaying, suddenly dropping out from under me?

Tuesday. It's been a week and a half since the storm began, a week and a half of martyrdom and torture.

In the afternoon I climb onto the bridge. Above us a tattered sky and the waves leaping at it in unceasing insane attacks; the water seems to be making a desperate effort to tear itself free from the earth, but however high the waves arch and leap, gravity drags them back, collapsing them with a crash into one another.

The speed with which the waves approach us is breathtaking. The breakers no longer have a crest of foam; even as each one forms, the storm snatches it away. The horizon has completely disappeared. I cannot endure this for more than half an hour. My hands are cramped from holding on. Water streams down the hollow of my spine and into my trousers.

The moment I am below, the boat resounds with the blows of a gigantic sledgehammer. The pressure hull quivers in every rib. It creaks and groans.

Wednesday. In the late afternoon I am perched with the Commander on the chart chest. From the tower down into the control room comes the sound of violent cursing. It goes on and on until the

Commander gets up, seizes the ladder to the tower hatch, and keeping his head at a safe distance from the continual trickle of water demands, "What the devil's going on?"

"Boat keeps swinging to port—hard to hold her on course."

"Don't get excited!" the Commander shouts up. He remains standing beside the tower hatch, then bends over the chart table. After a short time he calls for the navigator. All I grasp is, "No longer any point—hardly any headway over the seabed."

The Commander still hesitates for a while, then over the loudspeaker system announces, "Stand by to dive!" The control-room mate, who has been crouching on the flood distributor like a tired fly, springs to his feet, heaving a sigh of relief. The Chief comes through the hatch and gives his orders. There is only the slurping of the bilge water to be heard and the drumbeat of the waves greatly magnified by the sudden stillness. A shower of water pours down through the tower; the bridge lookouts climb down dripping. Two of them immediately take charge of the hydroplanes; the First Watch Officer is already ordering, "Flood!"

Hissing, the air escapes from the diving cells. We quickly tilt downward. The bilge water shoots gurgling forward. A shattering blow smacks into the tower, but the next wave only sounds dull, and the following ones meet no resistance whatever. More roaring and gurgling, then silence.

We stand around stiffly, bemused by the sudden peace. The stillness is like a great wall of insulation between us and the chaotic symphony above.

The face of the First Watch Officer looks scalded. His lips are bloodless, his eyes deep in their sockets. There is caked salt on his cheekbones. Panting, he frees himself from the water-logged towel around his neck.

The depth manometer shows 130 feet. But the hand moves further over the dial: 160, 190. This time we have to go deeper to find quiet. Only after 210 feet does the Chief balance the boat to an even keel. The bilge water rips through the stern, then back again. Gradually it settles down: the roaring and slapping cease. A tin can that has been rolling over the floor plates now lies motionless.

"Boat in balance," the Chief reports to the Commander.

The First Watch Officer sinks onto the chart chest and dangles his white, bleached hands between his knees, too exhausted to take off his wet clothing.

Two hundred ten feet of water over the boat.

We are now as safe from the blows of the waves as though we were lying in the dead angle of a cannon. The sea protects us from itself.

The Commander turns to me. "No need to keep hanging on." And I realize that I'm still clinging tightly to a pipe.

The steward brings in the dishes for the evening meal and starts to assemble the table railings.

"Down with the railings, you there!" the Chief snaps at him and like lightning reaches to do it himself.

The loaf of bread that the steward brings in has been almost entirely destroyed by the damp. Admittedly, the green islands of mold that spring up every day through the brown crust have been wiped away by Cookie with his stinking dishcloth—but that hasn't helped much. The bread is penetrated by green mold—like Gorgonzola. In addition, yellow sulfur-like deposits have made their appearance.

The Chief says, "Don't say anything against mold. Mold is healthy." He waxes enthusiastic. "Mold is a noble plant, of the same family as the hyacinth! In this place we should be thankful for anything that grows."

We apply the same patience we would bring to bear on complicated jigsaws to whittle out the small halfway-healthy cores of the thick slices. Out of a whole loaf only a fragment remains—smaller than a child's fist.

"Sunday art," says the Commander contemptuously.

The Second Watch Officer, however, maintains that this bread sculpture gives him pleasure. While he zealously cuts irregular stars out of gray slices of bread, he tells us about sailors who have nourished themselves for months on worms, mouse droppings, and biscuit crumbs. He embellishes his description with so many details that you could believe he has experienced it all himself.

Finally the Chief interrupts him. "We know all that, you old Aztec. That was when you were roaming around the Pacific with Lieutenant-Commander Magellan, just because the old trophy-hunter wanted some straits named after him. I see it all. Must have been a hard life!"

Thursday. Exhausted. Done for. No lessening of the storm. Deliverance, finally, toward evening, when the Commander gives the order to submerge because of limited visibility.

Gradually it falls quiet in the boat again. The Berliner is sitting

close to the control-room hatch, taking a pair of binoculars apart
—water between the lenses.

The radio shack is empty. The radioman is next door in the sound
room. He's put on the headset and is casually turning the wheel of
the sound detector.

In the Officers' Mess the First Watch Officer is busy with his
loose-leaf notebooks—what else! He has even got out a stapler. Funny
that we should have a stapler on board. There's a pencil sharpener as
well. Apparently we're fitted out as a complete office. At least he
leaves the typewriter alone.

The Chief is looking at photos. The Second Engineer appears to
be in the engine room. The Commander is dozing.

Quite unexpectedly the Chief says, "At home they must have
had snow by now."

"Snow!"

The Commander opens his eyes. "Could be—we're already well
into November. Funny thing, it's years since I've seen snow."

The Chief passes his photographs around: snowy landscapes.
Figures like dark blots on pure white. The Chief with a girl, hills
with ski tracks; a fence runs across the left side of the picture. At the
base of the pickets the snow has melted away.

While I stare at the picture, memories return. A mountain town,
shortly before Christmas. The warm security of low-ceilinged rooms.
Tireless hands using all sorts of knives and chisels to carve figures
out of soft pine for the great revolving mechanical Christmas mountain. The smell of the wood, the warmth of the stove envelop me,
along with the odor of paints and glues, and the sharp aroma of
schnapps from the huge glass in the middle of the table, called the
"riding school" because it goes around and around. The church
smell of incense rising in smoking blue columns from the mouths of
the little carved mineworkers and dwarfs in leather pants, and the
wild mountain goblins sculpted out of turnips. And outside, snow
and cold—so piercing it made your nostrils burn when you breathed.
Horse-drawn sleds tinkling with many-toned bells. Steam from the
horses' nostrils white in the light of the harness lanterns. Illuminated
angels everywhere in the windows between banks of moss . . .

"Yes," says the Old Man. "Real snow for once—that's what I'd
like to see."

The Chief puts his photos away thoughtfully.

The Commander has the time of the evening meal moved up.

"It's specially for the Second Watch Officer," he says. "He's to be
allowed to eat in peace!"

Hardly has the Second Watch Officer washed down his last

mouthful, when the command rings through the boat, "Stand by to surface!"

Immediately my muscles tense.

In the middle of the night the engines are stopped again. I sit up suddenly, confused, in a half-sleep. The drone of the diesels keeps on in my head. A single bulb is burning in the compartment. Through the hatch I hear orders from the control room, spoken low, as though the men were involved in some secret activity. I hear a hissing. The boat slants forward. The glow of the lamp moves upward above the hatch. The waves, still breaking against the body of the boat, sound as if someone were beating on tightly stretched canvas. Then silence. The breathing of the off-duty watch is clearly audible.

A man taps his way from the control room through the compartment.

Frenssen catches hold of him. "What's up?"

"No idea!"

"Tell us what's going on—c'mon."

"Nothing special. No visibility now. Black as a bear's ass."

"So that's it," says Frenssen.

I settle myself properly and go to sleep with a feeling of deep satisfaction.

It must be five o'clock when I wake up again. It's very hot in the compartment and the fumes from the resting diesels have penetrated the room. The ventilators are humming. I stretch out comfortably. The bunk doesn't move. I feel this blessing all the way down to the pit of my stomach.

Friday. The Commander doesn't surface until breakfast is over. Even at 130 feet the boat is being moved by the groundswell. We soon break out into the tearing whirlpool and the first waves crash against the tower. So much water comes down that the bilge is instantly full. And there's no position in which your muscles can relax.

The direction of the waves must have changed again. Although the boat has maintained the same course underwater it's now rolling more to port. At times it holds at an extreme angle for frightening periods of time.

The navigator reports that the wind has shifted and is now west-southwest. That explains it!

"A beam sea—we won't be able to take it for long!" says the Commander.

But at lunch, while we are laboriously trying to keep ourselves at the table, he speaks reassuringly. "The waves are coming at a bit of an angle now. The wind will soon shift. If it comes from astern everything will be all right."

I decide to stay at the table after the meal. I discover a book sliding up and down the floor in front of the Second Watch Officer's locker. I reach for it awkwardly and open it at random. I perceive only individual words: "Squaresail yard—inner jib—top gallant sail—back brace—jack block . . ."

Professional vocabulary from the era of sailing ships: beautiful, proud words. We have nothing to compare with them.

The roaring of the waves along our steel skin swells again and again in a furious crescendo.

Suddenly the boat heels to port. I am thrown out of my seat, and the bookcase empties itself completely. Whatever was left between the railings on the table falls crashing to the floor. The Old Man has braced himself sideways like a tobogganer putting on the brakes. The Chief has slid to the floor. We all remain like this for some minutes as though posing for an old-fashioned camera. The boat will never right itself from this extreme roll. My god, we can't get out of it!

But after several minutes the compartment tilts back to the horizontal. The Chief exhales with a shrill siren wheeze. In slow motion the Commander props himself upright and says, "Man alive!"

"Oha!" someone roars in the bow compartment.

I want to stay huddled on the floor. The room immediately heels to starboard. The din is even wilder. My god, how can they survive up there on the bridge!

I pretend to read, but thoughts are whirling through my head. The boat is sure to make it, says the Commander. More seaworthy than any other vessel. A ballast keel one yard wide, half a yard deep, filled with iron bars. A long-armed lever, balanced in the middle. No superstructures. Center of gravity lies below the structural center. No other kind of ship could withstand this.

"What's that?" asks the Old Man, looking over at my book.

"Something about sailing ships."

"Hah!" he answers. "A full storm on a sailing ship, there's something you ought to live through. On a boat like this you don't feel a thing."

"Thanks!"

"Make fast the tower hatch—that's all we have to worry about. But on sailing ships—good god! Reefing and furling sails, spare gear lashed fast to the spars, storm jibs bent on, handlines rigged on deck, hatches battened down—the work never stops. And then nothing to do but sit in the cabin and trust to the Lord God. Nothing to eat. And up in the shrouds again, torn sails to clew up and unreef. New ones to lash on while you're standing on the jackstays. And then the braces every time the wind shifts . . ."

There it is again, that precise, vigorous, powerful language; we're poorer now that it's gone.

As the room heels to port I get to my feet. I want to go and see the inclination indicator in the control room.

The inclination indicator is a simple pendulum with a scale. The pendulum has now swung a full fifty degrees, so the boat is heeling fifty degrees to starboard. The pendulum remains stationary at fifty, as though nailed at this extreme, because the boat hasn't righted itself. I can only explain this by supposing that a second wave must have crashed over her before she could free herself from the first. Now the pendulum moves even further—to sixty degrees. And for an instant it reaches sixty-five!

The Commander has followed me. "Looks impressive," he says behind me, "but you have to subtract something, because the pendulum's own momentum carries it too far." For the Commander to be really disconcerted, the boat would probably have to be sailing keel up.

The men on duty in the control room are now wearing oilskins, and the bilge has to be bailed almost continuously. It seems to me that the pumps are running nonstop.

The navigator lurches into the room, like a man with a broken foot.

"Well?" The Commander turns to him.

"Since midnight a drift of fifteen miles may be assumed."

"You could really express yourself a little less tentatively. You're always right." The Commander adds under his breath, for my benefit, "He's always that cautious, but in the end his calculations work out almost exactly. It happens every time."

A radiogram has arrived; the Commander is handed the slip of paper. Bending over his arm, I read the message with him. "Impossible to reach area of operations at designated time because of weather—UT."

"We'll copy that and sign it with our own initials," says the Commander. Then he pushes himself to his feet and, calculating how much the boat will heel, staggers forward. Soon he's back with a half unfolded chart that he spreads out on the chart chest.

"This is where UT is—almost directly in our line of advance. And here is where we are."

I can see that these two points are some hundreds of miles apart. The Commander looks morose. "If it's all part of the same depression, then good night! It looks like an enormously extended storm system, and there's no indication it's going to move on soon."

Thoughtfully he folds up the chart and pushes back the sleeve of his sweater so that he can read his watch. "Not long till dinner," he says, as though to sum up the whole point of the radiogram and his reactions.

When dinner time comes and the Commander appears in the Officers' Mess I can't believe my eyes—he's wearing oilskins. The others stare at him as if there's a stranger on board. We can hardly see anything of his face, he has wrapped himself up so completely.

"This evening's dinner dress will be oilskins," the Old Man murmurs and grins at us from between the collar of his oilskin jacket and the lowered brim of his sou'wester as though through the slit in a visor. "Well, gentlemen?" he asks impatiently. "Not hungry today? Just when the cook has brought off this magnificent coup: soup in this weather!"

It takes a while for us to rouse ourselves, and then like obedient children we tumble into the control room where the foul-weather gear is hanging. The famous statue of Laocöon conjures itself up before my eyes as I watch the contortions and corkscrew maneuvers the engineers and Watch Officers have to perform to get into their still-wet gear.

Finally we sit down around the table, looking like carnival figures. The Commander is bursting with mischievous pride.

Suddenly there's a crash in the gangway: the steward has landed on his stomach. His hands are above his head, still clutching the soup tureen. Not a drop has been spilled.

"It's never got the better of him yet!" says the Commander, unmoved, and the Chief nods in agreement.

"And no rehearsal—a performance like that first time around—he's really something!"

The Second Watch Officer serves the soup—consisting of potatoes, meat, and vegetables—while I hold on to the safety belt under his oilskin jacket. Nevertheless, he's only got to the second man before he empties a whole ladleful onto the table.

"Goddammit!"

Whereupon the Chief lets his half-full plate spill, substantially increasing the pond of soup in front of us. Pale chunks of potato float about in the dark-brown brew between the railings—blocks of ice from a glacier that's just calved. The next time the boat heels, only the potato is left on the table; the soup has found its way under the railings, slopping into the laps of the Commander and the Chief.

The Commander casts a triumphant glance around the table. "You see?" He can hardly wait for more soup to overflow.

The Second Watch Officer's gurgling laughter is interrupted by a dull crash. The Commander's grin freezes. Immediately he's all attention. The Chief springs up to get out of his way as word comes from the control room: "Chart chest overturned."

Through the hatch I can see four men struggling to put the heavy iron box back in its place.

The Commander looks disconcerted, then mutters to himself, "Incredible. That chest has been there since this boat was commissioned and has never moved so much as an inch."

"No one at home will believe it," the Chief remarks. "They simply can't imagine it. On our next leave we ought to invent a U-boat game. Go without shaving or washing for months. No change of linen, into bed with boots and stinking leather clothes on. Brace your knee against the table while eating, and instead of serving spinach on a plate, plop it down on the table top . . ."

The Chief gulps a couple of mouthfuls and goes on elaborating his plan. "And if the telephone rings, yell 'Alarm!' like a madman, knock over the table, and rush for the door like greased lightning."

Saturday. The gusts have once again become a single prolonged blast that pummels the boat head on.

The barograph is drawing a steep line downward.

"I'd just like to know," says the Old Man, "how the Tommies keep their scows together in such heavenly weather. They can't make the whole damn convoy heave to. And the boys on those tin can destroyers—they'll be having quite a time of it!"

I remember trips on destroyers at force five. That was enough. Full speed was out of the question. At six our destroyers don't leave the harbor at Brest. Time off. But the British destroyers can't pick and choose their weather. They have to furnish convoy protection in any storm—even this one.

In the afternoon I disguise myself as a great seadog and climb the ladder. I wait close under the hatch cover until the water has gushed away, push the lid open, and climb out. Kicking the hatch shut and fastening the snap of my safety belt I do in one motion.

A wave like the back of a gigantic whale rises obliquely in front of the boat. It gets bigger and bigger, loses its hump and straightens up into a wall. The wall becomes concave, rushes toward us, gleaming glassy-green. And now our bow plunges into it. "No longer—" The Second Watch Officer has hardly begun when the wave crashes against the tower. The boat reels.

"—any use," the Second Watch Officer completes his sentence a minute later.

I know of times when the whole deck crew has been torn out of a bridge cockpit by an oversized wave, without anyone in the boat knowing a thing about it. Such murderous waves are created at random from the piling of one swell upon another. Against a giant of that kind no safety belt holds.

What must it feel like to lie there in the water, in your sodden gear, and see the boat moving away—smaller and smaller, hidden momentarily behind the waves and then gone for good. You're done for, *fini*. And the expression on the face of the first man to discover that the whole bridge watch has disappeared, that the boat is wandering blindly through the seas . . .

We're making slow speed; more would be dangerous. The boat could dive involuntarily. There have been instances of boats running too fast in a heavy sea and being driven at an angle down one mountainous wave and into the next, like a dowel, carried by their own momentum to a depth of a hundred feet or more. The bridge watch came close to being drowned. And if too much water were to pour in through the diesel intake pipes, a boat could actually sink.

The Second Watch Officer turns his red face toward me. "I'd like to know how much progress we're really making!"

Suddenly he shouts, "Heads down!"

Which means: duck and hold your breath.

I just have time to see the open-mouthed Officer, the green mountain that's rising to the left in front of our tower, and the great white paw that extends from it hesitating. Then it strikes with thundering force on the side of the foreship. The boat sags way over under the blow. Down with your head! A boiling surge hisses over the bridge, submerges it. We no longer have a ship under our feet.

But now the same wave lifts the boat up. The bow extends clean out of water and hangs for a while in midair until the wave lets the boat fall. Water rushes off through the scuppers and the open after-end of the cockpit. Foaming whirlpools tear at our legs.

"Too damn much," growls the Second Watch Officer. Then just as the next wave is running through under the boat he has the hatch opened and word passed down. "To the Commander: Visibility much impaired by breaking waves. Request alteration of course three hundred degrees."

For a moment radio music rises from the open tower hatch. Then a voice from below. "Three hundred degrees course authorized."

"Alter course to three hundred degrees," the Second Watch Officer orders the helmsman. Slowly the boat turns until the waves are coming obliquely from astern. Now it will perform like a rocking horse.

"Heading three hundred degrees," comes the voice of the helmsman from below. The tower hatch is closed again.

My face burns if I rub my sleeve over it. I've no idea how often I've been caught by the whiplashes. I'm only surprised that my eyes aren't swollen shut. Every blink is painful. My eyelids seem to have puffed up double. My god, what punishment!

I nod wordlessly to the Second Watch Officer, wait for a swirling whirlpool to subside, pull open the hatch, and disappear below.

Bottomless depression overwhelms me. This martyrdom is a test of endurance, an exercise to determine the limits of our capacity for pain.

The radioman picks up SOS calls from several ships.

"The cargo hatches on the freighters must be getting smashed, and the holds filling with water. The waves'll be making matchwood of the lifeboats too."

The Old Man describes various kinds of storm damage that can afflict an ordinary ship. "If the steering mechanism breaks down on one of those barges or they lose a screw, there's nothing the crew can do but pray."

The roar of the water, the rattling of spray, and the hissing of the bilge form background music to the dull resounding thump of the waves on the foreship.

I can only marvel that this wild upheaval hasn't rent our seams, that the boat hasn't begun to buckle. Some dishes and a few bottles of apple juice are all that have been broken so far. It seems that the waves can do nothing to the ship itself. But they are forcing *us* gradually to our knees. The machines hold up—only we mere men are poorly constructed for such torment.

I can tell by the paucity of radio activity how unsuccessful the U-boats are being. Requests for position reports, routine signals, test transmissions—that's all.

I'm suddenly reminded of a passage in Joseph Conrad's *Youth*, when the bark *Judea*, with a cargo of coal for Bangkok, runs into an Atlantic winter storm which little by little destroys the ship: the bulwark, the stays, the lifeboats, the ventilators, the deckhouse, along with the galley and the crew's quarters! And how they man the pumps, from captain down to cabin boy, slaving for their lives, lashed to the mast—day and night. The sentence, "We had forgotten what it was like to feel dry," remains in my mind.

This memory brings me comfort now: The sea cannot drown us. No other kind of ship is as seaworthy as this one.

Sunday. Before taking even the most trivial action I have to struggle with myself. Should I even bother—or would it be just as well not to?

It's the lack of sleep that undermines our strength most of all. The only real peace comes when there's no visibility at all and the Commander orders a dive. Once the boat is balanced, you rarely hear so much as a raised voice. Decks of playing cards lie idle. During the hour or two that we're underwater, everyone tries to get some sleep.

The quiet in the submerged boat disconcerts me every time. When all the men are lying in their bunks or on the floor overcome by exhaustion, it's as though the boat had been deserted by her crew.

Monday. I summon up enough energy to note in my diary: "Impossible to serve meals. Whole thing meaningless. Dive shortly before two o'clock. Marvelous: We stay down. More and more inflammations. Carbuncles of the worst kind. Inflamed scabs. Icthyol ointment on everything."

Tuesday. The Commander writes up the day just past in the war log:

13.00 *Both engines turning over fast enough to achieve half speed. But we remain almost stationary.*
13.55 *Dive on account of bad weather.*
20.00 *Surface. Still heavy sea. Use of weapons limited.*
22.00 *Proceeding submerged because of weather conditions.*
01.31 *Surface. Heavy seas. Limited visibility.*
02.15 *Boat hove to because of very heavy seas.*

Wednesday. The wind shifts to the southeast. Its strength has increased again to eleven. "Very heavy seas from east to southeast. Barometer falling sharply."

In the control room the navigator is braced with spread legs against the chart table. As I try to look over his shoulder he glances up moodily and growls, "Ten days with no fixed bearing. And these crazy waves and winds must have pushed us miles off course."

Thursday. In the half-light of dawn the navigator decides to try his luck once more. Visibility has in fact somewhat improved. Here and there the sky is torn open to reveal a few stars. The horizon can be glimpsed when it's not being cut off by the humps of wandering waves. Then it looks like a straight furrow interrupted by large hummocks.

But whenever the navigator gets ready and has located a known star, spray comes shooting over the bridge and makes the sextant unusable. He has to hand the instrument down to the control room and wait for it to be dried and handed up again. After a quarter of an hour he gives up. "An inaccurate navigational reading is just as bad as none at all!" he says as he climbs down. He'll try again at dusk.

Friday. "A shitty life!" the Chief announces at breakfast.

"Our search methods," I tell the Old Man, "remind me of certain fishing techniques they use in Italy." I pause for effect the way he does after tossing out one of his lures. Not until he says, "Really?" do I go on. "I've seen fishermen around Venice let down huge square nets from the piers over a kind of framework of poles. They wait a while and then hoist the nets up by pulleys—in the hope that some fish or other will be dimwitted enough to stick around."

"That sounds like criticism of the High Command!" the Chief breaks in.

"Clear case of undermining military discipline!" remarks the Old Man. And the Chief announces, "What we need is brains in the right places. Out with those clowns in High Command and let's have you on the Staff instead to get things done!"

"And we can install the Chief in the National Museum!" I'm able to shout after him just as he disappears into the control room.

Saturday. It's six forty in the morning when a vessel is reported on our port quarter. Wind eight to nine, sea eight. Visibility wretched. It's remarkable that the bridge watch was able to make the ship out so soon in the uniformly gray pea soup. Probably a lone vessel tacking sharply.

We're in luck. We're ahead of this dark shadow that rises

momentarily from behind a foaming sea and then disappears for long minutes at a stretch as though by magic.

"He probably thinks he's traveling faster than he is. Can't be making more than fourteen knots! He'd have to take a huge tack in the wrong direction to get away from us," says the Old Man. "Let's edge up a little closer. He certainly can't see us against the clouds."

Not more than ten minutes go by before the Commander orders a dive. The torpedo watch is sent to battle stations.

Engine-room orders. Hydroplane orders. And then, "Stand by for single shots, tubes one and three!"

How is the Commander going to attack in this sea? Bet everything on a single card is probably his strategy now—come hell or high water he wants to score.

The Commander himself gives the firing data without betraying the slightest excitement. "Enemy speed fourteen. Bearing one hundred. Distance three thousand feet."

The First Watch Officer reports, "Tubes ready," almost as casually. But suddenly the Old Man bursts out cursing and orders reduced speed, probably to cut down on periscope vibration.

The periscope motor hums and hums, stopping only for brief intervals. The Old Man is doing his best to keep the enemy in sight despite the high waves. Apparently he's now extending the asparagus stalk still farther. In these waves he's not running much risk. Who aboard the steamer could conceivably guess that a U-boat might attack in this chaos? Experience and theory both teach that in weather like this a U-boat can't use its weapons. We tumble through the waves.

The Commander calms down. "Easily ten thousand tons. Has a murderous cannon—aft. Goddam these rain squalls!"

"No good," we suddenly hear from the tower. "Surface!" The Chief reacts quickly. The first heavy wave that hits us hurls me straight across the control room, but I'm able to catch hold of the chart table and keep my footing.

The Commander calls me to the bridge.

Low-hanging, dark-gray curtains all around us over the raging sea. No trace of the steamer. It has disappeared in the rain squalls.

"Careful!" the Old Man warns as a bottle-green wave rushes toward us.

When it's roared by, he shouts in my face, "They couldn't possibly have seen us!"

He orders us to push on in the general direction of the steamer. To do this we have to run at high speed against the waves. The wind lashes our faces. I manage to endure this for barely ten minutes and then go below in a gush of water. The Chief has to bale every few minutes. "Senseless," he announces shortly. "They've got away after all!"

Despite the dousing spray I venture a sidelong glance into the tower. Little Benjamin is at the helm. A good man—he has to use every effort to keep the boat on course. Even out of sight of the rolling waves I can feel the bow being constantly forced off course. The hatch is sealed again. The only connection from the bridge to the interior is the speaking tube.

The Old Man orders us down to listen. He's determined not to give up. The sonar should reach farther than our sight.

Dripping wet, with lobster-red faces, the bridge watch comes down.

We descend to 130 feet. It gets still as death in the boat. Only the bilge slops back and forth, from the groundswell. All of us except the two bridge lookouts sitting at the hydroplane controls have our eyes on the sound man. But no matter how diligently he turns his wheel—nothing! The Old Man orders, "Course sixty degrees!"

After half an hour he has us surface again. Has he finally given up? I go on deck with the navigator's watch. The Commander remains below.

The kind of view we have of the stormy waves is usually reserved for shipwrecked men. We might as well be on a raft.

"Bone-grinders," roars the navigator. "Watch out—a lookout on a boat once . . ." That's as far as he gets because there in front of us is a wave preparing to strike. I brace myself diagonally against the bulwark, pressing my chin against my chest.

The water has barely gurgled away when the navigator goes on in the same hoarse shout. ". . . he had three ribs broken—safety belt tore—hurled aft—straight onto the machine gun—lucky for him!"

After the boat has taken on the next three waves he whirls around, removes the stopper from the speaking tube, and shouts down, "To the Commander: No more visibility!"

The Commander listens to reason. Another dive, another full sonar search. Still nothing.

Is it worthwhile to peel off our dripping clothes? The hydroplane operators have even kept on their sou'westers. Within half an hour they're proved right. The Commander has us surface again.

"There's only one chance left: If he makes a big tack—a major alteration in course—it'll lose him his head start," says the Old Man.

For a good half hour he sits still, frowning, his eyes half-closed. Then something suddenly brings him to his feet. His abruptness makes me jump. He must have heard something from the bridge. Even before the report comes that the steamer's in sight again, he's at the hatch.

Alarm again. Dive.

When I get to the control room he's sitting in the tower behind the periscope eyepiece. I hold my breath. When the raging sea lets up for a moment I hear him cursing under his breath. He's having his troubles again. How can he keep the steamer in the periscope for more than seconds at a time in an ocean like this?

"There he is!"

The cry from above startles me. We stand firmly braced, waiting, but nothing more is heard from above.

The Old Man bursts into loud curses because he can't see anything. Then orders to the helmsman. And now—I can't believe my ears—the Old Man wants both E-motors at full speed. In this weather?

Another three or four minutes, then, "Crash dive to two hundred feet!" We stare at one another. The control-room mate looks dumbfounded.

What does this mean?

It takes the Old Man to relieve our uncertainty; he climbs down the ladder, announcing, "Hard to believe—they saw us! The scow turned directly at us; they were going to ram us. What a nerve—and what a dirty trick. Incredible!"

He struggles for self-control, and loses. Furiously he slams a glove down on the floor plates. "This filthy weather—this goddam . . ." Completely out of breath, he sits down on the chart chest and sinks into apathetic silence.

I stand around, feeling embarrassed and hoping against hope that we're not going to surface again too soon.

Sunday. We're proceeding underwater. The crew is probably secretly praying for bad visibility; bad visibility means staying under and staying under means peace.

We have become haggard old men, half-starved Robinson Crusoes, though there's no shortage of food. It's just that nobody has the faintest desire to touch the stuff.

The engineers have had the worst of it. They no longer get any fresh air at all. For more than fourteen days now it's been impossible to go on deck. Admittedly, the Commander has permitted smoking in the tower, "under the spreading chestnut tree," but the first man who tried to light a cigarette there instantly had his match blown out. The draft is impossible when the diesels are sucking air out of the boat.

Even Frenssen has become monosyllabic. The evening "uproar in the cable locker," the gabble and singing in the bow compartment, have also ceased.

Only the sound room and the hydroplane stations are in action. The control-room mate and his two assistants are on duty, along with the E-motor personnel. The helmsman in the tower has to fight against falling asleep.

One of the motors is humming. I've long since given up trying to figure out which one. The boat's making five knots, much slower than a bicycle rider and yet faster than we'd be doing on the surface.

Our lack of success weighs heavily on the Old Man, who's getting moodier each day. He never was all that loquacious, but he's hardly approachable at all now. You'd think from his depression that the success or failure of the entire U-boat campaign was his responsibility.

The humidity in the boat still seems to be worsening daily.

A vintage season for mold: it's already taken possession of my spare shirts. It's different from the variety that produces such spectacular growth on the sausages: less virulent, it forms big black-green stains instead. The leather of my sports shoes is filmed with green, and the bunks reek of it. They must be rotting from the inside out. If I leave my seaboots off for a single day, they turn greenish-gray from mold and salt.

Monday. Unless I'm very much deceived, the storm has abated a little.

"Perfectly normal," says the Old Man at breakfast. "No reason to rejoice. We may even have reached a fairly quiet zone—depends if we've hit the eye of the storm. But if we have, it's absolutely certain that the whole performance will start up again once we hit the other side."

The waves are just as tall as yesterday, but the bridge lookouts are no longer being constantly whiplashed by flying spray. Now and again they can even venture to use their binoculars.

Tuesday. I no longer have to look around for handholds whenever I want to cross the control room. We can even eat without table rails and we no longer have to brace the pots painstakingly between our knees. There's a real meal: Navy bacon with potatoes and brussels sprouts. I can feel my appetite returning as I eat.

After the change of the night watch, I drag myself out of my bunk. The circle of the sky framed in the tower hatch glows barely brighter than the black rim of the hatch itself. I wait a good ten minutes in the control room propped against the navigator's table before asking, "Permission to come on the bridge?"

"*Jawohl!*" The voice of the Second Watch Officer.

Bommschtjwumm—the waves are booming against the boat, the sounds interspersed with a sharp hissing and then a dull roar. Pale braids of foam gleam on either side and blend into the darkness.

The water shimmers green down the length of the boat, as if lit up from within, making a silhouette of the boat's hull against the darkness.

"Damn phosphorescence!" the Second Watch Officer growls. Moonlight floods down behind the scattered bands of mist. Now and again a star sparkles and is gone.

"Black as hell," mutters Dorian. Then shouts to the stern lookouts, "Look alive, you men!"

As I climb down into the control room at about 23.00 I see two control-room mates at work over the water distributor. On closer inspection, I see they are grating potatoes.

"What in the world?"

Then the Old Man's voice comes from behind me. "Potato pancakes, or whatever the things are called."

He takes me with him into the galley. There he asks for a frying pan and some fat. A seaman comes from the control room with a bowl of grated potatoes. Happy as a schoolboy, the Commander lets the fat melt in the frying pan, which he raises to let the hissing lard run from side to side. Then the mixture is dropped in from a height. Hot fat spatters onto my trousers. "Almost time to launch the first one!" The Old Man wrinkles his nose, inhales the rising aroma, strikes an attitude. The great moment has come. A flip, and the pancake flies through the air, performs a somersault and lands back in the pan again, perfectly flat, and golden brown.

Each of us tears a piece from the first one that's done and holds it between bared teeth until it's cooled a little. "Neat, eh?" the Commander asks. Cookie has to get up out of his bunk and fetch big cans of apple sauce.

Gradually the finished pancakes pile up into a respectable heap. It's midnight: change of watch in the engine room. The door flies open and the Gigolo comes into the galley, smeared with oil. Disconcerted, he stares at the Commander and is about to rush on through, but the Commander shouts, "Halt! Stop!" The Gigolo freezes as though riveted to the floor.

Now he's commanded to close his eyes and open his mouth and the Commander stuffs in a rolled-up potato pancake, then smears a spoonful of apple sauce on top. The Gigolo's chin gets a layer as well.

"About face! Next!"

The procedure is repeated six times. The watch coming on duty gets exactly the same treatment. We eat so fast that the pancakes are gone in no time. Already the bottom of the bowl is bare.

"Next batch for the sailors!"

It's one o'clock before the Commander stretches and rubs the sweat from his face with the sleeve of his jacket. "Go ahead, eat it up!" he says, pushing the last pancake my way.

Wednesday. In the afternoon I go up with the second watch. The waves have changed completely. No more mountain ridges advancing with long, unbroken slopes to windward and abrupt declivities in the lee. The ordered phalanx of waves has given way to mad confusion; as far as the narrowed eye can see through the blowing spray, the watery landscape is in upheaval. Huge masses of water are being hurled aloft in every direction, and the waves have no lines at all. The wind must have raised a new groundswell over the old one, making mountainous rollers collide with powerful cross-seas.

Hardly any visibility. No horizon. Only watery vapor right before our eyes. "These damn seas!" the navigator growls. The boat executes a kind of reeling dance, starting and stumbling, wavering back and forth, unable to find any rhythm at all.

New torment. It's turned cold again. The icy blasts of the wind cut my wet face like knives.

Thursday. The wind's blowing from the northwest; the barometer's still falling. I become obsessed with the crazy hope that it's going to rain oil—a downpour of oil to smooth the seas.

The Commander appears at dinner, looking morose. For a long time there's silence. Then he smiles with clenched teeth. "Four weeks! Not bad going!"

We've been taking this pounding for a good four weeks.

The Old Man strikes the table with his left fist; he takes a deep breath, holds it, finally blows it out noisily through closed lips, closes his eyes, and lets his head hang to one side: a picture of resignation. We sit around, wallowing in our misery.

The navigator reports that the horizon is clearing, so the northwest wind must have blown away the low-hanging clouds and given us back our sight.

Friday. The sea is a huge, green tattered quilt, shedding its white lining at every tear. The Commander tries every possible trick to protect the boat from the waves—sealing the watertight forecastle, blowing the diving cells—but nothing helps. Finally there is nothing left but to alter course.

With aching eyes I scan holes, trenches, folds, gullies, and channels out into the distance—but there's no darker spot—nothing! We no longer even think about aircraft. What plane could stay aloft in this storm? Whose eye could spot us in this tumult? We aren't even leaving a wake, so there's no trail to betray us.

Once more we shoot into a valley while the next wave rises diagonally behind us. The Second Watch Officer stares at it but doesn't duck—he just stands there stiffly as if smitten with lumbago.

"Something there . . ." I hear him roar, but the sea has already hit the tower. I press my chin against my chest, hold my breath, brace myself, become a dead weight to prevent the sucking whirlpool from dragging me off my feet. Then up with the head again to search the heaving waves. One trough after the other.

Nothing.

"There was something there!" the Second Watch Officer shouts again. "At two hundred sixty degrees!"

He bawls at the port lookout aft: "Hey—you—see anything?"

Once again we are carried upward by a roaring elevator. I'm standing shoulder to shoulder with the Second Watch Officer, and there! A dark shape suddenly heaves up under the blowing spray—next moment it's gone.

A barrel? And how far off?

The Second Watch Officer pulls out the plug and presses the speaking tube to his mouth. Ordering binoculars. The hatch is thrust open from below and the glasses handed out just in time to avoid the next flood. The Second Watch Officer hastily kicks the hatch shut. The binoculars remain more or less dry.

I duck down beside him as he protects the glasses from the spray with his left hand, waiting tensely for the floating object to rise again. But there's nothing to be seen except a tumult of white-striped hills. We're in a deep trough.

As we rise again, we narrow our eyes, try to concentrate.

"Goddammit, dammit, dammit!" Abruptly the Second Watch Officer claps the glasses to his eyes. I stare at him. Suddenly he roars, "There!" No doubt about it. He's right: there *was* something! And again! A dark shape. It soars up, pauses for a couple of heartbeats, and sinks out of sight again.

The Second Watch Officer puts the glasses down and shouts, "That was actually . . ."

"What?"

The Second Watch Officer bites off a syllable between his teeth. Then he turns his face full at me and bursts out, "That—must be—a submarine!"

A submarine? That corkscrewing barrel a submarine? Am I hearing things? He must be crazy!

"Fire a recognition rocket?" asks the bosun's mate.

"No—not yet—wait a bit—not absolutely certain!" The Second Watch Officer bends over the speaking tube again. "Leather cloths to the bridge! And fast!"

He hunches down behind the bulwark, like a harpooner on a whaling ship preparing to strike, and waits for us to be lifted up again. I fill my lungs to their bursting point and hold my breath— as if this would improve my sight as I stare out over the boiling waves.

Nothing!

The Second Watch Officer hands me the binoculars. I brace myself like a mountain climber in a rock chimney and swing the glasses through 260 degrees. A circular section of gray-white sea. Nothing more.

"There!" roars the Second Watch Officer and flings out his right hand. I hastily hand him the glasses. He stares doggedly then puts the glasses down. One leap and he's at the speaking tube. "To the Commander: submarine on our port quarter!"

The Second Watch Officer hands me the binoculars. I don't dare lift them because a huge wave is rising astern. I cling fast and try to protect them with my body, but the swirling flood rises to my navel.

"Dammit!"

The gigantic wave is taking us up. I put the glasses to my eyes, search for two to three seconds across the raging watery waste—and there I have it. No doubt about it: the Second Watch Officer is right. A conning tower. A few seconds, and it's gone like a ghost.

As the wave drains away the hatch flies open. The Commander pushes himself up and gets the details from the Second Watch Officer.

"You're right!" he mutters from under the binoculars.

Then: "They aren't diving, are they? Surely they can't be. Quick, bring up the signal lamp!"

The seconds pass, but despite three pairs of eyes, there's nothing more to be seen. I catch a distracted look on the Commander's face. Then a speck appears in the light greenish gray—the up-ended barrel!

The Old Man orders an approach with both engines. What does he intend to do? Why isn't he firing a recognition signal? Why hasn't the other boat? Can they have missed us?

Spray and foam are dashing heavily across the bridge, but I push myself higher. An alpine ridge with snow-covered summits is bearing down on us from astern. For a couple of heartbeats I'm petrified: The first gigantic wave could rise at the wrong moment and break over us. Then there's a sharp hissing: It's running past, under the boat—but the next instant it's thrown up a huge wall in front of our eyes, as high as a house. And the next wave cuts us off from astern.

Suddenly the tower of the other boat appears, high over the foaming crests, like a cork shot out of a bottle. The cork dances for a while, then disappears. Minutes pass, and there's nothing to be seen.

The Second Watch Officer is shouting—not words, just an inarticulate roar. The Commander raises the hatch cover and bellows down: "How long do I have to wait for that lamp?"

It's handed up. The Commander wedges himself between the periscope housing and the bulwark and grips the lamp with both hands. I brace myself against his thighs to give him more support and leverage. I can already hear him pressing the key: *dot—dot—dash*. He stops. That's it. I steal a quick glance around. The other boat is gone; it might as well have been sucked into an abyss. Nothing to be seen but a watery gray wilderness.

"Crazy! Absolutely crazy!" I hear the Commander say.

Then, before I can spot the tower of the other boat again, there's a flash in the heaving gray: A white sun glares at us through the flying spray, goes out, glares again: *dot—dash—dash*. For a while, nothing; then more glare in the general chaos.

"That's Thomsen!" roars the Old Man.

Braced at an angle, I hang onto his left thigh with all my strength; the Second Watch Officer is now beside me, hanging onto the right. Our lamp is in action again. The Commander is sending a message, but I have to keep my head down, so I can't see what he's tapping out. However, I can hear him dictating loudly. "Maintain—course—and—speed—we—will—come—closer . . ."

A mountain of water greater than any we've seen is overtaking us. White spindrift whirls from its crest in plumes like clouds of powdered snow. The Commander hands down the lamp and quickly lowers himself, using our shoulders for support.

My breath is cut short. The roaring and hissing of this four-story wall drowns out the noise of all the others. We press our backs against the forward bulwark. The Second Watch Officer has his forearm in front of his face for protection, like a boxer.

No one has eyes for the other boat. We stare at this gigantic wave that is approaching us with unearthly deliberation, heavy as lead, slowed down by its own monstrous bulk. On its back the foam glints wickedly. The nearer it comes, the more it swells, rising higher and again higher above the gray-green tumult. Suddenly the wind ceases. Little waves splash aimlessly around the boat. Then it dawns on me: This father of all waves has thrown up a great barrier against the storm. We are in its lee against the wind.

"Hold hard!—Watch out!—Duck!" roars the Commander at the top of his voice.

I shrink down still farther, tense every muscle so as to clamp myself viselike between the bulwark and the column of the TBT. My heart turns over. If this wave breaks—God help us! The boat will never get out from under.

All other sounds are now lost in a single sharp, evil hissing. For the space of a few oppressive moments I don't even breathe. Then I feel the boat being heaved up from astern; on and on it rises, transfixed at an angle against the crumpled ridges of the slope, higher than ever before. The stranglehold of fear is beginning to relax its grip on me—and then the crest breaks. A monstrous cudgel strikes the tower and makes it ring, sending a shudder through the whole boat. I hear a shrill, gurgling whine, and a maelstrom of water shoots swirling into the bridge.

I clamp my mouth shut and hold my breath. There's green glass in front of my eyes. I make myself as heavy as I can so that the solid current won't tear me off my feet. God—are we going to drown? The whole bridge cockpit is full to overflowing.

Finally the tower tips sideways. I bob up and gulp for air, but at once my breath is cut short. The bridge is heeling even farther. Can a U-boat capsize? What about our ballast keel? Can it withstand this sort of fury?

The whirlpool is trying to rip the clothes from my body. I open my mouth wide, breathe hard, and pull first my right foot and then my left out of the vortex, as though out of a snare. Now I can venture to look up. Our stern is vertical! Quickly I turn my head front, force my bent knees to straighten, allow myself a quick glance over the bulwark. I glimpse the face of the Second Watch Officer: his mouth is wide open and he looks as if he's yelling at the top of his voice. But nothing seems to be coming out.

Water drips from the Commander's face. The rim of his sou'wester is streaming like a roof gutter. Stiff and unmoved, he's staring straight ahead. I follow the direction of his eyes.

The other craft must now be on our port bow. Suddenly its whole length is laid bare. The same wave that ran under us is lifting it skyward. This takes no more than a moment, then its bow is buried in a flood of foam. It looks as if they'd gone to sea with only half a boat. A column of spray shoots straight up from their tower, like ocean rollers colliding with a cliff. They disappear completely in the gray spindrift.

The Second Watch Officer roars something that sounds like "poor devils!" Poor devils! Has he gone mad? Has he forgotten that we're being shaken and thrown around in exactly the same way?

We swing around farther. The angle between our course and the running of the sea grows steadily less. Soon we'll be able to take the waves head on.

"Good work—oh, hell!" roars the Second Watch Officer. "If only that bunch—over there—doesn't go and try—something fancy!"

I too am afraid that they won't be able to hold their boat on course in this sea. Our turning circle quickly carries us closer to them. Already the waves thrown off by their bow, which is acting like a snowplow, are colliding with the choppy cross-current stirred up by our own. Sheets of water shoot into the air—dozens of geysers, small, large, gigantic . . .

Then we're on our way up again. An insane wave surging out of the depths like some fabled leviathan has taken us on its back. We rise—a Submarine Ascension—*Kyrie eleison!* As if struggling to free ourselves from the earth we soar like a black zeppelin, higher and higher. Our foreship is right out of the water.

I might as well be on the roof of a building as I look down into the bridge of the other boat—god! Hasn't the Old Man cut it too fine? We could be slammed down on top of them!

But no commands come. I can now recognize each of the five men who are bracing themselves against the starboard bulwark and staring up at us. Thomsen is in the middle.

They're all gaping like the wooden dolls with mouths you try to pop cloth balls into—or like a brood of nestlings waiting for their mother to return.

So that's the way it looks! That's how the Tommies would see us if they were around just now: a barrel with five men lashed down tight inside—a black kernel in a patch of foam, a pit in the white flesh of a fruit. Only when the wave subsides does the image change —and a steel tube comes rolling out of the water.

Now the whale lets us slide sideways off his back, and we're on our way down again. Down and down.

My god—why doesn't the Old Man do something?

I catch sight of his face. He's grinning. The maniac can grin at a time like this.

"Heads down!"

Quick, arch your back like a cat. Hold tight, knees against the bulwark, back against the periscope housing. Tense your muscles. Tighten your belly. The wall, the wall of water, bottle-green and heraldically decorated, rises before us like Hiroshige's *Great Wave off Kanagawa*.

It becomes concave, curves toward us—get your head out of the way! Still time to gasp a lungful of air and huddle up, press the binoculars against your belly—and the hammer strikes again. Hold your breath, count. Fight down the choking and go on counting till the tearing flood recedes.

I'm amazed: our terrible sideways slide didn't happen this time.

The Old Man—hardened skipper that he is—knew how the whale would behave. He can sense what the water will do, predict the behaviors of sea monsters.

Now it's Thomsen's turn to wobble on the crest of a mountainous wave, pushed upward by a gigantic fist. Peering through the glasses, I see his diving tanks come completely free, glistening brightly. The boat hangs there for an eternity—then is suddenly slung into the next valley. A torn white comb shoots up between us, and the others disappear as though they had never existed. A dozen heartbeats later and I still see nothing but gray-white boiling waves, wind-whipped mountains of snow. They look primeval, having swallowed up the other boat.

To think that down there in the belly of the other boat, in the midst of this wild dance, there's the watch standing by the engines, the radioman crouching in his shack, and men braced in their bunks in the bow compartment trying to read or sleep; lights are burning down there and human beings are alive . . .

See here, I tell myself, you're acting like the Second Watch Officer. You're completely forgetting that we're traveling in the same sort of boat. Our men are putting up with the very same treatment as the ones over there.

The Commander calls for signal flags. Signal flags? He's gone completely nuts! How can anyone signal here?

But he grasps them like two relay runners' batons, and as we hurtle up again toward the sky he quickly unsnaps his safety belt, braces himself against the periscope housing, high over the bulwark, and keeping himself firmly wedged unrolls the hand flags; with complete composure, as though we were on an outing on the Wannsee, he sends his message: W-h-a-t-h-a-v-e-y-o-u-s-u-n-k.

Hard to believe: a man on the other boat actually makes the arm signal for "Understood." And as we're being swept down again on our conveyor belt, the other lunatic over there signals: T-e-n-t-h-o-u-s-a-n-d-t-o-n-s.

Like people in the cars of two ferris wheels turning in opposite directions, we exchange information in deaf and dumb language through the flying spray. For seconds at a time the boats hang level with each other. As we rise again the Old Man gives the other boat one more signal: G-o-o-d-l-u-c-k-y-o-u-b-a-s-t-a-r-d-s.

The other lot have now got out their flags. We read aloud in chorus: R-e-g-a-r-d-s-b-r-o-k-e-n-m-a-s-t-s-a-n-d-s-h-r-o-u-d-s-t-o-y-o-u.

Suddenly the wave lets us drop, and we are pitched downward at racing speed. Heeling to the limit, we sink into a valley filled with spindrift.

High above us the bow of the other boat is pushed free, way out over the abyss; it's left hanging—both torpedo tube doors on the port side clearly visible, as is every individual flood slit and the whole underwater hull—until the overhanging foreship drives into the valley like a falling ax blade. With a fury that could split steel it slices into the wave. The water is suddenly hurled aside to left and right in huge, glassy, green masses. The waves meet over it again, cover it with boiling eddies, and wash over the bridge. Only a few dark flecks remain visible in the raging foam: the heads of the bridge watch and one arm waving a red signal flag.

I intercept a dumbfounded glance from the Second Watch Officer to the Commander, and then I see the face of the Chief, distorted in ecstasy; he must have been on the bridge for some time.

I hug the periscope with one arm and hoist myself higher. The other boat remains hidden astern in the trough of the waves. Then suddenly a barrel is there, tossed high, then sunk; after that there's only a dancing cork, and a few minutes later nothing whatever.

The Old Man orders a resumption of course. Up with the tower hatch—keep your eye on a passing wave—and down through the gullet.

The helmsman in the tower squeezes out of the way, but the boat heels to starboard, so he gets a dash of water just the same.

"What was going on?"

"Met another boat—U-Thomsen—pretty close!"

The hatch is kicked shut from above. Pale faces emerge from the darkness as if picked out by miners' lamps. We're underground again. I suddenly realize that not even the helmsman saw what was going on.

I undo my sou'wester from under my chin, laboriously pull off my rubber jacket. The control-room mate is hanging on my every word. For better or worse I have to throw him a scrap or two— "Hard to believe the way the Commander handled her—honest— it was a model exercise!"

The excitement seems to have loosened my muscles: I get out of my soaking clothes much faster than the day before. Next to me the Chief is meticulously drying himself.

Ten minutes later we're assembled in the Officers' Mess.

I'm still wound up, but I try to behave casually: "Wasn't that all rather informal?"

"What d'you mean?" the Old Man asks.

"Our meeting."

"How so?"

"Weren't we supposed to fire a recognition signal?"

"Oh god," says the Commander. "*That* tower—you could recognize it at first glance! They'd have had a fit if we'd shot off a rocket. It would have meant they'd have had to answer at once. And who knows whether they'd have had the shells ready in weather like this? Why go around embarrassing our friends?"

"And just because recognition signals are never to be used in doubtful cases, we get rousted out of our seats a couple of times a day while someone fetches them!"

"No grumbling," says the Old Man. "A must is a must—regulations."

Ten minutes later he comes back to my criticism. "In weather like this we don't have to bother about the Tommies' subs anyway. What would they be looking for? A *German* convoy?"

Saturday. The excitement is over. At lunchtime we sit tightly braced around the table and chew. The off-duty lookouts are gradually sinking into their old lethargy.

The meal is over before the Old Man finally opens his mouth. "They got through fast!"

"They" must mean Thomsen and his crew. The Old Man is astonished that Thomsen turned up in our area. "After all, he only got in a short time before we put to sea—and the damage!"

Got through fast—that means a short time in dock.

"The C-in-C's in a hurry these days!"

Shortened dock time—sketchier repairs. Can't allow the patient to lie about in bed instead of getting back on his feet. No more malingering.

A good quarter of an hour goes by before the Old Man talks again. "There's something wrong about this. Even if we're supposed to be well equipped with boats in the Atlantic, that can't mean more than a dozen. A dozen boats between Greenland and the Azores—and yet we're practically tripping over each other here. Something's not quite right! Oh well—nothing to do with me."

Nothing to do with him! Yet he racks his brains from dawn till dusk and probably through the night as well, brooding over the obvious dilemma: too large a field of operations—too few boats—no supporting aircraft.

"It's time they came up with something."

When I wake up on the third morning after our meeting in the storm, the movement of the boat tells me that the sea's running lower.

I clamber into my oilskins as fast as I can and head for the bridge. It's not yet fully light.

The horizon has been blown clean. Only an occasional crest breaks on the high groundswell. The waves are running almost as high as in recent days, but their motion is far less violent—the boat is no longer being shaken and jarred.

The wind is steady. Once in a while it moves uneasily a few points from its main direction, which is northwest. It blows cold.

Toward midday the wind drops almost completely. Instead of its howl there is only a subdued hissing and rustling. The wild uproar still echoes in my ears and the unaccustomed quiet makes me uncomfortable, almost as if the soundtrack had stopped in a movie theater. The waves are still high, an endless white-maned herd sweeping past the boat, solemn, awe-inspiring.

For all their movement it's hard to realize that the waves aren't actually advancing—that the whole surface of the ocean isn't speeding past us. I have to summon up the image of a wheatfield waving in the wind in order to make myself see that these enormous masses of water are as anchored as the wheat stalks.

"Rarely seen a groundswell this size," says the navigator. "It must stretch a good thousand miles."

We pick up a radio report from Flossmann: "Lone ship sunk with triple salvo."

"He'll make admiral yet," says the Old Man. He sounds more disgusted than envious. "Up there in the Danish Strait."

The Old Man's bitterness finds relief in an outburst of rage. "They can't keep us hacking around like this—on nothing but a hunch! The whole thing's futile!"

For diversion I rearrange my tiny locker. Everything's a mess: gray-black spots of mildew on all my shirts, belt turned green with mold, all my clothes smelling of damp rot. A marvel that we ourselves haven't decayed—gradually watched our living bodies turn putrid.

With some of us, admittedly, the process seems to have set in already. Zörner's face is completely disfigured by crimson boils with yellow cores. The contrast with his pasty complexion makes the inflammation look all the more evil. The seamen are the worst off because their constant contact with salt water keeps their cuts and carbuncles from healing.

But the storm is over. Once again the bridge is a place where we can recuperate.

Nothing breaks the circle of the horizon. A flawless line where sky and water meet and merge into one.

I perceive the sea as a great flat disk supporting a gray glass bell jar. Whichever way we move, the bell moves with us, so that we always remain at the center of the disk. Its radius is only sixteen miles, so the disk is thirty-two miles in diameter—a mere nothing compared to the endless Atlantic.

vii CONTACT

THE FIRST MESSAGE our radioman picks up today is a request for Thomsen to report his position.

"Where is he now?" I ask the Old Man.

"He hasn't reported," the Old Man says. "And there've been two more requests since then."

Images of disaster: boats under aircraft attack, bombs exploding around them like gigantic incandescent cauliflowers.

I tell myself that Thomsen must have his own reasons for not replying. Situations certainly exist in which even the briefest radio signal can be a giveaway.

Next morning at breakfast I inquire, as casually as I can, "Anything from Thomsen?"

"No!" says the Old Man, and goes on chewing, staring stolidly ahead. Must be damage to the antenna, I tell myself. Or trouble with the transmitter. Radio mast carried away, something like that.

Herrmann comes in with the daybook. The Old Man reaches for it impatiently, reads the signals, signs, and snaps the book shut. I take it and hand it back. The Old Man says nothing.

Recently there've been cases of boats being bombed so badly that they couldn't even get off a distress signal.

"He should have reported long ago," says the Old Man. "Without having to be asked."

Next day no mention of Thomsen. The subject is taboo. No theorizing, but it's easy to see what the Old Man thinks. Before long, Headquarters is going to be issuing another three-star report.

Around midday, just as lunch is about to be served, there's a report from the control room. "To the Commander. Trails of smoke at one hundred forty degrees!"

The Commander is on his feet in an instant. We rush after him into the control room. On my way, I grab a pair of binoculars from their hook and reach the bridge close behind the Old Man.

"Where?"

The navigator points. "There, on the port beam under the right-hand bulge of the big cumulus cloud—very faint."

No matter how hard I look, I can't make anything out in the direction indicated. The navigator certainly wouldn't mistake a galleon made of cloud for a smoke trail! The area in question is like a crowded stage set, with screen after screen of cloud coming up over the horizon in a rich display of gray and mauve.

The Commander bends his head to the binoculars. I work the horizon again inch by inch, while it dances violently in my glasses. Nothing but close-packed clouds, and every single one of them potentially a trail of smoke. I strain my eyes as hard as I can. Already they're watering.

What a witch's cauldron! Finally I spot a thin pipe, a shade darker than the mauve-colored background and flaring out toward the top like a tuba. Close beside it the same shape repeats itself like a reflection—a little dimmer and more blurred perhaps, but unmistakable all the same. And there—a whole row of tiny pine trees, their thin trunks reaching down below the horizon. The Commander lowers his glasses. "Convoy! No doubt about it. What's our course?"

"Two hundred fifty degrees!"

The Old Man doesn't hesitate for a second. "Steer two hundred thirty!"

"Course two hundred thirty degrees."

"Both engines half speed ahead!"

He turns to the navigator, who has kept his eyes glued to his glasses. "Do they seem to be running on a southerly course, navigator?" "That's my guess," says Kriechbaum, still staring through his glasses.

"Got to get ahead of them first and find out exactly where they're headed," says the Commander and orders the helmsman "Port ten degrees!"

No excited outburst. No fever of the hunt. Expressionless faces.

Wichmann is the only one to betray excitement: He was the first to discover the smoke clouds.

"Third watch. Told you so. Leave it to the third watch!" he

mutters to himself with self-satisfaction from under his glasses. But when he notices out of the corner of his eye that the Commander has heard him, he blushes and falls silent.

As yet, the tiny pine trees tell us nothing about the ships' course. South was only an assumption. The convoy may be heading toward the boat. Or it may just as well be going away. The ships with their telltale plumes of smoke may be moving below the horizon in any direction on the compass rose.

My glasses remain fixed on our target as the boat slowly turns under me.

"Rudder neutral!"

The helmsman in the tower now brings the helm to midship position.

The boat continues to turn.

"How far has she swung?" asks the Commander.

"One hundred seventy degrees!" the answer comes from below.

"Steer one hundred sixty-five!"

The turn of the boat slackens until the tiny pines stand precisely over our bow. Squinting suspiciously, the Commander inspects the skies with their heavy cover of gray clouds. He tilts his head back and pivots almost a full circle on his axis. Please god, no planes!

A report from below: "Lunch on the table!"

"No time! Bring it up," the Commander orders gruffly.

The plates are put on small fold-down seats attached to the bridge bulwark. The food just sits there. No one touches it.

The Commander asks the navigator what time the moon sets. So he's going to wait until nightfall before attacking. For the time being there's nothing for us to do but stay alert and keep contact—come hell or high water—so that other U-boats can be brought up.

The smoke clouds gradually push their way higher above the horizon and move slightly to starboard.

"I think they're shifting to the right!" says the navigator.

"A returning convoy," the Commander agrees. "Probably sailing in ballast. Too bad, really. One headed east would have been better."

"Twelve mastheads visible already," Wichmann reports.

"That'll do for the time being," the Commander retorts and shouts below, "Helmsman, what's our course?"

"One hundred sixty-five degrees!"

The Commander starts muttering calculations. "Convoy bearing twenty degrees to starboard—so its true course is one hundred eighty-five degrees. Distance? Probably average-sized steamers—means about sixteen miles."

Our wake bubbles like lemon soda. Little white clouds like bursts of shrapnel are blowing aimlessly across the sky. The boat charges ahead through the gray sea, wet-muzzled, slavering.

"Probably close enough now—won't slip through our fingers!" says the Commander. And immediately qualifies his statement. "Provided nothing gets in the way." And to the helmsman: "Hard a-starboard! Course two hundred fifty-five degrees!"

Slowly the smoke clouds swing over until they're on our port beam. The boat is now running on a course we assume is parallel to the convoy.

The Commander lowers his glasses for no more than seconds at a time. Now and again he murmurs something. I hear snatches. "Never get it . . . just the way . . . you want it . . . They're going the wrong way."

So: a fully laden convoy headed for England would be better. Not just because the cargo would be lost, but also because chasing an eastbound convoy would bring us closer to home. The enormous consumption of fuel at high speed is worrying the Old Man. If the pursuit were to bring us nearer to home base, our situation would look a lot better.

"Fuel?" I hear the navigator say. Ordinarily he avoids the word like an obscenity. The Commander resembles a police detective as he confers with him in whispers. Finally the Chief is summoned. He's looking bleak.

"Have everything double-checked," the Old Man orders, and the Chief nimbly disappears below.

It must be a good half hour until the Commander orders both engines run at full speed. He wants to be far enough ahead of the convoy before twilight.

The booming of the engines soars until the repeated firing of the individual cylinders blends into a single rumbling roar. Spray shoots out of the slits in the grating and comes flying at us like shaving lather. The bow wave is suddenly huge.

The Chief promptly reappears. Worried about fuel.

"Supplies are pretty low, Herr Kaleun!" is his sepulchral warning. "We can't keep this up for more than three hours at most!"

"How much d'you reckon we'll need if we really crawl home?" the Commander asks casually. The Chief leans over and cups his hands around his mouth, like a man lighting a cigarette in the wind, so I can't hear his answer. In any case, he has his figures all ready.

About a thumb's breadth above the horizon the ragged, brownish balls of smoke gradually coalesce into an oily, ochre-brown bank of mist. The mastheads beneath look like slowly-sprouting beard stubble.

The Old Man puts his binoculars down, pushes the leather shield over the lenses, and turns to the First Watch Officer, who at some point has taken over. "Under no circumstances allow those mastheads to rise any higher than they are now!" Then he disappears through the tower hatch. Not quite as agilely as the Chief, I see. I climb down behind him.

Down in the control room, the navigator has copied all our maneuvers onto a large sheet of graph paper. He's just entering a new bearing for the enemy and correcting the distance.

"Give it here!" the Commander interrupts. "So that's where he is right now! Looks all right." And, turning to me, "His exact course will gradually become clear from the graphs in the next few hours." But there's an urgent undertone in his voice as he says to the navigator, "Unfold the big chart so we can see where he's coming from." Bending over it, he carries on a kind of monologue. "Coming from the North Channel! What's his over-all course likely to be? Well, we'll soon have that . . ." He lays his protractor between the position of the convoy and the North Channel and reads off the angle. "Two hundred fifty degrees, more or less!" He thinks for a moment. "But they can't have steered that course straight through. They have to have made a long detour north to outflank suspected U-boat patrols. Didn't do them much good . . . that's the way it goes!"

The droning roar of the two diesels fills every crevice of the boat. It works on us like a tonic: we hold our heads higher again—our bodies are suddenly more supple. My pulse seems to beat faster.

The Old Man has changed most conspicuously of all. He looks relaxed, almost cheerful, and now and again the corners of his mouth curl in a smile. The engines are running flat out and already the world looks rosy—as if all we'd been longing for was to hear the muffled roaring throb of the diesels again. For a while no one speaks. Then the Commander says, "In any case, we can't open up before dark. They may have some surprises up their sleeve."

Before dark—it's hours till then.

I can only stand being in my bunk for a quarter of an hour. I get up to see how things are going in the engine room, astern. The after hatch won't open. I have to use the whole weight of my body to overcome the suction of the racing engines. The noise is like a box on the ears. Mouth and eyes open wide. The pushrods on the sides of the diesels are visible only as a waving blur. The needles on the dials of the manometers jerk feverishly back and forth. Oil fumes fill the room like thick fog.

Johann is on duty. Frenssen's there too. He gives a broad grin when he sees me—that usual look of weariness is gone. His eyes are proud. Everything in order. Now we'll see what his two diesels are capable of!

Johann is rubbing black oil from his hands with colored cotton waste. It's a wonder he hasn't gone deaf in here. But this infernal roar is probably like the rustling of trees in a forest to him. He brings his mouth close to my ear and bellows, "What's up?"

I roar back right in his ear. "Pro—ceeding against—a—convoy. Waiting—till—dark!" The chief mechanic blinks twice, nods, and turns back to his manometers. It takes me several seconds to realize that the men here in the stern don't even know *why* we're running at full speed. The bridge is far away. When you're standing here on the iron grids, the world beyond the hatch ceases to exist. The engine telegraph, the signal lights, the public-address system are the only connections with the outside. If the Old Man doesn't see fit to announce over the loudspeaker why we're changing speed, no one here knows what's going on.

Once again, as always happens when I set foot in the engine room, the uniform rumble of the explosions takes possession of me completely. I'm stunned, and immediately assailed by lurid visions. Obsessive, tormenting images: the engine rooms of great ships—targets for our torpedoes! Huge halls with high- and low-pressure turbines, heavily insulated pipelines under great pressure, highly vulnerable boilers, driving shafts, and the many auxiliary engines. No partitions. If they take a hit, they fill quicker than any other compartment of the ship, and with a flooded engine room, no ship can be kept afloat.

A series of pictures rushes through my mind. A hit amidships triggers the chain reaction: the boilers explode, releasing high-pressure steam, and pipelines are torn apart; the ship immediately loses power; the silvery gleaming iron stairs, so narrow there's only room for one man at a time—but everyone is fighting at once, trying to find a way up them in the dark, through the searing steam, toward the deck.

What a job! Working in the engine room ten feet below the water line, knowing that at any second a torpedo may tear open the ship's side without the slightest warning! How often while on convoy the men must measure the thin plates that divide them from the sea. How often they must surreptitiously try out the quickest route to the deck, always with the taste of panic in their mouths, and in their ears the rending scream of iron, the blast of the explosion, and the roaring inrush of the sea. Not one second's feeling of security. Always scared shitless, always waiting for the clanging of the alarm bell. A hell of fear—three, four weeks at a stretch.

On the tankers it's even worse. A torpedo amidships and the boat rapidly becomes a single flaming inferno. Every square foot white hot from bow to stern. If the compressed gases explode, the ship blows up in a belch of fire and smoke—a gigantic torch.

Something flickers in Johann's face, jerking me out of my nightmares. His expression of watchful concentration remains for a moment, then dissolves: everything in order. The door to the motor room is standing open. Oil-heavy, hothouse warmth fills the compartment. The motor is turning over without charging. A quick beat indicates that the air-compressors are working. Rademacher is engaged at the moment in feeling the temperature of the shaft bearings. Zörner the E-stoker is sitting on a pile of oilskins, reading. He's too immersed to notice me looking over his shoulder:

The Junker was holding the woman in his arms, bending her backward so that the light fell on her face in its circle of black curls; he encountered a look of fierce challenge, such as he felt on his own face burning down on her, as though each of them was seeking assurance that her surrender would sweep them ever more fiercely to the very end, to a roaring destruction, a return to that darkness from which they had emerged into the singing, golden hall of a life menaced on all sides, and the terrible futility of their fleeting moments together. The Junker's features were frozen in a threatening and paralyzing mask of overweaning power, then they slowly and painfully relaxed and he stammered into the roaring stillness, as if his tongue were reluctant to obey him, that he wished to kill her . . .

The bridge is a long way off. I have to feel my way back into reality along an Ariadne's thread. As I let the hatch slam against its frame, the noise of the diesels is cut short as at the stroke of a knife, but in my skull the dull roar continues. I shake my head, but some minutes go by before I can silence the dull thrumming in both ears.

"They must have a pretty complicated tacking system," the Old Man says to me when I'm on the bridge again.

"Astonishing how they manage it. They don't just run their general course with a touch of routine tacking thrown in. Nothing so simple. They build all sorts of deviations into the system to stop us getting the hang of it too quickly. It's driving the navigator crazy. Right now he's working nonstop, poor bastard: presumed enemy course, our course, collision course. It can't be easy, keeping a circus like that going!" It takes me a few seconds to realize that this last sentence no longer refers to our navigator but to the English convoy commander. "It used to be that they only altered course in regular tacks; never took us long to see what their over-all intention was. But recently they've learned to make life tough for us, the bastards. Well, we all do the best we can. Must be a fascinating job, convoy commander. Keeping a herd of sheep like that together straight across the Atlantic, always on the alert . . ."

Now *we* have become the contact boat. *We* must see to it that we're neither driven off nor forced to submerge. We have to be as persistent as our ship's fly. If you strike at her and miss, she immediately sits down again in exactly the same place. The fly—the symbol of persistence, and so a genuine heraldic animal. Why don't any of us have one in our conning tower? Commanders have had wild boars and snorting bulls painted on, but no one has yet hit upon the fly.

Ought to propose it to the Old Man sometime: a big fly on the tower! Only not right now. Hands jammed deep in his trouser pockets, he's doing his lumbering dance around the open hatch. A bridge lookout ventures a bewildered glance. Immediately the Old Man snaps at him. "What're you doing with your eyes, sailor?"

I've never seen him like this before. He keeps slamming the tower bulwark with his fist, a regular drumroll, until the bridge resounds with it. Then he roars, "Navigator, have to have the radio message ready. I'll take another quick bearing so we can give them an accurate general course report."

The direction finder is brought onto the bridge. The Commander places it on the bridge compass, takes a bearing on the smoke trails, and reads off the degrees. Then he calls down, "Navigator: True bearing one hundred fifty-five degrees—distance fourteen miles!"

After a while the navigator reports, "Convoy course two hundred forty degrees!"

"Well, just as we suspected," the Commander says to himself and nods at me, then calls below: "Can you make any estimate of speed?"

The navigator's face appears in the hatch. "Between seven point five and eight point five knots, Herr Kaleun!"

Hardly a minute passes before a slip with the radio message is handed up. "Convoy in Square AX three hundred fifty-six, course two hundred forty degrees—speed about eight knots—UA." The Old Man signs the radio message with a stump of a pencil and hands it down again.

The Chief comes on deck, looking worried, and peers up at the Commander like a kicked dog.

"Here you are again!" The Commander's trying to head him off. "Whoever wants to play has to pay! Or are there any *serious* problems?"

"Not on account of the diesels, Herr Kaleun! Only the voyage home."

"Ach, Chief, stop your Doomsday nonsense! Praise the Lord and keep your powder dry. Or don't you believe in the Lord God, Father of Heaven and Earth? She's running pretty, isn't she?"

Once the Chief has disappeared, however, the Commander does start doing some calculations with the navigator. "When will it be dark?"

"At 19.00."

"So we won't have to run full speed very much longer. At least we've got enough for the first attack! After that we'll have to draw on the secret reserves that Their Highnesses the Chiefs like to keep squirreled away."

The smoke clouds now look like captive balloons on short strings, stretched out along the horizon. I count fifteen.

With forced indifference the Commander says, "We'd better give some thought to their protective screen. Edge up a bit closer. It could be very useful tonight to know what kind of escorts we have to reckon with."

The First Watch Officer immediately shifts course two points to port. Number One, who has charge of the forward starboard section, mutters audibly, "This time we're about due for something . . ."

The Commander really cuts him short. "Careful, gentlemen! Anything can happen between now and dusk!"

Taking the dim view. But I'm convinced that down deep the Old Man is absolutely confident. The old superstition: don't jinx the attack.

The C-in-C's radiograms reveal that five boats in all have already been turned loose on the convoy. Five—that's a real pack. One of them, as we discover from his position report, arrived during the night. It's Flechsig—and he's to the west of us.

The First Watch Officer is sitting in the Officers' Mess, and it's clear that he's nervous. I see him moving his lips noiselessly.

Probably memorizing his "prayer before battle," the words of command for firing the torpedoes. Since no enemy came within torpedo range on his last patrol, this is his first attack. In any event, we're safe from his typewriter for the time being.

I bump into the Chief in the control room. He may be looking quite self-possessed, but he's on hot bricks. I watch him silently but with a meaningful grin until he inquires furiously what I find so interesting.

"Come, come," says the Old Man, suddenly bobbing up out of nowhere.

"Let's hope the gas exhaust pipes hold up," says the Chief. "There's damage in the one from the port diesel."

It's only a few hours since Johann was telling me a story. "We were keeping contact once on UZ, when the diesel exhaust pipes broke. God, what a shambles! All the exhaust gas was venting into the diesel compartment. Couldn't see your hand in front of your face. Had to get the hell out of there and come back with escape gear. Two of the stokers keeled over on us. Had to be relieved. The Old Man himself came down. Question was: Give up and let the scows go or put up with the gas until we attacked? It was touch and go—for three whole hours! The walls were completely black and we looked like niggers."

The Chief gets restless. He disappears aft without a word. Five minutes later he's back again. ——

"Well, how does it look?"

"*Comme ci, comme ça*," is his sibylline reply.

The Commander is busy at the chart table and seems to be paying no attention.

The radioman comes in with the daybook to be signed. Which means two more hours have gone by.

"Our newspaper," says the Old Man. "A message for Merkel, nothing special, simply an order to report his position. He sailed the same day we did."

The fact that old Merkel, alias Catastrophe Merkel, is still alive amazes us all. His First Watch Officer had told me what he got away with during his last patrol when he met a tanker in an unusually heavy sea. "The tanker had bad luck. She altered course and ran straight in front of our sights. The sea was running so high that we couldn't get her in our periscope. We had to close right in so that the tanker couldn't take evasive action after we fired our torpedoes. Merkel ordered a single shot, tube three. We heard the detonation as it hit, immediately followed by another one. The Chief did all he could to keep us at periscope depth, but we still couldn't get a glimpse of the tanker. It was minutes before the periscope came clear and when it did—there was the side of tanker looming over us. They'd circled. Too late to get away. They rammed us when we were only fifty feet down. Both periscopes in the ashcan, but the pressure hull held—amazing! It really was a matter of inches. We couldn't surface: our tower hatch was completely jammed shut from the impact of the collision. Not very pleasant if you can't look around, let alone get out. Disagreeable feeling. Eventually we made it through the galley hatch and opened the tower hatch from outside with a hammer and chisel. But we were in no shape for emergency dives . . ."

At the time no one dared ask Merkel how he had managed to make his way back two thousand miles to base with his tower smashed up and his periscope gone. But Merkel's hair was gray before that anyway.

While I'm trying to get my cameras ready in the petty officers' compartment, I run into a noisy conversation among the inhabitants. Despite the closeness of the convoy, they're back on subject number one.

"You really should've seen his last lady friend. Born in 1870. First you had to sweep the cobwebs out of the way . . ."

Zeitler emits a deafening belch that comes from the pit of his stomach.

"Long-distance record!" says Pilgrim applaudingly.

I take refuge in the bow compartment. The off-duty lookouts, five or six of them, are sitting under the swaying hammocks on the floor plates, some cross-legged, some sprawled out. All they need is a small campfire.

I'm besieged. "Well, how does it look?"

"Everything seems to be going according to schedule."

The Gigolo is stirring his teacup with a greasy knife.

"Godawful bouillon," Ario grins, "but nourishing."

The bridge johnny comes in and pretends amazement. "What kind of a campsite is this supposed to be?"

Then he tries to find a place in the circle, and Ario promptly loses his temper. "Don't be so cool about walking off with my bread and butter! You did the same thing yesterday. Next time I'm going to bash your head in!"

The bridge johnny helps himself to another slice of bread, settles himself comfortably, and addresses the company at large. "Let me tell you a little secret—you're all simple-minded swine."

Nobody takes this amiss.

Tension keeps me on the move. Back in the petty officers' quarters I hardly need to listen to know what they're talking about. Zeitler has the floor. "We had the same sort of a pig on board when I was with the minesweepers."

"If by any chance the pig you're talking about is me, you're about due for accident compensation!" Frenssen announces. "And fast."

"Bullshit, you heinie! Who's talking about you?"

"If the shoe fits . . ." Pilgrim pipes up.

I take a look around the room. Rademacher has pulled his curtain shut. Zeitler seems to be acting offended; apparently he's imitating Frenssen, waiting to be spoken to.

The door to the galley opens. The one beyond, leading to the engine room, is also open. The noise from the diesels drowns all conversation. "Ten minutes till time!" I hear a voice call. Confusion, complaints, curses: getting ready to change the engine-room watch. It must be 18.00 now.

Back on to the bridge. Twilight soon. Dark clouds have come up under gray skies.

The sucking roar of the intake nozzles for the superchargers on both sides of the bridge silences the diesels.

"I wouldn't care to be their convoy commander when our pack hits," the Old Man says in a loud voice from under his binoculars. "They're going at a crawl! After all, they can't move any faster then the slowest steamer. And no chance to maneuver. Some of the captains are bound to be real dummies—and trying to follow a fixed tacking system with a mob like that—oh my god! They're all used to steering straight ahead, and to hell with the regulations for avoiding collisions at sea . . ."

After a while he begins again. "Anyone who ships on one of those gasoline tankers must be either superhuman—or subnormal. Spending weeks on end crawling along with a shipful of gasoline, just waiting for the torpedoes to hit! No thank you!"

For a good while he stares silently through his glasses. "They're tough fellows," he growls eventually. "I heard about one man who'd been fished out of the drink for the fourth time by the crew of a destroyer. He'd been sunk three times, rescued three times, and he shipped out again for the fourth—that's really something. Of course, they get lots of cash—love of country plus a fat paycheck—maybe that's the best mix of soil for breeding heroes." Then he adds dryly, "Sometimes the booze is enough."

The loop antenna has been up for some time. We're now sending directional signals for the other boats in the area. The flag pushers at Command Headquarters in Kernével are also getting short signals sent out at hourly intervals, prearranged combinations of letters from which they can deduce all they need to know about the convoy: position, course, speed, number of ships, escort system, our own fuel situation, and even the weather. Our changes in course allow them to form a picture of the convoy's movement too. We are forbidden to attack until more boats have been brought up.

The mood in the boat has changed. It's remarkably quiet in the compartments. The excitement seems to have subsided. Most of the men are lying down, trying to get some sleep during these last few hours before we attack.

In the control room all systems have long since been made ready, the connections tested again and again. Now there's nothing further for the control-room mates to do. One of them is working on a crossword puzzle and asks me whether I know a city in France that begins with Ly—"

"Lyon."

"Thanks. Perfect."

The Chief appears from aft. "Well, how do things look?" he asks.

"Good, as far as I can tell."

The Chief seems to have no pressing problems aside from his concern about fuel. He has weaseled his way around the boat to his own satisfaction, so he sits down on the chart chest to chat for a bit. "Looks as if all that calculating's paid off: I'd stopped believing in it. Dear god, the shitty times we have to put up with nowadays! Used to be *veni, vidi, vici*: In the old days you could take a position right on course and sit there until someone came along. Now Their Highnesses make themselves scarce—quite right, of course, from their point of view."

19.00. The optical system for the night direction-finder lies ready in the control room with three men bustling around it: The torpedo-firing mechanism is being inspected.

I'm vaguely aware of someone saying, "A whole string of tubs—we *have* to get some of them!"

Up on the bridge again. Now it's 19.30 hours. All the officers are assembled except for the apprentice engineer. The Chief is sitting

on the TBT column like a hunter in his tree blind. Our course is
180 degrees. Behind the trails of smoke the sky has separated into
blood-red horizontal stripes. It looks like a huge marquee. The sun
has sunk away behind the clouds. The red fades slowly into a pale
silky green. A few clouds with tattered edges drift close to the horizon, still tinged with the afterglow. Moving slowly, bathed and
flecked with rose, they look like some exotic species of fantailed
goldfish. Their scales catch the light, sparkle and gleam, then fade
again. Dark patches suddenly appear on them like fingerprints.

Night is now rising in the east. Stretch after stretch of the sky is
overrun by the darkness we have been awaiting so eagerly.

"Navigator, write down: '19.30 hours—twilight—horizon somewhat closer—convoy formation clearly discernible in four columns—
intend to attack by night.' That way we have something ready for the
war log."

The Old Man gives an order to the engine room. The roar of
the diesels immediately fades and falters. Back to the sound of that
interminable frigging around. The white mane of our wake collapses
and turns into a bright green trail behind us.

Now we're far enough ahead of the convoy. The idea is that
despite the rapidly decreasing visibility we should have time to
register their every change of course and adjust our own accordingly
so as to keep the superstructures of the steamers low on the horizon.

The sky is already hung with the chalky-white disk of the moon,
which gradually begins to glow.

"May take a while yet," the Old Man says to me. He's hardly
finished speaking when the stern starboard lookout reports, "Masthead astern!" Our glasses all swing in the same direction. I find
nothing. "Goddammit!" the Old Man mutters.

I glance sideways to see where his glasses are pointing. Then
I aim my binoculars at the horizon and move them slowly along it to
the left, trying to find his angle. The horizon is barely distinguishable from the evening sky. I keep searching—there! A real mast!
Hair-thin! No plume of smoke—has to be an escort vessel. Corvette?
Destroyer? A sweeper making its big evening swing to clear the
neighborhood before nightfall?

Have they spotted us already? They always have their best men
in the crow's nest!

Anyway, they have us straight in front of them in the west,
where it's nowhere near dark enough yet. We're silhouetted much
too clearly against the horizon.

Why doesn't the Old Man take action? He's crouching like a
harpooner waiting behind his cannon for the whale to blow again.

Without putting down his glasses he orders "Both engines full ahead!"

No hydroplane orders. No order to dive.

The blowers roar. The boat leaps forward. My god, this seething white wake is bound to betray us to the Tommies! Our hull of course is camouflaged gray, but the white trail and the blue cloud of exhaust gas over it . . . The diesels are now pouring out as many fumes as a defective tractor. Blotted out by this thick banner of gas, the horizon disappears completely astern, together with the needle-thin mast. I can't see whether it's growing taller or shrinking.

If we can't see him, I think, perhaps he can't see us either.

The noise of the diesels is infernal. They're really eating into the Chief's fuel supply.

The Chief, I notice, has disappeared from the bridge. The Old Man keeps his glasses pointed astern. We haven't varied from our course by so much as one degree. The navigator is staring off along with him.

After a while the Old Man orders both diesels slow speed ahead. The wake dwindles. Gradually the blue haze lifts. Intently the Old Man and the navigator search the horizon. I do the same, inch by inch. Nothing.

"Hm," says the Old Man. The navigator is silent. He's got his binoculars balanced between outstretched thumbs and middle fingers. Finally he says, "Nothing, Herr Kaleun!"

"Have you a record of when she came in sight?"

"*Jawohl*, Herr Kaleun, 19.52 hours!"

The Old Man steps over to the hatch and calls down, "For the record: '19.52 hours. Escort vessel in sight.' Have you got that? 'Evasive action using maximum speed on surface—escort fails to spot us through cover of our exhaust gas'—have you got that?—'Through cover of our exhaust gas.'"

So that was it. The Old Man was using the fumes deliberately.

My heart is pounding.

"Exciting, isn't it?" he says. Then there's a new shock. In the west a rocket bursts high above the horizon; it hangs there for a while, then describes a curve like the crook of a cane as it falls and is extinguished.

The Commander is the first to set down his glasses. "What's that all about?"

"They're changing course!" says the navigator.

"Maybe—and maybe they're calling up destroyers," the Commander growls. "We don't want them peering down our necks right now. Eyes peeled, gentlemen, no daydreaming." And after a while, "A rocket—they must be out of their minds!"

The navigator calls down, "For the record: 'Light rocket over convoy at ten degrees'—add the time!"

"Funny!" mutters the Old Man again. Then he turns his face to the moon. "Let's hope we get rid of that bastard before long!" I'm standing close to him, following the direction of his glance. The moon shows a man's face: fat, round, baldheaded. "Just like a contented old customer in a whorehouse," remarks the Second Watch Officer.

"Two men contemplating the moon," I murmur to myself.

"How's that?"

"Oh—nothing. The title of a picture by Friedrich."

"What Friedrich's that?"

"Caspar David Friedrich—German romantic painter."

"I get it! A nature-lover . . ."

"Mastheads higher!" reports the navigator.

The convoy must have tacked toward us.

"Veer away again!"

The new rudder setting is reported from below. "Bearing two hundred degrees!"

The moon adorns itself with a wide rainbow halo.

"Let's hope they leave us alone," the Commander mutters testily. Aloud, he inquires about fuel consumption.

The Chief appears so quickly he must have been lying in wait. He reports, "We checked everything out at 18.00, Herr Kaleun. Up to now, given the high rate of speed, we've used about fourteen hundred gallons. We've practically no reserves left!"

"Number One still has a supply of cooking oil," jeers the Old Man. "And if there's nothing else to do, we'll just have to *sail* home."

I sit down on a spray-damp ledge beside the platform for the anti-aircraft gun. White foam streaks past beneath me in constantly changing patterns. The moon's reflection in the wake is shattered. The myriad tiny splinters are shaken together into a kaleidoscope of new formations. The sea is transparent, illuminated from within by tiny greenish dots. The shape of the boat's hull shows clearly against the glimmer: plankton. The iron bars of the railing throw stark shadows along the gratings, cutting across the lines of black between the individual bars to form a sharply defined pattern of diamonds. The pattern moves. The shadows of the railing fall across my boots: the boat must be turning in the direction of the convoy.

All at once thin clusters of rays, fan-shaped and pale-green, shoot across the sky.

"Northern lights!—On top of everything else!" from the Commander.

A curtain of glittering glass rods like the ones that hung from our lamp at home is now suspended across the sky. Brilliant greenish-white light sweeps through the glass curtain in waves. Gleaming lances shoot up in bursts from beyond the horizon, die, blaze up again, dim a little, grow longer as they brighten. The water around the boat sparkles as if studded with fireflies. Our wake becomes a glittering train.

"Quite a fireworks display," says the Commander. "Pretty, but not what we wanted."

From the brief exchanges between Commander and navigator I gather that they're debating whether or not to have us charge into the midst of the convoy from a forward position. The navigator swings his head thoughtfully from right to left and back again. The Old Man seems equally uncertain.

"Better not!" he says finally, and turns toward the moon. It's an almost circular hole punched in the inky cloth of the sky, a splendid blaze of white that falls like gaslight, chalky but extraordinarily luminous. A few clouds drift across the horizon like gray lumps of ice. As soon as they cross the path of the moon they light up; in places they sparkle as if covered with sapphires.

Under the moon the sea becomes a huge plane of crumpled silver paper, gleaming and sparkling, mirroring the lunar radiance a thousand times over. It's as if the sea had jelled into immobility in the moonlight. No waves—only this frozen brilliance. I'm suddenly reminded of the scene in the Bar Royal on the night of our departure —Thomsen. Don't think about that now.

Despite the moonlight the Old Man tries to edge a little closer to the convoy, trusting to our dark background and probably also relying on the lack of watchfulness among the sailors in the convoy.

Of course we show very little above the water, and we haven't much of a bow wave at this speed. If only we could present our narrow silhouette, bow or stern, to the enemy, we would be almost invisible. This, however, is impossible right now: we have to pursue a course parallel to—and slightly in advance of—the convoy's.

Why doesn't a convoy this size have more of an outlying escort? I ask myself. Was that one ship all the Tommies were able to provide by way of protection for their flanks? Or are we already between the outer ring and the convoy itself?

The Old Man will know what to do. This isn't his first convoy.

He has a thorough knowledge of enemy tactics. Once he even used his periscope to observe a depth bomb pursuit aimed at himself. The commander of the destroyer had presumed that the boat was lying deep in an estimated position that the Old Man had long since abandoned. The Old Man had all motors stopped, suspended the boat from the periscope, and watched the destroyer making its runs and laying down a whole carpet of depth charges. He's even said to have played at being a sports commentator, giving a running commentary on the proceedings so that the men could share in the fun.

Right now he's silent. "Four columns," is all he says in the course of the next fifteen minutes.

Our high-speed escape from the picket boat has apparently brought us too far ahead of the convoy, which explains why we've been running at slow speed for some time. Headquarters will no doubt have summoned a number of other boats that haven't yet arrived. For the time being, our job is to keep signaling the course of the convoy.

"Perhaps we might close in a little more?"

The Commander's question is addressed to Kriechbaum.

"Mm!" is all the navigator says, and keeps his binoculars fixed on the convoy. The Old Man takes this as sufficient assent. He gives the helmsman an order that brings our bow diagonally across the course of the convoy.

Once more we stand stiff and silent. Excited? God forbid! Like landlubbers, runs through my mind. Lubbers? What are lubbers? But at once administer my own rebuke: The hell with it, better concentrate on keeping a proper lookout!

"Man battle stations!" The Old Man's voice sounds rusty. He has to cough to free his vocal cords. From below, one loud roar after another. "Chief Engineer: Engine room on battle stations!" The Chief to the bridge, "Below deck on battle stations!" But that's not the end of it. "First Watch Officer: Torpedo crew on battle stations!" And now the unmistakable high voice of the First Watch Officer: "Torpedo crew on battle stations!"

The direction finder is handed up. The First Watch Office places it carefully on its column as if it were a raw egg.

As seen from the convoy, we are right in the path of the moon. I can't understand why the Old Man stays on this side and not in the shadow. Probably he's thinking the way they would: Sea as bright as silver paper in the moonlight, more brilliant than full noonday sun, so why should any German submarines be plowing around here?

Clearly the Old Man is counting on the enemy's defenses being weaker on the moonlit side. And he's probably right, for if there weren't any holes in the defense on this side, we would have been discovered long ago.

I can picture the deployment of the ships and the escort vessels as clearly as in an aerial reconnaissance photograph: four columns in an extended rectangle; in the middle the most valuable ships, the tankers; two corvettes—the sweepers—as advance guards, racing in wide circles directly in front of the convoy, in order to prevent any U-boats from swinging back among the steamers from an advanced position. Guarding the flanks, destroyers or corvettes speeding up and down—in the lee of the moon, of course. Then, at a great distance from the herd, the rearguard defense, the killers: escort ships that are not specifically defending the convoy, because U-boats could hardly attack from a position astern. They are there to take on any U-boats that have been spotted by the convoy corvettes, work them over while the convoy moves on.

20.00. It occurs to me that I should have a second night film ready. In my hasty descent I make a mess of things. I've hardly arrived in the control room when a confusion of cries reaches me from above. Abandoning my film I hastily climb up again. "Vessel approaching." The Commander. "There—coming from outside—you can see her edging up!"

I stop breathing. Ahead, four points to port, I catch sight of the mastheads of the steamers. But the Old Man is facing aft. I search in that direction. There it is: a narrow shadow pointing over the horizon.

What do we do now? Dive? Make a getaway? Give up? Say the hell with it?

"Both engines full ahead!" The Commander's voice is a monotone. Will he try the old trick again and just keep on going?

"One point to port!"

So that's not it.

A minute passes, then the Old Man makes his intentions clear. "Closing in on the convoy!"

As I direct my glasses toward the steamers again, the navigator announces "Mastheads getting bigger!" in a voice less than matter of fact.

We must either dive to escape the approaching destroyer or run much too close to the convoy.

Our wake whips back and forth like a huge tail. Over it spread the diesel fumes, screening us in mist; with luck it'll work this time too. In any case, I can no longer see the shadow of the destroyer through the veil of gas.

I swing the glasses back. The convoy is now directly in front of our bow.

"Dammit to hell!" from the Commander.

"Destroyer appears to be falling back," reports the navigator. Long minutes of tense uncertainty before he breaks the spell: "Distance increasing!"

The Commander hasn't given another glance to the destroyer. All his attention is focused on the hummocks on the horizon—directly over our bow.

"What's our course?"

"Bearing fifty degrees!"

"Fifteen points to starboard, steer one hundred forty degrees."

I'm still paralyzed with fear.

The Commander says, "They're running in rather loose formation . . ." Only then does he come back to the destroyer. "Good thing we didn't dive. Close thing this time."

Abruptly he asks the navigator, "Kriechbaum, what sort of feeling d'you have?"

The navigator leaves his elbow propped in position, simply turns his head from behind the binoculars, and says, "It's a sure thing, Herr Kaleun! Absolutely. Has to work!"

"Perfectly straightforward."

Funny sort of conversation, I think. Are they reassuring each other?

I sneak a look into the tower. Covers have been removed from the target-position calculator, the deflection calculator, and the torpedo-firing mechanism. Bluish light gleams from the dials.

"Time!" the Commander asks below.

"20.10 hours!"

Unbelievable that we should be allowed to travel unchallenged beside the convoy as though we actually belong to it.

"I don't like the look of that shadow," the Commander murmurs to the navigator.

I turn in the same direction and pick up the thing in my glasses. Its angle to us is very sharp. Approaching or receding—we can't tell. Thirty degrees or one hundred fifty! It's certainly no steamer! But the Old Man is already turning away again.

The First Watch Officer is fumbling nervously with the direction finder. He peers through the telescopic sight, then straightens up again momentarily and takes his bearing direct, over the bulwark in the direction of the convoy. The Old Man, sensing his restlessness, asks in a derisive undertone, "Visibility suit you, First Watch Officer?"

Again and again the Old Man turns his face to the moon. Then he gives voice to his annoyance. "Wish we could use the thing for target practice . . ."

I place my hopes in the clouds, which are lying in deep piles on the horizon and gradually rising—so slowly, admittedly, that it may take a good while before they reach the moon.

"They're tacking to starboard!" says the Old Man, and is seconded by the navigator: "Just what I was thinking."

The shadows have indeed grown flatter.

The Old Man orders a ten-point turn to starboard.

"They're not going to try some new trick?"

I'm standing so close to the TBT that I can hear the First Watch Officer every time he breathes out. I'm uneasy: the paler shadow is no longer to be seen.

"Time?"

"20.28 hours!"

viii SECOND ATTACK

THE MOON has turned even whiter, icier. All around its sharply defined halo the sky is clear. But one of the clouds on the horizon is advancing on it, looking like the vanguard of a whole horde.

I only have eyes for this particular one. It's moving in the right direction, but after a while it slows down until it's hardly rising at all; then it turns threadbare and starts to unravel. As we watch, it dissolves. All that's left is a veil of vapor.

"For chrissake!" hisses the navigator.

But then another cloud prepares to free itself from the horizon, even heavier and fuller than the first.

The wind pushes it a little sideways, exactly the way we want it to go. No one is cursing any longer, as if cursing might upset it.

I abandon the cloud to concentrate on the horizon. In my glasses I can make out the bow, stern, and midship superstructures of the freighters.

The Commander tells the First Watch Officer his plan. "Charge them and fire. After firing, turn instantly to port. If that cloud keeps rising, I'll go in for the main attack!"

The First Watch Officer gives the instructions for the calculator, which is operated by one man in the tower and a second in the control room.

"Tubes one to four stand by for surface firing!"

All four torpedo tubes are flooded.

The bow compartment reports over the speaking tube: "Tubes one to four clear for surface firing!"

"Connect TBT and target position calculator. Firing will take place from bridge!" orders the First Watch Officer.

The words come smoothly. So he can do it. He's got that much by heart.

The mate at the calculator in the tower acknowledges the orders.

The Old Man behaves as though all this liturgical antiphony has nothing to do with him. Only the tension in his stance betrays his acute awareness of everything that's going on.

The First Watch Officer now reports to the mate in the tower: "Enemy position bow right—angle fifty—enemy speed ten knots—range ten thousand feet—torpedo speed thirty—depth ten—position changing."

The First Watch Officer doesn't need to worry about the proper lead angle for the torpedoes. The position calculator computes that. The calculator is connected directly with the gyrocompass and the TBT column, along with the torpedoes, whose steering mechanism is thus continuously adjusted. Every change in the boat's course is automatically translated for the torpedoes. All the First Watch Officer has to do is keep the target in the crosshairs of the glasses on the TBT column.

He bends over the eyepiece. "Ready for comparison reading! . . . Variation . . . Zero!"

"*Must* work," the Commander murmurs. Once more he glances up at the moon. The second cloud has stopped, like a captive balloon that has reached its predetermined height. Three handbreadths below the moon: There it hangs, and doesn't budge.

"One good push!" The navigator shakes his clenched fist; an outburst of feeling from so quiet a man as Kriechbaum amazes me. But there's no time to muse over the navigator; the Commander jerks his face sharply around and orders: "Full speed ahead! Hard a-port! Commence attack! Open torpedo doors!"

From below come the shouted repetitions of the commands. The bow is already beginning to swing along the horizon—seeking the shadows.

"Midships!—Steady as she goes! Hold ninety degrees!" The boat is racing straight at the dark shapes, which are growing larger by the second.

The plowshare of the bow cuts into the shining sea, hurling aside great masses of sparkling water. The wave surges, glints with a thousand facets. The foreship rises. Immediately spray sweeps over us. The diesels are running at full speed. The bulwark quivers.

"Find your target!" the Commander orders.

The First Watch Officer remains bent over the sight.

"There, those two overlapping ones, we'll take them. Have you got them? To the left, beside the single freighter! The big one will need a double shot, the others singles. Fire a double, one at the forward edge of the bridge and one just ahead of the aftermast!"

I'm standing close behind the Commander.

"Tubes one to four clear!"

My heart is hammering in my throat, and I can't think straight. The roaring engines, the shadows, the silver sea, the moon, the final charge! We're meant to be a U-boat—let's pray everything goes right.

The First Watch Officer keeps the target in his sights. His mouth is downturned, his voice matter of fact and dry. He's constantly revising his figures. He already has his right hand on the firing lever.

"Connect tubes one and two—angle sixty-five—follow changing angle!"

"Request angle!"

"Angle seventy . . . angle eighty!"

Close beside me I hear the Commander say, "Tubes one and two, permission to fire!"

Seconds later the First Watch Officer orders, "Tubes one and two fire!"

I strain all my senses: no report—no jolt—nothing! The boat races on, even closer to the freighters.

They've noticed nothing!—nothing!

"Connect tube three!"

"Tube three—fire!"

"Port ten!" orders the Commander.

Once more the bow moves, searching, along the chain of ships.

"Connect tube four!" from the First Watch Officer. He waits until the new target is in position and orders, "Tube four—fire!"

It's at this moment, close beside the target steamer, that I discover a long, low ship—a shadow that's not as dark as the others—probably painted gray.

"Hard a-port! Connect stern tube!" That was the Commander. The boat heels heavily as she turns. The shadows move to starboard.

The navigator calls, "Vessel veering this way!"

I see that our stern is now aimed at the shadows. But I also see that the light-colored shape is narrowing. I can even see the thread of her bow wave.

"Tube five—fire! Hard a-starboard!" shouts the Commander. The boat has barely swung toward the other side when orange-red lightning blazes up, followed in a fraction of a second by another flash. A mighty fist strikes me in the knees, and a sharp whistling goes through me like cold steel.

"They're firing, the bastards! ALARM!" roars the Old Man.

With one jump I'm in the hatch and let myself fall through. Seaboots land on my shoulders. I leap away, jammed up against the chart table, doubled over with pain. Someone goes rolling across the floor in front of me.

"Flood!" shouts the Commander, and immediately afterward, "Hard a-port!" There's a dash of water from above. Our high speed is forcing the boat down at a steeper angle than usual, but the Commander still orders, "All hands forward!"

"That was damned good!" he exclaims as he catches up with us.

I have some difficulty realizing that this is praise for the enemy artillery. The cavalcade of men goes stumbling through the compartment. I catch terrified looks. Everything begins to slide. The leather jackets and the binoculars on their hooks to right and left of the hatch are standing out from the walls.

The needle of the depth manometer sweeps over the scale, till the Chief finally orders the hydroplanes reversed. The jackets and binoculars sink slowly—very gradually—back toward the walls. The boat returns to an even keel.

I can't catch the Commander's eye. "That was damned good"— anything better and we'd have been done for. I can think of only one thing: the torpedoes—what about the torpedoes?

"Just as I thought—it was a destroyer," says the Commander. He sounds short of breath. I can see his chest heaving. He looks us over as if to assure himself that everyone's present, then mutters, "The return engagement is about to begin."

The destroyer! At such close range! The Old Man must have known for some time that the pale shadow was no freighter. The Tommies' destroyers are light gray, just like ours.

There's a destroyer coming hell for leather straight at our diving point! "The return engagement!" It's going to be a pretty explosive one.

"Take her down to three hundred feet—slowly," orders the Old Man.

The Chief repeats the order in a low voice. He's crouching behind the hydroplane operators, his eyes fixed on the manometer.

A whisper: "Now we're in for it!"

Make yourself heavy, make yourself small, shrink!

Our torpedoes! Did they all miss? Can that happen? Five of them? A double and two singles and the stern tube as well while we were turning. Admittedly the shot from tube five was hastily aimed, but the others! Why no explosion?

The Chief brings his head even closer to the round eye of the manometer. On his forehead, sweat sparkles like pearls of dew. I see the single drops link up, making trails down his face like snail tracks. He wipes his forehead impatiently with the back of his hand.

We've barely moved an inch.

They'll be above us any moment now.

What went wrong? Why no explosions?

Everyone stands silent, brooding. The needle of the depth manometer moves another ten divisions.

I try to think clearly. How long since we dived?—How fast was that destroyer moving?—Misses!—All misses!—These shitty torpedoes!—The familiar suspicions—Sabotage! What else could it be? Faulty steering mechanisms, the bastards! And any minute now the Tommies will be ripping our asses up! The Old Man must have been out of his mind. What he did was a torpedo boat attack! On the surface! Straight up and at 'em. They can't have believed their eyes! How many yards' range was it, anyway? How many seconds for a destroyer to reach us at top speed? Those garbled steering orders! The turn!—Crazy: The Old Man had ordered hard a-port just as we were diving. That's something you never do. What can he have been up to? Then I get it: The Tommies saw us diving away to starboard. The Old Man was trying to fool them—let's hope they're not as crafty as we are!

The Old Man rests one thigh on the chart chest. All I see of him is his bent back and the dim white of his cap over the upturned collar of his fur-lined vest.

The navigator's eyes are almost completely closed: slits carved in wood with a sharp chisel. He's sucking his lips between his teeth. His right hand holding fast to the housing of the sky periscope. Six feet away, the control-room mate's face is no more than a pale blob.

A dull, smothered sound breaks the silence—like a stick hitting a slack drumhead.

"That one got it!" whispers the Commander. He raises his head abruptly, and I can see his face. His eyes are squinting, his mouth stretched wide.

Another dull concussion.

"And that one too! Damned slow running time," he adds dryly.

What is he talking about? Torpedoes? Have two of them hit?

The Second Watch Officer has straightened up. His fists are knotted and he's baring his clenched teeth like an ape. It's obvious he wants desperately to shout. But he only swallows and chokes. The grimace stays frozen on his face.

The needle of the depth manometer keeps moving slowly over the dial.

Another drumbeat.

"Number three!" says someone.

These dull detonations—is that all there is to it? I squeeze my eyes shut. All my nerves seem to be concentrated in my ear canals. Is that all there's going to be?

Then there's a sound like a sheet being slowly torn in two, followed by a second sheet being rapidly ripped to shreds. After that, a violent rasping of metal, and now all around us nothing but tearing, grating, knocking, cracking.

I've been holding my breath so long that I have to fight for air. Dammit. What's happening now?

The Old Man raises his head.

"Two of them going down, navigator—there *are* two, wouldn't you say?"

The noise—is that the bulkheads bursting?

"They've—had—it!" The Old Man drags the words out in long breaths.

No one moves. No one gives a victory yell. The control-room mate is standing beside me, motionless, in his usual position, one hand on the ladder, head turned to face the depth manometer. The two hydroplane operators: stiff folds in rubber suits, sou'westers gleaming with moisture. The pale eye of the manometer: the pointer steady now. Then I register: The hydroplane operators are actually still wearing their sou'westers!

"Damned slow running time. I'd already given up." The Commander's voice is back to its usual dark growl. The breaking and cracking, roaring and tearing show no sign of coming to an end.

"Now *there's* a couple of boats you can write off for good."

Then a shattering blow knocks me off my feet. In the nick of time I catch hold of a pipe to break my fall. There's a crash of breaking glass.

I pull myself upright, automatically stagger forward a couple of steps, jostle against someone, collide with a hard corner, and collapse into the hatch frame.

This is it. The reckoning! Mustn't let yourself go! I press my left shoulder hard against the metal frame of the hatch and make myself as heavy as I can. I use both hands to seize the pipe that runs under my thighs. My own special place. My hands touch the smooth enamel paint and feel the rust on the underside of the pipe. An iron grip. Like a vise. I stare intently at the back of my left hand, then my right, as though staring could make them grip all the harder.

Where's the next?

I raise my hunched head very slowly, like a turtle, ready to retract it instantly when the expected blow comes. All I hear is someone sniffing violently.

My eyes seem to be drawn magnetically to the Commander's cap. He takes a step—and his cap and the red and white scales on either side of the water gauge become part of a single image: clowns' striped whips. Or the oversized lollipops that stand like flowers in jars in the windows of Parisian confectioners. All-day suckers. Or the beacon lighthouse that we saw on the port bow as we left the harbor. That was painted red and white too.

The hatch frame almost bucks me out. An enormous detonation tries to shatter my eardrums. Then blow after blow, as if the sea were a mass of huge powder kegs being set off in quick succession.

A multiple drop.

Christ, that was accurate! That was their second charge. They're no fools, and they didn't fall for our bluff.

My guts contract.

Outside, nothing but rearing, gurgling, rumbling! Undersea whirlpools seize the boat, tossing it violently this way and that. Luckily, I'm so firmly wedged I might as well be in a gyrowheel.

Suddenly the gurgling of the water, pouring back on itself to fill the vacuum left by the explosions, ebbs away, but we can still hear the dull roaring, knocking, and breaking up of the other boats.

The Commander laughs like a madman. "They're certainly going down—well, that saves us a parting shot. Too bad we can't watch the tubs go under, though."

I blink in exasperation. But already the Old Man's voice is matter of fact again. "That was the second strike!"

I become aware of the voice of the hydrophone operator. My powers of perception must have been partially suspended. The operator must have been giving continuous reports, but I haven't heard a word.

"Destroyer bearing thirty degrees to port. Getting louder fast!"

The Commander's eyes are fixed on the operator's lips. "Any change?"

The operator hesitates. Finally he reports, "Sound receding astern!"

The Commander immediately orders an increase in speed. Now I can finally clear the fog from my brain, follow what is going on, and think with the others. The hope is that the destroyer will cross our course a good way astern, which is obviously what the Old Man's after.

We still don't know which way the destroyer will turn in its renewed attempt to pass overhead—the Old Man must be guessing that it'll be to port, for he has the helm put hard to starboard.

The chief mechanic Franz comes into the room. His face is chalk-white. Beads of sweat gleam like glycerin on his forehead. Although there are no waves to worry about, he hangs on first with his left hand, then with his right. "They've got us!" he blurts out. Then he shouts for safety cassettes for the gyrocompass.

"Stop that racket!" the Commander rounds on him angrily.

Four detonations in quick succession, almost a single blow. But the deep whirlpools don't reach us.

"Astern—way astern!" the Old Man jeers. "Not as easy as all that."

He props his left leg against the chart table, then undoes the buttons of his collar. He's making himself comfortable. He pushes his hands into the pockets of his leather trousers and turns to the navigator.

Another single detonation—not close, but the echo is remarkably long. The bubbling and roaring seem never-ending.

Through the dull hubbub comes the Old Man's voice. "They're spitting in the wrong corner."

The destroyer certainly seems to have faulty bearings—another couple of distant detonations. But we're still tormented by the acoustical aftermath of every bomb—even those that explode several thousand yards away. The enemy knows how demoralizing this can be, even if the bombs fall wide of the mark.

"Take this down, navigator."

"*Jawohl*, Herr Kaleun."

" '22.40 hours proceed to attack'—22.40 hours is right, isn't it, navigator?—'proceed to attack. Columns running in close formation' —yes, close formation. How many columns we don't need to say. 'Destroyers clearly visible up ahead and on the moonlit side . . .' "

How's that? Clearly visible? Destroyers clearly visible up ahead . . . So there's more than one? My mouth goes dry. The Old Man didn't say a word about it. On the contrary, he was acting the whole time as if there were no escort on the side we were attacking.

" '. . . clearly visible.' Have you got that? 'Attack on starboard side of second column'—got that too?"

"*Jawohl,* Herr Kaleun."

" 'Moon very bright . . .' "

"You can say that again," murmurs the Second Watch Officer, but so softly the Commander can't hear him.

" '. . . very bright—but not bright enough to necessitate underwater attack . . .' "

I have to get up to make way for the men who ended up in the bow compartment when "All hands forward!" was ordered, and who now want to get back through the hatch. They tiptoe past like tightrope walkers to avoid making any noise.

The Old Man orders the boat down farther and to hold depth and course for about five minutes. And when the hydrophone operator announces a new attack he takes us deeper still. He's betting that the people in the destroyer won't have caught this second maneuver and therefore that they'll be setting their canisters to go off at the previous depth . . . the one we were holding just long enough to make sure their sound men got a good reading.

New reports from the operator. No doubt about it: the destroyer is on our heels.

Despite the urgency in the operator's voice the Old Man gives no new orders to the helmsman. I know: he's postponing any change in course until the last moment, so the destroyer that's speeding after us won't have time to copy our maneuver. Hare and hound! Only when the dog is about to snap—when he's sure the hare is already in his jaws—does the hare swerve, but the dog can't make the turn: His own momentum is too great.

The analogy doesn't totally fit our case, I admit—we're not as fast as the hare, and our turning circle is too big. Indeed, it doesn't fit at all: The destroyer can always turn faster than we can. But if it's running full speed and wants to change course, it too is thrown off. A tin can like that simply has too little draft.

"Not bad shooting. Azimuth damned good. They just aimed a little too high . . ." Then the Old Man orders, "Hard a-starboard. Port motor full speed ahead!"

All the auxiliary machines have long since been turned off: the radio transformer, the ventilators, even the gyrocompass. I hardly dare breathe. Quiet as a mouse. What does that mean, "Quiet as a mouse"? The cat up there—we mice down here? Anyway, don't move!

They really should have got us on the first attack—they were so close to our diving point. But the Old Man was too clever for them. First he turned our narrow silhouette toward theirs. And then the turn to starboard—and the dive, but with the rudder hard a-port. Like a player taking a goal kick who looks at one corner of the net and kicks at the other.

The Old Man favors me with a nod. "We're not through with them yet. Tough lot. They're no beginners."

"Really," is all I manage.

"Though they must be getting a trifle annoyed by now," he adds.

He orders us down farther; five hundred feet. Going by the operator's reports, the destroyer must be following us around on a leash. At any moment they can signal their engines full speed ahead and start attacking. What we need is a faster boat.

The Old Man orders higher speed. This involves all sorts of risks, because the faster the motors run the more racket they make. The Tommies must be able to hear our E-motors just by using their ears. But the Commander's prime concern is probably to get out of range of the enemy's direction finder.

"Destroyer getting louder!" the operator announces in a low voice.

The Commander whispers an order for us to reduce speed again. So it didn't work. We didn't manage to break away. They're still after us. They're not going to let themselves be shaken off; they'd rather let their scows wallow along without protection. After all, positive location of a U-boat is no everyday occurrence.

A gigantic sledgehammer hits the boat. At almost the same instant, the Old Man orders the bilge pumps turned on and the speed increased. As soon as the tumult outside ebbs away he has the pumps stopped and the motors reduced to slow. "Thirteen—fourteen," the navigator counts, and makes two new marks on his slate. So that was two bombs. I count: first we had four. Then the second drop, the multiple ejection, was counted as six. Does that check? I recalculate.

Another three, four blows—so violent that the floor plates clatter. I feel the detonations right down to my stomach. Cautiously I turn my head. The navigator's chalking up four.

The Old Man hasn't budged an inch. He holds his head so that he has one eye on the depth manometer and his left ear turned toward the sound room.

"They really don't seem to like us." That from the ensign. Unbelievable: He actually said something. Now he's staring at the floor plates: The sentence must have escaped him involuntarily. Everyone heard. The navigator is grinning, and the Old Man turns his head. For an instant there's a trace of amusement on his face.

The pebbles. At first it sounds like no more than a handful of coarse sand thrown against our port side. But now it's garden gravel, three, four scoops, one after the other. Their Asdic. It feels like being suddenly lit up from all sides, as if we were lying exposed on a huge stage in full view of the audience.

"Swine!" mutters the control-room mate half to himself. For a moment I hate them too, but after all, who or what are "they": the hard singing of the screws, the hornet buzz, the rattle of gravel against the boat's side? That shadow, the narrow silhouette that was only a shade brighter than the freighters—that's all I've been able to see of the enemy . . .

The whites of their eyes! For us, that's pure rubbish! We've lost our sight. No more seeing—only listening. Ear against the wall! So why no new report from our eavesdropper-in-chief? The Commander is blinking impatiently. Nothing?

All ears harken unto Thee, O Lord, for Thou wilt bring great joy to those who trust in Thy word—or something like that. The Bible Scholar would have the exact quote; he's hardly recognizable in the dusky light. The hydrophone operator raises his eyebrows. That's another sign: won't be long before everyone's ears are busy again.

They have ears, and hear not. One of the Psalms of David. I'm all ears. I am one gigantic ear, all my nerves a single listening knot; they've twined themselves like fine elfin hair around hammer, anvil, and stirrup.

A box on the ears—we've had plenty of those—lend a willing ear —walls have ears—pull the wool over someone's ears . . . Of course, *that's* it: they want to skin us, pull our hide over our ears.

How do things look on the surface now?

There's sure to be a murderous amount of illumination. All searchlights on, and the sky studded with parachute flares so that the archenemy can't escape. All cannon barrels lowered and ready to be fired at once if they succeed in forcing us to the surface.

The operator reports, "Destroyer bearing twenty degrees. Getting louder fast!" And after a short hesitation, "Commencing attack!"

Two ax blows hit the boat broadside. More wild roaring and gurgling. Then two more blows in the midst of the raging tumult.

I've opened my mouth the way artillery men do so that my eardrums won't burst. After all, I was trained as a naval gunner. But now I'm not next to a cannon; I'm on the other end, in the midst of the bursting shells.

There's no getting away from here. No use throwing yourself flat. Digging in—that's a laugh: what we have under our feet are iron floor plates covered with cunt patterns, as Zeitler calls the thousand little shapes. I exert all my self-control to suppress claustrophobia, the damnable urge to flee in any direction. Keep your feet nailed to the floor! I pray for lead in the soles of my shoes, like those bright, barrel-shaped toy figures that always bob up again however you knock them down. Thank god, I can remember what they're called. Standup men . . . standup men, incense men, humming tops, fancy nutcrackers. Bright pretty toys.

When you think about it, I'm well off. I can't be knocked over either. The frame of the hatch in which I'm crouching is the best place to be at a time like this.

I loosen my grip on the pipe. Apparently it's safe to relax. Ease the muscle cramp, move the jawbone, rest the skeleton, relax the belly muscles, let the blood circulate. For the first time I realize how painful my contortions have been.

Our every move is defined by our opponents. The Tommies can even decide what positions we must assume. We draw our heads in, huddle waiting for the impact of the detonation, and stretch and loosen up once the roaring begins outside. Even the Old Man is careful not to unleash his derisive laughter except during the gurgling that follows the explosions.

The operator half opens his mouth. Immediately I catch my breath again. What now? If only I knew where the last series fell, just how far from the boat the bombs exploded or how far we are from our diving point! After our first unsuccessful attempt to break away, it seems as though the pursuit has gone around and around in circles—first to the right, then to the left, up and down, like a rollercoaster ride. We haven't made any ground at all. Every attempt so far to break out sideways and find cover has been spotted by the enemy.

The operator closes his mouth and opens it again. He looks like a carp in a tank at the fish store. Open, shut, and then open again. He announces a new attack.

And then immediately calls "Asdic!" hoarsely from the sound room. He could have saved himself the trouble. Everyone in the control room has heard the *ping-ping*. As have the men in the bow compartment on top of the torpedoes, and aft in the motor room and diesel room.

The enemy has got us trapped in the tentacles of the direction finder. Right now they're turning steel hand wheels and searching through three dimensions with pulsing beams—*zirp—zirp—ping—ping* . . .

The Asdic, I remind myself, is only effective up to a speed of about thirteen knots. During a fast attack the destroyer no longer has directional contact. At higher speeds the Asdic suffers major interference from the destroyer's own noises and the commotion of its screws, which is an advantage for us, since it gives us a last-minute opportunity to make minor changes in our position. But the Commander up there is also capable of figuring out that we won't stand still and wait for the attack. Only: which way we move is the one thing his directional boys can't tell him. There he has to use his intuition.

One break for us is that our enemy and his clever machine can't tell exactly how deep we are. In this, nature is on our side: water is not simply water; right down through our present depth it forms layers like sedimentary rock. The salt content and the physical characteristics of the individual layers are never the same. And they scatter the Asdic. All we have to do is move suddenly from a layer of warm water into a cold one and the Asdic becomes inaccurate. A layer of dense plankton will influence it too. And the people up there with their apparatus can't correct their plotting of our position with any confidence because they don't know where these damn layers are.

Herrmann is working away at his wheel.

"Report!" says the Old Man in the direction of the sound room.

"Sounds bearing three hundred fifty degrees."

In less than five minutes the screws are audible to the naked ear.

Ritschipitschipitschipitschi—that's no full-speed attack. The destroyer is moving just fast enough to be able to go on tracking us, and the Asdic echoes loud and clear.

A fresh attack. Four, five detonations. Close. Against closed eyelids I project jets of flame, towering St. Elmo's fire, the flickering gleam of chrysoprase, cascading sparks around dark-red central cores, dazzling white naphtha flames, whirling Chinese pinwheels, blinding surges, amethyst beams piercing the darkness, an enormous fiery holocaust loosed from rainbow-haloed fountains of bronze.

"Exercise maneuvers," whispers the Old Man.

I wouldn't call them that.

A gigantic fist comes down and shakes the boat. I feel the thrust in my knees as we're jolted upward. The needle of the depth indicator jerks back. The light goes out, and there's the sound of breaking glass. My heart is pounding—finally the emergency light goes on.

I see the Old Man biting his lower lip. It's the moment of decision. Does he take the boat down to the depth where the last bombs exploded or up a few hundred feet?

He orders a turn and a simultaneous dive. Back down the roller-coaster again. One—two—three—but where? Up? Down? Left? The last surge made it sound as if the bombs had been forward and to port of us. But were they above or below the boat? Here we go again. The operator resumes his reports.

The blow hits me right on the third dorsal vertebra. Followed by another—and another: two straight punches to the back of the head and the neck.

Smoke is beginning to swirl out from the helmsman's station. To crown everything else, are we going to have a fire? Are those cables beginning to smolder? And won't that cause short circuits?

Calm down! Nothing can happen to this scow: *I* am on board. *I* am immortal. With me on board the boat is immune.

No doubt about it—the instrument panel is on fire! The sign on the Minimax: *Keep calm! Fight fire from below.* My brain keeps repeating: immune—immune—immune.

The control-room mate springs into action and almost disappears in the flames and smoke. Two or three men go to his assistance. I notice that the boat is bow heavy—more and more so. I hear, "Valve —bilge duct broken." But that can't be all there is to it! Why doesn't the Chief trim toward the stern? What else are our trim tanks for, if not to act as a balancing rod?

Although the destroyer must be quite close, the Old Man orders full speed ahead. Of course! We already have too much water in the boat; we can no longer manage to keep her buoyant. We need the power of the screws and their pressure on the hydroplanes to make the boat stern heavy fast. Otherwise the Old Man would never create such a racket: at this speed it's like having a cowbell around our neck. Dilemma: to sink or speed up. The Tommies up there must be able to hear us—motors, screws, and bilge pump—with their own ears. They might just as well turn off their Asdic and save the current.

In addition to his complicated course calculations, the Old Man now has to worry constantly about the boat's depth. We're in a tricky situation. If it were only a question of surfacing, that wouldn't take much: "Don rescue gear," and blow the tanks with everything we've got. Don't even think about it!

Everything's wet, covered in condensation.

"Driving-shaft gaskets making water!" someone shouts from the stern. Immediately followed, from forward, by ". . . valve leaking!" I'm no longer paying much attention. Why bother worrying about which valve it might be.

Four detonations in quick succession, then the mad gurgle and roar of the black flood rushing back into the huge hollows torn out by the bombs.

"Thirty-three—four—five—thirty-six," the navigator counts in a loud voice. That time it was close!

We're now at four hundred feet.

The Old Man takes us deeper and turns the boat to port.

The next detonation slams my teeth together. I can hear sobbing. The new control-room assistant? Surely he's not going to have a fit of hysterics?

"Nice shooting!" the Old Man jeers loudly as the next detonations surge over us.

I tense my stomach muscles as if to protect my organs against a ton of pressure. It's some minutes before I dare release my left hand from its grip on the pipe. It rises of its own volition and brushes across my forehead: cold sweat. My whole back feels equally clammy. Fear?

I seem to be seeing the Commander's face through a fog.

It's the smoke from the helmsman's station still hanging in the room, although the smoldering has stopped. There's a sour taste in my mouth and a dull pressure somewhere in my head. I hold my breath; it only makes the pressure worse.

Any moment and it'll be time again—the destroyer will have completed its circle. The pack of hounds has to grant us this brief respite whether they want to or not.

There's the Asdic again. Two or three sharp rattles of pebbles. A cold hand creeps under my collar and runs down my back. I shudder.

The pressure in my head becomes unbearable. What now? Why is nothing happening? Every whisper has died away. The condensation pitter-patters at steady one-second intervals. Silently I count them. At twenty-two the blow lands, doubling me over with my head crumpled against my chest.

Am I deaf? I see the floor plates dancing, but it's seconds before I hear their metallic clatter, mixed with a yowling, groaning sound and a high-pitched screech. The pressure hull! It can't be anything else. The boat heaves and pitches in the rearing eddies. Men stagger against one another.

Another double blast. The boat groans. Clattering scraping sounds.

The Tommies are being economical. No more carpeting—instead, always two bombs at a time, probably set for different depths. I dare not relax my muscles—the hammer lands again with enormous force.

A gurgling, coughing gasp quite close to me turns into a moan.

Sounds as if someone has been hit. It confuses me momentarily, but then reality reasserts itself: don't be crazy, no one gets shot down here.

The Old Man has got to think up something new. No chance of sneaking away. The Asdic won't let us go. They've got first-class men sitting up there at the controls, and they're not easily bluffed. How much time do we have left? How much do the Tommies need to circle?

Lucky for us that they can't drop their bombs overboard whenever they want. They have to be running at full speed before they fire. If those bastards could use their Asdic to sneak up right over the boat before dropping their cans, this cat and mouse game would have been over long ago. As it is, they have to attack at high speed so as not to blow themselves out of the water when their bombs go off.

What's the Old Man up to now? It's making him frown. I can tell from the way his brows are twitching that he's deep in concentration. How long will he go on waiting? Can he pull off another last-minute swerve to escape the advancing destroyer?—and in the right direction?—at the right speed?—and the right depth?

It's high time he opened his mouth and gave an order. Or has he given up? Thrown in the sponge?

Suddenly a sound like canvas being ripped. The Commander's voice crackles out at the same moment: "Bail!—Hard a-port! And gun those goddam motors!"

The boat leaps forward. The noise of the bilge pump is drowned in the roar that fills the sea around us. Men stagger and clutch the pipes. The Old Man doesn't budge. The navigator clings to his table.

The Old Man's gamble suddenly dawns on me. He's ordered us to hold a straight course, even though we've been spotted. A new wrinkle. A variation he hasn't tried on the Tommies before. Obvious: The Commander of the destroyer wasn't born yesterday. He doesn't come rushing blindly to the spot where they've located us. They know our tricks. They know that we know they're attacking; they know that we know they can't use their Asdic at high speed, that we'll try to escape their line of attack and also change depth. Whether we feint to port or to starboard, whether we head up or down is something they can only guess at. They have to rely on luck.

And so the Old Man stops playing tricks for once and simply holds his course and depth until the next drop. Bluff and double bluff. And just when you think you're lucky—bang! You get it up the ass!

"Time?" asks the Commander.

"01.30 hours," the navigator replies.

"Really?" There's astonishment in his voice. Even he seems to be finding the dance a trifle drawn out.

"Most unusual," he murmurs. "But they probably want to be absolutely sure."

For a while nothing stirs. The Old Man orders us deeper. Then deeper still.

"Time."

"01.45 hours!"

Unless my ears are really playing tricks on me, even the compass motor has been shut off. Not a sound in the boat. Only the pitter-patter of condensation ticking off the seconds.

Have we made it? How far have we gone in a quarter of an hour's silent running? Then the stillness is broken again by the hideous noises that the Old Man calls "creaking in the beams": Our steel cylinder is being brutally tested for resistance by the pressure at these depths. The steel skin is bulging inward between the ribs. The interior woodwork groans.

We're down at 650 feet again, more than twice the shipyard guaranty, creeping along through the blackness at a speed of four knots with this vast column of water sitting on top of us.

Operating the hydroplanes becomes a balancing trick. If the boat sinks any lower, its tortured fabric may no longer be able to withstand the external pressure. A matter of inches could be crucial. Is the Old Man counting on the Tommies not knowing our maximum diving depth? We ourselves never mention this magic number in feet but say, "Three times *r* plus sixty." An incantation. Could the Tommies really not know how much *r* is? Every stoker knows; probably fifty thousand Germans do, all told.

No reports from the operator. I can't believe we've escaped. The bastards are probably lying in wait, engines stopped. They know that they were almost directly above us. The only thing they couldn't calculate was our depth, and the Old Man has taken extreme measures about that. The Chief moves his head back and forth uneasily. Nothing seems to rasp on his nerves so much as the creaking in the woodwork.

Two detonations. Bearable. The gurgling is cut short at a stroke. But our bilge pump keeps going for several seconds more! They must have heard the damn thing. You'd think someone could build quieter ones.

The longer we remain at these depths, the more tormenting the thought of how thin our steel hull is. We aren't armor-plated. All we have to withstand the pressure of the water and the shock waves of the explosions is a mere inch of steel. The circular ribs—two every three feet—are all that give our thin-walled tube the meager powers of resistance that enable us to stay alive down here.

"They're taking one helluva time to get ready," whispers the Old Man. We must be dealing with some really clever bastards if even he admits it.

I try to picture what's going on up there. I have my own memories to help me, for after all it's not so long since I was one of the hunters, on a destroyer myself. It's the same game on both sides except that the Tommies have their highly perfected Asdic and we have nothing but our sound gear. It's the difference between electronics and acoustics.

Listen—make a run—drop the bombs—circle—listen—make a run—drop more bombs—try setting them for shallow depths—then for deeper ones—then the star act: the spread—launch at least a dozen canisters simultaneously—like drumfire. The same thing the Tommies do.

Each one of our depth charges contained four hundred pounds of amatol. So a dozen bombs had more than two tons of high explosive. When we had a good directional indication on the S-apparatus, all the ejectors were fired at once: starboard, port, and aft. I can still hear the Captain's voice: "Not very sporting, this king of thing."

Very odd that nothing is happening. Marking time—given up? Perhaps I can ease the tension in my muscles. But careful—mustn't jump if it begins again. Annihilation by whirlpool, with time out now and again. Fear of the next onslaught begins to grow. Quick—think about something else.

The time we made sonar contact close to the southwest corner of England. On the destroyer *Karl Galster*—nothing but guns and machines. The frightened voice from the starboard wing of the bridge: "Torpedo trail three points to the starboard!" The voice still rings in my ears: hoarse, yet piercing. Unforgettable, if I live to be a hundred.

The trail of bubbles—crystal clear. An eternity before the pale track of our wake finally curved to one side.

I have to swallow. Fear grips me by the throat—double fear—both remembered and actual. My thoughts race. Must be careful not to get them mixed up. "Torpedo trail three points to starboard." That was on the *Karl Galster*. The overpowering, mind-numbing tension. And then the voice of salvation. "Torpedo trail passed astern!"

Just endure, last out each round. How long has it been so far? I still don't dare move. This time I'm one of the hunted. Trapped in the deep. On a boat with no more torpedoes in its tubes. Defenseless, even if we manage to surface.

How the Captain of the *Karl Galster* pulled it off! He must have got clear by a matter of inches. Full rudder and engines going full speed until the ship swung round parallel to the torpedo's course. The vibrations! As if she were about to fly to pieces. And then the shrill bell: a warning for the men in the engine room to expect an explosion. Then the torpedo officer's voice on the ship's phone: "Fire two charges!" And the breathless waiting, until a double blow made the ship shiver in every seam. Nothing to be seen but two white, shimmering splashes astern, to left and right of the fading glimmer of our wake—as if two great lumps of rock had fallen into the water.

Then the order: "Hard a-port!" And the Captain reduced speed so that the men below in the belly of the ship could get a more accurate bearing: the same tactics used by the Tommies, precisely the same. Full ahead again—a perceptible leap forward—and off toward the echo we'd picked up on our sonar.

The Captain ordered a spread to be dropped at the point where the equipment reacted most strongly. Canisters all set for the same shallow depth. Short, sharp thunderclaps. Then a rumbling as if we'd hit a mine. I can still see the huge, gleaming white geysers standing poised majestically for seconds before they collapsed in spray. And the foam that came blowing over us like wet curtains.

The Old Man keeps staring at the manometers, as if his eyes could control the play of the needles. But the needles don't move. No Asdic either. The sound man looks like someone lost in pious meditation. I wonder why they're not on the move up there, why nothing is happening. At four knots per hour we can't possibly have escaped the net of their direction finder.

"Steer two hundred twenty degrees," the Old Man orders.

More silence.

"Heading two hundred twenty degrees," comes the helmsman's whispered response after a considerable lag.

"Propeller sounds bearing twenty degrees, fading," is the next hushed report. It brings a mocking grin to the Old Man's face.

I put myself back on the bridge of the *Karl Galster*: pale moonlight on cold, expressionless faces. No matter how hard we stared, no sign of the enemy. Just orders, the splash of the canisters, the third of the explosions. Cross-bearings and new drops. Seething white patches disrupting the pale filigree of our wake.

And then an oil slick on the black water. Once again I see the sharply-etched, thin white finger of the searchlight pointing it out. The ship swings toward it. There's no mercy: "Port bombs away! Starboard bombs away!"

All guns trained on the oil slick, muzzles lowered.

I can still see all the fish with ruptured air bladders floating on the surface of the water in the beam of the searchlight. Fish and more fish—but no sign of wreckage, only the fleck of oil. Suddenly our sound equipment fell silent.

No time for a search. Cruisers might appear at any moment and bar our passage home. The Captain had to head for Brest whether he wanted to or not. And that was when he said, "Not very sporting, this kind of thing."

The operator's voice suddenly penetrates my consciousness. If I understood him correctly, the destroyer is swinging toward us. So they're attacking again. They were just playing us on a line. Cat and mouse stuff. No hope of escape. We didn't fool them.

The operator is grimacing again. I start counting silently, and then the blows begin, one after the other. We're flung around, jolted. The whole sea is a single exploding powder keg.

And again the gushing roar that will not stop, and more propeller noises! But why no pause between them? Where are the propellers coming from again so quickly? That's the easygoing paddling of slow screws, not the quick ringing whirl with its wicked, whistling, underlying howl that indicates top speed.

In the back of my mind I realize what's been going on: this can't be the destroyer that attacked us first—she couldn't be back so soon. She needs time to circle. After all, she can't be coming at us stern-first . . .

There's no delay about the next bombs. They come in triplets.

The light has gone out. Someone calls for emergency light. The Chief shines the beam of his pocket flashlight on the depth manometer. He doesn't dare let his eyes leave the dial for so much as a second: We're so deep that any further descent is dangerous.

"Report sound bearings!"

"Nine points to port," the operator replies.

"Hard a-starboard, steer three hundred ten degrees."

The Commander is trying to make use of our narrow silhouette, exactly as he did on the surface. He wants to present our stern to the enemy so as to give the Asdic beams the smallest possible surface to work on.

"Propeller sounds bearing two hundred degrees—getting stronger!"

The directional beam hits us again. I'm rigid, totally unable to relax; my head will soon crack like glass. My skull seems under the same extreme pressure as our steel skin. The slightest touch now would be too much. My heartbeats ring magnified in my ears. I try shaking my head, but the pounding goes on just the same.

"Brace yourself," I whisper to myself. Fear bordering on hysteria seems to be literally destroying my mind. Yet at the same time it's sharpening my powers of perception. I see and feel everything going on around me with astounding clarity.

"Range? . . . And what about the second sound?" The Old Man's voice is no longer indifferent.

So—I wasn't making it up. Damn, damn, and double damn, the Old Man's calm is gone. Was it the second sound that disconcerted him? But everything depends on him keeping a clear head. Instead of working with precision instruments he has to use his own system of perception, which is probably located in the seat of his pants, or in his stomach.

He's pushed his cap up and runs the back of his hand over his forehead. His sauerkraut hair springs out from under the visor like stuffing out of a torn mattress. His forehead is a washboard and his sweat a stream of bleach. He bares his teeth and snaps them sharply three times. In the silence it sounds like the faint clicking of castanets.

My left leg is asleep. Pins and needles. I lift it cautiously. The moment I'm balancing on my right leg, a series of frightful explosions rocks the boat. This time I find no handhold and fall full length to the floor on my back.

Painfully I manage to turn over. I force my arms up, raise my shoulders, and manage to get on all fours, but keep my head down ready for the next blow.

I hear screams that seem to be coming from a long way off.

Water breach? Didn't I just hear "water breach"? Is that why we're sinking aft? First forward, now aft . . .

"Aft up ten—both E-motors full ahead!"

That was the Old Man. Loud and clear. So I haven't gone deaf after all. Full speed ahead. In this situation! Isn't that much too loud? My god, the boat's still shuddering and groaning continuously. Sounds as if it's battling its way through an immensely deep groundswell.

I want to lie down and hide my head in my arms.

No light. The crazy fear of drowning in the dark, unable to see the green-white torrent of water as it comes bursting into the boat . . .

A beam darts over the walls and finds its goal: the depth manometer. A sharp singing note from astern like a circular saw eating into wood. Two or three men shake themselves out of their daze. Orders are hissed. Another beam strikes the Old Man's face, which looks like a gray cardboard cutout. The stern heaviness is getting worse: I can feel it in my whole body. How long will the Old Man keep the motors running full speed? The roar of the depth charge has long since died away. Now anyone can hear us—anyone in the belly of the ship up there. Or can they? Certainly they can if their ship's engines are stopped.

"Where are the reports?" I hear the Old Man growl.

I can feel with my elbow that the man standing slightly to the left in front of me is shivering. I can't see who he is.

Once again the old temptation to let myself slump down onto the floor. Mustn't give in.

Someone stumbles. "Silence!" the Old Man hisses.

It's now that I notice the E-motors are no longer running at full speed. The emergency lighting goes on. So that isn't the Chief's back over there—the Second Engineer has taken over the hydroplanes. The Chief is nowhere to be seen. He's probably astern for the moment; all hell seems to have been let loose back there. The evil sawmill-shriek is unrelenting.

But we're moving. Not on an even keel, to be sure, but at least we aren't sinking any deeper. So the pressure hull must have held. And the motors are working.

An odd scraping sound makes me lift my head. It sounds like a cable being dragged along outside. Sweep wires? But that's impossible! They can't be working with sweep wires at depths like these. Perhaps it's something new, some special kind of probing impulse.

The scraping stops. In its place we have the chirping *ping-ping* once again. They've got us!

How late is it? I can't make out the hands of my watch. Probably two o'clock.

"Bearing one hundred forty degrees. Getting louder!"

Again the vicious sound of the Asdic beam hitting the boat. Now it's like pebbles being shaken in a tin can—not even loud. But loud enough to send visions of horror darting through my mind. Cascades of blood dripping over the diving tanks. Red-tinged waves. Men clutching white rags in uplifted hands. I'm well aware of what goes on when a boat is forced to the surface. The Tommies want to see red, as much juice as possible. They let fly with every gun they've got. They mangle the tower while we poor bastards are scrambling up into it; they smash the bridge to bits, make mincemeat of anything that moves, concentrating on the diving tanks so as to make the gray whale blow the last of its air. And then ram her down! Use their sharp bow to slash into the boat with a howling screech. No one can blame them: There at last is the enemy for whom they've been staring themselves blind—for days, weeks, months on end—the treacherous tormentor who's denied them a moment's peace, even when he was hundreds of miles away. They've never been able to be sure for so much as a second that they weren't being spied upon from the trough of a wave by that Polyphemus eye. And here she is finally, the tarantula that drew blood. The blood lust won't subside until fifteen or twenty men have been murdered.

The pressure hull creaks, crunches, and grates again. The Old Man has been taking us deeper without my being aware of it. The Chief's eyes are glued to the dial of the manometer, then he suddenly darts a glance at the Old Man, but the latter behaves as if he hasn't noticed.

"What bearing now?"

"Two hundred eighty degrees—two hundred fifty-five degrees—two hundred forty degrees—getting louder!"

"Hard a-port!" the Commander whispers after a brief pause for thought, and this time gives the change of course to the hydrophone operator as well: "To sound room: We're turning to port!" And as a commentary for us, "The usual!"

And that second noise?

Perhaps they've long since changed places, I tell myself; perhaps the ship above us isn't the same one that attacked us with her guns. After all, escort vessels each have different duties. The destroyer that fired on us was carrying out flank protection. She most probably turned over the task of finishing us off to a sweeper some time ago.

We have no idea who's attacking us.

It's fishing with dynamite: Rip open the air bladders of the fish so that they float up from the depths—our air bladders are our diving tanks. The fish have theirs *in* their bellies; with us the great air bladders are outside, not even pressure-resistant. For a fraction of a second I see a huge drifting gray fish that has been driven to the surface, white belly up, rolling heavily from side to side in the waves . . .

This infernal dripping condensation! *Pitter-patter—pitter-patter* —every single damn drop sounds like a hammer blow.

Finally the Old Man turns his head toward us: His body doesn't move an inch. He simply twists his head as far as it will go on the turntable of his fur collar and grins. As if invisible surgical hooks were drawing the corners of his mouth diagonally upward—a trifle crookedly, so we can see a fraction of an inch of white tooth in the left-hand corner.

What's going to happen now? They can't have given up and called it a day. A day! What time is it anyhow? About 04.00? Or only 02.15? They've had us hooked since 22.53.

But what was that second sound? Complete mystery.

Does the operator still have no new bearings? Herrmann's mouth looks sewn shut. He's thrust his face out of the sound room but for once his eyes are open—his face looks empty, as if he'd died and someone had neglected to close his eyes.

The Old Man's contemptuous grin has become a trace more human, no longer quite so deadly. The relaxation in his face is like a laying-on of hands. Take up your bed and walk! Yes, walk—how about a pleasure stroll around the ship—on the promenade deck. That would make for an amusing interlude now. But no one ever considered our need for freedom of movement; we have no more room than tigers in a traveling cage.

I suddenly see the tiger cage on wheels at Ravenna Beach, that filthy wagon with iron bars. The giant cats, limp and thirsty in the blazing midday heat, crowded together in three square feet of shade along the back wall. On the ground immediately in front of the cage, some fishermen had laid out dead tuna fish: gleaming steel-blue projectiles, almost as slim as torpedoes. The fat horseflies were already at them. They go for the eyes first with tuna fish, just as they did with Swoboda. Accompanying this miserable sight was the tattoo of African drumming, a sharp, rhythmic staccato that was sent sweeping across the empty courtyard from a distant corner. The source of the African music was a dark-brown man in torn overalls who was thrusting thin slabs of ice about three feet long into a metal box; inside which was a cylinder studded with spikes, rotating madly. It threw the ice into the air, snapped at it, threw it into the air again, bit once more. Hurled and crunched and ground up the slabs of ice to the thud and roll of drums. This barbaric uproar, the dead tuna fish, the five tigers—tongues hanging out—in their inferno: that's all I can remember of Ravenna Beach.

Softly, softly the Old Man orders a change of course. The helmsman presses a button: a dull click. So we're doubling back, or at least turning a little.

If only we had some idea of what this latest pause means. They probably want to cradle us into a feeling of security.

But why no more Asdic beams? First two of them, then nothing at all!

Have we managed to sneak away after all? Or can't the Asdic reach us at these depths? Are the layers of the water finally protecting us?

In the highly charged silence the Commander whispers, "Pencil and paper over here."

The navigator is slow to grasp that the request is being made to him.

"Suppose we might as well get a radio report ready," murmurs the Old Man.

The navigator is unprepared for this. He reaches awkwardly for a pad that's lying on the chart table, and his fingers grope for a pencil with blind uncertainty.

"Take it down," the Commander orders. "'Scored hit on eight thousand GRT and five thousand five hundred GRT—heard to sink —Probable hit on eight thousand GRT—' Well, go on. Write it down!"

The navigator bends over his table.

The Second Watch Officer turns around, his mouth open with astonishment.

When the navigator is finished and swivels around again, his face is as expressionless as ever; it betrays nothing at all. This doesn't cost him much effort: nature has endowed him with wooden facial muscles. Nor is there anything to be read in his eyes, they lie so deep in the shadow of his brows. "After all, that's all they want to know," says the Old Man in a low voice. The navigator holds the slip of paper in the air, arm extended. I approach him on tiptoe and hand the paper on to the operator, who's meant to preserve it carefully so that it will be ready in the event we should ever be able to transmit again.

The Old Man's just murmuring to himself, ". . . the last hit . . ." when the sea is shaken by four explosions.

He shrugs his shoulders, makes a contemptuous gesture, and grumbles to himself, "Ah well!" And after a while, "Precisely!"

You'd think he was being forced against his will to listen to the insistent self-justifications of a drunkard. But when the roar ebbs away, he says not a word; the silence again becomes tense.

The operator reports his figures in a subdued tone, half whispered, like the formula for an invocation: he's picked up a clear bearing again.

No Asdic noises! I mock myself by thinking, "Our friends have turned their Asdic off to spare our nerves . . ."

The moon—the fucking moon!

If someone unexpectedly came through the hatch right now, he'd be astounded to see us standing around like idiots, not uttering a syllable. Speechless idiots would be the right description. A snatch of laughter wells up in me; I choke it back. Unexpectedly through the hatch! Some joke!

"Time?"

"02.30 hours," the Commander is informed by the navigator.

"It's been some time," the Commander acknowledges.

I have no idea what's normal. How long can we keep this up? What's the state of our oxygen supply? Is the Chief already releasing precious gas from his cylinders so that we can breathe?

The navigator is holding his stopwatch, following its jerking second hand as attentively as if our lives depended on his observations. Has he been keeping a dead-reckoning chart of our dive, all our attempted evasions? They must make a crazy pattern.

The Old Man is uneasy. How can he trust this quiet? He can't let his mind wander the way I can. For him there's only the enemy and his tactics.

"Well?" he drawls expectantly, the word long-drawn-out and derisive, as he glances theatrically upward. I wonder why he doesn't add, "Ready, darling?"

He grins at me, head to one side. I try to grin back but feel my smile stiffen. My cheek muscles harden of their own accord.

"We really got them, didn't we?" he says softly, and stretches himself comfortably against the periscope housing. You'd think he was savoring the attack in retrospect. "Amazing, the way the hatches burst. Sounded really fabulous. The first one must have sunk damn fast."

"Death rattle." Just where did I get that from? Must have been out of some PR report. That kind of inflated rhetoric couldn't come from anywhere else: death rattle.

"Dying"—a funny word: everyone seems to avoid it. No one ever "dies" in obituaries. The Lord takes unto Himself. The dear departed enters into eternal peace, putting an end to his earthly pilgrimage— but there's no dying. The straightforward verb "to die" is avoided like the plague.

Silence in the boat. Only the soft shifting of the hydroplanes, and now and then a change of course.

"Propeller sounds getting louder fast," reports the operator. There's the Asdic again! This time it sounds like someone writing on a slate with chalk, but pressing much too hard.

"Sounds getting louder."

I notice the sausages hanging from the ceiling. All coated with white. Isn't doing them any good, the stench and the damp. But salami will stand a good deal. Certainly still edible. Smoked meat too. Dead flesh—living flesh. My blood races. My ears respond. Loud beating of my heart: they've got us!

"Time?"

"02.40 hours!"

A yowling sound! What was that? And was it inside the boat? Or outside?

A definite bearing! The destroyer with the white bone in her teeth! Coming at top speed!

The Old Man puts his feet up and unbuttons his vest. He might be making himself comfortable to tell a joke or two.

I wonder what becomes of sunken boats. Do they just stay there, crumpled up, a grotesque armada, perpetually suspended at a depth where the water corresponds precisely to the weight of the collapsed lump of steel? Or do they go on being compressed until they sink thousands upon thousands of feet and drop to the bottom? I must ask the Commander sometime. After all, he's on intimate terms with pressure and displacement. He must know. Rate of descent, twenty-five miles per hour—I ought to know too.

The Old Man grins his usual slightly crooked grin. But his eyes roam watchfully. He gives the helmsman a muttered order: "Hard a-port, steer two hundred seventy degrees!"

"Destroyer attacking!" the operator reports.

I keep my eyes fixed on the Old Man. Don't look now.

The white bone . . . they're coming for us at top speed!

We're still as deep as we can go.

A moment's suspended animation. Then the operator makes a face. No doubt about what that means.

The seconds stretch out: the bombs are on their way. Breathe deep, tense your muscles. A series of shattering blows almost throws me off my feet.

"Do you mind!" the Old Man exclaims. Someone shouts, "Breach above the depth gauge!"

"Not so loud," snaps the Commander.

It's the same thing as last time. A weak spot. A jet of water, stiff as a rod, shoots straight across the control room, dividing the Old Man's face in two; in one half, his mouth gaping in surprise, in the other, his raised eyebrows and the deep-curving creases in his forehead.

A shrill whistling and clattering. Incomprehensible shouting back and forth. My blood seems to be turning to ice. I catch the fluttering glance of the Bible Scholar.

"I'll fix it!" The control-room mate. He's at the point of the leak in a single bound.

Suddenly I'm overwhelmed with rage: goddam swine! All we can do is wait for the bastards to drown us in our own boat like rats.

The control-room mate is dripping. He's turned off some valve or other. The stream falters and splashes in a curve onto the floor plates.

I notice that the boat has become stern heavy again. The Chief takes advantage of the next explosion to trim forward. The boat very slowly returns to an even keel.

That jet of water shooting into the boat under unimaginable pressure has shaken me to the core; a foretaste of catastrophe. Only finger-thick, but horrifying enough. Worse than the worst storm wave.

More blows.

Unless I'm totally confused, some of the men have gathered under the tower hatch. As if there were any point!

It hasn't gotten to the point yet where we have to surface. The Old Man, sitting there so relaxed, doesn't look at all as though he were at the end of his tether. But the grin has gone from his face.

The operator whispers, "More propeller sounds at one hundred twenty degrees."

"Now we're in for it!" the Old Man mutters. There's no doubt about it.

"What's its present bearing—the second sound?"

His voice has become urgent. Yet more computations to be made in his head.

A report from astern: "Diesel air valves making water badly!" The Old Man exchanges a glance with the Chief, who disappears aft. The Old Man takes over the hydroplanes.

"Forward up ten," I hear him order in a murmur.

I become aware of a strong pressure in my bladder. The sight of the stream of water must have prompted it. But I don't know where I can relieve myself.

The Chief reappears in the control room. Aft, there have been two or three breaks around the flanges. His head seems to have developed a nervous tic. A leak—and he can't pump: the enemy up there have seen to that. The auxiliary pump must be kaput anyway. "Glass case of the auxiliary bilge pump cracked," I hear amid the roaring chaos. The glass in the water gauge has broken, too. It's madness.

The Old Man orders both motors full ahead again. All our high-speed evasive maneuvers are doing is reducing the capacity of our batteries. The Old Man's gambling with our supplies. If we have no more battery juice, if we run out of compressed air or oxygen, the boat *has* to surface. The game will be up—nothing more we can do . . . The Chief has blown compressed air into the diving cells again and again in order to give us the buoyancy he could no longer achieve with the bilge pump alone.

Compressed air has an extremely high market value: Given our present circumstances, we're in no position to start manufacturing more. Using the compressor is out of the question.

And how about the oxygen? How long can we go on breathing the stench that permeates the boat?

The sound man gives one report after another. I too can hear the Asdic rattle again.

But it's still not really clear whether we have two pursuers now in place of one.

The Old Man pushes a hand under his cap. He probably doesn't have much grasp of the situation either. Hydrophone reports give practically no information about the enemy's intentions.

Or could they in turn be fooling us with their own noises? Technically it would be possible. Our having to rely completely on the operator's perceptions is preposterous.

The destroyer seems to be making a wide circle. No further word about the second series of noises, but this could mean that a second ship has just been lying there silent for some time.

The pause continues. The First Watch Officer glances round uncertainly. Crumpled face. Sharp nose, white about the nostrils.

The control-room mate is trying to pee into a big can. He fumbles about laboriously trying to get his cock out through his leather trousers.

Then—without warning—a crash. The half-filled can drops from Tin-ear Willie Isenberg's hand and spills onto the floor plates. The place instantly stinks of urine. I'm surprised the Old Man doesn't start cursing.

I breathe very shallowly so as not to encounter the steel band around my chest, not to inhale too much of the stench. The air is terrible: the hot smell of diesels running at full speed . . . the stink of fifty men . . . our sweat—the sweat of fear. God knows what else has gone into this miasma of odors. Now the air smells of shit too. Someone must have lost control. Sweat and piss and shit and bilge—unendurable.

I can't help thinking of the poor bastards in the stern. They can't see the Commander, draw comfort from his presence. They are really caged in. No one to signal when the infernal din is going to break out again. I'd rather die than be stuck back there between the reeking, hot engine blocks.

So it does matter, after all, where one's battle station is. Even here there are the privileged and the underprivileged.

Hacker and his crew working in the bow compartment at the tubes—no one tells them our course either. They hear neither the orders to the helmsman nor the signals to the engine room. They don't know what the sound man reports. They have no notion which way we're moving—or whether we're moving at all. It's only when an explosion suddenly hurls the boat upward or slams it deeper down that they feel it in their stomachs; and if we go very deep indeed they can hear the telltale "creaking of the beams."

Three detonations. This time the gigantic sledgehammer came from below. I catch a glimpse of the depth manometer in the beam of a flashlight. It jumps backward. I can feel it in the pit of my stomach. We are being hurled upward in a high-speed elevator.

If the boat is five hundred feet or so down, the pressure waves from depth charges are supposed to be at their worst if they go off another hundred feet below that. How deep are we now? Six hundred feet.

There is no flexible steel underneath us. Nothing really to protect the engines! They are the most vulnerable to explosions from below.

Six more bombs. Again so close under our keel that I can feel the twisting force in my knee joints. I'm standing on one end of a seesaw while someone drops blocks of stone on the other end. The needle jerks backward again. Up and down—just what the Tommies want.

This attack has cost them at least a dozen bombs. There must be a mass of fish up there, floating on their sides, their air bladders torn apart. The Tommies could collect them by the netful. Something fresh for the galley.

I try to take long, regular breaths. For a good five minutes I breathe deeply, then four bombs explode. All astern. The sound man reports a decrease in strength.

I concentrate on imagining how one could reproduce all of this, this entire scene, in papier mâché for the stage. Everything very exact. Scale one to one. It would be easy: just remove the port wall—that's where the audience would sit. No elevated stage. Everything face to face. Direct view of the hydroplane station. Shift the sky periscope up front to give the whole thing perspective. I fix in my mind the positions and attitudes of the actors: the Old Man leaning against the periscope shaft—solid, heavy-set, in his ragged sweater, his fur-lined vest, his salt-flecked boots with their thick cork soles, the stubborn tangle of hair escaping from under his old battered cap with its tarnished trim. Color of his beard: sauerkraut, slightly rotten sauerkraut.

The hydroplane operators in their rubber jackets—in the heavy unyielding folds of their foul-weather gear—are two stone blocks that might have been hewn out of dark basalt and polished.

The Chief in half profile: olive-green shirt with rolled-up sleeves, crumpled dark olive-green linen trousers. Sneakers. Valentino hair slicked back. Thin as a whippet. Expressionless as a wax doll. Only his jaw muscles constantly working. Not a syllable, only the play of the jaw.

The First Watch Officer has turned his back to the audience. One senses he doesn't want to be observed because he isn't in complete control of himself.

Not much of the Second Watch Officer's face to be seen. He's too heavily muffled up, standing motionless, his eyes darting everywhere, as if searching for an escape hatch—as if they're trying to get away, to be free of him, to abandon him, leave him eyeless, while standing rigid by the periscope.

The navigator keeps his head down and pretends to be checking his stopwatch.

Only some minor sound effects: a low humming and the occasional drip of water on the metal plates.

All easy to reproduce. Minutes of silence, complete immobility. Only the constant hum and the dripping. Just keep everyone standing there frozen—until the audience becomes uneasy . . .

Three detonations, no doubt astern.

The navigator apparently has a new method of keeping score. Now he draws the fifth mark diagonally through the first four. That saves space and makes it easier to follow. He's already on his sixth row. I can't remember just how our conscientious scorekeeper tallied the last salvos.

The Old Man goes on calculating uninterruptedly: our course, the enemy's course, an escape course. With every report from the sound room, the basic factors in his calculations change.

What's he doing now? Will he have us steer straight ahead? No, this time he's trying another turn: hard a-port.

Let's hope he's made the right choice, that the Commander of the destroyer hasn't decided on port too—or on starboard, should he be steering toward us. That's the way it is: I don't even know whether the destroyer is attacking from forward or astern.

The figures that the operator is calling out are becoming jumbled in my head.

"Dropping cans!" The operator has heard the splash of more bombs hitting the surface of the water.

I hold tight.

"Man the bilge pump," the Old Man orders, enunciating with great care although the explosion hasn't yet come.

The noise! But it doesn't seem to bother the Old Man.

A whirlpool of detonations.

"Saturation pattern!" he says.

If it doesn't work with single charges or with series of them, they simply lay down a carpet.

Unshrinkable!

With half my mind I ask myself where I dug up the English word "unshrinkable." Finally I see it machine-stitched, in gold thread, on the label of my swimming trunks, under the words "pure wool."

A carpet! A spool begins unwinding in my head: hand-knotted, exquisite Afghan design—flying carpet—Harun al Rashid—Oriental bullshit!

"Much too good for us!" sneers the Old Man. In the worst of the noise he orders the speed increased. "Now they're reloading!" Contemptuously, he explains the absence of new detonations. "The more you use, the more you lose."

A golden maxim, like something straight out of the messroom calendar. The quintessential lesson of a dozen depth-charge attacks: "The more you use, the more you lose."

The Commander orders us up. What does that mean? Are we going to surface? Is the next order to be: "Prepare escape gear!"?

Atlantic Killer—a title for a film. Show a hairline crack in an egg. That's all it would take on our eggshell—just one crack. The enemy can leave the sea to do the rest.

The efforts we used to make to get rid of garden snails. The black shiny giants, the night snails, we would collect in buckets to be emptied into toilets and flushed away. Drowned in the cesspool— that did the job. Stepping on them is as disgusting as chopping them up. An explosion of green slime.

As children we played the cremation game. Away with the hearth fender, little pails of rainworms dumped onto the red coals—and in a second the worms were transformed with a loud hiss into twists of black ash.

Rabbits. You hold them firmly with your left hand and give them a blow on the back of the neck. Neat and clean: only a little twitching—as though electrocuted. Carp you hold with your left hand sideways on the board and give them a heavy blow on the snout with a stick. It makes a crunching sound. Quickly slit open their stomachs. Careful with the gall bladder, the gall mustn't spill out. The swollen air bladders gleam like Christmas tree ornaments. Funny thing about carp: even when they're cut in two there's still life in them. It used to frighten us as children when the halves went on jerking for hours on end.

I could never bring myself to kill doves, even though it's easy to do. You simply tear their heads off. Clamp them between index and middle fingers—a small twisting motion and crack and away! Roosters and hens you hold high on the wings with your left hand, directly under the shoulder blades, as it were. And then quickly press them sideways on the block and guillotine them with the ax. Let them bleed, but be sure to keep a firm hold, or they'll fly away without their heads. A bloody mess.

New sounds: propeller noises—a high whistling, audible throughout the boat. I see the new control-room assistant trembling all over. He's slumped down over the water distributor. Someone else—who is it?—sits down on the floor plates. Doubled up, a dark lump of flesh and fear. The others are huddled in a variety of postures, making themselves as small as possible. As though hiding would do any good now.

Only the Old Man sits in his usual way, casual and relaxed.

A new detonation! My left shoulder hits something so hard that I nearly cry out.

Two more.

"Start pumping!" the Old Man orders above the roar. We can't lose the destroyer. Damnation, we can't shake her off!

The Chief stares glassily out of the corners of his eyes. He looks as if he can hardly wait for the next series of bombs. Perverse: he *wants* to bail, and to do that he *needs* the bombs.

The boat can no longer be held without continuous bailing. Bilge pump on when there's roaring outside, bilge pump off when it stops. Again and again—on and off—on and off.

Waiting—waiting—waiting.

Still nothing? Nothing at all? I open my eyes but keep them firmly fixed on the floor plates.

A double blow. Pain in the back of my neck. What was that? Cries—the floor shudders—the floor plates jump—the whole boat vibrates—the steel howls like a dog. The lights have gone again. Who cried out?

"Permission to blow tanks?" I hear the Chief's voice as though through wool.

"No!"

The beam of the Chief's pocket flashlight wavers over the Commander's face. No mouth. No eyes.

Tearing, shrieking, shrill screaming—then more shattering blows. The orgy of noise has hardly ebbed when the chirp of the Asdic is back again. In our deep-sea aviary, the chirp that rings of betrayal. Rasps the nerves more than anything else. They couldn't have come up with a worse sound to torment us. Like our own Stuka's siren scream. I hold my breath.

Three o'clock plus how many minutes? I can't quite make out the big hand.

Reports. Fragments of words both from forward and aft. *What* is leaking badly? A drive-shaft gasket? Of course, I understand, both shafts go through the pressure hull.

The emergency lights go on. In the half-darkness I see that the control room is full of men. What now? What is happening? Which men are these? They must have come in through the after hatch. I've been sitting in the forward one. They couldn't have got through *here*. Damn this dim light. I can't recognize any of them. Two men —the control-room mate and one of the assistants—half block my view. They're standing as stiff as ever, but everything behind them is in motion. I hear the scuffling of boots, panting breath, sharp snorts, a few mumbled curses.

The Old Man hasn't noticed yet. He keeps his eyes on the depth manometer. Only the navigator turns his head.

"Breach in the diesel room," someone shouts from the stern.

"Propaganda!" says the Old Man without even turning around, and then once more with deliberate clarity, "Prop-a-gan-da!"

The Chief starts in the direction of the diesel room but stops short and looks at the manometer.

"I demand a report!" snaps the Commander, turning away from the manometers and seeing the crowd in the semi-darkness around the after hatch.

As though by reflex he draws his head in and bends forward slightly. "Chief, just give me your light," he orders in a whisper.

There's a stir among the men who have come into the control room from astern. They shrink back like tigers in front of their trainer. One of them even succeeds in raising his leg behind him and groping his way back through the hatch. It looks like a circus act. The flashlight in the Commander's hand catches only the receding back of a man hastening through the hatch toward the stern, rescue kit under his arm.

The face of the control-room mate is close to mine. His mouth a dark hole. His eyes wide—I can see the full circle of his pupils. He seems to be screaming but there is no sound.

Have my powers of perception gone mad? I don't see the control-room mate as frightened, but as an actor imitating the fear of a control-room mate.

The Commander orders both motors half speed ahead.

"Half speed ahead both!" comes the voice of the helmsman from the tower.

The control-room mate seems to be coming out of his coma. He begins to glance around furtively but won't look anyone straight in the face. His right foot feels its way cautiously over the floor plates. His tongue moistens his gray lower lip.

In a soft voice the Old Man sneers, "Wasting their tin cans . . ."

The navigator has come to a dead stop, his hand holding its piece of chalk. He looks frozen in mid-movement, but it's only hesitation. He doesn't know how many marks to jot down for the last attack. His bookkeeping could get scrambled. One error—and the whole thing would be down the drain.

He blinks as if to shrug off a dream, then makes five bold strokes. Four straight up and down, and one through the middle.

The next explosions come singly—sharp, ripping bursts but with little after-roar. The Chief has to shut down the pumps quickly. The navigator starts on the next group of chalk marks. As he is drawing the last one, the chalk falls from his hand.

Another great blast. Once more, a rattling over badly laid rails. Rumbling across switches, then bumping through broken stone. Metal screams and shrills.

If a rivet should give way now, it could—as I well know—plow straight through my skull like a bullet. The pressure! A stream of water breaking into the boat could saw a man in half.

The sour smell of fear! Now they've got us in the wringer, by the short hairs. We've had it. *It's our turn now.*

"Sixty degrees—getting stronger—more sounds at two hundred degrees!" Two, then four explosions in my head. They're going to rip open our hatches, the filthy swine!

Groans and hysterical sobbing.

The boat is jouncing like an airplane in a pocket of turbulence.

They're carpeting us.

The impact has knocked two men down. I see a mouth shrieking, flailing feet, two faces masked in terror.

Two more explosions. The sea is a single raging mass.

Subsiding roar and then suddenly silence. Only essential sounds: the sonorous insect hum of the motors, men breathing, the steady drip of water.

"Forward up ten," whispers the Chief.

The whine of the hydroplane motors pierces me to the bone. Must *everything* make so much noise?

Isn't the Old Man going to change course? Aren't we going to turn again? Or will he try to break out of the circling pattern by steering straight ahead?

Why doesn't the sound man say something?

If he has nothing to report, it can only mean that there are no engines running on the surface. But the bastards can't have gone so quickly that he didn't catch them at it. So they're lying there doggo. We've seen that happen a couple of times before. Still, the noise of the destroyer's engines has never been absent this long . . .

The Old Man maintains depth and course.

Five minutes pass, then the operator's eyes suddenly open wide, and he turns his hand wheel furiously. His forehead is deeply furrowed. They're about to attack again. I no longer listen to his reports but try to concentrate on nothing but keeping my seat. A sharp double crack.

"Boat making water!" A cry comes from astern in the roar following the explosion.

"Express yourself properly," the Commander orders the invisible man in a hiss.

Making water! This miserable naval jargon! Sounds like manufacturing something: "creating" it, and yet making water is about the worst thing that can happen in our situation.

The next one seems to hit me below the belt. Don't scream! I clench my teeth until my jaws ache. Someone else cries out for me, in a falsetto that goes right through me. The beam of a flashlight sweeps around in search of the man who screamed. I hear a new noise; the chattering of teeth like the quick rattle of castanets, then sniffling, snorting. There are men sobbing too.

A body lands against my knee and almost knocks me over. I feel someone hauling himself up, seizing me by the leg. But the first man, the one who fell against my knee, seems to be staying flat on the floor plates.

The emergency light over the navigator's table has not gone on again. The darkness provides a cover under which panic can secretly spread.

More racking sobs. They come from someone crouching on the water distributor. I can't see who he is. The control-room mate is suddenly there, giving him such a blow on the back that he cries out.

The Old Man swings around as though bitten by a tarantula and snaps in the direction of the water distributor, "Report to me when this is over!"

Who? The control-room mate? The man he hit?

When the light improves I see the new control-room assistant is silently weeping.

The Old Man orders half speed.

"Half speed ahead both!" the helmsman acknowledges.

This means that the boat's buoyancy can no longer be maintained at slow speed. Too much water has seeped in astern.

The propeller noises can be heard more clearly than ever. A roaring rhythmic beat. As counterpoint, the sound of a milk cooler, and over that a whirring egg beater and the buzz of a drill. Full speed!

The needle of the depth manometer moves a few marks further. The boat is slowly sinking. The Chief can no longer stop it—blowing the tanks would make far too much noise and pumping is out of the question.

"One hundred ninety degrees!" the operator reports. "One hundred seventy degrees!"

"Steer sixty degrees!" orders the Commander and pushes home the tight-drawn steel cable of the sky periscope. "Let's hope we're not leaving an oil slick," he remarks as if by accident. Oil slick! The words flash through the room, echo in my mind, and at once leave iridescent streaks on my closed eyelids. If oil is rising from the boat, the enemy has as good a target as he could possibly wish for.

The Commander bites his lower lip.

It's dark up there, but oil smells even in the dark—for miles.

There's a whisper from the sound room. "Destroyer sounds very close!"

The Commander whispers back, "Slow ahead both—minimum hydroplanes!"

He takes off his cap and lays it beside him on the chart chest. A sign of resignation? Have we reached the end?

The operator leans way out of his compartment as though about to make a report. But his mouth remains shut. His face is rigid with tension. Suddenly he takes his earphones off. I know what that means: noises everywhere, so there's no longer any point in trying to determine where they're coming from.

Now I can hear them myself.

A crashing, exploding roar, as though the sea itself were collapsing. Finished! Darkness!

"Are there ever to be any proper reports?" I hear an unrecognizable voice say before I open my eyes again.

The boat is becoming perceptibly stern heavy. In the beam of a flashlight the telephone cable and some oilskins swing out from the wall.

A few more heartbeats, then a voice penetrates the stillness. "Motor room—shipping water!" Immediately followed by more reports: "Bow compartment flanges holding—diesel room flanges holding fast." Finally the emergency light. The needle of the depth manometer moves with terrifying speed over the dial.

"Full ahead both!" the Old Man orders. Despite the desperation implicit in this command, his voice is matter of fact and calm.

The boat lunges forward: the batteries have connected up, one after the other.

"Forward hydroplane full up! Aft full down!" the Chief orders the operators. But the indicator doesn't move. It's frozen.

"Aft hydroplane out of action," reports the control-room mate. Ashen-faced, he turns toward the Commander with a look of complete trust.

"Recouple for manual," the Chief orders, so calmly that we might as well be on maneuvers. The hydroplane operators rise and throw their entire weight against the hand wheels. The white needle of the indicator suddenly trembles—thank god, it's moving! The mechanism isn't damaged and the hydroplane isn't jammed; only the electrical control has failed.

The loud humming of the motors. Full speed—that's insanity! But what else is left for us to try? Running silently, we can no longer hold our present level. The motor room is making water—an inrush of water at our most vulnerable point.

"Both E-motors falling below full power!"

The Old Man reflects no more than a second, then commands, "Examine both batteries! Test the accumulator bilges for acid!" No doubt about it: some of the battery cells must have cracked and run dry. What next? What more can happen?

My heart almost stops as the First Watch Officer moves to one side, revealing the depth manometer. The needle is still moving slowly forward. The boat is sinking, even though the motors are running on all the power still available.

It's only seconds before there is a sharp hissing sound. The control-room mate has released the compressed air. Our buoyancy tanks are filling.

"Blow them full!"

The Chief has sprung to his feet. He's breathing in short gasps. His voice vibrates. "Trim forward! Move, move!"

I don't dare stand up for fear my legs will fail me. My muscles are like jelly, my nerves are quivering. Let the final blow fall! Give up! Call it a day! This is unendurable!

I realize that I'm slipping into dazed indifference. Nothing matters. Just get it over with—one way or another. I summon up all my strength to pull myself together.

Damn it all, don't let go.

We have risen 175 feet. The indicator comes to a halt. The Commander orders, "Open exhaust three!"

Terror wells up in me. I know what this order means. A surge of air is now rising toward the surface and forming a bubble that will betray our position. A torrent of fear. To ward it off, I murmur, "Immune! Immune!"

My heart keeps pounding! My breath comes in gasps. I hear a muffled command: "Shut off the exhaust!"

The navigator turns his head to the Old Man. I can see his full face: a wood carving. Pale, polished linden wood. He sees me and thrusts out his lower lip.

"Hysterical women," growls the Old Man.

If the E-motors aft are swamped, if there should be a short circuit . . . how could the screws turn? Without propellers and hydroplanes both working, we're done for.

The Commander impatiently demands reports from the motor room.

I catch only fragments: ". . . made watertight with wooden wedges—sole-plate broken—lots of water, cause unknown."

I hear a high whimpering sound. Seconds pass before I realize that it's not coming from the enemy. It's coming from somewhere forward. A high undulating wail.

The Old Man turns a disgusted face in that direction. He looks as if he might explode with rage at any moment.

"One hundred fifty degrees—getting louder!"

"And the other—the first one?"

"Ninety degrees; sixty degrees; holding steady!"

Christ, now the fuckers have got together. They're tossing the ball back and forth, and the ball is the Asdic bearing. Our original pursuer is no longer acting under any handicap. While he's attacking at top speed—which puts his own Asdic out of action—his colleague can idle along, taking bearings for him. And then radio the figures to him.

The Old Man's face is contorted, as though he had taken too long to swallow an especially bitter pill. "This is a crime!"

For the first time, the sound man shows signs of nervousness. Or does he _have_ to turn his wheel so violently to find out which of the two sounds is getting louder?

If the second Commander up there is an old hand, if the two of them have worked together before, they'll exchange roles as often as possible in order to outfox us.

Unless I'm completely mistaken, the Old Man is steering toward the enemy in a tight curve.

Rollercoaster! The thought keeps coming back. Rollercoaster. Up, down, gliding, rising and falling curves, looping back on ourselves, sudden dives and jarring ascents.

Two crashes shake the boat. Four, five more follow. Two of them from underneath. Only a couple of seconds, and the face of the chief mechanic Franz appears in the frame of the after hatch, completely distorted in terror.

He emits a sort of cackling high-pitched "hee hee hee," which sounds like a bad imitation of the destroyer's screws. The Commander, who has closed his eyes again, turns toward him. Meanwhile the mechanic has climbed through the frame of the hatch and stands, escape apparatus in hand, half crouched behind the periscope shaft in the control room. He bares his teeth, looking like a monkey. They gleam brightly out of his dark beard. A spasmodic sobbing now compounds the "hee hee hee."

How does he do it? Then I realize that the sobbing is coming from another corner.

The Old Man stiffens. For a fraction of a second he sits rigidly upright. Then he draws his head in again and turns around slowly. He sees the chief mechanic. Seconds pass and then he snarls, "Are you crazy? Back to your battle station! At once!"

According to regulations the chief mechanic should say, "*Jawohl,* Herr Kaleun!" But he simply opens his mouth wide as if he were at the point of screaming hysteria.

Loss of hearing, I think to myself: He's shouting and I can't hear a thing. But my ears are working! I can hear the Old Man spit out, "Goddammit, pull yourself together!"

He's on his feet.

The sobbing stops.

"Destroyer bearing one hundred twenty degrees," reports the operator. The Old Man blinks irritably.

The chief mechanic starts to writhe in a wordless struggle—as if under the spell of a hypnotist. I can see the spasm begin to pass. If only he doesn't collapse!

"Return to battle station at once!" and immediately thereafter, in a threatening undertone, "At once, I said!"

"One hundred ten degrees. Getting louder!" The operator's whispering voice sounds like the monotone of a priest.

The Old Man hunches his head down even farther, then relaxes again and moves two or three steps forward. I get up to make room for him. Where does he mean to go?

The chief mechanic finally pulls himself together with a jerk and gasps out, "*Jawohl,* Herr Kaleun!"

Then he throws a lightning glance around him, bends over double, and disappears through the after hatch without the Old Man seeing him.

The Commander, who is just on the point of putting his left leg through the forward hatch frame, stops and looks back with an odd expression on his face.

"Herr Kaleun, he's gone," stammers the Chief.

The Commander withdraws his leg. It looks as if a film were suddenly being run backwards. Like a slightly dazed boxer whose vision had been blurred for a minute or two, the Commander walks stiffly and silently back to his place.

"I'd have finished him off!"

The pistol in his cubbyhole!

"Starboard full rudder! Steer two hundred thirty degrees!" he says in his normal voice. "Take her down one hundred seventy-five feet, Chief!" The operator reports, "Propeller sounds bearing ten degrees."

"Acknowledged!" says the Old Man.

The Asdic beams rattle and rasp along the boat.

"Revolting," he whispers.

Everyone in the control room knows that it's not the Asdic he's referring to but the chief mechanic. "Franz of all people! Disgraceful!" He shakes his head in disgust, as though he'd seen a sexual exhibitionist. "Lock him up. I'll have him locked up!"

"Destroyer attacking," reports the operator in a drone.

"Steer two hundred degrees. Both motors slow ahead!"

The Old Man is up to his tricks again: dodging aside into the underbrush. How many times does this make?

Through the forward hatch drifts a sour smell. Some of the men must have vomited.

The operator starts squinting again. Whenever he makes this face I turn my head away and hunch up my shoulders.

A tattoo on the boat, then an immense blow, and soon the infernal resounding gurgle and roar of the water, like a mighty rolling echo.

Five thunderclaps punctuate the echo. A matter of seconds. Everything that is lying around loose comes sliding and rolling toward the stern. The Chief has increased speed during the detonations and in the ensuing roar he shouts, "Pump!" He remains behind the hydroplane operators, crouched as if to leap.

The thundering and roaring goes on and on. We crash through a raging waterfall. The bilge pumps work throughout the noise.

Before the Chief can shut them off, three more explosions shake the boat.

"Continue bailing!" The Chief sucks in his breath, throws a quick look at the Commander. Could there be a touch of satisfaction in it? Can he actually be feeling *proud* because his bilge pumps are still functioning?

"They're doing their best for you, Chief," says the Old Man. "Superb service!"

04.00. Our attempts to break away have lasted—how many hours? I've lost count. Most of the men in the control room are sitting down: elbows on knees, heads in their hands. No one even looks up any longer. The Second Watch Officer is staring at the floor as if he could see mushrooms growing out of the floor plates. The graduated circle of the sky periscope has been torn loose and dangles on a wire. There is the tinkle of falling glass.

But wonders never cease!—The boat remains watertight. We're still moving, still buoyant. The motors are running, our screws turning. We're making headway, and we still have power for the rudder. The Chief can hold the boat: it's actually on an even keel again.

The navigator is bent over the chart table as though he is fascinated by it; his head is close to it, and the points of the dividers—which are clasped in his right hand—have bored into the linoleum.

The control-room mate has stuck two fingers into his mouth, apparently about to whistle on them.

The Second Watch Officer is trying to imitate the Commander's equanimity. But his fists betray him: they're firmly clenched around his binoculars—he still has the glasses hanging around his neck—and he's flexing them very slowly at the wrists, first one way, then the other. His knuckles are white with strain.

The Commander turns to the operator, who has his eyes closed and is twisting the wheel of his apparatus from side to side. Having apparently singled out the sound he was looking for, his maneuverings taper off almost to nothing.

In a subdued voice he announces, "Destroyer noises receding at one hundred twenty degrees!"

"They think they've finished us off!" says the Commander. That's the last of one of them—but what about the other?

The Chief is in the stern, so the Commander himself is still in charge of the hydroplanes.

The whining has ceased. All that comes from the bow compartment is an occasional spasmodic sobbing.

The Chief reappears, his hands and forearms black with oil. Snatches of his half-whispered report reach me. "Flange of outer gas vent . . . condenser . . . two foundation bolts broken . . . already replaced . . . firmly wedged with wooden pegs . . . flange still leaking—but it's minor."

Beside the Commander's desk lies a carton of syrup, mashed and trodden all over the floor. The accordion is spread open in this disgusting mess. All the pictures have fallen off the walls. I take a cautious step over the face of the C-in-C.

In the Officers' Mess, books lie strewn among towels and spilled bottles of apple juice. The silly straw dog with glass eyes that's supposed to be our mascot has landed on the floor too. This is where I probably ought to start cleaning up—do something to occupy my hands. I bend over; stiff joints; I go down on my knees. Christ! I can actually move my hands. I'm making myself useful! Quietly, quietly, be careful. Don't hit anything. It must be way past four o'clock.

I've been cleaning up for a good ten minutes when the Chief comes through: greenish rings under his eyes. Pupils dark as lumps of coal, cheeks sunken. He's at the end of his tether.

I hand him a bottle of fruit juice. It's not just his hand; his whole body is trembling. He perches on a ledge while he's drinking. But as he puts the bottle down he's already on his feet, staggering slightly like a boxer, badly shaken and completely exhausted, but pulling himself up out of his corner one more time. ". . . It won't work," he mutters as he disappears.

Suddenly there are three more explosions, but this time they sound like beats on a slack drumskin. "Miles away," I hear the navigator say.

"Two hundred seventy degrees—moving away slowly!" the operator reports.

To think that somewhere there is dry land, hills and valleys . . . people are still asleep in their houses. In Europe, that is. In America they're still sitting up with the lights burning, and we're probably closer to America than we are to France. We've come too far west.

Absolute silence in the boat. After a while the operator whispers, "Destroyer bearing two hundred sixty degrees. Very faint. Slow revs—seems to be moving away."

"They're running silent," says the Commander. "Dawdling as slow as they can. And listening! Where in hell's the second one? Watch it!"

This is addressed to the hydrophone operator. So the Old Man no longer knows precisely where the enemy is.

I can hear the chronometer ticking and the condensation dripping into the bilge. The operator does a full sweep—and another, and another—but gets no bearing in his instrument.

"I don't like it," the Commander mutters to himself. "Don't like it at all."

A trick! It has to be. Something's wrong: it sticks out a mile.

The Old Man stares straight ahead, expressionless, then blinks quickly once or twice and swallows hard. Apparently he can't decide on a course of action.

If I only knew what the game was. No more explosions—no more Asdic—the Commander's continued play-acting—what to make of it?

If only I could ask the Old Man straight out, in four plain words, "How do things stand?"

But my mouth seems to be riveted shut. I'm incapable of thought. Head's a volcanic crater, bubbling evilly.

I feel thirsty. There must still be some apple juice left in the locker. I open it carefully, but shards of china fall out. All that damn banging around. Most of the cups and saucers are broken. A coffee pot has lost its spout. Looks idiotic without it. Fortunately the bottle of apple juice is intact. Apparently it was what smashed everything else. Quite right too: Smash everything around you so as to stay whole yourself.

The framed photograph of our launching is still lying under the table, broken. Sharp slivers of glass still sticking in the frame. I must have missed it while I was cleaning up. I manage to get hold of it but can't be bothered to loosen the glass daggers, so it goes back on its hook just as it is.

"No more noises?" asks the Commander.

"No, Herr Kaleun!"

Slowly it gets to be 05.00.

No noise. Hard to understand. Have they really given up the chase? Or are they considering us as sunk already?

I feel my way back into the control room. The Commander is consulting in whispers with the navigator. I hear, "In twenty minutes we surface!"

I hear it, but I can't believe my ears. Do we *have* to surface? Or are we really safely out of the shit?

The operator starts to say something; he's about to make a report—but he stops in mid-syllable and keeps turning his wheel. He must have caught a faint sound, which he's now trying to track by fine-tuning his apparatus.

The Old Man stares into the operator's face. The operator moistens his lower lip with his tongue. In a very low voice he reports, "Noise bearing sixty degrees—very faint."

Abruptly the Old Man climbs through the hatch and crouches

down beside him in the gangway. The operator passes him the headset. The Old Man listens and the operator turns his wheel very gently back and forth along the scale, and gradually the Old Man's face grows stern.

Minutes pass. The Old Man remains tied to the hydrophone by the cord of the headset. He looks like a fish on a line. His orders to the helmsman are to bring the bow around so that he can hear better.

"Stand by to surface!"

His voice, grating and determined, has startled others than myself. The Chief's eyelids twitch.

Stand by to surface! He must know what is and isn't possible! Noises still audible in the hydrophone and he's getting ready to go up?

The hydroplane operators sit hunched over their tables. The navigator has finally taken off his sou'wester. His mask-like face looks years older, the lines in it carved even deeper.

The Chief stands behind him, his left thigh resting on the chart chest, his right hand on the pillar of the sky periscope, his torso bent forward as though to bring him as close as possible to the needle of the depth manometer that is slowly moving backward over the scale. With every mark it passes we are three feet closer to the surface. It moves very slowly, as if to give us time to experience these minutes at leisure.

"Radio clear by now?" asks the Commander.

"*Jawohl*, Herr Kaleun!"

The watch is already assembled in oilskins and sou'westers under the tower hatch. Binoculars are being polished—much too vigorously, or so it seems. No one says a word.

My breathing has steadied. I've regained the use of my muscles. I can stand without being afraid of staggering, but at the same time I can single out every muscle, every bone in my body. The flesh on my face feels frozen.

The Old Man intends to surface. We're going to breathe sea air again. We are alive. The bastards didn't kill us.

No sudden outbursts of joy. I'm still in the grip of terror. Letting our tense shoulders droop, holding our heads a little higher—that's about all we can manage.

The crew is completely exhausted. Even after the order to surface has been given, both control-room assistants sit apathetically on the flooding and bailing distributors. And as for the control-room mate, he's trying to look casual, but I can still see the horror in his face.

I suddenly long for a periscope ten times the length of this one. If only the Old Man could take a single quick look around from the safety of our present position, so that we would know what's going on up there—what that damn bunch is really up to!

The boat has risen to periscope depth. We're close to the surface. The Chief has the boat firmly in hand. No trace of excessive buoyancy.

The Old Man sticks the asparagus stalk out. I hear the periscope motor spring into action and stop again, and then the soft snap and click of the clutch. The Old Man is riding his merry-go-round.

The tension in the room is almost unbearable. Without intending to, I hold my breath until I have to gasp for air like a drowning man. No word from above.

So things do look bad! If it were all clear, the Old Man would tell us at once.

"Take this down!"

Thank god, the Old Man's voice.

The navigator thinks the words are for him. He reaches for a pencil. My god, are we going to have this all over again? Literary composition for the war log?

"Here we go: 'Periscope reveals—destroyer, corrected bearing one hundred degrees, lying motionless—range about sixty-five hundred yards.' Got that?"

"Jawohl, Herr Kaleun!"

" 'Moon still very bright.' Got that?"

"Jawohl, Herr Kaleun!"

" 'Remaining submerged.' " So that's that!

No further word from above.

Three or four minutes pass, then the Commander gropes his way down. "Thought they could fool us! Same old tricks! Idiots! Every time they think we'll bite. Chief, take her down to two hundred feet again! We'll just move a little to one side and reload the torpedoes in our own good time."

The Old Man is behaving as if everything were going according to plan. I want to grasp my head in my hands: he sounds as if he's reading some boring company report from the business section of a newspaper. "Navigator, take this down: 'Running silent to get clear of destroyer. Presume that destroyer—that destroyer has lost us . . . No sound in immediate vicinity.' "

"Presume" is good! So he doesn't even know for sure. He narrows his eyes. Apparently he's not yet through with his dictation.

"Navigator!"

"*Jawohl*, Herr Kaleun!"

"Add this. 'Conflagration—brilliant conflagration, corrected bearing two hundred fifty degrees. Assume it to be tanker hit by us.'" The Old Man gives an order to the helmsman. "Steer two hundred fifty degrees!"

I stare around from one to another and see nothing but impassive faces. Only the Second Watch Officer betrays a slight frown. The First Watch Officer is gazing expressionlessly into space. The navigator is writing at the chart table.

Aft, and in the bow compartment, they're making repairs. Now and then a man comes through the control room with oil-smeared hands and reports to the First Watch Officer, who has taken charge of the hydroplanes. They always do it in a whisper. No one apart from the Old Man dares use his normal voice.

"Another half hour and we'll reload the torpedoes," he says, and then to me, "This would be a good time for a drink."

He makes no move to leave the control room, so I hurriedly go in search of a bottle of apple juice. I don't seem to want to move. Every muscle aches as I clamber through the hatch. Limping past Herrmann, I see that he's totally intent on his hydrophone wheel. But right now I don't give a damn what he picks up with it.

Whatever the report was, after half an hour the Old Man gives the order to reload the torpedoes.

They're working like madmen in the bow compartment. Wet clothes, sweaters, leather suits, and all kinds of junk are piled up close to the hatch, and the floor boards are gone.

"Praise the Lord with trumpets and cymbals," intones the torpedo mechanic Hacker. "Finally we'll get some room in here," he adds for my benefit, wiping the sweat from his neck with a filthy rag of a towel. He urges his coolies on. "Get with it, boys, get with it—up with the hoists!"

"A smear of Vaseline and straight into the crack!" Ario hangs suspended from the chains of the hoist in mock ecstasy, as he hauls away in time to Hacker's calls of *hau-ruck.* "Fuck me—fuck me—you horny goat, oh, oh, oh, you bastard—oh, you—that's it—deeper—go on! More—more!"

I'm amazed that he can find the breath for it in this madhouse. A seaman who's also hauling away at the tackle, has an embittered expression on his face. He's pretending to be deaf.

When the first torpedo is in its tube, the Berliner spreads his legs and dries the sweat from his torso with a hand towel, then hands the dirty rag to Ario.

The First Watch Officer appears to check the time. The men work on doggedly. Aside from Hacker's *hau-rucks* and subdued curses there's nothing to be heard.

Back in the Officers' Mess I see the Old Man in his usual corner of the Chief's bunk, legs stretched out in front of him, leaning back at an angle like a man at the end of a very long train ride. His face is upturned, his mouth half open. A thread of saliva dangles from one corner, disappearing into his beard.

I wonder what to do. He can't just lie here like this, with people coming and going. I cough loudly, as if to clear a frog in my throat —and instantly the Old Man is wide awake, sitting up straight again. But he says nothing, just gestures toward a seat.

Finally he asks haltingly, "How do things look forward?"

"One fish is already in its tube. They're just about finished! The men, I mean—not the work."

"Huh. And have you been aft?"

"No—too much work going on."

"Tsch, it looks pretty shitty back there. But the Chief will manage; he's a helluva dancing master." Then he calls into the gangway, "Food! For the officers of the watch as well." And to me, "Never pass up the chance for a celebration—even if it's only with a piece of bread and a sour pickle!"

Plates and knives and forks are brought in. Soon we're sitting around a properly set table.

I'm blabbering away silently to myself like an idiot. "Crazy— absolutely crazy." There in front of my eyes are a smooth clean table, plates, knives, forks, cups, the familiar lamplight. I stare at the Old Man stirring his tea with a polished spoon, the First Watch Officer dissecting a sausage, the Second Watch Officer splitting a spiced pickle lengthwise.

The steward asks me whether I want more tea. "Me? Tea? Yes!" I stammer. A hundred depth charges are still exploding in my head. Every muscle aches from the desperate tension. I have a cramp in my right thigh; I can even feel my jaw muscles at every bite. That comes from grinding my teeth.

"Why are you goggling like that?" the Commander asks, his mouth full, and I hastily spear a slice of sausage on my fork. Keep your eyes open. Don't begin to think. Chew, chew thoroughly, the way you usually do. Move your eyes. Blink.

"Another pickle?" asks the Old Man.

"Yes, please—thanks!"

From the gangway comes a dull thumping. Is Hinrich, who has relieved Herrmann in the sound room, trying to call attention to himself? A loud stamping of boots, then he announces, "Exploding depth charges, bearing two hundred thirty degrees."

His voice sounds much higher than Herrmann's, a tenor as opposed to a bass.

I try to relate his report to our course. Two points to port.

"Well, it's about time we surfaced," says the Old Man, his mouth full. "Ship's time?"

"06.55 hours!" is the report from the navigator in the control room.

The Old Man gets up, still chewing, stands there while he washes down his mouthful with a great gulp of tea, and reaches the end of gangway in three determined strides. "We surface in ten minutes. Add a note to the log: '06.00, torpedoes reloaded. 06.55, depth charge detonations at two hundred thirty degrees.'"

Then he comes back and wedges himself into his corner again.

Hacker appears, gasping for air. He has to take a couple of deep breaths before he can get a word out. My god, look at him! The sweat is pouring down him in rivulets. He can hardly stay on his feet as he stammers out his report. "Four bow torpedoes loaded. Stern tube . . ."

He tries to go on, but the Old Man interrupts him. "Very good, Hacker; it's obvious we can't reach it for the time being."

Hacker tries to do a snappy about-face, but loses his balance. He's just able to save himself from falling by clutching the top of the lockers.

"These youngsters!" says the Old Man. "They really are amazing!" And then, "It certainly feels different having torpedoes in the tubes again!"

I know that all he wants to do now is attack the destroyer that's been tormenting us. He'd be betting everything on a single card again, but no doubt he has something else in mind . . .

He gets up resolutely, does up three buttons on his fur-lined vest, jams his cap down harder on his head, and heads for the control room.

The Chief appears and announces that the damages aft have been repaired with shipboard materials. Shipboard materials—that means only temporary repairs.

I climb into the control room behind the Old Man.

The bridge watch is already standing by. The Second Engineer has stationed himself behind the hydroplane operators. The boat is rising rapidly. We'll soon be at periscope level.

Without wasting a word the Old Man climbs into the tower. The periscope motor begins to run. More clicks and pauses. I have difficulty breathing again until his voice comes down loud and clear. "Surface."

The equalization of pressure is like a blow. I want to roar and gulp all at once, instead of which I simply stand there like all the others. Only my lungs are in action, pumping in the fresh sea air. Down comes the voice of the Commander, "Both diesels!"

Astern in the diesel room the compressed air rushes into the cylinders. The pistons begin to move up and down. And now the ignition! The diesels fire. A shudder runs through the boat as violent as the first jerk of a tractor. The bilge pumps hum, the ventilators pump aid through the boat—a stream of sound to make the nerves relax—like a soothing bath.

I climb onto the bridge behind the lookouts.

Christ! A monstrous conflagration over the horizon.

"That must be the third steamer!" roars the Commander.

Against the dark heavens I can make out a black cloud above the red inferno: smoke winding upward like a gigantic worm. We head toward it. Soon the bow and stern of the vessel grow clearly visible, but her midship is almost invisible.

The wind brings the acrid, suffocating smell of fuel oil.

"Broke their back," the Commander raps out. He orders full speed ahead and changes course. Our bow is now pointing straight at the conflagration.

The glare of the fire flickers, lighting the gigantic smoke clouds from underneath, and through the smog we can make out tongues of flame.

Now and again the entire cloud is shot through from inside with flashes of yellow, and individual bursts soar up into the darkness like star shells. Real rockets explode, rose-blood red, through the welter of smoke. Their reflections snake across the dark water between us and the burning ship.

A single mast stands out black against the reflection of the fire, rising up out of the flames like an admonitory finger. The wind forces the smoke in our direction, as if the ship wanted to shroud herself and go down unseen. Only the stern of the tanker is visible as a dark hulk. It must have heeled toward us; when the wind blows the smoke away I recognize the tilted deck, a few super-structures, the stump of what was once a loading crane.

"No need to fire again!" The Commander's voice is harsh and husky. His words turn into a hoarse gurgle which seems to die away in drunken laughter.

Nevertheless, he doesn't order the boat to turn aside; on the contrary, we slowly draw closer and closer to the inferno.

All around the stern of the tanker dark-red flames are licking up out of the sea: the water itself is on fire. Spilled fuel oil.

"Perhaps we can find out her name!" says the Commander.

The rumbling and cracking of a brush fire reaches us, followed by a sharp hissing and snapping. The sea is now yellow with the reflection of the burning stern and red from the flaming oil.

Then we in turn are flooded with the same crimson glare. Every slit in the grating stands out in the light of the leaping flames.

I turn my head. Everyone's face is red—distorted red masks.

Now there is the thud of another explosion. And then—I prick up my ears—wasn't that a hoarse cry? Could there still be people on board? Didn't I just see a gesticulating arm? I squint—but there's nothing in the binoculars but flames and smoke. Nonsense, no human sound could make itself heard through this inferno.

What will the Old Man do? Now and again he gives an order to the helmsman. I know: stay head on—don't be silhouetted against the conflagration. "Look sharp!" says the Old Man, and then, "She'll be going down any minute now!"

I barely hear him. We stand there rooted. Madmen, desperadoes, staring into a hell of flames.

How far is it? Eight hundred yards?

The significance of its being such a big ship gnaws at me. How many men would such a vessel carry as minimum crew? How many dead this time?—twenty, thirty? British ships are certainly sailing with as few men as possible these days. Perhaps they even divide their watches in two instead of three. But they couldn't manage with less than ten seamen, plus eight for engines, wireless, officers, and stewards. Has a destroyer picked them up? But to do that it would have to stop—can a destroyer run such a risk, with a U-boat in the immediate vicinity?

Over there a cluster of glaring red beams of fire shoots into the sky: the still-floating stern spits out trails of sparks. And then a distress rocket. So there *are* still people on board! God in heaven—in that inferno!

"That went off by itself. There's no one left on board. It's impossible!" the Old Man says in his ordinary voice.

Once more I use the binoculars to grope my way through the smoke. There! No doubt of it: people! Crowded together on the stern. For a second I see them sharp against the blazing backdrop. Now some are jumping into the water; only two or three are left, still running about up there on the deck. One of them is hurled into the air. I see him clearly, like a disjointed doll, against the reddish-yellow glare.

The navigator roars, "There are some over there, too!" and points to the water in front of the burning tanker. I snatch up my glasses: a raft with two people on it.

I keep my binoculars on them for half a minute. No sign of movement. Undoubtedly dead.

But there! The black humps—they must be swimmers!

The Second Watch Officer turns his glasses in that direction too. The Old Man explodes. "Look out! For god's sake, you're supposed to be keeping watch astern."

Aren't those screams I'm hearing through the crackling? One of the swimmers raises an arm for an instant. The others, seven—no, ten—men are recognizable only as floating black balls.

The wind forces the banners of oily smoke down once more and I lose sight of the swimmers. Then they're there again. No doubt about it—they're making for our boat. Behind them the red tongues of spreading oil reach out in an ever-widening front.

I glance sideways at the Commander. "Damn risky," I hear him murmur, and I know what he means. We've come too close. It's getting hot.

For two or three minutes he says nothing. He picks up his binoculars, puts them down again, struggling to come to a decision; then in a voice so husky it almost cracks he calls down the order for both diesels to be reversed.

The men in the engine room will be wide-eyed. Reverse—we haven't had that one before. Nasty: Now we can't crash dive—the boat has no steerageway.

The burning oil spreads faster than the men can swim. They haven't a chance. The fire on the water devours the oxygen. To suffocate, to burn to death, to drown—whoever is caught will die in all three ways at once.

Luckily the crackling of the conflagration and the dull roar of minor explosions render their screams inaudible.

The red-tinged face of the Second Watch Officer wears a look of horror.

"Can't understand it," the Old Man says dully. "No one came to pick them up . . ." I too find it incomprehensible. All those hours! Were they trying at first to save the ship? Perhaps she was still manageable after the hit; perhaps the engines were still good for a few knots. Possibly they tried to put the fire out in the hope that they could still escape an enemy submarine. I shudder at what that crew must have gone through.

"Now we won't even find out her name!" I hear the Old Man say. He's trying to be ironic.

Nausea in my throat. I have a vision of the man I helped to rescue out of the huge pool of fuel oil in the harbor basin after an air attack. He stood there on the pier, vomiting and shaken with convulsive cramps and groans. The burning oil had scorched his eyes. Luckily a sailor appeared with a fire hose. He washed off the slime at such high pressure that the poor wretch was knocked down and rolled over the stones like a shapeless black bundle.

Suddenly the stern of the tanker rises, looming up as if it were being thrust out of the water from underneath. For a while it stands, steep as a cliff, in the burning sea; then with two or three muffled explosions it plunges, roaring, out of sight.

In seconds the sea closes over the spot where it sank, sucking in the huge ship as though it had never existed. Of the swimmers there is nothing more to be seen.

Our men who are below must now be able to hear the music of destruction, the terrifying groaning, cracking, and tearing, the explosions of the boilers, the breaking up of the holds. How deep is the Atlantic here? Sixteen thousand feet? Thirteen thousand at least.

The Commander orders us to turn away.

"Nothing more for us to do here!"

The bridge lookouts are back in their usual positions, motionless, their binoculars to their eyes. Forward above the horizon there's a dim reddish glow, such as big cities cast against the sky at night. And now in the southwest something brightens and flares almost up to the zenith.

"Navigator, take this down. 'Glow of flames visible at two hundred thirty degrees.' And add ship's time. Other boats are in action over there. We'll just take a look and see what kind of neon sign it is," he mutters in my direction and orders the bow turned toward the flickering light.

What now? Is this going to go on until we're left drifting somewhere with empty tanks? Haven't we had enough? The Old Man's probably itching to pull himself down a destroyer. As repayment, revenge for our ordeal.

The Chief disappears from the bridge.

"So it goes," says the Old Man. "But it's high time we sent that signal! Navigator—paper and pencil. We'd better begin again. Now we can describe the whole thing properly . . ."

I know what he means: the risk of being spotted if we send more than a brief radio signal is now irrelevant. By this time the Tommies are well aware that we're active in this vicinity. No further need to worry about their taking bearings on our transmitter.

"Just take it down—as follows: 'Depth charge pursuit—by destroyers.' 'Sophisticated depth bomb pursuit' might be better. 'Numerous attacks'—but who cares about that? They can just as well find it in the war log. So let's leave it at that: 'Numerous attacks.' They're a lot more interested in what we sank, navigator, so we'll keep it absolutely simple: 'Depth charge pursuit by destroyers.' Leave out the 'numerous attacks' as well. To continue: 'Depth bomb attack. Five torpedoes fired. Four hits. Passenger liner eight thousand GRT and freighter five thousand five hundred GRT. Sinkings clearly audible. Hit on eight thousand GRT tanker. Sinking observed— UA.' "

"Passenger liner," the Old Man had dictated. Was that one of the ones re-equipped as troop transports? I don't want to picture the effect of a torpedo hitting a fully loaded troop transport . . . The drunken loudmouth in the Bar Royal: "Destroy the enemy, not just his ships!"

From below comes the report that the radioman has picked up SOS calls from British steamers. "Well, well," says the Old Man. Not a word more.

At 07.30 hours we pick up a signal from one of our own boats. The navigator reads it aloud, quite carried away. "Sank three steamers. Fourth ship probable. Four hours depth charge pursuit during attack. Convoy broken into groups and lone ships. Contact broken off. Pursuing southwest—UZ."

I stare at the glow over the horizon, which is punctuated now and again by bright flashes.

A frenetic jumble of sequences races through my mind: The projector's running too fast. Pieces of film have been spliced together meaninglessly, at random, and there are a lot of double exposures. Again and again I see clouds from explosions, which remain frozen for a few instants and then collapse, dropping a rain of planks and fragments of iron. I see the black smoke of oil darkening the sky like a gigantic skein of wool. Then the crackling of the blaze, the flame of oil on water—and the struggling black balls in front of it.

I'm overwhelmed with horror at what we have done with our torpedoes. Delayed reaction. One stab at the firing lever! I close my eyes to blot out the haunting visions, but I continue to see the sea of flames spreading out over the water and men swimming for their lives.

How does the Old Man feel when he visualizes the mass of ships that he himself has destroyed? And when he thinks of the crowds of men who were traveling on those ships and went down with them, or were blown up by the torpedoes—scalded, maimed, dismembered, burned to death, smothered, drowned, smashed. Or half scalded and half smothered and then drowned. Almost two hundred thousand tons: a medium-sized harborful of ships chalked up by him alone.

After a while there's a report from below that messages have been received. Kupsch is in contact with the same convoy; Stackmann has scored a hit on a six thousand GRT.

I'm hit by waves of weariness. I must not lean against the bulwark or the TBT—otherwise I'll go to sleep standing up. Dull emptiness in my skull. And I can feel a spastic writhing in my guts. And pressure in my bladder. Stiff-legged, I climb down into the boat.

The chief mechanic Franz is not in the Quarters. Since making such a fool of himself, he's kept out of sight. Actually this ought to be his time off. He's probably afraid to set foot out of the engine room.

As I emerge from the head, the Second Watch Officer is at the door. So he feels the same need. My god, what a sight: the face of an elderly dwarf, creased and petulant. Has the stubble of his beard actually turned darker? I stare at him disconcertedly until I realize it's an illusion—the result of his chalk-white skin. The stubble simply stands out more than before.

When he reappears, he asks the steward for coffee.

"I think lemonade might be better," I say.

The steward pauses, irritated. The Second Watch Officer sprawls in the corner of the sofa without bothering to reply.

"Lemonade," I decide. "For me too."

Sleep would do us both good. So what's the point of coffee?

I'm just stretching, seeing what it feels like, when the Old Man appears and says, "Quick, something to eat!"

The steward comes in with the lemonade and two cups.

"Strong coffee and cold cuts for me, and make it fast!" says the Old Man.

The steward is back in no time. The cook must have had the food ready and waiting.

The Old Man chews, pauses, and chews some more, staring straight ahead. The silence becomes oppressive.

"Three more ships gone," he says, but without a trace of triumph in his voice; on the contrary, it sounds sullen and grating.

"Damn nearly us too!" The words slip out.

"Rubbish," says the Old Man and stares holes in the air. He

chews for a minute or two and then I hear him say, "At least we always carry our own respectable coffin around with us. We're just like snails."

This banal image seems to please him. "Just like snails," he repeats, nodding to himself with a weary grin.

So that's all there was to it: the enemy—just a few shadows above the horizon. Firing the torpedoes—not even a perceptible jolt. The unearthly flames—our victory bonfire. Nothing seems to fit together any more: first the hunting fever, then the attack, the depth charges, the hours of torture. But even before that the sounds of the sinking ships—and then when we surfaced, the burning hulk—the third victim! Four torpedoes scored direct hits—and we're deep in depression.

The Old Man seems to come out of a kind of trance. He straightens up and shouts into the gangway, "Ship's time?"

"07.50 hours!"

"Navigator!"

He appears instantly from the control room.

"Can we get at them again?"

"Difficult!" says the navigator. "Unless . . ." The navigator pauses and begins again. "That is, unless they change their general course."

"We can hardly count on that . . ."

The Old Man follows him into the control room. I hear fragments of dialogue and the Old Man thinking aloud. "Dived at 22.53 hours, let's say 23.00—now it's 07.50, so we've lost a good eight hours. How fast are they moving? Probably about eight knots, so they've made sixty-four miles—at a very rough guess. To get where they are now we'd need more than four hours at full speed. But the fuel situation! It's too long at full speed; and, besides, the convoy will be that much farther ahead."

Nevertheless, he still seems unwilling to make any preparations to reverse our course.

The Chief turns up in the control room. He doesn't say a word, but the very way he stands there is a question in itself: When do we turn back?

Despite my exhaustion I can't sleep. I might as well be full of pep pills. Excitement is making me restless. No one in the Quarters. Uproar in the bow compartment. Must be some sort of half-hearted victory celebration. I push the hatch open. In the murky light I can make out a circle of men sitting on the floor plates, which are now back in place. I hear ragged singing. They drag out the last line until it sounds like a chorale. It's all very well for them to holler—they didn't see a thing, poor devils.

If they hadn't been told that the detonations and shrieking of rending metal came from the water pressure smashing the sides and holds of sinking ships—our targets—they wouldn't have been able to make head or tail of the deafening underwater uproar.

The navigator is on watch. The glow has died down but is still clearly visible. Suddenly he calls, "Something moving!" His right arm is pointing out over the dark sea ahead. He sends word below. Within seconds the Old Man is on the bridge.

It looks like a raft, with a bunch of men on it.

"Megaphone on deck," orders the Old Man and then, "Closer!" He props himself high against the bulwark and roars, "*What's the name of your ship?*" in English.

The men down there are quick to answer, as if this might buy them the reward of a rescuing hand: "*Arthur Allee!*"

"Just as well to know," says the Old Man.

One of the men tries to cling on to our boat, but we've already picked up speed. He hangs between us and the raft. And then he lets go and sinks into our foaming wake. Teeth—all I can make out is two rows of teeth, not even the whites of his eyes.

Will anyone find the others?

We haven't been going another quarter hour before a strange twinkling appears on the water in the pale light. Tiny flashing points—like fireflies. As we approach, they turn out to be little lamps dancing up and down. More survivors, hanging in their life preservers. I can clearly see them waving their arms. Trying to attract our attention? They're probably shouting too, but none of it reaches us because the wind is against them.

Stony-faced, the Old Man orders reduce speed and gives commands to the helmsman that will prevent the boat from coming too close to the drifting men. But we're still moving so fast that our bow wave catches two or three of them, slamming them up and then down again. Are they really waving at us or is that a threat, a last impotent gesture against the enemy who has turned them over to the deadly grasp of the sea?

We all stand there frozen—six men with fear clawing at our hearts, each knowing that any one of those men thrashing in the sea might be us. What will become of them? They escaped immediate catastrophe when their ship sank. But is there any hope for them? How cold is the water in December? Does the Gulf Stream reach this far? How long have they already been floating there? It's hard to believe: the ships guarding the convoy's rear must have passed the disaster area hours ago.

The Old Man stands motionless: a sailor who dares not help another in distress because an order from the C-in-C forbids rescuing surviving personnel! There's only one exception: flyers who have been shot down. They have valuable information. Apparently they're worth their weight in gold.

I can still see the little lights like will-o'-the-wisps. "Port five!" the Old Man orders. "Those were Navy men, probably from a corvette."

The Second Watch Officer appears. "Looks like an erupting volcano," he says to himself, meaning the fiery glow. The little lights have vanished.

There's a flash through the smoke. After a while an explosion rolls across the water like dull thunder, followed by yet another. A report comes up: "Sound room to bridge: Depth charges at two hundred sixty degrees!"

All hell must have broken loose in the convoy. The wind brings us the smell of burning oil: the stench of death.

Pale morning light is rising over the horizon. The glow of the fire gradually subsides.

I'm dead on my feet, almost ready to drop, when the bridge reports, "Burning vessel ahead!" It's 09.00. No choice but to struggle up to the bridge again.

"She's been hit," says the Old Man. "A straggler. We'll finish her off!"

He puts the binoculars to his eyes and his voice emerges from between gloved hands as he addresses the navigator. "First get a forward position. She's probably slowed down. About five knots, I'd say."

The Old Man gives a change of course: "Two points to port." The cloud of smoke grows rapidly larger and slowly moves to starboard. We should be able to see masts and even superstructures by now, but the smoke has shrouded everything.

Another five minutes, then the Old Man orders the boat to dive and level off at periscope depth: forty-five feet.

After a while he gives a kind of battle report from the tower: "Mustn't let her get away—she's tacking—well, if we hold on for a while, she'll tack again—just wait . . . Ship has two masts, four loading hatches, nice little scow—about eight thousand—riding low at the stern—fire aft. Think she's also been burning amidships."

His voice becomes a snarl. "Chief! She's turning this way!"

The periscope must have been underwater for a moment, blocking his view.

The Chief makes a face. Now it's up to him to trim ship precisely so that the Commander can operate as much as possible without moving the periscope. The Chief cocks his head forward and to one side, toward the Papenberg.

A series of rudder maneuvers. Suddenly the Old Man has the motors run full speed. The boat gives a palpable leap forward.

Then I hear the First Watch Officer above me reporting that the tubes are ready. The lateral directional angles are being transmitted to the lead-angle calculator in the tower, and from the lead-angle calculator to the torpedoes.

The First Watch Officer has long since pulled the safety catch from the firing mechanism. He's waiting there in the tower for the Old Man to get us lined up for the shot.

Is all this never to end? My mind is reeling. Am I dreaming? Did I hear: "Open torpedo doors"?

"Tube one stand by!" Two seconds pause: "Tube one fire!"— "Connect tube two!"

I seem to be living in some vivid waking dream. The sound of dull detonations, immediately followed by a much sharper one.

The Commander's voice seems to be coming from a great distance. "Lying dead in the water now!"

And then, almost subconsciously, I hear, "Seems to be sinking slowly."

Yet another! Will that be added to our score? The fog in my head is getting thicker. Weakness in the knees. Just keep on your feet. I hold on to the chart table, work my way slowly to the after hatch. My bunk seems miles away.

Was it a noise that woke me so suddenly?

Peace reigns in the petty officers' quarters. I clamber out of my bunk. Feel my way into the control room like a blind man. Pain in every limb as if I were just out of traction.

There's some life in the control room. Tin-ear Willie and the Bible Scholar are fussing about. I still can't make out what happened. Did I keel over? Pass out? Am I awake or dreaming?

Then I happen to see the war log. It's lying open on the desk.

12/13—yes, that must be right. Crazy: in a month Christmas will be long past. No longer any sense of the time of year. Completely lost. I read:

09.00 *Battle-damaged tanker. Running at slow speed, five knots. Course about 120 degrees. Attain forward position to determine firing data.*

10.00 *Dive for underwater attack. Tanker turns toward us, making range very close.*

10.25 *Fire torpedo. Hit scored amidships. Simultaneous major explosion of fuel oil. Great quantities of smoke and flame. Escaping oil burning on water. Huge smoke cloud in sky. Strong blaze. Steamer sinks deeper but continues to make headway. Some of crew still on board. Three guns on superstructure aft. Cannot be used on account of smoke and heat. No lifeboats visible.*

The fact that the tanker had guns is something the Old Man didn't tell us. When in God's name did he write all this? How late is it now?

10.45 *Propeller sounds. Moving forward.*

10.52 *Renewed attack. Waiting too dangerous. May be a trap. Hit scored below after mast. Another blaze. Tanker stops. Settles deeper astern. Flank blown out at point of impact. Fire on water spreading quickly. Must reverse engines fast.*

11.10 & 11.12 *Detonations on board. Apparently compartments exploding. Gasoline containers or munitions. Tanker lying dead in the water.*

11.40 *Propeller noises. Turbines. Suspect destroyer. Not visible in periscope.*

11.55 *Surface. Tanks not blown. Destroyer lying motionless beside wreck.*

I was present during all that. But the second torpedo shot . . . ? Everything is a jumble: just how did I come to be lying in my bunk?

11.57 *Crash dive. Silent running. Retreat.*

12.10 *Surface. Intend to remain motionless and wait to see whether tanker sinks. Batteries charged. Destroyer's mast visible on horizon from time to time in neighborhood of wreck.*

13.24–14.50 *Remain stopped. Tanker staying afloat. Fire slowly dying out.*

15.30 *Decide to approach again and give coup de grâce. Tanker is broken in two at point of impact forward of the after superstructures. Parts connected only by gangways. Complete loss certain. Foreship twisted sideways and awash. Lifeboats drifting empty. Destroyer has obviously abandoned tanker.*

16.40 *Approach closer and shoot holes in bow and stern with machine gun.*

20.00 *Return voyage begun. Other boats in contact. Dispatched radiogram: "Sank damaged tanker 8000 GRT. Returning to base—UA."*

23.00 *Radiogram received: "From UX: Two large freighters 00.31 Square Max Red. General course east. Ten knots. Have been out of contact*

*for an hour. Am pursuing. Wind west-northwest 7. Sea 5, barometer
1027 and rising. Use of weapons still curtailed by weather."*

So: three torpedoes for that scow! A copybook periscope attack.
Plus machine guns. I certainly heard their chattering. Just when did
I pass out?

I stare at the page. Even the last entry is in the Old Man's handwriting. Slowly the whole thing begins to seem uncanny. He even
had the energy to write up the war log during the night. I can still
hear him say: "Nothing more now but home to Kassel," and his
order to steer a course of forty-five degrees. And I realize I knew
that we were headed northeast.

It's hard, pulling myself together. The diesel sounds . . . oddly
irregular. Of course—economy speed!

Economy speed! If I understood the Chief correctly, he knows
he can do his damnedest to figure out the "most favorable" speed
for the return voyage; but the fuel oil still won't last us to Saint
Nazaire.

The navigator has unfolded a big sea chart that shows coastal
lines as well. I'm astonished to see how far south we've come. The
Old Man doesn't seem to be worried about fuel, or does he really
believe that the Chief has secret reservoirs to tap in time of need?

The green curtain in front of the Old Man's cubbyhole is drawn.
Asleep. Instinctively I start to tiptoe. I have to steady myself with
both hands, my limbs ache so.

The bunks in the officer's quarters are occupied too. The first
time we've actually had a full sleeping car. I feel like a conductor,
checking that everything's all right.

Everyone asleep—that means the navigator has the watch. The
third—so it must be after eight p.m.

My watch has stopped.

The next compartment is quiet too. Chief mechanic Franz's
bunk is empty. Of course: the engine room watch has been on duty
since six o'clock.

The Old Man hasn't said another word about the Franz incident. Will he have forgotten it entirely, or does he intend to follow
it up with a court-martial?

Not a sound through the bow compartment hatch.

A sleeping boat. No one awake, no one to talk to. I sit down on
the chart chest, stare blankly ahead, and fall prey to tormenting
visions.

ix PRO-VISIONING

HERRMANN YELLS, "Communications Officer!"

Ordinary signals are deciphered by the radioman, using the code machine, and entered in plain text in the radio log, which is shown to the Commander every two hours.

When Herrmann put this particular message through his machine, it made no sense. Only the first words, "Officer's signal," were comprehensible. Hence the Communications Officer (who is otherwise known as our Second Watch Officer).

He must have heard the report come in, for he scrambles out of his bunk with tousled hair, looking self-important, and sets up the decoding machine on the table. The Commander gives him today's code-setting on soluble paper. (The connecting pins of the machine are soluble in salt water too, so there can be no accidents with the enemy.)

Communications Officer! That's all we need. It must be about some new and special operation, something really tricky, supersecret.

"Hurry it up!" says the Old Man.

The first word the Second Watch Officer deciphers is "Commander." That means that when he puts the entire message through his decoding machine he'll get nothing out of it. In other words, this is in triple code. The Commander himself must now do the whole job again, using a setting known only to himself.

Significant glances: absolutely unprecedented. Never happened before on this patrol. What's in store for us? The Old Man disappears into his hole with the decoding machine and summons the First Watch Officer. The two rummage about among the papers for a good five minutes. The atmosphere is tense. When the Old Man finally reappears, he says not a word. Everyone is silent.

"Interesting," he murmurs finally. Nothing else, though all eyes are fixed on him. Another several minutes go by before he finally speaks. "We've been assigned a new port of call."

His voice is not quite as calm as he obviously would like. There must be something fishy about this new destination.

"Really?" the Chief says casually, as if he didn't give a damn where he was meant to provision the boat next.

"La Spezia."

"What's that?"

"Exactly what I said—La Spezia. Have you just gone deaf, Chief?"

The Commander pushes himself to his feet, steers his way back to his cubbyhole, and disappears behind the curtain. We can hear him rummaging around again.

I can see the map of Europe—every indentation of it. At school, nobody could beat me at drawing the map of Europe freehand. La Spezia—Italy. What a mess! There's an empty feeling in the pit of my stomach. Deep-down terror; I blink and gasp like a fish out of water.

The Second Watch Officer stammers, "But that means—"

"Yes, the Mediterranean!" the Chief interrupts sharply. "We seem to be needed there." He swallows, his Adam's apple jerking conspicuously. "So it's off to Gibraltar!"

"Gibraltar . . ." echoes the Second Watch Officer, looking at me open-mouthed.

"Dshebel al Tarik!"

"What?"

"Gibraltar in Arabic: Tarik's Mountain."

Gibraltar: a rock inhabited by apes. Closeup of an ape mother with infants clinging to her stomach. Glint of bared teeth. A British crown colony. The Pillars of Hercules. A bridge for the migration of peoples between Europe and Asia. Africa olé! Tangier! Tang, tangier, tangiest! The Gibraltar convoys! Half the British fleet is around Gibraltar. Somewhere in my head there's a phonograph needle stuck in a groove: Gibraltar—Gi-bral-tar—plaster altar, plaster altar, plaster altar.

This won't go down very well with the Old Man either. He can hardly be itching to explore the Mediterranean. Let alone a trashy harbor somewhere in Italy. The Führer decrees—and we're stuck with the consequences! That's the motto we need: it should be burned in capital letters on the lid of a lemon crate and hung in the control room.

Now I begin to make sense of the radio news reports of the last few weeks. North Africa, the heavy fighting at Tobruk. The British advance westward along the coast road. The Mediterranean must be teeming with British convoy freighters and fighting ships. And now the U-boats are supposed to go in and mop up?

I visualize every detail of the map of the Strait of Gibraltar, and on it I project a hideously tangled system of direction finders, anti-shipping nets, dense cordons of patrol boats, mines, and every imaginable kind of nasty surprise.

I'm still stunned, unable to think straight. But repeating themselves somewhere in the back of my head are the persistent words: DUE FOR REPAIR. Our scow is certainly due for repair after all the punishment we've taken. What can be the meaning of this madness? If only the Old Man would be frank for once.

"Fuel oil—fuel oil," is the next thing I hear from the control room. And again, "Fuel oil." Once from the Old Man and once from the navigator.

Then, "New course ninety degrees!"

Ninety degrees? Due east? I don't grasp that at all.

When the Old Man comes back from the control room and sits down at the table with a scowl on his face, as though he's still lost in his course calculations, it should be up to the Chief to ask the question we all want answered: Where do we get the fuel oil?

But the Chief's mouth might as well be closed with surgical tape. The Old Man spends a good five minutes clawing at his beard. Then he growls, "Provisioning at Vigo."

Vigo—Vigo—Vigo! Why there? Vigo—that's in Spain, or is it Portugal? Where the hell *is* Vigo?

The Chief is sucking his lips so hard that he's making creases in his cheeks. "Mhm," is all that comes out of him.

"Very considerate of High Command," the Commander says derisively. "They think of just about everything, after their *own* worries, that is. Two hundred fifty miles—or thereabouts. I suppose we can manage that without sails—eh, Chief—what do you say?"

The calendar shows December 14, the day we were supposed to put in at our base port. Now, instead of returning in French they want us to do it Spanish; after that, in Italian. Real cosmopolitan stuff. Reception with castanets instead of with Greater Germany's brass band; hundred-year-old sherry instead of beer.

Spanish gardens, Spanish fly, what else is there that's Spanish?

"Impeccable arrangements," says the Old Man. "No need to goggle like that, Chief. You'll get plenty of fuel oil and torpedoes. And food, of course—a full-scale provisioning, just like home port!"

How does he know all this, I wonder. After all, the coded signal was quite short.

"What More Could Heart Desire?" says the Chief.

The Old Man merely looks at him disapprovingly.

It occurs to me that this was to have been the Chief's last patrol. It's certainly his twelfth, and this is his second boat. There aren't many these days who've survived twelve patrols. And now—at the very end—they're offering him a special treat. Let's call a spade a spade: It's a superb chance to drown—one minute before closing time.

I pull myself together and climb through the hatch.

As yet the crew has no notion of what lies ahead. They'll be pretty goddam surprised. Instead of the channel at Saint Nazaire and a brass band, a Macaroni port with a whole load of trouble and grief before we get there.

But the "lords" seem to have got wind of the fact that something's up. Suddenly every face is tense, questioning. The silence after the signal could only mean that some crucial message had come in. And the order to the helmsman soon after would be perfectly self-explanatory to anyone who used his head. In any case, we're no longer on course for our home port.

All conversation ceases immediately whenever I enter a room. Anxious faces. But as long as the Old Man makes no announcement, I must do my best to look casual.

His expression is eloquent enough: Is it even possible to break through into the Mediterranean in the first place? And if so, what next? The enemy has the advantage of a number of nearby land bases, which means that its aerial surveillance over the Mediterranean is incomparably tighter than over the Atlantic. Can boats operate there at all during the daytime? Given really good lighting conditions and angle of vision, they say a plane can spot a U-boat as much as two hundred feet down—as a kind of shadow.

The bosun's broad forehead is distinguished by a diagonal scar running from his right eyebrow to the base of his nose. It turns reddish whenever he's excited. Right now it's gone puce.

The navigator has no such reliable "index of emotions." He's got the perfect poker face: a classic example of a fixed type. He changes places with the Commander at the chart table and starts behaving like a tiger with his prey, growling at anyone who even comes near him, so no one can see which chart he's working on with his protractor and dividers.

"We've been running on a different course for the last hour now," says Turbo in a low voice as he comes through the control room from astern.

"Bright boy, you don't miss a thing!" Hacker sneers. "They ought to use you for airplane cover."

An hour *already!* A whole hour, sixty minutes? Don't make me laugh! What does an hour mean to us? How many have we spent wallowing around aimlessly, how many have we wasted just to get us through the routine. Of course, their value began to rise the moment we started for home. Right now it would still be a hundred forty hours before we put in—assuming normal conditions. A hundred forty units of time—sixty minutes each—at fuel-hoarding cruising speed, and always hoping there'll be no enemy aircraft. At full speed we'd probably make it in no more than thirty. But full speed is out of the question. Everything's out of the question, as a matter of fact—gone to hell. Change of plan!

Cruising speed. The crew spends the second hour racked with nervous curiosity. The Old Man continues to maintain his silence.

On my way into the petty officers' quarters to fetch some writing materials I hear, "Funny kind of course . . ."—"Well yes, maybe the powers-that-be want us to admire the sunset in the Bay of Biscay." —"Putting it to a girl in Saint Nazaire, a really good fuck; you can write that all off. The whole thing's beginning to stink."

Silence.

Then I hear the familiar crackling of the loudspeaker. Finally— the Commander!

"Attention. We've been given a new port of call. La Spezia. As you know, that lies in the Mediterranean. Provisioning in Vigo. On the coast of Spain."

No comment, not a syllable of explanation, no excuses— nothing. He simply says, "End," and there's another last crackle.

The off-duty mates stare dumbly into space. The E-mate Rademacher looks at his piece of buttered bread as though it had been forced on him by a stranger. Finally Frenssen breaks the spell. "Oh, shit!"

"My ass!" is the next exclamation.

The meaning of the order is gradually dawning on them: no return to the base that has become a second home to them all. No chance of a stylish landing maneuver, to show off in front of the the news hounds and the carbolic brigade all standing there waiting with big bunches of flowers clutched in front of their stiffly starched aprons. Christmas leave? That's overboard too.

They're getting angry. "A helluva way to treat us!"—"What they need is a kick in the ass!"—"If you don't like it you can get out and walk!"—"Jesus, who'd have thought it!"

I look for the ensign. He's crouched on his bunk, hands hanging down between his knees, face as white as a sheet, and eyes staring vacantly in front of him.

"It'll make the Chief happy," says Frenssen; "we've used up almost all our supplies. Almost no oil left and practically no fish, so why should we fuss?"—"But Spain's neutral."—"Drop it. Someone else can worry about that!"—"Looks like red tape to me!"—"You could tell something like this was sure to happen just by sticking a finger up your own ass!"—"We're going to have some real fun!"

Stricken silence still reigns in the bow compartment. The rattling of a bucket between the torpedo tubes sounds unnaturally loud.

"It simply won't work," Ario says finally.

"Don't try to do the thinking for High Command," replies Dunlop. "Have you never heard of provisioning?"

"But what's it all got to do with Spain? What's the name of that dump?"

"Vigo."

"Shit!" says Bockstiegel. "Shit, shit!" And then, "Shit on horseback."

"But they're—they really are—stark, raving mad!" The Gigolo is stuttering with indignation. "The Mediterranean!" He puts so much disgust into the word you'd think he was discussing a stinking sewer.

Turbo is worried. "They've probably written us off completely in Saint Nazaire. What's to become of our duffel bags?"

"They'll be delivered with the rest of our estate!" Ario reassures him.

"Shut your trap!" shouts the Gigolo. No one can take that joke.

"Christmas with the Macaronis! Who'd have guessed it?"

"How d'you mean, with the Macaronis? If you get leave, it doesn't matter a shit whether you travel straight through France or straight through Italy . . ."

"Up through Italy," Hagen corrects him.

"Well yes," says Ario resignedly. He's obviously thinking what no one dares say aloud: If we ever get that far . . .

"Gibraltar—what's so bad about that?" the Bible Scholar inquires tentatively.

"Stupid stays stupid; pills won't help," is the answer he gets from one of the hammocks. And from a lower bunk, "A creature like that's still alive—and Schiller had to die!"

"Hasn't an inkling of geography; he's pathetic! You've probably never noticed the way Gibraltar's constructed. Man, it's as narrow as a virgin's slit. We'll have to smear our scow with Vaseline to get through."

"It's been known to happen," Hagen says finally.

"What d'you mean?"

"A fellow getting stuck and not being able to get out again. Happened to a classmate of mine. There he was jammed, like in a vise."

"You're kidding!"

"I promise you, it's true!"

"What happened next?"

"Nothing works, so they get the doctor. He has to give the lady a shot . . ."

Turbo, always a stickler for precision, isn't satisfied. "And how d'you get a doctor if you're stuck inside the lady?"

For the moment Gibraltar has lost its terrors.

"No idea. Scream?"

"Or wait till the snow falls!"

I find the Commander in the control room.

"A change is as good as a rest," I remark.

"Terrific!" he says morosely, then turns toward me and stares. As usual, he's chewing on the stem of his cold pipe. We stand facing each other like statues for a while until he beckons me to sit down beside him on the chart chest.

"Protecting our supply lines is probably what they call it. Africa's burning and we're supposed to play firemen. It's lunacy—U-boats in the Mediterranean when we haven't even enough in the Atlantic right now . . ."

I try to be sarcastic. "Hardly the right season for the Mediterranean. The C-in-C slipped up . . ."

"This doesn't seem to have been his idea. After all, he did everything he could to keep us from being used for weather reporting. We need *every* boat for front-line combat. Why else did they build the VII-C's, except for the Battle of the Atlantic?"

Up to now, I think, we've been lording it over the world as a self-reliant fighting ship. Now we're no more than a pawn of higher strategy—our nose turned toward Spain by remote control; our plans for the trip home, along with everything that hinges on them, reduced to nothing . . .

"He's having quite a time of it, the Chief," the Commander begins again haltingly. "It's his wife—she's expecting a child some time in the next few days. We had everything so well worked out for his leave. Even allowing for a long patrol. But of course we never figured on something like this. They don't even have their own apartment. Completely bombed out while he was on the patrol before last. They live with his wife's parents in Rendsburg. Now he's afraid things may go wrong. Understandable. There's something the matter with his wife. She almost died in labor the last time, and the child was stillborn."

It's the first time that anyone's private life has been discussed. Why is the Old Man telling me all this? It isn't at all his style.

An hour after dinner I get the answer. The Old Man is busy writing up the war log when he notices that I'm trying to get past him. He says, "Just a minute!" and pushes me onto his berth. "I intend to put you ashore in Vigo—you and the Chief. The Chief's due to leave the boat after this patrol anyway—that's official."

"But—"

"Let's not have any heroics. I'm working on the signal right now. *Somehow*, you and the Chief are going to be guided through Spain— disguised as gypsies for all I care."

"But—"

"No buts. It's too chancy for anyone to try singly. I've thought it all out. We have agents there who'll get you through all right."

My thoughts are in chaos. Leave the boat now? How will that look? Straight through Spain? What does he think he's up to?

I find the Chief in the control room. "I suppose you know already—the Old Man's going to put us both ashore."

"What on earth are you talking about?"

"We're being put off at Vigo—you and I."

"How so?" The Chief sucks in his cheeks. I can see the idea working in him. Finally he just says matter of factly, "All I want to know is how the Old Man's going to make out with that mutton-head—especially now!" He says no more, and it takes me a few moments to realize that the muttonhead in question is his successor.

And the ensign, I think—if only we could take the ensign along too.

Next time I come through the control room, the navigator's at the chart table. Now at last our route can give him straight lines to draw on his chart again. Everyone's busy. No one looks up; they're all privately trying to come to terms with their disappointment and their fears.

By the second day the fear has subsided. There are still four days at cruising speed between us and the actual approach to the Spanish coast. The crew has got hold of themselves much quicker than might have been expected, considering the low level of their morale. From my berth I hear the familiar chatter resume.

"Last time I had real luck: all the way from Savenay to Paris in a compartment with no one but a girl from the signal corps. It was really something: no need to work up a sweat, once you're in—you just let the train do the banging for you. But when we went through the junction, I was almost flung out of her."

"I never do it in cars. No room for action. It's much better if I get her to squat on the front seat, while I ram it in from behind—standing up outside, get it?"

I looked through the crack in the curtain right into Frenssen's face, alight with memories. "It rained once. My little chick stayed nice and dry but I was soaking wet. It came down off the roof like out of a drainpipe. But that way I could wash my cock off right away!"

"Did you go bareback?"

"Sure. The mouse knows how to be careful."

Later I hear: ". . . and then he went and got himself a girl despite the fact he'd already been married for three years. Word of honor, they're living together, all three of them."

"Well, well."

"He can't be a very sensitive type."

"Who needs sensitivity?"

It's shortly before noon on the third day after the Gibraltar order, near the end of his watch, when the navigator calls down to report a floating object. I climb onto the bridge behind the Commander. "Forty-five degrees to starboard," says the navigator.

The object is still about three thousand feet away. The Commander orders us to steer for it. It's not a lifeboat—more like a formless, flat lump. The sea is calm. The thing seems to be moving toward us. Over it hangs a strange cloud like a swarm of wasps. Seagulls? The Commander's mouth tightens and he inhales sharply; otherwise he makes no sound. He lowers his glasses: "Yellow spots— that's a raft!"

Now I can recognize it in my own glasses. An unmanned raft with barrels along the sides. Barrels? Or are they fenders?

"There are people on it!" the navigator says from under his binoculars.

"So there are."

The Old Man gives a change of course. Our bow is now pointing exactly toward the raft.

"No one moving over there!"

I stare through my binoculars. The drifting object grows steadily larger. Aren't those seagull cries I hear?

The Commander sends both lookouts down from the bridge.

"Navigator, take over their sectors! No sight for the crew," he murmurs to me.

He orders the helm to port, and we approach in an extended left-hand curve. Our bow wave brushes the corpses that hang in the water around the raft. One after another, they begin nodding like mechanical dolls in a store window.

Five dead, all bound tight to the raft. Why aren't they lying on it? Why are they hanging in the ratlines? The wind! Were they seeking protection from the biting wind?

Cold and fear, how long can one endure them? How long does one's body warmth resist the icy paralysis that grips the heart? How quickly do one's hands die?

There's one of the corpses that keeps rising higher out of the water than the others, making stiff bows that seem to go on and on.

"No name on the raft," says the Old Man.

Another of the dead seamen is floating, bloated, on his back. There's no flesh left on the bones of his face. The seagulls have pecked away everything soft. On his skull there remains only a small scrap of scalp covered with black hair.

"Seems we got here too late." The Old Man gives orders to the engine room and helmsman, sounding hoarse. ". . . the hell out of here," I hear him mutter.

The gulls sweep over us, shrill and evil. I wish I had a shotgun.

"Those were people from a liner!"

Good thing the Old Man's talking.

"They were wearing those old-fashioned life jackets. You don't usually find them on warships any more." And after a while he mutters, "Bad omen," and gives an order to the helmsman. He waits another ten minutes before ordering the lookouts back on deck.

I feel ill and climb below. Barely ten minutes later and the Commander comes down too. He sees me sitting on the chart chest and says, "That's almost always the way it is with gulls. Once we found two lifeboats. Everyone in them dead too. Frozen, probably. And all of them had lost their eyes."

How long had they been drifting with the raft? I don't dare ask him.

"The best thing," he says, "is to hit a gasoline tanker. That way everything blows up at once. These problems don't arise. With crude oil, unfortunately, it's different."

Although the bridge lookouts couldn't have seen much before the Commander sent them below, there has obviously been talk in the boat. The men speak in monosyllables. The Chief must have noticed something. He stares questioningly at the Old Man, then quickly lowers his eyes.

In the wardroom there's no discussion at all. Not even one of the hard-nosed comments that usually disguise the men's true feelings. You might think that this was a particularly thick-skinned, unfeeling bunch, that other men's fate left them cold. But the silence that has suddenly fallen, the irritability that hangs in the air, prove otherwise. They're probably seeing themselves hanging helplessly on a raft or drifting in a boat. Everyone on board knows how small the chances are of a raft being discovered in this area, and what fate awaits it even if the sea is calm. Men who lose their ship in a convoy can cherish some hope of being picked up—search units go to work; it's known where the disaster occurred, and rescue operations are begun at once. But these were not men from a convoy. Otherwise we would have seen wreckage.

The approach to Vigo isn't easy. For days we've been unable to get a proper fix on our position. Persistent fog. No sun, no stars. The navigator has done his dead reckoning as well as he possibly can, but it's impossible for him to estimate the drift—heaven knows how far we are from our calculated position. Swarms of gulls accompany the boat. They have black wing sheaths and narrower and longer pinions than the Atlantic gulls. I have the impression that I can already smell land.

Suddenly I'm choked with longing for terra firma. How does it look now? Late autumn—early winter. The only way to judge how late in the season we are, here on board, is by watching the nights draw in. As children we used to make potato fires at this time of the year and fly homemade kites that were bigger than we were . . .

Then I realize how wrong I am. Potato fire time is long past. Indeed, I've lost all real sense of time. But still I see the milky-white smoke from our fire, winding its way over the damp earth like a gigantic maggot. The brushwood won't burn properly: it takes the rising wind to make the fire glow red. We let our potatoes bake in the hot ashes . . . the impatient testing with hard sticks to see whether they're done . . . the black skin that crackles as it splits open . . . and then the first bite into their mealy insides . . . the taste of smoke on our tongues . . . the smell of smoke that clings to our clothes for days afterward! Chestnuts in all our trouser pockets. Fingers yellow from cracking walnuts. The bits of white meat that taste good only if you're careful to peel the yellow skin out of all the crevices. Otherwise they're bitter.

06.00.

The dark circle of the tower hatch sways back and forth; I can tell its motion by the wandering of the stars. Squeezing past the helmsman, who's jammed in among his instruments along the wall on the forward side of the tower, I climb up.

"Permission to come on the bridge?"

"*Jawohl!*" The voice of the Second Watch Officer.

Sunrise.

The sea today is a miniature range of foothills, all round, smooth, undulating hummocks and intersecting lines. The hills roll past under the boat, cradling us up and down. A good dozen seagulls circle us on motionless wings. They stretch out their heads and look at us with stony eyes.

It turns foggy during the navigator's watch. He looks worried. This close to the coast, not knowing the ship's precise position, and now fog to boot—there couldn't be a worse combination. Since we have to have a bearing of some kind, whatever the cost, the Old Man orders the diesels slow ahead and we creep closer to the coast.

The First Watch Officer is also on the bridge. We all peer forward intently into the watery milk soup. Something solidifies into a lump in the gray gloom and quickly takes shape: a fishing boat cutting across our bow.

"We could always ask him where we are," growls the Old Man. "First Watch Officer, d'you know Spanish?"

"*Jawohl*, Herr Kaleun!"

It takes a while for the First Watch Officer to realize the Old Man's joking.

Gradually the wind rises, the fog thins out, and a rocky cliff suddenly rises in front of us.

"Goddammit!" the Old Man says, "Stop engines—stop!"

We've come much too close.

"Let's hope there are no Spaniards out there," he mutters. "Well, it's hardly the weather for an outing."

Our bow wave collapses. The sudden silence takes my breath away. The bridge begins to sway. The Old Man is staring through his binoculars, and Kriechbaum too is searching the coast intently.

"Good work, navigator!" the Old Man says finally. "We seem to be almost exactly where we wanted to be—except a bit too close! Well now, let's worm our way nice and quietly up to the entrance and then take a look at the traffic. Both engines slow speed ahead! Steer thirty degrees!"

The helmsman acknowledges the order.

"Water depth?" the Commander asks.

The First Watch Officer bends over the hatch and repeats the question.

"Two hundred fifty feet!" comes the answer from below.

"Continuous soundings!"

The veils of mist are sweeping in once more.

"Perhaps not altogether unfavorable," says the Commander. "A kind of camouflage overcoat. Look sharp, men; see that we don't smash anyone to bits!"

We've made landfall on this coast a good two hours earlier than originally calculated.

"The best thing, it seems to me," the Old Man begins slowly, "is to use the northern entrance—underwater—then maybe out the same way again. Spend the night provisioning and then beat it before daybreak, say around four o'clock. Navigator, if possible, I want to be beside the provision ship by 22.00. Six hours—that should be enough. We'll just have to hurry like hell with the transfers!"

No lights, no bearings, no entrance buoys. Nothing. Even in the easiest harbors there's a pilot to help every steamer enter and depart; even with the most up-to-date charts and the clearest possible weather, there must always be a pilot on board—only for us, these regulations are totally irrelevant.

The veils of mist rise again.

"Neither here nor there. Better to wait till dark . . ." I hear the Old Man say.

I leave the bridge.

Shortly thereafter the Old Man orders us down to periscope depth.

Using the electric motors we worm our way gradually closer and closer to the harbor entrance.

The Old Man sits in the tower in the periscope saddle, his cap turned backward the way old-fashioned motorcycle riders used to wear them.

"What's that noise?" he asks urgently. We all listen. I can clearly hear a high-pitched, uniform swishing, overlaid by a dull, hammering sound.

"No idea!" says the navigator.

"Odd!"

The Old Man lets the periscope motor run for a second and then stops it, so as to leave our asparagus stalk sticking the minimum distance out.

"To the sound room: What do you have, bearing one hundred twenty degrees?"

"A small diesel!"

"Probably some little coastal vessel. And another—and another—and yet another, must be a gathering of the clans. But that one's moving—Duck!" And after a while: "Bad visibility again. Can hardly see a damn thing, we'll have to find some tub and follow her in."

"A hundred twenty-five feet!" reports the mate at the hydrophone.

"How would it be if we just anchored here?" the Old Man asks through the hatch.

The navigator is silent. Obviously he's not taking the question seriously.

Anchor? Actually, we do carry one of those symbols of hope around with us, just like a steamer. I wonder if a U-boat has ever used one.

The Commander calls the First Watch Officer to relieve him at the periscope and climbs down heavily. "In two hours it'll be dark; that's when we'll run in—one way or another!"

"How are we going to proceed after that?" I ask.

"Exactly according to plan," is the dry answer.

The "p" of plan is spat out from between his teeth—his way of expressing contempt for the whole arrangement.

Later on, however, he does finally condescend to explain. "Among the secret documents we brought with us are instructions to cover precisely this contingency. We've been radioed our exact arrival time. Our agents in Vigo will take care of what's necessary—if they haven't done so already."

"Nice work," murmurs the Chief.

"You can say that again."

"Time to surface," the navigator announces.

"Okay, then, let's go!" The Old Man gets to his feet.

Blue-gray evening twilight. The wind comes off the coast, bringing the smell of land. I raise my nose like a dog sniffing quickly to identify the layers of odor, the jumbled smells: rotting fish, fuel oil, rust, burned rubber, tar—but over and through it all there's something more: the smell of dust, the smell of earth, the smell of leaves.

The diesels spring to life. The Commander has apparently decided to push on regardless.

A pair of running lights appears, twinkling. Red, green, then white as well—and higher than the others—that one must be at the masthead.

The Second Watch Officer reports a ship edging toward us.

The Old Man turns his glasses, stands motionless for a while, then orders our speed reduced. "Well, doesn't look—doesn't look at all bad. She's planning to run in, no question about that! What would you say—hmm? Let's just follow her for a while—seems to be another of those small coastal steamers but a sturdy one. Makes a lot of smoke. Must be using old felt boots for fuel. Wish it were a little darker!"

The Old Man hasn't had the tanks completely blown, so our upper deck barely rises above the water. Unless someone sees us from the side, we could hardly be recognized as a U-boat.

The Old Man turns the bow toward the starboard running light of the approaching vessel. Seen from the steamer, we're lying against a stretch of coast that obscures the outline of our tower: always remember your background—the old rule!

The Old Man has the helm put slowly farther to starboard, so as to keep the green light over our net guard until the stern light of the steamer also comes into view. Only then does the Old Man increase our speed by one notch. We're traveling directly in her wake. I can smell the smoke.

"Phew!" exclaims the Old Man. "For god's sake, keep a sharp lookout, in case anything cuts across our bow! There must be ferries and other boats like that around!"

He's searching with his glasses. Suddenly there's a shadow to starboard. No time to turn aside! We pass by so close that we can see a spot of light: no doubt about it—it's a man smoking a cigarette. If he'd been paying any attention he'd have seen us, a strange shadow half hidden in smoke.

Now we have three or four large shadows in front of us. Are they approaching? Or going away? What's going on?

"All kinds of traffic," mutters the Old Man from under his glasses.

Lights—stern lanterns—a distant rumbling.

"They seem to be lying at anchor," I hear the navigator say.

"D'you think we've already reached the inner roadstead?"

"Seems so!"

A whole necklace of lights springs up in the distance, strung delicately along the horizon, but broken here and there; that could mean a pier with ships lying alongside—and the shadows of the ships causing the dark spaces.

Steamers to starboard, too. Their position is hard to make out. If they were all swinging from their anchors in the same direction, it would be simple. But one vessel lies with her stern toward us, while the one next door is showing her bow. Despite the darkness, their silhouettes are clear against the distant lights.

"Lying between freighters, apparently," mutters the Old Man.

I've no notion how he expects to find the right steamer—the one that's to provision us, the German ship *Weser*.

"Ship's time?"

"21.30 hours!"

"It's all going perfectly."

The Old Man gives two full-rudder orders in quick succession. There seem to be difficult currents just here. The helmsman's working hard.

Jesus! If only we could use our searchlight. Stumbling about in a strange house in the dark is sheer madness.

In any case, there are steamers by the dozen and apparently warships too. Over there, three points to starboard, is something that has to be a gunboat or small destroyer.

The Old Man orders the engines stopped. We keep moving for a while under our own momentum, and as we move, our bow swings around to starboard.

"Now all we have to do is find the right tub!" I hear the Old Man say.

More engine-room commands, then steering orders, then more engine-room commands, and another staccato stream of steering orders. A zigzag course between the big shadows.

Orders to the helmsman and the engine room come spitting out like machine-gun fire.

"I'm going mad!" mutters the Second Watch Officer.

"That won't get the job done," growls the Old Man.

"There's a streetcar!" exclaims the Second Watch Officer.

Yes—a blue lightning flash, a streetcar! As though to prove the point, the trolley strikes two or three more sparks from the overhead cable.

In front of us lies a huge dark mass. It must be the overlapping silhouettes of two or three ships.

"Someone's flashing!" the navigator reports.

"Where?"

I stare hard. For a fraction of a second a tiny point of light flares up in the midst of the huge shadows.

The Old Man observes it silently. The cigarette glow reappears, goes out, comes on again.

"The signal!" says the Old Man and takes a deep breath.

Incredulously, I stand with my eyes riveted to the constantly blinking dot. It can't be more than a small flashlight!

"The things they expect of us!" I exclaim involuntarily.

"Anything brighter would be conspicuous," says the Old Man.

Our boat edges slowly closer to the dark mass that gradually resolves itself into three shadows: three ships in a row. The light is flashing from the middle one. The shadows steadily begin to draw apart. We steer directly for the center one. It's lying at one hundred twenty degrees, then one hundred. Gradually it rises, becomes a barrier wall. The Old Man orders us to turn. Suddenly I hear German voices. "Watch out! Fender! Get a move on!"—"Don't go overboard there, man!"—"Another fender here!"

The strip of black water between the bulge of our port buoyancy tank and the ship's steep side is steadily shrinking. Now we have to tilt our heads to see the figures of the men bending over the railing above us.

Our bosun is on the upper deck, herding his men back and forth with half-muted curses. Four or five fenders are lowered from above.

"At least they know how to tie up!" says the Old Man.

"Maybe they've had some practice. Or d'you think we're the first?"

No answer.

A ship is anchored nearby in a blaze of floodlights, making a murderous din as it loads cargo from some lighter-ships. The thudding of the winches marks the beat.

"Just as well there's all that noise," says the Old Man.

The dim light from the *Weser*'s portholes is the only illumination allowed us.

A dull bump.

"Wonder how we're supposed to get up!"

Then a Jacob's ladder is dropped over the side. I'm allowed up directly after the Commander. Christ, I'm stiff—no exercise! Hands reach down to me from above. Iron plates resound under my feet. Someone seizes my right hand. "A cordial welcome, Herr Kapitän-leutnant!"

"No, no—I'm not—that's the Commander!"

Dazzled, we stand in the doorway to the saloon. Snow-white

tablecloths, two bunches of flowers, paneled walls polished like mirrors, attractively draped curtains over the portholes, thick carpet . . . I move in a kind of dream. Ornamental plants everywhere—in pots on the floor, suspended by chains from the ceiling. My god! Upholstered furniture, and bunches of grapes in a bowl on the table.

Profound distrust settles in the pit of my stomach. Any minute now there will be a loud bang, and this whole apparition will disappear.

I stare into the beaming parson's face of the strange Captain as if he were a creature from another planet: white goatee, monk-like tonsure surrounding a tanned bald spot, collar and tie.

Someone else shaking my hand. A sonorous voice that seems to come from a great distance. More confusion. God knows the Old Man might have put on something other than that eternal, disgusting sweater! After all, we're in different surroundings. How can the Captain of the *Weser* know that this old-clothes peddler is our Commander? I can feel myself blushing, but the Old Man and the Captain of the *Weser* immediately get together: vigorous shaking of hands, grins, animated conversation.

We're urged to sit down. The officers of the *Weser* appear. Christ! All in full dress uniform. More handshaking and grinning. The Old Man might have worn his decorations for once.

The *Weser*'s Captain is positively overflowing with kindness. Like a captain in a picture book: wrinkled, crafty, with big reddish ears. He wants to do it all for us as well as he possibly can. The ship's bakery has been hard at work since morning. There's everything: cakes, fresh bread, whatever we want. My mouth begins to water.

"Christmas cakes too, and, of course, fresh rolls," says the Captain.

I can still hear the Chief's description of his dream food: fresh rolls, melting yellow butter, and hot cocoa.

The Captain's voice goes on in a ghostly chant: "Fresh sausages, boiled pork—slaughtered just this morning—fried sausages. Every kind of fruit, even pineapples. Unlimited supplies of oranges, fresh figs, bunches of grapes, almonds . . ."

God in heaven! We've landed in the Garden of Eden. It's been years since I've seen oranges or pineapples, and never in my life have I eaten fresh figs.

The Captain relishes our speechless astonishment. Then he motions across the table like a magician and in less than a minute great platters of sausage and ham are carried in.

Tears start in my eyes. The Old Man is just as flabbergasted. He rises from his chair as if all this prodigality is too much for him and stammers, "I'll just go and take a quick look—see how things are going."

"Everything's going just fine—it's all moving along—everything's going splendidly!" he's reassured from all sides, and the Captain pushes him back into his seat.

The Old Man sits there embarrassed and stutters, "Fetch the First Watch Officer—and the Chief . . ." I'm already on my feet.

"The Second Watch Officer and the Second Engineer are to stay on board for the time being!"

"All the crew can bathe," the *Weser* Captain shouts after me, "in two shifts. Everything's ready."

When I reappear in the unaccustomed glare of the saloon, the Old Man is still grinning with embarrassment. He fidgets uncertainly in his chair, apparently uneasy at such peace and quiet.

The Captain wants to know how the boat's mission worked out. The Old Man squirms.

"Yes, well. This time they really had their hooks in us. But it's incredible what a boat like ours can stand!"

The Captain nods as if these few words are enough to explain everything. An array of beer bottles is set up on the big table. It's beer from Bremen, plus German whiskey, French Martell, Spanish Cognac, Spanish red wine.

There's a knock at the door. What now? Two men in trench coats appear, they take off their felt hats and glance rapidly from one of us to the next as if they're after a criminal. Enter the police?

"Herr Seewald, representative of the naval attaché," I hear.

The second man seems to be some kind of agent. The First Watch Officer and the Chief come in behind them. The saloon is filling up.

My heart is pounding. Any minute now we'll know whether the patrol has come to an end for the Chief and me, or whether it will lead on to Gibraltar.

More chairs are brought in. The Old Man is already leafing through the papers that the taller of the two has handed him with a formal bow.

There's silence for a few moments, apart from the shuffling of papers and the rising and falling howl of the wind.

The Old Man raises his eyes over the packet of papers and says, "Turned us down, Chief. High Command has turned us down!"

I don't dare glance at the Chief. My own mind is racing: This means I don't go either. Well then, it just won't happen; so be it! It's probably all for the best.

I force a grin.

After all, the Old Man can't leave the boat either—nobody can— and without the Chief, he'd be sunk. Am I afraid? The Old Man is sure to win out. But then there's the opposing argument: The scow needs an overhaul. All that damage—and repaired with nothing but material we had on board. How can the thing hold up? How will we manage?

Vigo; for the time being we're right here in Spain. Around midnight. The fact only sinks in by degrees. I have to put up a good front.

Would I have been so hard hit if I hadn't been so sure that the Old Man's plan would really work out? Naturally, I'd been betting that the patrol would end in Vigo for both of us. I simply didn't want to admit it to myself.

Not having shown any enthusiasm for the Old Man's plan right from the beginning, I can act as though I'd expected nothing but a turndown all along. No emotionalism. Refused—that's okay with me. But the Chief! This is a bitter blow, hitting him much harder than it hits me.

In any case, the Old Man has trouble digesting the news. That much is clear. He seems glad when the two men in trench coats present him with something else that demands his attention, but he still sits there thunderstruck. These two oily henchmen, ready to bow and scrape and rub their hands, turn the scene into a midnight horror play directed for the crudest effects. The contrasts are too obvious, too gross: the Weser's dignified Captain and these drunken vultures.

But how do we look ourselves? I stare at the Old Man as if I were seeing him for the first time. I, after all, am still more or less decently dressed with my salt-encrusted leather trousers and my half-washed sweater, but the Old Man looks as if he'd been thrown out of a poorhouse in the middle of the night. His beard is as shaggy as his hair. On board, we'd all got used to his rotting sweater, but here in the bright lights of this paneled room, even I am exasperated by this frayed, unraveled knitted rag. Only the V neck is still intact. To the right, over his ribs, there's a hole almost as big as the one for his head. And his rumpled shirt, the ancient cap, his scarecrow's trousers . . .

For the first time I notice how pale, hollow-eyed, and emaciated he looks. The Chief too. He wouldn't need any makeup job to play Mephistopheles. The last few days have really worn him out. This thirteenth patrol, coming right after the twelfth without any leave, was a little much for an exhausted man who has far more responsibilities to bear than any other member of the crew.

The Old Man is openly at pains to demonstrate his refusal to have anything to do with the two civilians. He's wearing his sour-pickle expression, declines the cigarettes they offer him, and barely answers them.

I hear that the *Weser* allowed herself to be interned here at the beginning of the war. She's now a kind of floating supply depot that is restocked from time to time with fuel oil and torpedoes. In absolute secrecy—there has to be strict regard for Spanish neutrality.

I can't get over the secret-agent faces of the two vultures. The taller is crafty, sly, his eyebrows a single line; low forehead, pomaded hair, Adolphe Menjou mustache, muttonchops extending below his earlobes. Much waving of his arms in the air so that his cuffs shoot out and show the gold cufflinks. The other one has close-set ears, a swarthy face, and a shifty air. The two of them stink of undercover work a mile off, even if one calls himself a representative of the naval attaché. Difficult, apparently, for a spy not to have a face that fits his profession.

I overhear odd snatches and tail ends of dialogue. To crown it all, we're not even going to be allowed to leave mail. Too risky! It's a secret operation . . . nothing must be allowed to leak out. We aren't even supposed to know exactly where Vigo is.

There will be dreadful worries at home. The patrol has already gone on longer than ever before and god knows how much longer it will be before we can send any mail. How will the men feel when they're told they have to hold on to the letters they've been writing so busily during the last few days?

And the ensign—how will he be able to stand it? I wish I'd never heard a word of his Romeo and Juliet story. But I can't just go over and comfort him—treat him as if he's a callow romantic boy.

The chatter of the two vultures seems to reach me through cotton wool. "One more, just to cure ourselves of the habit, Herr Kapitän-leutnant!"—"That must have been an interesting mission. Herr Kapitänleutnant."

I'd be missing my guess about the Old Man if he utters anything more than a mumbled "Yes."

Not even their direct questions about our boat's successes can elicit any response from the Old Man. He simply narrows his eyes and glares from one to the other, waits for his silence to unnerve them, and then says, "Yes."

I can see that his mind is working the whole time, and I can imagine what's bothering him. Involuntarily, I glance at his hands. He's clenched them together, the way he always does when he feels uncomfortable.

Then he signals me with a nod of the head.

"Just stretch my legs a bit," he says to the company.

The sudden change from the warmth of the saloon to the cold night air takes my breath away. I smell oil—our provisioning. The Old Man hurries toward the stern with such long strides that I'm barely able to keep up. When he can go no farther, he turns around abruptly and leans against the railing. Between the bow of a lifeboat and the black supports of some iron structure, whose purpose I can't make out, I see the flickering glow of Vigo: yellow lights, white lights, a few red ones. Two sparkling necklaces run upward, gradually drawing together—that must be a street leading up the hill from the harbor.

At the pier lies a destroyer, all its decks lit up. Floodlights blaze down on a freighter. You can clearly see that her loading cranes are at work.

A circle of yellow light shines up from below us—the open torpedo supply hatch. The galley hatch is open too. I hear voices. "They'll never be any use to me again, these good clothes!"—"Oh, cut the rubbish—get going. Grab that!"

That was unmistakably the Berliner.

Subdued singing echoes from below decks in the *Weser*.

I'm excited by the sparkling lights, the rosy-red halos around the streetlamps over there on the shore. They're surrounded by an aura of sex. I smell bed, the warm milky smell of skin, the sweetish smell of powder, the anchovy-sharp smell of cunt, Eau de Javel, sperm.

Interrupted shouts, fragments of commands, the loud banging of metal.

"What a racket," says the Old Man.

The situation obviously disturbs him. "Those people on the fishing boat—they must have seen us," he says finally. "And the men on the ship. Who knows whether they're all reliable? It would be easy enough to flash a signal from here to shore. In any case, we're going to put to sea earlier. Not as arranged. And we'll take the same way out. Not the southern passage they recommended. If only we had more water under our keel around here . . ."

Blue sparks flash on the shore like a short circuit. Another trolley. Sounds of chattering borne on the wind, then the honking of cars and the dull clanking from other ships. Suddenly a deep silence.

"Just where do they get the torpedoes?" I ask the Old Man.

"Other boats deposit them here—the ones on return voyage that didn't use up their whole quota. They drop in here on a visit, as suppliers, so to speak. Return voyages are very useful for that. It's the same for any superfluous fuel oil in their tanks."

"How well has it worked up to now? After all, we aren't the first."

"That's just it . . . Three boats have already been supplied here. Two were lost."

"Where?"

"That's what's not clear. It's perfectly possible there's a Tommy destroyer on duty, waiting for us off the southern entrance. I don't like any of this!"

From below we can hear a kind of communal singsong. The First Watch Officer should be here. Then by way of climax we get the melody of the "Internationale," but with new words:

> *Brothers of freedom and sunlight!*
> *Buy condoms cheap at the co-op!*

In the pale glow of the distant floodlights I can see the Old Man grinning. He listens a while longer, then goes on. "They're not nearly careful enough around here! This is hardly a reliable operation!"

A stab of memory: I realize that somewhere before I've seen a box of Spanish matches like the ones lying in there on the table.

"Those Spanish matches," I say. "I recognize them."

The Old Man doesn't seem to be listening. I begin again. "A box of Spanish matches like those, just like the ones on the table in the saloon, I've seen one before . . ."

"Really?" he says.

"Yes, in La Baule on the table in the Royal. It belonged to Merten's First Watch Officer."

"So Merten has already been here once—interesting!"

"The box of matches suddenly vanished. But no one admitted to taking it."

"Interesting," says the Old Man again. "I don't like it at all!"

"And then a box like that turned up another time . . ." But this doesn't seem to matter to the Old Man. It's enough for him to know that our method of provisioning hasn't remained as secret as the gentlemen sitting around the green table imagine. The boxes of matches—perhaps none of it is that important. Perhaps I'm only imagining things. But Spanish matches—you can't help noticing—Spanish matches in France.

I suddenly remember the ensign. Let's hope Ullmann doesn't try anything silly. Better have a look and see where he is. I pretend that I have to take a leak and climb over the tower down into the boat. How shabby it suddenly looks down here!

I encounter Ullmann in the control room. He's helping to stow away fresh bread. The net that hung low in front of the radio shack when we put out is being filled up again.

I'm suddenly embarrassed, and can't think what to say to him. "Well, Ullmann," I manage, and then add, "A pretty mess!"

I'm notoriously unsuited to the role of comforter. The ensign looks pathetic. How often must he have told himself in the last few hours that there's no way back from La Spezia to La Baule? What I would really like to do is take him by the shoulders and give him a thorough shaking. Instead of which, I do what he's doing, and stare at the pattern of the floor plates, only able to stammer out, "This is just—this is just miserable!" The ensign blows his nose. Jesus, he has to pull himself together. I have an idea. "Ullmann, quick, fetch me your letter . . . Or do you want to add a line to it? No, better write it over again as of now with no giveaways in it—got it? I'll see you in ten minutes in the control room."

It'd be ridiculous, I think, if I can't persuade the Captain of the *Weser* . . .

The Old Man is still brooding at the railing, and I stand silent beside him. Soon a squat shadow appears: the Captain of the *Weser*. The Old Man goes through his customary trampling dance, and says, "I've never been to Spain before."

My thoughts are with Ullmann.

The Captain of the *Weser* is not a voluble man. He speaks in an agreeable, cautious fashion, his deep voice tinged with a North German accent. "We have a Flettner rudder—designed by the same Flettner who invented the rotor ship. The rotors were a flop, but the rudder has been a great success. We can turn on a coin. In a narrow harbor that's a big advantage."

A queer bird—giving us a lecture on his special rudder at a moment like this.

A dull bumping disturbs the Old Man. The First Watch Officer turns up. "Just see whether the lines and fenders are properly cleared!" the Old Man orders.

The wind is freshening quite perceptibly.

"Would the Commander not like to take a bath?" asks the Captain of the *Weser*.

"Thank you, no."

A man comes up to announce that the meal is served in the saloon.

"Let's enjoy it!" says the Old Man, and moves after the Captain.

Once again the change from darkness to the blinding light of the saloon makes me pause for a moment. The two vultures seem to have got themselves plastered. Their faces are flushed, their eyes no longer as alert as they were around midnight.

I steal a glance at my wristwatch: two thirty. I have to sneak out again and look for the ensign. He slips his letter into my hand, like a pickpocket passing something to his sidekick.

Meantime the First Watch Officer and the Chief have relieved the Second Watch Officer and the assistant engineer. It'll probably be five o'clock before we're ready for departure.

I wish I could stretch out and sleep, but I go back to the saloon.

The two civilians are now being hail-fellow-well-met. The Old Man has to permit the taller of the two to slap him on the shoulder and babble, "Sieg Heil and fat booty!"

I almost sink through the floor in humiliation.

Fortunately, when the time comes, there's a companionway instead of the Jacob's ladder on the way back. Everything has been carefully blacked out, so I manage to exchange a few words with the Captain of the *Weser*, thereby detaining him so that we lag some way behind the others. I don't say much. He takes the letter without any fuss. "I'll see to it," he says.

A gangway has been extended from a lower deck to our bridge. With one hand propped on the TBT I let myself drop into the bridge cockpit. There wells up in me a kind of affection for the boat, and I lay both hands flat against the damp metal of the bulwark. The steel is vibrating: the diesels are beginning to run.

Commands to cast off. Shouts from above.

The Old Man sees to it that we get away quickly. Already I can barely make out the waving figures on the *Weser*.

The port running light of a steamer is suddenly very close. The Old Man calls for the signal light. What is he up to?

He himself signals over, "Anton, Anton." A hand-held searchlight flashes back from the steamer.

"B-u-e-n-v-i-a-j-e," the Old Man reads out.

And then he replies, "G-r-a-c-i-a-s."

"Yes, I have foreign languages too!" says the Old Man. And then, "They saw us—no doubt about it. Now perhaps they'll assume we're polite Tommies or something of the sort."

Our course is one hundred seventy degrees—almost due south.

The provisioning in Vigo has cheered the men up.

"Went off pretty well—but they could have rounded up some

dames while they were at it!" I hear in the wardroom. "A quick one on the gangplank!"

"Those guys were absolutely shattered by us! The Old Man in that sweater of his—it was an act in itself!"

The consternation that reduced them to silence after the Gibraltar signal seems to have vanished. Now they sound as though they'd wanted the Mediterranean all along, just to make a change.

Frenssen claims to have had a brother who was in the Foreign Legion. He describes a desert landscape with date palms and oases, fata morganas, desert fortresses, and luxuriously equipped whorehouses "with a thousand women—and boys too—something for everyone!"

Pilgrim starts reminiscing too.

"I had a girl once who was crazy about pants with zippers. Couldn't control herself, even on the streetcar. Kept grinding her hip against my fly, zipping it up and down, up and down . . . like the guillotine—makes a man nervous!"

"So what did you do?" asks Wichmann.

"Do? What the hell *can* you do? It's like the Grand Old Duke of York in the nursery rhyme—'when you're up, you're up' . . ."

"Well, easy come, easy go!"

"You're a real gorilla—no class at all."

Wichmann suddenly gets dreamy. "One of those real leisurely afternoon fucks—a bit of music—a little something to drink—that's still the best. You and your slam-bam-thank-you-ma'ams!"

Memories come to mind: lazy lovemaking on rainy afternoons. The doorbell rings, but we pay no attention. In another world—far from everyday reality. Curtains half drawn. Landlady out shopping. Only us and the cat in the apartment.

Later Frenssen and Zeitler quietly and matter of factly discuss the varying merits of certain postures during intercourse.

"It can drive you crazy sometimes," Frenssen says. "I laid a doll on the heath once . . . straight up a slope. Christ, was that a job—uphill, you know—but finally, just as I was coming, I turned the lady around a hundred and eighty degrees."

He makes a scooping motion with both hands to illustrate the turn.

Later there is whispering back and forth between two bunks. "How do you feel?"

"How do you think I feel? Doesn't matter a damn where they send us, does it?"

"Come on, admit it! Do you think I don't know why you've been so down in the mouth? But, that's all over with now! Don't worry about it. Your little girl will be taken care of. After all, she's a very presentable doll, something like that doesn't get dusty . . ."

The next day a thoughtful atmosphere prevails in the petty officers' quarters, a few swaggering speeches by Zeitler and Frenssen notwithstanding. No chitchat from bunk to bunk. It's not going to be child's play—everyone has realized that by now.

At the midday meal the Old Man begins to talk about the way he plans our passage past Gibraltar—hesitantly, trying our patience as usual; anyone would think he was putting his thoughts together for the first time like pieces of a jigsaw puzzle—that he hadn't spent hour after hour concocting his plan, weighing the risks, then discarding the whole project, recombining the elements, weighing the advantages and disadvantages.

"We'll use the nighttime approach—on the surface. As close as we possibly can. It'll be a real obstacle race."

Obstacles like destroyers and other patrols, I add silently.

"Then we'll simply dive and let ourselves sink our way past."

I don't dare expose my curiosity with so much as a glance, so I pretend to understand: perfectly clear—let ourselves sink our way past. That's the latest style.

The Old Man simply continues to stare straight ahead. He pretends to be thinking and says no more, as if he'd explained himself fully.

Sink! Not exactly an attractive expression. Makes for a feeling in the pit of the stomach like a falling elevator. But if the Delphic oracle wants it that way, that's what we'll do: sink!

The Second Watch Officer doesn't have as good a control over his face as I do. He seems to have a nervous tic in his eye—it makes him look as if he's asking questions with his eyelashes—a new, unobtrusive way of gathering information.

But the Old Man simply leans his head back in his barber-chair posture. Finally, after two or three minutes, he directs a few explanations to the finely grained plywood on the ceiling. "You see, there are two currents in the Strait of Gibraltar: a surface current from the Atlantic into the Mediterranean and a deeper one that flows in the opposite direction. And there's quite a bit of push behind them."

He thrusts out his lower lip and sucks in his cheeks, then looks down and just sits there in silence again.

"Seven-knot current," he finally tosses in, like a tidbit for us to chew on a while.

Then I see the light. Sink—this time he means horizontally, not in the usual up and down sense.

Perfectly obvious—and brilliant!

Nothing simpler: Dive, and let yourself be carried through the strait by the current—no noise, and it saves fuel.

The rules of the game demand that we appear bored. No astonishment. Don't nod; don't move an eyelash. The Old Man thrusts out his lower lip again and nods deliberately. The Chief allows himself a sort of lopsided grin. The Old Man registers this, takes a deep breath, returns to his barber-chair posture, and asks in unexpectedly official tones, "Well, Chief, everything clear?"

"*Jawohl*, Herr Kaleun," the Chief replies, nodding vigorously, as if sheer zeal might keep him at it forever.

There's a tense pause. What the Old Man needs now is an opponent, a doubter. The Chief gladly obliges. Admittedly, all he says is, "Hm, hm," but that's enough to indicate certain reservations. Although all of us—except the Commander—are now staring expectantly at the Chief, he simply cocks his head on one side like a blackbird searching for nightcrawlers in the short grass. He wouldn't think of voicing his doubts—he's just allowing them to flicker through. That's enough to begin with. He's an old hand—he takes his time, he dallies—something he learned from the Old Man.

Our company devotes a good five minutes to this silent game. Finally the Old Man seems to have had enough. "Well, Chief?" he says encouragingly. But the Chief's holding up remarkably well. He shakes his head very gently and delivers his dry curtain line. "Absolutely first rate, Herr Kaleun! Inspired idea."

I'm amazed at this cold-blooded bastard! And to think that I was afraid he was close to a nervous breakdown during the last attack.

On the other hand, the Old Man's doing well too. He betrays no visible reaction whatever; he simply lowers his head and observes his Chief out of the corner of his eye, as though he had to check on a patient's state of mind without the patient noticing it. A raising of the left eyebrow expresses his concern about the invalid: pure drawing-room comedy.

The Chief pretends to be unaware of the Commander's psychiatric examination. With superbly mimed indifference he raises his right leg, clasps his hands under his knee and looks absolutely blank while casually observing the veins in the woodwork.

Just as the silence threatens to become oppressive, the steward appears. Even the extras are in good form today, providing the action when it's time to put an end to the dumb show.

The soup makes its rounds. We spoon it, chew, and are silent.

Once again I notice the fly. She's walking across the photograph of the C-in-C. Right into his wide-open mouth. Too bad it's not happening in real life: a black fly the size of a small dumpling straight down his throat—right at the climax of one of his stemwinding speeches. "Attack—onward and up . . . ugh—" The fly takes wing and the C-in-C utters only the first syllable before he chokes. Our fly didn't disembark in Vigo: she resisted all temptations to become a Spanish fly. Spanish flies—there are such things! She stayed on board, proved her loyalty. *No one* deserted. We're all still aboard, all present and accounted for, our fly included. At the same time she's probably the only creature that can come and go as she pleases. Not bound by the C-in-C's orders the way we are. An example of spectacular loyalty. Through thick and thin. Very commendable.

Up in the bow, a kind of opera evening seems to be in progress. Through the closed hatch come scraps of song. When the hatch clicks open, there is rousing noise from the compartment:

> *Here comes the sheik*
> *He's on the make . . .*

This is repeated ad infinitum. Just as I've given up all hope of textual change, some of them get together on the next verse:

> *Through the wide, wide wastes of the Sahara*
> *There wanders a sex-crazy crone,*
> *Along comes a filthy old Bedouin*
> *First she screams, then he roars, then they moan.*

"It's Arabian week! Probably something to do with the fact that we're headed south," says the Old Man. "They're singing to pluck up their courage."

Because the Old Man seems to have some free time after breakfast, I ask him for some explanations. "This strong current flowing into the Mediterranean—I don't understand it. Where does all the water come from?" I have to make up my mind to be patient. The Old Man is never quick off the mark. First he tilts his head to one side and frowns—I can see the sentences taking shape.

"Well . . . yes . . . there *are* quite remarkable conditions there."

Pause. Now the rules require that I fix my eyes on his face to keep his remarks staggering on.

"You already know that the Mediterranean not only has a current that flows *in* but also one that flows *out*. Two of them, one above the other: upper one in, lower one out. The reason is that there's practically no rainfall anywhere in the area. There's endless sunshine, though—so a lot of water evaporates. And as the salt obviously doesn't evaporate along with the water, the salt content increases. The saltier the water, the heavier it is. All clear and logical, isn't it?"

"So far—yes."

The Old Man hangs fire. Dragging on his cold pipe, he behaves as if the whole theorem were now resolved—QED. Only when I start to get to my feet does he go on. "The salt solution sinks; it forms the deep water of the Mediterranean and, with its tendency to seek even greater depth, flows out through the strait into the Atlantic and settles at about three thousand feet, where it has the same specific gravity as the surrounding water. Meanwhile equalization is taking place up above. Less salty water is flowing from the Atlantic into the Mediterranean, replacing the water lost through evaporation."

". . . and the deep water that has flowed out."

"Exactly!"

"And what we intend to do is to profit by this sensible arrangement—i.e., to slip in with the less salty replacement water?"

"It's the only way . . ."

On the Commander's orders I'm standing watch as an additional lookout.

"Tricky, being this close to land!"

In less than half an hour the port lookout aft roars: "Aircraft at seventy degrees!"

The Second Watch Officer whirls around to stare in the same direction as the outstretched arm of the lookout.

I'm already at the tower hatch. As I drop through, I hear the alarm, immediately followed by the shrilling of the bell. The Chief comes through the forward hatch in a single bound.

The emergency air exhausts are opened, the red and white hand wheels spun.

From above, the voice of the Second Watch Officer: "Flood!"

Slowly, as if in the teeth of fierce resistance, the needle of the depth manometer begins to move.

"All hands forward!" orders the Chief. Falling rather than running, the crew storms through the control room toward the bow.

The Commander is sitting hunched over the chart chest. I can see nothing but his bent back. He's the first to move again: He gets up and, like an angry director, makes a gesture of dismissal with his left hand while he pushes his right deep into his trouser pocket. "Nothing! Stay underwater for the time being!" And, to the Second Watch Officer, "Good work, Second Watch!"

He turns to me. "Good start! We're beginning just fine! We'll make great progress if it goes on like this."

There's just enough room for me at the chart table for once. I get a good view of the Gibraltar chart. From the African coast to the British docks is about seven miles. These docks are the only ones at which the British Mediterranean fleet can put in for repairs, the only ones that damaged commercial vessels have at their disposal. The British will do everything to protect these facilities.

Only seven miles from coast to coast—a narrow corridor, but we have to slink through it.

The Pillars of Hercules: in the north the Rock of Gibraltar, the Mountain of Saturn; in the south, on the coast of Spanish Morocco, the Rock of Avila close to Ceuta.

We will probably have to stick close to the south coast, steal our way in along the wall, so to speak.

But would that really be a good idea? The Tommies can figure out for themselves that a German U-boat would hardly sail straight through their wartime harbor; they'll take measures to protect the other side accordingly. The Old Man, of course, must have made his plan long ago. I'm curious to know what course he's worked out.

The Second Watch Officer appears and bends over the chart table beside me.

"The enchanted meeting place of two seductive climates, where the mildness and beauty of the Mediterranean world encounter the strength and sheer immensity of the Atlantic!"

I look at him in amazement.

"That's what it says in the sea manual!" he says indifferently, as he goes to work with the protractor.

"Seven miles—well, we'll have room!"

"Depth?" I ask.

"Up to thirty-two hundred feet. That's plenty!"

The Chief joins us.

"Once a pack of us attacked a Gibraltar convoy. The ones that were left must have felt pretty good when they finally saw the Rock. There were twenty of them when the freighters put to sea. And after we'd finished, there were only eight left. It was somewhere around here—perhaps a little to the west."

The lighthouses I find on the chart have foreign names. One is called Zem Zem. Then there's Cape Saint Vincent. What was that about Nelson and Cape Saint Vincent?

An hour later we surface again. The First Watch Officer has hardly mounted his watch when the alarm bell jolts me once more.

"Suddenly came from way up—don't know what type!" Zeitler blurts out, breathing hard.

"They must have spotted us," the Commander remarks. "We'll stay underwater a while."

He doesn't leave the control room again, and he's visibly uneasy. The moment he squats on the chart chest, he seems impelled to get up again. He's looking his most morose. "Probably it's all part of the outer defenses."

Another half hour goes by, then the Old Man climbs into the tower and orders us to surface.

The engines have been running a bare ten minutes when the alarm bell shrieks again. Its ugly tone no longer pierces me to the very marrow but it still gives me a violent start.

"If it goes on like this, we'll be stuck here the whole day going up and down!"

The Old Man continues to pretend indifference, but he knows the difficulties. Conditions are about as unfavorable as they could possibly be. After that long period of bad weather, there's barely so much as a ripple to disturb the surface of the sea. Which means that aircraft will have no trouble finding us, even without a moon.

The British may not be able to close the strait with underwater nets, but they'll be putting in every tub they've got that floats. They've probably known for some time what our Command has in mind. *Their* secret service, after all, works.

Letting ourselves drift through the narrows sounds perfectly plausible, but its only advantage is that the enemy can't actually *hear* us. It gives us no protection against Asdic.

I witness the control-room mate getting out his escape gear from behind his bunk. He's visibly upset that I've seen him, and, looking indignant, immediately throws the gear down on top of his bunk. As if it had got into his hands by mistake!

Pilgrim comes through, trying to use his body to conceal what he's carrying. I can hardly believe my own eyes. More escape gear. Funny how differently people react. Forward in the bow compartment, the "lords" are acting as though nothing special were afoot, and here the escape gear is being dug out.

I notice that the bananas we strung up across the control room are getting yellow. The people over in La Spezia would be delighted. And all that red wine the crew of the *Weser* put aboard! The Old Man swore a blue streak when he discovered the bottles. But he didn't have the heart to order them thrown over the side.

I decide to take a quick look at things topside. I've hardly stuck my head out when a fishing boat emerges from a low fogbank.

"Damn close. Must have seen us!"

This is an act we've all sat through before.

The Old Man snorts. Silence for a while. Then he starts theorizing: "Has to have been a Spaniard."

Let's hope so, I say to myself.

"Well, anyway, there's nothing we can do about it!"

The Portuguese coast looms up. Over the reddish rocks I see a white house. Looks like Brittany, like the Côte Sauvage at Le Croisic, where a storm can make the surf explode like shells from the big guns. First a couple of hollow booms, immediately followed by geysers shooting up between the black rocks. When the sea is calm and the tide is out, tiny yellow beaches stretch between the cliffs. Pale-yellow rustling sedge in the damp bays. Prickly gorse garlanded and festooned with spindrift when the northwest wind rages against the coast. Deep-worn roads buried in foam like snow. Pale silver stars of thistles on the sand. Sometimes, too, a cast-up paravane lost from a mine sweeper. High two-wheeled carts the farmers use to gather half-dried seaweed together into great piles. And to seaward the lighthouse painted red and white like our Papenberg.

And now the box of Spanish matches is in my mind again. I knew it all the time, of course, without being willing to admit it to myself: The same box with the blazing sun on it—bright yellow on hot red—Simone kept one in the crocodile handbag she always carried around with her to hold "*ma vie privée*," as she called it. Once she was rummaging around in it for a photo she wanted to show me and out fell the match box. She snatched it up again much too quickly. Why shouldn't I see it? The First Watch Officer from Franke's boat, who often came into her parents' café, had given it to her—no, left it behind—no, she had begged it from him . . . suspicion flares again. Simone and the Maquis! Was she disloyal after all—despite all her assurances? Her constant questioning: "*Quand est-ce que vous partez?—vers quelle heure?*"—"Oh, ask your friends. They know our timetable better than we do!"—And then the outbursts of tears, the pathetic whimpers, the sudden rage. "Mean, mean—*tu es méchant—méchant—méchant!*" Smeared make-up, sniffling. The picture of misery.

But why didn't she get one of those pretty little black-lacquered toy coffins in the mail the way her friends in the house did? Why was Simone the only person not to get one? Her sorrowful face—all pretense? No one can put on as good a show as that. Or can they?

I see the wide low bed, the loud rose pattern on the cover, the twisted fringes, smell Simone's fragrant dry skin. Simone never perspires. How she loves her delicate taut body, how aware she is of her every movement.

I sit in the middle of the café not daring to meet her glance. But when she's moving back and forth between the tables with the agility of a weasel, looking after her customers, I follow her with my eyes. Light and graceful as a matador in the ring. The layout of the chairs determines her figures and passes, gives her the opportunity for constantly new variations. She avoids these obstacles as she would the horns of a bull, swaying her hips to one side or drawing in her stomach a little. She handles her white serving napkin like a cape. I notice that she never bumps into anything, never so much as touches the corner or the back of a seat. And her laughter! Tossed out like sparkling coins. Again and again the violet of her sweater flits into view. In vain I try to keep my eyes on the newspaper. Who suggested to her this sophisticated combination of violet sweater and gray slacks—this quite remarkable violet, neither reddish nor bluish—like a painting by Braque? And on top of it, the ochre-brown of her face and the blackness of her hair.

A lot of guests in the inn now. They come in thirsty from the beach. The waitress can't keep up. It's fun to see how Simone catches up with her at the desk between trips and reproves her, unobtrusively, like a silently threatening cat.

I can still hear her voice. "We have to be careful!"—"Ach, always being careful!"—"You must beware; and so must I!"—"Who can stop us?"—"Don't be stupid. There's so much they can do without 'stopping' us!"—"But none of it matters!"—"Yes, but we want to survive!"—"Ach, no one's going to survive!"—"*We* are."

She meets me at the train in Savenay, has a car from god knows where, won't let me say a word because she knows I'll start swearing, drives like a maniac, asks, "Are you afraid? If a military policeman shows up, I'll step on the gas. They can never shoot straight!"

I hear her on the morning before we put to sea. "*Si tu ne* turn over right now and get up—*je te pousse dehors avec mon cul*—with my ass, *compris?*"

With a lighted cigarette she singes the hair on the calf of my right leg. "It smells so nice, of a little *cochon!*" She reaches for a fur-trimmed belt, clamps the end of it under her nose with her curled upper lip to resemble a mustache, looks in the mirror, and bursts out laughing. Then she plucks some wool from the fringes of the bedcover and stuffs it into her nose and ears. And now she tries German. "I am ready for misleading—I am noxious—*je suis d'accord* —I am very happy for it—with it—over it—how do you say that? I could become a nice little cannibal—*j'ai envie d'être* seduced. *Et toi?* And now I'm going to sing something for you:

> *Monsieur de Chevreuse ayant declaré que tous*
> *les cocus devraient être noyés,*
> *Madame de Chevreuse lui a fait demander*
> *s'il était bien sûr de savoir nager!"**

All play-acting? Pure deception? The Mata Hari of La Baule?

And again, the morning we left. Simone crouching motionless at the table, shoulders hunched, staring at me: eyes swimming, mouth filled with half-chewed roll, butter, and honey.

"Go ahead and eat!"

Obediently she begins to chew. Tears pour down her cheeks. One hangs from her nose. It's cloudy. I notice that especially. Probably the salt. Salt tears. "Now eat. Be good!" I take her by the back of the neck like a rabbit, pushing her hair up with the back of my hand. "Come on now, eat, for heaven's sake. Stop worrying!"

The heavy sweater—thank god for the white sweater with its cable pattern. Gives me something to talk about. "Lucky you finished the sweater. I'll be able to make good use of it. It's really cold outside these days!"

She sniffles. "It's fantastic—the wool—absolutely the exact amount. Only one little piece left over." She shows me how much by spreading her thumb and index finger. "Not even four sous' worth! What do you say to sweaters in the Navy? Something like happy? Or faithful? Are you happy with your sweater? Will you be faithful to it?"

She sniffles again, holds her breath, laughs through her tears. Brave. She's well aware that it's not going to be any picnic. You can't feed her tall stories the way you can to the women at home. She always knows when a boat is missing. But how? By accident? The evidence? There are, after all, a hundred "legitimately" possible

---

* "Monsieur de Chevreuse, having declared that all cuckolds ought to be drowned, Madame de Chevreuse put the question to him as to whether he was perfectly sure he knew how to swim!"

ways of finding out. "Lords" who once used to be regular customers all of a sudden don't turn up any more. And of course the French cleaning women in the billets know when a crew has gone to sea and when, according to all expectations, they should be back. There is far too much talk everywhere. And yet, and yet . . .

The old Breton clock shows six thirty. But it's ten minutes fast. A reprieve. The driver will be here in ten minutes. Simone goes to work on my jacket. "You have a spot here, *cochon!*"

She cannot grasp that I'm going aboard dressed this way.

"What d'you think it is? A pleasure boat?"

I have stored up every word. "I come with you to the channel!" "No, you mustn't do that. Besides, it's cordoned off!"—"I'll get through just the same, I'll borrow a nurse's pass. I want to see you run out!"—"Please don't. It could cause trouble. You know when we're leaving. You can see us from the beach half an hour later."— "But you'll be no more than a matchstick!"

Again the word "match." The red and yellow box. I strain my memory, seize hold of something: the bridge table with the brown cigarette holes burned in the light plumwood veneer. It's easy to recall the *trompe-l'oeil* pattern of the tiles on the floor, which either make clearly defined cubes placed on end or negative geometric indentations, depending on whether you look at a white or a black tile first . . . The gray ashes in the hearth . . . Outside the squealing of brakes. Then a horn. The driver in field gray—naval artillery.

Simone runs the flat of her hands over the new sweater. She huddles up so small against me that she doesn't even reach my chin. Also, I'm wearing my big seaboots.

"Why do you have such big boots?"

"They have cork soles and are lined and besides . . ." I hesitate for a moment but her laughter and her amazement encourage me to go on. "Besides, they have to be big enough to let you kick them off in the water without any trouble." I quickly clasp her head and run my fingers through her hair. "Well now, don't make a scene!"— "Your bag? Where is your bag? Have you noticed all the things I packed into it? The parcel is something you mustn't open until you're at sea, *ja?* Promise!"—"I promise!"—"And you'll wear your sweater, too?"—"Every day, whenever we're outside. And when I go to sleep I'll pull the collar up and feel at home!"

I'm thankful everything is so down to earth.

"D'you need hand towels?"—"No, they have them on board. And leave half of that soap out. They have saltwater soap on board."

I look at the clock. The car has been standing outside for five minutes. We still have to pick up the Chief. If only it were all over!

. . . It ends very fast. The garden gate at hip level, the turpentine smell of pine trees. Turn around one more time. Slam the gate. Over —*fini!*

Night is falling quickly. The last light from the sky shimmers and fades in our wake.

"Well, Kriechbaum, what sort of feeling d'you have about this?" the Commander asks the navigator.

"Good!" he says without hesitation. But didn't his voice sound forced?

Another half hour—then the Commander sends me below, along with the three lookouts. He wants no one but the navigator up there. That must mean we're already very close to where he assumes the ring of defenses are.

I hear the electric motors being put into gear. The pounding of the diesels stops; now we're running on the surface with our motors, something we've never done before.

"Ship's time?" the Commander calls down.

"20.30 hours," the helmsman calls back.

I remain in the control room. A half hour passes. The motors run with so little noise that all I have to do is stand under the tower, and I can hear everything the Commander says.

"Good god—the Tommies've actually called up half the fleet! They can't *all* be going to the casino in Tangier! Watch that one over there, Kriechbaum. Let's hope we don't run anyone over."

The Chief appears beside me, also glancing upward.

"Damned difficult!" he says.

Going by nothing but their navigation lights, the Old Man has to figure out the course and speed of the enemy ships, present our narrow silhouette to one patroling vessel after another and try to outmaneuver them. Damn hard to know at once which light belongs to which ship, whether the scow has stopped or is going away at an angle of a hundred ten degrees—or perhaps coming toward us at seventy.

Nor can the helmsman relax for an instant. He makes his return report in hushed tones. But the Old Man's voice has relaxed. I know him: He's in his element now.

"Such a decent bunch of people; they've set their navigation lights properly—nice of them! Kriechbaum, what's your little tub doing? Getting closer?"

The boat seems to be going round in circles. I must pay more attention to the orders to the helmsman.

"Shit! That was a close one!"

The Commander is silent for a while. Sticky work. A pulse beats high in my throat.

"That's right, my boy, just run along that way!" I hear at last. "What a mob! But they're doing the best they can! Whoops, who's that coming over there? Steer ninety degrees to port."

I'd give a lot to be on the bridge now.

"Navigator, keep your eye on that vessel headed across our bow —yes, that one over there!—report if she changes course!"

Suddenly he orders both motors stopped. I strain my ears. The Chief snorts. What now?

The slapping of the waves against the buoyancy tanks sounds much too loud. Like wet wash cloths. The boat rocks back and forth. My questioning glance at the Chief remains unanswered. All the lights in the control room have been shaded, so I can only see his face as a pale slab.

I hear him shift his weight twice in sheer excitement.

Tschjumm—tschjumm: the waves slap against the side.

Relief: the Old Man finally has the port motor started. For a good ten minutes we make very little headway; we seem to be sneaking along on tiptoe.

"We'd have caught that one!" comes from above. The Chief lets out his breath.

The Old Man orders the starboard motor started too. Have we already wormed our way through the heavy outer defenses? And what if the Tommies have set up a whole series of systems, not just one? "They can hardly have set up boom blockades," says the Old Man. "Far too much current." Where are we anyway? A glance at the chart? No, not now. No time for it.

"Well, Kriechbaum, exciting, isn't it?"

The Old Man is talking loudly up there, totally unconcerned.

"Steady as we are! What's our interloper doing now?"

Unfortunately, I can barely hear the navigator. Tension must have constricted his breathing; he answers in a whisper.

The Old Man changes course yet again. "Just a little closer! It's working out all right. They probably aren't reckoning on us turning up! Be sure the scow over there stays well clear of us—okay?"

For a good five minutes there's nothing from above but two orders to the helmsman.

Then: "In ten minutes we dive!"

"All right with me," murmurs the Chief.

For the time being, however, despite the Old Man's announcement, the Chief stays put. Is he trying to demonstrate how sure of himself he is? There's no question about it: the boat has been perfectly trimmed. All the systems that are his responsibility have been carefully tested during the last few hours. The control-room mate hasn't had any rest at all.

". . . well, who says . . . that's the way . . . now behave yourselves . . ."

The Old Man sounds as if he's talking to a child who won't finish his food.

"Well, we'll just take a look!" says the Chief at last and disappears.

I have a sudden thought: Quick! Get to the can! Opportunities may become rare.

I'm in luck—stateroom H is free.

In the can it's like squatting inside a machine. There's no woodwork in here to conceal the mind-boggling tangle of pipes. You can barely move between the narrow walls. And to make things even more difficult, the bosun has crammed canned goods from the *Weser* into every inch of space between the mops and pails.

While I'm exerting myself, I remember the description of a seaman in the latrine of a damaged vessel during a storm, whose job was to keep slowly pouring oil: This oil would flow out through the drain and supposedly calm the surface of the waves. The steamer was listing heavily, so the latrine lay just about at the water line. Whenever the ship heeled too far over, water rushed through the drain into the latrine and kept on rising. The door wouldn't open, because a bolt on the outside had slid shut, and the seaman knew that he would drown if the ship rolled any farther. He couldn't even hope that air would be trapped near the ceiling and resist the water pressure, for latrines are traditionally well ventilated—normal ships' latrines, that is, not a U-boat's.

So there he was, caught like a mouse in a trap, and he went on pouring oil whenever the drainpipe stopped spouting sea water: a lonely man on an abandoned post fighting for his ship.

Instantly I'm seized by the most humiliating claustrophobia. We might have a diving accident. The batteries might explode, and this damned heavy iron catch never open again—bent by the explosion. I see myself banging on the door in despair: no one to hear me.

Scenes from movies flash through my mind: a car hurtling into a river, trapping its passengers. Agonized faces behind the bars of a burning penitentiary. A theater gangway jammed with panic-stricken mobs. My bowels seize up; I get to my feet and try to concentrate on the drips of condensation hanging from the lower edge of a gleaming silver potash cartridge that's stored in a container behind the toilet.

I pretend to be calm and pull up my trousers with deliberate slowness. But then my hands begin to work faster than I want them to, pumping the toilet empty. Get the door open fast! Get out! Breathe deep! Jesus!

Fear? Was that just fear, common, ordinary fear, or was it claustrophobia? When have I experienced real fear? In the air raid shelter? Not really. After all, there was no question but that we'd be dug out eventually. Once in Brest—when the bombers suddenly came—I ran like a rabbit. It was quite a performance. But genuine fear?

In Dieppe, on the mine sweeper? That crazy rise and fall of the tide. We'd already picked up one mine; when the alarm suddenly went off, the wall of the pier was as high as a four-story house, and we were lying in the mud on the bottom of the harbor basin, with the bombs beginning to fall and nowhere to go.

But all of that was nothing compared to my fear in the endless echoing corridors of the boarding school on Sundays, when most of the students had gone home—hardly anyone in the huge building. People chasing me, knives in their hands, fingers curling to seize me by the neck from behind. Pursuing footsteps pounding after me in the corridor. Horror behind my back—unceasing fear. The torment of school: In the middle of the night I'd start up out of my sleep, sticky between my thighs, positive I must be bleeding to death. No light. There I'd lie, rigid with terror, paralyzed by the fear that I'd be murdered if I so much as moved.

x GIBRALTAR

CHANGEOVER. There's a lot of pushing and shoving because men from the second watch are still standing around in the control room, while those on the third are beginning to turn up. The Berliner can't understand why we still haven't dived. "With the Old Man it's all or nothing. No half measures!"

Tension has loosened their tongues. Three or four of them are talking at once. "Boy, that's quite an idea!"—"It's really working out!"—"How are things in the shop?"—"We're making out."

Zeitler runs his comb through his hair.

"That's it—fix yourself up," says the Berliner. "They say a lot of the Tommies are queer."

Zeitler pays no attention.

Turbo sings softly to himself.

I stand under the hatchway, sou'wester fastened under my chin, right hand on the ladder, looking up. "Permission to come on the bridge?"

But the Commander roars, "ALARM!"

The navigator comes sliding down the ladder. His seaboots land close beside me with a bang. Uproar from above.

The Commander—where in the world is the Commander?

I'm about to open my mouth when a dreadful explosion catches me in the knees. God, my eardrums! I stagger against the chart chest. Someone shouts, "The Commander! The Commander!" And someone else, "We've been hit! Artillery shell!"

A heavy cascade descends on us. No more light. Ears deafened. Fear.

The boat has already started to tilt. Then the Commander lands smack in the middle of us like a heavy sack. Groaning with pain, all he manages to say is, "Hit, right beside the tower!"

In the beam of a flashlight I see him bent over backward, his hands pressed against his kidneys.

"Cannon's gone!—Almost blew me out!"

Somewhere in the darkness in the after half of the control room, someone is screaming shrilly—like a woman.

"It was a bee—direct attack," the Commander gasps.

I feel the boat sinking fast. A bee? A bee? In the middle of the night? Not an artillery shell but a plane—impossible!

An emergency light goes on.

"Blow the tanks!" roars the Commander. "Blow them all!" And then in a whiplash voice, "Surface at once! Break out life-saving gear!"

I stop breathing. Two, three terrified faces in the half darkness of the after-hatch frame. All movement ceases.

The Commander groans, panting.

In the same hour came forth fingers of a man's hand, and wrote upon the plaster of the wall of the king's palace . . . A bee—that's impossible!

Bow heavy? Much too bow heavy? Cannon gone! How can the cannon have vanished?

"A hit beside the tower," like an oath from the Old Man, and then louder, "What's wrong now? God Almighty! When am I going to get some reports?"

In answer there's a chorus of cries from astern. "Breach in the diesel room!"—"Breach in the motor room!"—Four, five times the dread word "breach" in the hubbub of shouting, half drowned by the hissing of compressed air streaming into the tanks.

Finally the hand of the depth manometer stops, trembles violently, and then slowly moves backward. We're rising.

The Commander is now standing under the tower. "Move it, Chief! Surface immediately! No periscope survey! I'm going onto the bridge alone. Keep everything at the ready!"

Icy terror. I don't have my escape gear with me. I stagger toward the after hatch, force my way between two men who don't want to move, then my hands reach the foot of my bunk and seize the thing.

The compressed air goes on hissing and there's wild confusion in the control room. So as not to be in the way, I crouch beside the forward hatch.

"Boat breaking surface—tower hatch free!" the Chief reports, his head tilted upward, so matter of factly he might as well be out on maneuvers. The Old Man is already in the tower. He pushes the hatch open and the commands begin. "Both diesels full speed ahead! Hard a-starboard! Steer one hundred eighty degrees!" His voice is harsh and grating.

Go overboard? Swim? I fasten my compressed-air tank, hastily fumble about with the catches on my life jacket. The diesels! This noise! How long can things keep on like this? I count the seconds half aloud amid the babble of voices coming through the after hatch.

What's the Old Man got in mind? One hundred eighty degrees— south! We're running straight for the African coast.

Someone roars, "Port diesel's failed!" All that mad noise of machinery—is it really just *one* diesel?

A sudden flash in the circle of the tower hatch makes me look up. Beside me the Chief's face is illuminated by the blinding magnesium glare.

"Star shells!" he snaps. It sounds like a bark.

The roar of the diesel is driving me mad. I want to block my ears and drown out the hammering of the explosions in the cylinders. Better still, open my mouth, the way I learned in the artillery; there may be another shot at any moment.

I hear myself counting. While I'm murmuring numbers, a new panic cry comes from astern. "E-motor bilge making water fast . . ."

I've never swum with escape gear. Not even in practice. How close are the patrol boats? Much too dark—no one will see us in the water. As for the current—it's powerful; the Old Man has said so himself. It'll drive us apart. If we have to swim, we've had it. The surface current flows out of the Mediterranean, so that means straight into the Atlantic. And no one will find us there. Nonsense. I'm all wrong: It pushes us into the Mediterranean. Surface current . . . undercurrent. Count—go on counting! Seagulls. Those hooked beaks. Gelatinous flesh. Skulls picked white and covered in slime . . .

Reeling off numbers I get to three hundred eighty when the Commanders roars "ALARM!" again.

He comes down the ladder, left foot, right foot, perfectly normal —normal, that is, except for his voice. "The bastards are shooting flares—shitting them!" He brings his voice under control. "It's like daylight up there!"

What now? Are we *not* going overboard after all? What's he got in mind? The reports from aft seem to make no impression on him.

The bow heaviness jams me back against the forward wall of the control room. With the palms of my hands I can feel the cold damp lacquer behind me. Am I wrong, or are we descending faster than usual? Sinking like a stone!

All hell breaks loose. Men stagger into the control room, slip, fall full length. One of them hits me in the stomach with his head as he goes down. I haul him to his feet. Don't recognize who he is. In the confusion have I missed the order "All hands forward!"?

The needle! It goes on turning . . . but the boat was balanced for a hundred feet. One hundred feet: It ought to have slowed down long ago. I concentrate on it—then it disappears into a blue haze. Puffs of smoke are forcing their way into the control room from aft.

The Chief jerks his head around. In that fraction of a second I see real horror in his face.

The needle . . . it's moving much too fast.

The Chief gives a hydroplane order. The old trick—hold the boat dynamically. Exert pressure on the hydroplanes with E-motors. But are they running full speed? I can't hear the usual humming. Are they running at all?

The nightmare pushing and sliding drowns out everything else. And the whimpering—who can that be? No one is recognizable in this miserable half-light.

"Forward hydroplane jammed!" the hydroplane operator reports without turning round.

The Chief is holding the beam of his inspection lamp trained on the depth manometer. Despite the smoke I can see that the pointer is moving quickly on: 160 . . . 190 . . . When it goes past 225 the Commander orders, "Blow the tanks!" The sharp hiss of compressed air soothes my jangled nerves. Thank god, now at last the scow will regain some of her buoyancy.

But the pointer continues to turn. Of course, it has to—that's normal: It'll keep turning until the boat's tendency to fall is changed into a tendency to rise. That always takes time.

But now—it *has* to stop! My eyes close tight shut, but I force them open, stare at the depth manometer. The pointer hasn't the slightest intention of coming to a halt. It goes right on . . . 250 . . . 300 feet.

I put all my will power into my stare, try to arrest the thin black strip of metal. No use: It passes the 325 mark and keeps going.

Perhaps the buoyancy from our compressed-air cylinders is not enough?

"Boat out of control, can't hold her," whispers the Chief.

What was that? Can't hold—can't hold? The breaches in the hull . . . Have we become too heavy? Are we finished? I go on crouching beside the hatch.

At what depth will the pressure hull be crushed? When will the steel skin between the ribs be ripped apart?

The pointer passes 375. I no longer dare look at it. I push myself up, searching for handholds. Pressure. One of the lessons the Chief has drummed into me shoots through my head: At great depths the pressure of the water reduces the actual volume of the boat. Hence the boat gains excess weight compared to the water it displaces. So the more we are compressed, the heavier we get. No more buoyancy, only gravitational pull, and an increased rate of descent.

"Six hundred!" the Chief announces. "Six twenty-five—six fifty . . ."

The report echoes in my skull: six hundred fifty, and we're still falling!

My breathing stops. Any moment now there'll be the screaming tear. And then the green cataracts.

Where will it start?

When water breaks through, something tells me, it starts with a single jet.

The whole boat groans and cracks: a sharp report like a pistol shot, then a hollow strident singing that makes my blood run cold. It gets shriller and shriller, a hellish sound, like a high-speed circular saw.

Again a sharp report and more cracking and groaning.

"Passing eight hundred!" a strange voice cries. My feet go out from under me. I'm just able to catch myself by the halyard of the sky periscope. The thin wire rope cuts painfully into the palm of my hand.

So this is the way it is.

The pointer will soon reach 825. Another crack of the whip. Realization dawns: Those are rivets popping. The boat is welded and riveted, and this pressure is more than such rivets and welding can stand.

The flanges! Those goddam outboard plugs!

A voice chants, "Turn not Thine eyes and Thy countenance from me." The Bible Scholar? Why the crowd in the control room? Who's fouling everything up around here?

Suddenly a hard blow knocks me off my feet. I roll forward, put my hand on someone's face, pull myself up against a body in a leather jacket. Out of the forward hatch come screams, and then, like an echo, more screams from aft. Cracking and clattering, the floor plates are repeatedly flung upward. Cascading noise of glass shattering, as if a Christmas tree had fallen over. Another heavy blow with a droning echo—and another. And now a high-pitched screech that saws straight through my body. The boat vibrates madly, shuddering under a series of dull blows as though we were being dragged across an enormous field of rubble. From outside comes a monstrous groaning howl—then a mad screeching, two more resounding blows. And suddenly it's all over. Except for a high-pitched whistle.

"We have arrived!" The clearly articulated words seem to be coming through a distant door. The Commander.

Lying on my back, I wriggle until my legs with their heavy boots are under me, wrestle myself up, twist, lose my footing, fall to my knees. A cry rises in my throat. I choke it back just in time.

Light! What's happened to the light? The emergency supply— why does no one turn it on? I can hear the gurgling of water. Is that the bilge? Water from the outside wouldn't gurgle.

I try to separate out the sounds and locate them. Cries, whispers, murmurs, the high note of panic, questions from the Old Man. "Where are my reports?" And immediately thereafter, imperiously, "I demand proper reports!"

Light at last! Half-light. Just what are all these people doing here? I blink, hood my eyes, try to penetrate the semi-darkness, catch fragments of words and a shout or two. The racket seems to be loudest aft. Christ! What exactly has happened?

Sometimes it's the Old Man's face in front of me, sometimes the Chief's. More snatches of reports. Sometimes a whole sentence, sometimes mere fragments of words. Men rush past me toward the stern, their eyes wide with terror. One bumps into me, almost knocking me down.

"A shovelful of sand"—where did those words come from? The Old Man, of course.

"A shovelful of sand under our keel!"

I try to understand: It must have been dark on the surface. Not pitch black, but not moonlit either. No flyer could possibly have discovered us in that gloom. Aerial bombardment at night—that never happens. Perhaps it was an artillery shell after all? Naval artillery? Land-based artillery? But the Old Man *did* roar, "A bee!" And the droning just before the detonation?

The Chief drives his men from pillar to post, barking out orders.

And then? "We have arrived!" Field of rubble—the pressure hull—we're as defenseless as a raw egg! The mad screeching—a streetcar rounding a curve. Of course: We ran full speed into the rocks on the bottom. What else could it have been? Both motors full speed ahead and our nose down. To think the boat could stand all that: the steel stretched to tearing point by the pressure, and then the impact itself.

Three, four men are lying on the floor. The Old Man stands like a dark mass under the tower, one hand on the ladder.

Clear as a bell over the confused roaring of orders, I hear the droning song of the Bible Scholar:

> Glorious, glorious that day,
> When, no more sin, no more dismay,
> We march into the Promised Land . . .

He gets no further. A flashlight blazes out. The control-room mate fetches him a jarring blow on the mouth with his right hand. It sounds as though the man's front teeth have been broken. Through the haze I see his wide, astonished eyes and blood streaming from his mouth.

The smallest movement hurts. Somewhere I must have struck my right shoulder as well as both my shinbones. Each time I move, I seem to be wading laboriously through water.

In my mind's eye I see a cross-section of the Strait of Gibraltar: on the right the African coast: tectonic plates descending toward the middle of the sea bed; and halfway down the slope between the African coast and the deepest part, our tiny tube.

The Old Man—that maniac—was he hoping against all better judgment that the British would be off-guard? Wasn't it obvious what massive defenses would have been prepared against our arrival? There he stands, one hand on the ladder, the crumpled cap on his head.

The First Watch Officer's mouth is open, his face a single, horrified question mark.

Where's the Chief? He's disappeared.

The sound man reports, "Sound gear's gone dead!"

The two hydroplane operators remain seated at the control table as though there were still something to control.

The graduated circle of the sky periscope dangles from its wire. Funny—that happened to us once before! There must be some better way of making them. This, let's face it, is a botched job.

For the first time I notice a sharp whistling and hissing from forward: water break in the foreship too? Cracked and leaking flanges! What sort of plugs are there in the foreship anyway? The pressure hull must have held, otherwise it would all be over by now. A leak through a tear—that goes faster.

Sank like a stone. A miracle that our back wasn't broken as we banged and rattled down. And that crash landing at some mad depth for which we were never designed! I feel a sudden respect for our tube and its powers of resistance. Thin steel, but first-class. Special quality. Superbly well made.

Suddenly I understand. The Old Man has got our leaking vessel into shallower water. Turning south! A short sprint in the direction of the coast and the Old Man has saved us. Hats off! Bet everything on one card and charge full ahead on one diesel. A moment's hesitation and the ground we're now resting on would have been unreachable.

But what's that? Instead of the high forced singing sound, I can now hear quite clearly a strange *vitschivitschivitsch*.

I strain my ears. That's the sound of propellers. No doubt about it—and getting closer.

The sound makes everyone stop dead as though touched by a magic wand. Now they've got us. The killers! They're directly overhead.

I lower my head, hunch my shoulders, and look at the rigid figures out of the corner of my eye. The Old Man is gnawing his lower lip. Forward and aft they must have heard it too: the sound of voices has stopped at a single stroke.

Under the gun! Looking straight into the muzzle of a pistol. When will the finger tighten around the trigger?

No motion, not the quiver of an eyelid. Like pillars of salt.

Vitschivitschivitschivitsch.

That's only a single propeller: *vitschivitschivitschivitsch*. Unchanged. The high-pitched singsong plucks at my nerves. The vessel up there is running at slow speed, otherwise we wouldn't be able to hear the splashing sounds. A turbine engine, no piston strokes.

But, after all, he can't just remain directly over our heads with his propeller going! After a while this swishing will have to fade. Christ, what does it mean?

I can't see the Old Man's face: that would involve pushing my way forward and I don't dare do it. Just stay still, muscles taut. Bated breath.

There—the Old Man has just muttered something in his deep bass. "Lap of honor—they're doing their lap of honor," and I understand. The vessel up there is turning in a circle, as tight as it possibly can, right over us. With full rudder. Marking out a funnel. And we are the point of that funnel.

They know exactly where we are.

The swishing grows no weaker, no stronger. Somewhere beside me, I hear a grinding of teeth, then a choked sigh. Then another—more of a smothered groan.

Lap of honor! The Old Man is right: they're waiting for us to come up. All they need now is some bit of proof—pieces of wreckage, oil, a few fragments of flesh.

But why don't the swine drop any bombs?

I hear water dripping. No one moves. Again the growling voice of the Old Man. "Lap of honor!" And again, "Lap of honor!" Someone whimpers. That must be the Bible Scholar again.

The words fill my skull. Long-distance bicycle races in Chemnitz. The mad thrashing of legs. Then the slow pedaling with uplifted, waving hand, a huge golden wreath slung over one shoulder and across the chest—the victor! Lap of honor! At the end, brilliant fireworks, and the crowd busily winding their way homeward to the streetcar station like a great black earthworm.

Vitschivitschivitsch . . .

Reports from astern, whispered from mouth to mouth. I don't catch them; all I hear is the beating of the propeller. It fills my whole body. I become a drum resonating under the unvarying throb of the screws.

The Bible Scholar keeps on whimpering. We all look away from one another, stare at the floor plates or the walls of the control room as though expecting pictures to be projected on them. Someone says, "Jesus!" and the Old Man laughs hoarsely.

Vitschivitschivitsch . . . Everything seems far away. A misty veil in front of my eyes. Or is it smoke? Are we on fire again someplace? My eyes focus. But the bluish haze remains. Yes, smoke! But god knows where from!

I hear the words, "oil spouting!" Good god, must there be an oil leak too? I see brilliant smears, serpentine Art Nouveau configurations, marbled end papers, Icelandic moss . . .

I try to calm myself. The current—it may be a blessing. Wash away the iridescent slick and disperse it.

But what good will that do? The Tommies know the current. They're at home here. They'll take it into account in their calculations; they weren't born yesterday. God knows how much oil has spouted up from our bunkers. But if a lot has escaped, perhaps it's a good thing. The more the better: the Tommies will think they've actually finished the job. Which tank can have cracked?

Once again everything inside me begins to spin. I want to escape, smash out of the encircling jungle of pipes and machinery, flee the valves and apparatus that are no longer of any use. I suddenly feel a bitter cynicism. After all, this is exactly what you wanted. You were up to your neck in easy living. You wanted to try something heroic for a change. "To stand for once before the ineluctable . . ." You got drunk on it all. ". . . where no mother cares for us, no woman crosses our path, where only reality reigns, grim in all its majesty . . ." Well, this is it, this is reality.

I can't keep this up for long. Already self-pity is mounting and I find myself muttering, "Shit, you goddam shit!"

The propeller scratching is so loud that no one can hear me. My heart is thumping in my throat. My skull is threatening to explode.

Waiting.

Wasn't that something scraping lightly along the boat—or am I raving?

Waiting—waiting—waiting.

Never before have I known what it's really like to be without some weapon in my hand. No hammer to strike out with, no wrench to throw my weight behind.

The *vitschivitsch* up there isn't getting any fainter. Unbelievable! Why no Asdic?

Perhaps they don't have it on board. Or perhaps we're lying in a hollow? In such a position that they can't single us out? In any case, we didn't land on sand, that's for sure. That howling and screeching came from scraping along rocks.

The Commander inhales loudly, then mutters, "Incredible! A straight dive, right out of the darkness!" So it's the airplane he's thinking about.

I hold my breath for as long as I can, then gulp spasmodically. My teeth are forcibly torn apart, and with a single wheezing inhalation I pump myself full of air. Once more I hold my breath, compress it, force it down—renewed choking in my throat.

When will the bombs come? How long are those swine going to go on playing with us? My stomach contracts. They wouldn't even need to use their ejector. They could simply roll a canister overboard—quite casually, like an unwanted barrel.

From the stern come whispered reports to the control room. The Old Man seems to be paying no attention.

". . . surface bomb—contact detonator—directly beside the boat—level with the cannon—incredible—so dark—and yet!" I hear him muttering to himself.

Madness, forcing us through these narrows. It had to go wrong . . . Anyone could work that much out. And the Old Man knew it! Has known it all along, ever since the radio orders to break through. The moment he read that signal, he knew we were already half done for. That was why he wanted to disembark the two of us in Vigo.

What's he talking about now?

Everyone in the control room has heard him. "Polite bunch—doing their victory march!"

The sarcasm works. The men raise their eyes, begin to move again. Gradually action resumes in the control room. Hunched over and on tiptoe, two men make their way, swaying, toward the stern.

I stare blankly at the Old Man: both hands deep in the pockets of his fur-lined vest, right foot on a rung of the ladder. Caught in the beam of a flashlight, he's visible to one and all, and it's obvious that he's lost none of his casualness. He even offers us a condescending shrug of the shoulders.

Somewhere there's a clatter of tools. "Quiet!" snaps the Commander. Gurgling in the bilge. It must have been going on for some time but this is the first time I've noticed it. It startles me: We're lying still. So how can the bilge be gurgling? Shit, the water must be rising under the floor plates.

The Old Man continues his repertory heroics. "They're taking care of us. What more can one ask?"

Then the gruesome whirring begins to fade. Unquestionably the vessel is moving away. The Commander turns his head this way and that, the better to pick up the fading sound. I'm just about to take a deep breath when the swish of the propeller comes back at its old strength.

"Interesting," mutters the Old Man, and nods his head at the Chief. All I hear of their whispering is, "Didn't withstand it—upsurge of oil—yes—"

Then the Old Man hisses to the navigator, "How long have they been riding that merry-go-round?"

"A full ten minutes, Herr Kaleun!" Kriechbaum whispers back. He doesn't move as he answers; only his head turns a few degrees to one side.

"Blessings be upon them!" says the Commander.

The Second Engineer, I now notice for the first time, is no longer here. Probably disappeared toward the stern. All hell must have broken loose there, but there were also disaster reports from the bow. I didn't catch them all. Lucky we have two engineers on board. That's rare: two on one boat. Luck—we're in luck! We plunge to the bottom, and the dear Lord slips a shovelful of sand under our keel. And on top of that, two engineers. Our cup overfloweth!

The Old Man makes a face. "Where's the Second Engineer?"

"In the motor room, Herr Kaleun!"

"Have him test the battery."

Suddenly there seems to be trouble in every quarter at once. I become conscious of a shrill whistling that has been in my ears for some time. It must be coming from the diesel room. The water leak. Our stern heaviness. After all, we hit bow on, but the ship is noticeably stern heavy, so water must be rising aft. Then why not trim forward? Normally we would be running the bilge pumps by now. But the main bilge pump is broken and, besides, would it be able to function against the enormous outside pressure? Nine hundred feet! *No boat has ever been this deep!* Our pump certainly wasn't built for it. I glance through the hatch toward the stern. What's wrong in the petty officers' quarters? Why is it so crowded? Emergency light . . . can't see a damn thing.

The Old Man is leaning against the shiny silver shaft of the sky periscope. I can see the horizontal expanse of his thigh but not what he's sitting on. His right hand is massaging his kneecap as though it hurt. His cap is perched halfway down the back of his neck, leaving his tangled hair free.

Suddenly his face goes tense. He puts both hands behind him and pushes himself to his feet. His voice is no longer a whisper as he asks the Chief, "How much water have we taken? Which buoyancy cells are damaged? Which can't be blown? Can we pump out the water already on board?"

The questions rain down. "What's wrong with the main bilge pump? Can it be fixed? If we blow out all undamaged buoyancy tanks and cells completely, will that give us enough buoyancy?"

The Old Man moves his shoulder as if trying to loosen his back muscles, then takes two or three aimless steps. The control-room mate also begins to move again.

I wrack my brains: we have three-compartment construction. Well and good. But what use is that now? If the Old Man were to have the control-room hatch toward the stern shut—just assuming, since it's no use to us right now—and if we then made the hatch airtight, the control room and foreship would stay nice and dry. No doubt about it. Then all we'd have to do is wait until the oxygen ran out. So much for that idea. Keep thinking, I tell myself. The main bilge pump—if it's out of order, we still have compressed air. But after that futile blowing we tried earlier, is there enough left? Who really knows whether the compressed air tanks have remained airtight? Without bilge pumps *and* compressed air we've had it. That much is clear: We have to be able to run pumps *and* blow. Reduce our weight *and* create buoyancy. And what happens if the buoyancy cells can no longer hold the compressed air at all—if it immediately rushes out through a leak or a loose connection the moment we begin to blow? What if it just bubbles up to the surface without providing any lift at all?

There's an infernal stench. No mistaking it—battery gas—so the battery cells must have gone. Battery cells are fragile. The explosion and then the impact as we hit bottom . . . Our very ability to move depends on our batteries. If the batteries are gone . . .

"Move it!" This from the Chief. "Faster, faster!" from the bosun. And constant whispered reports, mostly from the stern. I hear them, but can no longer take anything in.

Men come through the control room swaying grotesquely as they try to keep their balance. I press myself against the periscope housing, tormented by the feeling of being superfluous. In the way.

The Second Watch Officer, quite close to me, is also pushed to one side. The seamen have nothing more to do. Normally there is plenty of work for the sailors on a ship that has gone aground. But we are a *sunken* ship. No work for sailors on sunken ships.

The gasping somewhere close to me is coming from the control-room mate. Tin-ear Willie. Deaf ears, perhaps they'd even be a blessing. See nothing, hear nothing, smell nothing; sink into the floor—but they're iron floor plates, not much good for sinking into. We have fuel oil to burn: granted. But who the hell knows whether we'll ever need it again. No use pretending: we're trapped. No creeping away this time, no evasive tactics. We might as well be nailed down. Our tube is holding, granted again, but they've turned it into a coffin. Without buoyancy we can lie here till Judgment Day. The resurrection of the body . . . from nine hundred feet. Wonder-boys of the German Navy!

Against the dim light at the hydroplane post I can see that the Commander's shoulders are sagging slightly. Apparently compelled to imitate him, I let myself go loose. I can feel the relief all the way down my back. The rhomboideus—that was what just uncramped itself. The great shoulder muscle, once learned, never forgotten. Anatomy classes in Dresden. The silly snipping away at corpses. Gas victims were good: they lasted better than people who had died of natural causes. The hall full of skeletons, all arranged like antique sculpture. A collection of ludicrous figures of bone: the Discus Thrower, the Votary, the Thorn Puller.

"Funny," I hear the Commander whisper in the direction of the manometer. He turns toward me and goes on: "He came at me like this, turned aside, sideslipped a little. All as clear as daylight!"

I can't see his hand motions; he confuses me completely. For him, this airplane is the only thing that seems to exist. "Perhaps there were two bombs—I couldn't make out exactly!"

The air hangs in smoky blue layers. Hard to breathe. Smell of gas. Two men in the Officers' Mess are taking off the cover of battery one. In the emergency light through the hatch I can see that one of them is holding a strip of blue litmus paper in his left hand and inserting a measuring stick with his right; he lifts the stick and wets the litmus paper. I stare at the two as if they are altar boys performing at High Mass.

Breathless orders from the Chief. "Get limewash in there right now. Then find out how many cells have run dry!"

So the bilge water in the battery compartment contains acid. A lot of battery cells must have cracked and run out, and the sulphuric acid has combined with sea water to form chlorine gas. That's what's stinking so hideously.

The Old Man bid too high, now he's being called. What can he do about it? That crazy crowd in Kernével, the gentlemen of the Staff, are the ones we can thank for this. We'll be on their conscience.

A voice in my head starts to jeer: "Conscience! Some conscience! In Kernével we're nothing but a number. Cross it out and that's it. The shipyard builds a new boat. Plenty of crews ready in the personnel reserve."

I see the Chief through the haze. His shirt is soaked and open to the navel, his hair hangs in a tangle over his face. There's a diagonal scratch across his left cheek.

The Second Engineer comes from astern. I gather from his whispering that the water is still slowly gaining in the motor-room bilge. Then the news is reduced to fragments. "Diesel room making water . . . a lot . . . flooding valve for torpedo cell one under tube five has burst . . . cold-water pipes . . . motor bearings . . . crack in the air-cooler pipe . . ."

He has to stop to catch his breath.

Boots scuffle over the floor plates.

Instantly the Old Man orders silence. Right, dammit—the little ship is still circling around up there.

Some of the breaches seem to be a complete mystery. The Second Engineer can't make out where the water is seeping in. It's rising in the control-room bilge too: The dull gurgling is clearly audible.

"What about the oil?" the Old Man asks. "Which fuel tank was hit?"

The Chief disappears aft. After a couple of minutes he returns to report. "At first there was a jet of oil out of the exhaust duct—but it turned to water."

"Strange," says the Old Man.

This is obviously against the rules. The exhaust duct, I learn, lies close to the diesels. If the tank there had been cracked, the jet of water should have shot out of the exhaust duct under much greater pressure than it actually did. The Commander and the Chief wrack their brains. The tank was still half full—so how could there be such a weak jet? Along with the ordinary fuel tanks, two of our buoyancy tanks were refilled with additional supplies pumped in from the *Weser*.

"Strange," the Chief echoes. "First oil, then water."

"Where does the connection from this fuel tank pass through the pressure hull to the outboard flange? And where are the plugs for the exhaust and intake?" Apparently there is still a chance that only the exhaust duct has been hit and that the tank itself has not been cracked.

The two of them can only guess, since the ducts lie so deeply hidden that no one can get at them.

The Chief disappears hastily toward the stern again.

I try to form a picture of the various tanks. In the saddle tanks, oil is floating on water, and the pressure is equalized. No empty spaces. So these tanks are less vulnerable than the fuel tanks. Very likely one of the outer tanks is cracked. But the measurements should show how much oil we have lost. The only question is whether the Chief knows exactly how much oil there should be in the tanks. In any case, the oil gauge is not that accurate. And the calculation of oil used per hour of running time is just as bad. Only the regular measurements give exact amounts. But when were all the tanks last measured?

The control-room mate arrives, soaked through, to report that a valve in a pipe was broken. He has repaired the damage. So that was the reason for all the water in the control-room bilge.

All at once I'm aware that the propeller noise has vanished. A trick? Perhaps they've stopped their engine? Do we dare breathe easy, or is the damned scow trying something new?

"Everything's busted!" I hear someone murmur. It must be Dorian. I strain to hear. Still no propeller.

"Now they've done their duty and retired," mutters the Old Man. "But he can't have seen us; it's impossible."

The lap-of-honor boys have lost their audience: no more noise, the Old Man's stopped thinking about them. It's the airplane he's obsessed with . . . "He *couldn't*. Absolutely out of the question—in that darkness . . . and those clouds. He was there much too suddenly. Flew straight at us." Then something like ". . . no radio—bad business. Damned important." I know what he means. Others must be told about the new device the British have. For some time there's been a rumor that the Tommies have a new electronic direction finder that's small enough to fit into a cockpit. We're proof positive that the rumor is true. If they can spot us from their airplanes, if we're no longer safe even at night, then it's "Lash the helm and start praying."

The Old Man wants to warn the other U-boats, but we're not exactly in a position to send out news bulletins.

In the control room there's such confusion now that I prefer to move into the Officers' Mess. But there's no room here either. Everything is covered with plans and blueprints and sketches. I become aware of the terrifying double meaning of the German word for "sketch": a break. A break in the pressure hull, a break in the ribs.

The ribs simply *cannot* have withstood that hideous impact. Nor the explosions before it. The steel skin may be somewhat elastic, but the ribs are in the form of rings and have no "give."

The Chief lays out an electrical diagram. He hastily draws lines with the broken stump of a pencil, murmuring constantly to himself, then with trembling hands he unbends a paper clip and uses that instead. He takes the wire to scratch a sketch in the linoleum of the table, which seems to imply that damage to our furniture— which is usually treated with such care—no longer matters at all.

The First Watch Officer sits beside him polishing his binoculars. Completely crazy. For the moment, seamanship is absurd—but he doesn't seem to have grasped this fact. Madness, as though clear vision was what mattered down here! His face, usually so smooth, has two deep folds running from his nostrils to the corners of his mouth. His long upper lip looks as if it's in parentheses. Blond stubble on his chin. This is no longer our dapper First Watch Officer.

A buzzing around the light. The fly! She too has survived. She'll probably outlive us all.

How late is it anyway? I discover that my watch is gone. A bad sign! I manage to get a look at the Chief's. A few minutes past midnight.

The Commander appears and directs a questioning glance at the Chief. "Can't be done with available materials," is what I make of the Chief's murmured reply.

Out of *what*, then? Are we supposed to order up some shipyard workers? Summon the specialists who built the boat?

All the floor plates have been taken up immediately in front of our table and in the gangway. Two men are working below in battery one. Lengths of cable and tools are being handed down to them from the control room.

"Fucking shit!" I hear a voice say from below. "Goddam filth!"

Suddenly Pilgrim appears in the opening. His eyes are streaming. Coughing heavily, he reports in the direction of the control room, since he can't see the Chief sitting in the Officers' Mess. "Total of twenty-four battery cells run out!"

Twenty-four out of how many? Will twenty-four cripple us, or is that tolerable? The Chief straightens up and orders Pilgrim and his helper to put on rescue gear. Two brown pouches are fetched from the control room. I hand them down.

While the two are still busy with the rescue gear, the Chief himself works his way down through the hole in front of our table. After a few minutes he twists himself out again, coughing, hastily fetches a plan of the batteries out of the locker, spreads it over the other plans, and studies it intently. He crosses out the individual battery cells—all twenty-four of them.

"The bridging bars won't be enough in any case." He doesn't even raise his face from the diagram. This means that the smashed cells can simply be taken out and thrown overboard. The Chief wants to bridge them and see whether the few cells remaining intact will function.

Finding the shortest way to connect the undamaged cells appears to be extremely complicated. The Chief begins to sweat; he draws a line, crosses it out again. Every few seconds he snuffles.

The Gigolo comes through the wardroom, balancing a big pail of white limewash that slops back and forth. This is to neutralize the sulphuric acid that has run out of the batteries, thereby preventing the formation of chlorine gas. I hear the Gigolo open the door of the can. In there is the drain for the washing faucet that will take the limewash into the battery bilge.

"Move it, men. *Move!*" yells the Chief. Then he gets up hesitantly. With the diagram still in his hand, he bends over the manhole to battery one and gives hushed directions to the man below, Pilgrim. I can't hear Pilgrim's reply. The Chief might as well be talking into a void. A weird muffled coughing and groaning comes out of the pit.

The Commander loudly orders white bread and butter. I must be having a stroke: white bread and butter? Now? He's certainly not hungry. He must be trying to indicate that everything's really all right, that the Commander has an appetite. And that whoever has an appetite can't be in serious trouble.

The steward actually arrives with acrobatic contortions, carrying a huge slice of white bread and a knife. Where can he have found the bread in all that confusion?

"Have half?" the Commander asks me.

"No thanks!"

He produces something like a grin, then leans back and gives a demonstration of how to chew. His lower jaw moves back and forth like that of a ruminating cow.

Two men manage to get over the opening in the floor by swinging hand-over-hand along a pipe, and see him eating. Which means the news will spread through the boat—exactly as he intended.

Little Zörner pushes himself up from below and pulls off his nose clip. Sweat is dripping from his bare torso. He sees the Old Man and his mouth falls open with astonishment.

The Old Man pushes bread and knife aside: end of act.

The Chief's exasperated voice comes up from below. "Goddammit! What's the matter *now*? Zörner, why's the light gone?"

"Shit," says someone.

Apparently they're short-handed below. I catch sight of a lamp in a corner of the mess, reach for it, test it. It works. With my arms braced behind me and the lamp pushed into the waist of my trousers I let myself down. The Chief is complaining again. "What the hell's the matter? Are we getting some light or aren't we?"

And now I appear as the Light of the World—like the Lord God with his halo. The Chief receives me silently. As if getting ready to repair the undersides of a car, I stretch myself out, half on my side, on the flat traveling platform that runs on rails under the floor. A tidy little place down here! I hope the Chief isn't kidding himself: If the motor dies on us, what we're doing here is futile. Even I understand that much. Funny that he doesn't say a word. I see his right leg beside me, lying there like a corpse's. Good thing I can hear his gasping breath. Now he's telling me how to hold the lamp, and I see his oil-covered fingers in the beam of light, curling, fanning out, reaching and coming together.

Silently I beseech him to keep going. Don't fumble around so nervously. Work cleanly, don't rush it. Everything depends on this.

Suddenly I see us from the outside, a picture seen a thousand times, handsome heroes smeared with oil and filth, posing stretched out; movie-star miners with distorted faces and thick beads of sweat on our foreheads.

Now my free hand is needed too. Pull this tight. All right, I've got it. Slowly now, so the wrench won't slip off. Shit, it did. Try again.

If only we could move! It's a mine gallery, except that instead of boring a passage, we work with wrenches, pliers, and bridging bars. The air is hardly bearable now. Pray god the Chief doesn't break down! He has a wrench in his mouth like an Indian stalking someone with a knife. He crawls forward a good ten feet. I follow him, scraping both my shins in the process.

I didn't have the faintest notion that the battery under the floor plates we walked on every day was so big. I'd always pictured a "battery" as being something much smaller. This is a gigantic enlargement of the automobile variety, but how much of it is usable? If there are more holes than knitting in a sock then it just isn't a sock any more and goes into the ragbag. What we have here is junk already—they've turned the whole boat into junk, the bastards.

Air! For god's sake, just send down some air! The steel clamps around my chest are squeezing me to death.

A face appears from above. I have a sudden impulse to seize hold of it. I can't make out whose it is, because it's turned a hundred eighty degrees: It's hard to recognize someone who's standing on his head.

The Chief gives me a sign. We have to get out of here. Helping hands are extended. I'm breathing in sharp, jerky gasps.

"Nice fuck-up, eh?" someone asks. I only dimly hear the voice. I can't even say "Yes!" No breath. My lungs heave. Fortunately there's a little space for me among all the diagrams on the Chief's sofa. I hear someone say it's two o'clock. Only two?

The Chief reports to the Old Man that we need wire. The bridging bars turned out to be insufficient even for this one half battery.

All at once it feels as though our real problem isn't getting to the surface, but hunting up wire: Wire is the Chief's solution to all our problems. Even the Second Watch Officer gets involved in the search.

Lovely, gleaming torpedoes in the tubes, in the bow compartment, and in the upper-deck compartment: twenty thousand marks apiece—but a bit of old wire? All we need is five marks' worth of the stuff. We're up to here in shells—but wire . . . It makes you laugh! We have plenty of ammunition for the damn fool cannon— both high explosive and incendiary! But the cannon's lying even deeper than we are, marking the spot where we'd be right now if the Old Man hadn't made his dash south. Ten high explosive shells for thirty feet of wire—it'd be a bargain!

The bosun has disappeared into the bow compartment. Lord knows where he expects to find wire there. And if the bosun doesn't find it in all his scrambling about, and if the Second Watch Officer

doesn't, and the navigator doesn't and the control-room mate doesn't
—what then?

I hear, "Tear out the electric wiring," and, "Twist them together."
That probably won't amount to anything very much. The wire has
to be of a certain diameter. So we braid a number of strands together? The only question is how long such a time-consuming repair
will take.

We're growing perceptibly more stern heavy. The stern torpedo
tube breach is reported to be two-thirds underwater. If the motor
is swamped, then this whole business about the wire is meaningless.

What day of the month is it? The calendar has vanished from
the wall. Gone, like my wristwatch. "A brief span of life was ap-
pointed us . . ."

A few minutes, and the Officers' Mess becomes unendurable. I
maneuver my way back over the open floor plates into the control
room. My whole body aches from my contortions. There's a stabbing
sensation between my shoulder blades and a rending pain all the
way down my back. Even my ass hurts.

On the floor plates, close to the periscope housing, lies the barograph, knocked out of the rim of the gimbals on which it rested.
Two of its glass plates are smashed. The recording hand has been
bent over like a hairpin. The rising and falling curve on the paper
drum has ended in a downward plunge and a thick ink blot. I'm
tempted to tear the paper off the drum and keep it. If we ever get
out of this, I'll frame the thing and hang it on my wall. A genuine,
documentary piece of graphic art!

The Chief has developed a system of priorities in his fight against
our disasters. First things first. Contain the fastest spreading damage.
Stamp out the growing fire before the wind catches it. Here on
board, every system is of vital importance—there are no superfluous installations—but our crisis has defined the difference between
the vital and the merely essential.

The Commander and the Chief are whispering together. The
chief mechanic Johann appears from astern; the control-room mate
joins in; even the chief mechanic Franz is allowed to participate.
The boat's technical braintrust is holding a meeting in the control
room—the only man missing is the Second Engineer, who's in the
motor room. As far as I can tell, work in the stern is going ahead
steadily and methodically. The Chief has turned over the trouble
with the battery to the two E-mates. Will they be able to cope?

The group disperses; only the Commander and Isenberg, the
control-room mate, remaining. For the benefit of the men inching
their way past, the Commander makes a show of settling himself

firmly on the chart chest, wrapped in his leather jacket, both arms pushed deep into the pockets, obviously at ease: the picture of a man who knows he can rely on his experts.

Pilgrim comes through and requests permission to go forward in search of wire.

"Go ahead!" says the Old Man. We need wire? Then wire will be provided, even if we have to reel it out of our own backsides.

The bosun pops up in the forward hatch, as ecstatic as a child under a Christmas tree, a few yards of old thick wire in his oil-smeared hands.

"Well, what do you know?" says the Old Man. "That's something, anyway!"

Number One goes splashing through the water that has now risen above the floor plates in the after half of the control room and climbs through the hatch into the petty officers' compartment, to where battery number two is situated under the floor plates.

"Great!" I hear the voice of the Chief from astern.

The bosun comes back, acting as if he'd discovered America all by himself. A simple soul. Doesn't seem to realize that a few feet of wire won't solve our problems.

"Go on looking!" the Old Man orders Number One. Then there's silence for a good ten minutes: no audience for him to play to.

"Let's hope they don't come back with sweepwires!" I hear him say finally.

Sweepwires? I think of the Breton mussel fishermen dragging their trawls over the sandy bottom to pull out the half-buried shells. But we're definitely not lying on a sandy bottom. We're between rocks. Which means that sweepwires would be no way to catch our boat—if they're what I think they are.

The Chief reappears. "How's it going?" the Commander asks.

"Fine. Almost done. Another three cells, Herr Kaleun."

"And astern?"

"So-so!" So-so. That means we're in pretty bad shape.

I collapse onto the leather sofa in the Officers' Mess and try to visualize our situation: While we were plummeting down, the Old Man ordered us to blow with everything we had. But it didn't do any good: We'd already shipped so much water that it couldn't be compensated for by forcing the water out of the buoyancy tanks. With all tanks blown, the boat still sank. It follows that we may be lying on the bottom, but there's still air in our buoyancy tanks— the same air we blew in. And this air could lift us statically—but only if we succeeded in reducing the weight of the boat. It's a bit like sitting in the gondola of a fully inflated balloon, kept anchored to the ground by excess ballast. Ballast has to be thrown out of the gondola so that the balloon can rise. Fair enough. But it only holds good for us on the assumption that the air vents in our buoyancy tanks are still watertight. If the valves have suffered too—that is, if they won't close—then presumably there's no air in the tanks and we can blow in as much more as we like—the entire contents of the compressed air cylinders—without the slightest effect.

Of course there's also the dynamic method of shifting the boat. With the engine going and both hydroplanes up, the boat can be raised diagonally like an airplane on takeoff. But this method is only possible with *slight* excess weight. It certainly won't work in our case: The boat's too heavy for that. And whether the juice we have left in the batteries is enough to turn our screws for even a few minutes is a big question. Does the Chief have any idea how much power the few undamaged cells can still supply?

We're probably stuck with the balloon method. So the water that has forced its way into the boat must be got rid of. Expelled. At all costs.

And then up! Up and overboard, and swim for it.

I can hang my films around my neck. I've made a watertight bundle. The ones of the storm have to go in. *They* at least must be saved. There've never been photographs like them.

The damned current in the Strait—if it weren't for that . . .

A shovelful of sand under our keel at the very last moment. A miracle.

The Old Man is chewing his lower lip. It's the Chief who's doing the thinking and directing. Everything depends on his decisions. How can he stand it? He hasn't been able to let up for a moment.

All breaches seem to have been stopped except for the odd trickle here and there, a few oozing wounds in our steel skin. But the water that's already in the boat? I have no idea how much of it there is. Two pints of water equals two pounds weight—weight I feel in every nerve of my body. We're heavy, heavy—monstrously heavy. We lie here on the bottom as if we've taken root.

"Stinks of shit in here!" That's Tin-ear Willie.

"So open the windows!" jeers Frenssen.

From the stern there's an explosive hiss like escaping steam. It goes right through me. For chrissake, what's happened now? The noise changes to that of an acetylene torch cutting steel. Impossible to get back there and see what it really is.

What does the Old Man have in mind? What's he thinking about as he sits there staring into thin air? Will he attempt to surface, run for the African coast, and beach the boat? That would seem the most likely, because he wants to surface before it's light. If all he had in mind was to surface and have us go overboard, he wouldn't care whether the men aft got their place clear before dawn or not. But that is exactly what he keeps asking about.

Swimming in the dark would be much too risky. The current would split us up in no seconds flat. Would the Tommies even notice us at all? We have no emergency blinkers on our life preservers. Not even red flares. Totally unequipped for special emergencies.

Not a sound from the Old Man. I can hardly question him. The first thing is obviously to try to free the boat from the bottom, get rid of ballast. But then, if that works, what do we do next?

At this moment he appears in the Officers' Mess. "He's bound to get a medal for this," I hear him say. "One of those nice jingling ones, the Victoria Cross or something."

I stare at him, moonstruck.

"He's certainly earned it. Perfect piece of work. No fault of his we're still lying around here instead of being blown to bits!"

I can see it now. A low barracks on Gibraltar. A crowd of pilots in their overalls, champagne glasses in hand, gathered to celebrate the sinking of a U-boat—a definite kill, confirmed by aerial reconnaissance, and with additional corroboration by the Navy.

"Naked fear," whispers the Commander, pointing at the back of the new control-room assistant. His sarcasm is like a laying-on-of-hands: *Come unto me, all ye that labour and are heavy laden, and I will give you rest.*

The navigator is standing in the gangway and reports, "Periscope top's cracked." It sounds as if he'd discovered a hole in his shoe. "Sky periscope's gone too!"

"So," is all the Old Man says. He sounds tired and resigned, as if a little destruction more or less no longer mattered.

Things must look worst aft. I wonder how the bomb could have worked so much havoc in the stern. The damage in the control room and in battery one is understandable, but that so much should have been broken aft is a mystery. Perhaps there were two bombs? Didn't it sound like a double explosion? I can't ask the Old Man.

The Chief comes through the aftership to report to the Old Man. From his outpourings I discover that almost all the outboard plugs have leaked. The whole electrical system has failed. As a result, the gunnery control is also out of commission. The bearings may also have been somewhat damaged. However, all that means is that they'd run hot if the driving shafts could turn.

What he's providing is a complete inventory of the damages. Not only the main bilge pump but all other bilge pumps have failed.

The cold-water pump ditto. The forward trim cell is no longer water-tight. The foundation bolts of the port diesel—miraculously—have held. But those of the starboard diesel are sheared off. The compressors have been torn from their bases. The forward hydroplane can hardly be moved—probably wrecked when the boat slammed into the rocks on the bottom. The compass system is ruined—magnetic, gyro, secondary—everything. The automatic log and the sounder system have been torn from their supports and are probably out of action. The radio has been badly hit. Even the engine room telegraph is out of order.

"Babel is not yet lost," mutters the Old Man. The Chief blinks and seems to have trouble recognizing him. What's the exact quotation? I rack my brains. Babel lost? That's not it.

Suddenly I hear a new sound. No question, it's coming from outside: a high, rhythmic singsong with a duller beat in it. There they are again! The Old Man heard it at the same instant I did. He listens with his mouth open and a scowl on his face. The vibration and whining increase. Turbines! The Asdic is sure to be next. Everyone freezes—sitting, standing, kneeling. I have trouble identifying the dark masses around me. To the left beside the periscope—that must be the navigator. Recognizable as usual, because his left shoulder is higher than his right. The hunched figure in front of the hydroplane table is the Chief. The man to his left must be the Second Watch Officer. Directly under the overhead hatch is the control-room mate.

Again the clamps around my chest, the choking in my throat.

My pulse is hammering. Everyone in the room must be able to hear it.

My ears pick up a whole range of tiny sounds, including all the ones they missed earlier: the squeaking of leather jackets, for example, and the tiny mouselike peeping of the soles of boots on iron floor plates.

Sweepwires? Asdic? Maybe the ship that was so fond of making the lap of honor had no depth charges on board, and this is its replacement. I tense every muscle, go totally rigid. Mustn't let anything show.

What's happening? Is the whining of the screws letting up a bit—or am I just fooling myself?

Pain in my lungs. Cautiously, gently, I let my chest expand. Breathe in unsteadily, then gasp for the next lungful. No doubt about it, the noises are getting weaker.

"Going away," mutters the Old Man. And immediately I go limp.

"Destroyer," he says expressionlessly. "It's teeming with ships around here. They've called up everything that can float!"

By which he means it was pure accident that a ship passed over us. A stone is lifted from my heart.

New sounds to jangle my nerves—this time the ringing and pounding of tools makes me jump. They're apparently hard at work again in the aftership. Only now does it dawn on me that once again there are more men in the control room than belong here. This attempt to get a place under the tower when the enemy is around is pure atavism. As if the "lords" didn't already know how deep we are. Down here the seamen have no advantage over the engine-room personnel. The rescue gear isn't worth a damn. Except, that is, for the oxygen cartridges, which contain half an hour of life if our oxygen cylinders give out.

The thought that the Tommies have long since written us off and that our presumed sinking has been reported hours ago to the British Admiralty fills me with something between contempt and horror. *Not yet*, you fuckers.

As long as *I* am aboard, this boat cannot perish. The lines of my hand say that I will have a long life. So we're *bound* to get through. Only, no one must find out that I'm immune, or I'd be a jinx. They haven't got us, not by a long shot! We're still breathing—under pressure and gasping, admittedly, but we're still alive.

If only we could send out a bulletin! But even if our radio hadn't gone to hell, we couldn't transmit from this depth. So no one at home will know how we met our end. "Died nobly in his country's service," the usual letter from the Commander in Chief to the next of kin. Our disaster will remain a mystery. That is, unless the British Admiralty relays over the Calais radio how they caught us.

They've developed death reports into a fine art: precise details, so that the people at home will believe them; name, birthdate, size of the Commander's cap. And what about H.Q.? They'll take their time before sending out the three-star report, as they usually do with the Dönitz Volunteer Corps. Besides, we might have valid reasons for not sending signals. We're sure to be ordered to report in the near future. Once, twice—the same old story.

But the way things stand, the gentlemen of the Staff will soon conclude—correctly—that we haven't achieved the requisite breakthrough. There was, after all, very little chance we would, as Kernével was well aware. Their mad slavedriver can gently break the news to himself that he's short one more boat, sunk off Gibraltar —British war port—a rock inhabited by apes—Mediterranean loca-

tion—the "enchanted meeting place of two seductive climates"—
that's what it said, after all! Christ! Don't go to pieces! I stare at the
bananas hanging from the ceiling over the sound room, quietly
ripening away. Two, three splendid specimens of pineapple among
them. But this only makes me feel worse: below, the smashed-up
batteries; up there, a Spanish garden!

The Chief appears again, opens the locker containing the rolled-
up diagrams, riffles through, pulls one out, and spreads it on the
table. I come to his assistance by weighting down the corners of the
diagram with books. It's a longitudinal section of the boat, with the
pipelines drawn in as black veins or red arteries.

The Second Engineer bobs up, tangled mop of hair, out of breath.
He bends over the plan beside the Chief. Not a word out of him
either. Silent movie stuff.

Everything hangs on their deliberations. They're sitting in judgment on our fate. I keep quiet. Don't disturb them. The Chief's
pencil points at a place on the diagram and he nods at his colleague,
who nods back—"understood." Both straighten up simultaneously.
It looks as though the Chief now knows how to go about getting
the water out of the boat. But how will he manage to make any
headway against the external pressure?

I catch sight of a piece of bread with a bite out of it on the table
in the Officers' Mess—fresh white bread from the *Weser*. Thickly buttered, with a chunk of sausage on it. Repulsive! My stomach turns.
Someone must have been eating just when the explosion came.
Amazing it didn't slide off the table when the boat stood on its head.

Breathing is getting harder by the minute. Why doesn't the
Chief release more oxygen? Pathetic that we're so dependent on air.
I need only hold my breath for a short time and the seconds begin
ticking in my ear, and then I get a choking sensation in my throat.
We have fresh bread, we're fully stocked with food—but what we
really need is air. It's being powerfully brought home to us that man
can't exist without it. When else have I ever dwelled on the fact
that I can't live without oxygen, that behind my ribs two flabby
lobes are unceasingly expanding and contracting. Lungs—I've only
seen them cooked. Boiled lungs—a favorite dog food! Lungs with
dumplings, an entrée for sixty *pfennigs* in the main depot, where
they kept the liver-dumpling soup warm in marmalade jars, inside
sauerkraut kettles along with all the sawdust from the floor—or did,
until the health squad shut the place down.

Nine hundred feet. What's the weight of the column of water
that's resting on the boat? I used to know: I had the figures im-

printed on my mind. But now they've faded. My brain is hardly functioning at all. I can't think with all this dull pressure inside my skull.

In my left-hand trouser pocket I feel my talisman—an oval piece of turquoise. I open my left fist and run my fingers lightly over the stone: like smooth, slightly rounded skin. Simone's belly! Immediately I hear her babbling in my ear, "That is my little *nombril*— what do you call it? Button in the belly? Belly button. Funny— *pour moi c'est ma boîte à ordure—regarde—regarde!*" She fingers some fluff out of the depths of her navel and holds it up with a giggle. If she could see me now, nine hundred feet down. Not just anywhere, somewhere out there in the Atlantic, but with a permanent address: Strait of Gibraltar, African Side Of. Here we are in our little tube with its cargo of fifty-one bodies: flesh, bone, blood, spinal jelly, pumping lungs and racing pulses, twitching eyelids—fifty-one minds, each with its own world of memories.

I try to picture her hair. How did she wear it toward the end? I rack my brains but can't remember. I try to bring her image closer, see her hair, but it remains indistinct. Doesn't matter. It'll come back suddenly. Mustn't try so hard. Memories return of their own accord.

I can see her violet sweater. And the yellow bandana and the mauve-colored blouse with the tiny pattern that, if you looked at it closely, read *"Vive la France"* a thousand times over. The orange-gold tone of her skin. And now I have her mad hairdo as well. The strands that always fell across her forehead were what excited me. It was important to Simone to look deliberately disheveled in an artistic way.

It wasn't right of her to swipe my new binoculars for her Herr Papa. He must have wanted to test them out to see whether the new design really is so much better than the old, must have been intrigued by the new blue tint that makes our glasses so much better for night work. And Simone? Did she simply want to show off? Monique got a toy coffin, Genevieve got one, Germaine too—but not Simone.

The Old Man turns up with the Chief. They bend over a diagram. I catch the words "by hand into the regulator tank." Aha, that must be about the water that has got in! By hand? Will that work? Anyway, both of them nod.

"Then outboard from the regulator tank by means of auxiliary pumps and compressed air . . ."

The Chief's voice has a distinct vibrato. A miracle that he's still

on his feet—he was already wiped out before this mess began. Anyone with a couple of dozen depth pursuits behind him is inevitably
used up. Which was why he was due to be relieved. Just one more
patrol!

And now this! He has big drops of sweat on his forehead, but his
brow is so furrowed and wrinkled that they can't run off. When he
turns his head, you can see his whole face shining with sweat.

". . . racket . . . can't be avoided . . . can't be done . . . buoyancy
cell three . . ."

What's he saying about buoyancy cell three? It can't have suffered any damage, it lies inside the pressure hull. What was it they
said: The boat can float on buoyancy cell three alone—but with so
much water aboard, the amount of lift this one cell can give is
naturally not enough—nothing like it. So it comes back to this: The
water has to be got out of the boat as quickly as possible. I haven't
the faintest idea how he intends to pump the water from the control
room into the regulator cells and then from the regulator cells overboard. But he's no fool. He never proposes anything if he's not sure
of his facts.

I gather that he's unwilling to try to free the boat from the
bottom until all necessary repairs have been made. Apparently one
attempt is all we've got.

"Boat . . . first get her . . . even keel!" The Old Man. Of course
the damned stern heaviness! But there's no question of pumping the
water forward now. So?

". . . water by hand from aft into the control room." "By hand."
For chrissake—by hand? In pans? Hand to hand? I stare at the Old
Man and wait for him to make his meaning clear, then I catch the
words, "bucket brigade." He really means it.

A fire brigade forms up through the petty officers' quarters and
the galley, and I join it. My place is beside the hatch. Hoarsely
whispered directions and curses. A bucket comes toward me—the
kind the steward uses to wash dishes. It's half full. I reach for it
and let it swing like a U-shaped dumbbell through the hatch; the
control-room mate has the job of taking it from me. I can hear him
empty it out into the control-room bilge level with the periscope.
The sharp gush and splash are suggestive, disgusting.

More and more pails and buckets are also being handed back in
the opposite direction to be passed through toward the stern. Instant
chaos. Hissing orders, the Chief straightens out the confusion of
empty and full.

The man who hands the pails to me is Zeitler, wearing a filthy,
torn shirt. With each bucket he shows me a grimly determined face.

From behind him come croaks and whispers of "Look out!": a particularly heavy bucket appears. I have to seize the handle with both hands. It still slops over. The swill soaks my trousers and shoes. My back is already wet—but that's sweat. Twice as I pass a bucket I get an encouraging grin from the Old Man. That at least is something.

Sometimes the procession stops because there's been a foul-up somewhere astern. A few half-suppressed curses and then the chain begins again.

The control-room mate doesn't have to be careful. He's the last in line and can let the water spill over onto the floor plates. I can see that the floor in the petty officers' compartment is also wet. But under the floor plates in that compartment is battery two. Won't it be damaged? I tell myself that the Chief is around: He'll take care of it.

Another slop—right over my stomach this time. Shit!

A dull bang, curses, the chain stops again; this time a bucket has apparently hit the hatch rim of the galley.

Am I wrong? Or has the boat already tilted back a couple of degrees toward the horizontal?

The water in the control room is now ankle deep.

How late is it? Must be at least four a.m. Too bad about my wristwatch. Of course the leather band was a dead loss—glued together, not sewn. Modern trash. But the works were good. I had it ten years without a single repair.

"Look out!" Zeitler snaps. Damn it, I must be careful. I no longer have to bend my arm. If Zeitler hands me the pail properly, I can save a lot of strength. He has a worse time of it: He has to heave the pails through the hatch, and he needs both hands to do it, I only have to use my right. I no longer even notice the way it reaches out and lets the pail swing through like a trapeze until it reaches the catcher on the other side.

"When's first light?" the Old Man asks the navigator. Kriechbaum thumbs through his tables. "Morning light begins at 07.30." So there's very little time left!

It may already be later than four o'clock. If we don't make our try soon, surfacing will be out for a whole day—we'll have to wait till evening. That means the people up there will have those hours of beautiful sunlight to play games with us.

"Take a break." The whispers from mouth to mouth. "Break—break—break."

If the Old Man is thinking of making a run for the coast—always assuming that the attempt to surface is successful—then he needs the protection of darkness. We hadn't even reached the narrowest spot in the Strait. The coast is still quite a stretch from here, so the time that remains to us, if we're to succeed, is even shorter. Will the bit of juice in the undamaged cells be enough for the motors? And what good is the whole patchwork on both batteries if the shaft bearings are damaged? The Chief's misgivings weren't just thin air.

Christ, look at the men! Green faces, yellow faces; green-black circles around the sockets of red-rimmed eyes. Mouths half open from lack of air, dark holes.

The Chief reappears to report that the motors are out of danger. However, he wants more water out of the main motor room.

"All right," says the Commander in his normal voice. "Carry on!"

The first time I reach for a pail again I realize how sore my muscles are. I can hardly manage to get back into the proper swing.

Choking, heaving lungs. No more air in the boat. But one thing is certain: We are definitely getting back onto an even keel.

The Commander sloshes over to the hatch. "Going okay?" he calls aft.

"*Jawohl*, Herr Kaleun!"

I could drop right here, in the muck all over the floor plates—I wouldn't give a damn. I count the pails. Just as I'm saying "fifty" to myself, the order comes from astern. "Belay the bailing!"

Thank god! I still have to take four or five buckets from Zeitler, but the empty pails no longer come back from the control-room mate: They're passed on farther forward.

Now to get my wet gear off. Chaos in the petty officers' compartment because everyone wants dry clothes. I get hold of my sweater, even manage to find my leather trousers on my bunk. Fantastic! Dry things! And now into my seaboots. Frenssen's elbow lands in my ribs, and Pilgrim tramples on my right foot, but finally I manage it. I splash through the control room, bouncing like a street urchin. In the Officers' Mess I can finally put my feet up.

Then I hear "oxygen." From mouth to mouth the order goes through the boat, "Adjust potash cartridges. All men off duty rest on their bunks!"

The Second Watch Officer stares at me in consternation.

Another message is passed from mouth to mouth. "Watch one another. Be sure no one's snorkel slips out of his mouth while he's asleep."

"Haven't used one of these for a long time," mutters the bosun next door.

Potash cartridges. That answers the question—it's going to take a long time. No rosy glow of dawn for us this time. The Second Watch Officer says nothing. He doesn't bat an eye, though the orders don't seem very welcome to him. I see by his watch that it's five o'clock.

I stagger back toward the stern again, splashing through the water in the control room, aware of the frozen faces of the personnel. Breaking out the potash cartridges means that there's no possibility of surfacing during the next few hours. Which also means: wait till dark. A whole day on the bottom. God Almighty! The engine-room crew will have ample time to put their shop in order again. No reason to hurry now.

With trembling hands I fish around in a corner at the head of my bed until I find my potash cartridge, a rectangular metal case twice the size of a cigar box.

The other inhabitants of the petty officers' compartment are already at work screwing in the tubes with the mouthpiece and getting the rubber nozzle—the snorkel—between their teeth. Only Zeitler hasn't got that far: He's swearing a blue streak. "Goddam shit—I've fucking well had enough!"

The black tubes are already hanging out of Pilgrim's and Kleinschmidt's mouths. I put on the nose clip, noticing as I do so how shaky my hands are. Cautiously I take the first gulp of air through the cartridge. Never done it before. Nervous about how it'll work. As I breathe out again, the valve in the mouthpiece rattles: that can't be right. Was I breathing too hard? Well then, slow down, do it more quietly. The air from the snout has a foul taste of rubber. Hope it won't go on like that.

The box is heavy. It hangs in front of my stomach like a street vendor's tray. Weighs a good two pounds. The contents are supposed to absorb the carbon dioxide we breathe out, or at least enough of it so that what we breathe in won't contain more than four per cent. More is dangerous. We could suffocate in our own exhalation. "When it gets chemical, it gets psychological," said the Chief. How right he was!

How long will the oxygen really last? The underwater endurance of a VII-C is supposed to be three days. So there must be enough oxygen in the tanks for three times twenty-four hours—without forgetting the period of grace contained in the steel cylinders of the life-saving gear.

If Simone could see me like this, with the snorkel in my mouth and the potash cartridge on my stomach . . .

I stare at Zeitler, taking him as my mirror image: wet matted hair; drops of sweat thick on his forehead; great, staring, feverish eyes with violet-black rings underneath; nose clamped shut by the clip. Under it his dark rubber proboscis protruding from a matted stubble of beard—a terrifying carnival figure.

Those ghoulish beards! How long have we actually been out? Try counting: seven, eight weeks? Or is it actually nine or ten?

Simone drifts in again. I see her on a movie screen, smiling, gesticulating, pushing down her shoulder straps. I blink—and she disappears.

Just a look around the control room, I say to myself, and clamber laboriously through the hatch. This damned street vendor's box! Now I see Simone projected directly onto pipes, shafts, and manometers. I see the tangle of ducts and hand wheels for shut-off valves, and over them Simone: breasts, thighs, fluff, her moist, half-open mouth. She rolls over on her stomach, raising her feet in the air, reaches for her ankles, and does the "swan." The striped shadows from the venetian blinds glide back and forth over her body as she rocks. Zebra-swan. I close my eyes.

Then right in front of me a double exposure: a face with a proboscis growing out of its mouth. I jump: It's the Second Watch Officer. He's staring at me. He seems to want to communicate. Awkwardly he pulls the rubber nozzle out of his mouth, dripping saliva. "Refrain from use of pistols. Danger of explosion!" he says nasally, lifting his eyebrows. Of course! The gas from the battery.

He sucks in his pacifier again, and winks his left eye before sitting down on his bunk. I can't even say, "Very funny, you idiot!"

Unsteady as a drunkard, I feel my way along the lockers, touch the Old Man's curtain, then more paneled walls. No contortions needed to get into the Officers' Mess. The floor plates have been laid down again. The battery's probably not a total write-off. In rudimentary form it may still be usable for a very short distance under power.

There's a light burning. If we left only this one bulb on it would probably keep burning forever. An electric bulb—forty watts—must use less current in a whole week than is needed for a single turn of the propellers. The Eternal Light—nine hundred feet down!

Someone has cleaned up—more or less. The pictures are back on the wall again, admittedly without glass. Even the books are in the shelf, in some kind of rough order. The First Watch Officer must be lying in his bunk. At any rate his curtain is closed. The Second Watch Officer is sitting in the left corner of the Chief's bunk, eyes tight shut. He'd do better to lie down properly instead of slumping in a corner like a wet sack. He's wormed his way in so firmly that he doesn't look as if he ever intends to move again.

It has never been so peaceful in here before. No traffic, no changing of the watch. Pictures and books. The familiar lamplight, the handsome veined woodwork, the black leather sofa. No pipes, no white ship's paint, not so much as a square inch of damaged hull. A green silk shade and glass bead fringe on the lamp and it would look just like home. A bunch of flowers on the table—artificial ones for all I care—and a fringed tablecloth, and it would be an honest-to-god living room. Of course the leather sofa should have a piece of wood over it with branded letters or a sampler in cross-stitch with the motto: "A poor thing, but mine own."

Admittedly, the Second Watch Officer spoils the picture. Or rather his snorkel does. No fancy-dress party in our living room!

This silence in the boat! It's as if the crew were no longer aboard, as if we two—the Second Watch Officer and I—were all alone between these four walls.

The Second Watch Officer has let his head sink down on his chest. He's succeeded in shutting out the surrounding world. No worries to trouble the Baby Officer, our Garden Gnome. How on earth has he managed, now of all times, to go dead to the world? Is he resigned to his fate, like most of the men? Or is his particular sleeping pill the Old Man's confidence act? Blind trust in the abilities of the Chief, in the skill of the repair crew? Or is it simply discipline? Sleep is the order, so sleep he does?

Now and again he grunts or chokes on his own saliva; he doesn't wake up but suckles away with smacking noises like a piglet at the tit of the mother sow.

Ready to drop. Sometimes I drowse for minutes at a time, then force myself back awake. It must be after six o'clock now. Now the Second Watch Officer looks like an exhausted fireman.

I ought to try to keep moving. Not just sit around here on my backside. Better to concentrate on everything that's going on in the boat right now. Fix the details. Focus on something. But none of *that* requires any movement at all. For example, I can fix my eyes on the Second Watch Officer's glittering rodent teeth. Then his left earlobe: properly developed, better formed than the First Watch Officer's. I observe the Second Watch Officer with scientific precision, divide up his head into separate sections. Make enlargements of his eyelashes, brows, lips.

I try to organize my thoughts. But it's like turning on a defective motor: It fires a few times and then goes dead.

How many hours have we actually been down here? It must have been around midnight when we sank, by ship's time in any case. But that doesn't correspond to our geographical location and is also off an hour; on board, we're on German Summer Time. Do I subtract or add? I can't decide. Not even something as simple as that. I'm completely off track. According to ship's time it must be at least 07.00. In any case we've lost any chance we had of attempting to surface in the gray of dawn. We'll have to wait till it's dark again up there.

The British cooks must have been up long ago, serving huge quantities of fried eggs and bacon, their standard breakfast for the fleet.

Hunger? For god's sake, don't even think about eating!

The Old Man was only suggesting that we try to surface before dawn in order to keep us on our feet. Clever of him not to make it definite. False optimism? Bullshit! It was just to keep the men going.

A whole day down here? Maybe even longer—and this eternal snorkel in your mouth. God!

In my sleep, I hear the Second Watch Officer clear his throat. I struggle back to consciousness, surface, and blink hard. Rub my eyes with the knuckle of my index finger. Heavy head. Lead in my skull. Pains behind the eyebrows—even worse farther back in my head. The snouted animal in the other corner is still the Second Watch Officer.

I wish I knew what time it is. Must be midday. My watch was a good one. Swiss. Seventy-five marks. Already lost it twice, but always found it again—a miracle each time. Where can it be lying around now?

And still this quiet! No humming of auxiliary machinery. The same deathly silence. The potash cartridge weighs on my stomach like a monstrous hot-water bottle.

Now and again a man with oil-smeared hands and arms comes through the compartment. Still something out of order back there? Hasn't our position improved at all while I was asleep? Is there new hope? No one to ask. Secretiveness everywhere.

But how do I know that the compass is functioning again—the whole system? Did I hear something while I was dozing? The hydroplane is only partially back in service, and hard to move. But that was already known before I fell asleep.

How about the water? The Chief had a plan. But does he still believe in it? Shouldn't have gone to sleep: lost track of everything, including time.

At some point I heard the Commander say, "We have to surface the moment it gets dark." But how long is it till then? Outrageous that my watch has gone.

I start looking for it, and discover that our straw dog has disappeared. No longer hanging from the ceiling. Nor under the table either. I let myself slide out of the bunk, crawl through the rubber boots and cans of food, and fumble about in the dark. Damnation, a splinter! The Chief's pillow. Then hand towels and leather gloves, but no dog. However tatty, he's our good-luck charm; he *can't* just disappear.

I'm about to sit down again when I notice the Second Watch Officer. He has the dog tucked under his left arm; he's clutching it the way a child clutches a doll, and he's fast asleep.

Another man comes through, stepping carefully, a heavy tool in his oil-smeared hands. I'm ashamed to be doing nothing. My only comfort is the fact that the Second Watch Officer and the entire naval contingent are also doing nothing. Orders to remain quiet, to sleep. In fact, we have the harder part: sitting here, lying here, staring straight ahead, having hallucinations.

This goddam snorkeling. Too much saliva in my mouth. Before, my gums were as dry as leather, and now this overproduction. Salivary glands simply aren't designed for this way of life.

Only two boats out of three survive their first patrol. That's the rule of thumb nowadays: Every third boat is sunk almost at once. Seen in this light, UA is one of the lucky ones. She has already inflicted all sorts of damage; she's bled the Tommies white, as they so elegantly put it. And now the Tommies have turned the tables on us. Another of those silly metaphors: "turn the tables"—"bleed them white."

Some of the men on the bunks already look as if they'd died in their sleep: still, peaceful, their nozzles in their mouths. As for the ones who are lying on their backs, all you'd have to do is fold their hands.

I have to keep talking to myself. To everything there is a season— even this ordeal. I shall put thee through the wringer, saith the Lord, and I shall rip open thy ass to the topmost vertebra so that howling and gnashing of teeth shall profit thee nothing.

There it is again: fear that rises from somewhere between my shoulder blades up into my throat, distends my rib cage, gradually fills my whole body. Even my cock. Hanged men often have an erection. Or does that come from something else?

The Commander of the *Bismarck* still had his Führer in mind when the time came to die. He even put it in words and had it dispatched as a radiogram: ". . . to the last shell . . . loyal to the death . . ." or some such elevating text. There was a man after our First Watch Officer's heart.

We're not very well equipped for this sort of nonsense down here. We can certainly compose noble texts, but we can't transmit them. The Führer will have to dispense with the UA's last words. There isn't even enough air to sing the national anthem.

Good old Marfels, he's had it already. It was a mistake to ship on the *Bismarck*. Really makes you laugh. Marfels, the badge collector, still short of a battle medal, so he had to step up and volunteer. Now his young widow can enjoy the hardware he left behind.

What must it have been like after they got that torpedo in the rudder mechanism and could only plow around in circles? The salvage ships *Castor* and *Pollux* were ordered out from Brest, but all that was left of the *Bismarck* by then had been reduced to scrap metal and mincemeat.

Dulce et decorum est pro patria . . . of all the crap!

I seek refuge from my nightmares in Simone. I repeat her name silently . . . once, twice, again and again. But this time the invocation fails.

All at once Charlotte appears instead of Simone. Her gourd-shaped tits. The way she could swing them back and forth when she was on her hands and knees.

Now other pictures force their way upward. Inge in Berlin. The assistant at Staff Headquarters. The room assigned by the station commandant. A Berlin room, or rather a hall, really. Don't put on the light: the blackout curtains are missing. I touch her. Thighs spread, she lets me fall into her. "For god's sake, don't stop! Go on! Don't stop. Like that!"

Brigitte, with her taste for turbans. "*J'aime Rambran . . . parce qu'il a son style!*" It took me a while to realize that she meant Rembrandt.

And the girl from Magdeburg, with the unwashed neck and freckles on her nose! The half-filled ashtray with the used condom. The goddam sluttishness of these schoolgirl whores! Appetite gone. Instant complaints. "What's wrong *now*? D'you expect me to wait till hell freezes over? Loosen up, will you!" And then, "Slow down—whaddaya trying to do—bang my fucking head off?"

The carousel keeps spinning, and I see the volunteer with the huge sagging breasts go sailing by. When asked why she did it free, gratis, and for nothing, her response was "showing the flag." You could crank her up, but none of the usual treatment ever got her going. What she wanted was gymnastics—brace yourself on hands and toes and give her a lightning demonstration of sexual push-ups.

I have a clear shot of a pane of frosted glass, the lowest of three in a white painted door. A phantom face: the exiled husband on all fours, ostrich-like in the conviction of his own invisibility. "Look at him—will you look at him! Mr. Peeping Tom himself!"

And now the spinner of fairy tales: knees drawn up, squatting on top of me chattering away as if she had no idea what was going on underneath. Didn't want me to move. Just played five years old and told fairy stories. Where on earth did I find that one?

The two naked whores in the shabby Paris hotel room. I don't want to look at them. Go away! I try to concentrate on Simone, but I can't summon her up. Instead I see one of the two whores washing herself between the legs, sitting on the bidet right under a bare lightbulb. Slack, pallid skin. The other one's no better. She's kept her stockings on and her grimy girdle. Gossiping away, she reaches into a battered shopping bag and pulls out half a pathetically small rabbit that's already been skinned. Wet newspaper sticks to it in dark-gray patches. The neck is half severed. There are dark-red trickles of blood around the ax mark. The whore who's still on the bidet with her face to the wall, working away with both hands splashing underneath her, keeps screeching every time she bends her head back toward the bluish white body of the rabbit, which the other one is holding out to her. She's so excited over this prize that she starts to sputter with laughter. The one with the rabbit in her hand has red pubic hair. Sticking next to it on her thigh there's a piece of the damp newspaper the rabbit had been wrapped in, as big as your hand. Her belly quivers as she laughs; the slack breasts wobble in unison.

I feel as nauseated as I did then.

If we don't move as much as a little finger, the consumption of oxygen must fall to almost zero. Lying stretched out, motionless, not even blinking our eyelids, we should be able to make our supply hold out much longer than the averages indicate.

Of course the motion of the lungs in itself uses up oxygen. So— breathe very shallowly, inhale only as much as the body needs for its basic functions.

But the oxygen we save here by staying still is being used up by the men who are exhausting themselves on the damaged engines aft. They're exploiting our reserves. Sucking the oxygen right out of our mouths.

Now and again a dull clang comes from astern. Each time it

makes me jump: Sounds are magnified five times in water. They're certainly doing all they can to avoid noise. But how can they work silently with those heavy tools?

The First Watch Officer comes back from an inspection tour. From time to time he has to make sure that all the sleepers still have their snorkels in their mouths. His blond hair, wet with sweat, is stuck to his forehead.

About all I can see of his face is the cheekbones—his eyes lie in shadow.

I haven't seen the Chief for a long time. I wouldn't want to be in his place. It's too much responsibility for one man. Let's hope he's up to it.

The Old Man appears on silent feet. He's still six feet away from the table when there's another clang from astern. He grimaces as though in sudden pain.

He's not wearing a potash cartridge. "Well, how goes it?" he asks, as though he didn't know that with the nozzle in my mouth I can't reply. I lift my shoulders slightly by way of an answer, then let them fall. The Old Man glances quickly into the forward compartment then disappears again.

I'm ready to drop with exhaustion, but sleep is impossible. Images float up like entries from a card index. The hairnet lady: hoity-toity Tante Bella, the Christian Scientist, the healer who'd taken a dip in all the sacred waters known to man. She did a roaring trade. The hairnets came in enormous bundles from Hong Kong. By the hundred gross. Tante Bella had elegant envelopes with transparent windows and uplifting texts printed on them, and there she sat with three little office drudges, all of them untangling the hairnets and putting each individual one into its pale violet-colored envelope—which made the hairnet instantly become fifty times more expensive than it had been a moment before. Tante Bella had a good dozen salesmen. Later I learned that she carried on exactly the same business with contraceptives—but all that happened late at night. I picture her sitting there in dead earnest, in front of a pile of pale, rose-colored condoms like a mountain of sheep's intestines, sorting out the mess with nimble fingers and slipping them into their little envelopes. Faber was Tante Bella's name—Bella Faber. Her son, Kurtchen, looked like a thirty-year-old hamster. He was the head of the sales force. Hairdressers were his principal clients. Meanwhile, Uncle Erich, Tante Bella's husband, installed automatic vending machines in the washrooms of rundown bars. "Three for one reichsmark." Uncle Erich had to have a drink with every barkeeper on his rounds to refill the machines. Then back onto his bicycle, one shabby saddlebag for the money and the other for the contraceptives; dismount, down another shot, out with the take, in with the condoms, down yet another shot. He couldn't keep it up for long, good old Uncle Erich with the silver bicycle clips on his trousers. He never removed them, not even indoors. One day he fell off his wheels between one vending machine and the next and was done for. The police carted him off. They must have been flabbergasted at the loads of coins and condoms they found in his bags.

All at once I notice that the Second Watch Officer's apparatus has fallen out of his mouth. How long has he been breathing without the snorkel? Was I dead to the world a while? I shake his shoulder but elicit no more than a rumble. I have to punch him hard before he gives a start and stares at me with horror, as though I were some grisly apparition. It takes a few seconds for him to pull himself together, grope for his snorkel, and begin to suck on it. Then he's asleep again.

I'll never understand how he manages it. If only he were pretending—but no, he really is dead to the world again. All that's lacking is a snore. I can't take my eyes off his pale, relaxed baby face. Envy? Or am I just tormented by my disappointment at not being able to communicate with him even by glance or gesture?

I can't stay here. My body is going to sleep of its own accord. Up and into the control room.

Repairs are still going on in the radio shack. Both mates are working by the light of a strong bulb they brought with them to screw into the socket, and they aren't wearing snorkels. Apparently they can't get the transmitter working. It's a job for a watchmaker. Probably the necessary replacement parts are lacking. "Can't be done with available materials," I hear Herrmann say. Always the same thing: "Not with available materials . . ." as if they had any choice.

The emergency bulb sheds an ugly light that barely penetrates the thick air. It doesn't even reach the walls, which are still in darkness. Three, four shadowy figures are working by the forward wall, bent over like miners at the end of a gallery. Wedged against the chart table with his forearms outstretched on it, the Old Man is staring fixedly at the chart. The machines have been stripped down, and the parts are still strewn at random around the darkened room. Even the flooding and bailing distributors are cluttered with pieces that don't belong there. Probably parts of the main bilge pump. In the background the beam of a pocket flashlight flits over the armatures and valves. I can just make out the pale eye of the manometer in the gloom. The pointer remains at nine hundred. I stare at it as if I can hardly believe my own eyes. No boat has ever been this deep before.

It's getting colder all the time. Certainly we're not radiating much body warmth, and heat is out of the question. Wonder how cold it is outside?

Plaster altar: Gibraltar—plaster altar.

Now, thank god, the Chief arrives. He's moving with his usual supple ease. Does that mean some kind of triumph? The Old Man turns to him and hmms and hahs.

As hard as I try, all I hear is that the breaches have been sealed. No sign of satisfaction from the Old Man.

"In any case, we can't surface before dark."

To this I can only nod. What I'd really like to toss in is "How about *after*?"

I'm afraid they're betting on their hopes rather than on realities.

The man who just came through the control room from the stern has doubtless heard what the Old Man said. It wouldn't surprise me if the Old Man had formulated his sentence with "surface" in it just for him, so that he can now go forward to report, "The Old Man just said something about surfacing."

I'm still not clear in my own mind how much of the Old Man's confidence is play-acting and how much conviction. In any case, whenever he thinks he's unobserved, he looks years older: a mess of wrinkles, all his face muscles slack, his reddened, swollen eyes half closed; at such moments his whole body speaks resignation. But now that his back's supported, he holds himself straight, arms folded on his chest, head tilted slightly backward, so still he might be posing for a sculptor. I can't even see whether he's breathing.

Without knowing exactly what I'm doing, I seem to have sat down in the ring of the forward hatch.

Suddenly the Old Man's face is bending over me. Has he said something? I must seem totally dazed as I pull myself to my feet, for he produces a calming, "There, there." Then with a motion of his head he urges me to accompany him astern. "Have to show our faces back there as well."

I dig out the rubber mouthpiece with my fingers, swallow my saliva, take a breath of air, and silently follow the Old Man. For the first time I notice someone sitting on the chart chest: Turbo. His head is flopping so loosely on his chest that his backbone might as well be broken. Someone is coming toward us: control-room mate Isenberg. Staggering like a drunk. In his left hand he has long metal rods and electric cables, and in his right a large pipe wrench that he's in the act of handing down to someone crouching on the floor.

The Old Man halts at the level of the deserted hydroplane station and surveys the dismal scene. The control-room mate hasn't yet noticed us. Suddenly, however, he looks round as he hears the splashing of my boots, and he straightens up, tries to stand, opens his mouth, and then shuts it again.

"Well, Isenberg?" says the Old Man. The control-room mate swallows but doesn't make a sound.

The Old Man takes a sideways step toward him and lays his right hand on his shoulder—just for a second; but Tin-ear Willie blossoms under it. He even manages a gratified grin. The Old Man gives two or three short nods and then moves heavily on.

I know that the control-room mate will now be exchanging glances with his men behind our backs. The Old Man! He's always managed . . .

The floor plates are still up in the petty officers' quarters. So they're still working on battery two, or giving it another go-around. A face streaked with sweat and oil pops up like an apparition from a stage trapdoor. The wide beard identifies him as Pilgrim, the E-mate. More dumbshow: for two or three seconds the Old Man and Pilgrim exchange glances, then Pilgrim grins all over his filthy face. The Old Man allows himself a questioning noise, then nods—and Pilgrim nods back eagerly: He too is comforted.

It's hard to get through aft. The nimble Pilgrim tries to prop up a piece of the floor plate from underneath so there will be room for us to put our feet down.

"Don't bother," says the Old Man; like a mountain climber, his belly pressed against the bunk railings, he traverses the narrow foot-ledge toward the stern. I accept Pilgrim's help.

The door to the galley is standing open. The galley itself has been cleaned up. "Excellent," murmurs the Old Man. "Just as I expected."

The next door, to the diesel room, is standing open too. Usually when the diesels are running and sucking in air, you have to exert all your strength to overcome what is virtually a vacuum in the diesel room. But the pulsing heart of the boat is dead.

Weak light from hand lamps; our eyes quickly adjust. My god, look at it! The duckboards have been removed, the shining floor plates too. For the first time I realize how far down the diesels extend. Between their bases I can make out a jumble of heavy machine parts—oil pans, tools, bushings. This is no longer a machine shop but a cannibal cave. Everything drips with black lubricating oil —the spilled black blood of machines. Repulsive pools of it have formed on all flat surfaces. Bunches of waste lie about. Everywhere tattered rags, dirty packings, bent pieces of pipe, asbestos boards black with finger marks, greasy nuts and bolts. Whispering voices, the dull clang of a tool.

While Johann is whispering with the Old Man, he goes on working with a gigantic wrench. I had no idea we had such heavy tools on board. Johann's movements are precisely measured: no nervous errors, no uncertain holds.

"Beam wedges in the leaks holding fast!"

The word "beam" sets me off again. Wood amid all this steel? Beam defenses—that's naval vocabulary. Where else are there "beams"?

Then I actually see them: square timbers—five by five. Driven tight with wedges like the supporting timbers in mines: exactly the same system. The sheer amount of carpentry among all this steel and iron! Where has the wood been stowed? I've never seen timber on board.

Where on earth does Johann get his calmness from? Does he simply forget that we have nine hundred feet of water over our heads, and that the oxygen will soon be running out? The Old Man peers here and there. He kneels in order to get closer to the people working below deck, contorted like fakirs. He says hardly a word, simply hums a little to himself and produces his usual drawling "Well-l-l?"

But out of their narrow pits the oil-smeared faces look at the Old Man as if he were a miracle worker. Their faith in his ability to get us out of here must be without limit.

At the after end of the starboard diesel, the lamplight reveals two or three men hunched over in cramped positions at the base of the diesels; they're cutting large gaskets.

"Well, how do things look in general?" the Old Man asks in a hushed voice, but warmly, the way he would inquire after the health of their wives and children.

He's standing propped on one elbow for support; in the angle between his arm and his body, I catch sight of the Chief. ". . . ribs broken by the dozen," I hear him whisper. ". . . can't really get at the problem anywhere!"

His face is thrown into exaggerated relief by one of the lamps. Extreme exhaustion has put greenish semi-circles under his eyes, which are burning feverishly. The lines in his face have deepened. He seems to have aged ten years overnight.

I can't see his body, only his floodlit face. I give a start as the pale, bearded head of John the Baptist speaks again. "Made a mess of the cooling-water system too. Pretty fair job actually—soldered—starboard diesel—Herr Kaleun—seems to be—complete wipe-out—not with available materials—otherwise it'll go to pot—not balanced—driveshaft bearings . . ."

There's something or other, as far as I can make out, that can only be put right by heavy hammering. The two of them agree that any work involving heavy hammering is out of the question.

Again the voice from below. "Thank god—that's halfway in working order—damned hair-splitting—more of a job for a watchmaker . . ."

The Old Man orders, "Put everything you've got into it—it'll be all right!" Then he turns to me as though he had a highly confidential communication to make, but what comes out is a stage whisper. "Good thing we've got a real specialist crew on board!"

The wrecked motor room is as horrifying as the diesel room: it's no longer our sterile, clean, electric workshop with all the machine parts hidden under steel hoods. The disguises have been torn away, the floor plates removed; the innards lie exposed, naked. Here too everything is a mass of oily waste, pieces of wood, tools. Wedges, cables, hand lamps, a wire net. And there's still water down there. There's something obscene about all this; something that looks like rape. The E-mate Rademacher is lying on his stomach, the veins in his neck bulging with the strain as he tries to tighten a base nut with an enormous wrench.

"A lot of field damage!" I say.

"Field damage: I like it," says the Old Man. "The paymaster will be around right away to have a look at the trampled lettuce, then he'll take care of our mere trifle out of his hip pocket—avoids bureaucracy!"

Rademacher hears his voice and starts to get up, but the Old Man holds him down, then nods and pushes his cap to the back of his head. Rademacher grins.

I discover a clock: twelve noon. So I *must* have slept, off and on. How could the clock have survived the explosion? My eyes fall on an empty bottle. Thirst! Where in the world can I get something to drink? How long is it since I've had anything? I'm not hungry: an empty belly, but no hunger. Just this hellish thirst.

There's still a bottle—half full. But I mustn't make off with Rademacher's juice.

The Old Man stands stiff as a post, thinking, his eyes fixed on the breach-lock of the stern torpedo tube. Is he making a résumé?

Finally he remembers me, jerks round, and murmurs, "Well, back we go again." Another pilgrim's progress past the halt, the blind, the needy, and the damned. A repeat performance to make sure the show's made its proper impact.

But this time the Old Man acts as if there were nothing special to notice; as though everything were in order. A couple of half-nods here and there, and we're back in the control room. He steps up to the chart table.

Oranges! Of course, we have oranges from the *Weser*. Two crates of them were put aboard in the bow compartment—perfect, ripe oranges. December, the best time for them. My mouth is trying to water, but my throat is choked: a single mass of mucus that has blocked my salivary glands completely. But oranges will clear all that away.

No one in the Quarters. The technicians are still aft. The navigator was last seen in the control room. But where has the bosun gone?

I try to open the hatch to the bow compartment as quietly as possible. Feeble light, as usual: a single weak bulb. It takes me a good minute to make out the scene in the gloom: men on bunks, men in hammocks; everyone asleep. Men on the floor plates too, almost up to the hatch; huddled close together like tramps trying to keep one another warm.

There've never been so many of them together in the bow compartment. Suddenly I realize that not only the men off watch but also the "lords" who would normally be on duty now are in here—so it's double occupancy.

The beam of my flashlight moves over the bodies. The place looks like a battlefield. Worse still, the aftermath of a gas attack: men lying in the half-darkness as if literally broken and twisted by pain, as if their masks had been no protection against some new gas introduced by the enemy.

It's reassuring to hear deep breathing and little smothered snores.

Probably no one would notice if the Chief turned off the oxygen supply. They would go on just as calmly, dozing away with their pig snouts over their faces and their potash cartridges on their stomachs. Sleep, my little ones, sleep . . . Passed away, dozing for Volk and Führer . . .

Isn't that someone moving over there, all hunched over? Hacker, the torpedo mechanic. Stepping cautiously over the bodies as if he were looking for someone in particular. He has to stay awake to see to it that no one lets the pig snout out of his mouth.

I begin to search for foot room. I have to force a way between the sleeping men, search out crevices, push my foot like a wedge between twisted bodies while taking care not to become entangled in the noose of a snorkel tube.

The oranges must be stowed all the way forward beside the floor breaches. I grope around until I touch first a crate and then a fruit, which I roll and heft in my hand. I gulp. I can't bear to wait any longer: standing there just as I am, both feet jammed between torsos, arms and legs, I dig the snorkel out of my mouth and plunge my teeth into the thick rind. It's not till my second bite that I get to the flesh of the fruit. Sucking loudly, I swallow the juice. A lot of it runs out of the corners of my mouth and drips onto the sleeping men. Bliss! I should have thought of it long ago.

Someone moves beside my left foot; a hand seizes my calf; I jump as though I'd been grabbed by an octopus. In this dim light I can't see who it is. A face rises: a grisly lemur with a trunk. Coming out of the half-darkness, the man scares me to death. I still can't recognize him: Schwalle or Dufte? I stammer, "Damned good oranges!" But there's no answer.

Hacker, who's still poking about, comes past, pulls out his mouth-piece, and growls, "Rotten acoustics." In the beam of my flashlight, long threads of spittle hang down from his chin. Dazzled, he closes his eyes.

"Excuse me!"

"I'm looking for the cook," he whispers.

I point to a dark corner near the hatch.

Hacker wobbles his way over two men, bends down, and says in a low voice, "Come on, up, up, Katter! Move. The men astern want something to drink."

Nothing has changed in the Officers' Mess. The Second Watch Officer is still asleep in his corner. I pull out one of the tattered volumes from the shelf and compel myself to read. My eyes feel their way along the lines. They move at their accustomed pace from left to right, registering every syllable, every individual letter, but meanwhile my thoughts drift away; peculiar connections take place in my brain. Disparate texts intrude themselves between my eyes and the printed page: sunken boats—what becomes of them? Does the shipwrecked U-boat armada come sailing home to harbor some day, washed in on the tide along with the mussels and the seaweed? Or do people lie here for the next ten thousand years preserved in some kind of salt-water alcohol? And if a way is eventually found to search the bottom of the sea and raise the ships? How will we look then if our boat is cut open with a blow torch?

Actually we would offer the recovery team a marvelously peaceful picture. In other sunken boats it would certainly look worse, with the crew probably locked together in chaos, or floating, bloated, between the diesel blocks. We are an exception. We'd be in a dry place.

No oxygen, so no rust, and above and beyond that, only the highest quality U-boat materials. The salvage would certainly pay for itself: We have any amount of valuable merchandise on board. And our provisions are certainly edible. Only the bananas, the pineapples, and the oranges would be too far gone.

And as for ourselves? In general, how much do corpses decay without oxygen? What becomes of fifty-one bladders full of urine, of the fricassee and potato salad in our intestines once the oxygen is all gone? Won't the fermentation process stop too? Do U-boat corpses become stiff and dry like dried codfish or like the bishops that one sees high above Palermo in Piana degli Albanesi? There they lie, under the altar pictures, in their glass caskets, adorned with brocaded silk, colored glass stones, and pearls: hideous but enduring. The difference is that the bishops had been disemboweled. But if it rained uninterruptedly for a couple of days, they stank just the same, as only codfish can stink, through their glass panes.

Our ship's fly comes into mind. I see the boat being raised years from now, covered with shaggy dark-green seaweed and thick clumps of mussels. The tower hatch is broken open and out swarm a million fat, greasy flies. Closeup of millions of *Battleship Potemkin* maggots, swarming over the hatch rim. And millions upon millions of crablice covering the corpses of the crew like mange . . .

"Twilight!" I hear from the control room. What does that mean, morning twilight or evening twilight? I'm totally confused.

The whispering voices come closer. The Old Man appears, and behind him, the Chief.

The Chief is reporting to the Old Man. He seems to have a new-found supply of strength, like a boxer getting his second wind after being almost counted out in the previous round. God knows how he does it. He hasn't had one moment away from the Second Engineer and his people. Now he and the Old Man are drawing up a kind of provisional account. I hear that the compressors have been rammed tight with wooden wedges. The thumb-thick bolts that fastened them to their base plates had been sheared off by the pressure wave of the explosion. Much depends on the compressors: they supply the air for blowing out the buoyancy tanks. Both periscopes are definitely in the ashcan. For the time being there's nothing to be done there. Too complicated . . .

I can see that the Chief is beginning to radiate hope as he makes his report.

Have our chances improved? I stop paying attention to detail. All I want to know is whether the Chief is certain he can force the water outboard and free the boat from the bottom. What do I care about the periscope? I have only one wish: to get to the surface. God knows what comes next. But first we have to get there. Just get there.

Not a word about bailing and outboard pumping. So what's the point of all our other successful repairs if we can't free ourselves from the bottom? Suddenly there are noises again, coming slowly closer. Unmistakable. Ship's propellers. Louder and louder.

"Propeller sounds in all directions!"

What does that mean—a whole convoy? The Old Man rolls his eyes like a tenant enraged by a brawl in the apartment overhead.

I look around helplessly. I am superfluous. I can only press myself farther into my corner. Every bone in my body feels tortured, tormented. That must be from swinging the buckets: a kind of violent charley horse.

The Old Man booms away in his usual voice. At first this terrifies me, then I understand that with the uproar overhead it's safe to talk aloud. No one can hear us. And the familiar hoarse growl is a comfort.

"Must be a traffic jam!" he says. The usual pretended indifference. But he can't fool me: I've seen him secretly massaging his back with both hands and heard him groan as he does so. He must have landed very awkwardly when he fell, but since then he has only snatched the odd fifteen minutes now and again to lie down.

The Chief isn't taking the din as well as the Old Man. When the rumble deepens overhead, the words stick in his throat, and his eyes dart this way and that. No one says a word. Dumbshow.

I wish the whole thing would reach its finale, so that the players could finally cross the footlights with their everyday faces again.

The propeller noise stops. The Old Man looks me straight in the face and nods in satisfaction, as though he had been the one to cut the noise off—just to please me.

The Chief takes a hasty gulp from the bottle of apple juice and disappears again.

I resolve to conquer my inhibitions and ask the Old Man straight out how things stand, but at that moment he gets to his feet, grimacing with pain, and plods heavily toward the stern.

After a while I can think of nothing better to do than follow him. Perhaps I can lure him into conversation in the control room. But he's disappeared. Must have gone farther astern. I have a nasty feeling that something is all fouled up aft. I should have listened more carefully.

The fog in my brain is getting thicker. The best thing would be for me to rest on my bunk. A man has to sleep sometimes. No point in just sitting around.

I must have felt my way into the petty officers' compartment in a trance. Now the trouble starts: I've had no practice wriggling into my bunk with a potash cartridge over my stomach; however, by dint of a kind of pole vault with a couple of very painful twists in it, I finally manage. Now to start unbuttoning my shirt, loosen my belt, unbutton the shirt further, all the way down, let my stomach swell as I breathe in, then flatten again—stretch out, exhale, lie there in a kind of sheath with my potash cartridge for a hot-water bottle; a mummy on a funeral bier.

Consciousness dissolves. Is it sleep, or another kind of oblivion? When I come to again, it's 17.00. Ship's time. I can tell from Isenberg's wristwatch.

I remain in my bunk. The borderline between waking and sleeping dissolves again. A dull booming echoes somewhere in my mind. Instead of getting up I try to take refuge in sleep, but the noise persists. Eyes closed, but awake, I listen. No doubt about it: depth charges. Trying to terrify us? Or are the Tommies harrying some other boat? But it must be broad daylight up there. No one would attempt a breakthrough in daylight. So? Are they on maneuvers? Keeping their men up to the mark?

I strain to hear, try to locate the rolling thunder. It's cascading all around us. Probably small units at work practicing encirclement. Now it's quiet again. I lean out of my bunk and stare into the control room.

The sound man reports propeller noises, several at once, from different directions. How can that be—the sound gear was supposed to be a wreck. Then I remember at one point that the Old Man had an earphone pressed to his head as I was squeezing past. So the sound gear is functioning again: We've got to the point where we can pick up acoustical information about the enemy. Is that some kind of an advantage?

The oil leak! The current must have carried it so far away that nobody up there can work out where it came from. Probably—cross fingers—there was one great bubble, and that was that. Luckily, oil doesn't float forever like cork. It emulsifies and gradually disappears. Viscosity—isn't that what they call it? Another word to add to my collection of spells and incantations.

"We must be lying in a good spot," I hear the Old Man say in the control room. Well, that's one way of looking at it: thank our lucky stars that we're jammed in the rocks; because they've saved us from the Asdic.

"Goddammit, if that noise doesn't stop, it'll drive me crazy!" Zeitler suddenly bursts out. Against orders: Zeitler's supposed to keep his pig's snout in his mouth and be quiet. Let's hope the Old Man didn't hear him.

Zeitler's left arm is hanging out of the bunk over there. If I squint hard, I can make out his wristwatch. 18.00 hours. No later? Losing my watch was a bad omen. Must simply have fallen off my wrist. Perhaps it's ticking away somewhere in the bilge. After all, it's *antimagnetic, waterproof, shockproof, stainless, made in Switzerland.*

The nose clip is hurting so much that I have to loosen it for a moment.

Christ, how it stinks! That's the gas from the battery! No, not just the gas. It stinks of shit and urine, too—as if someone had had the trots in here. Did someone's sphincter go while he was asleep? Or is there a piss bucket standing around somewhere?

Piss: immediately I feel the desperate pressure in my own bladder. The urge subsides, only to be succeeded by ominous stomach cramps. I squeeze my thighs together. What if we all get the trots? The can is unusable at these depths—no good trying to expel the stuff with compressed air. The stench is becoming almost unbearable.

Better to put the clip back on my nose and breathe through the rattling cartridge! Lucky that nature gave us a choice: nose or mouth. I can simply opt for breathing by the second method; mercifully there are no olfactory nerves in my jaws. The Lord of Heaven and Earth had more foresight in kneading his clay than the designers of our scow did.

I can certainly hold out for a while longer. Stay flat, don't move, relax your belly muscles, think of something else. Anything but piss and shit.

In the whorehouse in Brest the smell was awful: sweat, perfume, sperm, piss, and Lysol—a stomach-churning mixture—the smell of lust gone rotten. *Eau de Javel*, they called the disinfectant, and no perfume, however sweet, could prevail against it. Nose clips would have been in order in that place too.

Rue d'Aboukir! When a big ship put in, the whores simply stayed on their backs between tricks. No more squatting on the bidet, panties on, being seductive, then panties off again: wornout cylinders of flesh with five dozen different pistons working up and down in them day after day.

I can see the steep alley: leprous, crumbling walls, charred timbers thrust into the air. A dead dog flattened on the broken pavement. Disgusting. A whole swarm of blowflies swirling up from the squeezed-out entrails. Fragments of tarboard. Bizarre wreckage of tile roofs like huge pieces of layered nougat. Every single garbage can overturned. Rats in broad daylight. Every other house damaged by bombs; even the ones partially intact are abandoned. Wooden window shutters piled up like barricades. There's barely a footpath between the ruins and the garbage.

Beside a wall, two sealords leaning against each other, face to face. "Come on, man, I'll pay for your fuck. You need it."

They're lined up at the bottom of the alley in front of the sanitation room. Two rows of stiff cocks. Everyone has to go through. From time to time the fat orderly shouts out of the door, "Next five . . . and get your rocks off fast! You've each got five minutes—and that's it!"

Idiotic grins. The bluejackets all have one hand in their trouser pockets holding their balls or their cocks. And they almost all have a cigarette in the other: nerves.

A miserable shed. All gray and shabby. Only the sanitation room is painted white. The rest's like greasy oil—light rancid yellow. Smell of semen and sweat. There's no bar. Not even the most primitive decoration.

The madam on her wooden throne has an obscene pug dog pressed against her bosom, right in the middle of the cleavage between her two massive tits. "Really looks like a fat ass," somebody remarks. "Boy, would I like to fuck her there!"

The old harridan produces the bits of German she's picked up. "No time. Move, move, don't break anything!"

Above her throne hangs a sign with a brightly colored rooster and the legend: "Quand ce coq chantera, crédit on donnera."

While each man is paying her, she tries to sell him one of her well-worn collection of photographs. Someone objects. "Auntie, nobody needs instructions. I'm ready to shoot as it is. They'll be humping today till nothing comes out but blue air."

Mattress squeaking through the stained wall.

A shrill nagging voice. "Come on, sweetheart, put the money right there."

And I was so stunned that she spoke German!

"Don't look so dumb! *Fais vite!* Sure, you're surprised!—I happen to come from Alsace! No—no—d'you think I want to be fired? Everyone has to pay in advance here, so let's see your money, darling. Paying is always worse when you have to do it afterward. Come on—and put a little extra for Lily on top—you're going to like her. Have you got another fifty? If you do, there're some pictures I could show you—" And from next door: "Come in, sweetie. God, talk about baby-snatching." Are they all from Alsace? "Does your kindergarten have the day off today? That all you can manage? No—keep your trousers on. And hurry up!"

At the bottom of the couch a strip of shabby oilcloth to go under your shoes: taking them off here is considered a waste of time.

"Man, that was quick. Well, that's that."

Behind a screen I hear her pissing in a chamber pot. No niceties.

Pale thighs. Wet pubic hair. Sickly face streaked with powder. Yellow teeth, one or two rotting and black. Breath reeking of Cognac. Red gash of mouth. Whitish intestinal ropes of used condoms tangled up in the wastebasket beside the bidet.

Cursing in the corridor. "Money back—too much beer—I can never get it up."

Downstairs a man is protesting against the injection.

"Then you won't get your paybook back!"

"Listen, I didn't go bareback!"

"Shut up. Everyone gets a shot here."

"I guess you get a free fuck, don't you?"

"Just be careful, man!"

"Oh kiss my ass!"

What a job! Injecting cocks all day long!

"There, you're done. Here's your paybook back. Double precaution: a rubber *and* a shot. They're real sticklers for etiquette in the Navy!"

The pressure in my bladder is driving me mad. Didn't the bosun set out buckets in the control room with a can of calcium chloride beside them? I struggle up and manage to get there, stiff-legged. Afterward, the Chief appears. Breathing heavily, he sits down beside me and stays very still. Only his chest moves. He purses his lips and inhales, which produces a whistle. He jumps, startled by the sound.

I pluck the pig snout out of my mouth. "Chief, I still have some glucose tablets." The Chief jerks himself back into reality. "No thanks, but a mouthful of apple juice wouldn't be bad."

I push myself up quickly, work my way through the hatch, stagger to the locker, and reach for the bottle. The Chief puts it to his mouth with one hand but then has to use the other because the bottle is rattling against his teeth. He takes huge gulps. A trickle runs over his lower lip and is caught in his beard. He doesn't even wipe it off.

Shall I ask him how things stand? Better not. From the way he looks, it might be the last straw.

In the petty officers' compartment the curtains of the bunks on the port side are open but the bunks aren't empty. Their occupants look like corpses laid out in their coffins. Zeitler, Ullmann, the Berliner, and Wichmann. Only the pig snouts don't belong.

The bunks of the engine-room crew are empty. So the diesel mates and the motor mates are still aft. I stretch out on the nearest lower bunk.

The First Watch Officer appears. Looking officiously concerned, he makes sure that everyone still has his snorkel in his mouth. As I stare after him I realize that I'm drifting off to sleep again.

When I come to, I recognize Frenssen. The way he looks, sitting there at the table, completely exhausted, goes straight to my heart. He has no snorkel. Of course—the men who have to work in the engine room can't wear this damnfool contraption. I make a noise rolling over, and Frenssen slowly turns his head. He stares at me blankly. His spine no longer seems able to support the weight of his torso. Instead of propping himself up on the table, he lets his shoulders sag and his arms dangle between his knees as though they had no joints but hung on strings, like primitive marionettes. He seems to be doubly prone to normal gravity. His mouth is open; his glassy stare is terrifying. God, he's going off the rails! Who knows how the others are holding out in this fetid air if Frenssen can no longer carry on. This bull of a man—and he's as weak as a fly.

Fly? Where's our fly?

The thought of an underwater Christmas returns. If the men aft don't get finished, we'll still be sitting here on Christmas Eve. There'll be an exchange of gifts. I'll catch the fly as my present to the Old Man. Put it in an empty match box, one with a pretty Spanish label, which the Old Man can hold against his ear, so that if the fly is buzzing, he can imagine that the motors are running again. Brilliant! And we'll make the Chief close his eyes and listen to the little box too. And if the Old Man agrees, it can even go the rounds and they can all listen to it for a whole minute—God's gift to our ears in all this silence, another blessing to celebrate along with the birth of our Lord.

I feel wretched, exhausted. I'd love to tell Frenssen, "I'll just see where the tea is," or some such nonsense, but with the snorkel I can't. He doesn't move an inch.

The tea! The pot must be in the control room; I must have seen it while I was in there.

I get up painfully. Frenssen hardly raises his eyes. In the control room the floor plates are still covered with water, so our worst problem hasn't been cleared up. No doubt the Chief will get around to it. He has his plan, of course, but the sight of this flood, and my boots splashing in it, fills me with horror just the same.

The tea: I look around, but the pot's nowhere to be seen. I do know where the apple juice is, however. I clamber through the hatch and shuffle to the locker, get a bottle out, tear off its top on a hinge, and bring it to Frennsen. Dear god, it takes him long enough to realize that it's for him. He could have spared himself the look of dog-like gratitude—after all, I'm not the Old Man.

Nothing more to do but go on sitting here conjuring up pictures.

Glückstadt comes to mind. That helps: immediately I turn bitter. The humiliations! Glückstadt—Happy City. The name itself was pure mockery. That's the way it always went: barracks, barrack rooms, barracks again. First fatigue duty and then the naval Mickey Mouse. Glückstadt was the worst—*nomen est omen*—a superstition.

The Greasy Spoon restaurant in town!—it had a different name, of course—where we spent our evenings eating fried potatoes by the plateful because we didn't get enough at camp. Three of us had to report because the owner heard about our name for his wretched dump. Confined to barracks; assigned to eternal Mickey Mouse—the main thing was to yell at the top of your voice. My specialty: leading a detachment into open country, and telling the men to disappear into the dugouts for a quick game of cards while I stood around roaring orders over the landscape like a maniac. I enjoyed that—and everyone else did too.

I see myself in the cutter, at the end of my strength, clinging to my oar and almost tumbling from the thwart. The mean, coarse faces of the mates, who made a kind of game out of pursuing, harassing, and bullying us new recruits. I see now.what they did to Flemming, poor, pathetic, nervous Flemming, who was handed over helpless to a collection of sadists in uniform. Into fatigues, out of fatigues! Rigging gear on, rigging gear off. Dress uniform on, dress uniform off, sports outfit on, sports outfit off. "Move it, move it, you shitheads!"

Five minutes later: locker inspection.

Poor Flemming never caught up. He began to have the wild look of a trapped rat. And if the bastards noticed someone who couldn't defend himself, they really went to town. On the double, three times around the barracks, once around crawling. A hundred yards' rabbit hop. Twenty push-ups. Up and over the walls on the assault course.

And then the special treats for all of us: to pull the cutter at full speed into the slime and then work it loose again, float it free—but only by hauling on the oars, pulling in rhythm on them for hours at a time until there was clear water under the cutter.

Poor Flemming didn't, couldn't, hold out.

One evening he was missing at roll call.

The mutilated corpse was washed up in the harbor, among the old fenders, bottles, pieces of wood, and puddles of lubricating oil.

It was a straight case of murder. Systematically harassed to death. He'd drowned himself in desperation, even though he could swim. His corpse wasn't a pretty sight: It had got caught in the propellers of a steamer. I had to go to Hamburg to the hearing. Now that it's gone this far, I thought to myself, the shit will really hit the fan. But what happened? His dear relatives, fine Hamburg ship-owners, found the idea of suicide unpalatable. So they stuck to the Navy version: accidental death in the course of duty! For Volk, Führer, and Vaterland. In loyal performance of his duty. Apparently they couldn't bear to forego the three salvos over the grave, so we fired our rifles over Flemming's hole in the ground. Salute—raise rifles—fire. And then again. And again. No one was even allowed to smile.

And then in France: the way I wrenched the pistol away from Obermeier, the radio announcer, when he was going to shoot himself on the beach in front of our requisitioned villa. What a farce, just because he'd had an affair in Paris with a lady who turned out to be half Jewish. Asshole Obermeier behaving like a madman, roaring, "I am a National Socialist! Give me my pistol, give me my pistol back!" It wouldn't have taken much for me to do him the favor.

I begin to choke. My mouth is swollen full; it tastes as bitter as gall. I can't stand the snorkel any longer. My mouth ejects it almost involuntarily. Saliva dribbles onto my shirt. I study it intently. I need a drink. Frenssen won't hold it against me if I reach for his bottle.

What the hell's that? My wristwatch lying on the table! Who put it there? I reach for it, feel as if my Christmas has come early. The sweep second hand is still hurrying around the dial. A good watch. It says a little after 20.00.

Which means we've already been down here almost twenty-four hours. The Commander wanted to try surfacing when it got dark. 20.00—then it must have been pitch black up there for a long time. At this time of year. But why did the Commander ask the navigator when the moon set? I'm not mixing this up. The Old Man asked twice, after all—just a couple of hours ago. But wasn't there a new moon a short time ago? That means almost no light at all, let alone setting. So what? The usual dilemma: no one to ask —neither the Old Man nor the navigator. Apparently it will only be really dark somewhere around four a.m.

That would mean the whole night to go. Another *whole* night— unendurable. The oxygen won't last that long. And what about the potash cartridges?

Restlessness forces me to move. I head for the Officers' Mess in a trance. My place on the Chief's bunk is unoccupied. The Second Watch Officer has disappeared. This day seems to have lasted a hundred hours already.

I don't know how long I've been dozing in the corner of the bunk when I wake up and recognize the Old Man in the gangway to the Officers' Mess. He's supporting himself with both hands as though we were in a surface vessel in a heavy sea. He must have come out of his cubbyhole. Feebly he lets himself onto the Chief's bunk beside me. He looks gray and exhausted, seems completely unaware of me, absentminded. For a good five minutes he doesn't utter a syllable. Then I hear him mutter, "I'm sorry."

I sit there as if turned to stone. "I'm sorry." The words echo in my head.

Two words, and the Commander has stamped out all hope. The renewed clutch of fear. No hope. That's what it must mean. Dream exploded. A few more charades, some stiff upper lip . . . and that's it. The whole exercise, all our efforts—nothing but bullshit. I knew it: We'll be stuck here till Judgment Day.

We might still have had a chance to swim for it. Overboard as soon as we surfaced. But now—what now? Slowly fall asleep as the oxygen gives out?

I take the snorkel out of my mouth although I don't want to talk. My hands do it automatically. Intelligent hands that say to them- selves: What's the point? Why this snorkeling if there's no chance left? Threads of saliva drip from my mouth, grow longer and longer. Like trumpeters emptying their U-shaped mouthpieces.

I turn to look directly at the Old Man. His face is a lifeless mask. I have a feeling that I could peel the mask away, but then I know for certain that I would have to look at raw flesh and sinews, like a picture from an anatomy book: spherical eyeballs, bluish-white; branching fibers; narrow tubes and veins; bands of muscle.

Have the Old Man's exertions finally done him in? It can't possibly be true! "I'm sorry." He can't have meant it seriously.

He doesn't move an inch. I can't catch his eye because he's staring down at the floor in front of him.

Fear of the emptiness in my head. I don't dare go to pieces now. Mustn't let myself go. Keep an eye on myself and don't let the Old Man out of my sight.

No doubt about it: He's all in. Why else would he say something like that?

Perhaps everything is starting to work for us, only the Old Man doesn't realize it. What can I do? Tell him that everything will still turn out all right? That when the need is greatest, the Lord is nigh?

Revolt. No! His two-word judgment can't take away my secret knowledge that I'm going to escape. Nothing can happen to *me. I* am taboo. Through me the whole boat is immune.

But doubt sets in again. I'd realized it before—only not admitted it: It's dark up there, has been for hours, and we were going to surface at dark. So we should have tried *long ago.* All that talk about the moon—nothing but pretext.

The Old Man continues to sit there motionless as though all the life had drained out of him. Not even the blink of an eye. I've never seen him this way before . . .

I try to shake off the stranglehold, try to swallow, try to choke down my fear.

A tapping sound.

I stare into the aisle. There stands the Chief, supporting himself left and right against the walls the way the Old Man just did. I try to read his face. But he's standing in semi-darkness, and his face remains a blur.

Why won't he come into the lamplight? Has everyone here gone mad? Why doesn't he sit down with us at the table? Surely not because his shirt is torn? Because his arms are smeared all the way up with filth?

His mouth is open. Probably wants to make a report. Waiting

for the Old Man to look up. Finally he moves his lips and takes his hands cautiously away from the walls. Must want his gestures to underline what he has to say. But the Old Man keeps his head down. Probably hasn't noticed him standing six feet away in the gangway.

I'm about to give him a push to bring him out of his trance, when the Chief clears his throat and the Old Man lifts his eyes irritably. Instantly the Chief is talking. "Respectfully report to Herr Kaleun —E-motors ready—water taken aboard has been pumped into regulator cells—possible to expel it outboard with compressed air— compass system ready—echo sounder ready . . ."

The Chief falters. His voice is hoarse. From now on I hear nothing but an endless echo. "Ready . . . ready . . . ready . . ."

"Good, Chief. Good, good!" stutters the Old Man. "Just get some rest now!"

I stagger to my feet to make room for the Chief. But he stammers ". . . still some problems—still a couple—to clear up," and takes two steps backward before executing a kind of aboutface. He's going to fall over any minute. No longer has the strength of an insect. One puff, and you could blow him over.

The Old Man has his elbows braced on the table and half his lower lip is between his teeth. Why doesn't he say something?

Finally he lets go and blows out hard. "Good men—simply have to have—good men!"

He lays the palms of both hands on the table, shifts his weight forward, and pushes himself heavily to his feet, then squeezes his way slowly past, hitches his belt up in the gangway, and sets off toward the stern wobbling like a drunk.

I sit there stunned, holding my mouthpiece in my lap with both hands. Did I just dream all that? But the Old Man really has vanished. Where to? He was sitting here just a moment ago . . . "I'm sorry." And then ". . . ready . . . ready . . . ready!"

Where is everyone? I'm about to shout when I hear voices from the control room. ". . . going to try! . . . have to see if it'll work!"— "When d'you think you'll be more or less ready?" That's the Old Man's voice. And it's sounding urgent. "Haven't much time left."

My head's spinning again. What am I doing still sitting around here? I replace my rubber mouthpiece. I'm wobbly too: I can hardly get to my feet. At each step it feels as if someone's hitting me in the back of the knees.

In the control room, the Old Man, the Chief, and the navigator, all with their heads together. A tight little group around the chart table.

The usual mocking voice starts whispering in my ear: here we go again, stretching out the action, spinning out the scene, milking it for everything it's got—a real crowd pleaser—the group of conspirators and their muffled whispers—always works.

Then I notice: no more water in the control room. Dry feet. Missed it before. Blackouts. Am I actually in my right mind now?

I hear the Old Man ask in a hushed voice, "What's it like up there now, navigator?"

"Been dark for some hours, Herr Kaleun!"

The Old Man obviously has himself under control again. And the navigator knew the answer. Nothing confuses him, he's right on the ball.

The control-room mate is fiddling about among the flooding and bailing distributors. I can see that he's straining to hear. He can't catch complete sentences either, but such fragments as we manage to pick up are sufficient tidings of salvation. I'm just surprised that I don't go to pieces and fall flat on my face.

"The one chance—all right!" mutters the Old Man. Then he looks at his watch, pauses, and his voice is steady. "In ten minutes we take her up!" It comes out like any casual announcement.

"We take her up." The four words repeat themselves in my brain like a mantra. I take the rubber mouthpiece out of my mouth again. The thread of saliva breaks and then forms again.

"I'm sorry" . . . "We take her up"!—it's enough to drive you mad.

I climb back into the Officers' Mess. The Second Watch Officer is lying in his bunk.

"Hey, Second Watch Officer!" I don't recognize my own voice. Somewhere between a croak and a sob.

He barely moves.

I try a second time. "Hey!" This time it sounds a bit better.

He feels with both hands for the tube of his mouthpiece, clasps it like a baby with its bottle. He obviously doesn't want to wake up. Doesn't want to lose the safety of sleep, wants to hold on to this barrier between him and insanity. I have to seize him by the arm and shake him. "Hey, buddy, wake up!"

His eyes open for a second, but he still refuses to be wakened. He tries to get away from me, to retreat into unconsciousness.

"We surface in ten minutes!" I whisper close to his face.

He blinks distrustfully but takes the snorkel out of his mouth.

"What?" he asks, bewildered.

"We're going to surface!"

"What did you say?"

"Yes, in ten minutes!"

"Honest?"

"Yes, the Commander . . ."

He doesn't leap to his feet. Not even a look of joy on his face. He simply leans back and closes his eyes again for a moment—but now he's smiling. He looks like someone who knows that a surprise party is being arranged for him—and who wasn't supposed to have found out about it yet.

xi RETURN VOYAGE

"PREPARE TO SURFACE!"

The order echoes through the boat.

The Commander: "First Watch Officer and navigator after me to the bridge!"

In the control room the First Watch Officer and the navigator pick out their oilskins, climb into their trousers, staggering as though we were rocking in a heavy sea, and pull their stiff jackets over their heads. They avoid looking at each other. Set faces, like hairdressers' dummies. The navigator seems to be demonstrating an exercise: He puts his sou'wester on very slowly—like a drillmaster, taking his time. He fastens the strings under his chin with deliberate care.

I realize for the first time what it is that I'm breathing—a stinking vapor suspended in dense layers throughout the boat, sour and suffocating. My lungs heave as they try to filter enough oxygen out of it.

Will the boat really come clear? And if she does, what then?

In answer to this unspoken question, the Old Man orders: "Prepare escape gear!"

So that's the idea: up, overboard, and swim for it. In the dark? In that racing current?

My film! I hurry to my bunk. Everything's lying ready, the escape gear and the film wrapped in a waterproof package, arranged so that I can hang it around my neck.

There's also a more deep-seated fear in me—worse than that of the darkness and the current—enemy fire. If the fingering search-light from one of their corvettes finds us, we might as well be lying center stage with all the lights up. Then more searchlights will be added, and the heavens will be festooned with star shells. Goddam Christmas trees! And then the machine guns will cut loose.

But of course we might be lucky. The craziest things happen: Perhaps they won't find us right away. But if we're in the water and they miss us at *that* point, we'll be swept away anyhow.

Distress lights! *We* have no distress blinkers. The Tommies are better equipped; they're all prepared to go overboard. But a situation like ours had no place in our leaders' calculations. The escape gear's our only equipment for disaster at sea.

I'm not very good at putting mine on. No practice. Never thought I'd have to use the thing. Frenssen helps me. Tentatively I insert the mouthpiece. Another snorkel. No end to them. Cautiously I turn on the oxygen tank and hear it hiss. Good: seems to be working.

Suddenly there is whispering and movement all around, and the terror subsides.

Everyone's wearing his escape gear, fumbling around with it, pretending to be frantically busy, just to keep from having to look up.

I catch the Second Watch Officer's eye. Trying to look calm but not succeeding. He makes a face to conceal his emotion.

The razor's edge: The Chief will release the compressed air, and we'll discover whether blowing the regulator cells and filling the buoyancy cells will provide enough lift to free us from the bottom. We still don't know whether the exhaust valves of the buoyancy tanks will remain airtight. We have only one shot at it. There will be no second chance.

In a clear voice the Commander orders: "Blow!" The control-room mate turns his valves. The compressed air hisses into the tanks. Will it force the water out? We stand there rigid, listening. Is the boat moving?

I flex my knees so that I can detect the slightest motion.

Nothing! Held fast. Heavy as lead!

The compressed air blows and blows.

Nothing!

Abandon hope, all ye who . . . the whole thing's been in vain! My legs start to wobble . . .

But. The boat definitely moved! And now there's a scraping contact on the outside like the impact of Asdic beams. A screech, shrill as a knife on porcelain, runs through me to the bone, and the needle of the depth manometer trembles.

There's a clearly perceptible jerk and the boat frees itself from the bottom. It scrapes groaning along a reef. More screeching and yowling. And then—silence.

I'm choking with joy.

I hold fast to the tower hatch ladder, my eyes fixed on the needle. For god's sake, *keep on* wobbling. I hypnotize it. It jerks three or four marks backward. The boat is floating, rising—under its own momentum—like a free balloon. We're actually buoyant.

I stare over the Commander's shoulder at the manometer needle. As does everyone else. Very slowly it creeps back over the dial. No movement in the control room. Not a word.

The needle turns with agonizing slowness. I want to take my hand and push the thing backward, as if that could keep the boat rising.

"Eight hundred feet!" says the Chief, as if we didn't all know already.

"Seven twenty-five!—Six fifty!—Six hundred!"

Periscope observation is out. Both periscopes wrecked. So the Commander won't even be able to make sure whether it's all clear or not. I quickly push this thought aside and concentrate on the depth manometer again. The boat is slowly continuing to rise.

"Five hundred fifty!"

The Commander is already under the tower when the indicator reaches the four hundred mark.

The minutes stretch out like slack elastic.

We stand around stiffly. I don't even dare shift my weight from one foot to the other. With his escape gear on over his fur-lined vest, the Old Man looks like a freak.

When the needle reaches two hundred, he orders the lights in the control room shaded. All that's left is the pale twilight that comes in from both sides through the open hatches, hardly enough to enable us to distinguish silhouettes.

We rise as slowly as an elevator being cranked up by hand after a power failure. Now I do shift from foot to foot. Slowly, cautiously. So no one will notice.

The sound gear is in action: Herrmann. He must be getting a mass of bearings; he'll only report if something is quite close. But there's nothing. Apparently we're in luck.

"Seventy feet—fifty feet!"

The water in the Papenberg column is already sinking. The Commander clambers heavily up the ladder.

"Tower hatch free!" the Chief reports.

I swallow. There are tears in my eyes.

The boat begins to move, rocking gently back and forth. And

then a slapping noise: *Tschjwumm—tschjwumm!* A wave hitting the side.

Now everything speeds up, as usual. The Chief reports, "Boat's clear!" And the Old Man shouts down, "Equalize pressure!"

A sharp bang. The tower hatch has sprung open. So the equalization was not complete. The air falls down on us in a solid mass. My lungs fill painfully, then they stop—the oxygen is too rich for them. I stagger. The pain literally forces me to my knees.

For god's sake, what's going on up there? The glare of parachute flares? Has the Old Man seen something? Why no orders?

The boat rocks gently back and forth. I hear the splashing of small waves. The boat resounds like a gong.

Finally the Old Man's bass voice. "Prepare to blow!"

Still darkness in the circle of the hatch. "Stand by to ventilate!" And then, "Diesel room, remain ready to dive!"

Diesel room ready to dive? But this gulp of air belongs to me. And this one too. Wet, dark, night air! I expand my ribcage, breathe my fill.

Again the splashing of the waves: *a Kyrie eleison.* I could hug the Chief.

Then from above, "Ready with the diesel!" I pass on the order, shouting louder than I have to.

The call goes from mouth to mouth to the engine room. The escape gas doors for the working diesel, the compressed-air cylinders, the test valves are now being opened; they're finding out whether the diesel has taken water, and putting it in gear on the driving shaft.

The engine room reports ready—and it's the Old Man again. "Port diesel half speed ahead!" The helmsman in the tower echoes the command; I shout it toward the stern.

The blowers snarl. The first shaking pulse runs through our frame.

The diesel sucks fresh air down into the boat in great waves. All the doors stand open so that it can reach into every corner.

The noise envelops me. I want to block my ears. They must be able to hear us from Africa to Spain. And the whole area must be crawling with lookouts. But what's the Old Man to do? We have no choice. We can't tiptoe.

If only I knew what it looked like up there!

The Old Man orders the navigator to the bridge. The First Watch Officer is beside me, also staring upward. He's holding onto a rung of the ladder with his right hand, I with my left. My mirror image.

Three, four orders to the helmsman in quick succession—then

a counter-order. "Belay hard a-port! Continue to steer two hundred fifty degrees!"

The helmsman no longer acknowledges the orders properly; he's getting muddled. But there's no rebuke.

"Well, well, well!" is all I hear from the Commander; the last "well" long drawn out. Not exactly a superfluity of information, but enough to tell us that we've just missed hitting something.

Clench your teeth. Hope the Old Man knows what he's doing. He's had practice, after all: mocking the enemy, flitting about right under their noses, showing them our narrow silhouette, always staying against a dark background, always according to the rules of the game.

The First Watch Officer sniffs hard, then breathes through his wide-open mouth. He might at least say something. Following *his* rules we'd have been up the creek. What the Old Man's doing isn't something you learn in training courses. He got us in this far on our quiet motors; now he has to use one racketing diesel and sneak us out again. The breakthrough into the Mediterranean has failed.

I seem to be sniffling too. We've all caught cold a little. I put my left foot on the lowest rung, using it like a bar rail. The First Watch Officer does the same with his right.

Once more the navigator's voice is too low. I can't catch more than half his reports. "Object . . . degrees!—object bearing thirty— edging our way—"

"Seems to be as much traffic here as on the Wannsee," from behind me. The Second Watch Officer! Our baby! He can play as tough as he likes, but he can't fool me. I'll always see him crouched in the corner of the bunk: out for the count, the straw dog in his arms.

He's moved very close: I can hear him breathing.

A crowd seems to be collecting in the control room. Understandable that the off-duty watch no longer feels like staying in their quarters. Too remote. Everyone who can find an excuse to be close to the tower is here. Fortunately no one notices them in the darkness. Despite the roar of the diesel I can clearly hear the hissing of compressed air from one of the little steel cylinders in the escape gear— and another one. Two men at least are now in position to go overboard.

My heart beats in my throat. Supposing they spot us—we can't dive.

A bewildering series of orders to the helmsman: "Port—starboard —midships—as she goes—hard a-port—" The Old Man's making the boat weave along like a snake.

I can't believe that we're still undetected—that the Tommies haven't raised a general alarm, that we're not being attacked on all sides by everything they've got. Someone *must* have heard us or seen us. They can't *all* be asleep. Or can the noise of the diesel actually be protecting us? Do the men on lookout take us for a British boat? But Tommy boats have different towers. Yes, I tell myself, that may be true, seen from the side, but from the front with a small silhouette, there certainly can't be much difference.

Again the short sharp hiss of an oxygen tank in the safety gear. If only we don't have to go overboard . . .

And if there's another airplane?

But that, after all, was no routine flight. We'd been reported. They could figure our course by dead reckoning and be ready at the right time. But nothing has been reported today. So the planes will remain grounded.

The Second Watch Officer clears his throat. His voice is squeaky. "First we have to get far enough westward, I imagine."

The Old Man is silent for a good five minutes. I visualize the chart: Yes, make a large arc toward the west in order to avoid the traffic around Cape Saint Vincent.

If only I were allowed onto the bridge! TO SEE!

The sky seems to sympathize: The cloud cover opens and a few stars appear. They move in the circle of the hatch from right to left, left to right. I wonder what their names are. The navigator would know. But he's above.

"Port twenty—new course two hundred seventy degrees!"

A minute, then the helmsman reports, "Two hundred seventy degrees it is."

"Ship's time?" the Commander calls down.

"21.30 hours!" the helmsman answers from the tower.

So, about an hour since we surfaced. What speed can we make on one diesel?

I don't even know exactly how fast it's running. With two diesels I would be able to tell from the sound. But I've had no practice deducing our speed from just one. And we're charging with the dynamo as we run. We need all the power we can get. With any luck, our remaining battery cells will store enough to get us through tomorrow. It's obvious, without anyone actually having to say it, that we'll have to give up running on the surface by first light. The Chief will have to keep us going at periscope depth, and hope for the best.

Finally a few fragments from above. ". . . well-l-l, navigator, he's going away. I'm sure of it. Just keep an eye on that approaching vessel. Way off—but nasty just the same."

After five minutes the Commander asks, "What's our course?"

"Two hundred seventy degrees!"

"Steady as she goes!"

"How many miles will we make before it gets light?" I ask the First Watch Officer.

He snorts. "Maybe twenty."

"Running quite well."

"Yes, seems to be."

I feel a hand on my upper arm, and jump.

"How does it look now?" asks the Chief.

"Someday I'll grab you in the dark too!" I blurt out. "Satisfactory is the way it looks—as far as I can tell."

"Pardon me, your worship!" says the Chief.

"And how are things with you, Chief?"

"Thanks for asking. *Comme ci, comme ça!*"

"An exhaustive report!"

"Just wanted to get a bit of air," he explains and disappears again.

"Seems we're not welcome with the Macaronis," I hear behind me. That must have been Isenberg. He's right: La Spezia! I'd forgotten all about our intention to go there. The beautiful blue Mediterranean. Now Rommel will have to figure out a way of getting his supplies across without us. After all, we're an Atlantic boat. It's up to the Italians to look out for Mediterranean convoys.

Are we the only boat? Or were there others they were trying to flog through?

If we succeed in getting far enough west—what then? One day underwater, at periscope depth, is all very well. But after that? We can't dive. The boat won't stand more than periscope depth. Is our transmitter working? There's been no talk of signaling. How many miles to the next French port? Or will the Old Man park our demolished scow at Vigo again and route-march us home through Spain—the whole crew this time?

If the weather gets worse, how are we going to get through Biscay? As it is, daylight travel is out of the question. We can no longer elude an airplane, and Biscay is teeming with them. Proceed at night and remain submerged by day? Granted, the nights are long, but will it work?

"Hold it . . . steady as she goes!" I hear from above.

The Old Man has changed course. He's heading farther south. The old game: he thinks the Tommies think—may think—that if more boats try to break through, they'll do it by the shortest route. Which is to say that if they're coming from the north or mid-Atlantic they won't go below thirty-six degrees. So we should stay south of thirty-six degrees. For the time being, that is.

If I've got it right, we must be in the neighborhood of Cape Spartel again. Or else farther west, but at the same latitude. The navigator hasn't time for his dead reckoning right now, and there's no one to take his place. So there'll be a pretty big hiatus on his course chart.

I notice that both Watch Officers have disappeared. I can hardly stay on my feet either. Fewer orders to the helmsman. So we must have got through the circle of patrols unscathed.

"Permission to come on the bridge?" I ask.

"*Jawohl*," from the Old Man.

I can hardly move a muscle. Been standing so long. Painfully I climb past the helmsman—the Berliner. Wind strikes me in the face before I can look over the bulwark.

"Well-l-l?" the Old Man asks in a drawl.

I can't say a word. Peer around—no shadows—nothing. There— on the port side a string of lights: nine or ten. What can that be? The African coast? Hard to believe!

I push myself up and take a look at the foreship. It shimmers in the pale moonlight. The upper deck looks so empty. Despite the darkness I can see that the gratings have been ripped apart in some bizarre fashion. Of the cannon nothing remains but the mounting. How must the forward side of our tower look? The fairing has certainly been torn to bits.

The Old Man, standing beside me, says, "Rather impressive, isn't it?"

"I'm sorry?"

"Impressive—all that." His voice subsides into a murmur. All I can hear is, "Jesus and his flock . . . sheep may safely graze."

The navigator interrupts. "Thought *He* was always with the Tommies—*they're* the ones with the whiskey."

Bad jokes! At a time like this!

More lights. The Old Man gives orders. We weave to and fro while maintaining a generally westerly course. First, just get away. Put space between us and them.

"How long can we keep it up, navigator?"

"A good hour still, Herr Kaleun!"

All I want to do is stand here and breathe easily, listen to the beating of my heart, let my eyes roam over the horizon, hear the hissing of the bow wave. I receive a dash of spray and taste it on my tongue: salty. Seeing, tasting, hearing, smelling the night air.

Feeling the motion of the boat. Responding with all my senses—I am alive!

I tip my head back. Here and there a few stars. Torn cloud cover that barely moves and shades the sickle moon. For us, resurrection has dawned—except that it was by night, and nobody else is even aware of it. In Kernével we count as sunk. The Tommies will have certainly reported that much promptly. *They* can use their radio as much as they like. We can't. Admittedly someone said that our transmitter might work, but we have to be very careful not to call attention to ourselves. The Tommies are too much on the alert; they can get bearings from even the briefest radio messages.

"All right then," mutters the Old Man. "Another hour and we'll pack it up! I think we can let the watch come on deck—eh, navigator?"

"Think so, Herr Kaleun!"

"Second watch, stand by!" the Commander calls below. "Well," he says to me.

"I can't understand it!"

"What can't you understand?"

"That they're letting us ramble around this way."

"Nor can I," the Old Man says dryly. "But it's typical of them. My old rule is: Keep going! This would never have happened with *me*."

"What wouldn't?"

"*We* wouldn't—be sailing around again, that is! Don't stop till the Commander's cap floats up—old rule."

My jaws drop open in sheer amazement. Professional criticism of enemy technique. If the Tommies had done things the Old Man's way, we'd have been totally wiped out by now.

"You ought to hit the sack for a while," he says. He sounds slurred, like one drunk giving another drunk advice, convinced that he's sober.

"I'm all right for a while," I say casually, but when I hear that the second watch is ready, I report down from the bridge all the same.

The stinking buckets have disappeared. The calcium chloride too. Situation normal. The ventilators are humming. Everything cleaned up. For a wonder, stateroom H is free.

All's quiet in the petty officers' compartment. Three curtains drawn. I clamber into my bunk just as I am, fully dressed, and push the escape gear to the foot of the bunk without repacking it. Now the potash cartridge and its pig snout are in my way. Where will it go? Overboard, preferably! I never want to see this aluminum box again. Where have the others stowed theirs? Up on edge against the wall. Yes, that works.

Explosions in my dreams. "What's that?" I stammer, pushing aside the curtain. Another three, four dull, echoing booms.

Someone is sitting at the table. He turns his face toward me. I blink and recognize the diesel mate Kleinschmidt.

"They're after someone!"

"Fucking bastards!"

"They can't be after us—it's been going on for half an hour!"

"How late is it now?"

"11.30 hours!"

"What's that? What did you say?"

"11.30 hours—right on the nose!"

With a twisting motion Kleinschmidt raises his right arm, so that I can see his watch.

Then I notice that I have my own watch again.

Chasing someone! But it must be daylight up there. 11.30— that's a.m. Can't rely on my feeling for time. I'm completely confused. Surely no one would try to get through during the day?

Another series of detonations! "Scare bombs perhaps," I say to Kleinschmidt. "I wish they'd be good enough to stop; it's driving me crazy!"

I push myself up, roll over the guardrail, and head for the control room to find out what's happening.

The control-room mate has taken over the job of keeping count of the depth charges, because the navigator's asleep.

"Thirty-three, thirty-four, thirty-five, thirty-six, thirty-eight."

The last two were simultaneous.

The First Watch Officer is there too. Sitting on the chart chest listening intently. In a drill-monkey jacket. Where in the world did he get that? It's not what we're used to seeing on him. His beard is still sprouting too. The light from the chart table makes deep shadowy hollows out of his eyes—a death's head. To complete the image, all he'd have to do is bare his teeth.

"Forty, forty-two, forty-four—that does it!"

"How far off?"

"Way off," says the control-room mate.

"At least fifteen miles," says the First Watch Officer.

"Thank you so much!"

The fact that the Commander is not in the control room makes me uneasy. And the Chief? Is he in the engine room? Or is he finally asleep? The two hydroplane operators perch motionless in front of their control buttons. Indifferent, as though they'd long since gone to sleep.

A whole series of detonations in a single grumbling drone.

"Way off!" I hear the Commander growl behind me. Wearing nothing but shirt and trousers. His face is twisted in professional disapproval. Behind him I see the navigator. And now the Chief.

"Shit!" mutters the Chief in every pause between bombs. "Shit —shit—shit!" Like a defiant child.

Have they by any chance been working over our oil slick? The bombs could hardly be intended for another boat. After all, it's broad daylight!

"Coming nearer," says the navigator.

That's all we need! The rudder motor is making much too much noise. Everything in this boat is too loud.

The Old Man dismisses this with a flick of his hand. "Foolishness!"

Just then the rumbling suddenly stops. You'd think the Old Man's hand had put an end to it.

"Probably unloading their surplus!" he says bitingly. "Had to get rid of them! So they're littering."

He disappears again.

I take a look at the chart. Amazing—the navigator has patched the hole in our course. It wouldn't surprise me if the ship's position, which was entered at 06.00, had been derived from astronomical observation. If I know him, he took a few quick shots at the stars before he left the bridge.

On the chart, everything looks quite simple. We've certainly performed more complicated maneuvers before: This is a mere reverse tack. I see by the Papenberg that we're sixty feet down.

Herrmann's on duty in the sound room. He favors me with a blank, owlish stare. I almost say "Good morning" into his empty face. But it's already midday. And I mustn't disturb him. He's supposed to be listening in all directions at once. His two earphones have to take the place of four pairs of binoculars; his two eardrums, eight eyes.

What was it the control-room mate said? "Limping home on crutches—not exactly my line." Back from the Beresina on crutches. And the Lord smote them with men and with horses, and with chariots. Faith, hope, and charity, these three. But the greatest of these is hope.

The Commander has closed his curtain. I tiptoe past.

In the Officers' Mess the Second Watch Officer is flat out. But the Chief isn't in his bunk. If he hasn't slept at all yet, he must be about ready for the madhouse. Twelve hours ago he was already practically a dead man. And this is the time his wife is due. A pretty state of affairs: his wife in a clinic in Flensburg, and the Chief in the Atlantic surrounded by demolished machinery, sixty feet down and on the verge of madness.

I'm ready to drop dead of exhaustion again. No strength to drag myself back to the petty officers' compartment. Half conscious, I collapse in a corner of the Chief's bunk.

The steward wakes me. Apparently he's been trying for some time. I knew someone was shaking me, but let myself float back into unconsciousness time after time. His mouth is close to my face. "Five minutes to midnight, Herr Leutnant!"

I squeeze my eyelids together as tight as I can, then wrench them open.

"Yes?"

"Five minutes to midnight, Herr Leutnant!"

"Is there something to eat?"

"*Jawohl!*"

I can hear the Commander next door, talking to the sound man. He's rasping like a drunk. Now he comes in.

"Well!" is all he has to say, as usual.

Reddened eyes, twitching eyelids, sallow skin, glistening hair, dark glistening beard: He's obviously put his whole head under a faucet.

Finally he opens his mouth. "What's on the menu?"

"Roulade of beef with red cabbage," the steward replies.

Cookie—he's a fucking genius! I'd been counting on canned sausage at best, not a Sunday dinner.

"Hm," says the Old Man. He's leaned back and is blinking at the ceiling.

"Where's the Chief?" I ask.

"With his beloved engines; where else? He fell asleep squatting right there between the diesels. They stretched him out on a bunk mattress. He's to stay there for the time being."

Three steaming dishes appear on the table. The Old Man savors the delicious smells that come wafting toward him.

Three, four dull detonations. Is that bombing never going to stop?

The Commander makes a face. Gnaws at his lower lip. Two explosions later he says, "These fireworks are getting to be a bore! Anyone would think it was New Year's Eve already!"

He shuts his eyes and massages his face. It doesn't improve his color for long.

"And the Second Engineer?"

The Commander yawns. But this one has words to it. ". . . In the engine room too. Seems there are still some things to be patched up there."

He yawns again, leans back, and pats his gaping mouth with the back of his right hand, thereby transforming the yawn into a tremolo.

"He's had a proper training course. Now at least he knows what it's all about!" He spears a piece of roulade, bares his teeth, and bites on it cautiously: hot.

"Propeller noise bearing ninety degrees!" calls the sound man.

The Old Man is up at once and beside the sound room.

"Louder or weaker?" he asks impatiently.

"Constant! Turbine engines! Still rather weak—now they're getting louder."

The loop of the headset arches between their two heads like a bracket as the two men share the earphones. Not a word.

Slowly I turn to look at our table again. My half of a roulade lies between a small heap of red cabbage and a small heap of potatoes. All at once it seems ridiculous.

"Moving away!" That was the sound man.

Groans and the cracking of joints announce that the Old Man is getting to his feet again.

"They might at least let us eat in peace," he says as he pushes himself back behind the narrow end of the table.

He's hardly sat down when the sound man announces new noises. "One hundred seventy degrees!"

"Just when it was getting nice and quiet," says the Commander with reproach in his voice—and then, "We'll just wait a bit!"

He takes two or three bites. I decide to go on eating too—very cautiously—in case I make any unnecessary clatter with my knife and fork.

Here we are, trying to swallow good roulades while the Tommies are playing the acoustics game. It strikes the Old Man as sheer spitefulness. "Cold," he says disgustedly, as he bites on the next mouthful. Annoyed, he stares at his food for a few minutes longer, then pushes the plate away.

The exploding depth charges plus the closeness of the propeller noises are making him visibly nervous. Possibly the Tommies really *are* focusing on our oil slick? Is there any way we can *know* whether we're leaving a trail behind us?

A couple of hours more sleep, that's the thing! Bliss! Stretch out, curl your toes, and then straighten them out again. Given the mess we're in, that amounts to pure happiness. I shudder at the thought that we'd have been swimming for hours by now if the Old Man hadn't been so stubborn. That ice-cold poker player knows what a floating vessel is worth, even if it's a wreck.

It's 17.30 hours when I wake up. Very odd—we're steering a course of thirty degrees. So the Old Man must want to bring us close to the coast again. If we hold to this course we'll run straight into Lisbon.

How long is it since I was called to the bridge one night because we were abreast of Lisbon?

Close under the coast is presumably the safest place for us. In case of need, run the scow ashore—that may be what he has in mind. Possible, yes. But if I know him, he'll do anything to hold out.

We are, after all, fully equipped. Quantities of oil—despite our losses due to leakage. Full quota of torpedoes and plenty of provisions. A provisioned boat is not something our Old Man would be likely to surrender.

For a voyage straight across Biscay, Cape Finesterre would be the starting point. Is that what he's after?

"Stand by to surface!" The order echoes from mouth to mouth. Since there's nobody moving in the next compartment, I get up, walk stiff-legged into the gangway, open the hatch to the bow compartment, and roar into the semi-darkness, "Stand by to surface!"

The customary ritual begins. The second watch is on duty. 18.00. Only two more hours of watch.

A crowd in the control room. Once again we have to surface blind.

"Tower free!"

"Equalize pressure!"

The hatch springs open. The Commander's the first one up. He immediately orders diesel power. The boat shudders. Course thirty degrees.

I go up onto the bridge behind the Second Watch Officer. A quick look around: We're alone within the circle of the horizon. The night-black sea contrasts sharply with a trace of brighter sky. Little wind.

"We'll soon have Lisbon abeam," says the Old Man.

"But this time to starboard," I say, and all the while I'm thinking: if that were the only difference!

The Chief appears for dinner. I hardly dare look at him, he's so worn.

"They must have had radar," the Old Man says to him.

Radar. All the big ships have it. Those huge maneuverable mattresses on the mast. The *Bismarck* caught the *Hood* with radar, before the *Hood* had shown so much as the tip of her mast. And now the Tommies must have succeeded in shrinking their huge systems the way the Japanese shrink trees. Dwarf trees, and now dwarf radars, so small the whole business fits into a cockpit. And you can bet your life we don't have any defense against it yet.

I'm curious to know when Simone will find out. Her people are very much on the alert. *Her people?* I'd give a lot to know whether she really is committed to the Maquis or not. We should have been back long ago. No boat in the last year has been out as long as this, even without the Gibraltar disaster.

Not a word about Gibraltar. Not the slightest reference to it. The hours we spent on the bottom are taboo.

The seamen are silent too. Gibraltar has left its mark on their faces. Naked fear is the most common expression. Everyone knows: We're unable to dive. The boat won't stand more than periscope depth. Many of the ribs are broken. The boat is as wobbly as a hammock, not much more than a traveling wreck. Everyone's afraid it's not up to the winter storms of Biscay. Our only piece of luck is that the Tommies are convinced they've smashed us. Which means they won't send out a search party.

The next day I wake up to feel a hand on my arm.

The shock of fear. "What's happened?"

The control-room assistant Turbo catches my horrified expression. No sound of the diesel, not a hum from the motors. Quiet in the boat.

"What's going on?"

Turbo's still staring at me.

"Man, can't you tell me what's going on?"

"We're lying dead."

Stopped? How can that be? Even while I was asleep, every change in speed was registering itself in my subconscious. And now the engine has stopped without my even hearing it?

A blow like a fist on a sandbag, then a sucking smack: waves striking against the buoyancy tanks. The boat rocks placidly back and forth.

"You're to come to the bridge."

The control-room mate is a considerate man. He's carved his news into bite-sized pieces and is waiting until I've swallowed the first before offering the next. "The Commander's topside—you're to come up too—fact is, we've stopped a liner."

As though to emphasize what he's saying, he nods, then withdraws from further questioning by walking backward.

Stopped a liner? The Old Man must have gone mad. What's all this nonsense about? A new act? Or a rehash of the old days when they captured enemy ships and sailed them home as booty?

So quiet! The curtain opposite is open, and the one underneath. No one around. Are they all out stopping ships?

Two men in the control room, thank god. Tilting my head back I ask, "Permission to come onto the bridge?"

"*Jawohl!*"

A wet wind. Sky full of stars. Chunky figures in the dark: the Commander, the navigator, the First Watch Officer. A quick glance over the bulwark: Oh my god—directly over our net guard a gigantic ship. Bearing ninety, bow left. Brilliantly lit up from stem to stern. A passenger liner. Easily twelve thousand gross registered tons, if not more! Just lying there! Dead in the water! A thousand tongues of yellow-white reflections on the black ocean: shimmering spangles.

"I've been busy with her for an hour now," the Old Man growls without turning around.

It's icy cold. I shiver. The navigator hands me his binoculars. After two or three minutes the Old Man speaks again. "We stopped her exactly fifty-five minutes ago."

He has his glasses to his eyes. The navigator begins a whispered explanation. "We used our lamp to signal her—" Then the Commander breaks in: "Signaled that we'd torpedo her if they used their radio. They probably haven't used it, either. And they were supposed to give us her name. But it doesn't check. *Reina Victoria*—something or other Spanish. The First Watch Officer couldn't find it in the register. Something's rotten in the State of Denmark!"

"But all those lights!" I say without thinking.

"What better camouflage than to keep all your lights on and claim to be a neutral?"

The navigator clears his throat. "Funny," he says, between the hands supporting his binoculars.

"Much too funny for my taste," growls the Commander. "If only we knew whether the scow's on record. I've asked. Message went out long ago."

So the Old Man has radioed after all! Damned dangerous. Was it really necessary?

"Still no answer. Maybe our transmitter is out of order."

This is too much! A signal—in our situation! Just to be sure they can get a fix on us!

The Old Man seems to have read my thoughts, because he says, "Have to be certain what I'm doing."

Once more the feeling of unreality, that this huge ship is an optical illusion, that at any minute there will be a bang—and then sighs of relief, laughter, end of performance.

"He's known for the last half hour that he'll be torpedoed if he doesn't send over a boat," says the Old Man.

The First Watch Officer also has his eyes glued to his glasses. Silence. This is pure madness. This gigantic liner towering over our bulwark. Playing pirates with our ruined scow! The Old Man's out of his mind!

"We're covering the wave length he uses. But god knows what all this is about. First Watch Officer, signal over again in English: If the boat isn't here in ten minutes, I'll open fire. Ship's time, navigator?"

"03.20 hours!"

"Report to me when it's 03.30."

For the first time I see the radioman Hinrich on the bridge. He's braced high up over the bulwark, with the heavy signal lamp in his hands, sending stabs of light darting through the darkness toward the liner.

"Damned impertinence!" the Old Man snorts, when there's no acknowledgment of the signal from the other side. "That really is . . . the fucking limit!"

The radioman has to repeat his call three times before a signal lamp finally shows between the bright portholes of the steamer. The First Watch Officer whispers each letter along with the radioman: short flash—long flash—short, long—another eternity before the answer is completed. The Old Man defiantly refuses to read the letters.

"Well?" he finally snaps at the First Watch Officer.

"He's hurrying the best he can, is what he signaled, Herr Kaleun."

"Hurrying the best he can! What's that supposed to mean? First he gives us a false name, then this rubbish. Ship's time, navigator?"

"03.25 hours."

"Nerve! Gives us a false name, then just sits there, not doing a fucking thing . . ."

The Commander shifts from one foot to the other, hands thrust deep into the side pockets of his leather jacket, head down.

No one ventures a word. Not a sound apart from the splashing of the waves against the buoyancy tanks till the Old Man cuts loose again, cursing hoarsely. "Hurrying the best they can—what the hell's that supposed to mean?"

From below, the Chief joins in. "What's wrong?"

"If there's no boat here in five minutes, I'm going to let them have it," the Old Man says in a tight voice.

I'm well aware that he's expecting the navigator to agree, but the navigator remains silent. He raises his glasses and puts them down again, but that's all. Minutes pass. The Commander turns to him: The navigator tries to raise his glasses, but too late. He has to express an opinion. "I—I—no idea, Herr Kaleun. You simply can't tell—"

"*What* can't you tell?" the Old Man interrupts.

"There's something not quite right," the navigator says haltingly.

"Exactly my opinion!" the Old Man answers. "The delay's intentional. They're sending for destroyers. Or aircraft."

He sounds as if he's trying to convince himself. The halting voice of the navigator makes itself heard again. ". . . worth waiting a bit."

After all, we *can't* play pirates with this ruined tub of ours. The Old Man can't possibly go on playing the heavy. Thank god the cannon's gone. Otherwise he'd be all set to fire away, just to get the people on the ghost ship moving.

"Flood tube one!"

That ice-cold voice! He's standing diagonally behind me. I can feel his impatience between my shoulder blades. This is no attack: This is a shooting gallery. Our opponent is lying still. So are we. Virtually point-blank range: We're holding our muzzle right up against the target, so to speak.

Two waves boom dully against the buoyancy tanks, one after the other. Then silence again. Only panting breath. Is that really the navigator? Suddenly the Old Man's voice is loud and cutting. "That's it, navigator: I've had enough! Anything to be seen?"

"No, Herr Kaleun," Kriechbaum replies from under his binoculars, his tone equally sharp. A few seconds pause, then he adds more calmly, "But I'm not happy . . ."

"What d'you mean, you're not happy, navigator? *Do* you see something—or don't you?"

"No, Herr Kaleun, nothing to be seen." Hesitantly.

"Then why the metaphysics?"

More silence, in which the splashing of the waves suddenly echoes loudly.

"All right then!" the Commander suddenly shouts, apparently in a rage, and gives his orders. "Tube one stand by for underwater shot!"

He takes a deep breath and then in a lowered voice—as if giving a running commentary on some trivial event—he gives the order to fire tube one.

A perceptible jolt runs through the hull as the torpedo leaves the boat.

"Tube one discharged!" comes the report from below.

The navigator puts down his binoculars, the First Watch Officer too. We stand rooted, all faces turned toward the glowing chain of portholes.

Christ, what happens next? It's a gigantic ship, this passenger liner. And it must be filled to bursting. Any moment now they'll be blasted sky high or drowned in their cabins. The torpedo can't possibly miss. The ship's lying still. No need to calculate the angle of fire. Smooth sea. The torpedo's set for six feet below the water line, aimed precisely midships. And the range is ideal.

I stare wide-eyed at the liner, already imagining a massive explosion: the whole ship rearing up, jagged fragments soaring into the air, a huge mushroom of smoke, a blaze of white and scarlet.

The air sticks in my throat. How much longer till the blow falls? The chains of light in the liner begin to dance—I must be straining my eyes.

Then I become aware that someone's making a report: "Torpedo not running!"

What? Who was that? The voice came from below—from the sound room. Not running! But I distinctly felt the jolt of its discharge.

"No wonder," says the navigator, with what sounds like a sigh of relief. The torpedo isn't running. Which means it's not functioning properly. The bomb from the plane! It must have wrecked the steering mechanism . . . the pressure wave, of course—no torpedo could have withstood it. An omen! And now?

Tube two, tube three, tube four?

"Then we'll just try tube five," I hear the Old Man say, immediately followed by the order: "Connect stern tube!"

Now he's giving the necessary engine and rudder orders to turn the boat—calmly, as if practicing maneuvers.

So he doesn't trust the other torpedoes in the bow tubes—but is counting on the fact that the one in the stern tube may still be undamaged.

So he won't let go. Won't leave it at that. Won't even heed the omens. He's waiting for a regular kick in the teeth. The boat slowly gains momentum and begins to turn. The bright lights of the ship that were ahead of us just a moment ago move gradually to starboard and then shift astern. Two or three minutes more and we'll have her right over our stern: in perfect position for tube five.

"*There they are!*"

I nearly jump out of my skin. The navigator shouts straight into my right ear.

"Where?" snaps the Commander.

"There—that has to be the boat!" He points with outstretched arm into the darkness.

My eyes are watering from staring at the night sea. And there —there actually *is* a blob—something black, something a shade darker than the rest of the water.

Soon it's between our stern and the flickering glow—a dark mass clearly outlined against the twinkling reflections.

"In a cutter! Are they out of their minds?" I hear the Old Man say. "A cutter. In this sea! And without light!"

I stare incredulously at the dark blob. For one brief instant I catch a glimpse of six figures.

"Number One and two men stand by on the upper deck! Searchlight to the bridge!"

From the tower, a confusion of voices.

"Move it!"

Apparently the electric cable has become tangled up in something, but the navigator reaches down and manages to get hold of the hand searchlight.

I think I can hear the splashing of oars.

Suddenly the bow of the cutter appears in the beam of the searchlight, high out of the water, unreal, projected on a movie screen; then it disappears again between the waves. Only the head of the man in the stern is visible; with his forearm he's shielding his eyes from the dazzling glare.

"Careful, Number One! Keep her well clear!" roars the Old Man.

"Christ almighty!" rings in my ear. I give another tremendous start. This time it's the Chief. I hadn't noticed him come on the bridge.

The cutter is up again. I make out six men plus the helmsman: shapeless creatures rowing furiously.

Number One thrusts out a boat hook like a lance.

Shouting, confusion of voices. Number One curses, and sends his men scurrying up and down on the upper deck with fenders. Now it sounds as though an oar has splintered. The helmsman on the cutter waves wildly with his free hand. Most of the shouting seems to be coming from him.

"Look out!" roars Number One. And again: "Look out! Goddammit, you crazy pigs . . ."

The Commander hasn't budged an inch. And he doesn't say a word.

"Searchlight to the upper deck! Don't blind them!" shouts Number One.

The cutter is carried away again; in a moment there are fifteen or twenty feet of open water between it and our upper deck. Two men have stood up, the helmsman and someone else I hadn't seen before; so there are eight of them.

Meanwhile Number One has been joined by some more of the crew. As the cutter swept toward us again, the two men succeed in jumping onto our upper deck, one after the other. The first one stumbles, almost falls, but is caught just in time by the bosun. The second jumps short and lands on his knees, but before he can fall back one of our men has grabbed him by the back of the neck like a rabbit. The first stumbles into the hole that the bomb tore in our upper deck; the second trips and falls against the gun mount. There's an audible thump.

"That'll put a nice gash in his face," someone behind me says. The bosun curses.

The two shapeless figures clamber stiffly up the iron ladder on the outside of the tower. Dear god, they're wearing old-fashioned kapok life jackets. No wonder they can hardly move.

"*Buenos noches!*" I hear.

"What was that the gentlemen just said?" the Chief asks.

The bridge is suddenly jammed. An incomprehensible torrent of talk. The smaller of the two men is gesturing like an epileptic marionette.

Sou'westers, pulled low, almost cover their faces. Their kapok life jackets have worked up so high during their climb that the arms of the second man—the one who's not motioning—stick out like two long handles.

"Take it easy gentlemen, and *downstairs please!*" says the Old Man in English, making quieting gestures as he points below.

"Spaniards," says the navigator.

They're small men, but they're wearing so much bulky clothing that they can hardly get through the hatch.

In the semi-darkness of the control room I finally get a look at them. One, the Captain, apparently is stout, with a short black beard that looks glued to his face. The other is a little taller and has a dark complexion. Both peer about as though searching for some means of escape. Now I notice that the Captain is bleeding from a flesh wound over his eye. Like a wounded boxer. The blood's running in streams down his cheek.

"Boy, they're at the end of their rope!" I hear the control-room mate Isenberg say.

He's right. I've never seen such fear.

Then I realize what a terrifying spectacle we must present: glittering eyes, sunken cheeks, unkempt beards, a barbarian horde loose in a world of machines. And we must stink like the plague. Most of us still have on the same tattered underwear we were wearing when we put to sea. And these two have come from a world of rosewood saloons and carpeted passageways: I bet there are even crystal chandeliers on the ceilings. Everything as fancy as the *Weser*.

Did we scare them up from the dinner table? Can't have. It's the middle of the night.

"They're acting as if we were about to butcher them," Isenberg murmurs.

The Old Man stares open-mouthed at the gesticulating Spanish Captain as if he's a visitor from outer space. Why doesn't he say something? We all stand round the two jumping jacks and stare: No one says a word. The fat Spaniard flails his arms and emits torrents of incomprehensible syllables.

Suddenly I'm wild with rage. I could jump at his throat, choke off his stream of gibberish, knee him in the balls. I no longer recognize myself: "You goddamned sonovabitch," I hear myself snarl, "getting us into this mess!"

The Old Man's flabbergasted.

"You can't wipe your ass on us like this!"

The Spaniard just stares at me, blank horror in his face. I can't articulate what has enraged me: but I know what it is. Turning us into executioners—not answering our signals; keeping the Old Man waiting for hours; arriving in this childish cutter instead of a motor launch; without running lights; simply wandering about.

The stream of Spanish has ceased abruptly. His eyes jerk around. Suddenly he stammers, "*Gutte Mann, Gutte Mann.*" He doesn't know whom to make this grotesque appeal to, so he turns on his heels in his life jacket, awkward as a bear, still clutching the oil-skin envelope with his ship's papers under his arm. Then he seizes them in his right hand and performs a kind of hands-up.

The Old Man screws up his face and reaches silently for the envelope. The Spaniard screeches in protest, but the Old Man interrupts him coldly. "Your ship's name?" He asks in English.

"*Reina Victoria—Reina Victoria—Reina Victoria!*"

Suddenly he's all eagerness to oblige; he bows and immediately rises on tiptoe to point out this name in the ship's papers, which the Old Man has pulled out of the envelope.

The First Watch Officer observes the scene expressionlessly, but he's beginning to look sick.

Suddenly, there's quiet. After a while the Old Man raises his eyes from the papers and looks at the First Watch Officer. "Tell this gentleman that his ship does not exist. After all, you speak Spanish."

The First Watch Officer comes out of his trance. He turns bright-red and begins to stammer out Spanish from behind the foreign Captain's back. The latter opens his eyes wide in amazement and snaps his head from side to side, trying to catch the First Watch Officer's eye, but no amount of head-turning can accomplish this—his life jacket's sitting much too high on him; he has to pivot his whole body. In so doing he ends up with his back to me. And it's a shock. Small stenciled letters on the under edge of his life jacket: *South Carolina*. I'm suddenly triumphant. Now we've got you! The Old Man was right. An American, disguised as a Spaniard!

I poke the Old Man and trace the lettering on the edge of the life jacket. "Interesting, this: look—*South Carolina!*"

The Spaniard whirls around as though bitten by a tarantula and pours out a torrent of words.

Got you, you bastard. Cut the Spanish jabber. You can talk English, you son of a bitch.

The Old Man stares nonplussed at the stuttering little man, then orders the First Watch Officer to tell us what the Spaniard is gabbling about.

"*South Carolina*—the ship—was actually named—*South Carolina*," stammers the First Watch Officer. The Spaniard is hanging on his words and nodding like a circus clown. "Now, however, it is *Reina Victoria*. It was—five years ago—bought from the Americans."

The Old Man and the Spaniard stare at each other, and look ready to spring at each other's throats. It's so quiet you can hear every drip of condensation as it falls.

"He's right," the navigator announces from the table. "Fourteen thousand gross tons." He's holding the register of ships.

The Old Man looks from the Spaniard to the navigator, and back again.

"Say that again," he says finally in a voice that cuts like a whip.

"The boat is entered in the supplement, Herr Kaleun." And when the Old Man still doesn't react, he adds in an undertone, "The Herr Oberleutnant didn't consult the supplement."

The Old Man clenches his fists and stares at the First Watch Officer. He's fighting a monumental battle for self-control. Finally he barks: "I—demand—an—explanation!"

The First Watch Officer turns uncertainly toward the navigator and reaches for the register. A couple of staggering steps toward the chart table, and he comes to a stop. The way he's propping himself up, you'd think he'd been wounded.

The Old Man is shaking as if in sudden horror. Before the First Watch Officer can say anything he turns back to the Spaniard, a twisted grin on his face. The Spanish Captain senses the change at once and becomes wildly voluble again. "*South Carolina* American ship—now *Reina Victoria* Spanish ship." Five, six times. Gradually the fear fades from his face.

"Navigator, take a look at these papers!" the Commander orders. But before he can begin to leaf through them, we get our briefing from the Spanish Captain. "*Dos mil pasaieros—por America del Sud —Buenos Aires!*"

The Old Man breathes in very loudly through his nose, then blows out hard through slack lips. His whole body sags. And now he slaps the Spaniard on the shoulder. The eyes of the Second Spaniard—he must be the First Officer—light up like candles on a Christmas tree.

The Commander is a changed man. He seems to have forgotten the First Watch Officer completely. A bottle of Cognac and three glasses appear as if by magic. "Never say no to an honest drop." The Spaniard considers this some kind of toast and won't be outdone. More crazy gibberish and cries of "*Eilitler! Eilitler! Eilitler!*"

The First Watch Officer is as white as a sheet. He stammers out a rough translation of the latest outburst. "Their Captain says—he thought *we* were—we were an English patrol boat. That's why— that's the reason that he—allowed himself so much time. It was only when—he realized we weren't British—that things went crazy. And then the first boat they sent—was, so he says, upset."

The Spaniard nods like a rocking horse and adds, "*Sí, sí,*" again and again. "*Sí, sí, sí!*"

". . . upset and drifted away. He apologizes."

"Apologizes is good!" says the Old Man. "He ought to be on his knees thanking us and the Tommy who ruined our first fish. And wouldn't you like to tell him that you almost had him standing around in a white nightgown by now? Him and his friend and his two thousand passengers as well! That *you* almost had the lot of them on your conscience. Why don't you tell him that?"

The First Watch Officer's lower jaw goes slack. He's finished; he can't even control his muscles any more.

When the Spaniards are back in the cutter, the Captain starts shouting offers of phonograph records and fruit: half an hour, and it'll all be here—very up to date! Spanish music! Flamenco! Marvelous fresh fruit, lots of it, for the whole crew!

"Push off, you old asshole!" roars one of the men on the upper deck, and shoves the Spanish cutter away from the buoyancy tank. Number One helps with the boat hook. The oars splash into the water. Fragments of Spanish words, and then something that sounds like "*Wiedersehen.*"

"Are you out of your mind?" roars the bosun. The Spaniards soon become a dark blob again.

"They must be! Not even carrying lights," the navigator scolds after them. "They were within sixty feet of us before we saw them. Completely mad!"

We all stare after them, but already there's no trace of the cutter: The night sea has swallowed it up.

The Old Man takes his time giving engine-room orders.

He finds the First Watch Officer in the control room.

"Do you have any idea—do you even have the brains to realize what you almost managed to commit? What *I* would have committed because my prize specimen of a First Watch Officer isn't even competent to do something as simple as consulting the register properly? I'll tell you something—you ought to be court-martialed!"

There's nothing left for the First Watch Officer to do but to shoot himself. But the only pistol on board is in possession of the Commander. Securely locked up.

Uproar in the petty officers' quarters: "The navigator knew something was screwy right from the start!"—"The First Watch Officer really got his balls chewed off!"—"We were nearly up the creek!"—"Trust the Old Man—jump in with both feet, *then* have second thoughts. But he really excelled himself this time."—"Christ, they don't know how lucky they were!"—"Damn great ship like that and no launch."—"Boy, what a horse's ass!" The last is a reference to the First Watch Officer.

Hours later the Old Man recapitulates. "Everything suddenly

went wrong at once. It was within a hair's breadth of being a second *Laconia* incident. If the torpedo's steering hadn't been ruined . . ."

Silence. Several minutes later, still chewing on his pipestem, he says: "It really shows you—life or death—sheer chance—oh, bullshit!" There's no doubt that the Old Man's feeling very uncomfortable about the whole thing, and he's trying to justify himself. "But the whole thing was so obvious—they *did* keep delaying—and we gave them more than enough time. They were behaving like maniacs!"

"Yes, but only because they were assuming they'd been stopped by a *British* patrol boat. We *did* hail them in English. Apparently they never even considered the possibility that we might be a German submarine."

"Well, that's what you get for showing off in foreign languages!"

"They must have been scared shitless when they recognized us!"

"Tsch!" says the Old Man. "That's the way things go. One thing leads to another and . . ."

He's silent for a good five minutes. They he says, "It's also a terrible disadvantage that we've no way of measuring the power of our transmitter. Perhaps our inquiry about them never even went out. After all, the antenna was sheared off, and all sorts of other equipment was ruined. A radio on the blink and an incompetent for a First Watch Officer—what more could you ask for?"

Quite apart from the state of our nerves, I add silently. It was the navigator who was right all along. Always rational, always cool, never flustered. He refused to be seduced by the Old Man's opinions when he disagreed with them.

The conciliatory gurgling of the Old Man's pipe is driving me out of my mind. "The whole thing would have caused the most god almighty stink!" I burst out, "and we'd have been right in the middle of it—"

"No, we wouldn't," the Old Man interrupts harshly.

I can't make head or tail of this. So I wait. There's obviously more to come. But the interval drags on and on, so finally I say: "I don't understand."

"Really? It's perfectly simple: We'd have had to wipe the slate clean. Typical case . . ."

He breaks off, then says in an undertone, "There would have been no survivors!"

What's he saying?

"It would have been the typical situation that you never find in the rules. In cases like this you're completely on your own. All the Navy does is tell you you have complete discretion. That you should use your own judgment."

The cold pipe in his right hand draws circles in the air. He's straining for words. "They didn't use their radio. Of course, they know that we can always monitor that, assuming things are normal. Suppose the torpedo's gyroscopic apparatus had been in order and had blown up its target, then the liner would have 'hit a mine.' Sunk so fast there wouldn't even have been time for a radio signal. In any case, a German U-boat couldn't let itself be seen as having anything to do with it. In situations like this there's no help for it. You have to wipe the slate whether you want to or not! You can't do these things by half-measures." He moves off heavily in the direction of the forward hatch.

The full implications of his gruesome use of the cliché begin to sink in, and I shiver. Instantly I'm assailed by images of lifeboats riddled by machine-gun fire, arms thrown up, waves reddened by streams of blood, faces filled with incredulous horror. I remember scraps of stories that have made my blood run cold. Half-heard babble in the Bar Royal. Only dead men tell no tales. Why did *they* get it? Why not *us*? They get us by the short hairs, too.

My teeth begin to chatter uncontrollably. What next? What else must happen before we're finally wiped out? A shuddering sob rises from somewhere deep inside me. I clench my fists and grit my teeth as hard as I can, choking it back until the whole lower half of my face is a single knot of pain. And just at that point the Chief turns up.

"Well, well, what's the matter now?" he asks, concern in his voice.

"Nothing," I manage to say. "Nothing—quite all right!"

He hands me a glass of apple juice. I seize it with both hands, take a great gulp, then say, "Lie down—I'd just like to lie down for a while."

In the bow compartment Dufte is almost beaten up when he says, "Biscay—let's hope we get through all right!" This is no time to tempt fate or jog the table that's supporting our house of cards. Who knows what else can collapse in this beat-up scow? The Old Man must have his reasons for laying a course so close to the coast. The order "Prepare safety gear" still haunts the air.

The thing we fear most is enemy flyers. If a plane spots us now, we're finished. Everyone knows that. Crash dives are out of the question. Times have changed: Now we actually pray for bad weather—but only moderately bad. Spare us the hurricane.

Tomorrow, everything will look even worse. At that point the coast will recede, and the voyage through Biscay begin. How can we cover this stretch without being spotted from the air? Biscay is under the tightest surveillance of all. And if the Old Man was right? If the British Air Force now have some kind of new equipment that makes us visible even on the darkest night?

What day is it today anyway? Just "today"; it's meaningless. When we're gliding along underwater, it's day. When we're surfaced and running on the diesel, it's night. Right now it's ten o'clock and we're underwater. So it must be ten a.m.

But what day of the week is it? My brain labors to work it out. I feel drugged. Finally a word takes shape: calendar. I wonder what day it's showing today. I can't get comfortable on this goddam chest I'm sitting on, so I might as well head for the Officers' Mess. That's where the calendar is too.

Wobbly as hell on my feet. Like walking on stilts. Well, get going! Pull yourself together.

The sound man is staring blankly as usual. Looks like a blowfish behind glass in an aquarium.

In the Officers' Mess I use my left hand to support myself on the table. Quite comfortable, standing this way.

What kind of date is that on the calendar? Ninth of December? We're way behind the times. Down with the ninth of December! I'll keep the sheet for my private notebook. Memorable. A kind of Bastille Day! The record from the barograph and the page from the calendar: evocative souvenirs, and as thrills go, cheap at the price. Eleventh of December. Down with that too. The thirteenth was Explosion Day. Keep that one too. Nineteenth of December. We were lying on the bottom. Twentieth—the same. Twenty-first, twenty-second. All those days! And now it's the twenty-third. Which is today. Which makes it Tuesday.

Then I hear someone say, "Christmas Eve tomorrow!" Some Christmas present! I gulp. Sentimentality? The usual Christmas emotions? The Festival of Love—at sea, on a bombed-out scow. It's certainly different! We are, of course, superbly equipped for the Festival of Love, thanks to the inimitable foresight of the Navy— there's the folding Christmas tree that came on board with the rest of the provisions. How will the Old Man handle it? He's certainly got more important things to worry about.

He's considering laying a course for La Rochelle. We could possibly head up the Gironde to Bordeaux, but although Bordeaux lies farther south, it's really no nearer. From our present position to La Rochelle is still about four hundred miles—four hundred miles straight across the Bay of Biscay: that means at least another thirty-five hours minimum. But since we have to submerge during the day, the calculation looks worse than that. We'll probably need as much as forty-eight hours. That's a long time, especially since we don't know what weather conditions we'll have to deal with in the next few days, or whether the diesel will hold out.

The Old Man and the navigator have still further worries. "There's the question of how we can get in—no notion—very narrow entrance —certain to be all kinds of barriers—coastal shelf very shallow— danger of mines."

Subdued voices everywhere. Everyone seems to be on tiptoe, as though the first loud noise would attract the enemy's attention.

I notice that everyone who comes through the control room tries to get a look at the chart, but no one dares ask how many miles it is to base; no one is willing to admit how shaky he is. At the same time they all have the same thought: Bay of Biscay, naval graveyard. The worst storms, the most intensive aerial surveillance.

When the navigator is back at his table I try the direct approach. "How many hours yet?" "Tsch!" is all I get by way of an immediate answer. Presently he'll start spinning conditional sentences that all begin with "if," I think to myself. But he's more diplomatic than that. "What can one say?"

I watch him out of the corner of my eye until he finally gets going again. "I calculate forty-six hours at least. Altogether, that is—not just counting the time at cruising speed."

In the bow compartment I discover that Ario was being tormented by worries of his own while the boat was on the bottom. Ario has a collection of contraceptives in his seabag. Plus some very expensive special items. He enumerates them: "Ones with rubber knobs, fancy ticklers, even a 'hedgehog' or two . . ." This was the embarrassment of riches that had been weighing on his mind the whole time. "Well, how would it look if stuff like that turned up among my things? And, besides, they'd be wasted on my next of kin . . . I can tell you one thing—before the next patrol, I'm going to blow up every single condom and pop the lot."

"You needn't have worried; the flotilla sees to it that they disappear. All our stuff is carefully sifted," Bockstiegel explains. "Filthy photos and rubbers, everything that might not amuse the widows and mourning relatives. I saw it done once; the paymaster has a whole team of specialists. Before your gear's turned over, it's as clean as a whistle. You can rely on that!"

For the bridge johnny, whose mind runs along economical lines, there are still open questions. "So what does the paymaster do with all those condoms? After all, they're private property, aren't they?"

"He puts them on a list, meathead. What else would he do? And someone makes two copies. And then they're all cross-referenced."

"Trust the Navy!" says Schwalle.

The Old Man spends his time commuting from the engine room to the bow compartment and back to the control room, always followed by the Chief, trying to form a realistic picture of the boat's condition, though he certainly won't be able to make an accurate assessment of everything that's out of order. The ribs, for instance, can't be examined because of the built-in installations.

"This boat is ready for the ashcan!" I hear him say as he passes.

The navigator reports that we're at the latitude of Cape Ortegal. So the crossing of Biscay is underway.

The Old Man includes the First Watch Officer in the consultation, perhaps out of some impulse of sympathy, so that the man won't feel completely annihilated. A precise sailing program is laid out, but the factors in the calculation must remain constant if the plan is to succeed. The prime requirement is that the diesel hold out.

The Old Man slumps on the sofa in the Officers' Mess; he starts to speak: "The Blessed Feast of Our Lord . . ." then falls silent. I can see he's fidgeting—it's not difficult to guess why he's troubled.

He clears his throat, trying to lure me into saying something. But what am I supposed to say? That nobody's exactly in the mood for a floating Christmas party?

"Oh, screw the whole thing!" he bursts out, while I'm still searching for words. "We'll simply postpone the festivities. Christmas Eve for us is when we have solid ground under our feet again. Or do you attribute some importance to this humbug? I suppose you'll be wanting to read aloud the Gospel according to Saint Luke?"

"No," is all I can say. Nothing witty occurs to me.

"Well then!" says the Old Man in relief. "We'll simply behave as though it isn't time yet."

Christmas. Since I turned fourteen something always went wrong. Sad Christmases, melodramatic Christmases, overdoses of emotional nonsense. Wailing and police in the house. And then the drunken Christmases . . .

The Old Man's right. What is all this wallowing in sentimentality? Just let the day run its normal course. A normal day, Christ! Better not throw days around like that. Better stick to thinking in terms of hours. Don't call down a jinx. No celebrations. Out of the question.

The Old Man is obviously feeling better. One problem less. I'm simply curious as to how he's going to communicate his postponement of festivities to the crew. Then I get my answer. "Tell the petty officers—it'll get around!"

Apparently the diesel isn't functioning as well as it seemed to be at first. There are bugs in it that are worrying the Chief. Nothing really ominous, just disturbing. For the next few hours he doesn't leave the engine room.

The men know that we're no longer close to shore, and the boat has become even quieter. Nerves show in fits of trembling at the most harmless noises. The Chief's the worst. Even at the best of times he reacts to the tiniest sound from the engines—sounds that no one else even registers—with the sensitivity of an exceptionally greedy dog hearing the faint rustling of a biscuit package. But this time he scared even me. As we were sitting side by side in the Officers' Mess, he leaped up so suddenly that I went cold; he listened for a fraction of a second with staring eyes, then dashed into the control room. Fiendish hubbub instantly broke out. The Chief's voice was cracking with rage. "Have you gone mad—damn and goddammit—since when—something like this—just take it away—get moving!"

He collapses in his corner again, panting. I don't dare ask him what was going on. Ten minutes later I make some inquiries of the control-room mate as offhandedly as possible.

The Bible Scholar had been working on the knives with polishing sand. This produced an odd gritty sound, and the Chief had been unable to identify it.

December twenty-fourth. Still afloat. We've covered a considerable stretch. As for the weather, we've had incredible good luck: Christmas weather. The December storms in Biscay are usually terrifying. But the most we've had have been winds of four to five, and sea three. The sea generally does remain one point below the wind. It couldn't have been better. We're almost halfway across, the diesel has held out, and we've had no pursuit group on our heels. That in itself is enough to provoke a small show of optimism.

But no! Everyone slouches about looking miserable. Even the Old Man is monosyllabic. This rubs off on the crew. He may simply be sticking to his maxim: "No reception before the church service." But unless he cheers them up, the crew quickly lapses into black pessimism. A bunch of depressives. I'll have to take a look in the bow compartment again. Perhaps it's better there.

The bow compartment looks appalling: There's more confusion than ever. Number One probably hasn't dared give the order to clean ship. The red-shaded lamps have disappeared. No further hint of whorehouse atmosphere. Apathetic, prostrate, the off-duty watch lies slumped on the floor plates, grown-up children with false beards. They hardly speak to one another. General surrender and fatalism seem to have taken hold.

A few hours later the whole boat has been cleaned up spick and span. The Commander put a rocket under Number One. Christmas house-cleaning.

"Can't let sloppiness take over!" he mutters to me.

A wise decision: Just stick to the ship's routine—no fuss, keep the tear ducts dry, distract the men from thoughts of home. I dread to think what total surrender to emotion might produce.

"La Spezia—would have fitted in perfectly," says the Old Man.

Dear god, is he off on Christmas again?

Memories of the orgies of food and drink laid on for the flotilla at the Hotel Majestic: long tables with white cloths, pine twigs instead of green fir for decoration. Everyone had a "fancy platter"— and a stamped-out star-shaped cardboard plate with spice cookies, Russian bread, pralines, a chocolate Saint Nicholas. Christmas carols roared out at full volume. Then the address by the Flotilla Chief—the enduring union of our beating hearts with those of our loved ones at home, the solicitous Führer, the old German Night of Dedication, the Great German Reich, and our splendid *Führer über alles*! And then, standing: "*Sieg Heil—Heil—Heil!*" Drunkenness and the descent into maudlin sentimentality, the blabbering and slobbering, the katzenjammer, the howling misery.

It's settled: We must try to put in at the nearest reachable base. Which means La Rochelle, not Saint Nazaire and home.

We're twenty-four hours away. The Old Man sticks rigidly to normal routine: forty-eight hours before entry into port, whorehouse regulations must be read aloud. This should have been done long ago. It's really the First Watch Officer's job, but the Old Man has relieved him—a kind of proof of grace, since this text is really something. It now devolves upon the Second Watch Officer to broadcast it to the crew over the ship's loudspeaker. Thus, instead of the Gospel according to Saint Luke, the whorehouse ordinance. The Second Watch Officer does it well. His tone of voice has the requisite seriousness for the reading of a flotilla order, while leaving no one in the slightest doubt that he considers the whole thing a piece of sublime lunacy.

The control-room mate is painting victory pennants. He has already finished one with the number eight thousand on it: That's for the first big scow in the convoy.

The First Watch Officer is sitting beside the Chief in the mess, doing paperwork: assignments for the shipyard, calculation of oil consumption, a report on the torpedoes fired. It wouldn't surprise me if he started pecking away at the typewriter again.

Almost hourly I sneak a look at the chart, and each time I itch to take a pencil and secretly extend the line that's inching toward La Rochelle.

Every mile we put behind us means that much less tension and fear.

Scraps of conversation echo through the half-open hatch to the bow compartment. The men's spirits seem to be rising again. I even hear someone in the next compartment ask who's going to be making out the leave permits. Hard to believe: We still have a whole night ahead of us, we're a long way from being able to relax in safety, and someone is getting excited about his leave permit.

Nothing I hear in the bow compartment would surprise me any more. "What kind of cathouses do they have in La Rochelle?"

The E-mate Pilgrim was apparently stationed there once.

"How would I know?" is all he says.

"Shit! It really is impossible to ask you a sensible question!"

Thank god—not a trace of Christmas spirit!

Around 01.00 I climb onto the bridge.

"Roughly another two and a half hours to the escort meeting point," the navigator reports to the Old Man.

Escort meeting point? Are we as close as that?

"Which means we'll be there nice and early," says the Old Man. "We'll tuck ourselves in for the time being and have a look at the traffic."

"*Jawohl*, Herr Kaleun," is all the navigator has to say.

"Well?" The Old Man turns to me. "No great hurry, I guess—or are you beginning to fidget?"

I can only sigh. What am I supposed to say?

The night air is silky. Am I simply imagining things, or does it smell of land—that delicate scent of damp foliage?

Perhaps we'll soon see a light from the coast. On second thought, no! La Rochelle, after all, isn't Lisbon. There's a blackout here. All along the French coast, the lighthouses were turned off long ago.

"Another hour's sleep?"

"Wouldn't hurt . . ."

I ask the navigator to rout me out when he's relieved and go below shortly after the Old Man.

"Sea's about two—hardly any wind," the navigator says as he wakes me, shaking me by the arm.

Once again I beat the Commander to the bridge.

I squint ahead. The horizon is clear, and the east is brightening already. The First Watch Officer is standing forward on the port side. "To the Commander: Dawn's breaking!" The Commander comes onto the bridge and silently checks in all directions.

"Well, it'll probably be all right for a little while longer," he says finally. But it doesn't take me long to sense how uneasy he is. Again and again he lifts his head to glance anxiously at the sky. In the east, a thread of pale yellow lies over the horizon. The darkness is thinning quickly. Another ten minutes and he says, "We must be just about there."

The sea is calm. We might as well be on a pond. The sounding gear is at work. Continuous reports from below. "One hundred feet, ninety feet . . ." It reaches the seventy-foot mark and stays there.

"Excellent!" says the Old Man. "Just what we need. All right, navigator, that'll do for now! We'll just tuck ourselves in for the time being. It's getting lighter all the time."

"Stand by to dive!" One more survey of the dark silky sea, then we climb down slowly, taking our time.

"Chief, just try to set us down nice and gently. Shouldn't be too hard here."

The bump when the boat touches bottom is no greater than that of an airplane touching the runway.

"Good," says the Old Man. "Now we'll let the dear Lord take over!"

"And his good Wife, the dear old white-haired lady . . . " That was the Chief. So he's found his voice again.

"Tiens, tiens!" The Old Man obviously feels he's back in France already. I must ask the navigator whether we're already on good

French sandy bottom or whether the seabed here is still international.

For some time my subconscious has been registering an odd bumping and scraping noise. Now there's a dull bang, like a fist hitting a wooden door, immediately followed by a second and third. They echo through the boat, the last almost drowned out by a shrill whistling before the bumping and scraping begin again.

"Hard to believe," says the Old Man. "That's quite some current."

"And the bottom isn't exactly all it's cracked up to be." The Chief.

So the bumping is being caused by rocks. We're not lying fast: We're being dragged over the bottom.

"Flood the tanks, Chief."

"*Jawohl*, Herr Kaleun!"

I hear water flowing into our regulator tanks: we're anchoring ourselves.

"Good, now let's hope our direction checks!"

Silence in the boat. Only the *ping-ping* of condensation. The off-duty watch have long since stretched themselves out on their bunks. As soon as it's really light, the Old Man will take us up to periscope depth—forty-five feet. He's not telling us what he'll do next. Approaching the coast without a boom-breaker and an escort will be a ticklish business. Impossible by day and extremely difficult by night.

Just as I lift my right leg to clamber through the after hatch, there's another bump.

"Goddammit to hell," mutters the Old Man. "We can't be lying parallel to the current. We'll have to try to reposition her."

With half an ear, I hear the blowing. Then another bump that echoes through the whole boat. Then an order first for the motors, then the hydroplane.

Hinrich is at the sound gear. His voice seems to come from a great distance. "Engine noises bearing three hundred degrees. Growing louder!"

The Old Man raises his eyebrows theatrically. He's standing in the middle of the control room, listening; the Chief is half concealed behind him. I don't dare make a move.

The Old Man swallows. I can see his Adam's apple jerking up and down.

"Piston engines!" the sound man reports.

The Old Man squats down in the gangway beside the sound room and puts on the headset. His rounded back is toward us. The sound man sticks his head out.

A mutter from the Old Man: "If that's not a submarine diesel I'll eat my hat."

He gives the headset back to the sound man, who listens for a couple of minutes, while the Old Man remains beside him. "Well, Hinrich?"

"Submarine diesels for sure!"

"German or English—that's the question. Get moving, First Watch Officer, ready with the recognition pistol. We'll surface and you fire at once. What's the bearing now?"

"Bearing remains two hundred seventy degrees."

"Stand by anti-aircraft guns! First Watch Officer, on the bridge immediately after me!" Instantly the control room is filled with turmoil. Someone opens the munitions locker. We're going to put on a fireworks display right outside our own front door? And throw in the machine guns just for good measure?

The Old Man already has his hand on a rung of the ladder. "All clear?"

"*Jawohl*, Herr Kaleun!"

"Surface!"

"Blow the tanks!"

I'm standing directly under the hatch when the recognition pistol goes off above me. Men are still climbing, so I only catch an occasional glimpse, between a thigh and the rim of the hatch, of the red and white magnesium flares. Pretty Christmas stars. Very appropriate. I wait, holding my breath.

"Fine!" That's the Old Man. "Signal returned. Take her closer, First Watch Officer. Let's have a look at our colleague."

"Incredible!" the Chief says behind me.

"Permission to come on the bridge?" I ask.

"Come ahead!"

It takes me a while to spot the other boat on the dark water. She's head on; you could mistake her for a floating barrel.

"Quick! Up with the signal light—move it! Now Zeitler, introduce us with all the proper courtesies!"

Zeitler directs the signal lamp at the other boat and taps away at his message.

From the other boat a light flashes out: message acknowledged. Then I hear our signal lamp again and the navigator reads off what's coming from over there: "UXW Oberleutnant Bremer."

"That's fantastic!" says the Old Man. "Someone has to be expecting them. All we need to do is follow them in!"

The navigator beams. A load off his mind: *He's* the one who would've had to figure out how to pilot us into La Rochelle.

"Now all we have to do is wait for their escort. Just ask them what time it's supposed to turn up."

The bosun's mate presses the key of the signal lamp; the answer comes in a matter of seconds. They must have a first-rate signal man. "08.00!"

"Now signal: 'We'll join you!' That'll give them a riddle to solve: How come *we're* turning up as unexpected guests? They must be wondering why we're putting in at another flotilla's home port—and today of all days."

The Old Man appears to have no intention of enlightening them.

During the exchange of signals we've moved closer together— within hailing distance. A loudspeaker booms: "What happened to your cannon?"

We gape at each other. The Old Man hesitates. Even I take a while to realize that the others can see us just as clearly as we can them, and that something has altered our silhouette.

"Damnfool question!" snarls the navigator.

But the Old Man puts the megaphone to his mouth and shouts, "I'll give you three guesses!"—then turns to the navigator and says in a normal voice: "He'd do better to make sure his own anti-aircraft guns are ready. It looks damned nasty to me around here!"

The navigator takes this as a direct injunction to shout at the bridge lookouts. "Keep your eyes peeled, men, for god's sake!"

Suddenly a violent, muffled explosion runs through the boat. I feel it as a blow to the back of my knees. Battery? Motors? Something gone wrong with the diesel? Hell, what *was* it?

The Old Man shouts down through the hatch. "Report! I want a report!"

Nothing from below. Questioning glances between the Old Man and the navigator. The Old Man raises his voice to a roar. "Report! Report at once!"

The Chief's face appears in the hatchway. "Nothing—nothing to report, Herr Kaleun!"

The Commander stares. Have we all gone crazy? There's just been an explosion—and a big one at that!

Then the signal lamp flashes out from the other boat. Three mouths spell out the message simultaneously: H-a-v-e-s-t-r-u-c-k-m-i-n-e.

"Move! Let's go closer!"

Mine, mine, mine. So we're dawdling over a minefield. They never come singly.

I focus my binoculars on the other boat. Nothing noticeable. She's simply lying a little stern heavy, as if badly trimmed. I had always pictured a mine casualty as looking quite different.

Our bow swings slowly round. The other boat is signaling again. "Read it out!" the Commander orders.

It's Zeitler who responds: H-i-t-i-n-s-t-e-r-n-m-a-k-i-n-g-w-a-t-e-r-f-a-s-t-u-n-a-b-l-e-t-o-d-i-v-e.

"One of those damned magnetic mines," says the Old Man. "Probably dropped by an aerial night patrol."

"And certainly not the only one . . ." the navigator says calmly.

"We can't change that, navigator. We *have* to stay on the surface and provide anti-aircraft protection."

And drift slowly through the minefield.

The navigator has nothing to say. His binoculars are trained on the other boat and he betrays not the slightest emotion.

"Just shout across, 'Will stay on surface and provide anti-aircraft protection!' "

The navigator puts the megaphone to his mouth. From the other side the message is acknowledged with a brief "Thanks!"

"Navigator, take a report: '06.15 hours. UXW hit by mine.' Tell the radioman to try again. Perhaps we'll be in luck. Have him send this message: 'Emergency. Emergency. UXW hit by mine. Unable to dive. All systems inoperative. Request immediate escort. Remaining at point of explosion—UA.' "

There's nothing left to do but wait and watch as it gets lighter.

"Seems to have bent their drive shaft," says the Old Man harshly. "If it had been the diesels, the motors would still be good for something, or *vice versa*."

I notice from the brightness behind us that the tide must have turned us around: we now have the east at our back. We all look gray in the pale morning light, as if smeared with ashes.

No engine noises, no motion, no vibration in the boat. We drift along like flotsam. The fear . . . and the silence. I hardly dare clear my throat. If only our diesel were running again—I'd give a lot to hear the noise.

"Ship's time?"

"07.10 hours!"

Fear. We avoid looking at one another, as though to intercept a glance would trigger a fatal explosion.

"Airplane! One hundred twenty degrees!"

"Ready anti-aircraft guns! Move it! Height?"

"Eight hundred! Looks like a Halifax!"

I disappear from the bridge, reach for ammunition, hand it on up. Our anti-aircraft gun is already blazing away. We're giving it everything we've got. But we're lying still. Playing target. Through the racket of our gun I hear a great explosion. Then sudden silence.

I rush onto the bridge and look around. Where in god's name is the other U-boat? Nothing but flat, opalescent sea. Only a couple of dark blobs drifting off our port beam.

Our bow swings toward them. Finally the navigator says, "Direct hit—just forward of the tower!"

I'm seeing things in a trance: a gray filter seems to have been intruded in front of the camera. I squint, blink hard, stare: The boat that was there a moment ago is gone. And the airplane? Disappeared. A single bomb? A single pass? A direct hit?

They're coming back, I tell myself, and there'll be a swarm of them. Fighter protection? Why don't we have any fighter protection? Fat pig Göring—him and his big mouth! *Where are our airplanes?*

The sea is flat, polished. No motion—not so much as a wrinkle. A knife-edge of horizon. And there, where the long hull of the boat was lying a moment ago, more of these blobs, a disturbing fault in smooth quicksilver. No whirlpool, no surge, nothing—no clatter of engines—silence.

Why does no one scream? The stillness is absurd. Gives me the feeling all this is unreal. Our bow has swung toward the drifting blobs. In the glasses they resolve themselves into individual entities, heads suspended in life jackets. The men manning our anti-aircraft gun are still standing there like statues, expressionless, as though they haven't yet grasped what has just happened. Only the heaving of their chests betrays them.

Number One is waiting on the upper deck with five men, to take aboard survivors.

"Goddammit—look out!" he roars.

On the starboard side the sea is red. Blood in salt water. What are we to do with these wretched creatures?

I don't dare look too closely. Better to watch the sky.

Close behind me, someone says, "Probably *they* pictured Christmas differently too!"

A man appears dripping on the bridge and stammers out some kind of report, his hand on his forehead: the other Commander, Bremer.

His face—innocent as a choirboy's—is twisted; in spasm. He actually howls. Stares straight ahead as if hypnotized. Clenches his teeth to try to stop his lower jaw clicking like a castanet, but can't do it. His whole body starts to tremble. A steady flood of tears runs down his twitching cheeks.

The Old Man looks at him coldly, in silence. Finally he speaks. "Why don't you go below!"

Bremer refuses with a violent shake of the head.

The Old Man issues an order. "Bring up the blankets!" And then, as if in a sudden rage: "Move it! I want blankets up here. *Now!*"

As the first blanket is handed up through the tower hatch he himself puts it around Bremer's shaking shoulders.

Not sufficient depth of water to dive; no boom-breaker; no anti-aircraft protection—what a fucking mess! This mirror-smooth sea. The Halifax. What was that all about? Was it really carrying just one bomb? A crate like that must carry a load of them.

"I felt—felt it—like a snake around my throat," Bremer goes on stammering.

This strange figure on the bridge wrapped in a blanket; the pathetic little handful of men on the upper deck; this silken, pastel sea. A masquerade. I feel I have to break through a membrane if I'm to reach reality.

"Look out!" yells a control-room assistant, heaving blankets through the hatch behind him. Bremer twitches violently. He's standing in the way.

He belongs to another flotilla, and none of our men know him.

The Old Man's voice is threatening to crack. He has to cough a couple of times to stop the croaking.

"Diving's out."

Too shallow, too much current. So we'll just have to go on drifting over the mines and wait till the Tommies come back. Still no fighter protection! But the other boat had been reported!—Nothing works right any more. Fucking Hermann Göring.

Anchor? Wouldn't it be better for us to ride at anchor? Nothing could be worse than letting the tide drag us over the mines.

The Old Man can't wait much longer. He has to decide now: to wait for the Tommies or be like Blücher at Waterloo—just charge straight ahead without boom-breaker or mine sweeper.

He screws up his face, the way he always does when he's thinking. But now we actually get orders to the engine room and the helmsman. Gradually the bow swings around toward the sun. Just as I thought: charge!

I'm absolutely wrong. The Old Man orders the diesel run at slow speed, just enough to hold the boat against the tide. We're running in place.

The most beautiful of all mornings at sea. I don't know whether it's the solemn grandeur of this Christmas morning or the misery on the upper deck that brings tears to my eyes. A sob rises in my throat. I try to choke it back. Mustn't let go.

If the sky had been dressed in mourning, in mist and darkness, the scene of the shipwrecked men might have been easier to bear. But this radiance of opal fire and gold that fills the sky and spreads out over the water is in such agonizing contrast to the half-drowned sailors who stand revealed on our upper deck that I want to cry out. They crowd together, huddled like sheep, each man wrapped in a dark-gray blanket. The morning light is too dazzling for me to pick out individual figures; they form a single dark mass. Two of them still have their caps on. One, a stringbean of a man, must be their First Watch Officer. The other is a petty officer, probably their Number One. The engine-room crew certainly didn't get out. That's the way it always goes. They seem to be barefoot. One of them has rolled up his trousers as though he were planning to go wading.

Our bosun and two of our men are trying to salvage an empty float. He's already piled up six or seven bright-yellow life rafts against the tower.

Apparently the Old Man won't take any of them below decks. There isn't any point. After all, we can't dive here. And then there are still the mines! Leave the poor beasts where they are.

It's high time the escort turned up. The enemy certainly isn't going to be content with dropping a single bomb. The Halifax must have reported, so the Tommies have known for some time that there's a second boat sitting waiting for another bomb. Our fucking Navy! The people on shore must have heard the explosion. Or have we no more forces at our disposal in these coastal waters? Aren't there any more patrol boats? Are we sheltering under the ass of the prophet?

Down there below the tower the radioman Herrmann, our orderly, and two seamen are busy with the wounded. An older man from the other boat was badly hit. Hands burned, head a ball of blood. Salt water on raw flesh!—A shudder runs through me. I can hardly bear to look.

Herrmann wraps the red head with gauze bandages, leaving only the eyes and the mouth showing—like a Tuareg. Then he lights a cigarette and puts it between the Tuareg's teeth. The Tuareg thanks him with a nod. The others are smoking too, some still sitting in their sodden clothes on the wreckage of our grating.

The other boat's First Watch Officer and their petty officer can't stop searching the skies, but their men seem indifferent. Two or three even let the air out of their life jackets so that they can sit more comfortably.

The Commander wants to know how many men have been rescued. I count: twenty-three on the foredeck; four aft—all severely wounded. That is barely more than half the crew.

How calm the sea is! Like unused metal foil. I've never seen it so smooth. Not the slightest breath of wind.

Then the navigator calls, "Object at two hundred seventy degrees!"

All binoculars swing toward the magnet: a tiny dark spot floating in the silky blue-gray. Impossible to make out what it is. I put down my glasses and squint. The navigator climbs up on the TBT, leans back at an angle, and raises his glasses again. Bremer—openmouthed—peers vaguely in the direction indicated.

"Recognize anything?" Impatience in the Old Man's voice.

"No, Herr Kaleun! But that must be the place where she sank, given the way the current's running now. It carried us quite a distance during all that rescue work."

"Hm."

Another two or three minutes, then the Old Man suddenly decides to have the bow turned about and to increase speed. We lay a course for the tiny dot.

What's he up to, tearing around in these mine-infested waters on account of a crate or an old oil barrel? Tempting fate? Hasn't he done enough of that?

Five minutes pass. Then the navigator, who hasn't lowered his glasses for so much as a second, says in an impassive voice: "Someone swimming over there!"

"Thought so!" the Old Man answers, just as coolly.

Someone swimming! It must be nearly an hour since Bremer's boat went down. We've been staring ourselves blind, all of us. And there was nothing, nothing at all to disturb the mirrored perfection of the sea.

The Old Man orders more speed. I have my binoculars to my eyes, and as we approach I too begin to make out the figure of a man. His head shows clearly above the bulge of his life jacket. And now he's lifting an arm.

The men on the upper deck have surged forward, until they are clutching the net guard. Hope no one goes overboard at this point. My heart is pounding. Someone really *is* moving out there! Our ace of a navigator knew right away that it was no flotsam he was looking at.

I climb down the iron rungs on the outside of the tower to the upper deck: I want to see the sailor they're about to pull out of the drink. God, I want to cry, you ought to be throwing your arms around the navigator's neck. That was one in a thousand. Only Kriechbaum could have pulled off something like this. He never stops using his eyes—or his head, for that matter.

Now they have him. Barefoot. Eighteen years old at most. Water pouring off him. He leans against the tower but manages to keep to his feet.

I nod encouragingly. Without saying a word. Now's not the time to ask how he managed to work his way out of the sunken boat.

Must be a stoker. Probably the only one who got out of the aftership. But why did it take so long? What went on? Who knows what his story is.

Nevertheless, I say, "Man alive—lucky, weren't you?"

The youngster pants, then nods.

Number One appears with blankets. Never thought he could be so tender: he wraps the boy up just like a mother. Jesus, he oughtn't to have done that. The youngster collapses, begins to sob, his teeth chattering.

"Hand over a cigarette," Number One orders one of our sailors. "Come on, light it! And fast!"

Cautiously he lowers the boy onto the gratings, props his back against the tower, and pushes the cigarette into his mouth. "Here, take the butt. Go on, smoke it!"

"Ship's time?"

"08.10 hours!"

The escort was due at 08.00. God!

My life jacket is beginning to bother me.

Lucky for the men on the upper deck that there's no wind and we have this mild weather. Christmas Day—and not cold. The sun will soon be up, but still we ought to see to it that they get something on their feet. After all, we don't need our seaboots. Number One has already had all available clothing carted up to them, sweaters especially.

I climb down to collect some footwear.

As I pass through the Officers' Mess I stop dead, thunderstruck. The First Watch Officer has got his typewriter out and is about to start pecking away. I'm speechless: This is too much! I snort disapprovingly, but he doesn't even look up, just jabs at the keys with his index finger and keeps his stony seagull eyes fixed straight down. I would really love to take his machine and beat him over the head with it. Instead of which I merely say, "You're nuts," work my way farther forward and roar, "Get going—move it, seaboots this way! Move it, man!"

What can he be pecking out right now? A report of our arrival? God only knows. Perhaps it's a receipt for Bremer, a properly typed acknowledgment that we've taken him aboard together with half his crew.

A chain is soon organized. The boots come up fast. I climb up after the last pair.

A shout from Bremer's navigator. "The escort!" He points forward.

And there, for a fact, are smoke clouds rising over the horizon. "Too late, gentlemen!" growls the Old Man.

Right next to my ear I hear a violent, staccato rattle. I turn my head. My god, it's the other Commander. His teeth are chattering.

The sun comes up and the sea is iridescent taffeta. The blue outline of the approaching boom-breaker and all her superstructures stands out sharply against the red ball. Over the river mouth hang swollen, misshapen clouds, shaded the subtle blue-gray of doves' feathers. A broken mauve-red spreads across the sky, and the highest clouds suddenly are bordered in brocade.

My eyes burn as I stare at the soaring disk of the sun. The Bible Scholar's Salvation Army jingle echoes in my head.

> *Glorious, glorious that day,*
> *When, no more sin, no more dismay,*
> *We march into the Promised Land . . .*

"Crazy the way things work out," says the Old Man—in an aside, so Bremer won't hear him. "Now everything checks again: Only *one* boat was expected and only *one* turns up."

He's been sizing up the boom-breaker. "Very pretty tub, a good eight thousand tons. Only two small derricks. Where d'you suppose they got them? . . . What in the world is that?" The last words are drawled out on a rising note.

Now I see it too: ship after ship coming over the horizon behind the boom-breaker.

"Gentlemen, you flatter us!" the Old Man says, to no one in particular.

Then on the boom-breaker a sun beams out. "Call from boom-breaker."

"Already noted, Second Watch Officer. Hurry up with the signal lamp. Let's see what they want."

The searchlight goes out, flashes again. The Second Watch Officer reads aloud: C-o-r-d-i-a-l-w-e-l-c-o-m-e.

"No doubt there's more to it than that!"

W-h-a-t-h-a-v-e-y-o-u-s-u-n-k.

"That's meant for you," the Commander says, turning to Bremer, who has opted to remain below in the bridge cockpit and now looks shrunken in contrast to the rest of us up here.

Bremer glances at us helplessly.

"Windbags," says the Second Watch Officer, his eyes fixed on the boom-breaker. "Next thing we know they'll be sending us Christmas greetings!"

"Oh the hell with it!" the Old Man says finally. "We'll simply consider the question addressed to us. Get moving, signal them 'Two fat freighters.' "

The key of the signal lamp clicks. A few seconds' pause, then back comes: H-e-a-r-t-y-c-o-n-g-r-a-t-u-l-a-t-i-o-n-s.

The Old Man makes a face and bites his lower lip.

"What do you think, shall we give them an explanation?" he asks the navigator.

"Just keep going, Herr Kaleun. They'll soon notice who it is they've brought in!"

If there are eyes behind those glasses, I think, they must have seen the sailors on our upper deck long ago. This kind of make-believe is unusual in the U-boat service. And the rubber rafts our Number One made such a neat pile of are hardly a usual feature of the upper decks of returning boats. They *must* be aware that something has been going on here. And that it may begin again at any moment. The Tommies will be back. They won't let us get off scot-free.

I try to calm down: In any case we'll soon be safe from the mines. And if an airplane chooses to attack now, it'll encounter considerably more fire power than two hours ago. The boom-breaker is well equipped with anti-aircraft guns, and the horde of escort vessels now arriving also have their own supply of popguns. But the Old Man doesn't seem to find this much comfort. Again and again he scowls as he searches the sky, which is gradually shading into blue.

"They always know when something's wrong," says the Second Watch Officer, meaning the seagulls, which are circling the boat in flocks.

The gulls catch the golden light on their feathers and emit shrill, plaintive cries. As they glide over us, they turn their heads searchingly from side to side.

I have no ear for the orders to the engine room and the helmsman. Hardly an eye for the approaching armada. I can't get over the way they're spewing out smoke so brazenly: in front of them there's a great thick wreath of it against the pastel background of the morning sky. Perhaps they're trying to divert attention if the enemy appears again—to concentrate it on themselves instead of us.

Once more I have my hands full, collecting and handing over a steady supply of blankets and shoes. I finally become aware of a fireboat, just as she arrives broad on our starboard beam. Her black flanks are covered with rashes of red lead. Minutes later there's a dark colossus to starboard. It's a dredge that works constantly around here to keep a channel open for major shipping.

Now finally I can find time to pick up a pair of binoculars and look out over our bow. The shore is still only a thin line, but there are cranes there, as small as toys; I can also see individual figures on the boom-breaker, which is now directly in front of us. And the course it's holding is taking us straight toward the coast.

We have to wait in the outer basin. Our sailors ready the lines on the upper deck, moving among the wounded with the utmost care.

A message from the signal tower. The navigator reads it out: "Enter immediately!" Through our binoculars we see a bridge opening in front of us. Already we can make out a crowd of people on the pier. Thank god, no brass bands.

A few seagulls screech, and the sound is deafening in the strange silence that descends as the boat creeps slowly between the moss-covered walls of the channel. From the pier small bouquets of flowers with twigs of fir tied around them are tossed down to us. No one picks them up.

The old revulsion against the people up there. I know that everyone standing here on the bridge feels the same way. We're like irritable animals, reacting violently to any false gesture.

Shrill whistling, a signal to the mooring crew on the upper deck. The hawsers lie neatly coiled and ready, fore and aft. Likewise our thick basket fenders.

Thin lines fly over to the pier, soldiers catch them and pull in the heavy hawsers attached to the other end. Sailors come to their aid and make fast the hawsers to the massive iron piles. The screws stir up the brackish water as they slowly draw the boat in.

"Stop engine! Crew fall in on the afterdeck!" the Commander's voice sounds hoarse.

The men up there can see our shattered upper deck, the shipwrecked men huddled together like sheep, the wounded. I find myself looking into horrified faces.

The gangway is pushed out. It slants sharply upward: **We're** united once more with solid earth.

Even before I hear the buzz, I can feel it as part of the very air I breathe: planes!

The sound is coming from the ocean: the swarm we've been expecting. All heads are raised. The humming grows louder, deepens into a steady thunder. Already the flak is cutting loose. There— out over the sea—tiny white clouds like wads of cotton hang in the sky. A flash of light: the wing of a plane. Now I can see black dots: five—six bombers. Seven. It's an armada!

A piercing snarl suddenly cuts into the furious barking of a four-barrel anti-aircraft gun. Shadows flit across the storehouses. Things fly apart.

The Old Man is shouting. "Quick, get out of here! Head for the bunker!" His voice cracks.

Already a hail of bullets is tearing into the paving stones, splintering them in all directions—pursuit planes!

They're not after us.

They're trying to silence the anti-aircraft posts. It's a combined attack by fighters and bombers.

Here and there the pier explodes into fountains of rubble. Fragments of stone sail through the air with a strange deliberation.

I'm still almost two hundred feet from the armored door of the bunker, which the people inside have pulled shut, leaving the narrowest possible entrance. I leap forward, my knees buckle again, I feel a sharp pain in my thighs. Legs like wobbly stilts that I can't control. I seem to have forgotten how to run.

Screams, little white puffs of cloud in the sky, howling sirens, the rattle and snap of machine-gun fire, and the sudden barking of the medium-sized flak, salvo after salvo crashing out in unending succession. Every kind of explosion following its own rhythm in a single, appalling cacophony. Smoke, mushrooms of dust, and in between the gray bodies of aircraft. Which are ours, which are the Tommies'? I recognize a double-tailed Lightning, and high up a hornet swarm of bombers.

I hear the sharp yapping of light flak, the clatter of machine guns, the chirping whine of splinters. Planes roar and scream. Farther off, the heavy flak rumbles at them like some mighty earthquake. They're coming in at every height.

In front of me is a grotesque ballet, choreographed by some madman on a paved stage with the mammoth structure of the U-boat bunker as a backdrop: figures throwing themselves to the ground, running zigzag, dropping to their knees, whirling into the air, sweeping together in tight formation, only to fly apart again, surging this way and that. One man throws his arms into the air, spins in a pirouette, and sinks down in a deep, court curtsy, his palms outstretched in reverence.

Again the roaring sweeps past. An invisible fist strikes me in the back of the knees. Slammed down on the paving stones, I try convulsively to make a word out of the only fragment in my brain: atro—atro . . . Renewed howling. A blast of air pins me to the ground as plane after plane roars over. Atrophy!

A bomber disintegrates in the sky. Fragments of wings tumble down. The tail lands with a crash behind the bunker. I can hardly breathe for dust and smoke. Arms flailing, I reach the concrete wall, squeeze through the slit in the bunker door, fall over someone lying on the floor, hit my forehead, roll to one side.

The rattle of gunfire sounds duller. I run my hand over my forehead, am not surprised at the sticky feel of blood. The man beside me is groaning and holding his stomach. As my eyes accustom themselves to the half-darkness I recognize him: gray oil-smeared clothes —must be from our boat—Zeitler.

Someone takes me under the shoulders from behind and tries to lift me to my feet.

"I'm all right, thanks!"

I stand up, stagger, eyes fogged, still supported by the man behind. The fog clears. I can stand alone. Then there is an enormous boom that almost shatters my eardrums. The whole bunker is one titanic, reverberating drum. The floor shakes under me. From the roof above the first of the flood docks—which I can just see into— huge lumps of concrete rain down, splash into the water, and pound the boat that's lying at the pier. Suddenly a brilliant light breaks through a hole in the bunker roof.

Light! I prop myself up.

The hole is a good ten feet by ten. Iron matting with thick lumps of concrete caught in it is left hanging where the roof once was. The matting moves, showering down more slabs of concrete.

The water in the dock continues to break against the piers. My god, twenty-four feet of solid concrete blasted into nothing! It's never happened before. Cries, orders. As much running about inside the bunker as there was outside.

Bunker roofs were supposed to be safe against bombs of any size.

Where's all the steam coming from?

Outside, the furious shooting and rolling thunder continue unabated, like some mighty, distant storm.

A huge cloud of dust settles. I have a furry taste on my tongue. No more air. A racking cough. I have to lean against the wall, my head resting on my forearm.

Air! All I want is air' I'm smothering. I force my way back to the armored door through a solid wall of humanity, knock aside two shipyard workers who try to bar my path, and push my way through the narrow opening. Nothing but black, oily smoke: something must have scored a hit on a fuel tank.

I'm wrong: The whole harbor basin is ablaze. Only the cranes rise unmoved out of the billowing clouds of fiery smoke. There's a sharp crackling and the wail of a steam siren that will not stop.

I look to the right, in the direction of the lock. The sky is clearer here. I see torn warehouse roofs, houses bombed to piles of rubble. Bent wires and jagged strips of iron tear at my feet. I almost fall into .a crater that I failed to see in the smoke. A man lying wounded raises himself up at me, madness in his eyes. Groans and whimpers everywhere. There must be hundreds more like him, hidden by the dust and smoke.

The boat! What has happened to the boat?

A gust of wind lifts the curtain of smoke. I climb through railings bent into hoops, swerve around two dead men, run past ruins of red-painted iron. A smoking pile of rocks slides into the water in front of me. God, that was the pier! And the boat? Where is it? I suddenly see a slab of steel towering out of the water like a gigantic plow-share—and attached to it a net guard. The bow! Wooden debris bobs about in the water. Water? It's oil! And the black lumps moving about in there: three—four—more—are all human beings. These strange water creatures in among the bursting bubbles must all be men from our boat. And the Old Man? What's happened to him? A banner of smoke streams across the scene. Shouts from behind me: a long, ragged line of soldiers and dockworkers is heading my way. Two trucks, sirens screaming, are racing toward me, swerving along between the craters in a mad slalom.

And there in the haze I see the Old Man, streaming with blood, his sweater and shirt torn to shreds. His eyes, which were always narrowed, are wide, wide open. At almost the same moment we sink to our knees, bracing our arms on the splintered stones, and face each other like two Sumo wrestlers. The Old Man opens his mouth as though to let loose a great shout. But all that gushes from his lips is blood.